Phantom Fortune, A Novel

M. E. Braddon

Contents

PHANTOM FORTUNE, A NOVEL

BY

M. E. Braddon

CHAPTER I.
PENELOPE.

People dined earlier forty years ago than they do now. Even that salt of the earth, the elect of society, represented by that little great world which lies between the narrow circle bounded by Bryanstone Square on the north and by Birdcage Walk on the south, did not consider seven o'clock too early an hour for a dinner party which was to be followed by routs, drums, concerts, conversazione, as the case might be. It was seven o'clock on a lovely June evening, and the Park was already deserted, and carriages were rolling swiftly along all the Westend squares, carrying rank, fashion, wealth, and beauty, political influence, and intellectual power, to the particular circle in which each was destined to illumine upon that particular evening.

Stateliest among London squares, Grosvenor--in some wise a wonder to the universe as newly lighted with gas--grave Grosvenor, with its heavy old Georgian houses and pompous porticoes, sparkled and shone, not alone with the novel splendour of gas, but with the light of many wax candles, clustering flower-like in silver branches and girandoles, multiplying their flame in numerous mirrors; and of all the houses in that stately square none had a more imposing aspect than Lord Denyer's dark red brick mansion, with stone dressings, and the massive grandeur of an Egyptian mausoleum.

Lord Denyer was an important personage in the political and diplomatic world. He had been ambassador at Constantinople and at Paris, and had now retired on his laurels, an influence still, but no longer an active power in the machine of government. At his house gathered all that was most brilliant in London society. To be seen at Lady Denyer's, evening parties was the guinea stamp of social distinction; to dine with Lord Denyer was an opening in life, almost as valuable as University honours, and more difficult of attainment.

It was during the quarter of an hour before dinner that a group of persons, mostly personages, congregated round Lord Denyer's chimney-piece, naturally trending towards the social hearth, albeit it was the season for roses and lilies rather than of fires, and the hum of the city was floating in upon the breath of the warm June evening through the five tall windows which opened upon Lord Denyer's balcony.

The ten or twelve persons assembled seemed only a sprinkling in the large lofty room, furnished sparsely with amber satin sofas, a pair of Florentine marble tables, and half an acre or so of looking glass. Voluminous amber draperies shrouded the windows, and deadened the sound of rolling wheels, and the voices and footfalls of western London. The drawing rooms of those days were neither artistic nor picturesque--neither Early English nor Low Dutch, nor Renaissance, nor Anglo-Japanese. A stately commonplace distinguished the reception rooms of the great world. Upholstery stagnated at a dead level of fluted legs, gilding, plate glass, and amber satin.

Lady Denyer stood a little way in advance of the group on the hearthrug, fanning herself, with her eye on the door, while she listened languidly to the remarks of a youthful diplomatist, a sprig of a lordly tree, upon the last *debut* at Her Majesty's Theatre.

'My own idea was that she screamed,' said her ladyship. 'But the new Rosinas generally do scream. Why do we have a new Rosina every year, whom nobody ever hears of afterwards? What becomes of them? Do they die, or do they set up as singing mistresses in second-rate watering-places?' hazarded her ladyship, with her eye always on the door.

She was a large woman in amethyst satin, and a gauze turban with a diamond aigrette, a splendid jewel, which would not have misbeseemed the head-gear of an Indian prince. Lady Denyer was one of the last women who wore a turban, and that Oriental head-dress became her bold and massive features.

Infinitely bored by the whiskerless attache, who had entered upon a disquisition on the genius of Rossini as compared with this new man Meyerbeer, her ladyship made believe to hear, while she listened intently to the confidential murmurs of the group on the hearthrug, the little knot of personages clustered round Lord Denyer. Hi 'Indian mail in this morning,' said one--'nothing else talked of at the club. Very flagrant case! A good deal worse than Warren Hastings. Quite clear there must be a public inquiry--House of Lords--criminal prosecution.'

'I was told on very good authority, that he has been recalled, and is now on his passage home,' said another man.

Lord Denyer shrugged his shoulders, pursed up his lips, and looked ineffably wise, a way he had when he knew very little about the subject under discussion.

'How will *she* take it, do you think?' inquired Colonel Madison, of the Life Guards, a man about town, and an inveterate gossip, who knew everybody, and everybody's family history, down to the peccadilloes of people's great grandmothers.

'You will have an opportunity of judging,' replied his lordship, coolly. 'She's to be here this evening.'

'But do you think she'll show?' asked the Colonel. 'The mail must have brought the news to her, as well as to other people--supposing she knew nothing about it beforehand. She must know that the storm has burst. Do you think she'll----'

'Come out in the thunder and lightning?' interrupted Lord Denver; 'I'm sure she will. She has the pride of Lucifer and the courage of a lion. Five to one in ponies that she is here before the clock strikes seven!'

'I think you are right. I knew her mother, Constance Talmash. Pluck was a family characteristic of the Talmashes. Wicked as devils, and brave as lions. Old Talmash, the grandfather, shot his valet in a paroxysm of *delirium tremens*,' said Colonel Madison. 'She's a splendid woman, and she won't flinch. I'd rather back her than bet against her.'

'Lady Maulevrier!' announced the groom of the chambers; and Lady Denyer moved at least three paces forward to meet her guest.

The lady who entered, with slow and stately movements and proudly balanced head, might have served for a model as Juno or the Empress Livia. She was still in the bloom of youth, at most seven-and-twenty, but she had all the calm assurance of middle-age. No dowager, hardened by the varied experiences of a quarter of a century in the great world, could have faced society with more perfect coolness and self-possession. She was beautiful, and she let the world see that she was conscious of her beauty, and the power that went along with it. She was clever, and she used her cleverness with unfailing tact and unscrupulous audacity. She had won her place in the world as an acknowledged beauty, and one of the leaders of fashion.

Two years ago she had been the glory and delight of Anglo-Indian society in the city of Madras, ruling that remote and limited kingdom with a despotic power. Then all of a sudden she was ordered, or she ordered her physician to order her, an immediate departure from that perilous climate, and she came back to England with her three-year-old son, two Ayahs, and four European servants, leaving her husband, Lord Maulevrier, Governor of the Madras Presidency, to finish the term of his service in an enforced widowhood.

She returned to be the delight of London society. She threw open the family mansion in Curzon Street to the very best people, but to those only. She went out a great deal, but she was never seen at a second-rate party. She had not a single doubtful acquaintance upon her visiting list. She spent half of every year at the family seat in Scotland, was a miracle of goodness to the poor of her parish, and taught her boy his alphabet.

Lord Denyer came forward while his wife and Lady Maulevrier were shaking hands, and greeted her with more than his usual cordiality. Colonel Madison watched for the privilege of a recognising nod from the divinity. Sir Jasper Paulet, a legal luminary of the first brilliancy, likely to be employed for the Crown if there should be an inquiry into Lord Maulevrier's conduct out yonder, came to press Lady Maulevrier's hand and murmur a tender welcome.

She accepted their friendliness as a matter of course, and not by the faintest extra quiver of the tremulous stars which glittered in a circlet above her raven hair did she betray her consciousness of the cloud that darkened her husband's reputation. Never had she appeared gayer, or more completely satisfied with herself and the world in which she lived. She was ready to talk about anything and everything--the newly-wedded queen, and the fortunate Prince, whose existence among us had all the charm of novelty--of Lord Melbourne's declining health--and Sir Robert Peel's sliding scale--mesmerism--the Oxford Tracts--the latest balloon ascent--the opera--Macready's last production at Drury lane--Bulwer's new novel--that clever little comic paper, just struggling into popularity--what do you call the thing--*Punch?*--yes, *Punch, or the London Charivari*--a much more respectable paper than its Parisian prototype.

Seated next Lord Denyer, who was an excellent listener, Lady Maulevrier's vivacity never flagged throughout the dinner, happily not so long as a modern banquet, albeit more ponderous and not less expensive. From the turtle to the pines and strawberries, Lady Maulevrier held her host or her right-hand neighbour in interested conversation. She always knew the particular subjects likely to interest particular people, and was a good listener as well as a good talker. Her right-hand neighbour was Sir Jasper Paulet, who had been allotted to the pompous wife of a court physician, a lady who had begun her married life in the outer darkness of Guildford Street, Bloomsbury, with a household consisting of a maid-of-all-work and a boy in buttons, with an occasional interregnum of charwoman; and for whom all the length and breadth of Harley Street was now much too small.

Sir Jasper was only decently civil to this haughty matron, who on the strength of a card for a ball or a concert at the palace once in a season affected to be on the most intimate terms with Royalty, and knew everything that happened, and every fluctuation of opinion in that charmed circle. The great lawyer's left ear was listening greedily for any word of meaning that might fall from the lips of Lady Maulevrier; but no such word fell. She talked delightfully, with a touch-and-go vivacity which is the highest form of dinner-table talk, not dwelling with a heavy hand upon any one subject, but glancing from theme to theme with airy lightness. But not one word did she say about the governor of Madras; and at this juncture of affairs it would have been the worst possible taste to inquire too closely after his lordship's welfare.

So the dinner wore on to its stately close, and just as the solemn procession of flunkeys, long as the shadowy line of the kings in 'Macbeth,' filed off with the empty ice-dishes, Lady Maulevrier said something which was as if a shell had exploded in the middle of the table.

'Perhaps you are surprised to see me in such good spirits,' she said, beaming upon her host, and speaking in those clear, perfectly finished syllables which are heard further than the louder accents of less polished speakers, 'but you will not wonder when I let you into the secret. Maulevrier is on his way home.'

'Indeed!' said Lord Denyer, with the most benignant smile he could command at such short notice. He felt that the muscles round his eyes and the corners of his mouth were betraying too much of his real sentiments. 'You must be very glad.'

'I am gladder than I can say,' answered Lady Maulevrier, gaily. 'That horried climate--a sky like molten copper--an atmosphere that tastes of red-hot sand--that flat barren coast never suited him. His term of office would expire in little more than a year, but I hardly think he could have lived out the year. However, I am happy to say the mail that came in to-day--I suppose you know the mail is in?' (Lord Denyer bowed)--'brought me a letter from his Lordship, telling me that he has sent in his resignation, and taken his passage by the next big ship that leaves Madras. I imagine he will be home in October.'

'If he have a favourable passage,' said Lord Denyer. 'Favoured by your good wishes the winds and the waves ought to deal gently with him.'

'Ah, we have done with the old days of Greek story, when Neptune was open to feminine influence,' sighed her ladyship. 'My poor Ulysses has no goddess of wisdom to look after him.'

'Perhaps not, but he has the most charming of Penelopes waiting for him at home.'

'A Penelope who goes to dinners, and takes life pleasantly in his absence. That is a new order of things, is it not?' said her ladyship, laughingly. 'I hope my poor Ulysses will not come home thoroughly broken in health, but that our Sutherland-shire breezes will set him up again.'

'Rather an ordeal after India, I should think,' said Lord Denyer.

'It is his native air. He will revel in it.'

'Delicious country, no doubt,' assented, his lordship, who was no sportsman, and who detested Scotland, grouse moors, deer forests, salmon rivers included.

His only idea of a winter residence was Florence or Capri, and of the two he preferred Capri. The island was at that time little frequented by Englishmen. It had hardly been fashionable since the time of Tiberius, but Lord Denyer went there, accompanied by his French chef, and a dozen other servants, and roughed it in a native hotel; while Lady Denyer wintered at the family seat among the hills near Bath, and gave herself over to Low Church devotion, and works of benevolence. She made herself a terror to the neighbourhood by the strictness of her ideas all through the autumn and winter; and in the spring she went up to London, put on her turban and her diamonds, and plunged into the vortex of West-End society, where she revolved among other jewelled matrons for the season, telling herself and her intimates that this sacrifice of inclination was due to his lordship's position. Lady Denyer was not the less serious-minded because she was seen at every aristocratic resort, and wore low gowns with very short sleeves, and a great display of mottled arm and dimpled elbow.

Now came her ladyship's smiling signal for the withdrawal of that fairer half of the assembly which was supposed to be indifferent to Lord Denyer's famous port and Madeira. She had been throwing out her gracious signals unperceived for at least five minutes before Lady Maulevrier responded, so entirely was that lady absorbed in her conversation with Lord Denyer; but she caught the look at last, and rose, as if moved by the same machinery which impelled her hostess, and then, graceful as a swan sailing with the current, she drifted down the room to the distant door, and headed the stately procession of matronly velvet and diamonds, herself at once the most regal and the most graceful figure in that bevy of fair woman.

In the drawing-room nobody could be gayer than Lady Maulevrier, as she marked the time of Signor Paponizzi's saltarello, exquisitely performed on the Signor's famed Amati violin--or talked of the latest scandal--always excepting that latest scandal of all which involved her own husband--in subdued murmurs with one of her intimates. In the dining-room the men drew closer together over their wine, and tore Lord Maulevrier's character to rags. Yea, they rent him with their teeth and gnawed the flesh from his bones, until there was not so much left of him as the dogs left of Jezebel.

He had been a scamp from his cradle, a spendthrift at Eton and Oxford, a black-leg in his manhood. False to men, false to women. Clever? Yes, undoubtedly, just as Satan is clever, and as unscrupulous as that very Satan. This was what his friends said of him over their wine. And now he was rumoured to have sold the British forces in the Carnatic provinces to one of the native Princes. Yes, to have taken gold, gold to an amount which Clive in his most rapacious moments never dreamt of, for his countrymen's blood. Tidings of dark transactions between the Governor and the native Princes had reached the ears of the Government, tidings so vague, so incredible, that the Government might naturally be slow to believe, still slower to act. There were whispers of a woman's influence, a beautiful Ranee, a creature as fascinating and as unscrupulous as Cleopatra. The scandal had been growing for months past, but it was only in the letters received to-day that the rumour had taken a tangible shape, and now it was currently reported that Lord Maulevrier had been recalled, and would have to answer at the bar of the House of Lords for his misdemeanours, which were of a much darker colour than those acts for which Warren Hastings had been called to account fifty years before.

Yet in the face of all this, Lady Maulevrier bore herself as proudly as if her husband's name were spotless, and talked of his return with all the ardour of a fond and trusting wife.

'One of the finest bits of acting I ever saw in my life,' said the court physician. 'Mademoiselle Mars never did anything better.'

'Do you really think it was acting?' inquired Lord Denyer, affecting a youthful candour and trustfulness which at his age, and with his experience, he could hardly be supposed to possess.

'I know it,' replied the doctor. 'I watched her while she was talking of Mau-levrier, and I saw just one bead of perspiration break out on her upper lip--an un-mistakable sign of the mental struggle.'

CHAPTER II.
ULYSSES.

October was ending drearily with north-east winds, dust, drifting dead leaves, and a steel-grey sky; and the Dolphin Hotel at Southampton was glorified by the presence of Lady Maulevrier and suite. Her ladyship's suite was on this occasion limited to three servants--her French maid, a footman, and a kind of factotum, a man of no distinct and arbitrary signification in her ladyship's household, neither butler nor steward, but that privileged being, an old and trusted servant, and a person who was supposed to enjoy more of Lady Maulevrier's confidence than any other member of her establishment.

This James Steadman had been valet to her ladyship's father, Lord Peverill, during the declining years of that nobleman. The narrow limits of a sick room had brought the master and servant into a closer companionship than is common to that relation. Lady Diana Angersthorpe was a devoted daughter, and in her attendance upon the Earl during the last three years of his life--a life which closed more than a year before her own marriage--she saw a great deal of James Steadman, and learned to trust him as servants are not often trusted. He was not more than twenty years of age at the beginning of his service, but he was a man of extraordinary gravity, much in advance of his years; a man of shrewd common-sense and clear, sharp intellect. Not a reading man, or a man in any way superior to his station and belongings, but a man who could think quickly, and understand quickly, and who always seemed to think rightly. Prompt in action, yet steady as a rock, and to all appearance recognising no earthly interest, no human tie, beyond or above the interests of his master. As a nurse Steadman showed himself invaluable. Lord Peverill left him a hundred pounds in acknowledgment of his services, which was something for Lord Peverill, who had very little ready cash wherewith to endow his only daughter. After his death the title and the estates went to a distant cousin; Lady Diana Angersthorpe was taken in hand by her aunt, the Dowager Marchioness of Carrisbrook; and James Steadman would have had to find employment among strangers, if Lady Diana had not pleaded so urgently with her aunt as to secure him a somewhat insignificant post in her ladyship's establishment.

'If ever I have a house, of my own, you shall have a better place in it, Steadman,' said Lady Diana.

She kept her word, and on her marriage with Lord Maulevrier, which happened about eighteen months afterwards, Steadman passed into that nobleman's service. He was a member of her ladyship's bodyguard, and his employment seemed to consist chiefly in poking fires, cutting the leaves of books and newspapers, superintending the footman's attendance upon her ladyship's household pets, and conveying her sentiments to the other servants. He was in a manner Lady Maulevrier's mouthpiece, and although treated with a respect that verged upon awe, he was not a favourite with the household.

And now the house in Mayfair was given over to the charge of caretakers. All the other servants had been despatched by coach to her ladyship's favourite retreat in Westmoreland, within a few miles of the Laureate's home at Rydal Mount, and James Steadman was charged with the whole responsibility of her ladyship's travelling arrangements.

Penelope had come to Southampton to wait for Ulysses, whose ship had been due for more than a week, and whose white sails might be expected above the horizon at any moment. James Steadman spent a good deal of his time waiting about at the docks for the earliest news of Greene's ship, the *Hypermnestra*; while Lady

Maulevrier waited patiently in her sitting-room at the Dolphin, whose three long French windows commanded a full view of the High Street, with all those various distractions afforded by the chief thoroughfare of a provincial town. Her ladyship was provided with a large box of books, from Ebers' in Bond Street, a basket of fancy work, and her favourite Blenheim spaniel, Lalla Rookh; but even these sources of amusement did not prevent the involuntary expression of weariness in occasional yawns, and frequent pacings up and down the room, where the formal hotel furniture had a comfortless and chilly look.

Fellside, her ladyship's place in Westmoreland, was the pleasure house which, among all her possessions, she most valued; but it had hitherto been reserved for summer occupation, or for perhaps two or three weeks at Easter, when the spring was exceptionally fine. The sudden determination to spend the coming winter in the house near Grasmere was considered a curious freak of Lady Maulevrier's, and she was constrained to explain her motives to her friends.

'His lordship is out of health,' she said, 'and wants perfect rest and retirement. Now, Fellside is the only place we have in which he is likely to get perfect rest. Anywhere else we should have to entertain. Fellside is out of the world. There is no one to be entertained.'

'Except your neighbour, Wordsworth. I suppose you see him sometimes?'

'Dear simple-minded old soul, he gives nobody any trouble,' said her ladyship.

'But is not Westmoreland very cold in winter?' asked her friend.

Lady Maulevrier smiled benignly, as at an inoffensive ignorance.

'So sheltered,' she murmured. 'We are at the base of the Fell. Loughrigg rises up like a cyclopean wall between us and the wind.'

'But when the wind is in the either direction?'

'We have Nabb Scar. You do not know how we are girdled and defended by hills.'

'Very pleasant,' agreed the friend; 'but for my own part I would rather winter in the south.'

Those terrible rumours which had first come upon the world of London last June, had been growing darker and more defined ever since, but still Lady Maulevrier made believe to ignore them; and she acted her part of unconsciousness with such consummate skill that nobody in her circle could be sure where the acting began and where the ignorance left off. The astute Lord Denyer declared that she was a wonderful woman, and knew more about the real state of the case than anybody else.

Meanwhile it was said by those who were supposed to be well-informed that a mass of evidence was accumulating against Lord Maulevrier. The India House, it was rumoured, was busy with the secret investigation of his case, prior to that public inquiry which was to come on during the next session. His private fortune would be made answerable for his misdemeanours--his life, said the alarmists, might pay the penalty of his treason. On all sides it was agreed that the case against Lord Maulevrier was black as Erebus; and still Lady Maulevrier looked society in the face with an unshaken courage, and was ready with smiles and gracious words for all comers.

But now came a harder trial, which was to receive the man who had disgraced her, lowered her pride to the dust, degraded the name she bore. She had married him, not loving him--nay, plucking another love out of her heart in order that she might give herself to him. She had married him for position and fortune; and now by his follies, by his extravagance, and by that greed of gold which is inevitable in the spendthrift and profligate, he had gone near to cheat her out of both name and fortune. Yet she so commanded herself as to receive him with a friendly air when he arrived at the Dolphin, on a dull grey autumn afternoon, after she had waited for him nearly a fortnight.

James Steadman ushered in his lordship, a frail attenuated looking figure, of middle height, wrapped in a furred cloak, yet shivering, a pale sickly face, light auburn whiskers, light blue eyes, full and large, but with no intellectual power in them. Lady Maulevrier was sitting by the fire, in a melancholy attitude, with the Blenheim spaniel on her lap. Her son was at Hastings with his nurses. She had nothing nearer and dearer than the spaniel.

She rose and went over to her husband, and let him kiss her. It would have been too much to say that she kissed him; but she submitted her lips unresistingly to his, and then they sat down on opposite sides of the hearth.

'A wretched afternoon,' said his lordship, shivering, and drawing his chair closer to the fire. Steadman had taken away his fur-lined cloak. 'I had really underrated the disagreeableness of the English climate. It is abominable!'

'To-day is not a fair sample,' answered her ladyship, trying to be cheerful; 'we have had some pleasant autumn days.'

'I detest autumn!' exclaimed Lord Maulevrier. 'a season of dead leaves, damp, and dreariness. I should like to get away to Montpellier or Nice as soon as we can.'

Her ladyship gave him a scathing look, half-scornful, half-incredulous.

'You surely would not dream of leaving the country,' she said, 'under present circumstances. So long as you are here to answer all charges no one will interfere with your liberty; but if you were to cross the Channel--'

'My slanderers might insinuate that I was running away,' interrupted Maulevrier, 'although the very fact of my return ought to prove to every one that I am able to meet and face this cabal.'

'Is it a cabal?' asked her ladyship, looking at him with a gaze that searched his soul. 'Can you meet their charges? Can you live down this hideous accusation, and hold up your head as a man of honour?'

The sensualist's blue eyes nervously shunned that look of earnest interrogation. His lips answered the wife's spoken question with a lie, a lie made manifest by the expression of his countenance.

'I am not afraid,' he said.

His wife answered not a word. She was assured that the charges were true, and that the battered rake who shivered over the fire had neither courage nor ability to face his accusers. She saw the whole fabric of her life in ruins, her son the penniless successor to a tarnished name. There was silence for some minutes. Lady Maulevrier sat with lowered eyelids looking at the fire, deep in painful thought. Two perpendicular wrinkles upon her broad white forehead--so calm, so unclouded in society--told of gnawing cares. Then she stole a look at her husband, as he reclined in his arm-chair, his head lying back against the cushions in listless repose, his eyes looking vacantly at the window, whence he could see only the rain-blurred fronts of opposite houses, blank, dull windows, grey slated roofs, against a leaden sky.

He had been a handsome man, and he was handsome still, albeit premature decay, the result of an evil life, was distinctly marked in his faded face. The dull, yellow tint of the complexion, the tarnished dimness of the large blue eyes, the discontented droop of the lips, the languor of the attitude, the pallid transparency of the wasted hands, all told of a life worn threadbare, energies exhausted, chances thrown away, a mind abandoned to despair.

'You look very ill,' said his wife, after that long blank interval, which marked so unnatural an apathy between husband and wife meeting after so long a severance.

'I am very ill. I have been worried to death--surrounded by rogues and liars--the victim of a most infernal conspiracy.' He spoke hurriedly, growing whiter and more tremulous as he went on.

'Don't talk about it. You agitate yourself to no purpose,' said Lady Maulevrier, with a tranquillity which seemed heartless yet which might be the result of suppressed feeling. 'If you are to face this scandal firmly and boldly next January, you must try to recover physical strength in the meanwhile. Mental energy may come with better health.'

'I shall never be any better,' said Lord Maulevrier, testily; 'that infernal climate has shattered my constitution.'

'Two or three months of perfect rest and good nursing will make a new man of you. I have arranged that we shall go straight from here to Fellside. No one can plague you there with that disguised impertinence called sympathy. You can give all your thoughts to the ordeal before you, and be ready to meet your accusers. Fortunately, you have no Burke against you.'

'Fellside? You think of going to Fellside?'

'Yes. You know how fond I am of that place. I little thought when you settled it upon me--a cottage in Westmoreland with fifty acres of garden and meadow--so utterly insignificant--that I should ever like it better than any of your places.'

'A charming retreat in summer; but we have never wintered there? What put it into your head to go there at such a season as this? Why, I daresay the snow is on the tops of the hills already.'

'It is the only place I know where you will not be watched and talked about,' replied Lady Maulevrier. 'You will be out of the eye of the world. I should think that consideration would weigh more with you than two or three degrees of the thermometer.'

'I detest cold,' said the Earl, 'and in my weak health----'

'We will take care of you,' answered her ladyship; and in the discussion which followed she bore herself so firmly that her husband was fain to give way.

How could a disgraced and ruined man, broken in health and spirits, contest the mere details of life with a high-spirited woman ten years his junior?

The Earl wanted to go to London, and remain there at least a week, but this her ladyship strenuously opposed. He must see his lawyer, he urged; there were steps to be taken which could be taken only under legal advice--counsel to be retained. If this lying invention of Satan were really destined to take the form of a public trial, he must be prepared to fight his foes on their own ground.

'You can make all your preparations at Fellside,' answered his wife, resolutely. 'I have seen Messrs. Rigby and Rider, and your own particular ally, Rigby, will go to you at Fellside whenever you want him.'

'That is not like my being on the spot,' said his lordship, nervously, evidently much disconcerted by her ladyship's firmness, but too feeble in mind and body for a prolonged contest.

'I ought to be on the spot. I am not without influence; I have friends, men in power.'

'Surely you are not going to appeal to friendship in order to vindicate your honour. These charges are true or false. If they are false your own manhood, your own rectitude, can face them and trample upon them, unaided by back-stairs influence. If they are true, no one can help you.'

'I think you, at least, ought to know that they are as false as hell,' retorted the Earl, with an attempt to maintain his dignity.

'I have acted as if I so believed,' replied his wife. 'I have lived as if there were no such slanders in the air. I have steadily ignored every report, every insinuation--have held my head as high as if I knew you were immaculate.'

'I expected as much from you,' answered the Earl, coolly. 'If I had not known you were a woman of sense I should not have married you.'

This was his utmost expression of gratitude. His next remarks had reference solely to his own comfort. Where were his rooms? at what hour were they to dine? And hereupon he rang for his valet, a German Swiss, and a servant out of a thousand.

CHAPTER III.
ON THE WRONG ROAD.

Lord and Lady Maulevrier left Southampton next morning, posting. They took two servants in the rumble, Steadman and the footman. Steadman was to valet his lordship, the footman to be useful in all emergencies of the journey. The maid and the valet were to travel by heavy coach, with the luggage--her ladyship dispensing with all personal attendance during the journey.

The first day took them to Rugby, whither they travelled across country by Wallingford and Oxford. The second day took them to Lichfield. Lord Maulevrier was out of health and feeble, and grumbled a good deal about the fatigue of the journey, the badness of the weather, which was dull and cold, east winds all day, and a light frost morning and night. As they progressed northward the sky looked grayer, the air became more biting. His lordship insisted upon the stages being shortened. He lay in bed at his hotel till noon, and was seldom ready to start till two o'clock. He could see no reason for haste; the winter would be long enough in all conscience at Fellside. He complained of mysterious aches and pains, described himself in the presence of hotel-keepers and headwaiters as a mass of maladies. He was nervous, irritable, intensely disagreeable. Lady Maulevrier bore his humours with unwavering patience, and won golden opinions from all sorts of people by her devotion to a husband whose blighted name was the common talk of England. Everybody, even in distant provincial towns, had heard of the scandal against the Governor of Madras; and everybody looked at the sallow, faded Anglo-Indian with morbid curiosity. His lordship, sensitive on all points touching his own ease and comfort, was keenly conscious of this unflattering inquisitiveness.

The journey, protracted by Lord Maulevrier's languor and ill-health, dragged its slow length along for nearly a fortnight; until it seemed to Lady Maulevrier as if they had been travelling upon those dismal, flat, unpicturesque roads for months. Each day was so horribly like yesterday. The same hedgerows and flat fields, and passing glimpse of river or canal. The same absence of all beauty in the landscape--the same formal hotel rooms, and smirking landladies--and so on till they came to Lancaster, after which the country became more interesting--hills arose in the background. Even the smoky manufacturing towns through which they passed without stopping, were less abominable than the level monotony of the Midland counties.

But now as they drew nearer the hills the weather grew colder, snow was spoken of, and when they got into Westmoreland the mountain-peaks gleamed whitely against a lead-coloured sky.

'You ought not to have brought me here in such weather,' complained the Earl, shivering in his sables, as he sat in his corner of the travelling chariot, looking discontentedly at the gloomy landscape. 'What is to become of us if we are caught in a snowstorm?'

'We shall have no snow worth talking about before we are safely housed at Fellside, and then we can defy the elements,' said Lady Maulevrier, coolly.

They slept that night at Oxenholme, and started next morning, under a clean, bright sky, intending to take luncheon at Windermere, and to be at home by night-fall.

But by the time they got to Windermere the sky had changed to a dark grey, and the people at the hotel prophesied a heavy fall before night, and urged the Earl and Countess to go no further that day. The latter part of the road to Fellside was rough and hilly. If there should be a snowstorm the horses would never be able to drag the carriage up the steepest bit of the way. Here, however, Lord Maulevrier's obstinacy came into play. He would not endure another night at an hotel so near his own house. He was sick to death of travelling, and wanted to be at rest among comfortable surroundings.

'It was murder to bring me here,' he said to his wife. 'If I had gone to Hastings I should have been a new man by this time. As it is I am a great deal worse than when I landed.'

Everyone at the hotel noticed his lordship's white and haggard looks. He had been known there as a young man in the bloom of health and strength, and his decay was particularly obvious to these people.

'I saw death in his face,' the landlord said, afterwards.

Every one, even her ladyship's firmness and good sense, gave way before the invalid's impatience. At three in the afternoon they left the hotel, with four horses, to make the remaining nineteen miles of the way in one stage. They had not been on the road half an hour before the snow began to fall thickly, whitening everything around them, except the lake, which showed a dark leaden surface at the bottom of the slope along the edge of which they were travelling. Too sullen for speech, Lord Maulevrier sat back in his corner, with his sable cloak drawn up to his chin, his travelling cap covering head and ears, his eyes contemplating the whitening world with a weary anger. His wife watched the landscape as long as she could, but the snow soon began to darken all the air, and she could see nothing save that blank blinding fall.

Half-way to Fellside there was a point where two roads met, one leading towards Grasmere, the other towards the village of Great Langdale, a cluster of humble habitations in the heart of the hills. When the horses had struggled as far as this point, the snow was six inches deep on the road, and made a thick curtain around them as it fell. By this time the Earl had dozed off to sleep.

He woke an hour after, let down the window, which let in a snow-laden gust, and tried to pierce the gloom without.

'As black as Erebus!' he exclaimed, 'but we ought to be close at home by this time. Yes, thank God, there are the lights.'

The carriage drew up a minute afterwards, and Steadman came to the door.

'Very sorry, my lord. The horses must have taken a wrong turn after we crossed the bridge. And now the men say they can't go back to Fellside unless we can get fresh horses; and I'm afraid there's no chance of that here.'

'Here!' exclaimed the Earl, 'what do you mean by here? Where the devil are we?'

'Great Langdale, my lord.'

A door opened and let out a flood of light--the red light of a wood fire, the pale flame of a candle--upon the snowy darkness, revealing the panelled hall of a neat little rustic inn: an eight-day clock ticking in the corner, a black and white sheepdog coming out at his master's heels to investigate the travellers. To the right of the door showed the light of a window, sheltered by a red curtain, behind which the chiefs of the village were enjoying their evening.

'Have you any post-horses?' asked the Earl, discontentedly, as the landlord stood on the threshold, shading the candle with his hand. 'No, sir. We don't keep post-horses.'

'Of course not. I knew as much before I asked,' said the Earl.

'We are fixed in this dismal hole for the night, I suppose. How far are we from Fellside?'

'Seven miles,' answered the landlord. 'I beg your pardon, my lord; I didn't know it was your lordship,' he added, hurriedly. 'We're in sore trouble, and it makes a man daft-like; but if there's anything we can do----'

'Is there no hope of getting on, Steadman?' asked the Earl, cutting short these civilities.

'Not with these horses, my lord.'

'And you hear we can't get any others. Is there any farmer about here who could lend us a pair of carriage horses?'

The landlord knew of no such person.

'Then we must stop here till to-morrow morning. What infernal fools those post-boys must be,' protested Lord Maulevrier.

James Steadman apologised for the postilions, explaining that when they came to the critical point of their journey, where the road branched off to the Langdales, the snow was falling so thickly, the whole country was so hidden in all-pervading whiteness, that even he, who knew the way so well, could give no help to the drivers. He could only trust to the instinct of local postilions and local horses; and instinct had proved wrong.

The travellers alighted, and were ushered into a not uncomfortable-looking parlour; very low as to the ceiling, very old-fashioned as to the furniture, but spot-lessly clean, and enlivened by a good fire, to which his lordship drew near, shivering and muttering discontentedly to himself.

'We might be worse off,' said her ladyship, looking round the bright little room, which pleased her better than many a state apartment in the large hotels at which they had stopped.

'Hardly, unless we were out on the moor,' grumbled her husband. 'I am sick to death of this ill-advised, unreasonable journey. I am at a loss to imagine your motive in bringing me here. You must have had a motive.'

'I had,' answered Lady Maulevrier, with a freezing look. 'I wanted to get you out of the way. I told you that plainly enough at Southampton.'

'I don't see why I should be hurried away and hidden,' said Lord Maulevrier. 'I must face my accusers, sooner or later.'

'Of course. The day of reckoning must come. But in the meantime have you no delicacy? Do you want to be pointed at everywhere?'

'All I know is that I am very ill,' answered her husband, 'and that this wretched journey has made me twenty years older.'

'We shall be safe at home before noon to-morrow, and you can have Horton to set you right again. You know you always believed in his skill.'

'Horton is a clever fellow enough, as country doctors go; but at Hastings I could have had the best physicians in London to see me,' grumbled his lordship.

The rustic maid-servant came in to lay the table, assisted by her ladyship's footman, who looked a good deal too tall for the room.

'I shan't dine,' said the Earl. 'I am a great deal too ill and cold. Light a fire in my room, girl, and send Steadman to me'--this to the footman, who hastened to obey. 'You can send me up a basin of soup presently. I shall go to bed at once.'

He left the room without another word to his wife, who sat by the hearth staring thoughtfully at the cheery wood fire. Presently she looked up, and saw that the man and maid were going on with their preparations for dinner.

'I do not care about dining alone,' said her ladyship. 'We lunched at Windermere, and I have no appetite. You can clear away those things, and bring me some tea.'

When the table furniture had been cleared, and a neat little tea-tray set upon the white cloth, Lady Maulevrier drew her chair to the table, and took out her pocket-book, from which she produced a letter. This she read more than once, meditating profoundly upon its contents.

'I am very sorry he has come home,' wrote her correspondent, 'and yet if he had stayed in India there must have been an investigation on the spot. A public inquiry is inevitable, and the knowledge of his arrival in the country will precipitate matters. From all I hear I much fear that there is no chance of the result being favourable to him. You have asked me to write the unvarnished truth, to be brutal even, remember. His delinquencies are painfully notorious, and I apprehend that the last sixpence he owns will be answerable. His landed estate I am told can also be confiscated, in the event of an impeachment at the bar of the House of Lords, as in the Warren Hastings case. But as yet nobody seems clear as to the form which the investigation will take. In reply to your inquiry as to what would have happened if his lordship had died on the passage home, I believe I am justified in saying the scandal would have been allowed to die with him. He has contrived to provoke powerful animosities both in the Cabinet and at the India House, and there is, I fear, an intention to pursue the inquiry to the bitter end.'

Assurances of the writer's sympathy followed these harsh truths. But to this polite commonplace her ladyship paid no attention. Her mind was intent on hard facts, the dismal probabilities of the near future.

'If he had died upon the passage home!' she repeated. 'Would to God that he had so died, and that my son's name and fortune could be saved.'

The innocent child who had never given her an hour's care; the one creature she loved with all the strength of her proud nature--his future was to be blighted by his father's misdoings-overshadowed by shame and dishonour in the very dawn of life. It was a wicked wish--an unnatural wish to find room in a woman's breast; but the wish was there. Would to God he had died before the ship touched an English port.

But he was living, and would have to face his accusers--and she, his wife, must give him all the help she could.

She sat long by the waning fire. She took nothing but a cup of tea, although the landlady had sent in substantial accompaniments to the tea-tray in the shape of broiled ham, new-laid eggs, and hot cakes, arguing that a traveller on such a night must be hungry, albeit disinclined for a ceremonious dinner. She had been sitting for nearly an hour in almost the same attitude, when there came a knock at the door, and, on being bidden to enter, the landlady came in, with some logs in her apron, under pretence of replenishing the fire.

'I was afraid your fire must be getting low, and that you'd be amost starved, my lady,' she said, as she put on the logs, and swept up the ashes on the hearth. 'Such a dreadful night. So early in the year, too. I'm thinking we shall have a gay hard winter.'

'That does not always follow,' said Lady Maulevrier. 'Has Steadman come downstairs?'

'Yes, my lady. He told me to tell your ladyship that his lordship is pretty comfortable, and hopes to pass a good night.'

'I am glad to hear it. You can give me another room, I suppose. It would be better for his lordship not to be disturbed, as he is very much out of health.'

'There is another room, my lady, but it's very small.'

'I don't mind how small, if it is clean and airy.'

'Yes, my lady. I am thankful to say you won't find dirt or stuffiness anywhere in this house. His lordship do look mortal badly,' added the landlady, shaking her head dolefully; 'and I remember him such a fine young gentleman, when he used to come down the Rothay with the otter hounds, running along the bank--joomping in and out of the beck--up to his knees in the water--and now to see him, so white and mashiated, and broken-down like, in the very prime of life, all along of living out in a hot country, among blackamoors, which is used to it--poor, ignorant creatures--and never knew no better. It must be a hard trial for you, my lady.'

'It is a hard trial.'

'Ah! we all have our trials, rich and poor,' sighed the woman, who desired nothing better than to be allowed to unbosom her woes to the grand looking lady in the fur-bordered cloth pelisse, with beautiful dark hair piled up in clustering masses above a broad white forehead, and slender white hands on which diamonds flashed and glittered in the firelight, an unaccustomed figure by that rustic hearth.

'We all have our trials--high and low.'

'That reminds me,' said Lady Maulevrier, looking up at her, 'your husband said you were in trouble. What did that mean?'

'Sickness in the house, my lady. A brother of mine that went to America to make his fortune, and seemed to be doing so well for the first five or six years, and wrote home such beautiful letters, and then left off writing all at once, and we made sure as he was dead, and never got a word from him for ten years, and just three weeks ago he drops in upon us as we was sitting over our tea between the lights, looking as white as a ghost. I gave a shriek when I saw him, for I was regular scared out of my senses. "Robert's ghost!" I cried; but it was Robert himself, come home to us to die. And he's lying upstairs now, with so little life in him that I expect every breath to be his last.'

'What is his complaint?'

'Apathy, my lady. Dear, dear, that's not it. I never do remember the doctor's foreign names.'

'Atrophy,' perhaps.

'Yes, my lady, that was it. Happen such crack-jaw words come easy to a scholar like your ladyship.'

'Does the doctor give no hope?'

'Well, no, my lady. He don't go so far as to say there's no hope, though Robert has been badly so long. It all depends, he says, upon the rallying power of the constitution. The lungs are not gone, and the heart is not diseased. If there's rallying power, Robert will come round, and if there isn't he'll sink. But the doctor says nature will have to make an effort. But I have my own idea about the case,' added the landlady, with a sigh.

'What is your idea?'

'That our Robert was marked for death when he came into this house, and that he meant what he said when he spoke of coming home to die. Things had gone against him for the last ten years in America. He married and took his wife out to a farm in the Bush, and thought to make a good thing out of farming with the bit of brass he'd saved at heeam. But America isn't Gert Langdale, you see, my lady, and his knowledge stood him in no stead in the Bush; and first he lost his money, and he fashed himself terrible about that, and then he lost a child or two, and then he lost his wife, and he came back to us a broken-hearted man, with no wish to live. The doctor may call it atrophy, but I will call it what the Scripture calls it, a broken and a wounded spirit.'

'Who is your doctor?'

'Mr. Evans, of Ambleside.'

'That little half-blind old man!' exclaimed her ladyship. 'Surely you have no confidence in him?'

'Not much, my lady. But I don't believe all the doctors in London could do anything for Robert. Good nursing will bring him round if anything can; and he gets that, I can assure your ladyship. He's my only brother, the only kith and kin that's left to me, and he and I were gay fond of each other when he was young. You may be sure I don't spare any trouble, and my good man thinks the best of his larder or his celler hardly good enough for Robert.'

'I am sure you are kind good people,' replied her ladyship gently; 'but I should have thought Mr. Horton, of Grasmere, could have done more than old Evans. However, you know best. I hope his lordship is not going to add to your cares by being laid up here, but he looked very ill this evening.'

'He did, my lady, mortal bad.'

'However, we must hope for the best. Steadman is a splendid servant in illness. He nursed my father for years. Will you tell him to come to me, if you please? I want to hear what he thinks of his lordship, and to discuss the chances of our getting home early to-morrow.'

The landlady retired, and summoned Mr. Steadman, who was enjoying his modest glass of grog in front of the kitchen fire. He had taught himself to dispense with the consolations of tobacco, lest he should at any time make himself obnoxious to her ladyship.

Steadman was closeted with Lady Maulevrier for the next half-hour, during which his lordship's condition was gravely discussed. When he left the sitting-room he told the landlord to be sure and feed the post-horses well, and make them comfortable for the night, so that they might be ready for the drive to Fellside early next morning.

'Do you think his lordship will be well enough to travel?' asked the landlord.

'He has made up his mind to get home--ill or well,' answered Steadman. 'He has wasted about a week by his dawdling ways on the road; and now he's in a fever to get to Fellside.'

CHAPTER IV.
THE LAST STAGE.

The post-horses--which had been well fed, but accommodated somewhat poorly in stable and barn--were quite ready to go on next morning; but Lord Maulevrier was not able to leave his room, where her ladyship remained in close attendance upon him. The hills and valleys were white with snow, but there was none falling, and Mr. Evans, the elderly surgeon from Ambleside, rode over to Great Langdale on his elderly cob to look at Robert Haswell, and was called in to see Lord Maulevrier. Her ladyship had spoken lightly of his skill on the previous evening, but any doctor is better than none, so this feeble little personage was allowed to feel his lordship's pulse, and look at his lordship's tongue.

His opinion, never too decidedly given, was a little more hazy than usual on this occasion, perhaps because of a certain awfulness, to unaccustomed eyes, in Lady Maulevrier's proud bearing. He said that his lordship was low, very low, and that the pulse was more irregular than he liked, but he committed himself no further than this, and went away, promising to send such pills and potions as were appropriate to the patient's condition.

A boy rode the same pony over to Langdale later in the afternoon with the promised medicines.

Throughout the short winter day, which seemed terribly long in the stillness and solitude of Great Langdale, Lady Maulevrier kept watch in the sick-room, Steadman going in and out in constant attendance upon his master--save for one half-hour only, which her ladyship passed in the parlour below, in conversation with the landlady, a very serious conversation, as indicated by Mrs. Smithson's grave and somewhat troubled looks when she left her ladyship; but a good deal of her trouble may have been caused by her anxiety about her brother, who was pronounced by the doctor to be 'much the same.'

At eleven o'clock that night a mounted messenger was sent off to Ambleside in hot haste to fetch Mr. Evans, who came to the inn to find Lady Maulevrier kneeling beside her husband's bed, while Steadman stood with a troubled countenance at a respectful distance.

The room was dimly lighted by a pair of candles burning on a table near the window, and at some distance from the old four-post bedstead, shaded by dark moreen curtains. The surgeon looked round the room, and then fumbled in his pockets for his spectacles, without the aid of which the outside world presented itself to him under a blurred and uncertain aspect.

He put on his spectacles, and moved towards the bed; but the first glance in that direction showed him what had happened. The outline of the rigid figure under the coverlet looked like a sculptured effigy upon a tomb. A sheet was drawn over the face of death.

'You are too late to be of any use, Mr. Evans,' murmured Steadman, laying his hand upon the doctor's sleeve and drawing him away towards the door.

They went softly on to the landing, off which opened the door of that other sick-room where the landlady's brother was lying.

'When did this happen?'

'A quarter of an hour after the messenger rode off to fetch you,' answered Steadman. 'His lordship lay all the afternoon in a heavy sleep, and we thought he was going on well; but after dark there was a difficulty in his breathing which alarmed her ladyship, and she insisted upon you being sent for. The messenger had hardly been gone a quarter of an hour when his lordship woke suddenly, muttered to himself in a curious way, gave just one long drawn sigh, and--and all was over. It was a terrible shock for her ladyship.'

'Indeed it must have been,' murmured the village doctor. 'It is a great surprise to me. I knew Lord Maulevrier was low, very low, the pulse feeble and intermittent; but I had no fear of anything of this kind. It is very sudden.'

'Yes, it is awfully sudden,' said Steadman, and then he murmured in the doctor's ear, 'You will give the necessary certificate, I hope, with as little trouble to her ladyship as possible. This is a dreadful blow, and she----'

'She shall not be troubled. The body will be removed to-morrow, I suppose.'

'Yes. He must be buried from his own house. I sent a second messenger to Ambleside for the undertaker. He will be here very soon, no doubt, and if the shell is ready by noon to-morrow, the body can be removed then. I have arranged to get her ladyship away to-night.'

'So late? After midnight?'

'Why not? She cannot stay in this small house--so near the dead. There is a moon, and there is no snow falling, and we are within seven miles of Fellside.'

The doctor had nothing further to say against the arrangement, although such a drive seemed to him a somewhat wild and reckless proceeding. Mr. Steadman's grave, self-possessed manner answered all doubts. Mr. Evans filled in the certificate for the undertaker, drank a glass of hot brandy and water, and remounted his nag, in nowise relishing his midnight ride, but consoling himself with the reflection that he would be handsomely paid for his trouble.

An hour later Lady Maulevrier's travelling carriage stood ready in the stable yard, in the deep shadow of wall and gables. It was at Steadman's order that the carriage waited for her ladyship at an obscure side door, rather than in front of the inn.

An east wind was blowing keenly along the mountain road, and the careful Stead-man was anxious his mistress should not be exposed to that chilly blast.

There was some delay, and the four horses jingled their bits impatiently, and then the door of the inn opened, a feeble light gleamed in the narrow passage with-in, Steadman stood ready to assist her ladyship, there was a bustle, a confusion of dark figures on the threshold, a huddled mass of cloaks and fur wraps was lifted into the carriage, the door was clapped to, the horses went clattering out of the yard, turned sharply into the snowy road, and started at a swinging pace towards the dark sullen bulk of Loughrigg Fell.

The moon was shining upon Elterwater in the valley yonder--the mountain ridges, the deep gorges below those sullen heights, looked back where the shadow of night enfolded them, but all along the snow-white road the silver light shone full and clear, and the mountain way looked like a path through fairyland.

CHAPTER V.
FORTY YEARS AFTER.

'What a horrid day!' said Lady Mary, throwing down her book with a yawn, and looking out of the deep bay window into a world of mountain and lake which was clouded over by a dense veil of rain and dull grey mist; such rain as one sees only in a lake district, a curtain of gloom which shuts off sky and distance, and nar-rows the world to one solitary dwelling, suspended amidst cloud and water, like another ark in a new deluge.

Rain--such rain as makes out-of-door exercise impossible--was always an af-fliction to Lady Mary Haselden. Her delight was in open air and sunshine--fishing in the lake and rivers--sitting in some sheltered hollow of the hills more fitting for an eagle's nest than for the occupation of a young lady, trying to paint those ever-varying, unpaintable mountain peaks, which change their hues with every change of the sky--swimming, riding, roving far and wide over hill and heather--pleasures all more or less masculine in their nature, and which were a subject of regret with Lady Maulevrier.

Lady Lesbia was of a different temper. She loved ease and elegance, the gra-

cious luxuries of life. She loved art and music, but not to labour hard at either. She
played and sang a little--excellently within that narrow compass which she had
allotted to herself--played Mendelssohn's 'Lieder' with finished touch and faultless
phrasing, sang Heine's ballads with consummate expression. She painted not at all.
Why should anyone draw or paint indifferently, she asked, when Providence has
furnished the world with so many great painters in the past and present? She could
not understand Mary's ardent desire to do the thing herself,--to be able with her
own pencil and her own brush to reproduce the lakes and valleys, the wild brown
hills she loved so passionately. Lesbia did not care two straws for the lovely lake district amidst which she had been reared,--every pike and force, every beck and gill
whereof was distinctly dear to her younger sister. She thought it a very hard thing
to have spent so much of her life at Fellside, a trial that would have hardly been endurable if it were not for grandmother. Grandmother and Lesbia adored each other.
Lesbia was the one person for whom Lady Maulevrier's stateliness was subjugated
by perfect love. To all the rest of the world the Countess was marble, but to Lesbia
she was wax. Lesbia could mould her as she pleased; but happily Lesbia was not the
kind of young person to take advantage of this privilege; she was thoroughly ductile
or docile, and had no desire, at present, which ran counter to her grandmother.

Lesbia was a beauty. In her nineteenth year she was a curious reproduction in
face and figure, expression and carriage, of that Lady Diana Angersthorpe who five
and forty years ago fluttered the dove-cots of St. James's and Mayfair by her brilliant beauty and her keen intelligence. There in the panelled drawing-room at Fellside hung Harlow's portrait of Lady Diana in her zenith, in a short-waisted, white
satin frock, with large puffed gauze sleeves, through which the perfect arm showed
dimly. Standing under that picture Lady Lesbia looked as if she had stepped out of
the canvas. She was to be painted by Millais next year. Lady Maulevrier said, when
she had been introduced, and society was beginning to talk about her: for Lady
Maulevrier made up her mind five or six years ago that Lesbia should be the reigning beauty of her season. To this end she had educated and trained her, furnishing
her with all those graces best calculated to please and astonish society. She was too
clever a woman not to discover Lesbia's shallowness and lack of all great gifts, save
that one peerless dower of perfect beauty. She knew exactly what Lesbia could be
trained to do; and to this end Lesbia had been educated; and to this end Lady Mau-

levrier brought down to Fellside the most accomplished of Hanoverian governesses, who had learned French in Paris, and had toiled in the educational mill with profit to herself and her pupils for a quarter of a century. To this lady the Countess entrusted the education of her granddaughters' minds, while for their physical training she provided another teacher in the person of a clever little Parisian dancing mistress, who had set up at the West-End of London as a teacher of dancing and calisthenics, and had utterly failed to find pupils enough to pay her rent and keep her modest *pot-au-feu* going. Mademoiselle Thiebart was very glad to exchange the uncertainties of a first floor in North Audley Street for the comfort and security of Fellside Manor, with a salary of one hundred and fifty pounds a year.

Both Fraeulein and Mademoiselle had been quick to discover that Lady Lesbia was the apple of her grandmother's eye, while Lady Mary was comparatively an outsider.

So it came about that Mary's education was in somewise a mere picking-up of the crumbs which fell from Lesbia's table, and that she was allowed in a general way to run wild. She was much quicker at any intellectual exercise than Lesbia. She learned the lessons that were given her at railroad speed, and rattled off her exercises with a slap-dash penmanship which horrified the neat and niggling Fraeulein, and then rushed off to the lake or mountain, and by this means grew browner and browner, and more indelibly freckled day by day, thus widening the gulf between herself and her beauty sister.

But it is not to be supposed that because Lesbia was beautiful, Mary was plain. This is very far from the truth. Mary had splendid hazel eyes, with a dancing light in them when she smiled, ruddy auburn hair, white teeth, a deeply-dimpled chin, and a vivacity and archness of expression, which served only in her present state of tutelage for the subjugation of old women and shepherd boys. Mary had been taught to believe that her chances of future promotion were of the smallest; that nobody would ever talk of her, or think of her by-and-by when she in her turn would make her appearance in London society, and that it would be a very happy thing for her if she were so fortunate as to attract the attention of a fashionable physician, a Canon of Westminster or St. Paul's, or a barrister in good practice.

Mary turned up her pert little nose at this humdrum lot.

'I would much rather spend all my life among these dear hills than marry a nobody in London,' she said, fearless of that grand old lady at whose frown so many people shivered. 'If you don't think people will like me and admire me--a little-- you had better save yourself the trouble of taking me to London. I don't want to play second fiddle to my sister.'

'You are a very impertinent person, and deserve to be taken at your word,' replied my lady, scowling at her; 'but I have no doubt before you are twenty you will tell another story.'

'Oh!' said Mary, now just turned seventeen, 'then I am not to come out till I am twenty.'

'That will be soon enough,' answered the Countess. 'It will take you as long to get rid of those odious freckles. And no doubt by that time Lesbia will have made a brilliant marriage.'

And now on this rainy July morning these two girls, neither of whom had any serious employment for her life, or any serious purpose in living, wasted the hours, each in her own fashion.

Lesbia reclined upon a cushioned seat in the deep embrasure of a Tudor window, her *pose* perfection--it was one of many such attitudes which Mademoiselle had taught her, and which by assiduous training had become a second nature. Poor Mademoiselle, having finished her mission and taught Lesbia all she could teach, had now departed to a new and far less luxurious situation in a finishing school at Passy; but Fraeulein Mueller was still retained, as watch-dog and duenna.

Lesbia's pale blue morning gown harmonised exquisitely with a complexion of lilies and roses, violet eyes, and golden-brown hair. Her features were distinguished by that perfect chiselling which gave such a haughty grace to her grandmother's countenance, even at sixty-seven years of age--a loveliness which, like the sculptured marble it resembles, is unalterable by time. Lesbia was reading Keats. It was her habit to read the poets, carefully and deliberately, taking up one at a time, and duly laying a volume aside when she found herself mistress of its contents. She had no passion for poetry, but it was an elegant leisurely kind of reading which suited her languid temperament. Moreover, her grandmother had told her that an easy familiarity with the great poets is of all knowledge that which best qualifies a woman to shine in conversation, without offending the superior sex by any assumption of scholarship.

Mary was a very different class of reader; capricious, omniverous, tearing out the hearts of books, roaming from flower to flower in the fields of literature, loving old and new, romance and reality, novels, travels, plays, poetry, and never dwelling long on any one theme. Perhaps if Mary had lived in the bosom of a particularly sympathetic family she might have been reckoned almost a genius, so much of poetry and originality was there in her free unconventional character; but hitherto it had been Mary's mission in life to be snubbed, whereby she had acquired a very poor opinion of her own talents.

'Oh,' she cried with a desperate yawn, while Lesbia smiled her languid smile over Endymion, 'how I wished something would happen--anything to stir us out of this statuesque, sleeping-beauty state of being. I verily believe the spiders are all asleep in the ivy, and the mice behind the wainscot, and the horses in the stable.'

'What could happen?' asked Lesbia, with a gentle elevation of pencilled brows. 'Are not these lovely lines--

"And coverlids gold-tinted like the peach,   Or ripe October's faded marigolds,   Fell sleek about him in a thousand folds."

Faded marigolds! Is not that intensely sweet?'

'Very well for your sleepy Keats, but I don't suppose you would have noticed the passage if marigolds were not in fashion,' said Mary, with a touch of scorn. 'What could happen? Why a hundred things--an earthquake, flood, or fire. What could happen, do you say, Lesbia? Why Maulevrier might come home unexpectedly, and charm us out of this death-in-life.'

'He would occasion a good deal of unpleasantness if he did,' answered Lesbia, coldly. 'You know how angry he has made grandmother.'

'Because he keeps race-horses which have an unlucky knack of losing,' said Mary, dubiously. 'I suppose if his horses won, grandmother would rather approve?'

'Not at all. That would make hardly any difference, except that he would not ruin himself quite so quickly. Grandmother says that a young man who goes on the turf is sure to be ruined sooner or later. And then Maulevrier's habits are altogether wild and foolish. It is very hard upon grandmother, who has such noble ambition for all of us.'

'Not for me,' answered Mary smiling. 'Her views about me are very humble.

She considers that I shall be most fortunate if a doctor or a lawyer condescend to like me well enough to make me an offer. He might make me the offer without liking me, for the sake of hearing himself and his wife announced as Mr. and Lady Mary Snooks at dinner parties. That would be too horrid! But I daresay such things have happened.'

'Don't talk nonsense, Mary,' said Lesbia, loftily. 'There is no reason why you should not make a really good marriage, if you follow grandmother's advice and don't affect eccentricity.'

'I don't affect eccentricity, but I'm afraid I really am eccentric,' murmured Mary, meekly, 'for I like so many things I ought not to like, and detest so many things which I ought to admire.'

'I daresay you will have tamed down a little before you are presented,' said Lesbia, carelessly.

She could not even affect a profound interest in anyone but herself. She had a narrowness of mental vision which prevented her looking beyond the limited circle of her own pleasures, her own desires, her own dreams and hopes. She was one of those strictly correct young women who was not likely to do much harm in the world but who was just as unlikely to do any good. Mary sighed, and went back to her book, a bulky volume of travels, and tried to lose herself in the sandy wastes of Africa, and to be deeply interested in the sources of the Congo, not, in her heart of hearts, caring a straw whether that far-away river comes from the mountains of the moon, or from the moon itself. To-day she could not pin her mind to pages which might have interested her at another time. Her thoughts were with Lord Maulevrier, that fondly-loved only brother, just seven years her senior, who had taken to race-horses and bad ways, and seemed to be trying his hardest to dissipate the splendid fortune which his grandmother, the dowager Countess, had nursed so judiciously during his long minority. Maulevrier and Mary had always been what the young man called 'no end of chums.'

He called her his own brown-eyed Molly, much to the annoyance of Lady Maulevrier and Lesbia; and Mary's life was all gladness when Maulevrier was at Fellside. She devoted herself wholly to his amusements, rode and drove with him, followed on her pony when he went otter hunting, and very often abandoned the pony to the care of some stray mountain youth in order to join the hunters, and go leaping from stone to stone on the margin of the stream, and occasionally, in moments of wild excitement, when the hounds were in full cry, splashing in and out of the water, like a naiad in a neat little hunting-habit.

Mary looked after Maulevrier's stable when he was away, and had supreme command of a kennel of fox-terriers which cost her brother more money than the Countess would have cared to know; for in the wide area of Lady Maulevrier's ambition there was no room for two hundred guinea fox-terriers, were they never so perfect.

Altogether Mary's life was a different life when her brother was at home; and in his absence the best part of her days were spent in thinking about him and fulfilling the duties of her position as his representative in stable and kennel, and among certain rustics in the district, chiefly of the sporting type, who were Maulevrier's chosen allies or *proteges*.

Never, perhaps, had two girls of patrician lineage lived a more secluded life than Lady Maulevrier's granddaughters. They had known no pleasures beyond the narrow sphere of home and home friends. They had never travelled--they had seen hardly anything of the outside world. They had never been to London or Paris, or to any city larger than York; and their visits to that centre of dissipation had been of the briefest, a mere flash of mild gaiety, a horticultural show or an oratorio, and back by express train, closely guarded by governess and footmen, to Fellside. In the autumn, when the leaves were falling in the wooded grounds of Fellside, the young ladies were sent, still under guardianship of governesses and footmen, to some quiet seaside resort between Alnwick and Edinburgh, where Mary lived the wild free life she loved, roaming about the beach, boating, shrimping, seaweed-gathering, making hard work for the governesses and footmen who had been sent in charge of her.

Lady Maulevrier never accompanied her granddaughters on these occasions. She was a vigorous old woman, straight as a dart, slim as a girl, active in her degree as any young athlete among those hills, and she declared that she never felt the need of change of air. The sodden shrubberies, the falling leaves, did her no harm. Never within the memory of this generation had she left Fellside. Her love of this mountain retreat was a kind of *culte*. She had come here broken spirited, perhaps broken hearted, bringing her dead husband from the little inn at Great Langdale forty years ago, and she had hardly left the spot since that day.

In those days Fellside House was a very different kind of dwelling from the gracious modern Tudor mansion which now crowned and beautified the hill-side above Grasmere Lake. It was then an old rambling stone house, with queer little rooms and inconvenient passages, low ceilings, thatched gables, and all manner of strange nooks and corners. Lady Maulevrier was of too strictly conservative a temper to think of pulling down an old house which had been in her husband's family for generations. She left the original cottage undisturbed, and built her new house at right angles with it, connecting the two with a wide passage below and a handsome corridor above, so that access should be perfect in the event of her requiring the accommodation of the old quaint, low ceiled rooms for her family or her guests. During forty years no such necessity had ever arisen; but the old house, known as the south wing, was still left intact, the original furniture undisturbed, although the only occupants of the building were her ladyship's faithful old house-steward, James Steadman, and his elderly wife.

The house which Lady Maulevrier had built for herself and her grandchildren had not been created all at once, though the nucleus dating forty years back was a handsome building. She had added more rooms as necessity or fancy dictated, now a library with bedrooms over it, now a music room for Lady Lesbia and her grand piano--anon a billiard-room, as an agreeable surprise for Maulevrier when he came home after a tour in America. Thus the house had grown into a long low pile of Tudor masonry--steep gables, heavily mullioned casements, grey stone walls, curtained with the rich growth of passion-flower, magnolia, clematis, myrtle and roses--and all those flowers which thrive and flourish in that mild and sheltered spot.

The views from those mullioned casements were perfect. Switzerland could give hardly any more exquisite picture than that lake shut in by hills, grand and bold in their varied outlines, so rich in their colouring that the eye, dazzled with beauty, forgot to calculate the actual height of those craggy peaks and headlands, the mind forgot to despise them because they were not so lofty as Mont Blanc or the Matterhorn. The velvet sward of the hill sloped steeply downward from Lady Maulevrier's drawing-room windows to the road beside the lake, and this road was so hidden by the wooded screen which bounded her ladyship's grounds that the lake seemed to lie in the green heart of her gardens, a lovely, placid lake on summer days, reflecting the emerald hue of the surrounding hills, and looking like a smooth green meadow, which invited the foot passenger to cross it.

The house was approached by a winding carriage drive that led up and up and up from the road beside the lake, so screened and sheltered by shrubberies and pine woods, that the stranger knew not whither he was going, till he came upon an opening in the wood, and the stately Italian garden in front of a massive stone porch, through which he entered a spacious oak-panelled hall, and anon, descending a step or two, he found himself in Lady Maulevrier's drawing-room, and face to face with that divine view of the everlasting hills, the lake shining below him, bathed in sunlight.

Or if it were the stranger's evil fate to come in wet weather, he saw only a rain-blotted landscape--the blurred outlines of grey mountain peaks, scowling at him from the other side of a grey pool. But if the picture without were depressing, the picture within was always good to look upon, for those oak-panelled or tapestried rooms, communicating by richly-curtained doorways from drawing room to library, from library to billiard room, were as perfect as wealth and taste could make them. Lady Maulevrier argued that as there was but one house among all the possessions of her race which she cared to inhabit, she had a right to make that house beautiful, and she had spared nothing upon the beautification of Fellside; and yet she had spent much less than would have been squandered by any pleasure-loving dowager, restlessly roving from Piccadilly to the Engadine, from Pontresina to Nice or Monaco, winding up with Easter in Paris, and then back to Piccadilly. Her ladyship's friends wondered that she could care to bury herself alive in Westmoreland, and expatiated on the eccentricity of such a life; nay, those who had never seen Fellside argued that Lady Maulevrier had taken in her old age to hoarding, and that she pigged at a cottage in the Lake district, in order to swell a fortune which young Maulevrier would set about squandering as soon as she was in her coffin. But here they were wrong. It was not in Lady Maulevrier's nature to lead a sordid life in order to save money. Yet in these quiet years that were gone--starting with that golden nucleus which her husband was supposed to have brought home from India, obtained no one knows how, the Countess had amassed one of the largest fortunes possessed by any dowager in the peerage. She had it, and she held it, with a grasp that nothing but death could loosen; nay, that all-foreseeing mind of hers might contrive to cheat grim death itself, and to scheme a way for protecting this wealth, even when she who had gathered and garnered it should be mouldering in her grave. The entailed estates belonged to Maulevrier, were he never such a fool or spendthrift; but this fortune of the dowager's was her own, to dispose of as she pleased, and not a penny of it was likely to go to the young Earl.

Lady Maulevrier's pride and hopes were concentrated upon her granddaughter Lesbia. She should be the inheritress of this noble fortune--she should spread and widen the power of the Maulevrier race. Lesbia's son should link the family name with the name of his father; and if by any hazard of fate the present Earl should die young and childless, the old Countess's interest should be strained to the uttermost to obtain the title for Lesbia's offspring. Why should she not be Countess of Maulevrier in her own right? But in order to make this future possible the most important factor in the sum was yet to be found in the person of a husband for Lady Lesbia--a husband worthy of peerless beauty and exceptional wealth, a husband whose own fortune should be so important as to make him above suspicion. That was Lady Maulevrier's scheme--to wed wealth to wealth--to double or quadruple the fortune she had built up in the long slow years of her widowhood, and thus to make her granddaughter one of the greatest ladies in the land; for it need hardly be said that the man who was to wed Lady Lesbia must be her equal in wealth and lineage, if not her superior.

Lady Maulevrier was not a miser. She was liberal and benevolent to all who came within the circle of her life. Wealth for its own sake she valued not a jot. But she lived in an age in which wealth is power, and ambition was her ruling passion. As she had been ambitious for her husband in the days that were gone, she was now ambitious for her granddaughter. Time had intensified the keen eagerness of her mind. She had been disappointed, cruelly, bitterly, in the ambition of her youth. She had been made to drink the cup of shame and humiliation. But to this ambition of her old age she held with even greater tenacity. God help her if she should be disappointed here!

It is not to be supposed that so astute a schemer as Lady Maulevrier had not surveyed the marriage market in order to discover that fortunate youth who should be deemed worthy to become the winner of Lesbia's hand. Years ago, when Lesbia was still in the nursery, the dowager had made herself informed of the age, weight, and colours of every likely runner in the matrimonial stakes; or, in plainer words, had kept herself, by her correspondence with a few intimate friends, and her close study of the fashionable newspapers, thoroughly acquainted with the characters and exploits, the dispositions and antecedents, of those half-dozen elder sons, among whom she hoped to find Lesbia's lord and master. She knew her peerage by heart, and she knew the family history of every house recorded therein; the sins and weaknesses, the follies and losses of bygone years; the taints, mental and physical; the lateral branches and intermarriages; the runaway wives and unfaithful husbands; idiot sons or scrofulous daughters. She knew everything that was to be known about that aristocratic world into which she had been born sixty-seven years ago; and the sum-total of her knowledge was that there was one man whom she desired for her granddaughter's husband--one man, and one only, and into whose hands, when earth and sky should fade from her glazing eyes, she could be content to resign the sceptre of power.

There were no doubt half-a-dozen, or more, in the list of elder sons, who were fairly eligible. But this young man was the Achilles in the rank and file of chivalry, and her soul yearned to have him and no other for her darling.

Her soul yearned to him with a tenderness which was not all on Lesbia's account. Forty-nine years ago she had fondly loved his father--loved him and had been fain to renounce him; for Ronald Hollister, afterwards Earl of Hartfield, was then a younger son, and the two families had agreed that marriage between paupers was an impudent flying in the face of Providence, which must be put down with an iron hand. Lord Hartfield sent his son to Turkey in the diplomatic service; and the old dowager Lady Carrisbrook whisked her niece off to London, and kept her there, under watch and ward, till Lord Maulevrier proposed and was accepted by her. There should be no foolishness, no clandestine correspondence. The iron hand crushed two young hearts, and secured a brilliant future for the bodies which survived.

Fifteen years later Ronald's elder brother died unmarried. Ha abandoned that career of vagrant diplomacy which had taken him all over Europe, and as far as Washington, and re-appeared in London, the most elegant man of his era, but thoroughly *blase*. There were rumours of an unhappy attachment in the Faubourg Saint

Germain; of a tragedy at Petersburg. Society protested that Lord Hartfield would die a bachelor, as his brother died before him. The Hollisters are not a marrying family, said society. But six or seven years after his return to England Lord Hartfield married Lady Florence Ilmington, a beauty in her first season, and a very sweet but somewhat prudish young person. The marriage resulted in the birth of an heir, whose appearance upon this mortal stage was followed within a year by his father's exit. Hence the Hartfield property, always a fine estate, had been nursed and fattened during a long minority, and the present Lord Hartfield was reputed one of the richest young men of his time. He was also spoken of as a superior person, inheriting all his father's intellectual gifts, and having the reputation of being singularly free from the vices of profligate youth. He was neither prig nor pedant, and he was very popular in the best society; but he was not ashamed to let it be seen that his ambition soared higher than the fashionable world of turf and stable, cards and pigeon matches.

Though not of the gay world, nor in it, Lady Maulevrier had contrived to keep herself thoroughly *en rapport* with society. Her few chosen friends, with whom she corresponded on terms of perfect confidence, were among the best people in London--not the circulators of club-house canards, the pickers-up of second-hand gossip from the society papers, but actors in the comedy of high life, arbiters of fashion and taste, born and bred in the purple.

Last season Lord Hartfield's absence had cast a cloud over the matrimonial horizon. He had been a traveller for more than a year--Patagonia, Peru, the Pyramids, Japan, the North Pole--society cared not where--the fact that he was gone was all-sufficient. Bachelors a shade less eligible came to the front in his absence and became first favourites. Lady Maulevrier, well informed in advance, had deferred Lesbia's presentation till next season, when she was told Lord Hartfield would certainly re-appear. His plans had been made for return before Christmas; and it would seem that his scheme of life was laid down with as much precision as if he had been a prince of the blood royal. Thus it happened, to Lesbia's intense disgust, that her *debut* was deferred till the verge of her twentieth birthday. It would never do, Lady Maulevrier told herself, for the edge to be taken off the effect which Lesbia's beauty was to make on society during Lord Hartfield's absence. He must be there, on the spot, to see this star rise gently and slowly above society's horizon, and to mark how everybody bowed down and worshipped the new light.

'I shall be an old woman before I appear in society,' said Lesbia, petulantly; 'and I shall be like a wild woman of the woods; for I have seen nothing, and know nothing of the civilised world.'

'You will be ever so much more attractive than the young women I hear of, who have seen and known a great deal too much,' answered the dowager; and as her granddaughter knew that Lady Maulevrier's word was a law that altered not, there was no more idle repinings.

Her ladyship gave no reason for the postponement of Lesbia's presentation. She was far too diplomatic to breathe a word of her ideas with regard to Lord Hartfield. Anything like a matrimonial scheme would have been revolting to Lesbia, who had grand, but not sordid views about matrimony. She thought it her mission to appear and to conquer. A crowd of suitors would sigh around her, like the loves and graces round that fair Belinda whose story she had read so often; and it would be her part to choose the most worthy. The days are gone when a girl would so much as look at such a fribble as Sir Plume. Her virgin fancy demands the Tennysonian ideal, the grave and knightly Arthur.

But when Lesbia thought of the most worthy, it was always of the worthiest in her own particular sphere; and he of course would be titled and wealthy, and altogether fitted to be her husband. He would take her by the hand and lead her to a higher seat on the dais, and place upon her head, or at least upon her letter-paper and the panels of her carriage, a coronet in which the strawberry leaves should stand out more prominently than in her brother's emblazonment. Lesbia's mind could not conceive an ignoble marriage, or the possibility of the most worthy happening to be found in a lower circle than her own.

And now it was the end of July, and the season which should have been glorified by Lady Lesbia's *debut* was over and done with. She had read in the society papers of all the balls, and birthdays, and race meetings, and regattas, and cricket matches, and gowns, and parasols, and bonnets--what this beauty wore on such an occasion, and how that other beauty looked on another occasion--and she felt as she read like a spell-bound princess in a fairy tale, mewed up in a battlemented tower, and deprived of her legitimate share in all the pleasures of earth. She had no patience with Mary--that wild, unkempt, ungraceful creature, who could be as happy as summer days are long, racing about the hills with her bamboo alpenstock, rioting with a pack of fox-terriers, practising long losers, rowing on the lake, doing all things unbecoming Lady Maulevrier's granddaughter.

That long rainy day dragged its slow length to a close; and then came fine days, in which Molly and her fox-terriers went wandering over the sunlit hills, skipping and dancing across the mountain streamlets--gills, as they were called in this particular world--almost as gaily as the shadows of fleecy cloudlets dancing up yonder in the windy sky. Molly spent half her days among the hills, stealing off from governess and grandmother and the stately beauty sister, and sometimes hardly being missed by them, so ill did her young exuberance harmonise with their calmer life.

'One can tell when Mary is at home by a perpetual banging of doors,' said Lesbia, which was a sisterly exaggeration founded upon fact, for Molly was given to impetuous rushing in and out of rooms when that eager spirit of hers impelled the light lithe body upon some new expedition. Nor is the society of fox-terriers conducive to repose or stateliness of movement; and Maulevrier's terriers, although strictly forbidden the house, were for ever breaking bonds and leaping in upon Molly's retirement at all unreasonable hours. She and they were enchanted to get away from the beautiful luxurious rooms, and to go roving by hill-side and force, away to Easedale Tarn, to bask for hours on the grassy margin of the deep still water, or to row round and round the mountain lake in a rotten boat. It was here, or in some kindred spot, that Molly got through most of her reading--here that she read Shakespeare, Byron, and Shelley, and Wordsworth--dwelling lingeringly and lovingly upon every line in which that good old man spoke of her native land. Sometimes she climbed to higher ground, and felt herself ever so much nearer heaven upon the crest of Silver Howe, or upon the rugged stony steep of Dolly Waggon pike, half way up the dark brow of Helvellyn; sometimes she disappeared for hours, and climbed to the summit of the hill, and wandered in perilous pathways on Striding Edge, or by the dark still water of the Red Tarn. This had been her life ever since she had been old enough to have an independent existence; and the hills and the lakes, and the books of her own choosing, had done a great deal more in ripening her mind than Fraeulein Mueller and that admirable series of educational works which has been provided for the tuition of modern youth. Grammars and geographies, primers and elementary works of all kinds, were Mary's detestation; but she loved books that touched her heart and filled her mind with thoughts wide and deep enough to reach into the infinite of time and space, the mystery of mind and matter, life and death.

Nothing occurred to break the placid monotony of life at Fellside for three long days after that rainy morning; and then came an event which, although commonplace enough in itself, marked the beginning of a new era in the existence of Lady Maulevrier's granddaughters.

It was evening, and the two girls were dawdling about on the sloping lawn before the drawing-room windows, where Lady Maulevrier read the newspapers in her own particular chair by one of those broad Tudor windows, according to her infallible custom. Remote as her life had been from the busy world, her ladyship had never allowed her knowledge of public life and the bent of modern thought to fall into arrear. She took a keen interest in politics, in progress of all kinds. She was a staunch Conservative, and looked upon every Liberal politician as her personal enemy; but she took care to keep herself informed of everything that was being said or done in the enemy's camp. She had an intense respect for Lord Bacon's maxim: Knowledge is power. It was a kind of power secondary to the power of wealth, perhaps; but wealth unprotected by wisdom would soon dwindle into poverty.

Lady Lesbia sauntered about the lawn, looking very elegant in her cream-coloured Indian silk gown, very listless, very tired of her lovely surroundings. Neither lake nor mountain possessed any charm for her. She had had too much of them. Mary roamed about with a swifter footstep, looking at the roses, plucking off a dead leaf, or a cankered bud here and there. Presently she tore across the lawn to the shrubbery which screened the lawn and flower gardens from the winding carriage drive sunk many feet below, and disappeared in a thicket of arbutus and Irish yew.

'What terribly hoydenish manners!' murmured Lesbia, with a languid shrug of her shoulders, as she strolled back to the drawing-room.

She cared very little for the newspapers, for politics not at all; but anything was better than everlasting-contemplation of the blue still water, and the rugged crest of Helm Crag.

'What was the matter with Mary that she rushed off like a mad woman?' inquired Lady Maulevrier, looking up from the *Times*.

'I haven't the least idea. Mary's movements are quite beyond the limits of my comprehension. Perhaps she has gone after a bird's-nest.'

Mary was intent upon no bird's-nest. Her quick ear had caught the sound of manly voices in the winding drive under the pine wood; and surely, yes, surely one was a clear and familiar voice, which heralded the coming of happiness. In such a moment she seemed to have wings. She became unconscious that she touched the earth; she went skimming bird-like over the lawn, and in and out, with fluttering muslin frock, among arbutus and bay, yew and laurel, till she stood poised lightly on the top of the wooded bank which bordered the steep ascent to Lady Maulevrier's gate, looking down at two figures which were sauntering up the drive.

They were both young men, both tall, broad-shouldered, manly, walking with the easy swinging movement of men accustomed to active exercise. One, the handsomer of the two in Mary's eyes, since she thought him simply perfection, was fairhaired, blue-eyed, the typical Saxon. This was Lord Maulevrier. The other was dark, bronzed by foreign travel, perhaps, with black hair, cut very close to an intelligentlooking head, bared to the evening breeze.

'Hulloa!' cried Maulevrier. 'There's Molly. How d'ye do, old girl?'

The two men looked up, and Molly looked down. Delight at her brother's return so filled her heart and mind that there was no room left for embarrassment at the appearance of a stranger.

'O, Maulevrier, I am so glad! I have been pining for you. Why didn't you write to say you were coming? It would have been something to look forward to.'

'Couldn't. Never knew from day to day what I was going to be up to; besides, I knew I should find you at home.'

'Of course. We are always at home,' said Mary; 'go up to the house as fast as ever you can. I'll go and tell grandmother.'

'And tell them to get us some dinner,' said Maulevrier.

Mary's fluttering figure dipped and was gone, vanishing in the dark labyrinth of shrubs. The two young men sauntered up to the house.

'We needn't hurry,' said Maulevrier to his companion, whom he had not taken the trouble to introduce to his sister. 'We shall have to wait for our dinner.'

'And we shall have to change our dusty clothes,' added the other; 'I hope that man will bring our portmanteaux in time.'

'Oh, we needn't dress. We can spend the evening in my den, if you like!'

Mary flew across the lawn again, and bounded up the steps of the verandah--a picturesque Swiss verandah which made a covered promenade in front of the house.

'Mary, may I ask the meaning of this excitement,' inquired her ladyship, as the breathless girl stood before her.

'Maulevrier has come home.'

'At last?'

'And he has brought a friend.'

'Indeed! He might have done me the honour to inquire if his friend's visit would be agreeable. What kind of person?'

'I have no idea. I didn't look at him. Maulevrier is looking so well. They will be here in a minute. May I order dinner for them?'

'Of course, they must have dinner,' said her ladyship, resignedly, as if the whole thing were an infliction; and Mary ran out and interviewed the butler, begging that all things might be made particularly comfortable for the travellers. It was nine o'clock, and the servants were enjoying their eventide repose.

Having given her orders, Mary went back to the drawing-room, impatiently expectant of her brother's arrival, for which event Lesbia and her grandmother waited with perfect tranquillity, the dowager calmly continuing the perusal of her *Times*, while Lesbia sat at her piano in a shadowy corner, and played one of Mendelssohn's softest Lieder. To these dreamy strains Maulevrier and his friend presently entered.

'How d'ye do, grandmother? how do, Lesbia? This is my very good friend and Canadian travelling companion, Jack Hammond--Lady Maulevrier, Lady Lesbia.'

'Very glad to see you, Mr. Hammond,' said the dowager, in a tone so purely conventional that it might mean anything. 'Hammond? I ought to remember your family--the Hammonds of----'

'Of nowhere,' answered the stranger in the easiest tone; 'I spring from a race of nobodies, of whose existence your ladyship is not likely to have heard.'

CHAPTER VI.
MAULEVRIER'S HUMBLE FRIEND.

That faint interest which Lady Lesbia had felt in the advent of a stranger dwindled to nothing after Mr. Hammond's frank avowal of his insignificance. At the very beginning of her career, with the world waiting to be conquered by her, a high-born beauty could not be expected to feel any interest in nobodies. Lesbia shook hands with her brother, honoured the stranger with a stately bend of her beautiful throat, and then withdrew herself from their society altogether as it were, and began to explore her basket of crewels, at a distant table, by the soft light of a shaded lamp, while Maulevrier answered his grandmother's questions, and Mary stood watching him, hanging on his words, as if unconscious of any other presence.

Mr. Hammond went over to the window and looked out at the view. The moon was rising above the amphitheatre of hills, and her rays were silvering the placid bosom of the lake. Lights were dotted here and there about the valley, telling of village life. The Prince of Wales's hotel yonder sparkled with its many lights, like a castle in a fairy tale. The stranger had looked upon many a grander scene, but on none more lovely. Here were lake and mountain in little, without the snow-peaks and awful inaccessible regions of solitude and peril; homely hills that one might climb, placid English vales in which English poets have lived and died.

'Hammond and I mean to spend a month or six weeks with you, if you can make us comfortable,' said Maulevrier.

'I am delighted to hear that you can contemplate staying a month anywhere,' replied her ladyship. 'Your usual habits are as restless as if your life were a disease. It shall not be my fault if you and Mr. Hammond are uncomfortable at Fellside.'

There was courtesy, but no cordiality in the reply. If Mr. Hammond was a sensitive man, touchily conscious of his own obscurity, he must have felt that he was not wanted at Fellside--that he was an excrescence, matter in the wrong place.

Nobody had presented the stranger to Lady Mary. It never entered into Maulevrier's mind to be ceremonious about his sister Molly. She was so much a part of himself that it seemed as if anyone who knew him must needs know her. Molly sat a little way from the window by which Mr. Hammond was standing, and looked at him doubtfully, wonderingly, with not altogether a friendly eye, as he stood with his profile turned to her, and his eyes upon the landscape. She was inclined to be jealous of her brother's friend, who would most likely deprive her of much of that beloved society. Hitherto she had been Maulevrier's chosen companion, at Fellside--indeed, his sole companion after the dismissal of his tutor. Now this brown, bearded stranger would usurp her privileges--those two young men would go roaming over the hills, fishing, otter-hunting, going to distant wrestling matches and leaving her at home. It was a hard thing, and she was prepared to detest the interloper. Even to-night she would be a loser by his presence. Under ordinary circumstances she would have gone to the dining-room with Maulevrier, and sat by him and waited upon him as he ate. But she dared not intrude herself upon a meal that was to be shared with a stranger.

She looked at John Hammond critically, eager to find fault with his appearence; but unluckily for her present humour there was not much room for fault-finding.

He was tall, broad-shouldered, well-built. His enemies would hardly deny that he was good-looking--nay, even handsome. The massive regular features were irreproachable. He was more sunburnt than a gentleman ought to be, Mary thought. She told herself that his good looks were of a vulgar quality, like those of Charles Ford, the champion wrestler, whom she saw at the sports the other day. Why did Maulevrier pick up a companion who was evidently not of his own sphere? Hoydenish, plain-spoken, frank and affectionate as Mary Haselden was, she knew that she belonged to a race apart, that there were circles beneath circles, below her own world, circles which hers could never touch, and she supposed Mr. Hammond to be some waif from one of those nethermost worlds--a village doctor's son, perhaps, or even a tradesman's--sent to the University by some benevolent busybody, and placed at a disadvantage ever afterwards, an unfortunate anomaly, suspended between two worlds like Mahomet's coffin.

The butler announced that his lordship's dinner was served.

'Come along, Molly,' said Maulevrier; 'come and tell me about the terriers, while I eat my dinner.'

Mary hesitated, glanced doubtfully at her grandmother, who made no sign, and then slipped out of the room, hanging fondly on her brother's arm, and almost forgetting that there was any such person as Mr. Hammond in existence.

When these three were gone Lady Lesbia expressed herself strongly upon Maulevrier's folly in bringing such a person as Mr. Hammond to Fellside.

'What are we to do with him, grandmother?' she said, pettishly. 'Is he to live with us, and be one of us, a person of whose belongings we know positively nothing, who owns that his people are common?'

'My dear, he is your brother's friend, and we have the right to suppose he is a gentleman.'

'Not on that account,' said Lesbia, more sharply than her wont. 'Didn't he make a friend, or almost a friend of Jack Howell, the huntsman, and of Ford, the wrestler. I have no confidence in Maulevrier's ideas of fitness.'

'We shall find out all about this Mr. Hamleigh--no Hammond--in a day or two,' replied her ladyship, placidly; 'and in the meantime we must tolerate him, and be grateful to him if he reconcile Maulevrier to remaining at Fellside for the next six weeks.'

Lesbia was silent. She did not consider Maulevrier's presence at Fellside an unmitigated advantage, or, indeed, his presence anywhere. Those two were not sympathetic. Maulevrier made fun of his elder sister's perfections, chaffed her intolerably about the great man she was going to captivate, in her first season, the great houses in which she was going to reign. Lesbia despised him for that neglect of all his opportunities of culture which had left him, after the most orthodox and costly curriculum, almost as ignorant as a ploughboy. She despised a man whose only delight was in horse and hound, gun and fishing-tackle. Molly would have cared very little for the guns or the fishing-tackle perhaps in the abstract; but she cared for everything that interested Maulevrier, even to the bagful of rats which were let loose in the stable-yard sometimes, for the education of a particularly game fox-terrier.

There was plenty of talk and laughter at the dinner-table, while the Countess and Lady Lesbia conversed gravely and languidly in the dimly-lighted drawing-room. The dinner was excellent, and both travellers were ravenous. They had eaten nothing since breakfast, and had driven from Windermere on the top of the coach in the keen evening air. When the sharp edge of the appetite was blunted, Maulevrier began to talk of his adventures since he and Molly had last met. He had not being dissipating in London all the time--or, indeed, any great part of the time of his absence from Fellside; but Molly had been left in Cimmerian, darkness as to his proceedings. He never wrote a letter if he could possibly avoid doing so. If it became a vital necessity to him to communicate with anyone he telegraphed, or, in his own language, 'wired' to that person; but to sit down at a desk and labour with pen and ink was not within his capacities or his views of his mission in life.

'If a fellow is to write letters he might as well be a clerk in an office,' he said, 'and sit on a high stool.'

Thus it happened that when Maulevrier was away from Fellside, no fair *chatelaine* of the Middle Ages could be more ignorant of the movements or whereabouts of her crusader knight than Mary was of her brother's goings on. She could but pray for him with fond and faithful prayer, and wait and hope for his return. And now he told her that things had gone badly with him at Epsom, and worse at Ascot, that he had been, as he expressed it, 'up a tree,' and that he had gone off to the Black Forest directly the Ascot week was over, and at Rippoldsau he had met his old friend and fellow traveller, Hammond, and they had gone for a walking tour together among the homely villages, the watchmakers, the timber cutters, the pretty peasant girls. They had danced at fairs--and shot at village sports--and had altogether enjoyed the thing. Hammond, who was something of an artist, had sketched a good deal. Maulevrier had done nothing but smoke his German pipe and enjoy himself.

'I was glad to find myself in a world where a horse was an exception and not the rule,' he said.

'Oh, how I should love to see the Black Forest!' cried Mary, who knew the first part of Faust by heart, albeit she had never been given permission to read it, 'the gnomes and the witches--der Freischuetz--all that is lovely. Of course, you went up the Brocken?'

'Of course,' answered Mr. Hammond; 'Mephistopheles was our *valet de place*, and we went up among a company of witches riding on broomsticks.' And then quoted,

'Seh' die Baeume hinter Baeumen, Wie sie schnell vorueberruecken, Und die Klippen, die sich buecken, Und die langen Felsennasen, Wie sie schnarchen, wie sie blasen!'

This was the first time he had addressed himself directly to Mary, who sat close to her brother's side, and never took her eyes from his face, ready to pour out his wine or to change his plate, for the serving-men had been dismissed at the beginning of this unceremonious meal.

Mary looked at the stranger almost as superciliously as Lesbia might have done. She was not inclined to be friendly to her brother's friend.

'Do you read German?' she inquired, with a touch of surprise.

'You had better ask him what language he does not read or speak,' said her brother. 'Hammond is an admirable Crichton, my dear--by-the-by, who was admirable Crichton?--knows everything, can twist your little head the right way upon any subject.'

'Oh,' thought Mary, 'highly cultivated, is he? Very proper in a man who was educated on charity to have worked his hardest at the University.'

She was not prepared to think very kindly of young men who had been successful in their college career, since poor Maulevrier had made such a dismal failure of his, had been gated and sent down, and ploughed, and had everything ignominious done to him that could be done, which ignominy had involved an expenditure of money that Lady Maulevrier bemoaned and lamented until this day. Because her brother had not been virtuous, Mary grudged virtuous young men their triumphs and their honours. Great, raw-boned fellows, who have taken their degrees at Scotch Universities, come to Oxford and Cambridge and sweep the board, Maulevrier had told her, when his own failures demanded explanation. Perhaps this Mr. Hammond had graduated north of the Tweed, and had come southward to rob the native. Mary was not any more inclined to be civil to him because he was a linguist. He had a pleasant manner, frank and easy, a good voice, a cheery laugh. But she had not yet made up her mind that he was a gentleman.

'If some benevolent old person were to take a fancy to Charles Ford, the wrestler, and send him to a Scotch University, I daresay he would turn out just as fine a fellow,' she thought, Ford being somewhat of a favourite as a local hero.

The two young men went off to the billiard-room after they had dined. It was half-past ten by this time, and, of course, Mary did not go with them. She bade her brother good-night at the dining-room door.

'Good-night, Molly; be sure you are up early to show me the dogs,' said Maulevrier, after an affectionate kiss.

'Good-night, Lady Mary,' said Mr. Hammond, holding out his hand, albeit she had no idea of shaking hands with him.

She allowed her hand to rest for an instant in that strong, friendly grasp. She had not risen to giving a couple of fingers to a person whom she considered her inferior; but she was inclined to snub Mr. Hammond as rather a presuming young man.

'Well, Jack, what do you think of my beauty sister?' asked his lordship, as he chose his cue from the well-filled rack.

The lamps were lighted, the table uncovered and ready, Carambole in his place, albeit it was months since any player had entered the room. Everything which concerned Maulevrier's comfort or pleasure was done as if by magic at Fellside; and Mary was the household fairy whose influence secured this happy state of things.

'What can any man think except that she is as lovely as the finest of Reynold's portraits, as that Lady Diana Beauclerk of Colonel Aldridge's, or the Kitty Fisher, or any example you please to name of womanly loveliness?'

'Glad to hear it,' answered Maulevrier, chalking his cue; 'can't say I admire her myself--not my style, don't you know. Too much of my lady Di--too little of poor Kitty. But still, of course, it always pleases a fellow to know that his people are admired; and I know that my grandmother has views, grand views,' smiling down at his cue. 'Shall I break?' and he began with the usual miss in baulk.

'Thank you,' said Mr. Hammond, beginning to play. 'Matrimonial views, of course. Very natural that her ladyship should expect such a lovely creature to make a great match. Is there no one in view? Has there been no family conclave--no secret treaty? Is the young lady fancy free?'

'Perfectly. She has been buried alive here; except parsons and a few decent people whom she is allowed to meet now and then at the houses about here, she has seen nothing of the world. My grandmother has kept Lesbia as close as a nun. She is not so fond of Molly, and that young person has wild ways of her own, and gives everybody the slip. By-the-by, how do you like my little Moll?'

The adjective was hardly accurate about a young lady who measured five feet six, but Maulevrier had not yet grown out of the ideas belonging to that period when Mary was really his little sister, a girl of twelve, with long hair and short petticoats.

Mr. Hammond was slow to reply. Mary had not made a very strong impression upon him. Dazzled by her sister's pure and classical beauty, he had no eyes for Mary's homelier charms. She seemed to him a frank, affectionate girl, not too well-mannered; and that was all he thought of her.

'I'm afraid Lady Mary does not like me,' he said, after his shot, which gave him time for reflection.

'Oh, Molly is rather *farouche* in her manners; never would train fine, don't you know. Her ladyship lectured till she was tired, and now Mary runs wild, and I suppose will be left at grass till six months before her presentation, and then they'll put her on the pillar-reins a bit to give her a better mouth. Good shot, by Jove!'

John Hammond was used to his lordship's style of conversation, and understood his friend at all times. Maulevrier was not an intellectual companion, and the distance was wide between the two men; but his lordship's gaiety, good-nature, and acuteness made amends for all shortcomings in culture. And then Mr. Hammond may have been one of those good Conservatives who do not expect very much intellectual power in an hereditary legislator.

CHAPTER VII.
IN THE SUMMER MORNING.

John Hammond loved the wild freshness of morning, and was always eager to explore a new locality; so he was up at five o'clock next morning, and out of doors before six. He left the sophisticated beauty of the Fellside gardens below him, and climbed higher and higher up the Fell, till he was able to command a bird's-eye view of the lake and village, and just under his feet, as it were, Lady Maulevrier's favourite abode. He was provided with a landscape glass which he always carried in his rambles, and with the aid of this he could see every stone of the building.

The house, added to at her ladyship's pleasure, and without regard to cost, covered a considerable extent of ground. The new part consisted of a straight range of about a hundred and twenty feet, facing the lake, and commandingly placed on the crest of a steepish slope; the old buildings, at right angles with the new, made a quadrangle, the third and fourth sides of which were formed by the dead walls of servants' rooms and coach-houses, which had no windows upon this inner enclosed side. The old buildings were low and irregular, one portion of the roof thatched, another tiled. In the quadrangle there was an old-fashioned garden, with geometrical flower-beds, a yew tree hedge, and a stone sun-dial in the centre. A peacock stalked about in the morning light, and greeted the newly risen sun with a discordant scream. Presently a man came out of a half glass door under a verandah which shaded one side of the quadrangle, and strolled about the garden, stopping here and there to cut a dead rose, or trim a geranium, a stoutly-built broad shouldered man, with gray hair and beard, the image of well-fed respectability.

Mr. Hammond wondered a little at the man's leisurely movements as he sauntered about, whistling to the peacock. It was not the manner of a servant who had duties to perform--rather that of a gentleman living at ease, and hardly knowing how to get rid of his time.

"Some superior functionary, I suppose," thought Hammond, "the house-steward, perhaps."

He rambled a long way over the hill, and came back to Fellside by a path of his own discovering, which brought him to a wooden gate leading into the stable-yard, just in time to meet Maulevrier and Lady Mary emerging from the kennel, where his lordship had been inspecting the terriers.

'Angelina is bully about the muzzle,' said Maulevrier; 'we shall have to give her away.'

'Oh, don't,' cried Mary. 'She is a most perfect darling, and laughs so deliciously whenever she sees me.'

Angelina was in Lady Mary's arms at this moment; a beautifully marked little creature, all thew and sinew, palpitating with suppressed emotions, and grinning to her heart's content.

Lady Mary looked very fresh and bright in her neat tailor gown, kilted kirtle, and tight-fitting bodice, with neat little brass buttons. It was a gown of Maulevrier's ordering, made at his own tailor's. Her splendid chestnut hair was uncovered, the short crisp curls about her forehead dancing in the morning air. Her large, bright; brown eyes were dancing, too, with delight at having her brother home again.

She shook hands with Mr. Hammond more graciously than last night; but still with a carelessness which was not complimentary, looking at him absently, as if she hardly knew that he was there, and hugging Angelina all the time.

Hammond told his friend about his ramble over the hills, yonder, up above that homely bench called 'Rest, and be Thankful,' on the crest of Loughrigg Fell. He was beginning to learn the names of the hills already. Yonder darkling brow, rugged, gloomy looking, was Nab Scar; yonder green slope of sunny pasture, stretching wide its two arms as if to enfold the valley, was Fairfield; and here, close on the left, as he faced the lake, were Silver Howe and Helm Crag, with that stony excrescence on the summit of the latter known as the 'Lion and the Lamb.' Lady Maulevrier's house stood within a circle of mountain peaks and long fells, which walled in the deep, placid, fertile valley.

'If you are not too tired to see the gardens, we might show them to you before breakfast,' said Maulevrier. 'We have three-quarters of an hour to the good.'

'Half an hour for a stroll, and a quarter to make myself presentable after my long walk,' said Hammond, who did not wish to face the dowager and Lady Lesbia in disordered apparel. Lady Mary was such an obvious Tomboy that he might be pardoned for leaving her out of the question.

They set out upon an exploration of the gardens, Mary clinging to her brother's arm, as if she wanted to make sure of him, and still carrying Angelina.

The gardens were as other gardens, but passing beautiful. The sloping lawns and richly-timbered banks, winding shrubberies, broad terraces cut on the side of the hill, gave infinite variety. All that wealth and taste and labour could do to make those grounds beautiful had been done--the rarest conifers, the loveliest flowering shrubs grew and flourished there, and the flowers bloomed as they bloom only in Lakeland, where every cottage garden can show a wealth of luxurious bloom, unknown in more exposed and arid districts. Mary was very proud of those gardens. She had loved them and worked in them from her babyhood, trotting about on chubby legs after some chosen old gardener, carrying a few weeds or withered leaves in her pinafore, and fancying herself useful.

'I help 'oo, doesn't I, Teeven?' she used to say to the gray-headed old gardener, who first taught her to distinguish flowers from weeds.

'I shall never learn as much out of these horrid books as poor old Stevens taught me,' she said afterwards, when the gray head was at rest under the sod, and governesses, botany manuals, and hard words from the Greek were the order of the day.

Nine o'clock was the breakfast hour at Fellside. There were no family prayers. Lady Maulevrier did not pretend to be pious, and she put no restraints of piety upon other people. She went to Church on Sunday mornings for the sake of example; but she read all the newest scientific books, subscribed to the Anthropological Society, and thought as the newest scientific people think. She rarely communicated her opinions among her own sex; but now and then, in strictly masculine and superior society, she had been heard to express herself freely upon the nebular hypothesis and the doctrine of evolution.

'After all, what does it matter?' she said, finally, with her grand air; 'I have only to marry my granddaughters creditably, and prevent my grandson going to the dogs, and then my mission on this insignificant planet will be accomplished. What new form that particular modification of molecules which you call Lady Maulevrier may take afterwards is hidden in the great mystery of material life.'

There was no family prayer, therefore, at Fellside. The sisters had been properly educated in their religious duties, had been taught the Anglican faith carefully and well by their governess, Fraeulein Mueller, who had become a staunch Anglican before entering the families of the English nobility, and by the kind Vicar of Grasmere, who took a warm interest in the orphan girls. Their grandmother had given them to understand that they might be as religious as they liked. She would be no let or hindrance to their piety; but they must ask her no awkward questions.

'I have read a great deal and thought a great deal, and my ideas are still in a state of transition,' she told Lesbia; and Lesbia, who was somewhat automatic in her piety, had no desire to know more.

Lady Maulevrier seldom appeared in the forenoon. She was an early riser, being too vivid and highly strung a creature, even at sixty-seven years of age, to give way to sloth. She rose at seven, summer and winter, but she spent the early part of the day in her own rooms, reading, writing, giving orders to her housekeeper, and occasionally interviewing Steadman, who, without any onerous duties, was certainly the most influential person in the house. People in the village talked of him, and envied him so good a berth. He had a gentleman's house to live in, and to all appearance lived as a gentleman. This tranquil retirement, free from care or labour, was a rich reward for the faithful service of his youth. And it was known by the better informed among the Grasmere people that Mr. Steadman was saving money, and had shares in the North-Western Railway. These facts had oozed out, of themselves, as it were. He was not a communicative man, and rarely wasted half an hour at the snug little inn near St. Oswald's Church, amidst the cluster of habitations that was once called Kirktown. He was an unsociable man, people said, and thought himself better than Grasmere folk, the lodging-house keepers, and guides, and wrestlers, and the honest friendly souls who were the outcome of that band of Norwegian exiles which found a home in these peaceful vales.

Miss Mueller, more commonly known as Fraeulein, officiated at breakfast. She never appeared at the board when Lady Maulevrier was present, but in her ladyship's absence Miss Mueller was guardian of the proprieties. She was a stout, kindly creature, and by no means a formidable dragon. When the gong sounded, John Hammond went into the dining-room, where he found Miss Mueller seated alone in front of the urn.

He bowed, quick to read 'governess' or 'companion' in the lady's appearance; and she bowed.

'I hope you have had a nice walk,' she said. 'I saw you from my bedroom window.'

'Did you? Then I suppose yours is one of the few windows which look into that curious old quadrangle?'

'No, there are no windows looking into the quadrangle. Those that were in the original plan of the house were walled up at her ladyship's orders, to keep out the cold winds which sweep down from the hills in winter and early spring, when the edge of Loughrigg Fell is white with snow. My window looks into the gardens, and I saw you there with his lordship and Lady Mary.'

Lady Lesbia came in at this moment, and saluted Mr. Hammond with a haughty inclination of her beautiful head. She looked lovelier in her simple morning gown of pale blue cambric than in her more elaborate toilette of last evening; such purity of complexion, such lustrous eyes; the untarnished beauty of youth, breathing the delicate freshness of a newly-opened flower. She might be as scornful as she pleased, yet John Hammond could not withhold his admiration. He was inclined to admire a woman who kept him at a distance; for the general bent of young women now-a-days is otherwise.

Maulevrier and Mary came in, and everyone sat down to breakfast. Lady Lesbia unbent a little presently, and smiled upon the stranger. There was a relief in a stranger's presence. He talked of new things, places and people she had never seen. She brightened and became quite friendly, deigned to invite the expression of Mr. Hammond's opinions upon music and art, and after breakfast allowed him to follow her into the drawing-room, and to linger there fascinated for half an hour, looking over her newest books, and her last batch of music, but looking most of all at her, while Maulevrier and Mary were loafing on the lawn outside.

'What are you going to do with yourself this morning?' asked Maulevrier, appearing suddenly at the window.

'Anything you like,' answered Hammond. 'Stay, there is one pilgrimage I am eager to make. I must see Wordsworth's grave, and Wordsworth's house.'

'You shall see them both, but they are in opposite directions--one at your elbow, the other a four mile walk. Which will you see first? We'll toss for it,' taking a shilling from a pocketful of loose cash, always ready for moments of hesitation. 'Heads, house; tails, grave. Tails it is. Come and have a smoke, and see the poet's grave. The splendour of the monument, the exquisite neatness with which it is kept, will astound you, considering that we live in a period of Wordsworth worship.'

Hammond hesitated, and looked at Lady Lesbia.

'Aren't you coming?' called Maulevrier from the lawn. 'It was a fair offer. I've got my cigarette case.'

'Yes, I'm coming,' answered the other, with a disappointed air.

He had hoped that Lesbia would offer to show him the poet's grave. He could not abandon that hope without a struggle.

'Will you come with us, Lady Lesbia? We'll suppress the cigarettes!'

'Thanks, no,' she said, becoming suddenly frigid. 'I am going to practice.'

'Do you never walk in the morning--on such a lovely morning as this?'

'Not very often.'

She had re-entered those frozen regions from which his attentions had lured him for a little while. She had reminded herself of the inferior social position of this person, in whose conversation she had allowed herself to be interested.

'*Filons!*' cried Maulevrier from below, and they went.

Mary would have very much liked to go with them, but she did not want to be intrusive; so she went off to the kennels to see the terriers eat their morning and only meal of dog biscuit.

CHAPTER VIII.
THERE IS ALWAYS A SKELETON.

The two young men strolled through the village, Maulevrier pausing to exchange greetings with almost everyone he met, and so to the rustic churchyard, above the beck.

The beck was swollen with late rains, and was brawling merrily over its stony bed; the churchyard grass was deep and cool and shadowy under the clustering branches. The poet's tomb was disappointing in its unlovely simplicity, its stern, slatey hue. The plainest granite cross would have satisfied Mr. Hammond, or a cross in pure white marble, with a sculptured lamb at the base. Surely the lamb, emblem at once pastoral and sacred, ought to enter into any monument to Wordsworth; but that gray headstone, with its catalogue of dates, those stern iron railings--were these fit memorials of one whose soul so loved nature's loveliness?

After Mr. Hammond had seen the little old, old church, and the medallion portrait inside, had seen all that Maulevrier could show him, in fact, the two young men went back to the place of graves, and sat on the low parapet above the beck, smoking their cigarettes, and talking with that perfect unreserve which can only obtain between men who are old and tried friends. They talked, as it was only natural they should talk, of that household at Fellside, where all things were new to John Hammond.

'You like my sister Lesbia?' said Maulevrier.

'Like her! well, yes. The difficulty with most men must be not to worship her.'

'Ah, she's not my style. And she's beastly proud.'

'A little *hauteur* gives piquancy to her beauty; I admire a grand woman.'

'So do I in a picture. Titian's Queen of Cyprus, or any party of that kind; but for flesh and blood I like humility--a woman who knows she is human, and not infallible, and only just a little better than you or me. When I choose a wife, she will be no such example of cultivated perfection as my sister Lesbia. I want no goddess, but a nice little womanly woman, to jog along the rough and tumble road of life with me.'

'Lady Maulevrier's influence, no doubt, has in a great measure determined the bent of your sister's character: and from what you have told me about her ladyship, I should think a fixed idea of her own superiority would be inevitable in any girl trained by her.'

'Yes, she is a proud woman--a proud, hard woman--and she has steeped Lesbia's mind in all her own pet ideas and prejudices. Yet, God knows, we have little reason to hold our heads high,' said Maulevrier, with a gloomy look.

John Hammond did not reply to this remark: perhaps there was some difficulty for a man situated as he was in finding a fit reply. He smoked in silence, looking down at the pure swift waters of the Rotha tumbling over the crags and boulders below.

'Doesn't somebody say there is always a skeleton in the cupboard, and the nobler and more ancient the race the bigger the skeleton?' said Maulevrier, with a philosophical air.

'Yes, your family secret is an attribute of a fine old race. The Pelopidae, for instance--in their case it was not a single skeleton, but a whole charnel house. I don't think your skeleton need trouble you, Maulevrier. It belongs to the remote past.'

'Those things never belong to the past,' said the young man. 'If it were any other kind of taint--profligacy--madness, even--the story of a duel that went very near murder--a runaway wife--a rebellious son--a cruel husband. I have heard such stories hinted at in the records of families. But our story means disgrace. I seldom see strangers putting their heads together at the club without fancying they are telling each other about my grandfather, and pointing me out as the grandson and heir of a thief.'

'Why use unduly hard words?'

'Why should I stoop to sophistication, with you, my friend. Dishonesty is dishonesty all the world over; and to plunder Rajahs on a large scale is no less vile than to pick a pocket on Ludgate Hill.'

'Nothing was ever proved against your grandfather.'

'No, he died in the nick of time, and the inquiry was squashed, thanks to the Angersthorpe interest, and my grandmother's cleverness. But if he had lived a few weeks longer England would have rung with the story of his profligacy and dish-onour. Some people say he committed suicide in order to escape the inquiry; but I have heard my mother emphatically deny this. My father told her that he had often talked with the people who kept the little inn where his father died, and they were clear enough in their assertion that the death was a natural death--the sudden collapse of an exhausted constitution.'

'Was it on account of this scandal that your father spent the best part of his life away from England?' Hammond asked, feeling that it was a relief to Maulevrier to talk about this secret burden of his.

The young Earl was light-hearted and frivolous by nature, yet even he had his graver moments; and upon this subject of the old Maulevrier scandal he was peculiarly sensitive, perhaps all the more so because his grandmother had never allowed him to speak to her about it, had never satisfied his curiosity upon any details of that painful story.

'I have very little doubt it was so--though I wasn't old enough when he died to hear as much from his own lips. My father went straight from the University to Vienna, where he began his career in the diplomatic service, and where he soon afterwards married a dowerless English girl of good family. He went to Rio as first secretary, and died of fever within seven years of his marriage, leaving a widow and three babies, the youngest in long clothes. Mother and babies all came over to England, and were at once established at Fellside. I can remember the voyage--and I can remember my poor mother who never recovered the blow of my father's death, and who died in yonder house, after five years of broken health and broken spirits. We had no one but the dowager to look to as children--hardly another friend in the world. She did what she liked with us; she kept the girls as close as nuns, so *they* have never heard a hint of the old history; no breach of scandal has reached *their* ears. But she could not shut me up in a country house for ever, though she did succeed in keeping me away from a public school. The time came when I had to go to the University, and there I heard all that had been said about Lord Maulevrier. The men who told me about the old scandal in a friendly way pretended not to believe it; but one night, when I had got into a row at a wine-party with a tailor's son, he told me that if his father was a snip my grandfather was a thief, and so he thought himself the better bred of the two. I smashed his nose for him, but as it was a decided pug before the row began, that hardly squared the matter.'

'Did you ever hear the exact story?'

'I have heard a dozen stories; and if only a quarter of them are true my grandfather was a scoundrel. It seems that he was immensely popular for the first year or so of his government, gave more splendid entertainments than had been given at Madras for half a century before his time, lavished his wealth upon his favourites. Then arose a rumour that the governor was insolvent and harassed by his creditors, and then a new source of wealth seemed to be at his command; he was more reckless, more princely than ever; and then, little by little, there arose the suspicion that he was trafficking in English interests, selling his influence to petty princes, winking at those mysterious crimes by which rightful heirs are pushed aside to make room for usurpers. Lastly it became notorious that he was the slave of a wicked woman, false wife, suspected murderess, whose husband, a native prince, disappeared from the scene just when his existence became perilous to the governor's reputation. According to one version of the story, the scandal of this Rajah's mysterious disappearance, followed not long after by the Ranee's equally mysterious death, was the immediate cause of my grandfather's recall. How much, or how little of this story--or other dark stories of the same kind--is true, whether my grandfather was a consummate scoundrel, or the victim of a baseless slander,--whether he left India a rich man or a poor man, is known to no mortal except Lady Maulevrier, and compared with her the Theban Sphinx was a communicative individual.'

'Let the dead bury their dead,' said Hammond. 'Neither you nor your sisters can be the worse for this ancient slander. No doubt every part of the story has been distorted and exaggerated in the telling; and a great deal of it may be pure invention, evolved from the inner consciousness of the slanderer. God forbid that any whisper of scandal should ever reach Lady Lesbia's ears.'

He ignored poor Mary. It was to him as if there were no such person. Her feeble light was extinguished by the radiance of her sister's beauty; her very individuality was annihilated.

'As for you, dear old fellow,' he said, with warm affection, 'no one will ever think the worse of you on account of your grandfather's peccadilloes.'

'Yes, they will. Hereditary genius is one of our modern crazes. When a man's grandfather was a rogue, there must be a taint in his blood. People don't believe in spontaneous generation, moral or physical, now-a-days. Typhoid breeds typhoid, and typhus breeds typhus, just as dog breeds dog; and who will believe that a cheat and a liar can be the father of honest men?'

'In that case, knowing what kind of man the grandson is, I will never believe that the grandfather was a rogue,' said Hammond, heartily.

Maulevrier put out his hand without a word, and it was warmly grasped by his friend.

'As for her ladyship, I respect and honour her as a woman who has led a life of self-sacrifice, and has worn her pride as an armour,' continued Hammond.

'Yes, I believe the dowager's character is rather fine,' said Maulevrier; 'but she and I have never hit our horses very well together. She would have liked such a fellow as you for a grandson, Jack--a man who took high honours at Oxford, and could hold his own against all comers. Such a grandson would have gratified her pride, and would have repaid her for the trouble she had taken in nursing the Maulevrier estate; for however poor a property it was when her husband went to India there is no doubt that it is a very fine estate now, and that the dowager has been the making of it.'

The two young men strolled up to Easedale Tarn before they went back to Fellside, where Lady Maulevrier received them with a stately graciousness, and where Lady Lesbia unbent considerably at luncheon, and condescended to an animated conversation with her brother's friend. It was such a new thing to have a stranger at the family board, a man whose information was well abreast with the march of progress, who could talk eloquently upon every subject which people care to talk about. In this new and animated society Lesbia seemed like an enchanted princess suddenly awakened from a spell-bound slumber. Molly looked at her sister with absolute astonishment. Never had she seen her so bright, so beautiful--no longer a picture or a statue, but a woman warm with the glow of life.

'No wonder Mr. Hammond admires her,' thought poor Molly, who was quite acute enough to see the stranger's keen appreciation of her sister's charms, and positive indifference towards herself.

There are some things which women find out by instinct, just as the needle turns towards the magnet. Shut a girl up in a tower till she is eighteen years old, and on the day of her release introduce her to the first man her eyes have ever looked upon, and she will know at a glance whether he admires her.

After luncheon the four young people started for Rydal Mount; with Fraeulein as chaperon and watch-dog. The girls were both good walkers. Lady Lesbia even, though she looked like a hot-house flower, had been trained to active habits, could walk and ride, and play tennis, and climb a hill as became a mountain-bred damsel. Molly, feeling that her conversational powers were not appreciated by her brother's friend, took half a dozen dogs for company, and with three fox-terriers, a little Yorkshire dog, a colley and an otter-hound, was at no loss for society on the road, more especially as Maulevrier gave her most of his company, and entertained her with an account of his Black Forest adventures, and all the fine things he had said to the fair-haired, blue-eyed Baden girls, who had sold him photographs or wild strawberries, or had awakened the echoes of the hills with the music of their rustic flutes.

Fraeulein was perfectly aware that her mission upon this particular afternoon was not to let Lady Lesbia out of her sight for an instant, to hear every word the young lady said, and every word Mr. Hammond addressed to her. She had received no specific instructions from Lady Maulevrier. They were not necessary, for the Fraeulein knew her ladyship's intentions with regard to her elder granddaughter,-- knew them, at least, so far as that Lesbia was intended to make a brilliant marriage; and she knew, therefore, that the presence of this handsome and altogether attractive young man was to the last degree obnoxious to the dowager. She was obliged to be civil to him for her nephew's sake, and she was too wise to let Lesbia imagine him dangerous: but the fact that he was dangerous was obvious, and it was Fraeulein's duty to protect her employer's interests.

Everybody knew Lord Maulevrier, so there was no difficulty about getting admission to Wordsworth's garden and Wordsworth's house, and after Mr. Hammond and his companions had explored these, they went back to the shores of the little lake, and climbed that rocky eminence upon which the poet used to sit, above the placid waters of silvery Rydal. It is a lovely spot, and that narrow lake, so poor a thing were magnitude the gauge of beauty, had a soft and pensive loveliness in the clear afternoon light.

'Poor Wordsworth' sighed Lesbia, as she stood on the grassy crag looking down on the shining water, broken in the foreground by fringes of rushes, and the rich luxuriance of water-lilies. 'Is it not pitiable to think of the years he spent in this monotonous place, without any society worth speaking of, with only the shabbiest collection of books, with hardly any interest in life except the sky, and the hills, and the peasantry?'

'I think Wordsworth's was an essentially happy life, in spite of his narrow range,' answered Hammond. 'You, with your ardent youth and vivid desire for a life of action, cannot imagine the calm blisses of reverie and constant communion with nature. Wordsworth had a thousand companions you and I would never dream of; for him every flower that grows was an individual existence--almost a soul.'

'It was a mild kind of lunacy, an everlasting opium dream without the opium; but I am grateful to him for living such a life, since it has bequeathed us some exquisite poetry,' said Lesbia, who had been too carefully cultured to fleer or flout at Wordsworth.

'I do believe there's an otter just under that bank,' cried Molly, who had been watching the obvious excitement of her bandy-legged hound; and she rushed down to the brink of the water, leaping lightly from stone to stone, and inciting the hound to business.

'Let him alone, can't you?' roared Maulevrier; 'leave him in peace till he's wanted. If you disturb him now he'll desert his holt, and we may have a blank day. The hounds are to be out to-morrow.'

'I may go with you?' asked Mary, eagerly.

'Well, yes, I suppose you'll want to be in it.' Molly and her brother went on an exploring ramble along the edge of the water towards Ambleside, leaving John Hammond in Lesbia's company, but closely guarded by Miss Mueller. These three went to look at Nab Cottage, where poor Hartley Coleridge ended his brief and clouded days; and they had gone some way upon their homeward walk before they were rejoined by Maulevrier and Mary, the damsel's kilted skirt considerably the worse for mud and mire.

'What would grandmother say if she were to see you!' exclaimed Lesbia, looking contemptuously at the muddy petticoat.

'I am not going to let her see me, so she will say nothing,' cried Mary, and then she called to the dogs, 'Ammon, Agag, Angelina;' and the three fox terriers flew along the road, falling over themselves in the swiftness of their flight, darting, and leaping, and scrambling over each other, and offering the spectators the most intense example of joyous animal life.

The colley was far up on the hill-side, and the otter-hound was still hunting the water, but the terriers never went out of Mary's sight. They looked to her to take the initiative in all their sports.

They were back at Fellside in time for a very late tea. Lady Maulevrier was waiting for them in the drawing-room.

'Oh, grandmother, why did you not take your tea!' exclaimed Lesbia, looking really distressed. 'It is six o'clock.'

'I am used to have you at home to hand me my cup,' replied the dowager, with a touch of reproachfulness.

'I am so sorry,' said Lesbia, sitting down before the tea-table, and beginning her accustomed duty. 'Indeed, dear grandmother, I had no idea it was so late; but it was such a lovely afternoon, and Mr. Hammond is so interested in everything connected with Wordsworth--'

She was looking her loveliest at this moment, all that was softest in her nature called forth by her desire to please her grandmother, whom she really loved. She hung over Lady Maulevrier's chair, attending to her small wants, and seeming scarcely to remember the existence of anyone else. In this phase of her character she seemed to Mr. Hammond the perfection of womanly grace.

Mary had rushed off to her room to change her muddy gown, and came in presently, dressed for dinner, looking the picture of innocence.

John Hammond received his tea-cup from Lesbia's hand, and lingered in the drawing-room talking to the dowager and her granddaughters till it was time to dress. Lady Maulevrier found herself favourably impressed by him in spite of her prejudices. It was very provoking of Maulevrier to have brought such a man to Fellside. His very merits were objectionable. She tried with exquisite art to draw him into some revealment as to his family and antecedents: but he evaded every attempt of that kind. It was too evident that he was a self-made man, whose intellect and good looks were his only fortune. It was criminal in Maulevrier to have brought such a person to Fellside. Her ladyship began to think seriously of sending the two girls to St. Bees or Tynemouth for change of air, in charge of Fraeulein. But any sudden proceeding of that kind would inevitably awaken Lesbia's suspicions;

and there is nothing so fatal to a woman's peace as this idea of danger. No, the peril must be faced. She could only hope that Maulevrier would soon tire of Fellside. A week's Westmoreland weather--gray skies and long rainy days, would send these young men away.

CHAPTER IX.
A CRY IN THE DARKNESS.

The peril had to be faced, for the weather did not favour Lady Maulevrier's hopes. Westmoreland skies forgot to shed their accustomed showers. Westmoreland hills seemed to have lost their power of drawing down the rain. That August was a lovely month, and the young people at Fellside revelled in ideal weather. Maulevrier took his friend everywhere--by hill and stream and force and gill--to all those chosen spots which make the glory of the Lake country--on Windermere and Thirlmere, away through the bleak pass of Kirkstone to Ullswater--on driving excursions, and on boating excursions, and pedestrian rambles, which latter the homely-minded Hammond seemed to like best of all, for he was a splendid walker, and loved the freedom of a mountain ramble, the liberty to pause and loiter and waste an hour at will, without being accountable to anybody's coachman, or responsible for the well-being of anybody's horses.

On some occasions the two girls and Miss Mueller were of the party, and then it seemed to John Hammond as if nothing were needed to complete the glory of earth and sky. There were other days--rougher journeys--when the men went alone, and there were days when Lady Mary stole away from her books and music, and all those studies which she was supposed still to be pursuing--no longer closely supervised by her governess, but on parole, as it were--and went with her brother and his friend across the hills and far away. Those were happy days for Mary, for it was always delight to her to be with Maulevrier; yet she had a profound conviction of John Hammond's indifference, kind and courteous as he was in all his dealings with her, and a sense of her own inferiority, of her own humble charms and little power to please, which was so acute as to be almost pain. One day this keen sense of humiliation broke from her unawares in her talk with her brother, as they two sat on a broad heathy slope face to face with one of the Langdale pikes, and with a deep valley at their feet, while John Hammond was climbing from rock to rock in the gorge on their right, exploring the beauties of Dungeon Ghyll.

'I wonder whether he thinks me very ugly?' said Mary, with her hands clasped upon her knees, her eyes fixed on Wetherlam, upon whose steep brow a craggy mass of brown rock clothed with crimson heather stood out from the velvety green of the hill-side.

'Who thinks you ugly?'

'Mr. Hammond. I'm sure he does. I am so sunburnt and so horrid!'

'But you are not ugly. Why, Molly, what are you dreaming about?'

'Oh, yes, I am ugly. I may not seem so to you, perhaps, because you are used to me, but I know he must think me very plain compared with Lesbia, whom he admires so much.'

'Yes, he admires Lesbia. There is no doubt of that.'

'And I know he thinks me plain,' said Molly, contemplating Wetherlam with sorrowful eyes, as if the sequence were inevitable.

'My dearest girl, what nonsense! Plain, forsooth? Ugly, quotha? Why, there are not a finer pair of eyes in Westmoreland than my Molly's, or a prettier smile, or whiter teeth.'

'But all the rest is horrid,' said Mary, intensely in earnest. 'I am sunburnt, freckled, and altogether odious--like a haymaker or a market woman. Grandmother has said so often enough, and I know it is the truth. I can see it in Mr. Hammond's manner.'

'What! freckles and sunburn, and the haymaker, and all that?' cried Maulevrier, laughing. 'What an expressive manner Jack's must be, if it can convey all that--like Lord Burleigh's nod, by Jove. Why, what a goose you are, Mary. Jack thinks you a very nice girl, and a very pretty girl, I'll be bound; but aren't you clever enough to understand that when a man is over head and ears in love with one woman, he is apt to seem just a little indifferent to all the other women in the world? and there is no doubt Jack is desperately in love with Lesbia.'

'You ought not to let him be in love with her,' protested Mary. 'You know it can only lead to his unhappiness. You must know what grandmother is, and how she has made up her mind that Lesbia is to marry some great person. You ought not to have brought Mr. Hammond here. It is like letting him into a trap.'

'Do you think it was wrong?' asked her brother, smiling at her earnestness. 'I should be very sorry if poor Jack should come to grief. But still, if Lesbia likes him--which I think she does--we ought to be able to talk over the dowager.'

'Never,' cried Mary. 'Grandmother would never give way. You have no idea how ambitious she is. Why, once when Lesbia was in a poetical mood, and said she would marry the man she liked best in the world, if he were a pauper, her ladyship flew into a terrible passion, and told her she would renounce her, that she would curse her, if she were to marry beneath her, or marry without her grandmother's consent.'

'Hard lines for Hammond,' said Maulevrier, rather lightly. 'Then I suppose we must give up the idea of a match between him and Lesbia.'

'You ought not to have brought him here,' retorted Mary. 'You had better invent some plan for sending him away. If he stay it will be only to break his heart.'

'Dear child, men's hearts do not break so easily. I have fancied that mine was broken more than once in my life, yet it is sound enough, I assure you.'

'Oh!' sighed Mary, 'but you are not like him; wounds do not go so deep with you.'

The subject of their conversation came out of the rocky cleft in the hills as Mary spoke. She saw his hat appearing out of the gorge, and then the man himself emerged, a tall well-built figure, clad in brown tweed, coming towards them, with sketch-book and colour-box in his pocket. He had been making what he called memoranda of the waterfall, a stone or two here, a cluster of ferns there, or a tree torn up by the roots, and yet green and living, hanging across the torrent, a rude natural bridge.

This round by the Langdale Pikes and Dungeon Ghyll was one of their best days; or, at least, Molly and her brother thought so; for to those two the presence of Lesbia and her chaperon was always a restraint.

Mary could walk twice as far as her elder sister, and revelled in hill-side paths and all manner of rough places. They ordered their luncheon at the inn below the waterfall, and had it carried up on to the furzy slope in front of Wetherlam, where they could eat and drink and be merry to the music of the force as it came down from the hills behind them, while the lights and shadows came and went upon yonder rugged brow, now gray in the shadow, now ruddy in the sunshine.

Mary was as gay as a bird during that rough and ready luncheon. No one would have suspected her uneasiness about John Hammond's peril or her own plainness. She might let her real self appear to her brother, who had been her trusted friend and father confessor from her babyhood; but she was too thorough a woman to let Mr. Hammond discover the depth of her sympathy, the tenderness of her compassion for his woes. Later, as they were walking home across the hills, by Great Langdale and Little Langdale, and Fox Howe and Loughrigg Fell, she fell behind a few paces with Maulevrier, and said to him very earnestly--

'You won't tell, will you, dear?'

'Tell what?' he asked, staring at her.

'Don't tell Mr. Hammond what I said about his thinking me ugly. He might want to apologise to me, and that would be too humiliating. I was very childish to say such a silly thing.'

'Undoubtedly you were.'

'And you won't tell him?'

'Tell him anything that would degrade my Mary? Assail her dignity by so much as a breath? Sooner would I have this tongue torn out with red-hot pincers.'

On the next day, and the next, sunshine and summer skies still prevailed; but Mr. Hammond did not seem to care for rambling far afield. He preferred loitering about in the village, rowing on the lake, reading in the garden, and playing lawn tennis. He had only inclination for those amusements which kept him within a stone's throw of Fellside: and Mary knew that this disposition had arisen in his mind since Lesbia had withdrawn herself from all share in their excursions. Lesbia had not been rude to her brother or her brother's friend; she had declined their invitations with smiles and sweetness; but there was always some reason--a new song to be practised, a new book to be read, a letter to be written--why she should not go for drives or walks or steamboat trips with Maulevrier and his friend.

So Mr. Hammond suddenly found out that he had seen all that was worth seeing in the Lake country, and that there was nothing so enjoyable as the placid idleness of Fellside; and at Fellside Lady Lesbia could not always avoid him without a too-marked intention, so he tasted the sweetness of her society to a much greater extent than was good for his peace, if the case were indeed as hopeless as Lady Mary declared. He strolled about the grounds with her; he drank the sweet melody of her voice in Heine's tenderest ballads; he read to her on the sunlit lawn in the lazy afternoon hours; he played billiards with her; he was her faithful attendant at afternoon tea; he gave himself up to the study of her character, which, to his charmed eyes, seemed the perfection of pure and placid womanhood. There might, perhaps, be some lack of passion and of force in this nature, a marked absence of that impulsive feeling which is a charm in some women: but this want was atoned for by sweetness of character, and Mr. Hammond argued that in these calm natures there is often an unsuspected depth, a latent force, a grandeur of soul, which only reveals itself in the great ordeals of life.

So John Hammond hung about the luxurious drawing-room at Fellside in a manner which his friend Maulevrier ridiculed as unmanly.

'I had no idea you were such a tame cat,' he said: 'if when we were salmon fishing in Canada anybody had told me you could loll about a drawing-room all day listening to a girl squalling and reading novels, I shouldn't have believed a word of it.'

'We had plenty of roughing on the shores of the St. Lawrence,' answered Hammond. 'Summer idleness in a drawing-room is an agreeable variety.'

It is not to be supposed that John Hammond's state of mind could long remain unperceived by the keen eyes of the dowager. She saw the gradual dawning of his love, she saw the glow of its meridian. She was pleased to behold this proof of Lesbia's power over the heart of man. So would she conquer the man foredoomed to be her husband when the coming time should bring them together. But agreeable as the fact of this first conquest might be, as an evidence of Lesbia's supremacy among women, the situation was not without its peril; and Lady Maulevrier felt that she could no longer defer the duty of warning her granddaughter. She had wished, if possible, to treat the thing lightly to the very last, so that Lesbia should never know there had been danger. She had told her, a few days ago, that those drives, and walks with the two young men were undignified, even although guarded by the Fraeulein's substantial presence.

'You are making yourself too much a companion to Maulevrier and his friend,' said the dowager. 'If you do not take care you will grow like Mary.'

'I would do anything in the world to avoid *that*,' replied Lesbia. 'Our walks and drives have been very pleasant. Mr. Hammond is extremely clever, and can talk about everything.'

Her colour heightened ever so little as she spoke of him, an indication duly observed by Lady Maulevrier.

'No doubt the man is clever; all adventurers are clever; and you have sense enough to see that this man is an adventurer--a mere sponge and toady of Maulevrier's.'

'There is nothing of the sponge or the toady in his manner,' protested Lady Lesbia, with a still deeper blush, the warm glow of angry feeling.

'My dear child, what do you know of such people--or of the atmosphere in which they are generated? The sponge and toady of to-day is not the clumsy fawning wretch you have read about in old-fashioned novels. He can flatter adroitly, and feed upon his friends, and yet maintain a show of manhood and independence. I'll wager Mr. Hammond's trip to Canada did not cost him sixpence, and that he hardly opened his purse all the time he was in Germany.'

'If my brother wants the company of a friend who is much poorer than himself, he must pay for it,' argued Lesbia. 'I think Maulevrier is lucky to have such a companion as Mr. Hammond.'

Yet, even while she so argued, Lady Lesbia felt in some manner humiliated by the idea that this man who so palpably worshipped her was too poor to pay his own travelling expenses.

Poets and philosophers may say what they will about the grandeur of plain living and high thinking; but a young woman thinks better of the plain liver who is not compelled to plainness by want of cash. The idea of narrow means, of dependence upon the capricious generosity of a wealthy friend is not without its humiliating influence. Lesbia was barely civil to Mr. Hammond that evening when he praised her singing; and she refused to join in a four game proposed by Maulevrier, albeit she and Mr. Hammond had beaten Mary and Maulevrier the evening before, with much exultant hilarity.

Hammond had been at Fellside nearly a month, and Maulevrier was beginning to talk about a move further northward. There was a grouse moor in Argyleshire which the two young men talked about as belonging to some unnamed friend of the Earl's, which they had thought of shooting over before the grouse season was ended.

'Lord Hartfield has property in Argyleshire,' said the dowager, when they talked of these shootings. 'Do you know his estate, Mr. Hammond?'

'Hammond knows that there is such a place, I daresay,' replied Maulevrier,
replying for his friend.

'But you do not know Lord Hartfield, perhaps,' said her ladyship, not arro-
gantly, but still in a tone which implied her conviction that John Hammond would
not be hand-in-glove with earls, in Scotland or elsewhere.

'Oh, yes! I know him by sight every one in Argyleshire knows him by sight.'

'Naturally. A young man in his position must be widely known. Is he popular?'

'Fairly so.'

'His father and I were friends many years ago,' said Lady Maulevrier, with a
faint sigh. 'Have you ever heard if he resembles his father?'

'I believe not. I am told he is like his mother's family.'

'Then he ought to be handsome. Lady Florence Ilmington was a famous beauty.'

They were sitting in the drawing-room after dinner, the room dimly lighted
by darkly-shaded lamps, the windows wide open to the summer sky and moonlit
lake. In that subdued light Lady Maulevrier looked a woman in the prime of life.
The classical modelling of her features and the delicacy of her complexion were
unimpaired by time, while those traces of thought and care which gave age to her
face in the broad light of day were invisible at night. John Hammond contemplated
that refined and placid countenance with profound admiration. He remembered
how her ladyship's grandson had compared her with the Sphinx; and it seemed to
him to-night, as be studied her proud and tranquil beauty, that there was indeed
something of the mysterious, the unreadable in that countenance, and that beneath
its heroic calm there might be the ashes of tragic passion, the traces of a life-long
struggle with fate. That such a woman, so beautiful, so gifted, so well fitted to shine
and govern in the great world, should have been content to live a long life of absolute seclusion in this remote valley was in itself a social mystery which must needs
set an observant young man wondering. It was all very well to say that Lady Maulevrier loved a country life, that she had made Fellside her earthly Paradise, and had

no desire beyond it. The fact remained that it was not in Lady Maulevrier's temperament to be satisfied with such an existence; that falcon eye was never meant to gaze for ever upon one narrow range of mountain and lake; that lip was made to speak among the great ones of the world.

Lady Maulevrier was particularly gracious to her grandson's friend this evening. Maulevrier spoke so decisively about a speedy migration northward, seemed so inclined to regret the time wasted since the twelfth of the month, that she thought the danger was past, and she could afford to be civil. She really liked the young man, had no doubt in her own mind that he was a gentleman in the highest and broadest sense of the word, but not in the sense which made him an eligible husband for either of her granddaughters.

Lesbia was in a pensive mood this evening. She sat in the verandah, looking dreamily at the lake, and at Fairfield yonder, a broad green slope, silvered with moonlight, and seeming to stretch far away into unfathomable distance.

If one could but take one's lover by the hand and go wandering over those mystic moonlit slopes into some new unreal world where it would not matter whether a man were rich or poor, high-born or low-born, where there should be no such things as rank and state to be won or lost! Lesbia felt to-night as if she would like to live out her life in dreamland. Reality was too hard, too much set round by difficulties and sacrifices.

While Lesbia was losing herself in that dream-world, Lady Maulevrier unbent considerably to John Hammond, and talked to him with more appearance of interest in his actual self, and in his own affairs, than she had manifested hitherto although she had been uniformly courteous.

She asked him his plans for the future--had he chosen a profession?

He told her that he had not. He meant to devote himself to literature and politics.

'Is not that rather vague?' inquired her ladyship.

'Everything is vague at first.'

'But literature now--as an amusement, no doubt, it is delightful--but as a profession--does literature ever pay?'

'There have been such cases.'

'Yes, I suppose so. Walter Scott, Gibbon, Macaulay, Froude, those made money

no doubt. But there is a suspicion of hopelessness in the idea of a young man starting in life intending to earn his bread by literature. One remembers Chatterton. I
should have thought that in your case the law or the church would have been better. In the latter Maulevrier might have been useful to you. He is patron of three or
four livings.'

'You are too good even to think of such a thing,' said Hammond; 'but I have set
my heart upon a political career. I must swim or sink in that sea.'

Lady Maulevrier looked at him with a compassionate smile Poor young man!
No doubt he thought himself a genius, and that doors which had remained shut to
everybody else would turn on their hinges directly he knocked at them. She was
sincerely sorry for him. Young, clever, enthusiastic, and doomed to bitterest disappointment.

'You have parents, perhaps, who are ambitious for you--a mother who thinks
her son a heaven-born statesman!' said her ladyship, kindly.

'Alas, no! that incentive to ambition is wanting in my case. I have neither father nor mother living.'

'That is very sad. No doubt that fact has been a bond of sympathy between you
and Maulevrier?'

'I believe it has.'

'Well, I hope Providence will smile upon your path.'

'Come what may, I shall never forget the happy weeks I have spent at Fellside,'
said Hammond, 'or your ladyship's gracious hospitality.'

He took up the beautiful hand, white to transparency, showing the delicate
tracing of blue veins, and pressed his lips upon it in chivalrous worship of age and
womanly dignity.

Lady Maulevrier smiled upon him with her calm, grave smile. She would have
liked to say, 'You shall be welcome again at Fellside,' but she felt that the man was
dangerous. Not while Lesbia remained single could she court his company. If Maulevrier brought him she must tolerate his presence, but she would do nothing to
invite that danger.

There was no music that evening. Maulevrier and Mary were playing billiards;
Fraeulein Mueller was sitting in her corner working at a high-art counterpane. Lesbia came in from the verandah presently, and sat on a low stool by her grandmoth-

er's arm-chair, and talked to her in soft, cooing accents, inaudible to John Hammond, who sat a little way off turning the leaves of the ***Contemporary Review***: and this went on till eleven o'clock, the regular hour for retiring, when Mary came in from the billiard-room, and told Mr. Hammond that Maulevrier was waiting for a smoke and a talk. Then candles were lighted, and the ladies all departed, leaving John Hammond and his friend with the house to themselves.

They played a fifty game, and smoked and talked till the stroke of midnight, by which time it seemed as if there were not another creature awake in the house. Maulevrier put out the lamps in the billiard-room, and then they went softly up the shadowy staircase, and parted in the gallery, the Earl going one way, and his friend the other.

The house was large and roomy, spread over a good deal of ground, Lady Maulevrier having insisted upon there being only two stories. The servants' rooms were all in a side wing, corresponding with those older buildings which had been given over to Steadman and his wife, and among the villagers of Grasmere enjoyed the reputation of being haunted. A wide panelled corridor extended from one end of the house to the other. It was lighted from the roof, and served as a gallery for the display of a small and choice collection of modern art, which her ladyship had acquired during her long residence at Fellside. Here, too, in Sheraton cabinets, were those treasures of old English china which Lady Maulevrier had inherited from past generations.

Her ladyship's rooms were situated at the southern end of this corridor, her bed-chamber being at the extreme end of the house, with windows commanding two magnificent views, one across the lake and the village of Grasmere to the green slopes of Fairfield, the other along the valley towards Rydal Water. This and the adjoining boudoir were the prettiest rooms in the house, and no one wondered that her ladyship should spend so much of her life in the luxurious seclusion of her own apartments.

John Hammond went to his room, which was on the same side of the house as her ladyship's; but he was in no disposition for sleep. He opened the casement, and stood looking out upon the moonlit lake and the quiet village, where one solitary light shone like a faint star in a cottage window, amidst that little cluster of houses by the old church, once known as Kirktown. Beyond the village rose gentle slopes, crowned with foliage, and above those wooded crests appeared the grand outline of the hills, surrounding and guarding Easedale's lovely valley, as the hills surrounded Jerusalem of old.

He looked at that delicious landscape with eyes that hardly saw its beauty. The image of a lovely face came between him and all the glory of earth and sky.

'I think she likes me,' he was saying to himself. 'There was a look in her eyes to-night that told me the time was come when----'

The thought died unfinished in his brain. Through the silent house, across the placid lake, there rang a wild, shrill cry that froze the blood in his veins, or seemed so to freeze it--a shriek of agony, and in a woman's voice. It rang out from an open window near his own. The sound seemed close to his ear.

CHAPTER X.
'O BITTERNESS OF THINGS TOO SWEET.'

Only for an instant did John Hammond stand motionless after hearing that unearthly shriek. In the next moment he rushed into the corridor, expecting to hear the sound repeated, to find himself face to face with some midnight robber, whose presence had caused that wild cry of alarm. But in the corridor all was silent as the grave. No open door suggested the entrance of an intruder. The dimly-burning lamps showed only the long empty gallery. He stood still for a few moments listening for voices, footsteps, the rustle of garments: but there was nothing.

Nothing? Yes, a groan, a long-drawn moaning sound, as of infinite pain. This time there was no doubt as to the direction from which the sound came. It came from Lady Maulevrier's room. The door was ajar, and he could see the faint light of the night-lamp within. That fearful cry had come from her ladyship's room. She was in peril or pain of some kind.

Convinced of this one fact, Mr. Hammond had not an instant's hesitation. He pushed open the door without compunction, and entered the room, prepared to behold some terrible scene.

But all was quiet as death itself. No midnight burglar had violated the sanctity of Lady Maulevrier's apartment. The soft, steady light of the night-lamp shone on the face of the sleeper. Yes, all was quiet in the room, but not in that sleeper's soul. The broad white brow was painfully contracted, the lips drawn down and distorted, the delicate hand, half hidden by the deep Valenciennes ruffle, clutched the coverlet with convulsive force. Sigh after sigh burst from the agitated breast. John Hammond gazed upon the sleeper in an agony of apprehension, uncertain what to do. Was this dreaming only; or was it some kind of seizure which called for medical aid? At her ladyship's age the idea of paralysis was not too improbable for belief. If this was a dream, then indeed the visions of Lady Maulevrier's head upon her bed were more terrible than the dreams of common mortals.

In any case Mr. Hammond felt that it was his duty to send some attendant to Lady Maulevrier, some member of the household who was familiar with her ladyship's habits, her own maid if that person could be unearthed easily. He knew that the servants slept in a separate wing; but he thought it more than likely that her ladyship's personal attendant occupied a room near her mistress.

He went back to the corridor and looked round him in doubt, for a moment or two.

Close against her ladyship's door there was a swing door, covered with red cloth, which seemed to communicate with the old part of the house. John Hammond pushed this door, and it yielded to his hand, revealing a lamp-lit passage, narrow, old-fashioned, and low. He thought it likely that Lady Maulevrier's maid might occupy a room in this half-deserted wing. As he pushed open the door he saw an elderly man coming towards him, with a candle in his hand, and with the appearance of having huddled on his clothes hastily.

'You heard that scream?' said Hammond.

'Yes. It was her ladyship, I suppose. Nightmare. She is subject to nightmare.'

'It is very dreadful. Her whole countenance was convulsed just now, when I went into her room to see what was wrong. I was almost afraid of a fit of some kind. Ought not her maid to go to her?'

'She wants no assistance,' the man answered, coolly. 'It was only a dream. It is not the first time I have been awakened by a shriek like that. It is a kind of nightmare, no doubt; and it passes off in a few minutes, and leaves her sleeping calmly.'

He went to her ladyship's door, pushed it open a little way, and looked in. 'Yes, she is sleeping as quietly as an infant,' he said, shutting the door softly as he spoke.

'I am very glad; but surely she ought to have her maid near her at night, if she is subject to those attacks.'

'It is no attack, I tell you. It is nothing but a dream,' answered Steadman impatiently.

'Yet you were frightened, just as I was, or you would not have got up and dressed,' said Hammond, looking at the man suspiciously.

He had heard of this old servant Steadman, who was supposed to enjoy more of her ladyship's confidence than any one else in the household; but he had never spoken to the man before that night.

'Yes, I came. It was my duty to come, knowing her ladyship's habits. I am a light sleeper, and that scream woke me instantly. If her ladyship's maid were wanted I should call her. I am a kind of watch-dog, you see, sir.'

'You seem to be a very faithful dog.'

'I have been in her ladyship's service more than forty years. I have reason to be faithful. I know her ladyship's habits better than any one in the house. I know that she had a great deal of trouble in her early life, and I believe the memory of it comes back upon her sometimes in her dreams, and gets the better of her.'

'If it was memory that wrung that agonised shriek from her just now, her recollections of the past must be very terrible.'

'Ah, sir, there is a skeleton in every house,' answered James Steadman, gravely.

This was exactly what Maulevrier had said under the yew trees which Wordsworth planted.

'Good-night, sir,' said Steadman.

'Good-night. You are sure that Lady Maulevrier may be left safely--that there is no fear of illness of any kind?'

'No, sir. It was only a bad dream. Good-night, sir.'

Steadman went back to his own quarters. Mr. Hammond heard him draw the bolts of the swing door, thus cutting off all communication with the corridor.

The eight-day clock on the staircase struck two as Mr. Hammond returned to his room, even less inclined for sleep than when he left it. Strange, that nocturnal disturbance of a mind which seemed so tranquil in the day. Or was that tranquillity only a mask which her ladyship wore before the world: and was the bitter memory of events which happened forty years ago still a source of anguish to that highly strung nature?

'There are some minds which cannot forget,' John Hammond said to himself, as he meditated upon her ladyship's character and history. 'The story of her husband's crime may still be fresh in her memory, though it is only a tradition for the outside world. His crime may have involved some deep wrong done to herself, some outrage against her love and faith as a wife. One of the stories Maulevrier spoke of the other day was of a wicked woman's influence upon the governor--a much more likely story than that of any traffic in British interests or British honour, which would have been almost impossible for a man in Lord Maulevrier's position. If the scandal was of a darker kind--a guilty wife--the mysterious disappearance of a husband-- the horror of the thing may have made a deeper impression on Lady Maulevrier than even her nearest and dearest dream of: and that superb calm which she wears like a royal mantle may be maintained at the cost of struggles which tear her heart-strings. And then at night, when the will is dormant, when the nervous system is no longer ruled by the power of waking intelligence, the old familiar agony returns, the hated images flash back upon the brain, and in proportion to the fineness of the temperament is the intensity of the dreamer's pain.'

And then he went on to reflect upon the long monotonous years spent in that lonely house, shut in from the world by those everlasting hills. Albeit the house was an ideal house, set in a landscape of infinite beauty, the monotony must be none the less oppressive for a mind burdened with dark memories, weighed down by sorrows which could seek no relief from sympathy, which could never become familiarised by discussion.

'I wonder that a woman of Lady Maulevrier's intellect should not have better known how to treat her own malady,' thought Hammond.

Mr. Hammond inquired after her ladyship's health next morning, and was told she was perfectly well.

'Grandmother is in capital spirits,' said Lady Lesbia. 'She is pleased with the contents of yesterday's *Globe*. Lord Denyer, the son of one of her oldest friends, has been making a great speech at Liverpool in the Conservative interest, and her ladyship thinks we shall have a change of parties before long.'

'A general shuffle of the cards,' said Maulevrier, looking up from his breakfast.

'I'm sure I hope so. I'm no politician, but I like a row.'

'I hope you are a Conservative, Mr. Hammond,' said Lesbia.

'I had hoped you would have known that ever so long ago, Lady Lesbia.'

Lesbia blushed at his tone, which was almost a reproach.

'I suppose I ought to have understood from the general tenor of your conversation,' she said; 'but I am terribly stupid about politics. I take so little interest in them. I am always hearing that we are being badly governed--that the men who legislate for us are stupid or wicked; yet the world seems to go on somehow, and we are no worse.'

'It is just the same with sport,' said Maulevrier. 'Every rainy spring we are told that all the young birds have been drowned, or that the grouse-disease has decimated the fathers and mothers, and that we shall have nothing to shoot; but when August comes the birds are there all the same.'

'It is the nature of mankind to complain,' said Hammond. 'Cain and Abel were the first farmers, and you see one of them grumbled.'

They were rather lively at breakfast that morning--Maulevrier's last breakfast but one--for he had announced his determination of going to Scotland next day. Other fellows would shoot all the birds if he dawdled any longer. Mary was in deep despondency at the idea of his departure, yet she laughed and talked with the rest. And perhaps Lesbia felt a little moved at the thought of losing Mr. Hammond. Maulevrier would come back to Mary, but John Hammond was hardly likely to return. Their parting would be for ever.

'You needn't sit quite in my pocket, Molly,' said Maulevrier to his younger sister.

'I like to make the most of you, now you are going away,' sighed Mary. 'Oh, dear, how dull we shall all be when you are gone.'

'Not a bit of it! You will have some fox-hunting, perhaps, before the snow is on the hills.'

At the very mention of fox-hounds Lady Mary's bright young face crimsoned, and Maulevrier began to laugh in a provoking way, with side-long glances at his younger sister.

'Did you ever hear of Molly's fox-hunting, by-the-by, Hammond?' he asked.

Mary tried to put her hand before his lips, but it was useless.

'Why shouldn't I tell?' he exclaimed. 'It was quite a heroic adventure. You must know our fox-hunting here is rather a peculiar institution,--very good in its way, but strictly local. No horse could live among our hills, so we hunt on foot, and as the pace is good, and the work hard, nobody who starts with the hounds is likely to be in at the death, except the huntsmen. We are all mad for the sport, and off we go, over the hills and far away, picking up a fresh field as we go. The ploughman leaves his plough, and the shepherd leaves his flock, and the farmer leaves his thrashing, to follow us; in every field we cross we get fresh blood, while those who join us at the start fall off by degrees. Well, it happened one day late in October, when there were long ridges of snow on Helvellyn, and patches of white on Fairfield, Mistress Mary here must needs take her bamboo staff and start for the Striding Edge. It was just the day upon which she might have met her death easily on that perilous point, but happily something occurred to divert her juvenile fancy, for scarcely had she got to the bottom of Dolly Waggon Pike--you know Dolly----'

'Intimately,' said Hammond, with a nod.

'Scarcely had she neared the base of Dolly Waggon when she heard the huntsman's horn and the hounds at full cry, streaming along towards Dunmail Raise. Off flew Molly, all among the butcher boys, and farmers' men, and rosy-cheeked squireens of the district--racing over the rugged fields--clambering over the low stone walls--up hill, down hill--shouting when the others shouted--never losing sight of the waving sterns--winding and doubling, and still going upward and upward, till she stood, panting and puffing like a young grampus, on the top of Seat Sandal, still all among the butcher boys and the farmer's men, and the guides and the red-cheeked squireens, her frock torn to ribbons, her hat lost in a ditch, her hair streaming down her back, and every inch of her, from her nose downwards, splashed and spattered with mire and clay. What a spectacle for gods and men, guides and butcher boys. And there she stood with the sun going down beyond Coniston Old Man, and a seven-mile walk between her and Fellside.

'Poor Lady Mary!' said Hammond, looking at her very kindly: but Mary did not see that friendly glance, which betokened sympathy rather than scorn. She sat silent and very red, with drooping eyelids, thinking her brother horribly cruel for thus publishing her foolishness.

'Poor, indeed!' exclaimed Maulevrier. 'She came crawling home after dark, footsore and draggled, looking like a beggar girl, and as evil fate would have it, her ladyship, who so seldom goes out, must needs have been taking afternoon tea at the Vicarage upon that particular occasion, and was driving up the avenue as Mary crawled to the gate. The storm that followed may be more easily imagined than described.'

'It was years and years ago,' expostulated Mary, looking very angry. 'Grandmother needn't have made such a fuss about it.'

'Ah, but in those days she still had hopes of civilising you,' answered Maulevrier. 'Since then she has abandoned all endeavour in that direction, and has given you over to your own devices--and me. Since then you have become a chartered libertine. You have letters of mark.'

'I don't care what you call me,' said Mary. 'I only know that I am very happy when you are at home, and very miserable when you are away.'

'It is hardly kind of you to say that, Lady Mary,' remonstrated Fraeulein Mueller, who, up to this point, had been busily engaged with muffins and gooseberry jam.

'Oh, I don't mean that any one is unkind to me or uses me badly,' said Mary. 'I only mean that my life is empty when Maulevrier is away, and that I am always longing for him to come back again.'

'I thought you adored the hills, and the lake, and the villagers, and your pony, and Maulevrier's dogs,' said, Lesbia faintly contemptuous.

'Yes, but one wants something human to love,' answered Mary, making it very obvious that there was no warmth of affection between herself and the feminine members of her family.

She had not thought of the significance of her speech. She was very angry with Maulevrier for having held her up to ridicule before Mr. Hammond, who already despised her, as she believed, and whose contempt was more galling than it need have been, considering that he was a mere casual visitor who would go away and return no more. Never till his coming had she felt her deficiencies; but in his presence she writhed under the sense of her unworthiness, and had an almost agonising consciousness of all those faults which her grandmother had told her about so often with not the slightest effect. In those days she had not cared what Lady Maulevrier or any one else might say of her, or think of her. She lived her life, and defied fortune. She was worse than her reputation. To-day she felt it a bitter thing that she had grown to the age of womanhood lacking all those graces and accomplishments which made her sister adorable, and which might make even a plain woman charming.

Never till John Hammond's coming had she felt a pang of envy in the contemplation of Lesbia's beauty or Lesbia's grace; but now she had so keen a sense of the difference between herself and her sister that she began to fear that this cruel pain must indeed be that lowest of all vices. Even the difference in their gowns was a source of humiliation to her how. Lesbia was looking her loveliest this morning, in a gown that was all lace and soft Madras muslin, flowing, cloud-like; while Mary's tailor gown, with its trim tight bodice, horn buttons, and kilted skirt, seemed to cry aloud that it had been made for a Tomboy. And this tailor gown was a costume to which Mary had condemned herself by her own folly. Only a year ago, moved by an artistic admiration for Lesbia's delicate breakfast gowns, Mary had told her grandmother that she would like to have something of the same kind, whereupon the dowager, who did not take the faintest interest in Mary's toilet, but who had a stern sense of justice, replied--

'I do not think Lesbia's frocks and your habits will agree, but you can have some pretty morning gowns if you like;' and the order had been given for a confection in muslin and lace for Lady Mary.

Mary came down to breakfast one bright June morning, in the new frock, feeling very proud of herself, and looking very pretty.

'Fine feathers make fine birds,' said Fraeulein Mueller. 'I should hardly have known you.'

'I wish you would always dress like that,' said Lesbia; 'you really look like a young lady;' and Mary danced about on the lawn, feeling sylph-like, and quite in love with her own elegance, when a sudden uplifting of canine voices in the distance had sent her flying to see what was the matter with the terrier pack.

In the kennel there was riot and confusion. Ahab was demolishing Angelina, Absalom had Agamemnon in a deadly grip. Dog-whip in hand, Mary rushed to the rescue, and laid about her, like the knights of old, utterly forgetful of her frock. She soon succeeded in restoring order, but the Madras muslin, the Breton lace had perished in the conflict. She left the kennel panting, and in rags and tatters, some of the muslin and lace hanging about her in strips a yard long, but the greater part remaining in the possession of the terriers, who had mauled and munched her finery to their hearts' content, while she was reading the Riot Act.

She went back to the house, bowed down by shame and confusion, and marched straight to the dowager's morning-room.

'Look what the terriers have done to me, grandmother,' she said, with a sob. 'It is all my own fault, of course. I ought not to have gone near them in that stupid muslin. Please forgive me for being so foolish. I am not fit to have pretty frocks.'

'I think, my dear, you can now have no doubt that the tailor gowns are fittest for you,' answered Lady Maulevrier, with crushing placidity. 'We have tried the experiment of dressing you like Lesbia, and you see it does not answer. Tell Kibble to throw your new gown in the rag-bag, and please let me hear no more about it.'

After this dismal failure Mary could not feel herself ill-used in having to wear tailor gowns all the year round. She was allowed cotton frocks for very warm weather, and she had pretty gowns for evening wear; but her usual attire was cloth or linsey woolsey, made by the local tailor. Sometimes Maulevrier ordered her a gown or a coat from his own man in Conduit Street, and then she felt herself smart and fashionable. And even the local tailor contrived to make her gowns prettily, having a great appreciation of her straight willowy figure, and deeming it a privilege to work for her, so that hitherto Mary had felt very well content with her cloth and linsey. But now that John Hammond so obviously admired Lesbia's delicate raiment, poor Mary began to think her woollen gowns odious.

After breakfast Mary and Maulevrier went straight off to the kennels. His lordship had numerous instructions to give on this last day, and his lieutenant had to receive and register his orders. Lesbia went to the garden with her book and with Fraeulein--the inevitable Fraeulein as Hammond thought her--in close attendance.

It was a lovely morning, sultry, summer-like, albeit September had just begun. The tennis lawn, which had been levelled on one side of the house, was surrounded on three sides by shrubberies planted forty years ago, in the beginning of Lady Maulevrier's widowhood. All loveliest trees grew there in perfection, sheltered by the mighty wall of the mountain, fed by the mists from the lake. Larch and mountain ash, and Lawsonian cyprus,--deodara and magnolia, arbutus, and silver broom, acacia and lilac, flourished here in that rich beauty which made every cottage garden in the happy district a little paradise; and here in a semi-circular recess at one end of the lawn were rustic chairs and tables and an umbrella tent. This was Lady Lesbia's chosen retreat on summer mornings, and a favourite place for afternoon tea.

Mr. Hammond followed the two ladies to their bower.

'This is to be my last morning,' he said, looking at Lesbia. 'Will you think me a great bore if I spend it with you?'

'We shall think it very nice of you,' answered Lesbia, without a vestige of emotion; 'especially if you will read to us.'

'I will do any thing to make myself useful. What shall I read?'

'Anything you like. What do you say to Tennyson?'

'That he is a noble poet, a teacher of all good; but too philosophical for my present mood. May I read you some of Heine's ballads, those songs which you sing so exquisitely, or rather some you do not sing, and which will be fresher to you. My German is far from perfect, but I am told it is passable, and Fraeulein Mueller can throw her scissors at me when my accent is too dreadful.'

'You speak German beautifully,' said Fraeulein. 'I wonder where you learned it?'

'I have been a good deal in Germany, and I had a Hanoverian valet who was quite a gentleman, and spoke admirably, I think I learned more from him than from grammars or dictionaries. I'll go and fetch Heine.'

'What a very agreeable person Mr. Hammond is,' said Fraeulein, when he was gone. 'We shall quite miss him.'

'Yes, I have no doubt we shall miss him,' said Lesbia, again without the faintest emotion.

The governess began to think that the ordeal of an agreeable young man's presence at Fellside had been passed in safety, and that her pupil was unscathed. She had kept a close watch on the two, as in duty bound. She knew that Hammond was in love with Lesbia; but she thought Lesbia was heart-whole.

Mr. Hammond came back with a shabby little book in his hand and established himself comfortably in one of the two Beaconsfield chairs.

He opened his book at that group of short poems called Heimkehr, and read here and there, as fancy led him. Sometimes the strain was a love-song, brief, passionate as the cry of a soul in pain; sometimes the verses were bitter and cynical; sometimes full of tenderest simplicity, telling of childhood, and youth and purity; sometimes dark with hidden meanings, grim, awful, cold with the chilling breath of the charnel-house. Sometimes Lesbia's heart beat a little faster as Mr. Hammond read, for it seemed as if it was he who was speaking to her, and not the dead poet.

An hour or more passed in this way. Fraeulein Mueller was charmed at hearing some of her favourite poems, asking now for this little bit, and anon for another, and expatiating upon the merits of German poets in general, and Heine in particular, in the pauses of the lecture. She was quite carried away by her delight in the poet, and was so entirely uplifted to the ideal world that, when a footman came with a message from Lady Maulevrier requesting her presence, she tripped gaily off at once, without a thought of danger in leaving those two together on the lawn. She had been a faithful watch-dog up to this point; but she was now lulled into a false sense of security by the idea that the time of peril was all but ended.

So she left them; but could she have looked back two minutes afterwards she would have perceived the unwisdom of that act.

No sooner had the Fraeulein turned the corner of the shrubbery than Hammond laid aside his book and drew nearer Lesbia, who sat looking downward, with her eyes upon the delicate piece of fancy work which had occupied her fingers all the morning.

'Lesbia, this is my last day at Fellside, and you and I may never have a minute alone together again while I am here. Will you come for a little walk with me on the Fell? There is something I must say to you before I go.'

Lesbia's delicate cheek grew a shade more pale. Instinct told her what was coming, though never mortal man had spoken to her of love. Nor until now had Mr. Hammond ever addressed her by her Christian name without the ceremonious prefix. There was a deeper tone in his voice, a graver look in his eyes, than she had ever noticed before.

She rose, and took up her sunshade, and went with him meekly through the cultivated shrubbery of ornamental timber to the rougher pathway that wound through a copse of Scotch fir, which formed the outer boundary of Lady Maulevrier's domain. Beyond the fir trees rose the grassy slope of the hill, on the brow of which sheep were feeding. Deep down in the hollow below the lawns and shrub-berries of Fellside the placid bosom of the lake shone like an emerald floor in the sunlight, reflecting the verdure of the hill, and the white sheep dotted about here and there.

There was not a breath in the air around them as those two sauntered slowly side by side in the pine wood, not a cloud in the dazzling blue sky above; and for a little time they too were silent, as if bound by a spell which neither dared to break. Then at last Hammond spoke.

'Lesbia, you know that I love you,' he began, in his low, grave voice, tremulous with feeling. 'No words I can say to-day can tell you of my love more plainly than my heart has been telling you in every hour of this happy, happy time that you and I have spent together. I love you as I never hoped to love, fervently, completely, believing that the perfection of earthly bliss will be mine if I can but win you. Dearest, is there such a sweet hope for me; are you indeed my own, as I am yours, heart and soul, and mind and being, till the last throb of life in this poor clay?'

He tried to take her hand, but she drew herself away from him with a frightened look. She was very pale, and there was infinite distress in the dark violet eyes, which looked entreatingly, deprecatingly at her lover.

'I dare not answer as you would like me to answer,' she faltered, after a painful pause. 'I am not my own mistress. My grandmother has brought me up, devoted herself to me almost, and she has her own views, her own plans. I dare not frustrate them!'

'She would like to marry you to a man of rank and fortune--a man who will choose you, perhaps, because other people admire you, rather than because he himself loves you as you ought to be loved; who will choose you because you are altogether the best and most perfect thing of your year; just as he would buy a yearling at Newmarket or Doncaster. Her ladyship means you to make a great alliances--coronets, not hearts, are the counters for her game; but, Lesbia, would you, in the bloom and freshness of youth--you with the pulses of youth throbbing at your heart--lend yourself to the calculations of age which has lived its life and forgotten the very meaning of love? Would you submit to be played as a card in the game of a dowager's ambition? Trust me, dearest, in the crisis of a woman's life there is one only counsellor she should listen to, and that counsellor is her own heart. If you love me--as I dare to hope you do--trust in me, hold by me, and leave the rest to

Heaven. I know that I can make your life happy.'

'You frighten me by your impetuosity,' said Lesbia. 'Surely you forget how short a time we have known each other.'

'An age. All my life before the day I saw you is a dead, dull blank as compared with the magical hours I have spent with you.'

'I do not even know who and what you are.'

'First, I am a gentleman, or I should not be your brother's friend. A poor gentleman, if you like, with only my own right arm to hew my pathway through the wood of life to the temple of fortune; but trust me, only trust me, Lesbia, and I will so hew my path as to reach that temple. Look at me, love. Do I look like a man born to fail?'

She looked up at him shyly, with eyes that were dim with tears. He looked like a demi-god, tall, straight as the pine trunks amongst which he was standing, a frame formed for strength and activity, a face instinct with mental power, dark eyes that glowed with the fire of intellect and passion. The sunlight gave an almost unearthly radiance to the clear dark of his complexion, the curly brown hair cut close to the finely shaped head, the broad brow and boldly modelled features.

Lesbia felt in her heart that such a man must be destined for success, born to be a conqueror in all strifes, a victor upon every field.

'Have I the thews and sinews of a man doomed to be beaten in the battle?' he asked her. 'No, dearest; Heaven meant me to succeed; and with you to fight for I shall not be beaten by adverse fortune. Can you not trust Providence and me?'

'I cannot disobey my grandmother. If she will consent----'

'She will not consent. You must defy Lady Maulevrier, Lesbia, if you mean to reward my love. But I will promise you this much, darling, that if you will be my wife--with your brother's consent--which I am sure of before I ask for it, within one year of our marriage I will find means of reconciling her ladyship to the match, and winning her entire forgiveness for you and me.'

'You are talking of impossibilities,' said Lesbia, frowning. 'Why do you talk to me as if I were a child? I know hardly anything of the world, but I do know the woman who has reared and educated me. My grandmother would never forgive me if I married a poor man. I should be an outcast.'

'We would be outcasts together--happy outcasts. Besides, we should not always be poor. I tell you I am predestined to conquer fate.'

'But we should have to begin from the beginning.'

'Yes, we should have to begin from the beginning, as Adam and Eve did when they left Paradise.'

'We are not told in the Bible that they had any happiness after that. It seems to have been all trouble and weariness, and toil and death, after the angel with the flaming sword drove them out of Eden.'

'They were together, and they must have been happy. Oh, Lesbia, if you do not feel that you can face poverty and the world's contempt by my side, and for my sake, you do not love me. Love never calculates so nicely; love never fears the future; and yet you do love me, Lesbia,' he said, trying to fold her in his arms; but again she drew herself away from him--this time with a look almost of horror--and stood facing him, clinging to one of the pine trunks, like a scared wood-nymph.

'You have no right to say that,' she said.

'I have the divine right of my own deep love--of heart which cries out to heart. Do you think there is no magnetic power in true love which can divine the answering love in another? Lesbia, call me an insolent coxcomb if you like, but I know you love me, and that you and I may be utterly happy together. Oh, why--why do you shrink from me, my beloved; why withhold yourself from my arms! Oh, love, let me hold you to my heart--let me seal our betrothal with a kiss!'

'Betrothal--no, no; not for the world,' cried Lesbia. 'Lady Maulevrier would cast me off for ever; she would curse me.'

'What would the curse of an ambitious woman weigh against my love? And I tell you that her anger would be only a passing tempest. She would forgive you.'

'Never--you don't know her.'

'I tell you she would forgive you, and all would be well with us before we had been married a year. Why cannot you believe me, Lesbia?'

'Because I cannot believe impossibilities, even from your lips,' she answered sullenly.

She stood before him with downcast eyes, the tears streaming down her pale cheeks, exquisitely lovely in her agitation and sorrow. Yes, she did love him; her heart was beating passionately; she was longing to throw herself on his breast, to be folded upon that manly heart, in trust in that brave, bright look which seemed to defy fortune. Yes, he was a man born to conquer; he was handsome, intellectual, powerful in all mental and physical gifts. A man of men. But he was, by his own admission, a very obscure and insignificant person, and he had no money. Life with him meant a long fight with adverse circumstances; life for his wife must mean patience, submission, long waiting upon destiny, and perhaps with old age and grey hairs the tardy turning of Fortune's wheel. And was she for this to resign the kingdom that had been promised to her, the giddy heights which she was born to scale, the triumphs and delights and victories of the great world? Yes, Lesbia loved this fortuneless knight; but she loved herself and her prospects of promotion still better.

'Oh, Lesbia, can you not be brave for my sake--trustful for my sake? God will be good to us if we are true to each other.'

'God will not be good to me if I disobey my grandmother. I owe her too much; ingratitude in me would be doubly base. I will speak to her. I will tell her all you have said, and if she gives me the faintest encouragement----'

'She will not; that is a foregone conclusion. Tell her all, if you like; but let us be prepared for the answer. When she denies the right of your heart to choose its own mate, then rise up in the might of your womanhood and defy her. Tell her, "I love him, and be he rich or poor, I will share his fate;" tell her boldly, bravely, nobly, as a true woman should; and if she be adamant still, proclaim your right to disobey her worldly wisdom rather than the voice of your own heart. And then come to me, darling, and be my own, and the world which you and I will face together shall not be a bad world. I will answer for that. No trouble shall come near you. No humiliation shall ever touch you. Only believe in me.'

'I can believe in you, but not in the impossible,' answered Lesbia, with measured accents.

The voice was silver-sweet, but passing cold. Just then there was a rustling among the pine branches, and Lesbia looked round with a startled air.

'Is there any one listening?' she exclaimed. 'What was that?'

'Only the breath of heaven. Oh, Lesbia, if you were but a little less wise, a little more trustful. Do not be a dumb idol. Say that you love me, or do not love me. If you can look me in the face and say the last, I will leave you without another word. I will take my sentence and go.'

But this was just what Lesbia could not do. She could not deny her love; and yet she could not sacrifice all things for her love. She lifted the heavy lids which veiled those lovely eyes, and looked up at him imploringly.

'Give me time to breathe, time to think,' she said.

'And then will you answer me plainly, truthfully, without a shadow of reserve, remembering that the fate of two lives hangs on your words.'

'I will.'

'Let it be so, then. I'll go for a ramble over the hills, and return in time for afternoon tea. I shall look for you on the tennis lawn at half-past four.'

He took her in his arms, and this time she yielded herself to him, and the beautiful head rested for a few moments upon his breast, and the soft eyes looked up at him in confiding fondness. He bent and kissed her once only, but a kiss that meant for life and death. In the next moment he was gone, leaving her alone among the pine trees.

CHAPTER XI.
'IF I WERE TO DO AS ISEULT DID.'

Lady Maulevrier rarely appeared at luncheon. She took some slight refection in her morning-room, among her books and papers, and in the society of her canine favourites, whose company suited her better at certain hours than the noisier companionship of her grandchildren. She was a studious woman, loving the silent life of books better than the inane chatter of everyday humanity. She was a woman who thought much and read much, and who lived more in the past than the present. She lived also in the future, counting much upon the splendid career of her beautiful granddaughter, which should be in a manner a lengthening out, a renewal of her own life. She looked forward to the day when Lesbia should reign supreme in the great world, a famous beauty and leader of fashion, her every act and word inspired and directed by her grandmother, who would be the shadow behind the throne. It was possible--nay, probable--that in those days Lady Maulevrier would herself reappear in society, establish her salon, and draw around her closing years all that is wittiest, best, and wisest in the great world.

Her ladyship was reposing in her low reading-chair, with a volume of Tyndall on the book-stand before her, when the door was opened softly and Lesbia came gliding in, and seated herself without a word on the hassock at her grandmother's feet. Lady Maulevrier passed her hand caressingly over the girl's soft brown hair, without looking up from her book.

'You are a late visitor,' she said; 'why did you not come to me after breakfast?'

'It was such a lovely morning, we went straight from the breakfast table to the garden; I did not think you wanted me.'

'I did not want you; but I am always glad to see my pet. What were you doing in the garden all the morning? I did not hear you playing tennis.'

Lady Maulevrier had already interrogated the German governess upon this very subject, but she had her own reasons for wishing to hear Lesbia's account.

'No, it was too warm for tennis. Fraeulein and I sat and worked, and Mr. Hammond read to us.'

'What did he read?'

'Heine's ballads. He reads German beautifully.'

'Indeed! I daresay he was at school in Germany. There are cheap schools there to which middle-class people send their boys.'

This was like a thrust from a rusty knife.

'Mr. Hammond was at Oxford,' Lesbia said, reproachfully; and then, after a longish pause, she clasped her hands upon the arm of Lady Maulevrier's chair, and said, in a pleading voice, 'Grandmother, Mr. Hammond has asked me to marry him.'

'Indeed! Only that? And pray, did he tell you what are his means of maintaining Lord Maulevrier's sister in the position to which her birth entitles her?' inquired the dowager, with crushing calmness.

'He is not rich; indeed, I believe, he is poor; but he is brave and clever, and he is full of confidence in his power to conquer fortune.'

'No doubt; that is your true adventurer's style. He confides implicitly in his own talents, and in somebody else's banker. Mr. Hammond would make a tremendous figure in the world, I daresay, and while he was making it your brother would have to keep him. Well, my dear Lesbia, I hope you gave this gentleman the answer his insolence deserved; or that you did better, and referred him to me. I should be glad to give him my opinion of his conduct--a person admitted to this house as your brother's hanger-on--tolerated only on your brother's account; such a person, nameless, penniless, friendless (except for Maulevrier's too facile patronage), to dare to lift his eyes to my granddaughter! It is ineffable insolence!'

Lesbia crouched by her grandmother's chair, her face hidden from Lady Maulevrier's falcon eye. Every word uttered by her ladyship stung like the knotted cords of a knout. She knew not whether to be most ashamed of her lover or of herself--of her lover for his obscure position, his hopeless poverty; of herself for her folly in loving such a man. And she did love him, and would fain have pleaded his cause, had she not been cowed by the authority that had ruled her all her life.

'Lesbia, if I thought you had been silly enough, degraded enough, to give this young man encouragement, to have justified his audacity of to-day by any act or word of yours, I should despise, I should detest you,' said Lady Maulevrier, sternly. 'What could be more contemptible, more hateful in a girl reared as you have been than to give encouragement to the first comer--to listen greedily to the first adventurer who had the insolence to make love to you, to be eager to throw yourself into the arms of the first man who asked you. That my granddaughter, a girl reared and taught and watched and guarded by me, should have no more dignity, no more modesty, or womanly feeling, than a barmaid at an inn!'

Lesbia began to cry.

'I don't see why a barmaid, should not be a good woman, or why it should be a crime to fall in love,' she said, in a voice broken by sobs. 'You need not speak to me so unkindly. I am not going to marry Mr. Hammond.'

'Oh, you are not? that is very good of you. I am deeply grateful for such an assurance.'

'But I like him better than anyone I ever saw in my life before.'

'You have seen to many people. You have had such a wide area for choice.'

'No; I know I have been kept like a nun in a convent: but I don't think when I go into the world I shall ever see anyone I should like better than Mr. Hammond.'

'Wait till you have seen the world before you make up your mind about that. And now, Lesbia, leave off talking and thinking like a child; look me in the face and listen to me, for I am going to speak seriously; and with me, when I am in earnest, what is said once is said for ever.'

Lady Maulevrier grasped her granddaughter's arm with long slender fingers which held it as tightly as the grasp of a vice. She drew the girl's slim figure round till they were face to face, looking into each other's eyes, the dowager's eagle countenance lit up with impassioned feeling, severe, awful as the face of one of the fatal sisters, the avengers of blood, the harbingers of doom.

'Lesbia, I think I have been good to you, and kind to you,' she said.

'You have been all that is kind and dear,' faltered Lesbia.

'Then give me measure for measure. My life has been a hard one, child; hard and lonely, and loveless and joyless. My son, to whom I devoted myself in the vigour of youth and in the prime of life, never loved me, never repaid me for my love. He spent his days far away from me, when his presence would have gladdened my difficult life. He died in a strange land. Of his three children, you are the one I took into my heart. I did my duty to the others; I lavished my love upon you. Do not give me cursing instead of blessing. Do not give me a stone instead of bread. I have built every hope of happiness or pleasure in this world upon you and your obedience. Obey me, be true to me, and I will make you a queen, and I will sit in the shadow of your throne. I will toil for you, and be wise for you. You shall have only to shine, and dazzle, and enjoy the glory of life. My beautiful darling, for pity's sake do not give yourself over to folly.'

'Did not you marry for love, grandmother?'

'No, Lesbia. Lord Maulevrier and I got on very well together, but ours was no love-match.'

'Does nobody in our rank ever marry for love? are all marriages a mere exchange and barter?'

'No, there are love-matches now and then, which often turn out badly. But, my darling, I am not asking you to marry for rank or for money. I am only asking you to wait till you find your mate among the noblest in the land. He may be the handsomest and most accomplished of men, a man born to win women's hearts; and you may love him as fervently as ever a village girl loved her first lover. I am not going to sacrifice you, or to barter you, dearest. I mean to marry you to the best and noblest young man of his day. You shall never be asked to stoop to the unworthy, not even if worthlessness wore strawberry leaves in his cap, and owned the greatest estate in the land.'

'And if--instead of waiting-for this King Arthur of yours--I were to do as Iseult did--as Guinevere did--choose for myself----'

'Iseult and Guinevere were wantons. I wonder that you can name them in comparison with yourself.'

'If I were to marry a good and honourable man who has his place to make in the world, would you never forgive me?'

'You mean Mr. Hammond? You may just as well speak plainly,' said Lady Maulevrier, freezingly. 'If you were capable of such idiocy as that, Lesbia, I would pluck you out of my heart like a foul weed. I would never look upon you, or hear your name spoken, or think of you again as long as I lived. My life would not last very long after that blow. Old age cannot bear such shocks. Oh, Lesbia, I have been father and mother to you; do not bring my grey hairs in sorrow to the grave.'

Lesbia gave a deep sigh, and brushed the tears from her cheeks. Yes, the very idea of such a marriage was foolishness. Just now, in the pine wood, carried away by the force of her lover's passion, by her own softer feelings, it had seemed to her as if she could count the world well lost for his sake; but now, at Lady Maulevrier's feet, she became again true to her training, and the world was too much to lose.

'What can I do, grandmother?' she asked, submissively, despairingly. 'He loves me, and I love him. How can I tell him that he and I can never be anything to each other in this world?'

'Refer him to me. I will give him his answer.'

'No, no; that will not do. I have promised to answer him myself. He has gone for a walk on the hills, and will come back at four o'clock for my answer.'

'Sit down at that table, and write as I dictate.'

'But a letter will be so formal.'

'It is the only way in which you can answer him. When he comes back from his walk you will have left Fellside. I shall send you off to St. Bees with Fraeulein. You must never look upon that man's face again.'

Lesbia brushed away a few more tears, and obeyed. She had been too well trained to attempt resistance. Defiance was out of the question.

CHAPTER XII.
'THE GREATER CANTLE OF THE WORLD IS LOST.'

The sky was still cloudless when John Hammond strolled slowly up the leafy avenue at Fellside. He had been across the valley and up the hill to Easedale Tarn, and then by rough untrodden ways, across a chaos of rock and heather, into a second valley, long, narrow, and sterile, known as Far Easedale, a desolate gorge, a rugged cleft in the heart of the mountains. The walk had been long and laborious; but only in such clambering and toiling, such expenditure of muscular force and latent heat, could the man's restless soul endure those long hours of suspense.

'How will she answer me? Oh, my God! how will she answer?' he said within himself, as he walked up the romantic winding road, which made so picturesque an approach to Lady Maulevrier's domain, 'Is my idol gold or clay? How will she come through the crucible? Oh, dearest, sweetest, loveliest, only be true to the instinct of your womanhood, and my cup will be full of bliss, and all my days will flow as sweetly as the burden of a song. But if you prove heartless, if you love the world's. wealth better than you love me--ah! then all is over, and you and I are lost to each other for ever. I have made up my mind.'

His face settled into an expression of indomitable determination, as of a man who would die rather than be false to his own purpose. There was no glow of hope in his heart. He had no deep faith in the girl he loved; indeed in his heart of hearts he knew that this being to whom he had trusted his hopes of bliss was no heroine. She was a lovely, loveable girl, nothing more. How would she greet him when they met presently on the tennis lawn? With tears and entreaties, and pretty little deprecating speeches, irresolution, timidity, vacillation, perhaps; hardly with heroic resolve to act and dare for his sake.

There was no one on the tennis lawn when he went there, though the hour was close at hand at which Lesbia had promised to give him his answer. He sat down in one of the low chairs, glad to rest after his long ramble having had no refreshment but a bottle of soda-water and a biscuit at the cottage by Easedale Tarn. He waited, calmly as to outward seeming, but with a heavy heart.

'If it were Mary now whom I loved, I should have little fear of the issue,' he thought, weighing his sweetheart's character, as he weighed his chances of success. 'That young termagant would defy the world for her lover.'

He sat in the summer silence for nearly half-an-hour, and still there was no sign of Lady Lesbia. Her satin-lined workbasket, with the work thrown carelessly across it, was still on the rustic table, just as she had left it when they went to the pine wood. Waiting was weary work when the bliss of a lifetime trembled in the balance; and yet he did not want to be impatient. She might find it difficult to get away from her family, perhaps. She was closely watched and guarded, as the most precious thing at Fellside.

At last the clock struck five, and Hammond could endure delay no longer. He went round by the flower garden to the terrace before the drawing-room windows, and through an open window to the drawing-room.

Lady Maulevrier was in her accustomed seat, with her own particular little table, magazines, books, newspapers at her side. Lady Mary was pouring out the tea, a most unusual thing; and Maulevrier was sitting on a stool at her feet, with his knees up to his chin, very warm and dusty, eating pound cake.

'Where the mischief have you been hiding yourself all day, Jack?' he called out as Hammond appeared, looking round the room as he entered, with eager, interrogating eyes, for that one figure which was absent.

'I have been for a walk.'

'You might have had the civility to announce your design, and Molly and I would have shared your peregrinations.'

'I am sorry that I lost the privilege of your company.'

'I suppose you lost your luncheon, which was of more importance,' said Maulevrier.

'Will you have some tea?' asked Mary, who looked more womanly than usual in a cream-coloured surah gown--one of her Sunday gowns.

She had a faint hope that by this essentially feminine apparel she might lessen the prejudicial effect of Maulevrier's cruel story about the fox-hunt.

Mr. Hammond answered absently, hardly looking at Mary, and quite unconscious of her pretty gown.

'Thanks, yes,' he said, taking the cup and saucer, and looking at the door by which he momently expected Lady Lesbia's entrance, and then, as the door did not open, he looked down at Mary, very busy with china teapots and a brass kettle which hissed and throbbed over a spirit lamp.

'Won't you have some cake,' she asked, looking up at him gently, grieved at the distress and disappointment in his face. 'I am sure you must be dreadfully hungry.'

'Not in the least, thanks. How came you to be entrusted with those sacred vessels, Lady Mary? What has become of Fraeulein and your sister?'

'They have rushed off to St. Bees. Grandmother thought Lesbia looking pale and out of spirits, and packed her off to the seaside at a minute's notice.'

'What! She has left Fellside?' asked Hammond, paling suddenly, as if a man had struck him. 'Lady Maulevrier, do I understand that Lady Lesbia has gone away?'

He asked the question in an authoritative tone, with the air of a man who had a right to be answered. The dowager wondered at his surpassing insolence.

'My granddaughter has gone to the seaside with her governess,' she said, haughtily.

'At a minute's notice?'

'At a minute's notice. I am not in the habit of hesitating about any step which I consider necessary for my grandchildren's welfare.'

She looked him full in the face, with those falcon eyes of hers; and he gave her back a look as resolute, and every whit as full of courage and of pride.

'Well,' he said, after a very perceptible pause, 'no doubt your ladyship has done wisely, and I must submit to your jurisdiction. But I had asked Lady Lesbia a question, and I had been promised an answer.'

'Your question has been answered by Lady Lesbia. She left a note for you,' replied Lady Maulevrier.

'Thanks,' answered Mr. Hammond, briefly, and he hurried from the room without another word.

The letter was on the table in his bedroom. He had little hope of any good waiting for him in a letter so written. The dowager and the world had triumphed over a girl's dawning love, no doubt.

This was Lesbia's letter:

'Dear Mr. Hammond,--Lady Maulevrier desires me to say that the proposal which you honoured me by making this morning is one which I   cannot possibly accept, and that any idea of an engagement between   you and me could result only in misery and humiliation to both. She   thinks it best, under these circumstances, that we should not again   meet, and I shall therefore have left Fellside before you receive   this letter.

'With all good wishes, very faithfully yours,
'LESBIA HASELDEN.'

'Very faithfully mine--faithful to her false training, to the worldly mind that rules her; faithful to the gods of this world--Belial and Mammon, and the Moloch Fashion. Poor cowardly soul! She loves me, and owns as much, yet weakly flies from me, afraid to trust the strong arm and the brave heart of the man who loves her, preferring the glittering shams of the world to the reality of true and honest love. Well, child, I have weighed you in the balance and found you wanting. Would to God it had been otherwise! If you had been brave and bold for love's sake, where is that pure and perfect chrysolite for which I would have bartered you?'

He flung himself into a chair, and sat with his head bowed upon his folded arms, and his eyes not innocent of tears. What would he not have given to find truth and courage and scorn of the world's wealth in that heart which he had tried to win. Did he think her altogether heartless because she so glibly renounced him? No, he was too just for that. He called her only half-hearted. She was like the cat in the adage, 'Letting I dare not, wait upon I would.' But he told himself with one deep sigh of resignation that she was lost to him for ever.

'I have tried her, and found her not worth the winning,' he said.

The house, even the lovely landscape smiling under his windows, the pastoral valley, smooth lake and willowy island, seemed hateful to him. He felt himself hemmed round by those green hills, by yonder brown and rugged wall of Nabb Scar, stifled for want of breathing space. The landscape was lovely enough, but it was like a beautiful grave. He longed to get away from it.

'Another man would follow her to St. Bees,' he said. 'I will not.'

He flung a few things into a Gladstone bag, sat down, and wrote a brief note to Maulevrier, asking him to make his excuses to her ladyship. He had made up his mind to go to Keswick that afternoon, and would rejoin his friend to-morrow, at Carlisle. This done, he rang for Maulevrier's valet, and asked that person to look after his luggage and bring it on to Scotland with his master's things; and then, without a word of adieu to anyone, John Hammond went out of the house, with the Gladstone bag in his hand, and shook the dust of Fellside off his feet.

He ordered a fly at the Prince of Wales's Hotel, and drove to Keswick, whence he went on to the Lodore. The gloom and spaciousness of Derwentwater, grey in the gathering dusk, suited his humour better than the emerald prettiness of Grasmere--the roar of the waterfall made music in his ear. He dined in a private room, and spent the evening roaming on the shores of the lake, and at eleven o'clock went back to his hotel and sat late into the night reading Heine, and thinking of the girl who had refused him.

Mr. Hammond's letter was delivered to Lord Maulevrier five minutes before dinner, as he sat in the drawing-room with her ladyship and Mary. Poor Mary had put on another pretty gown for dinner, still bent upon effacing Mr. Hammond's image of her as a tousled, frantic creature in torn and muddy raiment. She sat watching the door, just as Hammond had watched it three hours ago.

'So,' said Maulevrier, 'your ladyship has succeeded in driving my friend away. Hammond has left Fellside, and begs me to convey to you his compliments and his grateful acknowledgment of all your kindness.'

'I hope I have not been uncivil to him,' answered Lady Maulevrier coldly. 'As you had both made up your minds to go to-morrow, it can matter very little that he should go to-day.'

Mary looked down at the ribbon and lace on her prettiest frock, and thought that it mattered a great deal to her. Yet, if he had stayed, would he have seen her frock or her? With his bodily eyes, perhaps, but not with the eyes of his mind. Those eyes saw only Lesbia.

'No, perhaps it hardly matters,' answered Maulevrier, with suppressed anger. 'The man is not worth talking about or thinking about. What is he? Only the best, truest, bravest fellow I ever knew.'

'There are shepherds and guides in Grasmere of whom we could say almost as much,' said Lady Maulevrier, 'yet you would scarcely expect me to encourage one of them to pay his addresses to your sister? Pray spare us all nonsense-talk, Maulevrier. This business is very well ended. You ought never to have brought Mr. Hammond here.'

'I am sure of that now. I am very sorry I did bring him.'

'Oh, the man will not die for love. A disappointment of that kind is good for a young man in his position. It will preserve him from more vulgar entanglements, and perhaps from the folly of a too early marriage.'

'That is a mighty philosophical way of looking at the matter.'

'It is the only true way. I hope when you are my age you will have learnt to look at everything in a philosophical spirit.'

'Well, Lady Maulevrier, you have had it all your own way,' said the young man, walking up and down the room in an angry mood. 'I hope you will never be sorry for having come between two people who loved each other, and might have made each other happy.'

'I shall never he sorry for having saved my granddaughter from an imprudent marriage. Give me your arm, Maulevrier, and let me hear no more about Mr. Hammond. We have all had quite enough of him,' said her ladyship, as the butler announced dinner.

CHAPTER XIII.
'SINCE PAINTED OR NOT PAINTED ALL SHALL FADE.'

Fraeulein Mueller and her charge returned from St. Bees after a sojourn of about three weeks upon that quiet shore: but Lady Lesbia did not appear to be improved in health or spirits by the revivifying breezes of the ocean.

'It is a dull, horrid place, and I was bored to death there!' she said, when Mary asked how she had enjoyed herself. 'There was no question of enjoyment. Grandmother took it into her head that I was looking ill, and sent me to the sea; but I should have been just as well at Fellside.'

This meant that between Lesbia and that distinctly inferior being, her younger sister, there was to be no confidence. Mary had watched the life-drama acted under her eyes too closely not to know all about it, and was not inclined to be so put off.

That pale perturbed countenance of John Hammond's, those eager inquiring eyes looking to the door which opened not, had haunted Mary's waking thoughts, had even mingled with the tangled web of her dreams. Oh, how could any woman scorn such love? To be so loved, and by such a man, seemed to Mary the perfection of earthly bliss. She had never been educated up to those wider and loftier views of life, which teach a woman that houses and lands, place and power, are the supreme good.

'I can't understand how you could treat that noble-minded man so badly,' she exclaimed one day, when she and Lesbia were alone in the library, and after she had sat for ever so long, staring out of the window, meditating upon her sister's cruelty.

'Of whom are you speaking, pray?'

'As if you didn't know! Of Mr. Hammond.'

'And pray, how do you know that he is noble-minded, or that I treated him badly?'

'Well, as to his being noble-minded, that jumps to the eyes, as French books say. As for your treatment of him, I was looking on all the time, and I know how unkind you were, and I heard him talking to you in the fir-copse that day.'

'You Were listening' cried Lesbia indignantly.

'I was not listening! I was passing by. And if people choose to carry on their love affairs out of doors they must expect to be overheard. I heard him pleading to you, telling you how he would work for you, fight the battle of life for you, asking you to be trustful and brave for his sake. But you have a heart of stone. You and grandmother both have hearts of stone. I think she must have taken out your heart when you were little, and put a stone in its place.'

'Really,' said Lesbia, trying to carry things with a high hand, albeit her very human heart was beating passionately all the time, 'I think you ought to be very grateful to me--and grandmother--for refusing Mr. Hammond.'

'Why grateful?'

'Because it leaves you a chance of getting him for yourself; and everybody can see that you are over head and ears in love with him. That jumps to the eyes, as you say.'

Mary turned crimson, trembled with rage, looked at her sister as if she would kill her, for a moment or so, and finally burst into tears.

'That is not true, and it is shameful for you to say such a thing,' she cried.

'Why, what a virago you are, Mary. Well, I'm very glad it is not true. Mr. Hammond is--yes, I will be quite candid with you--he is the only man I am ever likely to admire for his own sake. He is good, brave, clever, all that you think him. But you and I do not live in a world in which girls are free to follow their own inclinations. I should break Lady Maulevrier's heart if I were to make a foolish marriage; and I owe her too much to set her wishes at naught, or to make her declining years unhappy. I must obey her, at any cost to my own feelings. Please never mention Mr. Hammond's name. I'm sure I've had quite enough unhappiness about him.'

'I see,' said Mary, bitterly. 'It is your own pain you think of, not his. He may suffer, so long as you are not worried.'

'You are an impertinent chit,' retorted Lesbia, 'and you know nothing about it.'

After this there was no more said about Mr. Hammond; but Mary did not forget him. She wrote long letters to her brother, who was still in Scotland, shooting, deer-stalking, fishing, killing something or other daily, in the most approved fashion of an Englishman taking his pleasure. Maulevrier occasionally repaid her with a telegram; but he was not a good correspondent. He declared that life was too short for letter-writing.

Summer was gone; the lake was no longer a shining emerald floor, dotted with the reflection of the flock upon the verdant slopes above it, but dull and grey of hue, and broken by white-edged wavelets. Patches of snow gleamed on the misty heights of Helvellyn, and the autumn winds howled and shrieked around Fellside in the evenings, when all the shutters were shut, and the outside world seemed little more than an idea: that mystic hour when the sheep are slumbering under the starry sky, and when, as the Westmoreland peasant believes, the fairies help the housewife at her spinning-wheel.

Those October evenings were very long and weary for Lesbia and her sister. Lady Maulevrier read and mused in her low chair beside the fire, with her books piled upon her own particular table, and lighted by her own particular lamp. She talked very little, but she was always gracious to her granddaughters and their governess, and she liked them to be with her in the evening. Lesbia played or sang, or sat at work at her basket-table, which occupied the other side of the fireplace; and Fraeulein and Mary had the rest of the room to themselves, as it were, those two places by the hearth being sacred, as if dedicated to household gods. Mary read immensely in those long evenings, devouring volume after volume, feeding her imagination with every kind of nutriment, good, bad, and indifferent. Fraeulein Mueller knitted a woollen shawl, which seemed to have neither beginning, middle, nor end, and was always ready for conversation, but there were times when silence brooded over the scene for long intervals, and when every sound of the light wood-ashes dropping on the tiled hearth was distinctly audible.

This state of things went on for about three weeks after Lesbia's return from St. Bees, Lady Maulevrier watchful of her granddaughter all the time, though saying nothing. She saw that Lesbia was not happy, not as she had been in the time before the coming of John Hammond. She had never been particularly gay or light-hearted, never gifted with the wild spirits and buoyancy which make girlhood so lovely a season to some natures, a time of dance and song and joyousness, a morning of life steeped in the beauty and gladness of the universe. She had never been gay as young lambs and foals and fawns and kittens and puppy dogs are gay, by reason of the well-spring of delight within them, needing no stimulus from the outside world. She had been just a little inclined to murmur at the dulness of her life at Fellside; yet she had borne herself with a placid sweetness which had been Lady Maulevrier's delight. But now there was a marked change in her manner. She was not the less submissive and dutiful in her bearing to her grandmother, whom she both loved and feared; but there were moments of fretfulness and impatience which she could not conceal. She was captious and sullen in her manner to Mary and the Fraeulein. She would not walk or drive with them, or share in any of their amusements. Sometimes of an evening that studious silence of the drawing-room was suddenly broken by Lesbia's weary sigh, breathed unawares as she bent over her work.

Lady Maulevrier saw, too, that Lesbia's cheek was paler than of old, her eyes less bright. There was a heavy look that told of broken slumbers, there was a pinched look in that oval check. Good heavens! if her beauty were to pale and wane, before society had bowed down and worshipped it; if this fair flower were to fade untimely; if this prize rose in the garden of beauty were to wither and decay before it won the prize.

Her ladyship was a woman of action, and no sooner did this fear shape itself in her mind than she took steps to prevent the evil her thoughts foreshadowed.

Among those friends of her youth and allies of her house with whom she had always maintained an affectionate correspondence was Lady Kirkbank, the fashionable wife of a sporting baronet, owner of a castle in Scotland, a place in Yorkshire, a villa at Cannes, and a fine house in Arlington Street, with an income large enough for their enjoyment. When Lady Diana Angersthorpe shone forth in the West End world as the acknowledged belle of the season, the star of Georgina Lorimer was beginning to wane. She was the eldest daughter of Colonel Lorimer, a man of good old family, and a fine soldier, who had fought shoulder to shoulder with Gough and Lawrence, and who had contrived to make a figure in society with very small means. Georgina's sisters had all married well. It was a case of necessity, the Colonel told them; they must either marry or gravitate ultimately to the workhouse. So the Miss Lorimers made the best use of their youth and freshness, and 'no good offer refused' was the guiding rule of their young lives. Lucy married an East India merchant, and set up a fine house in Porchester Terrace. Maud married wealth personified in the person of a leading member of the Tallow Chandlers' Company, and had her town house and country house, and as fine a set of diamonds as a duchess.

But Georgina, the eldest, trifled with her chances, and her twenty-seventh birthday beheld her pouring out her father's tea in a small furnished house in a street off Portland Place, which the Colonel had hired on his return from India, and which he declared himself unable to maintain another year.

'Directly the season is over I shall give up housekeeping and take a lodging at Bath,' said Colonel Lorimer. 'If you don't like Bath all the year round you can stay with your sisters.'

'That is the last thing I am likely to do,' answered Georgina; 'my sisters were barely endurable when they were single and poor. They are quite intolerable now they are married and rich. I would sooner live in the monkey-house at the Zoological than stay with either Lucy or Maud.'

'That's rank envy,' retorted her father 'You can't forgive them for having done so much better than you.'

'I can't forgive them for having married snobs. When I marry I shall marry a gentleman.'

'When!' echoed the parent, with a sneering laugh. 'Hadn't you better say "if"'?

At this period Georgina's waning good looks were in some measure counterbalanced by the cumulative effects of half a dozen seasons in good society, which had given style to her person, ease to her manners, and sharpness to her tongue. Nobody in society said sharper or more unpleasant things than Miss Lorimer, and by virtue of this gift she got invited about a great deal more than she might have done had she been distinguished for sweetness of speech and manner. Georgie Lorimer's presence at a dinner table gave just that pungent flavour which is like the faint suspicion of garlic in a fricassee or of tarragon in a salad.

Now in this very season, when Colonel Lorimer was inclined to speak of his daughter, as Sainte Beuve wrote of Musset, as a young woman with a very brilliant past, a lucky turn of events gave Georgina a fresh start in life, which may be called a new departure. Lady Diana Angersthorpe, the belle of the season, took a fancy to her, was charmed with her sharp tongue and acute sense of the ridiculous. The two became fast friends, and were seen everywhere together. The best men all flocked round the beauty, and all talked to the beauty's companion: and before the season was over, Sir George Kirkbank, who had had half made up his mind to propose to Lady Diana, found himself engaged to that uncommonly jolly girl, Lady Diana's friend. Georgina spent August and September with Lady Di, at the Marchioness of Carisbroke's delightful villa in the Isle of Wight, and Sir George kept his yacht at Cowes all the time, and was in constant attendance upon his fiancee. It was George and Georgie everywhere. In October Colonel Lorimer had the profound pleasure of giving away his daughter, before the altar in St. George's, Hanover Square, and it may be said of him that nothing in his relations with that young lady became him better than his manner of parting with her.

So the needy Colonel's daughter became Lady Kirkbank, and in the following spring Diana Angersthorpe was married at the same St. George's to the Earl of Maulevrier. The friends were divided by distance and by circumstance as the years rolled on; but friendship was steadily maintained; and a regular correspondence with Lady Kirkbank, whose pen was as sharp as her tongue, was one of the means by which Lady Maulevrier had kept herself thoroughly posted in all those small events, unrecorded by newspapers, which make up the secret history of society.

It was of her old friend Georgie that her ladyship thought in her present anxiety. Lady Kirkbank had more than once suggested that Lady Maulevrier's grand-daughters should vary the monotony of Fellside by a visit to her place near Doncaster, or her castle north of Aberdeen; but her ladyship had evaded these friendly suggestions, being very jealous of any strange influence upon Lesbia's life. Now, however, there had come a time when Lesbia must have a complete change of scenery and surroundings, lest she should pine and dwindle in sullen submission to fate, or else defy the world and elope with John Hammond.

Now, therefore, Lady Maulevrier decided to accept Lady Kirkbank's hospitality. She told her friend the whole story with perfect frankness, and her letter was immediately answered by a telegram.

'I start for Scotland to-morrow, will break my journey by staying a night at Fellside, and will take Lady Lesbia on to Kirkbank with me next day, if she can be ready to go.'

'She shall be ready,' said Lady Maulevrier.

She told Lesbia that she had accepted an invitation for her, and that she was to go to Kirkbank Castle the day after to-morrow. She was prepared for unwillingness, resistance even; but Lesbia received the news with evident pleasure.

'I shall be very glad to go,' she said, 'this place is so dull. Of course I shall be sorry to leave you, grandmother, and I wish you would go with me; but any change will be a relief. I think if I had to stay here all the winter, counting the days and the hours, I should go out of my mind.'

The tears came into her eyes, but she wiped them away hurriedly, ashamed of her emotion.

'My dearest child, I am so sorry for you,' murmured Lady Maulevrier. 'But believe me the day will come when you will be very glad that you conquered the first foolish inclination of your girlish heart.'

'Yes, I daresay, when I am eighty,' Lesbia answered, impatiently. She had made up her mind to submit to the inevitable. She had loved John Hammond--had been as near breaking her heart for him as it was in her nature to break her heart for anybody; but she wanted to make a great marriage, to be renowned and admired. She had been reared and trained for that; and she was not going to belie her training.

A visitor from the great London world was so rare an event that there was naturally a little excitement in the idea of Lady Kirkbank's arrival. The handsomest and most spacious of the spare bedrooms was prepared for the occasion. The housekeeper was told that the dinner must be perfect. There must be nothing old-fashioned or ponderous; there must be mind as well as matter in everything. Rarely did Lady Maulevrier look at a bill of fare; but on this particular morning she went carefully through the menu, and corrected it with her own hand.

A pair of post-horses brought Lady Kirkbank and her maid from Windermere station, in time for afternoon tea, and the friends who had only met twice within the last forty years, embraced each other on the threshold of Lady Maulevrier's morning-room.

'My dearest Di,' cried Lady Kirkbank, 'what a delight to see you again after such ages; and what a too lovely spot you have chosen for your retreat from the world, the flesh, and the devil. If I could be a recluse anywhere, it would be amongst just such delicious surroundings.'

Without, twilight shades were gathering; within, there was only the light of a fire and a shaded lamp upon the tea table; there was just light enough for the two women to see each other's faces, and the change which time had wrought there.

Never did womanhood in advanced years offer a more striking contrast than that presented by the woman of fashion and the recluse. Lady Maulevrier was almost as handsome in the winter of her days as she had been when life was in its spring. The tall, slim figure, erect as a dart, the delicately chiselled features and alabaster complexion, the soft silvery hair, the perfect hand, whiter and more transparent than the hand of girlhood, the stately movements and bearing, all combined to make Lady Maulevrier a queen among woman. Her brocade gown of a deep shade of red, with a border of dark sable on cuffs and collar, suggested a portrait by Velasquez. She wore no ornaments except the fine old Brazilian diamonds which flashed and sparkled upon her slender fingers.

If Lady Maulevrier looked like a picture in the Escurial, Lady Kirkbank resembled a caricature in *La Vie Parisienne*. Everything she wore was in the very latest fashion of the Parisian *demi-monde*, that exaggerated elegance of a fashion plate which only the most exquisite of women could redeem from vulgarity. Plush, brocade, peacock's feathers, golden bangles, mousquetaire gloves, a bonnet of purple plumage set off by ornaments of filagree gold, an infantine little muff of lace and wild flowers, buttercups and daisies; and hair, eyebrows and complexion as artificial as the flowers on the muff.

All that art could do to obliterate the traces of age had been done for Georgina

Kirkbank. But seventy years are not to be obliterated easily, and the crow's feet showed through the bloom de Ninon, and the eyes under the painted arches were glassy and haggard, the carnation lips had a withered look. Age was made all the more palpable by the artifice which would have disguised it.

Lady Maulevrier suffered an absolute shock at beholding the friend of her youth. She had not accustomed herself to the idea that women in society could raddle their cheeks, stain their lips, and play tricks before high heaven with their eyebrows and eyelashes. In her own youth painted faces had been the ghastly privilege of a class of womankind of which the women of society were supposed to know nothing. Persons who showed their ankles and rouged their cheeks were to be seen of an afternoon in Bond Street; but Lady Diana Angersthorpe had been taught to pass them by as if she saw them not, to behold without seeing these creatures outside the pale. And now she saw her own dearest friend, a person distinctly within the pale, plastered with bismuth and stained with carmine, and wearing hair of a colour so obviously false and inharmonious, that child-like faith could hardly accept it as reality. Forty years ago Lady Kirkbank's long ringlets had been darkest glossiest brown, to-day she wore a tousled fringe of bright yellow, piquantly contrasting with Vandyke brown eyebrows.

It took Lady Maulevrier some moments to get over the shock. She drew a chair to the fire and established her friend in it, and then, with a little gasp, she said:

'I am charmed to see you again, Georgie!'

'You darling, I was sure you would be glad. But you must find me awfully changed--awfully.'

For worlds Lady Maulevrier could not have denied this truth. Happily Lady Kirkbank did not wait for an answer.

'Society is so wearing, and George and I never seem to get an interval of quiet. Kirkbank is to be full of men next week. Your granddaughter will have a good time.'

'There will be a few women, of course?'

'Oh, yes, there's no avoiding that; only one doesn't reckon them. Sir George only counts his guns. We expect a splendid season. I shall send you some birds of my own shooting.'

'You shoot!' exclaimed Lady Maulevrier, amazed.

'Shoot! I should think I do. What else is there to amuse one in Scotland, after the salmon fishing is over? I have never missed a season for the last thirty years, unless we have been abroad.'

'Please, don't innoculate Lesbia with your love of sport.'

'What! you wouldn't like her to shoot? Well, perhaps you are right. It is hardly the thing for a pretty girl with her fortune to make. It spoils the delicacy of the skin. But I'm afraid she'll find Kirkbank dull if she doesn't go out with the guns. She can meet us with the rest of the women at luncheon. We have some capital picnic luncheons on the moor, I can assure you.'

'I know she will enjoy herself with you. She has been accustomed to a very quiet life here.'

'It is a lovely spot; but I own I cannot understand how you can have lived here exclusively during all these years--you who used to be all life and fire, loving change, action, political and diplomatic society, to dance upon the crest of the wave, as it were. Your whole nature must have suffered some curious change.'

Their close intimacy of the past warranted freedom of speech in the present.

'My nature did undergo a change, and a severe one,' answered Lady Maulevrier, gloomily.

'It was that horrid--and I daresay unfortunate scandal about his lordship; and then the sad shock of his death,' murmured Lady Kirkbank, sympathetically. 'Most women, with your youth and beauty, would have forgotten the scandal and the husband in a twelvemonth, and would have made a second marriage more brilliant than the first. But no Indian widow who ever performed suttee was more worthy of praise than you, or even that person of Ephesus, whose story I have heard somewhere. Indeed, I have always spoken of your life as a long suttee. But you mean to re-appear in society next season, I hope, when you present your granddaughter?'

'I shall certainly go up to London to present her, and possibly I may spend the season in town; but I shall feel like Rip Van Winkle.'

'No, no, you won't, my dear Di. You have kept yourself *au courant*, I know. Even my silly gossiping letters may have been of *some* use.'

'They have been most valuable. Let me give you another cup of tea,' said Lady Maulevrier, who had been officiating at her own exquisite tea-table, an arrangement of inlaid woods, antique silver, and modern china, which her friend pronounced a perfect poem.

Indeed, the whole room was poetic, Lady Kirkbank declared, and there are many highly praised scenes which less deserve the epithet. The dark red walls and cedar dado, the stamped velvet curtains, of an indescribable shade between silver-grey and olive, the Sheraton furniture, the parqueterie floor and Persian prayer-rugs, the deep yet brilliant hues of crackle porcelain and Chinese cloisonne enamel, the artistic fireplace, with dog-stove, low brass fender, and ingle-nook recessed under the high mantelpiece, all combined to form a luxurious and harmonious whole.

Lady Kirkbank admired the ***tout ensemble*** in the fitful light of the fire, the dim grey of deepening twilight.

'There never was a more delicious cell!' she exclaimed, 'but still I should feel it a prison, if I had to spend six weeks in the year in it. I never stay more than six weeks anywhere out of London; and I always find six weeks more than enough. The first fortnight is rapture, the third and fourth weeks are calm content, the fifth is weariness, the sixth a fever to be gone. I once tried a seventh week at Pontresina, and I hated the place so intensely that I dared not go back there for the next three years. But now tell me. Diana, have you really performed suttee, have you buried yourself alive in this sweet spot deliberately, or has the love of retirement grown upon you, and have you become a kind of lotus-eater?'

'I believe I have become a kind of lotus-eater. My retirement here has been no sentimental sacrifice to Lord Maulevrier's memory.'

'I am glad to hear that; for I really think the worst possible use a woman can make of her life is in wasting it on lamentation for a dead and gone husband. Life is odiously short at the best, and it is mere imbecility to fritter away any of our scanty portion upon the dead, who can never be any the better for our tears.'

'My motive in living at Fellside was not reverence for the dead. And now let us talk of the gay world, of which you know all the secrets. Have you heard anything more about Lord Hartfield?'

'Ah, there is a subject in which you have reason to be interested. I have not forgotten the romance of your youth--that first season in which Ronald Hollister used to haunt every place at which you appeared. Do you remember that wet afternoon at the Chiswick flower-show, when you and he and I took shelter in the orange house, and you two made love to each other most audaciously in an atmosphere of orange-blossoms that almost stifled me? Yes, those were glorious days!'

'A short summer of gladness, a brief dream,' sighed Lady Maulevrier. 'Is young Lord Hartfield like his father?'

'No, he takes after the Ilmingtons; but still there is a look of your old sweet-heart--yes, I think there is an expression. I have not seen him for nearly a year. He is still abroad, roaming about somewhere in search of adventures. These young men who belong to the Geographical and the Alpine Club are hardly ever at home.'

'But though they may be sometimes lost to society, they are all the more worthy of society's esteem when they do appear,' said Lady Maulevrier. 'I think there must be an ennobling influence in Alpine travel, or in the vast solitudes of the Dark Continent. A man finds himself face to face with unsophisticated nature, and with the grandest forces of the universe. Professor Tyndall writes delightfully of his Alpine experiences; his mind seems to have ripened in the solitude and untainted air of the Alps. And I believe Lord Hartfield is a young man of very high character and of considerable cultivation, is he not?'

'He is a splendid young fellow. I never heard a word to his disparagement, even from those people who pretend to know something bad about everybody. What a husband he would make for one of your girls!'

'Admirable! But those perfect arrangements, which seem predestined by heaven itself, are so rarely realised on earth,' answered the dowager, lightly.

She was not going to show her cards, even to an old friend.

'Well, it would be very sweet if they were to meet next season and fall in love with each other,' said Lady Kirkbank. 'He is enormously rich, and I daresay your girls will not be portionless.'

'Lesbia may take a modest place among heiresses,' answered Lady Maulevrier. 'I have lived so quietly during the last forty years that I could hardly help saving money.'

'How nice!' sighed Georgie. 'I never saved sixpence in my life, and am always in debt.'

'The little fortune I have saved is much too small for division. Lesbia will therefore have all I can leave her. Mary has the usual provision as a daughter of the Maulevrier house.'

'And I suppose Lesbia has that provision also?'

'Of course.'

'Lucky Lesbia. I only wish Hartfield were coming to us for the shooting. I would engage he should fall in love with her. Kirkbank is a splendid place for match-making. But the fact is I am not very intimate with him. He is almost always travelling, and when he is at home he is not in our set. And now, my dear Diana, tell me more about yourself, and your own life in this delicious place.'

'There is so little to tell. The books I have read, the theories of literature and art and science which I have adopted and dismissed, learnt and forgotten--those are the history of my life. The ideas of the outside world reach me here only in books and newspapers; but you who have been living in the world must have so much to say. Let me be the listener.'

Lady Kirkbank desired nothing better. She rattled on for three-quarters of an hour about her doings in the great world, her social triumphs, the wonderful things she had done for Sir George, who seemed to be as a puppet in her hands, the princes and princelings she had entertained, the songs she had composed, the comedy she had written, for private representation only, albeit the Haymarket manager was dying to produce it, the scathing witticisms with which she had withered her social enemies. She would have gone on much longer, but for the gong, which reminded her that it was time to dross for dinner.

Half-an-hour later Lady Kirkbank was in the drawing-room, where Mary had retired to the most shadowy corner, anxious to escape the gaze of the fashionable visitor.

But Lady Kirkbank was not inclined to take much notice of Mary. Lesbia's brilliant beauty, the exquisite Greek head, the faultless complexion, the deep, violet eyes, caught Georgina Kirkbank's eye the moment she had entered the room, and she saw that this girl and no other must be the beauty, the beloved and chosen grandchild.

'How do you do, my dear?' she said, taking Lesbia's hand, and then, as if with a gush of warm feeling, suddenly drawing the girl towards her and kissing her on both cheeks. 'I am going to be desperately fond of you, and I hope you will soon contrive to like me--just a little.'

'I feel sure that I shall like you very much,' Lesbia answered sweetly. 'I am prepared to love you as grandmother's old friend.'

'Oh, my dear, to think that I should ever be the old friend of anybody's grand-mother!' sighed Lady Kirkbank, with unaffected regret. 'When I was your age I used to think all old people odious. It never occurred to me that I should live to be one of them.'

'Then you had no dear grandmother whom you loved,' said Lesbia, 'or you would have liked old people for her sake.'

'No, my love, I had no grandparents. I had a father, and he was all-sufficient--anything beyond him in the ancestral line would have been a burden laid upon me greater than I could bear, as the poet says.'

Dinner was announced, and Mary came shyly out of her corner, blushing deep-ly.

'And this is Lady Mary, I suppose?' said Lady Kirkbank, in an off-hand way, 'How do you do, my dear? I am going to steal your sister.'

'I am very glad,' faltered Mary. 'I mean I am glad that Lesbia should enjoy her-self.'

'And some fine day, when Lesbia is married and a great lady, I shall ask you to come to Scotland,' said Lady Kirkbank, condescendingly, and than she murmured in her friend's ear, as they went to the dining-room, 'Quite an English girl. Very fresh and frank and nice,' which was great praise for such a second-rate young person as Lady Mary.

'What do you think of Lesbia?' asked Lady Maulevrier, in the same under-tone.

'She is simply adorable. Your letters prepared me to expect beauty, but not such beauty. My dear, I thought the progress of the human race was all in a downward line since our time; but your granddaughter is as handsome as you were in your first season, and that is going very far.'

CHAPTER XIV.
'NOT YET.'

Lady Kirkbank carried off Lesbia early next day, the girl radiant at the idea of seeing life under new conditions. She had a few minutes' serious talk with her grandmother before she went.

'Lesbia, you are going into the world,' said Lady Maulevrier; 'yes, even a coun-try house is the world in little. You will have many admirers instead of one; but I think, I believe, that you will be true to me and to yourself.'

'You need not fear, grandmother. I have been an idiot; but--but it was only a passing folly, and I shall never be so weak again.'

Lesbia's scornful lips and kindling eyes gave intensity to her speech. It was evident that she despised herself for that one touch of womanly softness which had made her as ready to fall in love with her first wooer as any peasant girl in Grasmere Vale.

'I am delighted to hear you speak thus, dearest,' said Lady Maulevrier. 'And if Mr. Hamilton--Hammond, I mean--should have the audacity to follow you to Kirkbank, and to intrude himself upon you there--perhaps to persecute you with clandestine addresses----'

'I do not believe he would do anything clandestine,' said Lesbia, drawing her-self up. 'He is quite above that.'

'My dear child, we know absolutely nothing about him. He has his way to make in the world unaided by family or connections. He is clever--daring. Such a man cannot help being an adventurer; and an adventurer is capable of anything. I warn you to beware of him.'

'I don't suppose I shall ever see his face again,' retorted Lesbia, irritably.

She had made up her mind that her life was not to be spoiled, her brilliant future sacrificed, for the sake of John Hammond; but the wound which she had suf-fered in renouncing him was still fresh, her feelings were still sore. Any contemptu-ous mention of him stung her to the quick.

'I hope not. And you will beware of other adventurers, Lesbia, men of a worse stamp than Mr. Hammond, more experienced in ruse and iniquity, men steeped to the lips in worldly knowledge, men who look upon women as mere counters in the game of life. The world thinks that I am rich, and you will no doubt take rank as an heiress. You will therefore be a mark for every spendthrift, noble or otherwise, who wants to restore his broken fortunes by a wealthy marriage. And now, my dearest, good-bye. Half my heart goes with you. Nothing could induce me to part with you, even for a few weeks, except the conviction that it is for your good.'

'But we shall not be parted next year, I hope, grandmother,' said Lesbia, affectionately. 'You said something about presenting me, and then leaving me in Lady Kirkbank's care for the season. I should not like that at all. I want you to go everywhere with me, to teach me all the mysteries of the great world. You have always promised me that it should be so.'

'And I have always intended that it should be so. I hope that it will be so,' answered her grandmother, with a sigh; 'but I am an old woman, Lesbia, and I am rooted to this place.'

'But why should you be rooted here? What charm can keep you here, when you are so fitted to shine in society? You are old in nothing but years, and not even old in years in comparison with women whom we hear of, going everywhere and mixing in every fashionable amusement. You are full of fire and energy, and as active as a girl. Why should you not enjoy a London season, grandmother?' pleaded Lesbia, nestling her head lovingly against Lady Maulevrier's shoulder.

'I should enjoy it, dearest, with you. It would be a renewal of my youth to see you shine and conquer. I should be as proud as if the glory were all my own. Yes, dear, I hope that I shall be a spectator of your triumphs. But do not let us plan the future. Life is so full of changes. Remember what Horace says----'

'Horace is a bore,' said Lesbia. 'I hate a poet who is always harping upon change and death.'

The carriage, which was to take the travellers to Windermere Station, was announced at this moment, and Lesbia and her grandmother gave each other the farewell embrace.

'You like Lady Kirkbank, I hope?' said Lady Maulevrier, as they went towards the ball, where that lady was waiting for them, with Lady Mary and Fraeulein Mueller in attendance upon her.

'She seems very kind, but I should like her better if she did not paint--or if she painted better.'

'My dear child I'm afraid it is the fashion of the day, just as it was in Pope's time, and we ought to think nothing about it.'

'Well, I suppose I shall get hardened in time.'

'My dearest Lesbia,' shrieked Lady Kirkbank from below, 'remember we have to catch a train.'

Lesbia hurried downstairs, followed by Lady Maulevrier, who had to bid her friend adieu. The luggage had been sent on in a cart, Lesbia's trunks and dress baskets forming no small item. She was so well furnished with pretty gowns of all kinds that there had been no difficulty in getting her ready for this sudden visit. Her maid was on the box beside the coachman. Lady Kirkbank's attendant, a Frenchwoman of five-and-thirty, who looked as if she had graduated at Mabille, was to occupy the back seat of the landau.

Lady Mary looked after her sister longingly, as the carriage drove down the hill. She was going into a new world, to see all kinds of people--clever people--distinguished people--musical, artistic, political people--hunting and shooting people--while Mary was to stay at home all the winter among the old familiar faces. Dearly as she loved these hills and vales her heart sank a little at the thought of those long lonely months, days and evenings that would be all alike, and which must be spent without sympathetic companionship. And there would be dreary days on which the weather would keep her a prisoner in her luxurious gaol, when the mountains, and the rugged paths beside the mountain streams, would be inaccessible, when she would be restricted to Fraeulein's phlegmatic society, that lady being stout and lazy, fond of her meals, and given to afternoon slumbers. Lesbia and Mary were not by any means sympathetic; yet, after all, blood is thicker than water; and Lesbia was intelligent, and could talk of the things Mary loved, which was better than total dumbness, even if she generally took an antagonistic view of them.

'I shall miss her dreadfully,' thought Mary, as she strolled listlessly in the gardens, where the leaves where falling and the flowers fading.

'I wonder if she will see Mr. Hammond at Lady Kirkbank's?' mused Mary. 'If he were anything like a lover he would find out all about her visit, and seize the opportunity of her being away from grandmother. But then if he had been much of a lover he would have followed her to St. Bees.'

Lady Maulevrier sorely missed her favourite grandchild. In a life spent in such profound seclusion, so remote from the busy interests of the world, this beloved companionship had become a necessity to her. She had concentrated her affections upon Lesbia, and the girl's absence made a fearful blank. But her ladyship's dignity was not compromised by any outward signs of trouble or loss.

She spent her mornings in her own room, reading and writing and musing at her leisure; she drove or walked every fine afternoon, sometimes alone, sometimes attended by Mary, who hated these stately drives and walks. She dined *tete-a-tete* with Mary, except on those rare occasions when there were visitors--the Vicar and his wife, or some wandering star from other worlds Mary lived in profound awe of her grandmother, but was of far too frank a nature to be able to adapt her speech or her manners to her ladyship's idea of feminine perfection. She was silent and shy under those falcon eyes; but she was still the same Mary, the girl to whom pretence or simulation of any kind was impossible.

Letters came almost every day from Kirkbank Castle, letters from Lesbia describing the bright gay life she was living at that hospitable abode, the excursions, the rides, the picnic luncheons after the morning's sport, the dinner parties, the dances.

'It is the most delightful house you can imagine,' wrote Lesbia; 'and Lady Kirkbank is an admirable hostess. I have quite forgiven her for wearing false eyebrows; for after all, you know, one must *have* eyebrows; they are a necessity; but why does she not have the two arches alike? They are *never* a pair, and I really think that French maid of hers does it on purpose.

'By-the-bye, Lady Kirkbank is going to write to you to beseech you to let me go to Cannes and Monte Carlo with her. Sir George insists upon it. He says they both like young society, and will be horribly vexed if I refuse to go with them. And Lady Kirkbank thinks my chest is just a little weak--I almost broke down the other night in that lovely little song of Jensen's--and that a winter in the south is just what I want. But, of course, dear grandmother, I won't ask you to let me be away so long if you think you will miss me.'

'If I think I shall miss her!' repeated Lady Maulevrier. 'Has the girl no heart, that she can ask such a question? But can I wonder at that? Of what account was I or my love to her father, although I sacrificed myself for his good name? Can I expect that she should be of a different clay?'

And then, meditating upon the events of the summer that was gone, Lady Maulevrier thought--

She renounced her first lover at my bidding; she renounces her love for me at the bidding of the world. Or was it not rather self-interest, the fear of making a bad marriage, which influenced her in her renunciation of Mr. Hammond. It was not obedience to me, it was not love for me which made her give him up. It was the selfishness engrained in her race. Well, I have heaped my love upon her, because she is fair and sweet, and reminds me of my own youth. I must let her go, and try to be happy in the knowledge that she is enjoying her life far away from me.'

Lady Maulevrier wrote her consent to the extension of Lesbia's visit, and by return of post came a letter from Lesbia which seemed brimming over with love, and which comforted the grandmother's wounded heart.

'Lady Kirkbank and I are both agreed, dearest, that you must join us at Cannes,' wrote Lesbia. 'At your age it is very wrong of you to spend a winter in our horrible climate. You can travel with Steadman and your maid. Lady Kirkbank will secure you a charming suite of rooms at the hotel, or she would like it still better if you would stay at her own villa. Do consent to this plan, dear grandmother, and then we shall not be parted for a long winter. Of course Mary would be quite happy at home running wild.'

Lady Maulevrier sighed as she read this letter, sighed again, and heavily, as she put it back into the envelope. Alas, how many and many a year had gone, long, mo-notonous, colourless years, since she had seen that bright southern world which she was now urged to revisit. In fancy she saw it again to-day, the tideless sea of deepest sapphire blue, the little wavelets breaking on a yellow beach, the white triangular sails, the woods full of asphodel and great purple and white lilies, the atmosphere steeped in warmth and light and perfume, the glare of white houses in the sun, the red and yellow blinds, the pots of green and orange and crimson clay, with olean-ders abloom, the wonderful glow of colour everywhere and upon all things. And then as the eyes of the mind recalled these vivid images her bodily eyes looked out upon the rain-blotted scene, the mountains rising in a dark and dismal circle round that sombre pool below, walling her in from the outer world.

'I am at the bottom of a grave,' she said to herself. 'I am in a living tomb, from which there is no escape. Forty years! Forty years of patience and hope, for what? For dreams which may never be realised; for descendants who may never give me the price of my labours. Yes, I should like to go to my dear one. I should like to revisit the South of France, to go on to Italy. I should feel young again amidst that eternal, unchangeable loveliness. I should forget all I have suffered. But it cannot be. Not yet, not yet!'

Presently with a smile of concentrated bitterness she repeated the words 'Not yet!'

'Surely at my age it must be folly to dream of the future; and yet I feel as if there were half a century of life in me, as if I had lost nothing in either mental or bodily vigour since I came here forty years ago.'

She rose as she said these words, and began to pace the room, with quiet, firm step, erect, stately, beautiful in her advanced years as she had been in her bloom and freshness, only with another kind of beauty--an empress among women. The boast that she had made to herself was no idle boast. At sixty-seven years of age her physical powers showed no signs of decay, her mental qualities were at their best and brightest. Long years of thought and study had ripened and widened her mind. She was a woman fit to be the friend and counsellor of statesmen, the companion and confidant of her sovereign: and yet fate willed that she should be buried alive in a Westmoreland valley, seeing the same hills and streams, the same rustic faces, from year's end to year's end. Surely it was a hard fate, a heavy penance, albeit self-imposed.

Lesbia went straight from Scotland to Paris with Sir George and Lady Kirkbank. Here they stayed at the Bristol for just two days, during which her hostess went all over the fashionable quarter buying clothes for the Cannes campaign, and assisting Lesbia to spend the hundred pounds which her grandmother had sent her for the replenishment of her well-provided wardrobe. It is astonishing how little way a hundred pounds goes among the dressmakers, corset-makers, and shoemakers of Lutetia.

'I had no notion that clothes were so dear,' said Lesbia, when she saw how little she had got for her money.

'My dear, you have two gowns which are absolutely *chien*,' replied Lady Kirkbank, 'and you have a corset which gives you a figure, which you must forgive me for saying you never had before.'

Lady Kirkbank had to explain that *chien* as applied to a gown or bonnet was the same thing as *chic*, only a little more so.

'I hope my gowns will always be *chien*,' said Lesbia meekly.

Next evening they were dining at Cannes, with the blue sea in front of their windows, dining at a table all abloom with orange flowers, tea roses, mignonette, waxen camellias, and pale Parma violets, while Lady Maulevrier and Mary dined *tete-a-tete* at Fellside, with the feathery snow flakes falling outside, and the world whitening all around them.

Next day the world was all white, and Mary's beloved hills were inaccessible.

Who could tell how long they might be covered; the winding tracks hidden; the narrow forces looking like black water or molten iron against that glittering whiteness? Mary could only walk along the road by Loughrigg to the bench called 'Rest and be thankful,' from which she looked with longing eyes across towards the Langdale Pikes, and to the sharp cone-shaped peak, known as Coniston Old Man, just visible above the nearer hills. Fraeulein Mueller suggested that it was in just such weather as this that a well brought up young lady, a young lady with *Vernunft* and *Anstand*, should devote herself to the improvement of her mind.

'Let us read German this *abscheulich* afternoon,' said the Fraeulein. 'Suppose we go on with the "Sorrows of Werther."'

'Werther was a fool,' cried Mary; 'any book but that.'

'Will you choose your own book?'

'Let me read Heine.'

Fraeulein looked doubtful. There were things in Heine--an all-pervading tone--which rendered him hardly an appropriate poet for 'the young person.' But Fraeulein compromised the matter by letting Mary read Atta Troll, the exact bearing of which neither of them understood.

'How beautifully Mr. Hammond read Heine that morning!' said Mary, breaking off suddenly from a perfectly automatic reading.

'You did not hear him, did you? You were not there,' said the Fraeulein.

'I was not *there*, but I heard him. I--I was sitting on the bank among the pine trees.'

'Why did you not come and sit with us? It would have been more ladylike than to hide yourself behind the trees.'

Mary blushed crimson.

'I had been in the kennels with Maulevrier; I was not fit to be seen,' she said.

'Hardly a ladylike admission,' replied the Fraeulein, who felt that with Lady Mary her chief duty was to reprove.

CHAPTER XV.
'OF ALL MEN ELSE I HAVE AVOIDED THEE.'

It was afternoon. The white hills yonder and all the length of the valley were touched here and there with gleams of wintry sunlight, and Lady Maulevrier was taking her solitary walk in the terrace in front of her house, a stately figure wrapped in a furred mantle, tall, erect, moving with measured pace up and down the smooth gravel path. Now and then at the end of the walk the dowager stopped for a minute or so, and stood as if in deep thought, with her eyes dreamily contemplating the landscape. An intense melancholy shadowed her face, as she thus gazed with brooding eyes on the naked monotony of those wintry hills. So had she looked in many and many a winter, and it seemed to her that her life was of a piece with those bleak hills, where in the dismal winter time nothing living trod. She stood gazing at the sinking sun, a fiery ball shining at the end of a long gallery of crag and rock, like a lamp at the end of a corridor; and as she gazed the red round orb dropped suddenly behind the edge of a crag, as if she had been an enchantress and had dismissed it with a wave of her wand.

'O Lord, how long, how long?' she said. 'How many times have I seen that sun go down from this spot, in winter and summer, in spring and autumn! And now that the one being I loved and cared for is far away, I feel all the weariness and emptiness of my life.'

As she turned to resume her walk she heard the muffled sound of wheels in the road below, that road which was completely hidden by foliage in summer, but which was now visible here and there between the leafless trees. A carriage with a pair of horses was coming along the road from Ambleside.

Lady Maulevrier stood and watched until the carriage drew up at the lodge gate, and then, when the gate had been opened, slowly ascended the winding drive to the house.

She expected no visitor; indeed, there was no one likely to come to her from the direction of Ambleside. Her heart began to beat heavily, with the apprehension of coming evil. What kind of evil she knew not. Bad news about her granddaughter, perhaps, or about Maulevrier. And yet that could hardly be. Evil tidings of that kind would have reached her by telegram.

Perhaps it was Maulevrier himself. His movements were generally erratic.

Lady Maulevrier hurried back to the house. She went through the conservatory, where the warm whiteness of azalia, and spirea, and arum lilies contrasted curiously with the cold white snow out of doors, to the hall, where a stranger was standing talking to the butler.

He was a man of foreign appearance, wearing a cloak lined with sables, and a sable cap, which he removed as Lady Maulevrier approached. He was thin and small, with a clear olive complexion, olive inclining to pale bronze, sleek raven hair, and black almond-shaped eyes. At the first glance Lady Maulevrier knew that he was an Oriental. Her heart sank within her, and seemed to grow chill as death at sight of him. Anything associated with India was horrible to her.

The stranger came forward to meet her, bowing deferentially. He had those lithe, gliding movements which she remembered of old, when she had seen princes and dignitaries of the East creeping shoeless to her husband's feet.

'Will your ladyship do me the honour to grant me an interview?' he said in very good English. 'I have travelled from London expressly for that privilege.'

'Then I fear you have wasted your time, sir, whatever your mission may be,' the dowager answered, haughtily. 'However, I am willing to hear anything you may have to say, if you will be good enough to come this way.'

She moved towards the library, the butler preceding her to open the door, and the stranger followed her into the spacious room, where coals and logs were heaped high upon the wide dog stove, deeply recessed beneath the old English mantel-piece.

It was one of the handsomest rooms of the house, furnished with oak bookcases about seven feet high, above which vases of Oriental ware and varied colouring stood boldly out against the dark oak wall. Richly bound books in infinite variety testified to the wealth and taste of the owner; while one side of the room was absorbed by a wide Gothic window, beyond which appeared the panorama of lake and mountain, beautiful in every season. A tawny velvet curtain divided this room from the drawing-room; but there was also a strong oak door behind the curtain, which was generally closed in cold weather.

Lady Maulevrier went over to this door, and took the precaution to draw the bolt, before she seated herself in her arm-chair by the hearth. She had her own particular chair in all the rooms she occupied--a chair which was sacred as a throne.

She drew off her sealskin gloves, and motioned with a slender white hand to the stranger to be seated.

'To whom have I the honour of speaking?' she asked, looking; him through and through with an unflinching gaze, as she would have looked at Death himself, had the grim skeleton figure come to beckon her.

He handed her a visiting card on which was engraved--

'Louis Asoph, Rajah of Bisnagar.'

'If my memory does not deceive me as to the history of modern India, the territory from which you take your title has been absorbed into the English dominion?' said Lady Maulevrier.

'It was trafficked away forty-three years ago, stolen, filched from my father! but so long as I have power to think and to act I will maintain my claim to that land; yes, if only by the empty mockery of a name on a visiting card. It is a duty I owe to myself as a man, which I owe still more to my murdered father.'

'Have you come all the way from London, and in such weather, only to tell me this story?'

She had twisted his card between her fingers as she listened to him, and now, with an action at once careless and contemptuous, she flung it upon the burning logs. Slight as the action was it was eloquent of scorn for the man.

'No, Lady Maulevrier, my mention of this story, with which you are no doubt perfectly familiar, is only a preliminary. I have come to claim my own, and to appeal to you as a woman of honour to do me justice. Nay, I will say as a woman of common honesty; since there is no nice point of honour in question, only the plain laws of mine and thine, which I believe are the same among all nations and creeds. I come to you, Lady Maulevrier, to ask you to restore to me the wealth which your husband stole from my father.'

'You come to my house, to me, an old woman, helpless, defenceless, in the absence of my grandson, the present Earl, to insult me, and insult the dead,' said Lady Maulevrier, white as statuary marble, and as cold and calm. 'You come to rake up old lies, and to fling them in the face of a solitary woman, old enough to be your mother. Do you think that is a noble thing to do? Even in your barbarous Eastern code of morals and manners is *that* the act of a gentleman?'

'We are no barbarians in the East, Lady Maulevrier. I come from the cradle of civilisation, the original fount of learning. We were scholars and gentleman, priests and soldiers, two thousand years before your British ancestors ran wild in their woods, and sacrificed to their unknown gods or rocky altars reeking with human blood! I know the errand upon which I have come is not a pleasant one, either for you or for me; but I come to you strong in the right of a son to claim the heritage which was stolen from him by an infamous mother and her more infamous paramour----'

'I will not hear another word!' cried Lady Maulevrier, starting to her feet, livid with passion. 'Do not dare to pronounce that name in my hearing--the name of that abominable woman who brought disgrace and dishonour upon my husband and his race.'

'And who brought your husband the wealth of my murdered father,' answered the Indian, defiantly. 'Do not ignore that fact, Lady Maulevrier. What has become of that fortune--two hundred thousand pounds in money and jewels. It was known to have passed into Lord Maulevrier's possession after my father was put away by his paid instruments.

'How dare you bring that vile charge against the dead?'

'There are men living in India who know the truth of that charge: men who were at Bisnagar when my father, sick and heartbroken, was shut up in his deserted harem, hemmed in by spies and traitors, men with murder in their faces. There are those who know tint he was strangled by one of those wretches, that a grave was dug for him under the marble floor of his zenana, a grave in which his bones were found less than a year ago, in my presence, and fitly entombed at my bidding. He was said to have disappeared of his own free will--to have left his palace under cover of night, and sought refuge from possible treachery in another province; but there were those, and not a few, who knew the real history of his disappearance--who knew, and at the time were ready to testify in any court of justice, that he had been got rid of by the Ranee's agents, and at Lord Maulevrier's instigation, and that his possessions in money and jewels had been conveyed in the palankins that carried the Ranee and her women to his lordship's summer retreat near Madras.

The Ranee died at that retreat six months after her husband's murder, not without suspicion of poison, and the wealth which she carried with her when she left Bisnagar passed into his lordship's possession. Had your husband lived, Lady Maulevrier, this story must have been brought to light. There were too many people in Madras interested in sifting the facts. There must have been a public inquiry. It was a happy thing for you and your race that Lord Maulevrier died before that inquiry had been instituted, and that many animosities died with him. Lucky too for you that I was a helpless infant at the time, and that the Mahratta adventurer to whom my father's territory had been transferred in the shuffling of cards at the end of the war was deeply concerned in hushing up the story.'

'And pray, why have you nursed your wrath in all these years? Why do you intrude on me after nearly half a century, with this legend of rapine and murder?'

'Because for nearly half a century I have been kept in profound ignorance of my father's fate--in ignorance of my race. Lord Maulevrier's jealousy banished me from my mother's arms shortly after my father's death. I was sent to the South of France under the care of an ayah. My first memories are of a monastery near Marseilles, where I was reared and educated by a Jesuit community, where I was baptised and brought up in the Roman Catholic faith. By the influence of the Jesuit Fathers I was placed in a house of commerce at Marseilles. Funds to provide for my education and establishment in life, under very modest conditions, were sent periodically by an agent at Madras. It was known that I was of East Indian birth, but little more was known about me. It was only when years had gone by and I was a merchant on my own account and could afford to go to India on a voyage of discovery--yes, as much a voyage of discovery as that of Vasco de Gama or of Drake--that I got from the Madras agent the clue which enabled me, at the cost of infinite patience and infinite labour, to unravel the mystery of my birth. There is no need to enter now upon the details of that story. I have overwhelming documentary evidence--a cloud of witnesses--to convince the most sceptical as to who and what I am. The documents are some of them in my valise, at your ladyship's service. Others are at my hotel in London, ready for the inspection of your ladyship's lawyers. I do not think you will desire to invite a public inquiry, or force me to recover my birthright in a court of justice. I believe that you will take a broader and nobler view of the case, and that you will restore to the wronged and abandoned son the fortune stolen from his murdered father.'

'How dare you come to me with this tissue of lies? How dare you look me in the face and charge my dead husband with treachery and dishonour? I believe neither in your story nor in you, and I defy you to the proof of this vile charge against the dead!'

'In other words you mean that you will keep the money and jewels which Lord Maulevrier stole from my father?'

'I deny the fact that any such jewels or money ever passed into his lordship's possession. That vile woman, your mother, whose infamy cast a dark cloud over Lord Maulevrier's honour, may have robbed her husband, may have emptied the public treasury. But not a rupee or a jewel belonging to her ever came into my possession. I will not bear the burden of her crimes. Her existence spoiled my life-- banished me from India, a widow in all but the name, and more desolate than many widows.'

'Lord Maulevrier was known to leave India carrying with him two large chests- -supposed to contain books--but actually containing treasure. A man who was in the Governor's confidence, and who had been the go-between in his intrigues, con- fessed on his death-bed that he had assisted in removing the treasure. Now, Lady Maulevrier, since your husband died immediately after his arrival in England, and before he could have had any opportunity of converting or making away with the valuables so appropriated, it stands to reason that those valuables must have passed into your possession, and it is from your honour and good feeling that I claim their restitution. If you deny the claim so advanced, there remains but one course open to me, and that is to make my wrongs public, and claim my right from the law of the land.'

'And do you suppose that any English judge or English jury would believe so wild a story--or countenance so vile an accusation against the defenceless?' de- manded Lady Maulevrier, standing up before him, tall, stately, with flashing eye and scornful lip, the image of proud defiance. 'Bring forward your claim, produce your documents, your witnesses, your death-bed confessions. I defy you to injure my dead husband or me by your wild lies, your foul charges! Go to an English law- yer, and see what an English law court will do for you--and your claim. I will hear no more of either.'

She rang the bell once, twice, thrice, with passionate hand, and a servant flew to answer that impatient summons.

'Show this gentlemen to his carriage,' she said, imperiously.

The gentleman who called himself Louis Asoph bowed, and retired without another word.

As the door closed upon him, Lady Maulevrier stood, with clenched hands and frowning brow, staring into vacancy. Her right arm was outstretched, as if she would have waved the intruder away. Suddenly, a strange numbness crept over that uplifted arm, and it fell to her side. From her shoulder down to her foot, that proud form grew cold and feelingless and dead, and she, who had so long carried herself as a queen among women, sank in a senseless heap upon the floor.

CHAPTER XVI.
'HER FACE RESIGNED TO BLISS OR BALE.'

Lady Mary and the Fraeulein had been sitting in the drawing-room all this time waiting for Lady Maulevrier to come to tea. They heard her come in from the garden; and then the footman told them that she was in the library with a stranger. Not even the muffled sound of voices penetrated the heavy velvet curtain and the thick oak door. It was only by the loud ringing of the bell and the sound of footsteps in the hall that Lady Mary knew of the guest's departure. She went to the door between the two rooms, and was surprised to find it bolted.

'Grandmamma, won't you come to tea?' she asked timidly, knocking on the oaken panel, but there was no reply.

She knocked again, and louder. Still no reply.

'Perhaps her ladyship is going to take tea in her own room,' she said, afraid to be officious.

Attendance upon her grandmother at afternoon tea had been one of Lesbia's particular duties; but Mary felt that she was an unwelcome substitute for Lesbia. She wanted to get a little nearer her grandmother's heart if she could; but she knew that her attentions were endured rather than liked.

She went into the hall, where the footman on duty was staring at the light snowflakes dancing past the window, perhaps wishing he were a snowflake himself, and enjoying himself in that white whirligig.

'Is her ladyship having tea in the morning-room?' asked Mary.

The footman gave a little start, as if awakened out of a kind of trance. The sheer vacuity of his mind might naturally slide into mesmeric sleep.

He told Lady Mary that her ladyship had not left the library, and Mary went in timidly, wondering why her grandmother had not joined them in the drawing-room when the stranger was gone.

The sky was dark outside the wide windows, white hills and valleys shrouded in the shades of night. The library was only lighted by the glow of the logs on the hearth, and in that ruddy light the spacious room looked empty. Mary was turning to go away, thinking the footman had been mistaken, when her eye suddenly lighted upon a dark figure lying on the ground. And then she heard an awful stertorous breathing, and knew that her grandmother was lying there, stricken and helpless.

Mary shrieked aloud, with a cry that pierced curtains and doors, and brought Fraeulein and half-a-dozen servants to her help. One of the men brought a lamp, and among them they lifted the smitten figure. Oh, God! how ghastly the face looked in the lamplight!--the features drawn to one side, the skin livid.

'Her ladyship has had a stroke,' said the butler.

'Is she dying?' faltered Mary, white as ashes. 'Oh, grandmother, dear grandmother, don't look at us like that!'

One of the servants rushed off to the stables to send for the doctor. Of course, being an indoor man, he no more thought of going out himself into the snowy night on such an errand than Noah thought of going out of the ark to explore the face of the waters in person.

They carried Lady Maulevrier to her bed and laid her there, like a figure carved out of stone. She was not unconscious. Her eyes were open, and she moaned every now and then as if in bodily or mental pain. Once she tried to speak, but had no power to shape a syllable aright, and ended with a shuddering sigh. Once she lifted her left arm and waved it in the air, as if waving some one off in fear or anger. The right arm, indeed the whole of the right side, was lifeless, motionless as a stone. It was a piteous sight to see the beautiful features drawn and distorted, the lips so accustomed to command mouthing the broken syllables of an unknown tongue. Lady

Mary sat beside the bed with clasped hands, praying dumbly, with her eyes fixed on her grandmother's altered face.

Mr. Horton came, as soon as his stout mountain pony could bring him. He did not seem surprised at her ladyship's condition, and accepted the situation with professional calmness.

'A marked case of hemiplegia,' he said, when he had observed the symptoms.

'Will she die?' asked Mary.

'Oh, dear, no! She will want great care for a little while, but we shall bring her round easily. A splendid constitution, a noble frame; but I think she has overworked her brain a little, reading Huxley and Darwin, and the German physiologists upon whom Huxley and Darwin have built themselves. Metaphysics too. Schopenhauer, and the rest of them. A wonderful woman! Very few brains could hold what hers has had poured into it in the last thirty years. The conducting nerves between the brain and the spinal marrow have been overworked: too much activity, too constant a strain. Even the rails and sleepers on the railroad wear out, don't you know, if there's excessive traffic.'

Mr. Horton had known Mary from her childhood, had given her Gregory's powder, and seen her safely through measles and other infantine ailments, so he was quite at home with her, and at Fellside generally. Lady Maulevrier had given him a good deal of her confidence during those thirty years in which he had practised as his father's partner and successor at Grasmere. He used to tell people that he owed the best part of his education to her ladyship, who condescended to talk to him of the new books she read, and generally gave him a volume to put in his pocket when he was leaving her.

'Don't be downhearted, Lady Mary,' he said; 'I shall come in two or three times a day and see how things are going on, and if I see the slightest difficulty in the case I'll telegraph for Jenner.'

Mary and the Fraeulein sat up with the invalid all that night. Lady Maulevrier's maid was also in attendance, and one of the menservants slept in his clothes on a couch in the corridor, ready for any emergency. But the night passed peacefully, the patient slept a good deal, and next day there was evident improvement. The stroke which had prostrated the body, which reduced the vigorous, active frame to an awful statue--like stillness--a quietude as of death of itself--had not overclouded the intellect. Lady Maulevrier lay on her bed in her luxurious room, with wide Tudor windows commanding half the circle of the hills, and was still the ruling spirit of the house, albeit powerless to move that slender hand, the lightest wave of which had been as potent to command in her little world as royal sign-manual or sceptre in the great world outside.

Now there remained only one thing unimpaired by that awful shock which had laid the stately frame low, and that was the will and sovereign force of the woman's nature. Voice was altered, speech was confused and difficult; but the strength of will, the supreme power of mind, seemed undiminished.

When Lady Maulevrier was asked if Lesbia should be telegraphed for, she replied no, not unless she was in danger of sudden death.

'I should like to see her before I go,' she said, labouring to pronounce the words.

'Dear grandmother,' said Mary, tenderly, 'Mr. Horton says there is no danger.'

'Then do not send for her; do not even tell her what has happened; not yet.'

'But she will miss your letters.'

'True. You must write twice a week at my dictation. You must tell her that I have hurt my hand, that I am well but cannot use a pen. I would not spoil her pleasure for the world.'

'Dear grandmother, how unselfish you are! And Maulevrier, shall he be sent for? He is not so far away,' said Mary, hoping her grandmother would say yes.

What a relief, what an unspeakable solace Maulevrier's presence would be in that dreary house, smitten to a sudden and awful stillness, as if by the Angel of Death!

'No, I do not want Maulevrier!' answered her ladyship impatiently.

'May I sit here and read to you, grandmother?' Mary asked, timidly. 'Mr. Horton said you were to be kept very quiet, and that we were not to let you talk, or talk much to you, but that we might read to you if you like.'

'I do not wish to be read to. I have my thoughts for company,' said Lady Maulevrier.

Mary felt that this implied a wish to be alone. She bent over the invalid's pillow and kissed the pale cheek, feeling as if she were taking a liberty in venturing so much. She would hardly have done it had Lesbia been at home; but she had a feeling that in Lesbia's absence Lady Maulevrier must want somebody's love--even hers. And then she crept away, leaving Halcott the maid in attendance, sitting at her work at the window furthest from the bed.

'Alone with my thoughts,' mused Lady Maulevrier, looking out at the panorama of wintry hills, white, ghost-like against an iron sky. 'Pleasant thoughts, truly! Walled in by the hills--walled in and hemmed round for ever. This place has always felt like a grave: and now I know that it *is* my grave.'

Fraeulein, and Lady Mary, and the maid Halcott, a sedate personage of forty summers, had all been instructed by the doctor that Lady Maulevrier was to be kept profoundly quiet. She must not talk much, since speech was likely to be a painful effort with her for some little time; she must not be talked to much by anyone, least of all must she be spoken to upon any agitating topic. Life must be made as smooth and easy for her as for a new-born infant. No rough breath from the outer world must come near her. She was to see no one but her maid and her granddaughter. Mr. Horton, a plain family man, took it for granted that the granddaughter was dear to her heart, and likely to exercise a soothing influence. Thus it happened that although Lady Maulevrier asked repeatedly that James Steadman should be brought to her, she was not allowed to see him. She whose will had been paramount in that house, whose word had been law, was now treated as a little child, while the will was still as strong, the mind as keen as ever.

'She would talk to him of business,' said Mr. Horton, when he was told of her ladyship's desire to see Steadman, 'and that cannot be allowed, not for some little time at least.'

'She is very angry with us for refusing to obey her,' said Lady Mary.

'Naturally, but it is for her own welfare she is disobeyed. She can have nothing to say to Steadman which will not keep till she is better. This establishment goes by clockwork.'

Mary wished it was a little less like clockwork. Since Lady Maulevrier had been lying upstairs--the voice which had once ruled over the house muffled almost to dumbness--the monotony of life at Fellside had seemed all the more oppressive. The servants crept about with stealthier tread. Mary dared not touch either piano or billiard balls, and was naturally seized with a longing to touch both. The house had a darkened-look, as if the shadow of doom overhung it.

During this regimen of perfect quiet Lady Maulevrier was not allowed to see the newspapers; and Mary was warned that in reading to her grandmother she was to avoid all exciting topics. Thus it happened that the account of a terrible collision between the Scotch express and a luggage train, a little way beyond Preston, an accident in which seven people were killed and about thirty seriously hurt, was not made known to her ladyship; and yet that fact would have been of intense interest and significance to her, since one of those passengers whose injuries were fatal bore the name of Louis Asoph.

CHAPTER XVII.
'AND THE SPRING COMES
SLOWLY UP THIS WAY.'

The wintry weeks glided smoothly by in a dull monotony, and now Lady Maulevrier, still helpless, still compelled to lie on her bed or her invalid couch, motionless as marble, had at least recovered her power of speech, was allowed to read and to talk, and to hear what was going on in that metropolitan world which she seemed unlikely ever to behold again.

Lady Lesbia was still at Cannes, whence she wrote of her pleasures and her triumphs, of flowers and sapphire sea, and azure sky, of all things which were not in the grey bleak mountain world that hemmed in Fellside. She was meeting many of the people whom she was to meet again next season in the London world. She had made an informal ***debut*** in a very select circle, a circle in which everybody was more or less ***chic***, or ***chien***, or ***zinc***, and she was tasting all the sweets of success. But in none of her letters was there any mention of Lord Hartfield. He was not in the little great world by the blue tideless sea.

There was no talk of Lesbia's return. She was to stay till the carnival; she was to stay till the week before Easter. Lady Kirkbank insisted upon it; and both Lesbia and Lady Kirkbank upbraided Lady Maulevrier for her cruelty in not joining them at Cannes.

So Lady Maulevrier had to resign herself to that solitude which had become almost the habit of her life, and to the society of Mary and the Fraeulein. Mary was eager to be of use, to sit with her grandmother, to read to her, to write for her. The warm young heart was deeply moved by the spectacle of this stately woman stricken into helplessness, chained to her couch, immured within four walls. To Mary, who so loved the hills and the streams, the sun and the wind, this imprisonment seemed unspeakable woe. In her pity for such a martyrdom she would have done anything to give pleasure or solace to her grandmother. Unhappily there was very little Mary could do to increase the invalid's sum of pleasure. Lady Maulevrier was a woman of strong feeling, not capable of loving many people. She had concentrated her affection upon Lesbia: and she could not open her heart to Mary all at once because Lesbia was out of the way.

'If I had a dog I loved, and he were to die, I would never have another in his place,' Lady Maulevrier said once; and that speech was the keynote of her character.

She was very courteous to Mary, and seemed grateful for her attentions; but she did not cultivate the girl's society. Mary wrote all her letters in a fine bold hand, and with a rapid pen; but when the letter-writing was over Lady Maulevrier always dismissed her.

'My dear, you want to be out in the air, riding your pony, or scampering about with your dogs,' she said, kindly. 'It would be a cruelty to keep you indoors.'

'No, indeed, dear grandmother, I should like to stay. May I stop and read to you?'

'No, thank you, Mary. I hate being read to. I like to devour a book. Reading aloud is such slow work.

'But I am afraid you must sometimes feel lonely,' faltered Mary.

'Lonely,' echoed the dowager, with a sigh. 'I have been lonely for the last forty years--I have been lonely all my life. Those I loved never gave me back love for love--never--not even your sister. See how lightly she cuts the link that bound her to me. How happy she is among strangers! Yes, there was one who loved me truly, and fate parted us. Does fate part all true lovers, I wonder?'

'You parted Lesbia and Mr. Hammond,' said Mary, impetuously. 'I am sure they loved each other truly.'

'The old and the worldly-wise are Fate, Mary,' answered the dowager, not angry at this daring reproach. 'I know your sister; and I know she is not the kind of woman to be happy in an ignoble life--to bear poverty and deprivation. If it had been you, now, whom Mr. Hammond had chosen, I might have taken the subject into my consideration.'

Mary flamed crimson.

'Mr. Hammond never gave me a thought,' she said, 'unless it was to think me contemptible. He is worlds too good for such a Tomboy. Maulevrier told him about the fox-hunt, and they both laughed at me--at least I have no doubt Mr. Hammond laughed, though I was too much ashamed to look at him.'

'Poor Mary, you are beginning to find out that a young lady ought to be ladylike,' said Lady Maulevrier; 'and now, my dear, you may go. I was only joking with you. Mr. Hammond would be no match for any granddaughter of mine. He is nobody, and has neither friends nor interest. If he had gone into the church Maulevrier could have helped him; but I daresay his ideas are too broad for the church; and he will have to starve at the bar, where nobody can help him. I hope you will bear this in mind, Mary, if Maulevrier should ever bring him here again.'

'He is never likely to come back again. He suffered too much; he was treated too badly in this house.'

'Lady Mary, be good enough to remember to whom you are speaking,' said her ladyship, with a frown. 'And now please go, and tell some one to send Steadman to me.'

Mary retired without a word, gave Lady Maulevrier's message to a footman in the corridor, slipped off to her room, put on her sealskin hat and jacket, took her staff and went out for a long ramble. The hills and valleys were still white. It had been a long, cold winter, and spring was still far off--February had only just begun.

Lady Maulevrier's couch had been wheeled into the morning-room--that luxurious room which was furnished with all things needful to her quiet life, her books, her favourite colours, her favourite flowers, every detail studiously arranged for her pleasure and comfort. She was wheeled into this room every day at noon. When the day was bright and sunny her couch was placed near the window: and when the day was dull and grey the couch was drawn close to the low hearth, which flashed and glittered with brightly coloured tiles and artistic brass.

To-day the sky was dull, and the velvet couch stood beside the hearth. Halcott sat at work in the adjoining bed-chamber, and came in every now and then to replenish the fire: a footman was always on duty in the corridor. A spring bell stood among the elegant trifles upon her ladyship's table; and the lightest touch of her left hand upon the bell brought her attendants to her side. She resolutely refused to have any one sitting with her all day long. Solitude was a necessity of her being, she told Mr. Horton, when he recommended that she should have some one always in attendance upon her.

As the weeks wore on her features had been restored to their proud, calm beauty, her articulation was almost as clear as of old: yet, now and then, there would be a sudden faltering, the tongue and lips would refuse their office, or she would forget a word, or use a wrong word unconsciously. But there was no recovery of power or movement on that side of the body which had been stricken. The paralysed limbs were still motionless, lifeless as marble; and it was clear that Mr. Horton had begun to lose heart about his patient. There was nothing obscure in the case, but the patient's importance made the treatment a serious matter, and the surgeon begged to be allowed to summon Sir William Jenner.

This, however, Lady Maulevrier refused.

'I don't want any fuss made about me,' she said. 'I am content to trust myself to your skill, and I beg that no other doctor may be summoned.'

Mr. Horton understood his patient's feelings on this point. She had a sense of humiliation in her helplessness, and, like some wounded animal that crawls to its covert to die, she would fain have hidden her misery from the eye of strangers. She had allowed no one, not even Maulevrier, to be informed of the nature of her illness.

'It will be time enough for him to know all about me when he comes here,' she said. 'I shall be obliged to see him whenever he does come.'

Maulevrier had spent Christmas and New Year in Paris, Mr. Hammond still his companion. Her ladyship commented upon this with a touch of scorn.

'Mr. Hammond is like the Umbra you were reading about the other day in Lord Lytton's "Last Days of Pompeii,"' she said to Mary. 'It must be very nice for him to go about the world with a friend who franks him everywhere.'

'But we don't know that Maulevrier franks him,' protested Mary, blushing.

'We have no right to suppose that Mr. Hammond does not pay his own expenses.'

'My dear child, is it possible for a young man who has no private means to go gadding about the world on equal terms with a spendthrift like Maulevrier--to pay for Moors in Scotland and apartments at the Bristol?'

'But they are not staying at the Bristol,' exclaimed Mary.

'They are staying at an old-established French hotel on the left side of the Seine. They are going about amongst the students and the workmen, dining at popular restaurants, hearing people talk. Maulevrier says it is delightfully amusing--ever so much better than the beaten track of life in Anglo-American Paris.'

'I daresay they are leading a Bohemian life, and will get into trouble before they have done,' said her ladyship, gloomily.

'Maulevrier is as wild as a hawk.'

'He is the dearest boy in the world,' exclaimed Mary.

She was deeply grateful for her brother's condescension in writing her a letter of two pages long, letting her into the secrets of his life. She felt as if Mr. Hammond were ever so much nearer to her now she knew where he was, and how he was amusing himself.

'Hammond is such a queer fellow,' wrote Maulevrier, 'the strangest things interest him. He sits and talks to the workmen for hours; he pokes his nose into all sorts of places--hospitals, workshops, poverty-stricken dens--and people are always civil to him. He is what Lesbia calls *sympatico*. Ah! what a mistake Lesbia and my grandmother made when they rejected Hammond! What a pearl above price they threw away! But, you see, neither my lady nor Lesbia could appreciate a gem, unless it was richly set.'

And now Lady Maulevrier lay on her couch by the fire, waiting for James Steadman. She had seen him several times since the day of her seizure, but never alone. There was an idea that Steadman must necessarily talk to her of business matters, or cause her mind to trouble itself about business matters; so there had been a well-intentioned conspiracy in the house to keep him out of her way; but now she was much better, and her desire to see Steadman need no longer be thwarted.

He came at her bidding, and stood a little way within the door, tall, erect, square-shouldered, resolute-looking, with a quiet force of character expressed in every feature. He was very much the same man that he had been forty years ago, when he went with her ladyship to Southampton, and accompanied his master and mistress on that tedious journey which was destined to be Lord Maulevrier's last earthly pilgrimage. Time had done little to Steadman in those forty years, except to whiten his hair and beard, and imprint some thoughtful lines upon his sagacious forehead. Time had done something for him mentally, insomuch as he had read a great many books and cultivated his mind in the monotonous quiet of Fellside. Altogether he was a superior man for the passage of those forty years.

He had married within the time, choosing for himself the buxom daughter of a lodgekeeper, whose wife had long been laid at rest in Grasmere churchyard. The buxom girl had grown into a bulky matron, but she was a colourless personage, and her existence made hardly any difference in James Steadman's life. She had brought him no children, and their fireside was lonely; but Steadman seemed to be one of those self-contained personages to whom a solitary life is no affliction.

'I hope I see you in better health, my lady,' he said, standing straight and square, like a soldier on parade.

'I am better, thank you, Steadman; better, but a poor lifeless log chained to this sofa. I sent for you because the time has come when I must talk to you upon a matter of business. You heard, I suppose, that a stranger called upon me just before I had my attack?'

'Yes, my lady.'

'Did you hear who and what he was?'

'Only that he was a foreigner, my lady.'

'He is of Indian birth. He claims to be the son of the Ranee of Bisnagar.'

'He could do you no harm, my lady, if he were twenty times her son.'

'I hope not. Now, I want to ask you a question. Among those trunks and cases and packages of Lord Maulevrier's which were sent here by heavy coach, after they were landed at Southampton, do you remember two cases of books?'

'There are two large cases among the luggage, my lady; very heavy cases, iron clamped. I should not be surprised if they were full of books.'

'Have they never been opened?'

'Not to my knowledge.'

'Are they locked?'

'Yes, my lady. There are two padlocks on each chest.'

'And are the keys in your possession?'

'No, my lady.'

'Where are the cases?'

'In the Oak Room, with the rest of the Indian luggage.'

'Let them remain there. No doubt those cases contain the books of which I have been told. You have not heard that the person calling himself Rajah of Bisnagar has been here since my illness, have you?'

'No, my lady; I am sure he has not been here.'

Lady Maulevrier gave him a scrutinising look.

'He might have come, and my people might have kept the knowledge from me, out of consideration for my infirmity,' she said. 'I should be very angry if it were so. I should hate to be treated like a child.'

'You shall not be so treated, my lady, while I am in this house; but I know there is no member of the household who would presume so to treat you.'

'They might do it out of kindness; but I should loathe such kindness,' said Lady Maulevrier, impatiently. 'Though I have been smitten down, though I lie here like a log, I have a mind to think and to plan; and I am not afraid to meet danger, face to face. Are you telling me the truth, Steadman? Have there been no visits concealed from me, no letters kept from me since I have been ill?'

'I am telling you nothing but the truth, my lady. No letter has been kept from you; no visitor has been to this house whose coming you have not been told of.'

'Then I am content,' said her ladyship, with a sigh of relief.

After this there followed some conversation upon business matters. James Steadman was trusted with the entire management of the dowager's income, the investment of her savings. His honesty was above all suspicion. He was a man of simple habits, his wants few. He had saved money in every year of his service; and for a man of his station was rich enough to be unassailable by the tempter.

He had reconciled his mind to the monotonous course of life at Fellside in the beginning of things; and, as the years glided smoothly by, his character and wants and inclinations had, as it were, moulded themselves to fit that life. He had easy duties, a comfortable home, supreme authority in the household. He was looked up to and made much of in the village whenever he condescended to appear there; and by the rareness of his visits to the Inn or the Reading-room, and his unwillingness to accept hospitality from the tradesmen of Grasmere and Ambleside, he maintained his dignity and exaggerated his importance. He had his books and his newspapers, his evening leisure, which no one ever dared to disturb. He had the old wing of the house for his exclusive occupation; and no one ventured to intrude upon him in his privacy. There was a bell in the corridor which communicated with his rooms, and by this bell he was always summoned. There were servants who had been ten years at Fellside, and who had never crossed the threshold of the red cloth door which was the only communication between the new house and the old one. Steadman's wife performed all household duties of cooking and cleaning in the south wing, where she and her husband took all their meals, and lived entirely apart from the other servants, an exclusiveness which was secretly resented by the establishment.

'Mr. Steadman may be a very superior man,' said the butler 'and I know that in his own estimation the Premier isn't in it compared with him; but I never was fond of people who set themselves upon pinnacles, and I'm not fond of the Steadmans.'

'Mrs. Steadman's plain and homely enough,' replied the housekeeper, 'and I know she'd like to be more sociable, and drop into my room for a cup of tea now and then; but Steadman do so keep her under his thumb: and because he's a misanthrope she's obliged to sit and mope alone.'

If Steadman wanted to drive, there was a dogcart and horse at his disposal; but he did not often leave Fellside. He seemed in his humble way to model his life upon Lady Maulevrier's secluded habits. It was growing dusk when Steadman left his mistress, and she lay for some time looking at the landscape over which twilight shadows were stealing, and thinking of her own life. Over that life, too, the shadows of evening were creeping. She had began to realise the fact that she was an old woman; that for her all personal interest in life was nearly over. She had never felt her age while her activity was unimpaired. She had been obliged to remind herself very often that the afternoon and evening of life had slipped away unawares in that tranquil retirement, and that the night was at hand.

For her the close of earthly life meant actual night. No new dawn, no mysterious after-life shone upon her with magical gleams of an unknown light upon the other side of the dark river. She had accepted the Materialist's bitter and barren creed, and had taught herself that this little life was all. She had learned to scorn the idea of a great Artificer outside the universe, a mighty spirit riding amidst the clouds, and ruling the course of nature and the fate of man. She had schooled herself to think that the idea of a blind, unconscious Nature, working automatically through infinite time and space, was ever so much grander than the old-world notion of a personal God, a Being of infinite power and inexhaustible beneficence, mighty to devise and direct the universe, with knowledge reaching to the farthest confines of space, with ear to listen to the prayer of His lowest creatures. Her belief stopped short even of the Deist's faith in an Almighty Will. She saw in creation nothing but the inevitable development of material laws; and it seemed to her that there was quite as much hope of a heavenly world after death for the infusoria in the pool as for man in his pride and power.

She read her Bible as diligently as she read her Shakespeare, and the words of the Royal Preacher in some measure embodied her own dreary creed. And now, in the darkening winter day, she watched the gloomy shadows creep over the rugged breast of Nabb Scar, and she thought how there was a time for all things, and that her day of hope and ambition was past.

Of late years she had lived for Lesbia, looking forward to the day when she was to introduce this beloved grandchild to the great world of London; and now that hope was gone for ever.

What could a helpless cripple do for a fashionable beauty? What good would it be for her to be conveyed to London, and to lie on a couch in Mayfair, while Lesbia rode in the Row and went to three or four parties every night with a more active chaperon?

She had hoped to go everywhere with her darling, to glory in all her successes, to shield her from all possibility of failure. And now Lesbia must stand or fall alone.

It was a hard thing; but perhaps the hardest part of it was that Lesbia seemed so very well able to get on without her. The girl wrote in the highest spirits; and although her letters were most affectionately worded, they were all about self. That note was dominant in every strain. Her triumphs, her admirers, her bonnets, her gowns. She had had more money from her grandmother, and more gowns from Paris.

'You have no idea how the people dress in this place,' she wrote. 'I should have been quite out in the cold without my three new frocks from Worth. The little

Princess bonnets I wear are the rage. Worth recommended me to adopt special flowers and colours; so I have worn nothing but primroses since I have been here, and my little primrose bonnets are to be seen everywhere, sometimes on hideous old women. Lady Kirkbank hopes you will be able to go to London directly after Easter. She says I must be presented at the May drawing-room--that is imperative. People have begun to talk about me; and unless I make my *debut* while their interest is fresh I shall be a failure. There is an American beauty here, and I believe she and I are considered rivals, and young men lay wagers about us, as to which will look best at a ball, or a regatta, what colours we shall wear, and so on. It is immense fun. I only wish you were here to enjoy it. The American girl is a most insolent person, but I have had the pleasure of crushing her on several occasions in the calmest way. In the description of the concert in last week's newspaper I was called *l'Anglais de marbre*. I certainly had the decency to hold my tongue while Faure was singing. Miss Bolsover's voice was heard ever so many times above the music. According to our English ideas she has most revolting manners, and the money she spends on her clothes would make your hair stand on end. Now do, dearest grandmother, make all your arrangements for beginning the campaign directly after Easter. You must take a house in the very choicest quarter--Lady Kirkbank suggests Grosvenor-place--and it *must* be a large house, for of course you will give a ball. Lady K. says we might have Lord Porlock's house--poor Lady Porlock and her baby died a few weeks ago, and he has gone to Sweden quite broken-hearted. It is one of the new houses, exquisitely furnished, and Lady K. thinks you might have it for a song. Will you get Steadman to write to his lordship's steward, and see what can be done?

'I hope the dear hand is better. You have never told me how you hurt it. It is very sweet of Mary to write me such long letters, and quite a pleasant surprise to find she can spell; but I want to see your own dear hand once more.'

CHAPTER XVIII.
'AND COME AGEN BE IT BY NIGHT OR DAY.'

Those winter months were unutterably dreary for Lady Mary Haselden. She felt weighed down by a sense of death and woe near at hand. The horror of that dreadful moment in which she found her grandmother lying senseless on the ground, the terror of that distorted countenance, those starting eyes, that stertorous breathing, was not easily banished from a vivid girlish imagination; seeing how few distractions there were to divert Mary's thoughts, and how the sun sank and rose again upon the same inevitable surroundings, to the same monotonous routine.

Her grandmother was kinder than she had been in days gone by, less inclined to find fault; but Mary knew that her society gave Lady Maulevrier very little pleasure, that she could do hardly anything towards filling the gap made by Lesbia's absence. There was no one to scold her, no one to quarrel with her. Fraeulein Mueller lectured her mildly from time to time; but that stout German was too lazy to put any force or fire into her lectures. Her reproofs were like the fall of waterdrops on a stone, and infinite ages would have been needed to cause any positive impression.

February came to an end without sign or token from the outer world to disturb the even tenor of life at Fellside. Mary read, and read, and read, till she felt she was made up of the contents of books, crammed with other people's ideas. She read history, or natural science, or travels, or German poetry in the morning, and novels or English poetry in the evening. She had pledged herself to devote her morning indoor hours to instructive literature, and to accomplish some portion of study in every day. She was carrying on her education on parole, as before stated; and she was too honourable to do less than was expected from her.

March came in with its most leonine aspect, howling and blustering; northeast winds shrieking along the gorges and wailing from height to height.

'I wonder the lion and the lamb are not blown into the lake,' said Mary, looking at Helm Crag from the library window.

She scampered about the gardens in the very teeth of those bitter blasts, and took her shivering terriers for runs on the green slopes of the Fell. The snow had gradually melted from the tides of the lowermost range of hills, but the mountain peaks were still white and ghostly, the ground was still hard and slippery in the early mornings. Mary had to take her walks alone in this bleak weather. Fraeulein had a convenient bronchial affection which forbade her to venture so much as the point of her nose outside the house in an east wind, and which justified her in occasionally taking her breakfast in bed. She spent her days for the most part in her arm-chair, drawn close to the fireplace, which she still insisted upon calling the oven, knitting diligently, or reading the **Rundschau**. Even music, which had once been her strong point, was neglected in this trying weather. It was such a cold journey from the oven to the piano.

Mary played a good deal in her desultory manner, now that she had the drawing-room all to herself, and no fear of Lady Maulevrier's critical ear or Lesbia's superior smile. The Fraeulein was pleased to hear her pupil ramble on with her favourite bits from Raff, and Hensel, and Schubert, and Mendelssohn, and Mozart, and was very well content to let her play just what she liked, and to escape the trouble of training her to that exquisite perfection into which Lady Lesbia had been drilled. Lesbia was not a genius, and the training process had been quite as hard for the governess as for the pupil.

Thus the slow days wore on till the first week in March, and on one bleak bitter afternoon, when Fraeulein Mueller stuck to the oven even a little closer than usual, Mary felt she must go out, in the face of the east wind, which was tossing the leafless branches in the valley below until the trees looked like an angry crowd, hurling its arms in the air, fighting, struggling, writhing. She must leave that dreary house for a little while, were it even to be lashed and bruised and broken by that fierce wind. So she told Fraeulein that she really must have her constitutional; and after a feeble remonstrance Fraeulein let her go, and subsided luxuriously into the pillowed depth of her arm-chair.

There had been a hard frost, and all the mountain ways were perilous, so Mary set out upon a steady tramp along the road leading towards the Langdales. The wind seemed to assail her from every side, but she had accustomed herself to defy the elements, and she only hugged her sealskin jacket closer to her, and quickened her pace, chirruping and whistling to Ahab and Ariadne, the two fox-terriers which she had selected for the privilege of a walk.

The terriers raced along the road, and Mary, seeing that she had the road all to herself, raced after them. A light snow-shower, large feathery flakes flying wide apart, fell from the steel-grey sky; but Mary minded the snow no more than she minded the wind. She raced on, the terriers scampering, rushing, flying before her, until, just where the road took a curve, she almost ran into a horse, which was stepping along at a tremendous pace, with a light, high dogcart behind him.

'Hi!' cried the driver, 'where are you coming, young woman? Have you never seen a horse till to-day?'

Some one beside the driver leapt out, and ran to see if Mary was hurt. The horse had swerved to one side, reared a little, and then spun on for a few yards, leaving her standing in the middle of the road.

'Why, it's Molly!' cried the driver, who was no less distinguished a whip than Lord Maulevrier, and who had recognised the terriers.

'I hope you are not hurt,' said the gentleman who had alighted, Maulevrier's friend and shadow, John Hammond.

Mary was covered with confusion by her exploit, and could hardly answer Mr. Hammond's very simple question.

She looked up at him piteously, trying to speak, and he took alarm at her scared expression.

'I am sure you are hurt,' he said earnestly, 'the horse must have struck you, or the shaft perhaps, which was worse. Is it your shoulder that is hurt, or your chest? Lean on me, if you feel faint or giddy. Maulevrier, you had better drive your sister home, and get her looked after.'

'Indeed, I am not hurt; not the least little bit,' gasped Mary, who had recovered her senses by this time. 'I was only frightened, and it was such a surprise to see you and Maulevrier.'

A surprise--yes--a surprise which had set her heart throbbing so violently as to render her speechless. Had horse or shaft-point struck her ever so, she would have hardly been more tremulous than she felt at this moment. Never had she hoped to see him again. He had set his all upon one cast--loved, wooed, and lost her sister. Why should he ever come again? What was there at Fellside worth coming for? And then she remembered what her grandmother thought of him. He was a hanger-on, a sponge, a led captain. He was Maulevrier's Umbra, and must go where his patron went. It was a hard thing so to think of him, and Mary's heart sank at the thought that Lady Maulevrier's worldly wisdom might have reckoned aright.

'It was very foolish of me to run into the horse,' said Mary, while Mr. Hammond stood waiting for her to recover herself.

'It was very foolish of Maulevrier to run into you. If he didn't drive at such a break-neck pace it wouldn't have happened.'

Umbra was very plain-spoken, at any rate.

'There's rank ingratitude,' cried Maulevrier, who had turned back, and was looking down at them from his elevated perch. 'After my coming all the way round by Langdale to oblige you with a view of Elterwater. Molly's all safe and sound. She wouldn't have minded if I'd run over her. Come along, child, get up beside me, Hammond will take the back seat.'

This was easier said than done, for the back of the dogcart was piled with Gladstone bags, fishing rods, and hat-boxes; but Umbra was ready to oblige. He handed Mary up to the seat by the driver, and clambered up at the back, when he hooked himself on somehow among the luggage.

'Dear Maulevrier, how delicious of you to come!' said Mary, when they were rattling on towards Fellside; 'I hope you are going to stay for ages.'

'Well, I dare say, if you make yourself very agreeable, I may stay till after Easter.'

Mary's countenance fell.

'Easter is in three weeks,' she said, despondingly.

'And isn't three weeks an age, at such a place as Fellside? I don't know that I should have come at all on this side of the August sports, only as the grandmother was ill, I thought it a duty to come and see her. A fellow mayn't care much for ancestors when they're well, you know; but when a poor old lady is down on her luck, her people ought to look after her. So, here I am; and as I knew I should be moped to death here----'

'Thank you for the compliment,' said Mary.

'I brought Hammond along with me. Of course, I knew Lesbia was safe out of the way,' added Maulevrier in an undertone.

'It is very obliging of Mr. Hammond always to go where you wish,' returned Mary, who could not help a bitter feeling when she remembered her grandmother's cruel suggestion. 'Has he no tastes or inclinations of his own?'

'Yes, he has, plenty of them, and much loftier tastes than mine, I can tell you. But he's kind enough to let me hang on to him, and to put up with my frivolity. There never were two men more different than he and I are; and I suppose that's why we get on so well together. When we were in Paris he was always up to his eyes in serious work--lectures, public libraries, workmen's syndicates, Mary Anne, the International--heaven knows what, making himself master of the political situation in France; while I was *rigolant* and *chaloupant* at the Bal Bullier.'

It was generous of Maulevrier to speak of his hanger-on thus; and no doubt the society of a well-informed earnest young man was a great good for Maulevrier, a good far above the price of those pounds, shillings, and pence which the Earl might spend for his dependent's benefit; but when a girl of Mary's ardent temper has made a hero of a man, it galls her to think that her hero's dignity should be sacrificed, his honour impeached, were it by the merest tittle.

Maulevrier made a good many inquiries about his grandmother, and seemed really full of kindness and sympathy; but it was with a feeling of profound awe, nay, of involuntary reluctance and shrinking, that he presently entered her ladyship's sitting-room, ushered in by Mary, who had been to her grandmother beforehand to announce the grandson's arrival.

The young man had hardly ever been in a sick room before. He half expected to see Lady Maulevrier in bed, with a crowd of medicine bottles and a cut orange on a table by her side, and a sick nurse of the ancient-crone species cowering over the fire. It was an infinite relief to him to find his grandmother lying on a sofa by the fire in her pretty morning room. A little tea-table was drawn close up to her sofa, and she was taking her afternoon tea. It was rather painful to see her lifting her tea-cup slowly and carefully with her left hand, but that was all. The dark eyes still flashed with the old eagle glance, the lines of the lips were as proud and firm as ever. All sign of contraction or distortion had passed away. In hours of calm her ladyship's beauty was unimpaired; but with any strong emotion there came a convulsive working of the features, and the face was momentarily drawn and distorted, as it had been at the time of the seizure.

Maulevrier's presence had not an unduly agitating effect on her ladyship. She received him with tranquil graciousness, and thanked him for his coming.

'I hope you have spent your winter profitably in Paris,' she said. 'There is a great deal to be learnt there if you go into the right circles.'

Maulevrier told her that he had found much to learn, and that he had gone into circles where almost everything was new to him. Whereupon his grandmother questioned him about certain noble families in the Faubourg Saint Germain who had been known to her in her own day of power, and whose movements she had observed from a distance since that time; but here she found her grandson dark. He had not happened to meet any of the people she spoke about: the plain truth being that he had lived altogether as a Bohemian, and had not used one of the letters of introduction that had been given to him.

'Your friend Mr. Hammond is with you, I am told,' said Lady Maulevrier, not altogether with delight.

'Yes, I made him come; but he is quite safe. He will bolt like a shot at the least hint of Lesbia's return. He doesn't want to meet that young lady again, I can assure you.'

'Pray don't talk in that injured tone. Mr. Hammond is a gentlemanlike person, very well informed, very agreeable. I have never denied that. But you could not expect me to allow my granddaughter to throw herself away upon the first adventurer who made her an offer.'

'Hammond is not an adventurer.'

'Very well, I will not call him so, if the term offends you. But Mr. Hammond is--Mr. Hammond, and I cannot allow Lesbia to marry Mr. Hammond or Mr. Any-body, and I am very sorry you have brought him here again. There is Mary, a silly, romantic girl. I am very much afraid he has made an impression upon her. She colours absurdly when she talks of him, and flew into a passion with me the other day when I ventured to hint that he is not a Rothschild, and that his society must be expensive to you.'

'His society does not cost me anything. Hammond is the soul of independence. He worked as a blacksmith in Canada for three months, just to see what life was like in a wild district. There never was such a fellow to rough it. And as for Molly, well, now, really, if he happened to take a fancy to her, and if she happened to like him, I wouldn't bosh the business, if I were you, grandmother. Take my word for it, Molly might do worse.'

'Of course. She might marry a chimney sweep. There is no answering for a girl of her erratic nature. She is silly enough and romantic enough for anything; but I shall not countenance her if she wants to throw herself away on a person without prospects or connections; and I look to you, Maulevrier, to take care of her, now that I am a wretched log chained to this room.'

'You may rely upon me, grandmother, Molly shall come to no harm, if I can help it.'

'Thank you,' said her ladyship, touching her bell twice.

The two clear silvery strokes were a summons for Halcott, the maid, who appeared immediately.

'Tell Mrs. Power to get his lordship's room ready immediately, and to give Mr. Hammond the room he had last summer,' said Lady Maulevrier, with a sigh of resignation.

While Maulevrier was with his grandmother John Hammond was smoking a solitary cigar on the terrace, contemplating the mountain landscape in its cold March greyness, and wondering very much to find himself again at Fellside. He had gone forth from that house full of passionate indignation, shaking off the dust from his feet, sternly resolved never again to cross the threshold of that fateful cave, where he had met his cold-hearted Circe. And now, because Circe was safe out of the way, he had come back to the cavern; and he was feeling all the pain that a man feels who beholds again the scene of a great past sorrow.

Was this the old love and the old pain again, he wondered, or was it only the sharp thrust of a bitter memory? He had believed himself cured of his useless love--a great and noble love, wasted on a smaller nature than his own. He had thought that because his eyes were opened, and he understood the character of the girl he loved, his cure must needs be complete. Yet now, face to face with the well-remembered landscape, looking down upon that dull grey lake which he had seen smiling in the sunshine, he began to doubt the completeness of his cure. He recalled the lovely face, the graceful form, the sweet, low voice--the perfection of gracious womanhood, manner, dress, movements, tones, smiles, all faultless; and in the absence of that one figure, it seemed to him as if he had come back to a tenantless, dismantled house, where there was nothing that made life worth living.

The red sun went down--a fierce and lurid face that seemed to scowl through the grey--and Mr. Hammond felt that it was time to arouse himself from gloomy meditation and go in and dress for dinner. Maulevrier's valet was to arrive by the coach with the heavier part of the luggage, and Maulevrier's valet did that very small portion of valeting which was ever required by Mr. Hammond. A man who has worked at a forge in the backwoods is not likely to be finicking in his ways, or dependent upon servants for looking after his raiment.

Despite Mr. Hammond's gloomy memories of past joys and disillusions, he contrived to make himself very agreeable, by-and-by, at dinner, and in the drawing-room after dinner, and the evening was altogether gay and sprightly. Maulevrier was in high spirits, full of his Parisian experiences, and talking slang as glibly as a student of the Quartier Latin. He would talk nothing but French, protesting that he had almost forgotten his native tongue, and his French was the language of Larchey's Dictionary of Argot, in which nothing is called by its right name. Mary was enchanted with this new vocabulary, and wanted to have every word explained to her; but Maulevrier confessed that there was a good deal that was unexplainable.

The evening was much livelier than those summer evenings when the dowager and Lady Lesbia were present. There was something less of refinement, perhaps, and Fraeulein remonstrated now and then about some small violation of the unwritten laws of 'Anstand,' but there was more mirth. Maulevrier felt for the first time as if he were master at Fellside. They all went to the billiard room soon after dinner, and Fraeulein and Mary sat by the fire looking on, while the two young men played. In such an evening there was no time for bitter memories: and John Hammond was surprised to find how little he had missed that enchantress whose absence had made the house seem desolate to him when he re-entered it.

He was tired with his journey and the varying emotions of the day, for it was not without strong emotion that he had consented to return to Fellside--and he slept soundly for the earlier part of the night. But he had trained himself long ago to do with a very moderate portion of sleep, and he was up and dressed while the dawn was still slowly creeping along the edges of the hills. He went quietly down to the hall, took one of the bamboos from a collection of canes and mountain sticks, and set out upon a morning ramble over the snowy slopes. The snow showers of yesterday had only sprinkled the greensward upon the lower ground, but in the upper regions the winter snows still lingered, giving an Alpine character to the landscape.

John Hammond was too experienced a mountaineer to be deterred by a little snow. He went up Silver Howe, and from the rugged breast of the mountain saw the sun leap up from amidst a chaos of hill and crag, in all his majesty, while the grey mists of night slowly floated up from the valley that had lain hidden below them, and Grasmere Lake sparkled and flashed in the light of the newly-risen sun.

The church clock was striking eight as Hammond came at a brisk pace down to the valley. There was still an hour before breakfast, so he took a circuitous path to Fellside, and descended upon the house from the Fell, as he had done that summer morning when he saw James Steadman sauntering about in his garden.

Within about a quarter of a mile of Lady Maulevrier's shrubberies Mr. Hammond encountered a pedestrian, who, like himself, was evidently taking a constitutional ramble in the morning air, but on a much less extended scale, for this person did not look capable of going far afield.

He was an old man, something under middle height, but looking as if he had once been taller; for his shoulders were much bent, and his head was sunk on his chest. His whole form looked wasted and shrunken, and John Hammond thought he had never seen so old a man--or at any rate any man who was so deeply marked with all the signs of extreme age; and yet in the backwoods of America he had met ancient settlers who remembered Franklin, and who had been boys when the battle of Bunker's Hill was fresh in the memory of their fathers and mothers.

The little old man was clad in a thick grey overcoat of some shaggy kind of cloth which looked like homespun. He wore a felt hat, and carried a thick oak stick, and there was nothing in his appearance to indicate that he belonged to any higher grade than that of the shepherds and guides with whom Hammond had made himself familiar during his previous visit. And yet there was something distinctive about the man, Hammond thought, something wild and uncanny, which made him unlike any of those hale and hearty-looking dalesmen on whom old age sate so lightly. No, John Hammond could not fancy this man, with his pallid countenance and pale crafty eyes, to be of the same race as those rugged and honest-looking descendants of the Norsemen.

Perhaps it was the man's exceeding age, for John Hammond made up his mind that he must be a centenarian, which gave him so strange and unholy an air. He had the aspect of a man who had been buried and brought back to life again.

So might look one of those Indian Fakirs who have the power to suspend life by some mysterious process, and to lie in the darkness of the grave for a given period, and then at their own will to resume the functions of the living. His long white hair fell upon the collar of his grey coat, and would have given him a patriarchal appearance had the face possessed the dignity of age: but it was a countenance without dignity, a face deeply scored with the lines of evil passions and guilty memories--the face of the vulture, with a touch of the ferret--altogether a most unpleasant face, Mr. Hammond thought.

And yet there was a kind of fascination about that bent and shrunken figure, those feeble movements, and shuffling gait. John Hammond turned to look after the old man when he had passed him, and stood to watch him as he went slowly up the Fell, plant his crutch stick upon the ground before every footstep, as if it were a third leg, and more serviceable than either of the other two.

Mr. Hammond watched him for two or three minutes, but, as the old man's movements had an automatic regularity, the occupation soon palled, and he turned and walked toward Fellside. A few yards nearer the grounds he met James Stead-man, walking briskly, and smoking his morning pipe.

'You are out early this morning,' said Hammond, by way of civility.

'I am always pretty early, sir. I like a mouthful of morning air.'

'So do I. By-the-bye, can you tell me anything about a queer-looking old man I passed just now a little higher up the Fell? Such an old, old man, with long white hair.'

'Yes, sir. I believe I know him.'

'Who is he? Does he live in Grasmere?'

Steadman looked puzzled.

'Well, you see, sir, your description might apply to a good many; but if it's the man I think you mean he lives in one of the cottages behind the church. Old Bar-low, they call him.'

'There can't be two such men--he must be at least a century old. If any one told me he were a hundred and twenty I shouldn't be inclined to doubt the fact. I never saw such a shrivelled, wrinkled visage, bloodless, too, as if the poor old wretch never felt your fresh mountain air upon his hollow cheeks. A dreadful face. It will haunt me for a month.'

'It must be old Barlow,' replied Steadman. 'Good day, sir.'

He walked on with his swinging step, and at such a pace that he was up the side of the Fell and close upon old Barlow's heels when Hammond turned to look after him five minutes later.

'There's a man who shows few traces of age, at any rate,' thought Hammond. 'Yet her ladyship told me that he is over seventy.'

CHAPTER XIX.
THE OLD MAN ON THE FELL.

Having made up his mind to stay at Fellside until after Easter, Maulevrier settled down very quietly--for him. He rode a good deal, fished a little, looked after his dogs, played billiards, made a devout appearance in the big square pew at St. Oswald's on Sunday mornings, and behaved altogether as a reformed character. Even his grandmother was fain to admit that Maulevrier was improved, and that Mr. Hammond's influence upon him must be exercised for good and not for evil.

'I plunged awfully last year, and the year before that,' said Maulevrier, sitting at tea in her ladyship's morning room one afternoon about a week after his return, when she had expressed her gracious desire that the two young men should take tea with her.

Mary was in charge of the tea-pot and brass kettle, and looked as radiant and as fresh as a summer morning. A regular Gainsborough girl, Hammond called her, when he praised her to her brother; a true English beauty, unsophisticated, a little rustic, but full of youthful sweetness.

'You see, I didn't know what a racing stable meant,' continued Maulevrier, mildly apologetic--'in fact, I thought it was an easy way for a nobleman to make as good a living as your City swells, with their soft goods or their Brummagem ware, a respectable trade for a gentleman to engage in. And it was only when I was half ruined that I began to understand the business; and as soon as I did understand it I made up my mind to get out of it; and I am happy to say that I sold the very last of my stud in February, and Tony Lumpkin is his own man again. So you may welcome the prodigal grandson, and order the fatted calf to be slain, grandmother!'

Lady Maulevrier stretched out her left hand to him, and the young man bent over it and kissed it affectionately. He felt really touched by her misfortunes, and was fonder of her than he had ever been before. She had been somewhat hard with him in his boyhood, but she had always cared for his dignity and protected his interests: and, after all, she was a noble old woman, a grandmother of whom a man might be justly proud. He thought of the painted harridans, the bare-shouldered skeletons, whom some of his young friends were obliged to own in the same capacity, and he was thankful that he could reverence his father's mother.

'That is the best news I have heard for a long time, Maulevrier,' said her ladyship graciously; 'better medicine for my nerves than any of Mr. Horton's preparations. If Mr. Hammond's advice has influenced you to get rid of your stable I am deeply grateful to Mr. Hammond.'

Hammond smiled as he sipped his tea, sitting close to Mary's tray, ready to fly to her assistance on the instant should the brazen kettle become troublesome. It had a threatening way of hissing and bubbling over its spirit lamp.

'Oh, you have no idea what a fellow Hammond is to lecture,' answered Maulevrier. 'He is a tremendous Radical, and he thinks that every young man in my position ought to be a reformer, and devote the greater part of his time and trouble to turning out the dirty corners of the world, upsetting those poor dear families who like to pig together in one room, ordering all the children off to school, marrying the fathers and mothers, thrusting himself between free labour and free beer, and interfering with the liberty of the subject in every direction.'

'All that may sound like Radicalism, but I think it is the true Conservatism, and that every young man ought to do as much, if he wants this timeworn old country to maintain its power and prosperity,' answered Lady Maulevrier, with an approving glance at John Hammond's thoughtful face.

'Right you are, grandmother,' returned Maulevrier, 'and I believe Hammond calls himself a Conservative, and means to vote with the Conservatives.'

Means to vote! An idle phrase, surely, thought her ladyship, where the young man's chance of getting into Parliament was so remote.

That afternoon tea in Lady Maulevrier's room was almost as cheerful as the tea-drinkings in the drawing-room, unrestrained by her ladyship's presence. She was pleased with her grandson's conduct, and was therefore inclined to be friendly to his friend. She could see an improvement in Mary, too. The girl was more feminine, more subdued, graver, sweeter; more like that ideal woman of Wordsworth's, whose image embodies all that is purest and fairest in womanhood.

Mary had not forgotten that unlucky story about the fox-hunt, and ever since

Hammond's return she had been as it were on her best behaviour, refraining from her races with the terriers, and holding herself aloof from Maulevrier's masculine pursuits. She sheltered herself a good deal under the Fraeulein's substantial wing, and took care never to intrude herself upon the amusements of her brother and his friend. She was not one of those young women who think a brother's presence an excuse for a perpetual *tete-a-tete* with a young man. Yet when Maulevrier came in quest of her, and entreated her to join them in a ramble, she was not too prudish to refuse the pleasure she so thoroughly enjoyed. But afternoon tea was her privileged hour--the time at which she wore her prettiest frock, and forgot to regret her inferiority to Lesbia in all the graces of womanhood.

One afternoon, when they had all three walked to Easedale Tarn, and were coming back by the side of the force, picking their way among the grey stones and the narrow threads of silvery water, it suddenly occurred to Hammond to ask Mary about that queer old man he had seen on the Fell nearly a fortnight before. He had often thought of making the inquiry when he was away from Mary, but had always forgotten the thing when he was with her. Indeed, Mary had a wonderful knack of making him forget everything but herself.

'You seem to know every creature in Grasmere, down to the two-year-old babies,' said Hammond, Mary having just stopped to converse with an infantine group, straggling and struggling over the boulders. 'Pray, do you happen to know a man called Barlow, a very old man?'

'Old Sam Barlow,' exclaimed Mary; 'why, of course I know him.'

She said it as if he were a near relative, and the question palpably absurd.

'He is an old man, a hundred, at least, I should think,' said Hammond.

'Poor old Sam, not much on the wrong side of eighty. I go to see him every week, and take him his week's tobacco, poor old dear. It is his only comfort.'

'Is it?' asked Hammond. 'I should have doubted his having so humanising a taste as tobacco. He looks too evil a creature ever to have yielded to the softening influence of a pipe.'

'An evil creature! What, old Sam? Why he is the most genial old thing, and as cheery--loves to hear the newspaper read to him--the murders and railway accidents. He doesn't care for politics. Everybody likes old Sam Barlow.'

'I fancy the Grasmere idea of reverend and amiable age must be strictly local. I can only say that I never saw a more unholy countenance.'

'You must have been dreaming when you saw him,' said Mary. 'Where did you meet him?'

'On the Fell, about a quarter of a mile from the shrubbery gate.'

'***Did*** you? I shouldn't have thought he could have got so far. I've a good mind to take you to see him, this very afternoon, before we go home.'

'Do,' exclaimed Hammond, 'I should like it immensely. I thought him a hateful-looking old person; but there was something so thoroughly uncanny about him that he exercised an absolute fascination upon me: he magnetised me, I think, as the green-eyed cat magnetises the bird. I have been positively longing to see him again. He is a kind of human monster, and I hope some one will have a big bottle made ready for him and preserve him in spirits when he dies.'

'What a horrid idea! No, sir, dear old Barlow shall lie beside the Rotha, under the trees Wordsworth planted. He is such a man as Wordsworth would have loved.'

Mr. Hammond shrugged his shoulders, and said no more. Mary's little vehement ways, her enthusiasm, her love of that valley, which might be called her native place, albeit her eyes had opened upon heaven's light far away, her humility, were all very delightful in their way. She was not a perfect beauty, like Lesbia; but she was a fresh, pure-minded English girl, frank as the day, and if he had had a brother he would have recommended that brother to choose just such a girl for his wife.

Mr. Samuel Barlow occupied a little old cottage, which seemed to consist chiefly of a gable end and a chimney stack, in that cluster of dwellings behind St. Oswald's church, which was once known as the Kirk Town. Visitors went downstairs to get to Mr. Barlow's ground-floor, for the influence of time and advancing civilisation had raised the pathway in front of Mr. Barlow's cottage until his parlour had become of a cellar-like aspect. Yet it was a very nice little parlour when one got down to it, and it enjoyed winter and summer a perpetual twilight, since the light that crept through the leaded casement was tempered by a screen of flowerpots, which were old Barlow's particular care. There were no finer geraniums in all Grasmere than Barlow's, no bigger carnations or picotees, asters or arums.

It was about five o'clock in the March afternoon, when Mary ushered John

Hammond into Mr. Barlow's dwelling, and, in the dim glow of a cheery little fire and the faint light that filtered through the screen of geranium leaves, the visitor looked for a moment or so doubtfully at the owner of the cottage. But only for a moment. Those bright blue eyes and apple cheeks, that benevolent expression, bore no likeness to the strange old man he had seen on the Fell. Mr. Barlow was toothless and nut-cracker like of outline; he was thin and shrunken, and bent with the burden of long years, but his healthy visage had none of those deep lines, those cross markings and hollows which made the pallid countenance of that other old man as ghastly as would be the abstract idea of life's last stage embodied by the bitter pencil of a Hogarth.

'I have brought a gentleman from London to see you, Sam,' said Mary. 'He fancied he met you on the Fell the other morning.'

Barlow rose and quavered a cheery welcome, but protested against the idea of his having got so far as the Fell.

'With my blessed rheumatics, you know it isn't in me, Lady Mary. I shall never get no further than the churchyard; but I likes to sit on the wall hard by Wordsworth's tomb in a warm afternoon, and to see the folks pass over the bridge; and I can potter about looking after my flowers, I can. But it would be a dull life, now the poor old missus is gone and the bairns all out at service, if it wasn't for some one dropping in to have a chat, or read me a bit of the news sometimes. And there isn't anybody in Grasmere, gentle or simple, that's kinder to me than you, Lady Mary. Lord bless you, I do look forward to my newspaper. Any more of them dreadful smashes?'

'No, Sam, thank Heaven, there have been no railway accidents.'

'Ah, we shall have 'em in August and September,' said the old man, cheerily. 'They're bound to come then. There's a time for all things, as Solomon says. When the season comes t'smashes all coom. And no more of these mysterious murders, I suppose, which baffle t'police and keep me awake o' nights thinking of 'em.'

'Surely you do not take delight in murder, Mr. Barlow?' said Hammond.

'No, sir, I do not wish my fellow-creatures to mak' awa' wi' each other; but if there is a murder going in the papers I like to get the benefit of it. I like to sit in front of my fire of an evening and wonder about it while I smoke my pipe, and fancy I can see the murderer hiding in a garret in an out-of-the-way alley, or as a stowaway on board a gert ship, or as a miner deep down in a coalpit, and never thinking that even there t'police can track him. Did you ever hear tell o' Mr. de Quincey, sir?'

'I believe I have read every line he ever wrote.'

'Ah, you should have heard him talk about murders. It would have made you dream queer dreams, just as he did. He lived for years in the white cottage that Wordsworth once lived in, just behind the street yonder--a nice, neat, lile gentleman, in a houseful of books. I've had many a talk with him when I was a young man.'

'And how old may you he now, Mr. Barlow?'

'Getting on for eighty four, sir.'

'But you are not the oldest man in Grasmere, I should say, by twenty years?'

'I don't think there's many much older than me, sir.'

'The man I saw on the Fell looked at least a hundred. I wish you could tell me who he is; I feel a morbid curiosity about him.'

He went on to describe the old man in the grey coat, as minutely as he could, dwelling on every characteristic of that singular-looking old person; but Samuel Barlow could not identify the description with any one in Grasmere. Yet a man of that age, seen walking on the hill-side at eight in the morning, could hardly have come from far afield.

CHAPTER XX.
LADY MAULEVRIER'S LETTER-BAG.

Although Maulevrier had assured his grandmother that John Hammond would take flight at the first warning of Lesbia's return, Lady Maulevrier's dread of any meeting between her granddaughter and that ineligible lover determined her in making such arrangements as should banish Lesbia from Fellside, so long as there seemed the slightest danger of such a meeting. She knew that Lesbia had loved her fortuneless suitor; and she did not know that the wound was cured, even by a season in the little-great world of Cannes. Now that she, the ruler of that household, was a helpless captive in her own apartments, she felt that Lesbia at Fellside would be her own mistress, and hemmed round with the dangers that beset richly-dowered beauty and inexperienced youth.

John Hammond might be playing a very deep game, perhaps assisted by Maulevrier. He might ostensibly leave Fellside before Lesbia's return, yet lurk in the neighbourhood, and contrive to meet her every day. If Maulevrier encouraged this folly, they might be married and over the border, before her ladyship--fettered, impotent as she was--could interfere.

Lady Maulevrier felt that Georgie Kirkbank was her strong rock. So long as Lesbia was under that astute veteran's wing there could be no danger. In that embodied essence of worldliness and diplomacy, there was an ever-present defence from all temptations that spring from romance and youthful impulses. It was a bitter thing, perhaps, to steep a young and pure soul in such an atmosphere, to harden a fresh young nature in the fiery crucible of fashionable life; but Lady Maulevrier believed that the end would sanctify the means. Lesbia, once married to a worthy man, such a man as Lord Hartfield, for instance, would soon rise to a higher level than that Belgravian swamp over which the malarian vapours of falsehood, and slander, and self-seeking, and prurient imaginings hang dense and thick. She would rise to the loftier table-land of that really great world which governs and admonishes the ruck of mankind by examples of noble deeds and noble thoughts; the world of statesmen, and soldiers, and thinkers, and reformers; the salt wherewithal society is salted.

But while Lesbia was treading the tortuous mazes of fashion, it was well for her to be guided and guarded by such an old campaigner as Lady Kirkbank, a woman who, in the language of her friends, 'knew the ropes.'

Lesbia's last letter had been to the effect that she was to go back to London with the Kirkbanks directly after Easter, and that directly they arrived she would set off with her maid for Fellside, to spend a week or a fortnight with her dearest grandmother, before going back to Arlington Street for the May campaign.

'And then, dearest, I hope you will make up your mind to spend the season in London,' wrote Lesbia. 'I shall expect to hear that you have secured Lord Porlock's house. How dreadfully slow your poor dear hand is to recover! I am afraid Horton is not treating the case cleverly. Why do you not send for Mr. Erichsen? It is a shock to my nerves every time I receive a letter in Mary's masculine hand, instead of in your lovely Italian penmanship. Strange--isn't it?--how much better the women of your time write than the girls of the present day! Lady Kirkbank receives letters from stylish girls in a hand that would disgrace a housemaid.'

Lady Maulevrier allowed a post to go by before she answered this letter, while she deliberated upon the best and wisest manner of arranging her granddaughter's future. It was an agony to her not to be able to write with her own hand, to be obliged to so shape every sentence that Mary might learn nothing which she ought not to know. It was impossible with such an amanuensis to write confidentially to Lady Kirkbank. The letters to Lesbia were of less consequence; for Lesbia, albeit so intensely beloved, was not in her grandmother's confidence, least of all about those schemes and dreams which concerned her own fate.

However, the letters had to be written, so Mary was told to open her desk and begin.

The letter to Lesbia ran thus:--

'My dearest Child,

'This is a world in which our brightest day-dreams generally end in mere dreaming. For years past I have cherished the hope of presenting you to your sovereign, to whom I was presented six and forty years ago, when she was so fair and girlish a creature that she seemed to me more like a queen in a fairy tale than the actual ruler of a great country. I have beguiled my monotonous days with thoughts of the time when I should return to the great world, full of pride and delight in showing old friends what a sweet flower I had reared in my mountain home; but, alas, Lesbia, it may not be.

'Fate has willed otherwise. The maimed hand does not recover, although Horton is very clever, and thoroughly understands my case. I am not ill, I am not in danger; so you need feel no anxiety about me; but I am a cripple; and I am likely to remain a cripple for months; so the idea of a London season this year is hopeless.

'Now, as you have in a manner made your _debut_ at Cannes, it would never do to bury you here for another year. You complained of the dullness last summer; but you would find Fellside much duller now that you have tasted the elixir of life. No, my dear love, it will be well for you to be presented, as Lady Kirkbank proposes, at the first drawing-room after Easter; and Lady Kirkbank will have to present you. She will be pleased to do this, I know, for her letters are full of enthusiasm about you. And, after all, I do not think you will lose by the exchange. Clever as I think myself, I fear I should find myself sorely at fault in the society of to-day. All things are changed: opinions, manners, creeds, morals even. Acts that were crimes in my day are now venial errors--opinions that were scandalous are now the mark of "advanced thought." I should be too formal for this easy-going age, should be ridiculed as old-fashioned and narrow-minded, should put you to the blush a dozen times a day by my prejudices and opinions.

'It is very good of you to think of travelling so long a distance to see me; and I should love to look at your sweet face, and hear you describe your new experiences; but I could not allow you to travel with only the protection of a maid; and there are many reasons why I think it better to defer the meeting till the end of the season, when Lady Kirkbank will bring my treasure back to me, eager to tell me the history of all the hearts she has broken.'

The dowager's letter to Lady Kirkbank was brief and business-like. She could only hope that her old friend Georgie, whose acuteness she knew of old, would divine her feelings and her wishes, without being explicitly told what they were.

'My dear Georgie,

'I am too ill to leave this house; indeed I doubt if I shall ever leave it till I am taken away in my coffin; but please say nothing to alarm Lesbia. Indeed, there is no ground for fear, as I am not dangerously ill, and may drag out an imprisonment of long years before the coffin comes to fetch me. There are reasons, which you will understand, why Lesbia should not come here till after the season; so please keep her in Arlington Street, and occupy her mind as much as you can with the preparations for her first campaign. I give you _carte blanche_. If Carson is still in business I should like her to make my girl's gowns; but you must please yourself in this matter, as it is quite possible that Carson is a little behind the times.

'I must ask you to present my darling, and to deal with her exactly as if she were a daughter of your own. I think you know all my views and hopes about her; and I feel that I can trust to your friendship in this my day of need. The dream of my life has been to launch her myself, and direct her every step in the mazes of town life; but that dream is over. I have kept age and infirmity at a distance, have even forgotten that the years were going by; and now I find myself an old woman all at once, and my golden dream has vanished.'

Lady Kirkbank's reply came by return of post, and happily this gushing epistle had not to be submitted to Mary's eye.

'My dearest Di,

'My heart positively bleeds for you. What is the matter with your hand, that you talk of being a life-long prisoner to your room? Pray send for Paget or Erichsen, and have yourself put right at once. No doubt that local simpleton is making a mess of your case. Perhaps while he is dabbing with lint and lotions the real remedy is the knife. I am sure amputation would be less melancholy than the despondent state of feeling which you are now suffering. If any limb of mine went wrong, I should say to the surgeon, "Cut it off, and patch up the stump in your best style; I give you a fortnight, and at the end of that time I expect to be going to parties again." Life is not long enough for dawdling surgery.

'As regards Lesbia, I can only say that I adore her, and I am enchanted at the idea that I am to run her myself. I intend her to be _the_ beauty of the season--not _one of the loveliest debutantes_, or any rot of that kind--but just the girl whom everybody will be crazy about. There shall be a mob wherever she appears, Di, I promise you that. There is no one in London who can work a thing of that kind better than your humble servant. And when once the girl is the talk of the town, all the rest is easy. She can choose for herself among the very best men in society. Offers will pour in as thickly as circulars from undertakers and mourning warehouses after a death.

'Lesbia is so cool-headed and sensible that I have not the least doubt of her success. With an impulsive or romantic girl there is always the fear of a _fiasco_. But this sweet child of yours has been well brought up, and knows her own value. She behaved like a queen here, where I need not tell you society is just a little mixed; though, of course, we only cultivate our own set. Your heart would swell with pride if you could see the way she puts down men who are not quite good style; and the ease with which she crushes those odious American girls, with their fine complexions and loud manners.

'Be assured that I shall guard her as the apple of my eye, and that the detrimental who circumvents me will be a very Satan of schemers.

'I can but smile at your mention of Carson, whose gowns used to fit us so well in our girlish days, and whose bills seem moderate compared with the exorbitant accounts I get now.

'Carson has long been forgotten, my dear soul, gone with the snows of last year. A long procession of fashionable French dressmakers has passed across the stage since her time, like the phantom kings in Macbeth; and now the last rage is to have our gowns made by an Englishman who works for the Princess, and who gives himself most insufferable airs, or an Irishwoman who is employed by all the best actresses. It is to the latter, Kate Kearney, I shall entrust our sweet Lesbia's toilettes.'

The same post brought a loving letter from Lesbia, full of regret at not being allowed to go down to Fellside, and yet full of delight at the prospect of her first season.

'Lady Kirkbank and I have been discussing my court dress,' she wrote, 'and we have decided upon a white cut-velvet train, with a border of ostrich feathers, over a satin petticoat embroidered with seed pearl. It will be expensive, but we know you will not mind that. Lady Kirkbank takes the idea from the costume Buckingham wore at the Louvre the first time he met Anne of Austria. Isn't that clever of her? She is not a deep thinker like you; is horribly ignorant of science, metaphysics, poetry even. She asked me one day who Plato was, and whether he took his name from the battle of Platoea; and she says she never could understand why people make a fuss about Shakespeare; but she has read all the secret histories and memoirs that ever were written, and knows all the ins and outs of court life and high life for the last three hundred years; and there is not a person in the peerage whose family history she has not at her fingers' ends, except my grandfather. When I asked her to tell me all about Lord Maulevrier and his achievements as Governor of Madras, she had not a word to say. So, perhaps, she draws upon her invention a little in talking about other people, and felt herself restrained when she came to speak of my grandfather.'

This passage in Lesbia's letter affected Lady Maulevrier as if a scorpion had wriggled from underneath the sheet of paper. She folded the letter, and laid it in the satin-lined box on her table, with a deep sigh.

'Yes, she is in the world now, and she will ask questions. I have never warned her against pronouncing her grandfather's name. There are some who will not be so kind as Georgie Kirkbank; some, perhaps, who will delight in humiliating her, and who will tell her the worst that can be told. My only hope is that she will make a great marriage, and speedily. Once the wife of a man with a high place in the world, worldlings will be too wise to wound her by telling her that her grandfather was an unconvicted felon.'

The die was cast. Lady Maulevrier might dread the hazard of evil tongues, of slanderous memories; but she could not recall her consent to Lesbia's *debut*. The girl was already launched; she had been seen and admired. The next stage in her career must be to be wooed and won by a worthy wooer.

CHAPTER XXI.
ON THE DARK BROW OF HELVELLYN.

While these plans were being settled, and while Lesbia's future was the all-absorbing subject of Lady Maulevrier's thoughts, Mary contrived to be happier than she had ever been in her life before. It was happiness that grew and strengthened with every day; and yet there was no obvious reason for this deep joy. Her life ran in the same familiar groove. She walked and rode on the old pathways; she rowed on the lake she had known from babyhood; she visited her cottagers, and taught in the village school, just the same as of old. The change was only that she was no longer alone; and of late the solitude of her life, the ever-present consciousness that nobody shared her pleasures or sympathised with her upon any point, had weighed upon her like an actual burden. Now she had Maulevrier, who was always kind, who understood and shared almost all her tastes, and Maulevrier's friend, who, although not given to saying smooth things, seemed warmly interested in her pursuits and opinions. He encouraged her to talk, although he generally took the opposite side in every argument; and she no longer felt oppressed or irritated by the idea that he despised her.

Indeed, although he never flattered or even praised her, Mr. Hammond let her see that he liked her society. She had gone out of her way to avoid him, very fearful lest he should think her bold or masculine; but he had taken pains to frustrate all her efforts in that direction; he had refused to go upon excursions which she could not share. 'Lady Mary must come with us,' he said, when they were planning a morning's ramble. Thus it happened that Mary was his guide and companion in all his walks, and roamed with him bamboo in hand, over every one of those mountainous paths she knew and loved so well. Distance was as nothing to them--sometimes a boat helped them, and they went over wintry Windermere to climb the picturesque heights above Bowness. Sometimes they took ponies, and a groom, and left their steeds to perform the wilder part of the way on foot. In this wise John Hammond saw all that was to be seen within a day's journey of Grasmere, except the top of Helvellyn. Maulevrier had shirked the expedition, had always put off Mary and Mr. Hammond when they proposed it. The season was not advanced enough--the rugged pathway by the Tongue Ghyll would be as slippery as glass--no pony could get up there in such weather.

'We have not had any frost to speak of for the last fortnight,' pleaded Mary, who was particularly anxious to do the honours of Helvellyn, as the real lion of the neighbourhood.

'What a simpleton you are, Molly!' cried Maulevrier. 'Do you suppose because there is no frost in your grandmother's garden--and if you were to ask Staples about his peaches he would tell you a very different story--that there's a tropical atmosphere on Dolly Waggon Pike? Why, I'd wager the ice on Grisdale Tarn is thick enough for skating. Helvellyn won't run away, child. You and Hammond can dance the Highland Schottische on Striding Edge in June, if you like.'

'Mr. Hammond won't be here in June,' said Mary.

'Who knows?--the train service is pretty fair between London and Windermere. Hammond and I would think nothing of putting ourselves in the mail on a Friday night, and coming down to spend Saturday and Sunday with you--if you are good.'

There came a sunny morning soon after Easter which seemed mild enough for June; and when Hammond suggested that this was the very day for Helvellyn, Maulevrier had not a word to say against the truth of that proposition. The weather had been exceptionally warm for the last week, and they had played tennis and sat in the garden just as if it had been actually summer. Patches of snow might still linger on the crests of the hills--but the approach to those bleak heights could hardly be glacial.

Mary clasped her hands delightedly.

'Dear old Maulevrier!' she exclaimed, 'you are always good to me. And now I shall be able to show you the Red Tarn, the highest pool of water in England,' she said, turning to Hammond. 'And you will see Windermere winding like a silvery serpent between the hills, and Grasmere shining like a jewel in the depth of the valley, and the sea glittering like a line of white light between the edges of earth and heaven, and the dark Scotch hills like couchant lions far away to the north.'

'That is to say these things are all supposed to be on view from the top of the mountain; but as a peculiar and altogether exceptional state of the atmosphere is essential to their being seen, I need not tell you that they are rarely visible,' said Maulevrier. 'You are talking to old mountaineers, Molly. Hammond has done Cotapaxi and had his little clamber on the equatorial Andes, and I--well, child, I have done my Righi, and I have always found the boasted panorama enveloped in dense fog.'

'It won't be foggy to-day,' said Mary. 'Shall we do the whole thing on foot, or shall I order the ponies?'

Mr. Hammond inquired the distance up and down, and being told that it involved only a matter of eight miles, decided upon walking.

'I'll walk, and lead your pony,' he said to Mary, but Mary declared herself quite capable of going on foot, so the ponies were dispensed with as a possible encumbrance.

This was planned and discussed in the garden before breakfast. Fraeulein was told that Mary was going for a long walk with her brother and Mr. Hammond; a walk which might last over the usual luncheon hour; so Fraeulein was not to wait luncheon. Mary went to her grandmother's room to pay her duty visit. There were no letters for her to write that morning, so she was perfectly free.

The three pedestrians started an hour after breakfast, in light marching order. The two young men wore their Argyleshire shooting clothes--homespun knickerbockers and jackets, thick-ribbed hose knitted by Highland lasses in Inverness.

They carried a couple of hunting flasks filled with claret, and a couple of sandwich boxes, and that was all. Mary wore her substantial tailor-gown of olive tweed, and a little toque to match, with a silver mounted grouse-claw for her only ornament.

It was a delicious morning, the air fresh and sweet, the sun comfortably warm, a little too warm, perhaps, presently, when they had trodden the narrow path by the Tongue Ghyll, and were beginning to wind slowly upwards over rough boulders and last year's bracken, tough and brown and tangled, towards that rugged wall of earth and stone tufted with rank grasses, which calls itself Dolly Waggon Pike. Here they all came to a stand-still, and wiped the dews of honest labour from their foreheads; and here Maulevrier flung himself down upon a big boulder, with the soles of his stout shooting boots in running water, and took out his cigar case.

'How do you like it?' he asked his friend, when he had lighted his cigarette. 'I hope you are enjoying yourself.'

'I never was happier in my life,' answered Hammond.

He was standing on higher ground, with Mary at his elbow, pointing out and expatiating upon the details of the prospect. There were the lakes--Grasmere, a disk of shining blue; Rydal, a patch of silver; and Windermere winding amidst a labyrinth of wooded hills.

'Aren't you tired?' asked Maulevrier.

'Not a whit.'

'Oh, I forgot you had done Cotapaxi, or as much of Cotapaxi as living mortal ever has done. That makes a difference. I am going home.'

'Oh, Maulevrier!' exclaimed Mary, piteously.

'I am going home. You two can go to the top. You are both hardened mountaineers, and I am not in it with either of you. When I rashly consented to a pedestrian ascent of Helvellyn I had forgotten what the gentleman was like; and as to Dolly Waggon I had actually forgotten her existence. But now I see the lady--as steep as the side of a house, and as stony--no, naught but herself can be her parallel in stoniness. No, Molly, I will go no further.'

'But we shall go down on the other side,' urged Mary. 'It is a little steeper on the Cumberland side, but not nearly so far.'

'A little steeper! I Can anything be steeper than Dolly Waggon? Yes, you are right. It is steeper on the Cumberland side. I remember coming down a sheer descent, like an exaggerated sugar-loaf; but I was on a pony, and it was the brute's look-out. I will not go down the Cumberland side on my own legs. No, Molly, not even for you. But if you and Hammond want to go to the top, there is nothing to prevent you. He is a skilled mountaineer. I'll trust you with him.'

Mary blushed, and made no reply. Of all things in the world she least wanted to abandon the expedition. Yet to climb Helvellyn alone with her brother's friend would no doubt be a terrible violation of those laws of maidenly propriety which Fraeulein was always expounding. If Mary were to do this thing, which she longed to do, she must hazard a lecture from her governess, and probably a biting reproof from her grandmother.

'Will you trust yourself with me, Lady Mary?' asked Hammond, looking at her with a gaze so earnest--so much more earnest than the occasion required--that her blushes deepened and her eyelids fell. 'I have done a good deal of climbing in my day, and I am not afraid of anything Helvellyn can do to me. I promise to take great care of you if you will come.'

How could she refuse? How could she for one moment pretend that she did not trust him, that her heart did not yearn to go with him. She would have climbed the shingly steep of Cotapaxi with him--or crossed the great Sahara with him--and feared nothing. Her trust in him was infinite--as infinite as her reverence and love.

'I am afraid Fraeulein would make a fuss,' she faltered, after a pause.

'Hang Fraeulein,' cried Maulevrier, puffing at his cigarette, and kicking about the stones in the clear running water. 'I'll square it with Fraeulein. I'll give her a pint of fiz with her lunch, and make her see everything in a rosy hue. The good soul is fond of her Heidseck. You will be back by afternoon tea. Why should there be any fuss about the matter? Hammond wants to see the Red Tarn, and you are dying to show him the way. Go, and joy go with you both. Climbing a stony hill is a form of pleasure to which I have not yet risen. I shall stroll home at my leisure, and spend the afternoon on the billiard-room sofa reading Mudie's last contribution to the comforts of home.'

'What a Sybarite,' said Hammond. 'Come, Lady Mary, we mustn't loiter, if we are to be back at Fellside by five o'clock.'

Mary looked at her brother doubtfully, and he gave her a little nod which seemed to say, 'Go, by all means;' so she dug the end of her staff into Dolly's rugged breast, and mounted cheerily, stepping lightly from boulder to boulder.

The sun was not so warm as it had been ten minutes ago, when Maulevrier flung himself down to rest. The sky had clouded over a little, and a cooler wind was blowing across the breast of the hill. Fairfield yonder, that long smooth slope of verdure which a little while ago looked emerald green in the sunlight, now wore a soft and shadowy hue. All the world was greyer and dimmer in a moment, as it were, and Coniston Lake in its distant valley disappeared beneath a veil of mist, while the shimmering sea-line upon the verge of the horizon melted and vanished among the clouds that overhung it. The weather changes very quickly in this part of the world. Sharp drops of rain came spitting at Hammond and Mary as they climbed the crest of the Pike, and stopped, somewhat breathless, to look back at Maulevrier. He was trudging blithely down the winding way, and seemed to have done wonders while they had been doing very little.

'How fast he is going!' said Mary.

'Easy is the descent of Avernus. He is going down-hill, and we are going upwards. That makes all the difference in life, you see,' answered Hammond.

Mary looked at him with divine compassion. She thought that for him the hill of life would be harder than Helvellyn. He was brave, honest, clever; but her grandmother had impressed upon her that modern civilisation hardly has room for a young man who wants to get on in the world, without either fortune or powerful connexions. He had better go to Australia and keep sheep, than attempt the impossible at home.

The rain was a passing shower, hardly worth speaking of, but the glory of the day was over. The sky was grey, and there were dark clouds creeping up from the sea-line. Silvery Windermere had taken a leaden hue; and now they turned their last fond look upon the Westmoreland valley, and set their faces steadily towards Cumberland, and the fine grassy plateau on the top of the hill.

All this was not done in a flash. It took them some time to scale Dolly's stubborn breast, and it took them another hour to reach Seat Sandal; and by the time they came to the iron gate in the fence, which at this point divides the two counties, the atmosphere had thickened ominously, and dark wreaths of fog were floating about and around them, whirled here and there by a boisterous wind which shrieked and roared at them with savage fury, as if it were the voice of some Titan monarch of the mountain protesting against this intrusion upon his domain.

'I'm afraid you won't see the Scottish hills,' shouted Mary, holding on her little cloth hat.

She was obliged to shout at the top of her voice, though she was close to Mr. Hammond's elbow, for that shrill screaming wind would have drowned the voice of a stentor.

'Never mind the view,' replied Hammond in the same fortissimo, 'but I really wish I hadn't brought you up here. If this fog should get any worse, it may be dangerous.'

'The fog is sure to get worse,' said Mary, in a brief lull of the hurly-burly, 'but there is no danger. I know every inch of the hill, and I am not a bit afraid. I can guide you, if you will trust me.'

'My bravest of girls,' he exclaimed, looking down at her. 'Trust you! Yes, I would trust my life to you--my soul--my honour--secure in your purity and good faith.'

Never had eyes of living man or woman looked down upon her with such tenderness, such fervent love. She looked up at him; looked with eyes which, at first bewildered, then grew bold, and lost themselves, as it were, in the dark grey depths of the eyes they met. The savage wind, hustling and howling, blew her nearer to him, as a reed is blown against a rock. Dark grey mists were rising round them like a sea; but had that ever-thickening, ever-darkening vapour been the sea itself, and death inevitable, Mary Haselden would have hardly cared. For in this moment the one precious gift for which her soul had long been yearning had been freely given to her. She knew all at once, that she was fondly loved by that one man whom she had chosen for her idol and her hero.

What matter that he was fortuneless, a nobody, with but the poorest chances of success in the world? What if he must needs, only to win the bare means of existence, go to Australia and keep sheep, or to the Bed River valley and grow corn? What if he must labour, as the peasants laboured on the sides of this rude hill? Gladly would she go with him to a strange country, and keep his log cabin, and work for him, and share his toilsome life, rough or smooth. No loss of social rank could lessen her pride in him, her belief in him.

They were standing side by side a little way from the edge of the sheer descent, below which the Bed Tarn showed black in a basin scooped out of the naked hill, like water held in the hollow of a giant's hand.

'Look,' cried Mary, pointing downward, 'you must see the Red Tarn, the highest water in England?'

But just at this moment there came a blast which shook even Hammond's strong frame, and with a cry of fear he snatched Mary in his arms and carried her away from the edge of the hill. He folded her in his arms and held her there, thirty yards away from the precipice, safely sheltered against his breast, while the wind raved round them, blowing her hair from the broad, white brow, and showing him that noble forehead in all its power and beauty; while the darkness deepened round them so that they could see hardly anything except each other's eyes.

'My love, my own dear love,' he murmured fondly; 'I will trust you with my life. Will you accept the trust? I am hardly worthy; for less than a year ago I offered myself to your sister, and I thought she was the only woman in this wide world who could make me happy. And when she refused me I was in despair, Mary; and I left Fellside in the full belief that I had done with life and happiness. And then I came back, only to oblige Maulevrier, and determined to be utterly miserable at Fellside. I was miserable for the first two hours. Memories of dead and gone joys and disappointed hopes were very bitter. And I tried honestly to keep up my feeling of wretchedness for the first few days. But it was no use, Molly. There was a genial spirit in the place, a laughing fairy who would not let me be sad; and I found myself becoming most unromantically happy, eating my breakfast with a hearty appetite, thinking my cup of afternoon tea nectar for love of the dear hand that gave it. And so, and so, till the new love, the purer and better love, grew and grew into a mighty tree, which was as an oak to an orchid, compared with that passion flower of earlier growth. Mary, will you trust your life to me, as I trust mine to you. I say to you almost in the words I spoke last year to Lesbia,' and here his tone grew grave almost to solemnity, 'trust me, and I will make your life free from the shadow of care--trust me, for I have a brave spirit and a strong arm to fight the battle of life--trust me, and I will win for you the position you have a right to occupy--trust me, and you shall never repent your trust.'

She looked up at him with eyes which told of infinite faith, child-like, unquestioning faith.

'I will trust you in all things, and for ever,' she said. 'I am not afraid to face evil fortune. I do not care how poor you are--how hard our lives may be--if--if you are sure you love me.'

'Sure! There is not a beat of my heart or a thought of my mind that does not belong to you. I am yours to the very depths of my soul. My innocent love, my clear-eyed, clear-souled angel! I have studied you and watched you and thought of you, and sounded the depths of your lovely nature, and the result is that you are for me earth's one woman. I will have no other, Mary, no other love, no other wife.'

'Lady Maulevrier will be dreadfully angry,' faltered Mary.

'Are you afraid of her anger?'

'No; I am afraid of nothing, for your sake.'

He lifted her hand to his lips, and kissed it reverently, and there was a touch of chivalry in that reverential kiss. His eyes clouded with tears as he looked down into the trustful face. The fog had darkened to a denser blackness, and it was almost as if they were engulfed in sudden night.

'If we are never to find our way down the hill; if this were to be the last hour of our lives, Mary, would you be content?'

'Quite content,' she answered, simply. 'I think I have lived long enough, if you really love me--if you are not making fun.'

'What, Molly, do you still doubt? Is it strange that I love you?'

'Very strange. I am so different from Lesbia.'

'Yes, very different, and the difference is your highest charm. And now, love, we had better go down whichever side of the hill is easiest, for this fog is rather appalling. I forgive the wind, because it blew you against my heart just now, and that is where I want you to dwell for ever!'

'Don't be frightened,' said Mary. 'I know every step of the way.'

So, leaning on her lover, and yet guiding him, slowly, step by step, groping their way through the darkness, Lady Mary led Mr. Hammond down the winding track along which the ponies and the guides travel so often in the summer season. And soon they began to descend out of that canopy of fog which enveloped the brow of Helvellyn, and to see the whole world smiling beneath them, a world of green pastures and sheepfolds, with a white homestead here and there amidst the fields, looking so human and so comfortable after that gloomy mountain top, round which the tempest howled so outrageously. Beyond those pastures stretched the dark waters of Thirlmere, looking like a broad river.

The descent was passing steep, but Hammond's strong arm and steady steps made Mary's progress very easy, while she had in no wise exaggerated her familiarity with the windings and twistings of the track. Yet as they had need to travel very slowly so long as the fog still surrounded them, the journey downward lasted a considerable time, and it was past five when they arrived at the little roadside inn at the foot of the hill.

Here Mr. Hammond insisted that Mary should rest at least long enough to take a cup of tea. She was very white and tired. She had been profoundly agitated, and looked on the point of fainting, although she protested that she was quite ready to walk on.

'You are not going to walk another step,' said Hammond. 'While you are taking your tea I will get you a carriage.'

'Indeed, I had rather hurry on at once,' urged Mary. 'We are so late already.'

'You will get home all the sooner if you obey me. It is your duty to obey me now,' said Hammond, in a lowered voice.

She smiled at him, but it was a weak, wan little smile, for that descent in the wind and the fog had quite exhausted her. Mr. Hammond took her into a snug little parlour where there was a cheerful fire, and saw her comfortably seated in an arm chair by the hearth, before he went to look after a carriage.

There was no such thing as a conveyance to be had, but the Windermere coach would pass in about half an hour, and for this they must wait. It would take them back to Grasmere sooner than they could get there on foot, in Mary's exhausted condition.

The tea-tray was brought in presently, and Hammond poured out the tea and waited upon Lady Mary. It was a reversal of the usual formula but it was very pleasant to Mary to sit with her feet on the low brass fender and be waited upon by her lover. That fog on the brow of Helvellyn--that piercing wind--had chilled her to the bone, and there was unspeakable comfort in the glow and warmth of the fire, in the refreshment of a good cup of tea.

'Mary, you are my own property now, remember,' said Hammond, watching her tenderly as she sipped her tea.

She glanced up at him shyly, now and then, with eyes full of innocent wonder. It was so strange to her, as strange as sweet, to know that he loved her; such a marvellous thing that she had pledged herself to be his wife.

'You are my very own--mine to guard and cherish, mine to think and work for,' he went on, 'and you will have to trust me, sweet one, even if the beginning of things is not altogether free from trouble.'

'I am not afraid of trouble.'

'Bravely spoken! First and foremost, then, you will have to announce your engagement to Lady Maulevrier. She will take it ill, no doubt; will do her utmost to persuade you to give me up. Have you courage and resolution, do you think, to stand against her arguments? Can you hold to your purpose bravely, and cry, no surrender?'

'There shall be no surrender,' answered Mary, 'I promise you that. No doubt grandmother will be very angry. But she has never cared for me very much. It will not hurt her for me to make a bad match, as it would have done in Lesbia's case. She has had no day-dreams--no grand ambition about me!'

'So much the better, my wayside flower! When you have said all that is sweet and dutiful to her, and have let her know at the same time that you mean to be my wife, come weal come woe, I will see her, and will have my say. I will not promise her a grand career for my darling: but I will pledge myself that nothing of that kind which the world calls evil--no penury, or shabbiness of surroundings--shall ever touch Mary Haselden after she is Mary Hammond. I can promise at least so much as that.'

'It is more than enough,' said Mary. 'I have told you that I would gladly share poverty with you.'

'Sweet! it is good of you to say as much, but I would not take you at your word. You don't know what poverty is.'

'Do you think I am a coward, or self-indulgent? You are wrong, Jack. May I call you Jack, as Maulevrier does?'

'May you?'

The question evoked such a gush of tenderness that he was fain to kneel beside her chair and kiss the little hand holding the cup, before he considered he had answered properly.

'You are wrong, Jack. I do know what poverty means. I have studied the ways of the poor, tried to console them, and help them a little in their troubles; and I know there is no pain that want of money can bring which I would not share willingly with you. Do you suppose my happiness is dependent on a fine house and powdered footmen? I should like to go to the Red River with you, and wear cotton gowns, and tuck up my sleeves and clean our cottage.'

'Very pretty sport, dear, for a summer day; but my Mary shall have a sweeter life, and shall occasionally walk in silk attire.'

That tea-drinking by the fireside in the inn parlour was the most delicious thing within John Hammond's experience. Mary was a bewitching compound of earnestness and simplicity, so humble, so confiding, so perplexed and astounded at her own bliss.

'Confess, now, in the summer, when you were in love with Lesbia, you thought me a horrid kind of girl,' she said, presently, when they were standing side by side at the window, waiting for the coach.

'Never, Mary. My crime is to have thought very little about you in those days. I was so dazzled by Lesbia's beauty, so charmed by her accomplishments and girlish graces, that I forgot to take notice of anything else in the world. If I thought of you at all it was as another Maulevrier--a younger Maulevrier in petticoats, very gay, and good-humoured, and nice.'

'But when you saw me rushing about with the terriers--I must have seemed utterly horrid.'

'Why, dearest There is nothing essentially horrible in terriers, or in a bright lively girl running races with them. You made a very pretty picture in the sunlight, with your hat hanging on your shoulder, and your curly brown hair and dancing hazel eyes. If I had not been deep in love with Lesbia's peerless complexion and Grecian features, I should have looked below the surface of that Gainsborough picture, and discovered what treasures of goodness, and courage, and truth and purity those frank brown eyes and that wide forehead betokened. I was sowing my wild oats last summer, Mary, and they brought me a crop of sorrow But I am wiser now--wiser and happier.

'But if you were to see Lesbia again would not the old love revive?'

'The old love is dead, Mary. There is nothing left of it but a handful of ashes, which I scatter thus to the four winds,' with a wave of his hand towards the open casement. 'The new love absorbs and masters my being. If Lesbia were to re-appear at Fellside this evening, I could offer her my hand in all brotherly frankness, and ask her to accept me as a brother. Here comes the coach. We shall be at Fellside just in time for dinner.'

CHAPTER XXII.
WISER THAN LESBIA.

Lady Mary and Mr. Hammond were back at Fellside at a quarter before eight, by which time the stars were shining on pine woods and Fell. They managed to be in the drawing-room when dinner was announced, after the hastiest of toilets; yet her lover thought Mary had never looked prettier than she looked that night, in her limp white cashmere gown, and with her brown hair brushed into a largo loose knot on the top of her head. There had been great uneasiness about them at Fellside when evening began to draw in, and the expected hour of their return had gone by. Scouts had been sent in quest of them, but in the wrong direction.

'I did not think you would be such idiots as to come down the north side of the hill in a tempest,' said Maulevrier; 'we could see the clouds racing over the crest of Seat Sandal, and knew it was blowing pretty hard up there, though it was calm enough down here.'

'Blowing pretty hard;' echoed Hammond, 'I don't think I was ever out in a worse gale; and yet I have been across the Bay of Biscay when the waves struck the side of the steamer like battering rams, and when the whole surface of the sea was white with seething foam.'

'It was a most imprudent thing to go up Helvellyn in such weather,' said Fraeulein Mueller, shaking her head gloomily as she ate her fish.

Mary felt that the Fraeulein's manner boded ill. There was a storm brewing. A scolding was inevitable. Mary felt quite capable of doing battle with the Fraeulein; but her feelings were altogether different when she thought of facing that stern old lady upstairs, and of the confession she had to make. It was not that her courage faltered. So far as resolutions went she was as firm as a rock. But she felt that there was a terrible ordeal to be gone through; and it seemed a mockery to be sitting there and pretending to eat her dinner and take things lightly, with that ordeal before her.

'We did not go up the hill in bad weather, Miss Mueller,' said Mr. Hammond. 'The sun was shining and the sky was blue when we started. We could not foresee darkness and storm at the top of the hill. That was the fortune of war.'

'I am very sorry Lady Mary had not more good sense,' replied Fraeulein with unabated gloom; but on this Maulevrier took up the cudgels.

'If there was any want of sense in the business, that's my look-out, Fraeulein,' he said, glaring angrily at the governess. 'It was I who advised Hammond and Lady Mary to climb the hill. And here they are, safe and sound after their journey I see no reason why there should be any fuss about it.'

'People have different ways of looking at things, replied Fraeulein, plodding steadily on with her dinner. Mary rose directly the dessert had been handed round, and marched out of the room: like a warrior going to a battle in which the chances of defeat were strong. Fraeulein Mueller shuffled after her.

'Will you be kind enough to go to her ladyship's room at once, Lady Mary,' she said. 'She wants to speak to you.'

'And I want to speak to her,' said Mary.

She ran quickly upstairs and arrived in the morning room, a little out of breath. The room was lighted by one low moderator lamp, under a dark red velvet shade, and there was the glow of the wood fire, which gave a more cheerful light than the lamp. Lady Maulevrier was lying on her couch in a loose brocade tea-gown, with old Brussels collar and ruffles. She was as well dressed in her day of affliction and helplessness as she had been in her day of strength; for she knew the value of surroundings, and that her stateliness and power were in some manner dependent on details of this kind. The one hand which she could use glittered with diamonds, as she waved it with a little imperious gesture towards the chair on which she desired Lady Mary to seat herself; and Mary sat down meekly, knowing that this chair represented the felon's dock.

'Mary,' began her grandmother, with freezing gravity, 'I have been surprised and shocked by your conduct to-day. Yes, surprised at such conduct even in you.'

'I do not think I have done anything very wrong, grandmother.'

'Not wrong! You have done nothing wrong? You have done something absolutely outrageous. You, my granddaughter, well born, well bred, reared under my roof, to go up Helvellyn and lose yourself in a fog alone with a young man. You could hardly have done worse if you were a Cockney tourist,' concluded her ladyship, with ineffable disgust.

'I could not help the fog,' said Mary, quietly. The battle had to be fought, and she was not going to flinch. 'I had no intention of going up Helvellyn alone with Mr. Hammond. Maulevrier was to have gone with us; but when we got to Dolly Waggon he was tired, and would not go any further. He told me to go on with Mr. Hammond.'

'*He* told you! Maulevrier!--a young man who has spent some of the best hours of his youth in the company of jockeys and trainers--who hasn't the faintest idea of the fitness of things. You allow Maulevrier to be your guide in a matter in which your own instinct should have guided you--your womanly instinct! But you have always been an unwomanly girl. You have put me to shame many a time by your hoydenish tricks; but I bore with you, believing that your madcap follies were at least harmless. To-day you have gone a step too far, and have been guilty of absolute impropriety, which I shall be very slow to pardon.'

'Perhaps you will be still more angry when you know all, grandmother,' said Mary.

Lady Maulevrier flashed her dark eyes at the girl with a look which would have almost killed a nervous subject; but Mary faced her steadfastly, very pale, but as resolute as her ladyship.

'When I know all! What more is there for me to know?'

'Only that while we were on the top of Helvellyn, in the fog and the wind, Mr. Hammond asked me to be his wife.'

'I am not surprised to hear it,' retorted her ladyship, with a harsh laugh. 'A girl who could act so boldly and flirtingly was a natural mark for an adventurer. Mr. Hammond no doubt has been told that you will have a little money by-and-by, and thinks he might do worse than marry you. And seeing how you have flung yourself at his head, he naturally concludes that you will not be too proud to accept your sister's leavings.'

'There is nothing gained by making cruel speeches, grandmother,' said Mary, firmly. 'I have promised to be John Hammond's wife, and there is nothing you nor anyone else can say which will make me alter my mind. I wish to act dutifully to you, if I can, and I hope you will be good to me and consent to this marriage. But if you will not consent, I shall marry him all the same. I shall be full of sorrow at having to disobey you, but I have promised, and I will keep my promise.'

'You will act in open rebellion against me--against the kinswoman who has reared you, and educated you, and cared for you in all these years!'

'But you have never loved me,' answered Mary, sadly. 'Perhaps if you had given me some portion of that affection which you lavished on my sister I might be willing to sacrifice this now deep love for your sake--to lay down my broken heart as a sacrifice on the altar of gratitude. But you never loved me. You have tolerated me, endured my presence as a disagreeable necessity of your life, because I am my father's daughter. You and Lesbia have been all the world to each other; and I have stood aloof, outside your charmed circle, almost a stranger to you. Can you wonder, grandmother, recalling this, that I am unwilling to surrender the love that has been given me to-day--the true heart of a brave and good man!'

Lady Maulevrier looked at her for some moments in scornful wonderment; looked at her with a slow, deliberate smile.

'Poor child!' she said; 'poor ignorant, inexperienced baby! For what a Will-o-the-wisp are you ready to sacrifice my regard, and all the privileges of your position as my granddaughter! No doubt this Mr. Hammond has said all manner of fine things to you; but can you be weak enough to believe that he who half a year ago was sighing and dying at the feet of your sister can have one spark of genuine regard for you? The thing is not in nature; it is an obvious absurdity. But it is easy enough to understand that Mr. Hammond without a penny in his pocket, and with his way to make in the world, would be very glad to secure Lady Mary Haselden and her five hundred a year, and to have Lord Maulevrier for his brother in-law?'

'Have I really five hundred a year? Shall I have five hundred a year when I marry?' asked Mary, suddenly radiant.

'Yes; if you marry with your brother's consent.'

'I am so glad--for his sake. He could hardly starve if I had five hundred a year. He need not be obliged to emigrate.'

'Has he been offering you the prospect of emigration as an additional inducement?'

'Oh, no, he does not say that he is very poor, but since you say he is penniless I thought we might be obliged to emigrate. But as I have five hundred a year--'

'You will stay at home, and set up a lodging-house, I suppose,' sneered Lady Maulevrier.

'I will do anything my husband pleases. We can live in a humble way in some quiet part of London, while Mr. Hammond works at literature or politics. I am not afraid of poverty or trouble, I am willing to endure both for his sake.'

'You are a fool!' said her grandmother sternly. 'And I have nothing more to say to you. Go away, and send Maulevrier to me.'

Mary did not obey immediately. She went over to her grandmother's couch and knelt by her side, and kissed the poor maimed hand which lay on the velvet cushion.

'Dear grandmother,' she said gently. 'I am very sorry to rebel against you. But this is a question of life or death with me. I am not like Lesbia. I cannot barter love and truth for worldly advantage--for pride of race. Do not think me so weak or so vain as to be won by a few fine speeches from an adventurer. Mr. Hammond is no adventurer, he has made no fine speeches--but, I will tell you a secret, grandmother. I have liked and admired him from the first time he came here. I have looked up to him and reverenced him; and I must be a very foolish girl if my judgment is so poor that I can respect a worthless man.'

'You *are* a very foolish girl,' answered Lady Maulevrier, more kindly than she had spoken before, 'but you have been very good and dutiful to me since I have been ill, and I don't wish to forget that. I never said that Mr. Hammond was worthless; but I say that he is no fit husband for you. If you were as yielding and obedient as Lesbia it would be all the better for you; for then I should provide for your establishment in life in a becoming manner. But as you are wilful, and bent upon taking your own way--well--my dear, you must take the consequence; and when you are a struggling wife and mother, old before your time, weighed down with the weary burden of petty cares, do not say, "My grandmother might have saved me from this martyrdom."'

'I will run the risk, grandmother. I will be answerable for my own fate.'

'So be it, Mary. And now send Maulevrier to me.'

Mary went down to the billiard room, where she found her brother and her lover engaged in a hundred game.

'Take my cue and beat him if you can, Molly,' said Maulevrier, when he had heard Mary's message. 'I'm fifteen ahead of him, for he has been falling asleep over his shots. I suppose I am going to get a lecture.'

'I don't think so,' said Mary.

'Well, my dearest, how did you fare in the encounter?' asked Hammond, directly Maulevrier was gone.

'Oh, it was dreadful! I made the most rebellious speeches to poor grandmother, and then I remembered her affliction, and I asked her to forgive me, and just at the last she was ever so much kinder, and I think that she will let me marry you, now she knows I have made up my mind to be your wife--in spite of Fate.'

'My bravest and best.'

'And do you know, Jack'--she blushed tremendously as she uttered this familiar name--'I have made a discovery!'

'Indeed!'

'I find that I am to have five hundred a year when I am married. It is not much. But I suppose it will help, won't it? We can't exactly starve if we have five hundred a year. Let me see. It is more than a pound a day. A sovereign ought to go a long way in a small house; and, of course, we shall begin in a very wee house, like De Quincey's cottage over there, only in London.'

'Yes, dear, there are plenty of such cottages in London. In Mayfair, for instance, or Belgravia.'

'Now, you are laughing at my rustic ignorance. But the five hundred pounds will be a help, won't it?'

'Yes, dear, a great help.'

'I'm so glad.'

She had chalked her cue while she was talking, but after taking her aim, she dropped her arm irresolutely.

'Do you know I'm afraid I can't play to-night,' she said.

'Helvellyn and the fog and the wind have quite spoilt my nerve. Shall we go to the drawing-room, and see if Fraeulein has recovered from her gloomy fit?'

'I would rather stay here, where we are free to talk; but I'll do whatever you like best.'

Mary preferred the drawing-room. It was very sweet to be alone with her lover, but she was weighed down with confusion in his presence. The novelty, the wonderment of her position overpowered her. She yearned for the shelter of Fraeulein Mueller's wing, albeit the company of that most prosaic person was certain death to romance.

Miss Mueller was in her accustomed seat by the fire, knitting her customary muffler. She had appropriated Lady Maulevrier's place, much to Mary's disgust. It irked the girl to see that stout, clumsy figure in the chair which had been filled by her grandmother's imperial form. The very room seemed vulgarised by the change.

Fraeulein looked up with a surprised air when Mary and Hammond entered together, the girl smiling and happy. She had expected that Mary would have left her ladyship's room in tears, and would have retired to her own apartment to hide her swollen eyelids and humiliated aspect. But here she was, after the fiery ordeal of an interview with her offended grandmother, not in the least crestfallen.

'Are we not to have any tea to-night?' asked Mary, looking round the room.

'I think you are unconscious of the progress of time, Lady Mary,' answered Fraeulein, stiffly. 'The tea has been brought in and taken out again.'

'Then it must be brought again, if Lady Mary wants some,' said Hammond, ringing the bell in the coolest manner.

Fraeulein felt that things were coming to a pretty pass, if Maulevrier's humble friend was going to give orders in the house. Quiet and commonplace as the Hanoverian was, she had her ambition, and that was to grasp the household sceptre which Lady Maulevrier must needs in some wise resign, now that she was a prisoner to her rooms. But so far Fraeulein had met with but small success in this endeavour. Her ladyship's authority still ruled the house. Her ladyship's keen intellect took cognisance even of trifles: and it was only in the most insignificant details that Fraeulein felt herself a power.

'Well, your ladyship, what's the row?' said Maulevrier marching into his grandmother's room with a free and easy air. He was prepared for a skirmish, and he meant to take the bull by the horns.

'I suppose you know what has happened to-day?' said her ladyship.

'Molly and Hammond's expedition, yes, of course. I went part of the way with them, but I was out of training, got pumped out after a couple of miles, and wasn't such a fool as to go to the top.'

'Do you know that Mr. Hammond made Mary an offer, while they were on the hill, and that she accepted him?'

'A queer place for a proposal, wasn't it? The wind blowing great guns all the time. I should have chosen a more tranquil spot.'

'Maulevrier, cannot you be serious? Do you forget that this business of to-day must affect your sister's welfare for the rest of her life?'

'No, I do not. I will be as serious as a judge after he has put on the black cap,' said Maulevrier, seating himself near his grandmother's couch, and altering his tone altogether. 'Seriously I am very glad that Hammond has asked Mary to be his wife, and still more glad that she is tremendously in love with him. I told you some time ago not to put your spoke in that wheel. There could not be a happier or a better marriage for Mary.'

'You must have rather a poor opinion, of your sister's attractions, personal or otherwise, if you consider a penniless young man--of no family--good enough for her.'

'I do not consider my sister a piece of merchandise to be sold to the highest bidder. Granted that Hammond is poor and a nobody. He is an honourable man, highly gifted, brave as a lion, and he is my dearest friend. Can you wonder that I rejoice at my sister's having won him for her adoring lover?'

'Can he really care for her, after having loved Lesbia?'

'That was the desire of the eye, this is the love of the heart. I know that he loves Mary ever so much better than he loved Lesbia. I can assure your ladyship that I am not such a fool as I look. I am very fond of my sister Mary, and I have not been blind to her interests. I tell you on my honour that she ought to be very happy as John Hammond's wife.'

'I am obliged to believe what you say about his character,' said Lady Maulevrier. 'And I am willing to admit that the husband's character has a great deal to do with the wife's happiness, from a moral point of view; but still there are material questions to be considered. Has your friend any means of supporting a wife?'

'Yes, he has means; quite sufficient means for Mary's views, which are very simple.'

'You mean to say he would keep her in decent poverty? Cannot you be explicit, Maulevrier, and say what means the man has, whether an income or none? If you cannot tell me I must question Mr. Hammond himself.'

'Pray do not do that,' exclaimed her grandson urgently. 'Do not take all the flavour of romance out of Molly's love story, by going into pounds, shillings, and pence. She is very young. You would hardly wish her to marry immediately?'

'Not for the next year, at the very least.'

'Then why enter upon this sordid question of ways and means. Make Hammond and Mary happy by consenting to their engagement, and trust the rest to Providence, and to me. Take my word for it, Hammond is not a beggar, and he is a man likely to make his mark in the world. If a year hence his income is not enough to allow of his marrying, I will double Mary's allowance out of my own purse. Hammond's friendship has steadied me, and saved me a good deal more than five hundred a year.'

'I can quite believe that. I believe Mr. Hammond is a worthy man, and that his influence has been very good for you; but that does not make him a good match for Mary. However, you seem to have settled the business among you, and I suppose I must submit. You had better all drink tea with me to morrow afternoon; and I will receive your friend as Mary's future husband.'

'That is the best and kindest of grandmothers.'

'But I should like to know more of his antecedents and his relations.'

'His antecedents are altogether creditable. He took honours at the University; he has been liked and respected everywhere. He is an orphan, and it is better not to talk to him of his family. He is sensitive on that point, like most men who stand alone in the world.'

'Well, I will hold my peace. You have taken this business into your hands, Maulevrier; and you must be responsible for the result.'

Maulevrier left his grandmother soon after this, and went downstairs, whistling for very joyousness. Finding the billiard-room deserted he repaired to the drawing-room, where he found Mary playing scraps of melody to her lover at the shadowy end of the room, while Fraeulein sat by the fire weaving her web as steadily as one of the Fatal Sisters, and with a brow prophetic of evil.

Maulevrier crept up to the piano, and came stealthily behind the lovers.

'Bless you, my children,' he said, hovering over them with outspread hands. 'I am the dove coming back to the ark. I am the bearer of happy tidings. Lady Maulevrier consents to your acquiring the legal right to make each other miserable for the rest of your lives.'

'God bless you, Maulevrier,' said Hammond, clasping him by the hand.

'Only as this sister of mine is hardly out of the nursery you will have to wait for her at least a year. So says the dowager, whose word is like the law of the Modes and Persians, and altereth not.'

'I would wait for her twice seven years, as Jacob waited, and toil for her, as Jacob toiled,' answered Hammond, 'but I should like to call her my own to-morrow, if it were possible.'

Nothing could be happier or gayer than the tea-drinking in Lady Maulevrier's room on the following afternoon. Her ladyship having once given way upon a point knew how to make her concession gracefully. She extended her hand to Mr. Hammond as frankly as if he had been her own particular choice.

'I cannot refuse my granddaughter to her brother's dearest friend,' she said, 'but I think you are two most imprudent young people.'

'Providence takes care of imprudent lovers, just as it does of the birds in their nests,' answered Hammond, smiling.

'Just as much and no more, I fear. Providence does not keep off the cat or the tax-gatherer.'

'Birds must take care of their nests, and husbands must work for their homes,' argued Hammond. 'Heaven gives sweet air and sunlight, and a beautiful world to live in.'

'I think,' said Lady Maulevrier, looking at him critically, 'you are just the kind of person who ought to emigrate. You have ideas that would do for the Bush or the Yosemite Valley, but which are too primitive for an over-crowded country.'

'No, Lady Maulevrier, I am not going to steal your granddaughter. When she is my wife she shall live within call. I know she loves her native land, and I don't think either of us would care to put an ocean between us and rugged old Helvellyn.'

'Of course having made idiots of yourselves up there in the fog and the storm you are going to worship the mountain for ever afterwards,' said her ladyship laughing.

Never had she seemed gayer or brighter. Perhaps in her heart of hearts she rejoiced at getting Mary engaged, even to so humble a suitor as fortuneless John Hammond. Ever since the visit of the so-called Rajah she had lived as Damocles lived, with the sword of destiny--the avenging sword--hanging over her by the finest hair. Every time she heard carriage wheels in the drive--every time the hall-door bell rang a little louder than usual, her heart seemed to stop beating and her whole being to hang suspended on a thread. If the thread were to snap, there would come darkness and death. The blow that had paralysed one side of her body must needs, if repeated, bring total extinction. She who believed in no after life saw in her maimed and wasting arm the beginning of death. She who recognised only the life of the body felt that one half of her was already dead. But months had gone by, and Louis Asoph had made no sign. She began to hope that his boasted documents and witnesses were altogether mythical. And yet the engines of the law are slow to put in motion. He might be working up his case, line upon line, with some hard-headed London lawyer; arranging and marshalling his facts; preparing his witnesses; waiting for affidavits from India; working slowly but surely, underground like the mole; and all at once, in an hour, his case might be before the law courts. His story and the story of Lord Maulevrier's infamy might be town talk again; as it had been forty years ago, when the true story of that crime had been happily unknown.

Yes, with the present fear of this Louis Asoph's revelations, of a new scandal, if not a calamity, Lady Maulevrier felt that it was a good thing to have her younger granddaughter's future in some measure secured. John Hammond had said of himself to Lesbia that he was not the kind of man to fail, and looking at him critically to-day Lady Maulevrier saw the stamp of power and dauntless courage in his countenance and bearing. It is the inner mind of a man which moulds the lines of his face and figure; and a man's character may be read in the way he walks and holds himself, the action of his hand, his smile, his frown, his general outlook, as clearly as in any phrenological development. John Hammond had a noble outlook: bold, without impudence or self-assertion; self-possessed, without vanity. Yes, assuredly a man to wrestle with difficulty, and to conquer fate.

When that little tea-drinking was over and Maulevrier and his friend were going away to dress for dinner, Lady Maulevrier detained Mary for a minute or two by her couch. She took her by the hand with unaccustomed tenderness.

'My child, I congratulate you,' she said. 'Last night I thought you a fool, but I begin to think that you are wiser than Lesbia. You have won the heart of a noble young man.'

CHAPTER XXIII.
'A YOUNG LAMB'S HEART AMONG THE FULL-GROWN FLOCKS.'

For three most happy days Mary rejoiced in her lover's society, Maulevrier was with them everywhere, by brookside and fell, on the lake, in the gardens, in the billiard-room, playing propriety with admirable patience. But this could not last for ever. A man who has to win name and fortune and a home for his young wife cannot spend all his days in the primrose path. Fortunes and reputations are not made in dawdling beside a mountain stream, or watching the play of sunlight and shadow on a green hill-side; unless, indeed, one were a new Wordsworth, and even then fortune and renown are not quickly made.

And again, Maulevrier, who had been a marvel of good-nature and contentment for the last eight weeks, was beginning to be tired of this lovely Lakeland. Just when Lakeland was daily developing into new beauty, Maulevrier began to feel an itching for London, where he had a comfortable nest in the Albany, and which was to his mind a metropolis expressly created as a centre or starting point for Newmarket, Epsom, Ascot and Goodwood.

So there came a morning upon which Mary had to say good-bye to those two companions who had so blest and gladdened her life. It was a bright sunshiny morning, and all the world looked gay; which seemed very unkind of Nature, Mary thought. And yet, even in the sadness of this parting, she had much reason to be glad. As she stood with her lover in the library, in the three minutes of *tete-a-tete* She stolen from the argus-eyed Fraeulein, folded in his arms, looking up at his manly face, it seemed to her that the mere knowledge that she belonged to him and was beloved by him ought to sustain and console her even in long years of severance. Yes, even if he were one of the knights of old, going to the Holy Land on a crusade full of peril and uncertainty. Even then a woman ought to be brave, having such a lover.

But her parting was to be only for a few months. Maulevrier promised to come back to Fellside for the August sports, and Hammond was to come with him. Three months--or a little more--and they were to meet again.

Yet in spite of these arguments for courage, Mary's face blanched and her eyes grew unutterably sad as she looked up at her lover.

'You will take care of yourself, Jack, for my sake, won't you, dear?' she murmured. 'If you should be ill while you are in London! If you should die--'

'Life is very uncertain, love, but I don't feel like sickness or death just at present,' answered Hammond cheerily. 'Indeed, I feel that the present is full of sweetness, and the future full of hope. Don't suppose, dear, that I am not grieved at this good-bye; but before we are a year older I hope the time will have come when there will be no more farewells for you and me. I shall be a very exacting husband, Molly. I shall want to spend all the days and hours of my life with you; to have not a fancy or a pursuit in which you cannot share, or with which you cannot sympathise. I hope you will not grow tired of me!'

'Tired!'

Then came silence, and a long farewell kiss, and then the voice of Maulevrier shouting in the hall, just in time to warn the lovers, before Miss Mueller opened the door and exclaimed,

'Oh, Mr. Hammond, we have been looking for you **everywhere**. The luggage is all in the carriage, and Maulevrier says there is only just time to get to Windermere!'

In another minute or so the carriage was driving down the hill; and Mary stood in the porch looking after the travellers.

'It seems as if it is my fate to stand here and see everybody drive away,' she said to herself.

And then she looked round at the lovely gardens, bright with spring flowers, the trees glorious with their young, fresh foliage, and the vast panorama of hill and dale, and felt that it was a wicked thing to murmur in the midst of such a world. And she remembered the great unhoped-for bliss that had come to her within the last four days, and the cloud upon her brow vanished, as she clasped her hands in child-like joyousness.

'God bless you, dear old Helvellyn,' she exclaimed, looking up at the sombre crest of the mountain. 'Perhaps if it had not been for you he would have never proposed.'

But she was obliged to dismiss this idea instantly; for to suppose John Hammond's avowal of his love an accident, the mere impulse of a weak moment, would be despair. Had he not told her how she had grown nearer and nearer to his heart, day by day, and hour by hour, until she had become part of his life? He had told her this--he, in whom she believed as in the very spirit of truth.

She wandered about the gardens for an hour after the carriage had started for Windermere, revisiting every spot where she and her lover had walked together within the last three days, living over again the rapture of those hours, repeating to herself his words, recalling his looks, with the fatuity of a first girlish love. And yet amidst the silliness inseparable from love's young dream, there was a depth of true womanly feeling, thoughtful, unselfish, forecasting a future which was not to travel always along the primrose path of dalliance--a future in which the roses were not always to be thornless.

John Hammond was going to London to work for a position in the world, to strive and labour among the seething mass of strugglers, all pressing onward for the same goal--independence, wealth, renown. Little as Mary know of the world by experience, she had at least heard the wiseacres talk; and that which she had heard was calculated to depress rather than to inspire industrious youth. She had heard how the professions were all over-crowded: how a mighty army of young men were walking the hospitals, all intent on feeling the pulses and picking the pockets of the rising generation: how at the Bar men were growing old and grey before they saw their first brief: how competitors were elbowing and hustling each other upon every road, thronging at every gate. And while masculine youth strove and wrestled for places in the race, aunts and sisters and cousins were pressing into the same arena, doing their best to crowd out the uncles and the brothers and the nephews.

'Poor Jack,' sighed Mary, 'at the worst we can go to the Red River country and grow corn.'

This was her favourite fancy, that she and her lover should find their first dwelling in the new world, live as humbly as the peasants lived round Grasmere, and patiently wait upon fortune. And yet that would not be happiness, unless Maulevrier were to come and stay with them every autumn. Nothing could reconcile Mary to being separated from Maulevrier for any lengthened period.

There were hours in which she was more hopeful, and defied the wiseacres. Clever young men had succeeded in the past--clever men whose hair was not yet grey had come to the front in the present. Granted that these were the exceptional men, the fine flower of humanity. Did she not know that John Hammond was as far above average youth as Helvellyn was above yonder mound in her grandmother's shrubbery?

Yes, he would succeed in literature, in politics, in whatever career he had chosen for himself. He was a man to do the thing he set himself to do, were it ever so difficult. To doubt his success would be to doubt his truth and his honesty; for he had sworn to her he would make her life bright and happy, and that evil days should never come to her; and he was not the man to promise that which he was not able to perform.

The house seemed terribly dull now that the two young men were gone. There was an oppressive silence in the rooms which had lately resounded with Maulevrier's frank, boyish laughter, and with his friend's deep, manly tones--a silence broken only by the click of Fraeulein Mueller's needles.

The Fraeulein was not disposed to be sympathetic or agreeable about Lady Mary's engagement. Firstly, she had not been consulted about it. The thing had been done, she considered, in an underhand manner; and Lady Maulevrier, who had begun by strenuously opposing the match, had been talked over in a way that proved the latent weakness of that great lady's character. Secondly, Miss Mueller, having herself for some reason missed such joys as are involved in being wooed and won, was disposed to look sourly upon all love affairs, and to take a despondent view of all matrimonial engagements.

She did not say anything openly uncivil to Mary Haselden; but she let the damsel see that she pitied her and despised her infatuated condition; and this was so unpleasant that Mary was fain to fall back upon the society of ponies and terriers, and to take up her pilgrim's staff and go wandering over the hills, carrying her happy thoughts into solitary places, and sitting for hours in a heathery hollow, steeped in a sea of summer light, and trying to paint the mountain side and the rush of the waterfall. Her sketch-book was an excuse for hours of solitude, for the indulgence of an endless day-dream.

Sometimes she went among her humble friends in the Grasmere cottages, or in the villages of Great and Little Langdale; and she had now a new interest in these visits, for she had made up her mind that it was her solemn duty to learn housekeeping--not such housekeeping as might have been learnt at Fellside, supposing she had mustered the courage to ask the dignified upper-servants in that establishment to instruct her; but such domestic arts as are needed in the dwellings of the poor. The art of making a very little money go a great way; the art of giving grace, neatness, prettiness to the smallest rooms and the shabbiest furniture; the art of packing all the ugly appliances and baser necessities of daily life, the pots and kettles and brooms and pails, into the narrowest compass, and hiding them from the aesthetic eye. Mary thought that if she began by learning the homely devices of the villagers--the very A B C of cookery and housewifery--she might gradually enlarge upon this simple basis to suit an income of from five to seven hundred a year. The house-mothers from whom she sought information were puzzled at this sudden curiosity about domestic matters. They looked upon the thing as a freak of girlhood which drifted into eccentricity, from sheer idleness; yet they were not the less ready to teach Mary anything she desired to learn. They told her those secret arts by which coppers and brasses are made things of beauty, and meet adornment for an old oak mantelshelf. They allowed her to look on at the milking of the cow, and at the churning of the butter; and at bread making, and cake making, and pie and pudding making; and some pleasant hours were spent in the acquirement of this useful knowledge. Mary did not neglect the invalid during this new phase of her existence. Lady Maulevrier was a lover of routine, and she liked her granddaughter to go to her at the same hour every day. From eleven to twelve was the time for Mary's duty as amanuensis. Sometimes there were no letters to be written. Sometimes there were several; but her ladyship rarely allowed the task to go beyond the stroke of noon. At noon Mary was free, and free till five o'clock, when she was generally in attendance, ready to give Lady Maulevrier her afternoon tea, and sit and talk with her, and tell her any scraps of local news which she had gathered in the day.

There were days on which her ladyship preferred to take her tea alone, and Mary was left free to follow her own devices till dinner-time.

'I do not feel equal even to your society to-day, my dear,' her ladyship would say; 'go and enjoy yourself with your dogs and your tennis;' forgetting that there was very seldom anybody on the premises with whom Lady Mary could play tennis.

But in these lonely days of Mary Haselden's life there was one crowning bliss which was almost enough to sweeten solitude, and take away the sting of separation; and that was the delight of expecting and receiving her lover's letters. Busily as Mr. Hammond must be engaged in fighting the battle of life, he was in no way wanting in his duty as a lover. He wrote to Mary every other day; but though his letters were long, they told her hardly anything of himself or his occupation. He wrote about pictures, books, music, such things as he knew must be interesting to her; but of his own struggles not a word.

'Poor fellow,' thought Mary. 'He is afraid to sadden me by telling me how hard the struggle is.'

Her own letters to her betrothed were simple outpourings of girlish love, breathing that too flattering-sweet idolatry which an innocent girl gives to her first lover. Mary wrote as if she herself were of the least possible value among created things.

With one of Mr. Hammond's earlier letters came the engagement ring; no half-hoop of brilliants or sapphires, rubies or emeralds, no gorgeous triple circlet of red, white, and green; but only a massive band of dead gold, on the inside of which was engraved this posy--'For ever.'

Mary thought it the loveliest ring she had ever seen in her life.

May was half over and the last patch of snow had vanished from the crest of Helvellyn, from Eagle's Crag and Raven's Crag, and Coniston Old Man. Spring--slow to come along these shadowy gorges--had come in real earnest now, spring that was almost summer; and Lady Maulevrier's gardens were as lovely as dreamland. But it was an unpeopled paradise. Mary had the grounds all to herself, except at those stated times when the Fraeulein, who was growing lazier and larger day by day in her leisurely and placid existence, took her morning and afternoon constitutional on the terrace in front of the drawing-room, or solemnly perambulated the shrubberies.

On fine days Mary lived in the garden, save when she was far afield learning the domestic arts from the cottagers. She read French and German, and worked conscientiously at her intellectual education, as well as at domestic economy. For she told herself that accomplishments and culture might be useful to her in her married life. She might be able to increase her husband's means by giving lessons abroad, or taking pupils at home. She was ready to do anything. She would teach the stupidest children, or scrub floors, or bake bread. There was no service she would deem degrading for his sake. She meant when she married to drop her courtesy title. She would not be Lady Mary Hammond, a poor sprig of nobility, but plain Mrs. Hammond, a working man's wife.

Lesbia's presentation was over, and had realised all Lady Kirkbank's expectations. The Society papers were unanimous in pronouncing Lord Maulevrier's sister the prettiest *debutante* of the season. They praised her classical features, the admirable poise of her head, her peerless complexion. They described her dress at the drawing-room; they described her 'frocks' in the Park and at Sandown. They expatiated on the impression she had made at great assemblies. They hinted at even Royal admiration. All this, frivolous fribble though it might be, Lady Maulevrier read with delight, and she was still more gratified by Lesbia's own account of her successes. But as the season advanced Lesbia's letters to her grandmother grew briefer--mere hurried scrawls dashed off while the carriage was at the door, or while her maid was brushing her hair. Lady Maulevrier divined, with the keen instinct of love, that she counted for very little in Lesbia's life, now that the whirligig of society, the fret and fever of fashion, had begun.

One afternoon in May, at that hour when Hyde Park is fullest, and the carriages move slowly in triple rank along the Lady's Mile, and the mounted constables jog up and down with a business-like air which sets every one on the alert for the advent of the Princess of Wales, just at that hour when Lesbia sat in Lady Kirkbank's barouche, and distributed gracious bows and enthralling smiles to her numerous acquaintance, Mary rode slowly down the Fell, after a rambling ride on the safest and most venerable of mountain ponies. The pony was grey, and Mary was grey, for she wore a neat little homespun habit made by the local tailor, and a neat little felt hat with, a ptarmigan's feather.

All was very quiet at Fellside as she went in at the stable gate. There was not an underling stirring in the large old stable-yard which had remained almost unaltered for a century and a half; for Lady Maulevrier, whilst spending thousands on the new part of the house, had deemed the existing stables good enough for her stud. They were spacious old stables, built as solidly as a Norman castle, and with all the virtues and all the vices of their age.

Mary looked round her with a sigh. The stillness of the place was oppressive, and within doors she knew there would be the same stillness, made still more oppressive by the society of the Fraeulein, who grew duller and duller every day, as it seemed to Mary.

She took her pony into the dusky old stable, where four other ponies began rattling their halters in the gloom, by way of greeting. A bundle of purple tares lay ready in a corner for Mary to feed her favourites; and for the next ten minutes or so she was happily employed going from stall to stall, and gratifying that inordinate appetite for green meat which seems natural to all horses.

Not a groom or stable-boy appeared while she was in the stable; and she was just going away, when her attention was caught by a flood of sunshine streaming into an old disused harness-room at the end of the stable--a room with one small window facing the Fell.

Whence could that glow of western light come? Assuredly not from the low-latticed window which faced eastward, and was generally obscured by a screen of cobwebs. The room was only used as a storehouse for lumber, and it was nobody's business to clean the window.

Mary looked in, curious to solve the riddle. A door which she had often noticed, but never seen opened, now stood wide open, and the old quadrangular garden, which was James Steadman's particular care, smiled at her in the golden evening light. Seen thus, this little old Dutch garden seemed to Mary the prettiest thing she had ever looked upon. There were beds of tulips and hyacinths, ranunculus, narcissus, tuberose, making a blaze of colour against the old box borders, a foot high. The crumbling old brick walls of the outbuildings, and that dungeon-like wall which formed the back of the new house, were clothed with clematis and wistaria, woodbine and magnolia. All that loving labour could do had been done day by day for the last forty years to make this confined space a thing of beauty. Mary went out of the dark stable into the sunny garden, and looked round her, full of admiration for James Steadman's work.

'If ever Jack and I can afford to have a garden, I hope we shall be able to make it like this,' she thought. 'It is such a comfort to know that so small a garden can be pretty: for of course any garden we could afford must be small.'

Lady Mary had no idea that this quadrangle was spacious as compared with the narrow strip allotted to many a suburban villa calling itself 'an eligible residence.'

In the centre of the garden there was an old sundial, with a stone bench at the base, and, as she came upon an opening in the circular yew tree hedge which environed this sundial, and from which the flower beds radiated in a geometrical pattern, Lady Mary was surprised to see an old man--a very old man--sitting on this bench, and basking in the low light of the westering sun.

His figure was shrunken and bent, and he sat with his chin resting on the handle of a crutched stick, and his head leaning forward. His long white hair fell in thin straggling locks over the collar of his coat. He had an old-fashioned, mummy-fied aspect, and Mary thought he must be very, very old.

Very, very old! In a flash there came back upon her the memory of John Hammond's curiosity about a hoary and withered old man whom he had met on the Fell in the early morning. She remembered how she had taken him to see old Sam Barlow, and how he had protested that Sam in no wise resembled the strange-looking old man of the Fell. And now here, close to the Fell, was a face and figure which in every detail resembled that ancient stranger whom Hammond had described so graphically.

It was very strange. Could this person be the same her lover had seen two months ago? And, if so, had he been living at Fellside all the time; or was he only an occasional visitor of Steadman's?

While she stood for a few moments meditating thus, the old man raised his head and looked up at her, with eyes that burned like red-hot coals under his shaggy white brows. The look scared her. There was something awful in it, like the gaze of an evil spirit, a soul in torment, and she began to move away, with side-long steps, her eyes riveted on that uncanny countenance.

'Don't go,' said the man, with an authoritative air, rattling his bony fingers upon the bench. 'Sit down here by my side, and talk to me. Don't be frightened, child. You wouldn't, if you knew what they say of me indoors.' He made a motion of his head towards the windows of the old wing--'"Harmless," they say, "quite harmless. Let him alone, he's harmless." A tiger with his claws cut and his teeth drawn--an old, grey-bearded tiger, ghastly and grim, but harmless--a cobra with the poison-bag plucked out of his jaw! The venom grows again, child--the snake's venom--but youth never comes back: Old, and helpless, and harmless!'

Again Mary tried to move away, but those evil eyes held her as if she were a bird riveted by the gaze of a serpent.

'Why do you shrink away?' asked the old man, frowning at her. 'Sit down here, and let me talk to you. I am accustomed to be obeyed'

Old and feeble and shrunken as he was, there was a power in his tone of command which Mary was unable to resist. She felt very sure that he was imbecile or mad. She knew that madmen are apt to imagine themselves great personages, and to take upon themselves, with a wonderful power of impersonation, the dignity and authority of their imaginary rank; and she supposed that it must be thus with this strange old man. She struggled against her sense of terror. After all there could be no real danger, in the broad daylight, within the precincts of her own home, within call of the household.

She seated herself on the bench by the unknown, willing to humour him a little; and he turned himself about slowly, as if every bone in his body were stiff with age, and looked at her with a deliberate scrutiny.

CHAPTER XXIV.
'NOW NOTHING LEFT TO LOVE OR HATE.'

The old man sat looking at Mary in silence for some moments; not a great space of time, perhaps, as marked by the shadow on the dial behind them, but to Mary that gaze was unpleasantly prolonged. He looked at her as if he could read every pulsation in every fibre of her brain, and knew exactly what it meant.

'Who are you?' he asked, at last.

'My name is Mary Haselden.'

'Haselden,' he repeated musingly, 'I have heard that name before.'

And then he resumed his former attitude, his chin resting on the handle of his crutch-stick, his eyes bent upon the gravel path, their unholy brightness hidden under the penthouse brows.

'Haselden,' he murmured, and repeated the name over and over again, slowly, dreamily, with a troubled tone, like some one trying to work out a difficult problem. 'Haselden--when? where?'

And then with a profound sigh he muttered, 'Harmless, quite harmless. You may trust him anywhere. Memory a blank, a blank, a blank, my lord!'

His head sank lower upon his breast, and again he sighed, the sigh of a spirit in torment, Mary thought. Her vivid imagination was already interested, her quick sympathies were awakened.

She looked at him wonderingly, compassionately. So old, so infirm, and with a mind astray; and yet there were indications in his speech and manner that told of reason struggling against madness, like the light behind storm-clouds. He had tones that spoke of a keen sensitiveness to pain, not the lunatic's imbecile placidity. She observed him intently, trying to make out what manner of man he was.

He did not belong to the peasant class: of that she felt assured. The shrunken, tapering hand had never worked at peasant's work. The profile turned towards her was delicate to effeminacy. The man's clothes were shabby and old-fashioned, but they were a gentleman's garments, the cloth of a finer texture than she had ever seen worn by her brother. The coat, with its velvet collar, was of an old-world fashion. She remembered having seen just such a coat in an engraved portrait of Count d'Orsay, a print nearly fifty years old. No Dalesman born and bred ever wore such a coat; no tailor in the Dales could have made it.

The old man looked up after a long pause, during which Mary felt afraid to move. He looked at her again with inquiring eyes, as if her presence there had only just become known to him.

'Who are you?' he asked again.

'I told you my name just now. I am Mary Haselden.'

'Haselden--that is a name I knew--once. Mary? I think my mother's name was Mary. Yes, yes, I remember that. You have a sweet face, Mary--like my mother's. She had brown eyes, like yours, and auburn hair. You don't recollect her, perhaps?'

'Alas! poor maniac,' thought Mary, 'you have lost all count of time. Fifty years to you in the confusion of your distraught brain, are but as yesterday.'

'No, of course not, of course not,' he muttered; 'how should she recollect my mother, who died while I was a boy? Impossible. That must be half a century ago.'

'Good evening to you,' said Mary, rising with a great effort, so strong was her feeling of being spellbound by the uncanny old man, 'I must go indoors now.'

He stretched out his withered old hand, small, semi-transparent, with the blue veins showing darkly under the parchment-coloured skin, and grasped Mary's arm.

'Don't go,' he pleaded. 'I like your face, child; I like your voice--I like to have you here. What do you mean by going indoors? Where do you live?'

'There,' said Mary, pointing to the dead wall which faced them. 'In the new part of Fellside House. I suppose you are staying in the old part with James Steadman.'

She had made up her mind that this crazy old man must be a relation of Steadman's to whom he gave hospitality either with or without her ladyship's consent. All powerful as Lady Maulevrier had ever been in her own house, it was just possible that now, when she was a prisoner in her own rooms, certain small liberties might be taken, even by so faithful a servant as Steadman.

'Staying with James Steadman,' repeated the old man in a meditative tone. 'Yes, I stay with Steadman. A good servant, a worthy person. It is only for a little while. I shall be leaving Westmoreland next week. And you live in that house, do you?' pointing to the dead wall. 'Whose house?'

'Lady Maulevrier's. I am Lady Maulevrier's granddaughter.'

'Lady Mau-lev-rier.' He repeated the name in syllables. 'A good name--an old title--as old as the conquest. A Norman race those Maulevriers. And you are Lady Maulevrier's granddaughter! You should be proud. The Maulevriers were always a proud race.'

'Then I am no true Maulevrier,' answered Mary gaily.

She was beginning to feel more at her ease with the old man. He was evidently mad, as mad as a March hare; but his madness seemed only the harmless lunacy of extreme old age. He had flashes of reason, too. Mary began to feel a friendly interest in him. To youth in its flush of life and vigour there seems something so unspeakably sad and pitiable in feebleness and age--the brief weak remnant of life, the wreck of body and mind, sunning itself in the declining rays of a sun that is so soon to shine upon its grave.

'What, are you not proud?' asked the old man.

'Not at all. I have been taught to consider myself a very insignificant person; and I am going to marry a poor man. It would not become me to be proud.'

'But you ought not to do that,' said the old man. 'You ought not to marry a poor man. Poverty is a bad thing, my dear. You are a pretty girl, and ought to marry a man with a handsome fortune. Poor men have no pleasure in this world--they might just as well be dead. I am poor, as you see. You can tell by this threadbare coat'--he looked down at the sleeve from which the nap was worn in places--'I am as poor as a church mouse.'

'But you have kind friends, I dare say,' Mary said, soothingly. 'You are well taken care of, I am sure.'

'Yes, I am well taken care of--very well taken care of. How long is it, I wonder--how many weeks, or months, or years, since they have taken care of me? It seems a long, long time; but it is all like a dream--a long dream. Once I used to try and wake myself. I used to try and struggle out of that weary dream. But that was ages ago. I am satisfied now--I am quite content now--so long as the weather is warm, and I can sit out here in the sun.'

'It is growing chilly now,' said Mary, 'and I think you ought to go indoors. I know that I must go.'

'Yes, I must go in now--I am getting shivery,' answered the old man, meekly. 'But I want to see you again, Mary--I like your face--and I like your voice. It strikes a chord here,' touching his breast, 'which has long been silent. Let me see you again, child. When can I see you again?'

'Do you sit here every afternoon when it is fine?'

'Yes, every day--all day long sometimes when the sun is warm.'

'Then I will come here to see you.'

'You must keep it a secret, then,' said the old man, with a crafty look. 'If you don't they will shut me up in the house, perhaps. They don't like me to see people, for fear I should talk. I have heard Steadman say so. Yet what should I talk about, heaven help me? Steadman says my memory is quite gone, and that I am childish and harmless--childish and harmless. I have heard him say that. You'll come again, won't you, and you'll keep it a secret?'

Mary deliberated for a few minutes.

'I don't like secrets,' she said, 'there is generally something dishonourable in them. But this would be an innocent secret, wouldn't it? Well, I'll come to see you somehow, poor old man; and if Steadman sees me here I will make everything right with him.'

'He mustn't see you here,' said the old man. 'If he does he will shut me up in my own rooms again, as he did once, years and years ago.'

'But you have not been here long, have you?' Mary asked, wonderingly.

'A hundred years, at least. That's what it seems to me sometimes. And yet there are times when it seems only a dream. Be sure you come again to-morrow.'

'Yes, I promise you to come; good-night.'

'Good-night.'

Mary went back to the stable. The door was still open, but how could she be sure that it would be open to-morrow? There was no other access that she knew of to the quadrangle, except through the old part of the house, and that was at times inaccessible to her.

She found a key--a big old rusty key--in the inside of the door, so she shut and locked it, and put the key in her pocket. The door she supposed had been left open by accident; at any rate this key made her mistress of the situation. If any question should arise as to her conduct she could have an explanation with Steadman; but she had pledged her word to the poor mad old man, and she meant to keep her promise, if possible.

As she left the stable she saw Steadman riding towards the gate on his grey cob. She passed him as she went back to the house.

Next day, and the day after that, and for many days, Mary used her key, and went into the quadrangle at sundown to sit for half an hour or so with the strange old man, who seemed to take an intense pleasure in her company. The weather was growing warmer as May wore on towards June, and this evening hour, between six and seven, was deliciously bright and balmy. The seat by the sundial was screened on every side by the clipped yew hedge, dense and tall, surrounding the circular, gravelled space, in the centre of which stood the old granite dial, with its octagonal pedestal and moss-grown steps. There, as in a closely-shaded arbour, Lady Mary and her old friend were alone and unobserved. The yew-tree boundary was at least eight feet high, and Mary and her companion could hardly have been seen even from the upper windows of the low, old house.

Mary had fallen into the habit of going for her walk or her ride at five o'clock every day, when she was not in attendance on Lady Maulevrier, and after her walk or ride she slipped through the stable, and joined her ancient friend. Stables and courtyard were generally empty at this hour, the men only appearing at the sound of a big bell, which summoned them from their snuggery when they were wanted. Most of Lady Maulevrier's servants had arrived at that respectable stage of long service in which fidelity is counted as a substitute for hard work.

The old man was not particularly conversational, and was apt to repeat the same things over and over again, with a sublime unconsciousness of being prosy; but he liked to hear Mary talk, and he listened with seeming intelligence. He questioned her about the world outside his cloistered life--the wars and rumours of wars--and, although the names of the questions and the men of the day seemed utterly strange to him, and he had to have them repeated to him again and again, he seemed to take an intelligent interest in the stirring facts of the time, and listened intently when Mary gave him a synopsis of her last newspaper reading.

When the news was exhausted, Mary hit upon a more childish form of amusement, and that was to tell the story of any novel or poem she had been lately reading. This was so successful that in this manner Mary related the stories of most of Shakespeare's plays; of Byron's Bride of Abydos, and Corsair; of Keats's Lamia; of Tennyson's Idylls; and of a heterogenous collection of poetry and romance, in all of which stories the old man took a vivid interest.

'You are better to me than the sunshine,' he told Mary one day when she was leaving him. 'The world grows darker when you leave me.'

Once at this parting moment he took both her hands, and drew her nearer to him, peering into her face in the clear evening light.

'You are like my mother,' he said. 'Yes, you are very like her. And who else is it that you are like? There is some one else, I know. Yes, some one else! I remember! It is a face in a picture--a picture at Maulevrier Castle.'

'What do you know of Maulevrier Castle?' asked Mary, wonderingly.

Maulevrier was the family seat in Herefordshire, which had not been occupied by the elder branch for the last forty years. Lady Maulevrier had let it during her son's minority to a younger branch of the family, a branch which had intermarried with the world of successful commerce, and was richer than the heads of the house. This occupation of Maulevrier Castle had continued to the present time, and was likely still to continue, Maulevrier having no desire to set up housekeeping in a feudal castle in the marches.

'How came you to know Maulevrier Castle?' repeated Mary.

'I was there once. There is a picture by Lely, a portrait of a Lady Maulevrier in Charles the Second's time. The face is yours, my love. I have heard of such hereditary faces. My mother was proud of resembling that portrait.'

'What did your mother know of Maulevrier Castle?'

The old man did not answer. He had lapsed into that dream-like condition into which he often sank, when his brain was not stimulated to attention and coherency by his interest in Mary's narrations.

Mary concluded that this man had once been a servant in the Maulevrier household, perhaps at the place in Herefordshire, and that all his old memories ran in one grove--the house of Maulevrier.

The freedom of her intercourse with him was undisturbed for about three weeks; and at the end of that time she came face to face with James Steadman as she emerged from the circle of greenery.

'You here, Lady Mary?' he exclaimed with an angry look.

'Yes, I have been sitting talking to that poor old man,' Mary answered, cheerily, concluding that Steadman's look of vexation arose from his being detected in the act of harbouring a contraband relation. 'He is a very interesting character. A relation of yours, I suppose?'

'Yes, he is a relation,' replied Steadman. 'He is very old, and his mind has long been gone. Her ladyship is kind enough to allow me to give him a home in her house. He is quite harmless, and he is in nobody's way.'

'Of course not, poor soul. He is only a burden to himself. He talks as if his life had been very weary. Has he been long in that sad state?'

'Yes, a long time.'

Steadman's manner to Lady Mary was curt at the best of times. She had always stood somewhat in awe of him, as a person delegated with authority by her grand-mother, a servant who was much more than a servant. But to-day his manner was more abrupt than usual.

'He spoke of Maulevrier Castle just now,' said Mary, determined not to be put down too easily. 'Was he once in service there?'

'He was. Pray how did you find your way into this garden, Lady Mary?'

'I came through the stable. As it is my grandmother's garden I suppose I did not take an unwarrantable liberty in coming,' said Mary, drawing herself up, and ready for battle.

'It is Lady Maulevrier's wish that this garden should be reserved for my use,' answered Steadman. 'Her ladyship knows that my uncle walks here of an afternoon, and that, owing to his age and infirmities, he can go nowhere else; and if only on that account, it is well that the garden should be kept private. Lunatics are rather dangerous company, Lady Mary, and I advise you to give them a wide berth wher-ever you may meet them.'

'I am not afraid of your uncle,' said Mary, resolutely. 'You said yourself just now that he is quite harmless: and I am really interested in him, poor old creature. He likes me to sit with him a little of an afternoon and to talk to him; and if you have no objection I should like to do so, whenever the weather is fine enough for the poor old man to be out in the garden at this hour.'

'I have a very great objection, Lady Mary, and that objection is chiefly in your interest,' answered Steadman, firmly. 'No one who is not experienced in the ways of lunatics can imagine the danger of any association with them--their consummate craftiness, their capacity for crime. Every madman is harmless up to a certain point--mild, inoffensive, perhaps, up to the very moment in which he commits some appalling crime. And then people cry out upon the want of prudence, the want of common-sense which allowed such an act to be possible. No, Lady Mary, I under-stand the benevolence of your motive, but I cannot permit you to run such a risk.'

'I am convinced that the poor old creature is perfectly harmless,' said Mary, with suppressed indignation. 'I shall certainly ask Lady Maulevrier to speak to you on the subject. Perhaps her influence may induce you to be a little more considerate to your unhappy relation.'

'Lady Mary, I beg you not to say a word to Lady Maulevrier on this subject. You will do me the greatest injury if you speak of that man. I entreat you--'

But Mary was gone. She passed Steadman with her head held high and her eyes sparkling with anger. All that was generous, compassionate, womanly in her nature was up in arms against her grandmother's steward. Of all other things, Mary Haselden most detested cruelty; and she could see in Steadman's opposition to her wish nothing but the most cold-hearted cruelty to a poor dependent on his charity.

She went in at the stable door, shut and locked it, and put the key in her pocket as usual. But she had little hope that this mode of access would be left open to her. She knew enough of James Steadman's character, from hearsay rather than from experience, to feel sure that he would not easily give way. She was not surprised, therefore, on returning from her ride on the following afternoon, to find the disused harness-room half filled with trusses of straw, and the door of communication completely blocked. It would be impossible for her to remove that barricade without assistance; and then, how could she be sure that the door itself was not nailed up, or secured in some way?

It was a delicious sunny afternoon, and she could picture the lonely old man sitting in his circle of greenery beside the dial, which for him had registered so many dreary and solitary hours, waiting for the little ray of social sunlight which her presence shed over his monotonous life. He had told her that she was like the sunshine to him--better than sunshine--and she had promised not to forsake him. She pictured him waiting, with his hand clasped upon his crutch-stick, his chin resting upon his hands, his eyes poring on the ground, as she had seen him for the first time. And as the stable clock chimed the quarters he would begin to think himself abandoned, forgotten; if, indeed, he took any count of the passage of time of which she was not sure. His mind seemed to have sunk into a condition which was between dreaming and waking, a state to which the outside world seemed only half real--a phase of being in which there was neither past nor future, only the insufferable monotony of an everlasting *now*.

Pity is so near akin to love that Mary, in her deep compassion for this lonely, joyless, loveless existence, felt a regard which was almost affection for this strange old man, whose very name was unknown to her. True that there was much in his countenance and manner which was sinister and repellant. He was a being calculated to inspire fear rather than love; but the fact that he had courted her presence and looked to her for consolation had touched Mary's heart, and she had become reconciled to all that was forbidding and disagreeable in the lunatic physiognomy. Was he not the victim of a visitation which entitled him to respect as well as to pity?

For some days Mary held her peace, remembering Steadman's vehement entreaty that she should not speak of this subject to her grandmother. She was silent, but the image of the old man haunted her at all times and seasons. She saw him even in her dreams--those happy dreams of the girl who loves and is beloved, and before whom the pathway of the future smiles like a vision of Paradise. She heard him calling to her with a piteous cry of distress, and on waking from this troubled dream she fancied that he must be dying, and that this sound in her dreams was one of those ghostly warnings which give notice of death. She was so unhappy about him, altogether so distressed at being compelled to break her word, that she could not prevent her thoughts from dwelling upon him, not even after she had poured out all her trouble to John Hammond in a long letter, in which her garden adventures and her little skirmish with Steadman were graphically described.

To her intense discomforture Hammond replied that he thoroughly approved of Steadman's conduct in the matter. However agreeable Mary's society might be to the lunatic, Mary's life was far too precious to be put within the possibility of peril by any such *tete-a-tetes*. If the person was the same old man whom Hammond had seen on the Fell, he was a most sinister-looking creature, of whom any evil act might be fairly anticipated. In a word Mr. Hammond took Steadman's view of the matter, and entreated his dearest Mary to be careful, and not to allow her warm heart to place her in circumstances of peril.

This was most disappointing to Mary, who expected her lover to agree with her upon every point; and if he had been at Fellside the difference of opinion might have given rise to their first quarrel. But as she had a few hours' leisure for reflection before the post went out, she had time to get over her anger, and to remember that promise of obedience given, half in jest, half in earnest, at the little inn beyond Dunmail Raise. So she wrote submissively enough, only with just a touch of reproach at Jack's want of compassion for a poor old man who had such strong claims upon everybody's pity.

The image of the poor old man was not to be banished from her thoughts, and on that very afternoon, when her letter was dispatched, Mary went on a visit of exploration to the stables, to see if by any chance Mr. Steadman's plans for isolating his unhappy relative might be circumvented.

She went all over the stables--into loose boxes, harness and saddle rooms, sheds for wood, and sheds for roots, but she found no door opening into the quadrangle, save that door by which she had entered, and which was securely defended by a barricade of straw that had been doubled by a fresh delivery of trusses since she first saw it. But while she was prowling about the sweet-scented stable, much disappointed at the result of her investigations, she stumbled against a ladder which led to an open trap-door. Mary mounted the ladder, and found herself amidst the dusty atmosphere of a large hayloft, half in shadow, half in the hot bright sunlight. A large shutter was open in the sloping roof, the roof that sloped towards the quadrangle, an open patch admitting light and air. Mary, light and active as a squirrel, sprang upon a truss of hay, and in another moment had swung herself in the opening of the shutter, and was standing with her feet on the wooden ledge at the bottom of the massive frame, and her figure supported against the slope of thick thatched roof. Perched, or half suspended, thus, she was just high enough to look over the top of the yew-tree hedge into the circle round the sundial.

Yes, there was the unhappy victim of fate, and man's inhumanity to man. There sat the shrunken figure, with drooping head, and melancholy attitude--the bent shoulders of feeble old age, the patriarchal locks so appealing to pity. There he sat with eyes poring upon the ground just as she had seen him the first time. And while she had sat with him and talked with him he had seemed to awaken out of that dull despondency, gleams of pleasure had lighted up his wrinkled face--he had grown animated, a sentient living instead of a corpse alive. It was very hard that this little interval of life, these stray gleams of gladness should be denied to the poor old creature, at the behest of James Steadman.

Mary would have felt less angrily upon the subject had she believed in Steadman's supreme carefulness of her own safety; but in this she did not believe. She looked upon the house-steward's prudence as a hypocritical pretence, an affectation of fidelity and wisdom, by which he contrived to gratify the evil tendencies of his own hard and cruel nature. For some reasons of his own, perhaps constrained

thereto by necessity, he had given the old man an asylum for his age and infirmity: but while thus giving him shelter he considered him a burden, and from
mere perversity of mind refused him all such consolations as were possible to his
afflicted state, mewed him up as a prisoner, cut him off from the companionship of
his fellow-men.

Two years ago, before Mary emerged from her Tomboyhood, she would have
thought very little of letting herself out of the loft window and clambering down
the side of the stable, which was well furnished with those projections in the way
of gutters, drain-pipes, and century-old ivy, which make such a descent easy. Two
years ago Mary's light figure would have swung itself down among the ivy leaves,
and she would have gloried in the thought of circumventing James Steadman so
easily. But now Mary was a young lady--a young lady engaged to be married, and
impressed with the responsibilities of her position, deeply sensible of a new dignity,
for the preservation of which she was in a manner answerable to her lover.

'What would *he* think of me if I went scrambling down the ivy?' she asked
herself; 'and after he has approved of Steadman's heartless restrictions, it would be
rank rebellion against him if I were to do it. Poor old man, "Thou art so near and
yet so far," as Lesbia's song says.'

She blew a kiss on the tips of her fingers towards that sad solitary figure, and
then dropped back into the dusty duskiness of the loft. But although her new ideas
upon the subject of 'Anstand'--or good behaviour--prevented her getting the better
of Steadman by foul means, she was all the more intent upon having her own way
by fair means, now that the impression of the old man's sadness and solitude had
been renewed by the sight of the drooping figure by the sundial.

She went back to the house, and walked straight to her grandmother's room.
Lady Maulevrier's couch had been placed in front of the open window, from which
she was watching the westward-sloping sun above the long line of hills, dark Helvellyn, rugged Nabb Scarr, and verdant Fairfield, with its two giant arms stretched out
to enfold and shelter the smiling valley.

'Heavens! child, what an object you are;' exclaimed her ladyship, as Mary drew
near. 'Why, your gown is all over dust, and your hair is--why your hair is sprinkled
with hay and clover. I thought you had learnt to be tidy, since your engagement.
What have you been doing with yourself?'

'I have been up in the hayloft,' answered Mary, frankly; and, intent on one idea, she said impetuously, 'Dear grandmother, I want you to do me a favour--a very great favour. There is a poor old man, a relation of Steadman's, who lives with him, out of his mind, but quite harmless, and he is so sad and lonely, so dreadfully sad, and he likes me to sit with him in the garden, and tell him stories, and recite verses to him, poor soul, just as if he were a child, don't you know, and it is such a pleasure to me to be a little comfort to him in his lonely wretched life, and James Steadman says I mustn't go near him, because he may change at any moment into a dangerous lunatic, and do me some kind of harm, and I am not a bit afraid, and I'm sure he won't do anything of the kind, and, please grandmother, tell Steadman, that I am to be allowed to go and sit with his poor old prisoner half an hour every afternoon.'

Carried along the current of her own impetuous thoughts, Mary had talked very fast, and had not once looked at her grandmother while she was speaking. But now at the end of her speech her eyes sought Lady Maulevrier's face in gentle entreaty, and she recoiled involuntarily at the sight she saw there.

The classic features were distorted almost as they had been in the worst period of the paralytic seizure. Lady Maulevrier was ghastly pale, and her eyes glared with an awful fire as they gazed at Mary. Her whole frame was convulsed, and she, the cripple, whose right limbs lay numbed and motionless upon the couch, made a struggling motion as she raised herself a little with the left arm, as if, by very force of angry will, she would have lifted herself up erect before the girl who had offended her.

For a few moments her lips moved dumbly; and there was something unspeakably awful in those convulsed features, that livid countenance, and those voiceless syllables trembling upon the white dry lips.

At last speech came.

'Girl, you were created to torment me;' she exclaimed.

'Dear grandmother, what harm have I done?' faltered Mary.

'What harm? You are a spy. Your very existence is a torment and a danger. Would to God that you were married. Yes, married to a chimney-sweep, even--and out of my way.'

'If that is your only difficulty,' said Mary, haughtily, 'I dare say Mr. Hammond would be kind enough to marry me to-morrow, and take me out of your ladyship's way.'

Lady Maulevrier's head sank back upon her pillows, those velvet and satin pillows, rich with delicate point lace and crewel-work adornment, the labour of Mary and Fraeulein, pillows which could not bring peace to the weary head, or deaden the tortures of memory. The pale face recovered its wonted calm, the heavy lips drooped over the weary eyes, and for a few moments there was silence in the room.

Then Lady Maulevrier raised her eyelids, and looked at her granddaughter imploringly, pathetically.

'Forgive me, Mary,' she said. 'I don't know what I was saying just now; but whatever it was, forgive and forget it. I am a wretched old woman, heart sick, heart sore, worn out by pain and weariness. There are times when I am beside myself; moments when I am not much saner than Steadman's lunatic uncle. This is one of my worst days, and you came bouncing in upon me, and tortured my nerves by your breathless torrent of words. Pray forgive me, if I said anything rude.'

'If,' thought Mary: but she tried to be charitable, and to believe that Lady Maulevrier's attack upon her was a new phase of hysteria, so she murmured meekly, 'There is nothing for me to forgive, grandmother, and I am very sorry I disturbed you.'

She was going to leave the room, thinking that her absence would be a relief to the invalid, when Lady Maulevrier called her back.

'You were asking me something--something about that old man of Steadman's,' she said with a weary air, half indifference, half the lassitude natural to an invalid who sinks under the burden of monotonous days. 'What was it all about? I forget.'

Mary repeated her request, but this time in measured tones.

'My dear, I am sure that Steadman was only properly prudent.' answered Lady Maulevrier, 'and that it would never do for me to interfere in this matter. It stands to reason that he must know his old kinsman's temperament much better than you can, after your half-hour interviews with him in the garden. Pray how long have these garden scenes been going on, by-the-by?' asked her ladyship, with a searching look at Mary's downcast face.

The girl had not altogether recovered from the rude shock of her grandmother's late attack.

'About three weeks,' faltered Mary. 'But it is more than a week now since I was in the garden. It was quite by accident that I first went there. Perhaps I ought to explain.'

And Mary, not being gainsayed, went on to describe that first afternoon when she had seen the old man brooding in the sun. She drew quite a pathetic picture of his joyless solitude, whilst all nature around and about him was looking so glad in the spring sunshine. There was a long silence, a silence of some minutes, when she had done; and Lady Maulevrier lay with lowered eyelids, deep in thought. Mary began to hope that she had touched her grandmother's heart, and that her request would be granted: but she was soon undeceived.

'I am sorry to be obliged to refuse you a favour, Mary, but I must stand by Steadman,' said her ladyship. 'When I gave Steadman permission to shelter his aged kinsman in my house, I made it a condition that the old man should be kept in the strictest care by himself and his wife, and that nobody in this establishment should be troubled by him. This condition has been so scrupulously adhered to that the old man's existence is known to no one in this house except you and me; and you have discovered the fact only by accident. I must beg you to keep this secret to yourself. Steadman has particular reasons for wishing to conceal the fact of his uncle's residence here. The old man is not actually a lunatic. If he were we should be violating the law by keeping him here. He is only imbecile from extreme old age; the body has outlived the mind, that is all. But should any officious functionary come down upon Fellside, this imbecility might be called madness, and the poor old creature whom you regard so compassionately, and whose case you think so pitiable here, would be carried off to a pauper lunatic asylum, which I can assure you would be a much worse imprisonment than Fellside Manor.'

'Yes, indeed, grandmother,' exclaimed Mary, whose vivid imagination conjured up a vision of padded cells, strait-waist-coats, murderously-inclined keepers, chains, handcuffs, and bread and water diet, 'now I understand why the poor old soul has been kept so close--why nobody knows of his existence. I beg Steadman's pardon with all my heart. He is a much better fellow than I thought him.'

'Steadman is a thoroughly good fellow, and as true as steel,' said her ladyship. 'No one can know that so well as the mistress he has served faithfully for nearly half a century. I hope, Mary, you have not been chattering to Fraeulein or any one else about your discovery.'

'No, grandmother, I have not said a word to a mortal, but----'

'Oh, there is a "but," is there? I understand. You have not been so reticent in your letters to Mr. Hammond.'

'I tell him all that happens to me. There is very little to write about at Fellside; yet I contrive to send him volumes. I often wonder what poor girls did in the days of Miss Austen's novels, when letters cost a shilling or eighteen pence for postage, and had to be paid for by the recipient. It must have been such a terrible check upon affection.'

'And upon twaddle,' said Lady Maulevrier. 'Well you told Mr. Hammond about Steadman's old uncle. What did he say?'

'He thoroughly approved Steadman's conduct in forbidding me to go and see him,' answered Mary. 'I couldn't help thinking it rather unkind of him; but, of course, I feel that he must be right,' concluded Mary, as much as to say that her lover was necessarily infallible.

'I always thought Mr. Hammond a sensible young man, and I am glad to find that his conduct does not belie my good opinion,' said Lady Maulevrier. 'And now, my dear, you had better go and make yourself decent before dinner. I am very weary this afternoon, and even our little talk has exhausted me.'

'Yes, dear grandmother, I am going this instant. But let me ask one question: What is the poor old man's name?'

'His name!' said her ladyship, looking at Mary with a puzzled air, like a person whose thoughts are far away. 'His name--oh, Steadman, I suppose, like his nephew's; but if I ever heard the name I have forgotten it, and I don't know whether the kinship is on the father's or the mother's side. Steadman asked my permission to give shelter to a helpless old relative, and I gave it. That is really all I remember.'

'Only one other question,' pleaded Mary, who was brimful of curiosity upon this particular subject. 'Has he been at Fellside very long?'

'Oh, I really don't know; a year, or two, or three, perhaps. Life in this house is all of a piece. I hardly keep count of time.'

'There is one thing that puzzles me very much,' said Mary, still lingering near her grandmother's couch, the balmy evening air caressing her as she leaned against the embrasure of the wide Tudor window, the sun drawing nearer to the edge of the hills, an orb of yellow flame, soon to change to a gigantic disk of lurid fire. 'I thought from the old man's talk that he, too, must be an old servant in our family. He talked of Maulevrier Castle, and said that I reminded him of a picture by Lely, a portrait of a Lady Maulevrier.

'It is quite possible that he may have been in service there, though I do not remember to have heard anything about it,' answered her ladyship, carelessly. 'The Steadmans come from that part of the country, and theirs is a hereditary service. Good-night, Mary, I am utterly weary. Look at that glorious light yonder, that mighty world of fire and flame, without which our little world would be dark and dreary. I often think of that speech of Macbeth's, "I 'gin to be aweary of the sun." There comes a time, Mary, when even the sun is a burden.'

'Only for such a man as Macbeth,' said Mary, 'a man steeped in crime. Who can wonder that he wanted to hide himself from the sun? But, dear grandmother, there ought to be plenty of happiness left for you, even if your recovery is slow to come. You are so clever, you have such resources in your own mind and memory, and you have your grandchildren, who love you dearly,' added Mary, tenderly.

Her nature was so full of pity that an entirely new affection had grown up in her mind for Lady Maulevrier since that terrible evening of the paralytic stroke.

'Yes, and whose love, as exemplified by Lesbia, is shown in a hurried scrap of a letter scrawled once a week--a bone thrown to a hungry dog,' said her ladyship, bitterly.

'Lesbia is so lovely, and she is so surrounded by flatterers and admirers,' murmured Mary, excusingly.

'Oh, my dear, if she had a heart she would not forget me, even in the midst of her flatterers. Good-night again, Mary. Don't try to console me. For some natures consolations and soothing suggestions are like flowers thrown upon a granite tomb. They do just as much and just as little good to the heart that lies under the stone. Good-night.'

Mary stooped to kiss her grandmother's forehead, and found it cold as marble. She murmured a loving good-night, and left the mistress of Fellside in her loneliness.

A footman would come in and light the lamps, and draw the velvet curtains, presently, and shut out the later glories of sunset. And then the butler himself would come and arrange the little dinner table by her ladyship's couch, and would himself preside over the invalid's simple dinner, which would be served exquisitely, with all that is daintiest and most costly in Salviati glass and antique silver. Yet better the dinner of herbs, and love and peace withal, than the choicest fare or the most perfect service.

Before the coming of the servants and the lamps there was a pause of silence and loneliness, an interval during which Lady Maulevrier lay gazing at the declining orb, the lower rim of which now rested on the edge of the hill. It seemed to grow larger and more dazzling as she looked at it.

Suddenly she clasped her left hand across her eyes, and said aloud--

'Oh, what a hateful life! Almost half a century of lies and hypocricies and prevarications and meannesses! For what? For the glory of an empty name; and for a fortune that may slip from my dead hand to become the prey of rogues and adventurers. Who can forecast the future?'

CHAPTER XXV.
CARTE BLANCHE.

Lady Kirkbank's house in Arlington Street was known to half fashionable London as one of the pleasantest houses in town; and it was known by repute only, to the other half of fashionable London, as a house whose threshold was not to be crossed by persons with any regard for their own dignity and reputation. It was not that Lady Kirkbank had ever actually forfeited her right to be considered an honest woman and a faithful wife. People who talked of the lady and her set with a contemptuous shrug of the shoulders and a dubious elevation of the eyebrows were ready, when hard pushed in argument, to admit that they knew of no actual harm in Lady Kirkbank, no overt bad behaviour.

'But--well,' said the punctilious half of society, the Pejinks and Pernickitys, the Picksomes and Unco-Goods, 'Lady Kirkbank is--Lady Kirkbank; and I would not allow my girls to visit her, don't you know.' 'Lady Kirkbank is received, certainly,' said a severe dowager. 'She goes to very good houses. She gets tickets for the Royal enclosure. She is always at private views, and privileged shows of all kinds; and she contrives to squeeze herself in at a State ball or a concert about once in two years; but any one who can consider Lady Kirkbank good style must have a very curious idea of what a lady ought to be.' 'Lady Kirkbank is a warm-hearted, nice creature,' said a diplomatist of high rank, and one of her particular friends, 'but her manners are decidedly--continental!'

About Sir George, society, adverse or friendly, was without strong opinions. His friends, the men who shot over his Scotch moor, and filled the spare rooms in his villa at Cannes, and loaded his drag for Sandown or Epsom, and sponged upon him all the year round, talked of him as 'an inoffensive old party,' 'a cheery soul,' 'a genial old boy,' and in like terms of approval. That half of society which did not visit in Arlington Street, in whose nostrils the semi-aristocratic, semi-artistic, altogether Bohemian little dinners, the suppers after the play, the small hours devoted to Nap or Poker, had an odour as of sulphur, the reek of Tophet--even this half of the great world was fain to admit that Sir George was harmless. He had never had an idea beyond the realms of sport; he had never had a will of his own outside his stable. To shoot pigeons at Hurlington or Monaco, to keep half a dozen leather-platers, and attend every race from the Craven to the Leger, to hunt four days a week, when he was allowed to spend a winter in England, and to saunter and sleep away all the hours which could not be given to sport, comprised Sir George's idea of existence. He had never troubled himself to consider whether there might not possibly be a better way of getting rid of one's life. He was as God had made him, and was perfectly satisfied with himself and the universe; save at such times as when a favourite horse went lame, or his banker wrote to tell him that his account was overdrawn.

Sir George had no children; he had never had a serious care in his life. He never thought, he never read. Lady Kirkbank declared that she had never seen him with a book in his hands since their marriage.

'I don't believe he would know at which end to begin,' she said.

What was the specific charge which the very particular people brought against Lady Kirkbank? Such charges rarely *are* specific. The idea that the lady belonged to the fast and furious section of society, the Bohemia of the upper ten, was an idea in the air. Everybody knew it. No one could quite adequately explain it.

From thirty to fifty Lady Kirkbank had been known as a flirty matron. Wherever she went, a train of men went with her; men young and middle-aged and elderly; handsome youths from the public offices; War, Admiralty, Foreign Office, Somerset House young men; attractive men of mature years, with grey moustachios, military, diplomatic, horsey, what you will, but always agreeable. At home, abroad, Lady Kirkbank was never without her court; but the court was entirely masculine. In those days the fair Georgie did not scruple to say that she hated women, and that girls were her particular abomination. But as the years rolled on Lady Kirkbank began to find it very difficult to muster her little court, to keep her train in attendance upon her. 'The birds were wild,' Sir George said. Her young adorers found their official duties more oppressive than hitherto; her elderly swains had threatenings of gout or rheumatism which prevented their flocking round her as of old at race meeting or polo match. They were loyal enough in keeping their engagements at the dinner table, for Lady Kirkbank's cook was one of the best in London; and the invited guests were rarely missing at the little suppers after opera or play: but Georgia's box was no longer crowded with men who dropped in between the acts to see what she thought of the singer or the piece, and her swains were no longer contented to sit behind her chair all the evening, seeing an empty corner of the stage across Georgia's ivory shoulder, and hearing the voices of invisible actors in the brief pauses of Georgie's subdued babble.

At fifty-five, Georgina Kirkbank told herself sadly enough that her day, as a bright particular star, all-sufficient in her own radiance, was gone. She could not live without her masculine circle, men who could bring her all the news, the gossip of the clubs; where everything seemed to become known as quickly as if each club had its own Asmodeus, unroofing all the housetops of the West End for inspection every night. She could not live without her courtiers; and to keep them about her she knew that she must make her house pleasant. It was not enough to give good dinners, elegant little suppers washed down by choicest wines; she must also provide fair faces to smile upon the feast, and bright eyes to sparkle in the subdued light of low shaded lamps, and many candles twinkling under coloured shades.

'I am an old woman now,' Lady Kirkbank said to herself with a sigh, 'and my own attractions won't keep my friends about me. *C'est trop connu ca.*'

And now the house in Arlington Street in which feminine guests had been as one in ten, opened its doors to the young and the fair. Pretty widows, lively girls, young wives who were not too absurdly devoted to their husbands, actresses of high standing and good looks, these began to be welcomed effusively in Arlington Street. Lady Kirkbank began to hunt for beauties to adorn her rooms, as she had hitherto hunted lions to roar at her parties. She prided herself on being the first to discover this or that new beauty. That lovely girl from Scotland with the large eyes--that sweet young creature from Ireland with the long eyelashes. She was always inventing new divinities. But even this change of plan, this more feminine line of politics failed to reconcile the strict and the stern, the Queen Charlotte-ish elderly ladies, and the impeccable matrons, to Lady Kirkbank and her sea. The girls who were launched by Lady Kirkbank never took high rank in society. When they made good marriages it was generally to be observed that they dropped Lady Kirkbank soon afterwards. It was not their fault, these ingrates pleaded piteously; but Edward, or Henry, or Theodore, as the case might be, had a most cruel prejudice against dear Lady Kirkbank, and the young wives were obliged to obey.

Others there were, however, the loyal few, who having won the prize matrimonial in Lady Kirkbank's happy hunting grounds, remained true to their friend ever afterwards, and defended her character against every onslaught.

When Lady Maulevrier told her grandson that she had entrusted Lady Kirkbank with the duty of introducing Lesbia to society, Maulevrier shrugged his shoulders and held his peace. He knew no actual harm in the matter. Lady Kirkbank's was rather a fast set; and had he been allowed to choose it was not to Lady Kirkbank that he would have delegated his grandmother's duty. In Maulevrier's own phrase it was 'not good enough' for Lesbia. But it was not in his power to interfere. He was not told of the plan until everything had been settled. The thing was accomplished; and against accomplished facts Maulevrier was the last to protest.

His friend John Hammond had not been silent. He knew nothing of Lady Kirkbank personally; but he knew the position which she held in London society, and he urged his friend strongly to enlighten Lady Maulevrier as to the kind of circle into which she was about to entrust her young granddaughter, a girl brought up in the Arcadia of England.

'Not for worlds would I undertake such a task,' said Maulevrier. 'Her ladyship never had any opinion of my wisdom, and this Lady Kirkbank is a friend of her own youth. She would cut up rough if I were to say a word against an old friend. Besides what's the odds, if you come to think of it? all society is fast nowadays, or at any rate all society worth living in. And then again, Lesbia is just one of those cool-headed girls who would keep herself head uppermost in a maelstrom. She knows on which side her bread is buttered. Look how easily she chucked you up because she did not think you good enough. She'll make use of this Lady Kirkbank, who is a good soul, I am told, and will make the best match of the season.'

And now the season had begun, and Lady Lesbia Haselden was circulating with other aristocratic atoms in the social vortex, with her head apparently uppermost.

'Old Lady K--has nobbled a real beauty, this time,' said one of the Arlington Street set to his friend as they lolled on the railings in the park, 'a long way above any of those plain-headed ones she tried to palm off upon us last year: the South American girl with the big eyes and a complexion like a toad, the Forfarshire girl with freckles and unsophisticated carrots. "Those lovely Spanish eyes," said Lady K----, "that Titianesque auburn hair!" But it didn't answer. Both the girls were plain, and they have gone back to their native obscurity spinsters still. But this is a real thorough-bred one--blood, form, pace, all there.'

'Who is she?' drawled his friend.

'Lord Maulevrier's sister, Lady Lesbia Haselden. Has money, too, I believe; rich grandmother; old lady buried alive in Westmoreland; horrid old miser.'

'I shouldn't mind marrying a miser's granddaughter,' said the other. 'So nice to know that some wretched old idiot has scraped and hoarded through a lifetime of deprivation and self-denial, in order that one may spend his money when he is under the sod.'

Lady Lesbia was accepted everywhere, or almost everywhere, as the beauty of the season. There were six or seven other girls who aspired to the same proud position, who were asserted by their own particular friends to have won it; just as there are generally four or five horses which claim to be first favourites; but the betting was all in favour of Lady Lesbia.

Lady Kirkbank told her that she was turning everyone's head, and Lesbia was quite willing to believe her. But was Lesbia's own head quite steady in this whirl-pool? That was a question which she did not take the trouble to ask herself.

Her heart was tranquil enough, cold as marble. No shield and safeguard so secure against the fire of new love as an old love hardly cold. Lesbia told herself that her heart was a sepulchre, an urn which held a handful of ashes, the ashes of her passion for John Hammond. It was a fire quite burned out, she thought; but that extinguished flame had left death-like coldness.

This was Lesbia's own diagnosis of her case: but the real truth was that among the herd of men she had met, almost all of them ready to fall down and worship her, there was not one who had caught her fancy. Her nature was shallow enough to be passing fickle; the passion which she had taken for love was little more than a girl's fancy; but the man who had power to awaken that fancy as John Hammond had done had not yet appeared in Lady Kirkbank's circle.

'What a cold-hearted creature you must be,' said Georgie. 'You don't seem to admire any of my favourite men.'

'They are very nice,' Lesbia answered languidly; 'but they are all alike. They say the same things--wear the same clothes--sit in the same attitude. One would think they were all drilled in a body every morning before they go out. Mr. Night-shade, the actor, who came to supper the other night, is the only man I have seen who has a spark of originality.'

'You are right,' answered Lady Kirkbank, 'there is an appalling sameness in men: only it is odd you should find it out so soon. I never discovered it till I was an old woman. How I envy Cleopatra her Caesar and her Antony. No mistaking one of those for the other. Mary Stuart too, what marked varieties of character she had an opportunity of studying in Rizzio and Chastelard, Darnley and Bothwell. Ah, child, that is what it is to *live*.'

'Mary is very interesting,' sighed Lesbia; 'but I fear she was not a correct person.'

'My love, what correct person ever is interesting? History draws a misty halo round a sinner of that kind, till one almost believes her a saint. I think Mary Stuart, Froude's Mary, simply perfect.'

Lesbia had begun by blushing at Lady Kirkbank's opinions; but she was now used to the audacity of the lady's sentiments, and the almost infantile candour with which she gave utterance to them. Lady Kirkbank liked to make her friends laugh. It was all she could do now in order to be admired. And there is nothing like audacity for making people laugh nowadays. Lady Kirkbank was a close student of all those delightful books of French memoirs which bring the tittle-tattle of the Regency and the scandals of Louis the Fifteenth's reign so vividly before us: and she had unconsciously founded her manners and her ways of thinking and talking upon that easy-going but elegant age. She did not want to seem better than women who had been so altogether charming. She fortified the frivolity of historical Parisian manners by a dash of the British sporting character. She drove, shot, jumped over five-barred gates, contrived on the verge of seventy to be as active us a young woman; and she flattered herself that the mixture of wit, audacity, sport, and good-nature was full of fascination.

However this might be, it is certain that a good many people liked her, chiefly perhaps because she was good-natured, and a little on account of that admirable cook.

To Lesbia, who had been weary to loathing of her old life amidst the hills and waterfalls of Westmoreland, this new life was one perpetual round of pleasure. She flung herself with all her heart and mind into the amusement of the moment; she knew neither weariness nor satiety. To ride in the park in the morning, to go to a luncheon party, a garden party, to drive in the park for half an hour after the garden party, to rush home and dress for the fourth or fifth time, and then off to a dinner, and from dinner to drum, and from drum to big ball, at which rumour said the Prince and Princess were to be present: and so, from eleven o'clock in the morning till four or five o'clock next morning, the giddy whirl went on: and every hour was so occupied by pleasure engagements that it was difficult to squeeze in an occasional morning for shopping--necessary to go to the shops sometimes, or one would not know how many things one really wants--or for an indispensable interview with the dressmaker. Those mornings at the shops were hardly the least agreeable of Lesbia's hours. To a girl brought up in one perpetual ***tete-a-tete*** with green hill-sides and silvery watercourses, the West End shops were as gardens of Eden, as Aladdin Caves, as anything, everything that is rapturous and intoxicating. Lesbia, the clear-headed, the cold-hearted, fairly lost her senses when she went into one of those exquisite shops, where a confusion of brocades and satins lay about in dazzling masses of richest colour, with here and there a bunch of lilies, a cluster of roses, a tortoise-shell fan, an ostrich feather, or a flounce of peerless Point d'Alencon flung carelessly athwart the sheen of a wine-dark velvet or golden-hued satin.

Lady Maulevrier had said Lesbia was to have *carte blanche*; so Lesbia bought everything she wanted, or fancied she wanted, or that the shop-people thought she must want, or that Lady Kirkbank happened to admire. The shop-people were so obliging, and so deeply obliged by Lesbia's patronage. She was exactly the kind of customer they liked to serve. She flitted about their showrooms like a beautiful butterfly hovering over a flower-bed--her eye caught by every novelty. She never asked the price of anything: and Lady Kirkbank informed them, in confidence, that she was a great heiress, with a millionaire grandmother who indulged her every whim. Other high born young ladies, shopping upon fixed allowances, and sorely perplexed to make both ends meet, looked with eyes of envy upon this girl.

And then came the visit to the dressmaker. It happened after all that Kate Kearney was not intrusted with Lady Lesbia's frocks. Miss Kearney was the fashion, and could pick and choose her customers; and as she was a young lady of good business aptitudes, she had a liking for ready money, or at least half-yearly settlements; and, finding that Lady Kirkbank was much more willing to give new orders than to pay old accounts, she had respectfully informed her ladyship that a pressure of business would prevent her executing any further demands from Arlington Street, while the necessity of posting her ledger obliged her to request the favour of an immediate cheque.

The little skirmish--per letter--occurred while Lady Kirkbank was at Cannes, and Miss Kearney's conduct was stigmatised as insolent and ungrateful, since had not she, Lady Kirkbank by the mere fact of her patronage, given this young person her chief claim to fashion?

'I shall drop her,' said Georgie, 'and go back to poor old Seraphine, who is worth a cartload of such Irish adventuresses.'

So to Madame Seraphine, of Clanricarde Place, Lady Lesbia was taken as a lamb to the slaughter-house.

Seraphine had made Lady Kirkbank's clothes, off and on for the last thirty years. Seraphine and Georgia had grown old together. Lady Kirkbank was always dropping Seraphine and taking her up again, quarrelling and making friends with her. They wrote each other little notes, in which Lady Kirkbank called the dressmaker her *cher ange*--her *bonne chatte*, her *chere vieille sotte*--and all manner of affectionate names--and in which Seraphine occasionally threatened the lady with the dire engines of the law, if money were not forthcoming before Saturday evening.

Lady Kirkbank within those thirty years had paid Seraphine many thousands; but she had never once got herself out of the dear creature's debt. All her payments were payments on account. A hundred pounds; or fifty--or an occasional cheque for two hundred and fifty, when Sir George had been lucky at Newmarket and Doncaster. But the rolling nucleus of debt went rolling on, growing bigger every year until the payments on account needed to be larger or more numerous than of old to keep Seraphine in good humour.

Seraphine was a woman of genius and versatility and had more than one art at her fingers' ends--those skinny and claw-shaped fingers, the nails whereof were not always clean. She took charge of her customer's figures, and made their corsets, and lectured them if they allowed nature to get the upper hand.

'If Madame's waist gets one quarter of an inch thicker it must be that I renounce to make her gowns,' she would tell a ponderous matron, with cool insolence, and the matron would stand abashed before the little sallow, hooked-nosed, keen eyed Jewess, like a child before a severe mother.

'Oh, Seraphine, do you really think that I am stouter?' the customer would ask feebly, panting in her tightened corset.

'Is it that I think so? Why that jumps to the eyes. Madame had always that little air of Reubens, even in the flower of her youth--but now--it is a Rubens of the Fabourg du Temple.'

And horrified at the idea of her vulgarised charms the meek matron would consent to encase herself in one of Seraphine's severest corsets, called in bitterest mockery *a la sante*--at five guineas--in order that the dressmaker might measure her for a forty-guinea gown.

'A plain satin gown, my dear, with an eighteenpenny frilling round the neck and sleeves, and not so much trimming as would go round my little finger. It is positive robbery,' the matron told her friends afterwards, not the less proud of her skin-tight high shouldered sleeves and the peerless flow of her train.

Seraphine was an artist in complexions, and it was she who provided her middle-aged and elderly customers with the lilies and roses of youth. Lady Kirkbank's town complexion was superintended by Seraphine, sometimes even manipulated by those harpy-like claws. The eyebrows of which Lesbia complained were only eyebrows *de province*--eyebrows *de voyage*. In London Georgie was much more particular; and Seraphine was often in Arlington Street with her little morocco bag of washes and creams, and brushes and sponges, to prepare Lady Kirkbank for some great party, and to instruct Lady Kirkbank's maid. At such times Georgie was all affection for the little dressmaker.

'*Ma chatte*, you have made me positively adorable,' she would say, peering at her reflection in the ivory hand-mirror, a dazzling image of rouge and bismuth, carmined lips, diamonds, and frizzy yellow hair; 'I verily believe I look under thirty--but do not you think this gown is a thought too *decolletee--un peu trop de peau, hein?*'

'Not for you, Lady Kirkbank, with your fine shoulders. Shoulders are of no age--*les epaules sont la vraie fontaine de jouvence pour les jolies femmes.*'

'You are such a witty creature, Seraphine, Fifine. You ought to be a descendant of that wicked old Madame du Deffand. Rilboche, give Madame some more chartreuse.'

And Lady Kirkbank and the dressmaker would chink their liqueur glasses in amity before the lady gathered up her satin train and allowed her peerless shoulders to be muffled in a plush mantle to go down to her carriage, fortified by that last glass of green chartreuse.

There were always the finest chartreuse and curacoa in a liqueur cabinet on Lady Kirkbank's dressing-table. The cabinet formed a companion to the dressing-case, which contained all those creamy and rose-hued cosmetics, powders, brushes, and medicaments, which were necessary for the manufacture of Georgie's complexion. The third bottle in the liqueur case held cognac, and this, as Rilboche the maid knew, was oftenest replenished. Yet nobody could accuse Lady Kirkbank of intemperate habits. The liqueur box only supplied the peg that was occasionally wanted to screw the superior mind to concert pitch.

'One must always be at concert pitch in society, don't you know, my dear,' said Georgie to her young protegee.

Thus it happened that, Miss Kearney having behaved badly, Lesbia was carried off to dear old Seraphine, and delivered over to that modern witch, as a sacrifice tied to the horns of the altar.

Clanricarde Place is a little nook of Queen Anne houses--genuine Queen Anne, be it understood--between Piccadilly and St. James's Palace, and hardly five minutes' walk from Arlington Street. It is a quiet little *cul de sac* in the very heart of the fashionable world; and here of an afternoon might be seen the carriages of Madame Seraphine's customers, blocking the whole of the carriage way, and choking up the narrow entrance to the street, which widened considerably at the inner end.

Madame Seraphine's house was at the end, a narrow house, with tall old-fashioned windows curtained with amber satin. It was a small, dark house, and exhaled occasional odours of garlic and main sewer: but the staircase was a gem in old oak, and the furniture in the triple telescopic drawing rooms, dwindling to a closet at the end, was genuine Louis Seize.

Seraphine herself was the only shabby thing in the house--a wizened little woman, with a wicked old Jewish face, and one shoulder higher than the other, dressed in a shiny black moire gown, years after moires had been exploded, and with a rag of old lace upon her sleek black hair--raven black hair, and the only good thing about her appearance.

One ornament, and one only, had Seraphine ever been guilty of wearing, and that was an old-fashioned half-hoop ring of Brazilian diamonds, brilliants of the first water. This ring she called her yard measure; and she was in the habit of using it as her Standard of purity, and comparing it with any diamonds which her customers submitted to her inspection. For the clever little dressmaker had a feeling heart for a lady in difficulties, and was in the habit of lending money on good security, and on terms that were almost reasonable as compared with the usurious rates one reads of in the newspapers.

Lesbia's first sensation upon having this accomplished person presented to her was one of shrinking and disgust. There was something sinister in the sallow face, the small shrewd eyes, and long hooked nose, the crooked figure, and claw-shaped hands. But when Madame Seraphine began to talk about gowns, and bade her acolytes--smartly-dressed young women with pleasing countenances--bring forth marvels of brocade and satin, embroideries, stamped velvets, bullion fringes, and ostrich feather flouncings, Lesbia became interested, and forgot the unholy aspect of the high priestess.

Lady Kirkbank and the dressmaker discussed Lesbia's charms as calmly as if she had been out of the room.

'What do you think of her figure?' asked Lady Kirkbank.

'One cannot criticise what does not exist,' replied the dressmaker, in French. 'The young lady has no figure. She has evidently been brought up in the country.'

And then with rapid bird-like movements, and with her head on one side, Seraphine measured Lesbia's waist and bust, muttering little argotic expressions **sotto voce** as she did so.

'Waist three inches too large, shoulders six inches too narrow,' she said decisively, and she dictated some figures to one of the damsels, who wrote them down in an order-book.

'What does that mean?' asked Lesbia, not at all approving of such cavalier treatment.

'Only that Seraphine will make your corsets the right size,' answered Lady Kirkbank.

'What? Three inches too small for my waist, and six too wide for my shoulders?'

'My love, you must have a figure,' replied Lady Kirkbank, conclusively. 'It is not what you are, but what you ought to be that has to be considered.'

So Lesbia, the cool-headed, who was also the weak-minded, consented to have her figure adjusted to the regulation mark of absolute beauty, as understood by Madame Seraphine. It was only when her complexion came under discussion, and Seraphine ventured to suggest that she would be all the better for a little accentuation of her eyebrows and darkening of her lashes, that Lesbia made a stand.

'What would my grandmother think of me if she heard I painted?' she asked, indignantly.

Lady Kirkbank laughed at her **naivete**.

'My dear child, your grandmother is just half a century behind the age,' she said. 'I hope you are not going to allow your life in London to be regulated by an oracle at Grasmere?'

'I am not going to paint my face,' replied Lesbia, firmly.

'Well, perhaps you are right. The eyebrows are a little weak and undecided, Seraphine, as you say, and the lashes would be all the better for your famous cosmetic; but after all there is a charm in what the painters call "sincerity," and any little errors of detail will prove the genuineness of Lady Lesbia's beauty. One *may* be too artistic.'

And Lady Kirkbank gave a complacent glance at her own image in one of the Marie Antoinette mirrors, pleased with the general effect of arched brows, darkened eyelids, and a daisy bonnet. The fair Georgie generally affected field-flowers and other simplicities, which would have been becoming to a beauty of eighteen.

'One is obliged to smother one's self in satin and velvet for balls and dinners,' said Lady Kirkbank, when she discussed the great question of gowns; 'but I know I always look my best in my cotton frock and straw hat.'

That first visit to Seraphine's den--den as terrible, did one but know it, as that antediluvian hyena-cave at Torquay, where the threshold is worn by the bodies of beasts dragged across it, and the ground paved with their bones--that first visit was a serious business. Later interviews might be mere frivolities, half-an-hour wasted in looking at new fashions, an order given carelessly on the spur of the moment; but upon this occasion Lady Kirkbank had to arm her young *protegee* for the coming campaign, and the question was to the last degree serious.

The chaperon and the dressmaker put their heads together, looked at fashion plates, talked solemnly of Worth and his compeers, of the gowns that were being worn by Bernhardt, and Pierson, and Croisette, and other stars of the Parisian stage; and then Lady Kirkbank gave her orders, Lesbia listening and assenting.

Nothing was said about prices; but Lesbia had a vague idea that some of the things would be rather expensive, and she ventured to ask Lady Kirkbank if she were not ordering too many gowns.

'My dear, Lady Maulevrier said you were to have *carte blanche*,' replied Georgie, solemnly. 'Your dear grandmother is as rich as Croesus, and she is generosity itself; and how should I ever forgive myself if I allowed you to appear in society in an inadequate style. You have to take a high place, the very highest place, Lesbia; and you must be dressed in accordance with that position.'

Lesbia said no more. After all it was Lady Kirkbank's business and not hers. See had been entrusted to Lady Kirkbank as to a person who thoroughly knew the great world, and she must submit to be governed by the wisdom and experience of her chaperon. If the bills were heavy, that would be Lady Kirkbank's affair; and no doubt dear grandmother was rich enough to afford anything Lesbia wanted. She had been told that she was to take rank among heiresses.

Lady Maulevrier had given her granddaughter some old-fashioned ornaments, topaz, amethysts, turquoise--jewels that had belonged to dead and gone Talmashes and Angersthorpes--to be reset. This entailed a visit to a Bond Street jeweller, and in the dazzling glass-cases on the counter of the Bond Street establishment Lesbia saw a good many things which she felt were real necessities to her new phase of existence, and these, with Lady Kirkbank's approval, she ordered. They were not important matters. Half-a-dozen gold bangles of real oriental workmanship, three or four jewelled arrows, flies and beetles, and caterpillars, to pin on her laces and flowers, a diamond clasp for her pearl necklace, a dear little gold hunter to wear when she rode in the park, a diamond butterfly to light up that old-fashioned amethyst *parure* which the jeweller was to reset with an artistic admixture of brilliants.

'I am sure you would not like the effect without diamonds,' said the jeweller. 'Your amethysts are very fine, but they are dark and heavy in tone, and want a good deal of lighting-up, especially for the present fashion of half-lighted rooms. If you will allow me to use my own discretion, and mix in a few brilliants, I shall be able to produce a really artistic *parure*; otherwise I would not recommend you to touch them. The present setting is clumsy and inelegant; but I really do not know that I could improve upon it, without an admixture of brilliants.'

'Will the diamonds add very much to the expense?' Lesbia inquired, timidly.

'My dear child, you are perfectly safe in leaving the matter in Mr. Cabochon's hands,' interposed Lady Kirkbank, who had particular reasons for wishing to be on good terms with the head of the establishment. 'Your dear grandmother gave you the amethysts to be reset; and of course she would wish it to be done in an artistic manner. Otherwise, as Mr. Cabochon judiciously says, why have the stones reset at all? Better wear them in all their present hideousness.'

Of course, after this Lesbia consented to the amethysts being dealt with according to Mr. Cabochon's taste.

'Which is simply perfect,' interjected Lady Kirkbank.

And now Lesbia's campaign began in real earnest--a life of pleasure, a life of utter selfishness and self-indulgence, which would go far to pervert the strongest mind, tarnish the purest nature. To dress and be admired--that was what Lesbia's life meant from morning till night. She had no higher or nobler aim. Even on Sunday mornings at the fashionable church, where the women sat on one side of the nave and the men on the other, where divinest music was as a pair of wings, on which the enraptured soul flew heavenward--even here Lesbia thought more of her bonnet and gloves--the *chic* or non-*chic* of her whole costume, than of the service. She might kneel gracefully, with her bent head, just revealing the ivory whiteness of a lovely throat, between the edge of her lace frilling and the flowers in her bonnet. She might look the fairest image of devotion; but how could a woman pray whose heart was a milliner's shop, whose highest ambition was to be prettier and better dressed than other women?

The season was six weeks old. It was Ascot week, the crowning glory of the year, and Lesbia and her chaperon had secured tickets for the Royal enclosure--or it may be said rather that Lesbia had secured them--for the Master of the Royal Buckhounds might have omitted poor old Lady Kirkbank's familiar name from his list if it had not been for that lovely girl who went everywhere under the veteran's wing.

Six weeks, and Lesbia's appearance in society had been one perpetual triumph; but as yet nothing serious had happened. She had had no offers. Half a dozen men had tried their hardest to propose to her--had sat out dances, had waylaid her in conservatories and in back drawing-rooms, in lobbies while she waited for her carriage--had looked at her piteously with tenderest declarations trembling on their lips; but she had contrived to keep them at bay, to strike them dumb by her coldness, or confound them by her coquetry; for all these were ineligibles, whom Lady Lesbia Haselden did not want to have the trouble of refusing.

Lady Kirkbank was in no haste to marry her *protegee*--nay, it was much more to her interest that Lesbia should remain single for three or four seasons, and that she, Lady Kirkbank, might have the advantage of close association with the young beauty, and the privilege of spending Lady Maulevrier's money. But she would have liked to be able to inform Lesbia's grandmother of some tremendous conquest--the subjugation of a worthy victim. This herd of nobodies--younger sons with courtesy titles and empty pockets, ruined Guardsmen, briefless barristers--what was the use of telling Lady Maulevrier about such barren victories? Lady Kirkbank therefore contented herself with expatiating upon Lesbia's triumphs in a general way: how graciously the Princess spoke to her and about her; how she had been asked to sit on the dais at the ball at Marlborough House, and had danced in the Royal quadrille.

'Has Lesbia happened to meet Lord Hartfield?' Lady Maulevrier asked, incidentally, in one of her letters.

No. Lord Hartfield was in London, for he had made a great speech in the Lords on a question of vital interest; but he was not going into society, or at any rate into society of a frivolous kind. He had given himself up to politics, as so many young men did nowadays, which was altogether horrid of them. His name had appeared in the list of guests at one or two cabinet dinners; but the world of polo matches and afternoon teas, dances and drums, private theatricals, and Orleans House suppers, knew him not. As a competitor on the fashionable race-course, Lord Hartfield was, in common parlance, out of the running.

And now on this glorious June day, this Thursday of Thursdays, the Ascot Cup day, for the first time since Lesbia's debut, Lady Kirkbank had occasion to smile upon an admirer whose pretensions were worthy of the highest consideration.

Mr. Smithson, of Park Lane, and Rood Hall, near Henley, and Formosa, Cowes, and Le Bouge, Deauville, and a good many other places too numerous to mention, was reputed to be one of the richest commoners in England. He was a man of that uncertain period of life which enemies call middle age, and friends call youth. That he would never see a five-and-thirtieth birthday again was certain; but whether he had passed the Rubicon of forty was open to doubt. It is possible that he was enjoying those few golden years between thirty-five and forty, which for the wealthy bachelor constitute verily the prime and summer-tide of life. Wisdom has come, experience has been bought, taste has been cultivated, the man has educated himself to the uttermost in the great school of daily life. He knows his world thoroughly, whatever that world is, and he knows how to enjoy every gift and every advantage which Providence has bestowed upon him.

Mr. Smithson was a great authority on the Stock Exchange, though he had ceased for the last three or four years to frequent the 'House,' or to be seen in the purlieus of Throgmorton Street. Indeed he had an air of hardly knowing his way to the City, of being acquainted with that part of London only by hearsay. He complained that his horses shied at passing Temple Bar. And yet a few years ago Mr. Smithson's city operations had been on a very extensive scale: It was in the rise and fall of commodities rather than of stocks and shares that Horace Smithson had made his money. He had exercised occult influences upon the trade of the great city, of the world itself, whereof that city is in a manner the keystone. Iron had risen or fallen at his beck. At the breath of his nostrils cochineal had gone up in the market at an almost magical rate, as if the whole civilised world had become suddenly intent upon dyeing its garments red, nay, as if even the naked savages of the Gold Coast and the tribes of Central Africa were bent on staining their dusky skins with the bodies of the female coccus.

Favoured by a hint from Smithson, his particular friends followed his lead, and rushed into the markets to buy all the cochineal that could be had; to buy at any price, since the market was rising hourly. And then, all in a moment, as the sky clouds over on a summer day, there came a dulness in the cochineal market, and the female coccus was being sold at an enormous sacrifice. And anon it leaked out that Mr. Smithson had grown tired of cochineal, and had been selling for the last week or two; and it was noised abroad that this rise and fall in cocci had brought Mr. Smithson seventy thousand pounds.

Mr. Smithson was said to have commenced life in a very humble capacity. There were some who declared he was the very youth who stooped to pick up a pin in a Parisian banker's courtyard, after his services as clerk had just been rejected by the firm, and who was thereupon recognised as a youth worthy of favour and taken into the banker's office. But this touching incident of the pin was too ancient a tradition to fit Mr. Smithson, still under forty.

Some there were who remembered him eighteen years ago as an adventurer in the great wilderness of London, penniless, friendless, a Jack-of-all-trades, living as the birds of the air live, and with as little certainty of future maintenance. And then Mr. Smithson disappeared for a space--he went under, as his friends called it; to reappear fifteen years later as Smithson the millionaire. He had been in Peru, Mexico, California. He had traded in hides, in diamonds, in silver, in stocks and shares. And now he was the great Smithson, whose voice was the voice of an oracle, who was supposed to be able to make the fortunes of other men by a word, or a wink, a nod, or a little look across the crowd, and whom all the men and women in London society--short of that exclusive circle which does ***not*** open its ranks to Smithsons-- were ready to cherish and admire.

Mr. Smithson had been in Petersburg, Paris, Vienna, all over civilised Europe during the last five weeks, whether on business or on pleasure bent, nobody knew. He affected to be an elegant idler; but it was said by the initiated that wherever Smithson went the markets rose or fell, and hides, iron, copper, or tin, felt the influence of his presence.

He came back to London in time for the Cup Day, and in time to fall desperately in love with Lesbia, whom he met for the first time in the Royal enclosure.

She was dressed in white, purest ivory white, from top to toe--radiant, dazzling, under an immense sunshade fringed with creamy marabouts. Her complexion--untouched by Seraphine--her dark and glossy hair, her large violet eyes, luminous, dark almost to blackness, were all set off and accentuated by the absence of colour in her costume. Even the cluster of exotics on her shoulder were of the same pure tint, gardenias and lilies of the valley.

Mr. Smithson was formally presented to the new beauty, and received with a cool contempt which riveted his chains. He was so accustomed to be run after by women, that it was a new sensation to meet one who was not in the least impressed by his superior merits.

'I don't suppose the girl knows who I am,' he said to himself, for although he had a very good idea of his intrinsic worth, he knew that his wealth ranked first among his merits.

But on after occasions when Lesbia had been told all that could be told to the advantage of Mr. Smithson, she accepted his homage with the same indifference, and treated him with less favour than she accorded to the ruined guardsmen and younger sons who were dying for her.

CHAPTER XXVI.
'PROUD CAN I NEVER BE OF WHAT I HATE.'

It was a Saturday afternoon, and even in that great world which has no occupation in life except to amuse itself, whose days are all holidays, there is a sort of exceptional flavour, a kind of extra excitement on Saturday afternoons, distinguished by polo matches at Hurlingham, just as Saturday evenings are by the production of new plays at fashionable theatres. There was a great military polo match for this particular Saturday--Lancers against Dragoons. It was a lovely June afternoon, and Hurlingham would be at its best. The cool greensward, the branching trees, the flowing river, would afford an unspeakable relief after the block of carriages in Bond Street and the heated air of London, where even the parks felt baked and arid; and to Hurlingham Lady Kirkbank drove directly after luncheon.

Lesbia leaned back in the barouche listening calmly, while her chaperon expatiated upon the wealth and possessions of Horace Smithson. It was now ten days since the meeting at Ascot, and Mr. Smithson had contrived to see a great deal of Lesbia in that short time. He was invited almost everywhere, and he had haunted her at afternoon and evening parties; he had supped in Arlington Street after the opera; he had played cards with Lesbia, and had enjoyed the felicity of winning her money. His admiration was obvious, and there was a seriousness in his manner of pursuing her which showed that, in Lady Kirkbank's unromantic phraseology, 'the man meant business.'

'Smithson is caught at last, and I am glad of it,' said Georgie.

'The creature is an abominable flirt, and has broken more hearts than any man in London. He was all but the death of one of the dearest girls I know.'

'Mr. Smithson breaks hearts!' exclaimed Lesbia, languidly. 'I should not have thought that was in his line. Mr. Smithson is not an Adonis, nor are his manners particularly fascinating.'

'My child how fresh you are! Do you suppose it is the handsome men or the fascinating men for whom women break their hearts in society? It is the rich men they all want to marry--men like Smithson, who can give them diamonds, and yachts, and a hunting stud, and half a dozen fine houses. Those are the prizes--the blue ribbons of the matrimonial race-course--men like Smithson, who pretend to admire all the pretty women, who dangle, and dangle, and keep off other offers, and give ten guinea bouquets, and then at the end of the season are off to Hombourg or the Scotch moors, without a word. Do you think that kind of treatment is not hard enough to break a penniless girl's heart? She sees the golden prize within her grasp, as she believes; she thinks that she and poverty have parted company for ever; she imagines herself mistress of town house and country houses, yachts and stables; and then one fine morning the gentleman is off and away! Do not you think that is enough to break a girl's heart?'

'I can imagine that girl steeped to the lips in poverty might be willing to marry Mr. Smithson's houses and yachts,' answered Lesbia, in her low sweet voice, with a faint sneer even amidst the sweetness, 'but, I think it must have been a happy release for any one to be let off the sacrifice at the last moment.'

'Poor Belle Trinder did not think so.'

'Who was Belle Trinder?'

'An Essex parson's daughter whom I took under my wing five years ago--a splendid girl, large and fair, and just a trifle coarse--not to be spoken of in the same day with you, dearest; but still a decidedly handsome creature. And she took remarkably well. She was a very lively girl, "never ran mute," Sir George used to say. Sir George was very fond of her. She amused him, poor girl, with her rather brainless rattle.'

'And Mr. Smithson admired her?'

'Followed her about everywhere, sent her whole flower gardens in the way of bouquets and Japanese baskets, and floral ***parures*** for her gowns, and opera boxes and concert tickets. Their names were always coupled. People used to call them Bel and the Dragon. The poor child made up her mind she was to be Mrs. Smithson. She used to talk of what she would do for her own people--the poor old father, buried alive in a damp parsonage, and struggling every winter with chronic bronchitis; the four younger sisters pining in dulness and penury; the mother who hardly knew what it was to rest from the continual worries of daily life.'

'Poor things!' sighed Lesbia, gazing admiringly at the handle of her last new sunshade.

'Belle used to talk of what she would do for them all,' pursued Lady Kirkbank. 'Father should go every year to the villa at Monte Carlo; mother and the girls should have a month in Park Lane every season, and their autumn holiday at one of Mr. Smithson's country houses. I knew the world well enough to be sure that this kind of thing would never answer with a man like Smithson. It is only one man in a thousand--the modern Arthur, the modern Quixote--who will marry a whole family. I told Belle as much, but she laughed. She felt so secure of her power over the man. "He will do anything I ask him," she said.'

'Miss Trinder must be an extraordinary young person,' observed Lesbia, scornfully. 'The man had not proposed, had he?'

'No; the actual proposal hung fire, but Belle thought it was a settled thing all the same. Everybody talked to her as if she were engaged to Smithson, and those poor, ignorant vicarage girls used to write her long letters of congratulation, envying her good fortune, speculating, about what she would do when she was married. The girl was too open and candid for London society--talked too much, "gave the view before she was sure of her fox," Sir George said. All this silly talk came to Smithson's ears, and one morning we read in the Post that Mr. Smithson had started the day before for Algiers, where he was to stay at the house of the English Consul, and hunt lions. We waited all day, hoping for some letter of explanation, some friendly farewell which would mean *a revoir*. But there was nothing, and then poor Belle gave way altogether. She shut herself up in her room, and went out of one hysterical fit into another. I never heard a girl sob so terribly. She was not fit to be seen for a week, and then she went home to her father's parsonage in the flat swampy country on the borders of Suffolk, and eat her heart, as Byron calls it. And the worst of it was that she had no actual justification for considering herself jilted. She had talked, and other people had talked, and among them they had settled the business. But Smithson had said hardly anything. He had only flirted to his heart's content, and had spent a few hundreds upon flowers, gloves, fans, and opera tickets, which perhaps would not have been accepted by a girl with a strong sense of her own dignity.'

'I should think not, indeed,' interjected Lesbia.

'But which poor Belle was only too delighted to get.'

'Miss Trinder must be very bad style,' said Lesbia, with languid scorn, 'and Mr. Smithson is an execrable person. Did she die?'

'No, my dear, she is alive poor soul!'

'You said she broke her heart.'

'"The heart may break, yet brokenly live on,"' quoted Lady Kirkbank. 'The disappointed young women don't all die. They take to district visiting, or rational dressing, or china painting, or an ambulance brigade. The lucky ones marry well-to-do widowers with large families, and so slip into a comfortable groove by the time they are five-and-thirty. Poor Belle is still single, still buried in the damp parsonage, where she paints plates and teacups, and wears out my old gowns, just as she is wearing out her own life, poor creature!'

'The idea of any one wanting to marry Mr. Smithson,' said Lesbia. 'It seems too dreadful.'

'A case of real destitution, you think. Wait till you have seen Smithson's house in Park Lane--his team, his yacht, his orchid houses in Berkshire.'

Lesbia sighed. Her knowledge of London society was only seven weeks old; and yet already the day of disenchantment had begun! She was having her eyes opened to the stern realities of life. A year ago when her appearance in the great world was still only a dream of the future, she had pictured to herself the crowd of suitors who would come to woo, and she had resolved to choose the worthiest.

What would he be like, that worthiest among the wooers, that King Arthur among her knights?

First and foremost, he would be of rank higher than her own--duke, a marquis, or one of the first and oldest among earls. Title and lofty lineage were indispensable. It would be a fall, a failure, a disappointment, were she to marry a commoner, however distinguished.

The worthy one must be noble, therefore, and of the old nobility. He must be young, handsome, intellectual. He must stand out from among his peers by his gifts of mind and person. He must have won distinction in the arena of politics or diplomacy, arms or letters. He must be 'somebody.'

She had been seven weeks in society, and this modern Arthur had not appeared. So far as she had been able to discover, there was no such person. The dukes and marquises were mostly men of advanced years. The young unmarried nobility were given over to sport, play, and foolishness. She had heard of only one man who at all corresponded with her ideal, and he was Lord Hartfield. But Lord Hartfield had given himself up to politics, and was no doubt a prig. Lady Kirkbank spoke of him with contempt, as an intolerable person. But then Lord Hartfield was not in Lady Kirkbank's set. He belonged to that serious circle to which Lady Kirkbank's house appeared about as reputable a place of gathering as a booth on a race-course.

And now Lady Kirkbank told Lesbia that this Mr. Smithson, a nobody with a great fortune, was a man whose addresses she, the sister of Lord Maulevrier, ought to welcome. Mr. Smithson, who claimed to be a lineal descendant of that Sir Michael Carrington, standard-bearer to Coeur de Lion in the Holy Land, whose descendants changed their name to Smith during the Wars of the Roses. Mr. Smithson bodily proclaimed himself a scion of this good old county family, and bore on his plate and his coach panels the elephant's head and the three demi-griffins of the Hertfordshire Smiths, who only smiled and shrugged their shoulders when they were complimented upon the splendid surroundings of their cousin. Who could tell? Some lateral branch of the standard-bearer's family tree might have borne this illustrious twig.

Lady Kirkbank and all Lady Kirkbank's friends seemed to have conspired to teach Lesbia Haselden one lesson, and that lesson meant that money was the first prize in the great game of life. Money ranked before everything--before titles, before noble lineage, genius, fame, beauty, courage, honour. Money was Alpha and Omega, the beginning and the end. Mr. Smithson, whose antecedents were as cloudy as those of Aphrodite, was a greater man than a peer whose broad acres only brought him two per cent., or half of whose farms were tenantless, and his fields growing cockle instead of barley.

Yes, one by one, Lady Lesbia's illusions were reft from her. A year ago she had fancied beauty all-powerful, a gift which must ensure to its possessor dominion over all the kingdoms of the earth. Rank, intellect, fame would bow down before that magical diadem. And, behold, she had been shining upon London society for seven weeks, and only empty heads and empty pockets had bowed down--the frivolous, the ineligible,--and Mr. Smithson.

Another illusion which had been dispelled was Lesbia's comfortable idea of her own expectations. Her grandmother had told her that she might take rank among heiresses; and she had held herself accordingly, deeming that her place was among the wealthiest. And now, since Mr. Smithson's appearance upon the scene, Lady Kirkbank had informed her young friend with noble candour that Lady Maulevrier's fortune, however large it might seem at Grasmere, would be a poor thing in London; and that Lady Maulevrier's ideas about money were as old-fashioned as her notions about morals.

'Life is about six times as expensive as it was in your grandmother's time.' said Lady Kirkbank, as the carriage rolled softly along the shabby road between Knightsbridge and Fulham. 'It is the pace that kills. Society, which used to jog along comfortably, like the old Brighton stage, at ten miles an hour, now goes as fast as the

Brighton express. In my mother's time poor Lord Byron was held up to the execration of respectable people as the type of cynical profligacy; in my own time people
talked about Lord Waterford; but, my dear, the young men now are all Byrons and
Waterfords, without the genius of the one or the generosity of the other. We are
all going at steeplechase rate. Social success without money is impossible. The rich
Americans, the successful Jews, will crowd us out unless we keep pace with them.
Ah, Lesbia, my dear girl, there would be a great future before you if you could only
make up your mind to accept Mr. Smithson.'

'How do you know that he means to propose to me?' asked Lesbia, mockingly.
'Perhaps he is only going to behave as he did to Miss Trinder.'

'Lady Lesbia Haselden is a very different person from a country parson's daughter,' answered her chaperon; 'Smithson told me all about it afterwards. He was really
taken with Belle's fine figure and good complexion; but one of her particular friends
told him of her foolish talk about her sisters, and how well she meant to get them
married when she was Mrs. Smithson. This disgusted him. He went down to Essex,
reconnoitered the parsonage, saw one of the sisters hanging out cuffs and collars in
the orchard--another feeding the fowls--both in shabby gowns and country-made
boots; one of them with red hair and freckles. The mother was bargaining for fish
with a hawker at the kitchen door. And these were the people he was expected to
import into Park Lane, under ceilings painted by Leighton. These were the people
he was to exhibit on board his yacht, to cart about on his drag. "I had half made
up my mind to marry the girl, but I would sooner have hung myself than marry
her mother and sisters so I took the first train for Dover, en route for Algiers," said
Smithson, and upon my word I could hardly blame the man,' concluded Lady Kirkbank.

They were driving up the narrow avenue to the gates of Hurlingham by this
time. Lesbia shock out her frock and looked at her gloves, tan-coloured mous-
quetaires, reaching up to the elbow, and embroidered to match her frock.

To-day she was a study in brown and gold. Brown satin petticoat embroidered
with marsh marigolds; little bronze shoes, with marsh marigolds tied on the la-
chets; brown stockings with marsh marigold clocks; tunic brown foulard smothered
with quillings of soft brown lace; Princess bonnet of brown straw, with a wreath
of marsh marigold and a neat little buckle of brown diamonds; parasol brown satin,

with an immense bunch of marsh marigolds on the top; fan to match parasol.

The seats in front of the field were nearly all full when Lady Kirkbank and Lesbia left their carriage; but their interests had been protected by a gentleman who had turned down two chairs and sat between them on guard. This was Mr. Smithson.

'I have been sitting here for an hour keeping your chairs,' he said, as he rose to greet them. 'You have no idea what work I have had, and how ferociously all the women have looked at me.'

The match was going on. The Lancers were scuffling for the ball, and affording a fine display of hog-maned ponies and close-cropped young men in ideal boots. But Lesbia cared very little about the match. She was looking along the serried ranks of youth and beauty to see if anybody's frock was smarter than her own.

No. She could see nothing she liked so well as her brown satin and buttercups. She sat down in a perfectly contented frame of mind, pleased with herself and with Seraphine--pleased even with Mr. Smithson, who had shown himself devoted by his patient attendance upon the empty chairs.

After the match was over the two ladies and their attendant strolled about the gardens. Other men came and fluttered round Lesbia, and women and girls exchanged endearing smiles and pretty little words of greeting with her, and envied her the brown frock and buttercups and Mr. Smithson at her chariot wheel. And then they went to the lawn in front of the club-house, which was so crowded that even Mr. Smithson found it difficult to get a tea-table, and would hardly have succeeded so soon as he did if it had not been for the assistance of a couple of Lesbia's devoted Guardsmen, who ran to and fro and badgered the waiters.

After much skirmishing they were seated at a rustic table, the blue river gleaming and glancing in the distance, the good old trees spreading their broad shadows over the grass, the company crowding and chattering and laughing--an animated picture of pretty faces, smart gowns, big parasols, Japanese fans.

Lesbia poured out the tea with the prettiest air of domesticity.

'Can you really pour out tea?' gasped a callow lieutenant, gazing upon her with goggling, enraptured eyes. 'I did not think you could do anything so earthly.'

'I can, and drink it too,' answered Lesbia, laughing. 'I adore tea. Cream and sugar?'

'I--I beg your pardon--how many?' murmured the youth, who had lost himself in gazing, and no longer understood plain English.

Mr. Smithson frowned at the intruder, and contrived to absorb Lesbia's attention for the rest of the afternoon. He had a good deal more to say for himself than her military admirers, and was altogether more amusing. He had a little cynical air which Lesbia's recent education had taught her to enjoy. He depreciated all her female friends--abused their gowns and bonnets, and gave her to understand, between the lines, as it were, that she was the only woman in London worth thinking about.

She looked at him curiously, wondering how Belle Trinder had been able to resign herself to the idea of marrying him.

He was not absolutely bad looking--but he was in all things unlike a girl's ideal lover. He was short and stout, with a pale complexion, and sunken faded eyes, as of a man who had spent the greater part of his life by candle light, and had pored much over ledgers and bank books, share lists and prospectuses. He dressed well, or allowed himself to be dressed by the most correct of tailors--the Prince's tailor--but he never attempted to lead the fashion in his garments. He had no originality. Such sublime flights as that of the man who revived corduroy, or of that daring genius who resuscitated the half-forgotten Inverness coat, were unknown to him. He could only follow the lead of the highest. He had small feet, of which he was intensely proud, podgy white hands on which he wore the most exquisite rings. He changed his rings every day, like a Roman Emperor; was reported to have summer and winter rings--onyx and the coolest looking intaglios set in filagree for warm weather--fiery rubies and diamonds in massive bands of dull gold for winter. He was said to devote half-an-hour every morning to the treatment of his nails, which were perfect. All the inkstains of his youth had been obliterated, and those nails which had once been bitten to the quick during the throes of financial study were now things of beauty.

Lady Lesbia surveyed Mr. Smithson critically, and shuddered at the thought that this person was the best substitute which the season had yet offered her for her ideal knight. She thought of John Hammond, the tall, strong figure, straight and square; the head so proudly carried on a neck which would have graced a Greek arena. The straight, clearly-cut features, the flashing eyes, bright with youth and hope and the promise of all good things. Yes, there was indeed a man--a man in all the nobility of manhood, as God made him, an Adam before the Fall.

Ah, if John Hammond had only possessed a quarter of Mr. Smithson's wealth how gladly would Lesbia have defied the world and married him. But to defy the world upon nothing a year was out of the question.

'Why didn't he go on the Stock Exchange and make his fortune?' thought Lesbia, pettishly, 'instead of talking vaguely about politics and literature.'

She felt angry with her rejected lover for having come to her empty-handed. She had seen no man in London who was, or who seemed to her, his equal. And yet she did not repent of having rejected him. The more she knew of the world and the more she knew of herself the more deeply was she convinced that poverty was an evil thing, and that she was not the right kind of person to endure it.

She was inwardly making these comparisons as they strolled back to the carriage, while Mr. Smithson and Lady Kirkbank talked confidentially at her side.

'Do you know that Lady Kirkbank has promised and vowed three things for you?' said Mr. Smithson.

'Indeed! I thought I was past the age at which one can be compromised by other people's promises. Pray what are those three things?'

'First, that you will come to breakfast in Park Lane with Lady Kirkbank next Wednesday morning. I say Wednesday because that will give me time to ask some nice people to meet you; secondly, that you will honour me by occupying my box at the Lyceum some evening next week; and thirdly, that you will allow me to drive you down to the Orleans for supper after the play. The drive only takes an hour, and the moonlight nights are delicious at this time of the year.'

'I am in Lady Kirkbank's hands,' answered Lesbia, laughing. 'I am her goods, her chattels; she takes me wherever she likes.'

'But would you refuse to do me this honour if you were a free agent?'

'I can't tell. I hardly know what it is to be a free agent. At Grasmere I did whatever my grandmother told me; in London I obey Lady Kirkbank. I was transferred from one master to another. Why should we breakfast in Park Lane instead of in Arlington Street? What is the use of crossing Piccadilly to eat our breakfast?'

This was a cool-headed style of treatment to which Mr. Smithson was not accustomed, and which charmed him accordingly. Young women usually threw themselves at his head, as it were; but here was a girl who talked to him as indifferently as if he were a tradesman offering his wares.

'What a dreadfully practical person you are?' he exclaimed. 'What is the use of crossing Piccadilly? Well, in the first place, you will make me ineffably happy. But perhaps that doesn't count. In the second place, I shall be able to show you some rather good pictures of the French school--'

'I hate the French school!' interjected Lesbia. 'Tricky, flashy, chalky, shallow, smelling of the footlights and the studio.'

'Well, sink the pictures. You will meet some very charming people, belonging to that artist world which is not to be met everywhere.'

'I will go to Park Lane to meet your people, if Lady Kirkbank likes to take me,' said Lesbia; and with this answer Mr. Smithson was bound to be content.

'My pet, if you had made it the study of your life how to treat that man you could not do it better,' said Lady Kirkbank, when they were driving along the dusty road between dusty hedges and dusty trees, past that last remnant of country which was daily being debased into London. 'Upon my word, Lesbia, I begin to think you must be a genius.'

'Did you see any gowns you liked better than mine?' asked Lesbia, reclining reposefully, with her little bronze shoes upon the opposite cushion.

'Not one--Seraphine has surpassed herself.'

'You are always saying that. One would suppose you were a sleeping partner in the firm. But I really think this brown and buttercups is rather nice. I saw that odious American girl just now--Miss--Miss Milwaukee, that mop-stick girl people raved about at Cannes. She was in pale blue and cream colour, a milk and water mixture, and looked positively plain.'

CHAPTER XXVII.
LESBIA CROSSES PICCADILLY.

Lady Kirkbank and Lady Lesbia drove across Piccadilly at eleven o'clock on Wednesday morning to breakfast with Mr. Smithson, and although Lesbia had questioned whether it was worth while crossing Piccadilly to eat one's breakfast, she had subsequently considered it worth while ordering a new gown from Seraphine for the occasion; or, it may be, rather that the breakfast made a plausible excuse for a new gown, the pleasure of ordering which was one of those joys of a London life that had not yet lost their savour.

The gown, devised especially for the early morning, was simplicity itself--rusticity, even. It was a Dresden shepherdess gown, made of a soft flowered stuff, with roses and forget-me-nots on a creamy ground. There was a great deal of creamy lace, and innumerable yards of palest azure and palest rose ribbon in the confection, and there was a coquettish little hat, the regular Dresden hat, with a wreath of rosebuds.

'Dresden china incarnate!' exclaimed Smithson, as he welcomed Lady Lesbia on the threshold of his marble hall, under the glass marquise which sheltered arrivals at his door. 'Why do you make yourself so lovely? I shall want to keep you in one of my Louis Seize cabinets, with the rest of my Dresden!'

Lady Kirkbank had considered the occasion suitable for one of her favourite cotton frocks and rustic hats--a Leghorn hat, with clusters Of dog-roses and honeysuckle, and a trail of the same hedge-flowers to fasten her muslin fichu.

Mr. Smithson's house in Park Lane was simply perfect. It is wonderful what good use a *parvenu* can make of his money nowadays, and how rarely he disgraces himself by any marked offences against good taste. There are so many people at hand to teach the *parvenu* how to furnish his house, or how to choose his stud. If he go wrong it must be by sheer perversity, an arrogant insistence upon being governed by his own ignorant inclinations.

Mr. Smithson was too good a tactician to go wrong in this way. He had taken the trouble to study the market before he went out to buy his goods. He knew that taste and knowledge were to be bought just as easily as chairs and tables, and he went to the right shop. He employed a clever Scotchman, an artist in domestic furniture, to plan his house, and make drawings for the decoration and furniture of every room--and for six months he gave himself up to the task of furnishing.

Money was spent like water. Painters, decorators, cabinet-makers had a merry time of it. Royal Academicians were impressed into the service by large offers, and the final result of Mr. MacWalter's taste and Mr. Smithson's bullion was a palace in the style of the Italian Renaissance, frescoed ceilings, painted panels, a staircase of sculptured marble, as beautiful as a dream, a conservatory as exquisite as a jewel casket by Benvenuto Cellini, a picture gallery which was the admiration of all London, and of the enlightened foreigner, and of the inquiring American. This was the house which Lesbia had been brought to see, and through which she walked with the calmly critical air of a person who had seen so many palaces that one more or less could make no difference.

In vain did Mr. Smithson peruse her countenance in the hope of seeing that she was impressed by the splendour of his surroundings, and by the power of the man who commanded such splendour. Lesbia was as cold as the Italian sculptor's Reading Girl in an alcove of Mr. Smithson's picture gallery; and the stockbroker felt very much as Aladdin might have done if the fair Badroulbadour had shown herself indifferent to the hall of the jewelled windows, in that magical palace which sprang into being in a single night.

Lesbia had been impressed by that story of poor Belle Trinder and by Lady Kirkbank's broad assertion that half the young women in London were running after Mr. Smithson; and she had made up her mind to treat the man with supreme scorn. She did not want his houses or his yachts. Nothing could induce her to marry such a man, she told herself; but her vanity fed upon the idea of his subjugation, and her pride was gratified by the sense of her power over him.

The guests were few and choice. There was Mr. Meander, the poet, one of the leading lights in that new sect which prides itself upon the cultivation of abstract beauty, and occasionally touches the verge of concrete ugliness. There were a newspaper man--the editor of a fashionable journal--and a middle-aged man of letters, playwright, critic, humourist, a man whose society was in demand everywhere, and who said sharp things with the most supreme good-nature. The only ladies whose society Mr. Smithson had deemed worthy the occasion were a fashionable actress, with her younger sister, the younger a pretty copy of the elder, both dressed picturesquely in flowing cashmere gowns of faint sea-green, with old lace fichus, leghorn hats, and a general limpness and simplicity of style which suited their cast of feature and delicate colouring. Lesbia wondered to see how good an effect could be produced by a costume which could have cost so little. Mr. Nightshade, the famous tragedian, had been also asked to grace the feast, but the early hour made the invitation a mockery. It was not to be supposed that a man who went to bed at daybreak would get up again before the sun was in the zenith, for the sake of Mr. Smithson's society, or Mr. Smithson's Strasbourg pie, for the manufacture whereof a particular breed of geese were supposed to be set apart, like sacred birds in Egypt, while a particular vineyard in the Gironde was supposed to be devoted wholly and solely to the production of Mr. Smithson's claret. It was a cabinet wine, like those rare vintages of the Rhineland which are reserved exclusively for German princes.

Breakfast was served in Mr. Smithson's smallest dining-room--there were three apartments given up to feasting, beginning with a spacious banqueting-room for great dinners, and dwindling down to this snuggery, which held about a dozen comfortably, with ample room and verge enough for the attendants. The walls were old gold silk, the curtains a tawny velvet of deeper tone, the cabinets and buffet of dark Italian walnut, inlaid with lapis-lazuli and amber. The fireplace was a masterpiece of cabinet work, with high narrow shelves, and curious recesses holding priceless jars of Oriental enamel. The deep hearth was filled with arum lilies and azalias, like a font at Easter.

Lady Kirkbank, who pretended to adore genius, was affectionately effusive to Miss Fitzherbert, the popular actress, but she rather ignored the sister. Lesbia was less cordial, and was not enchanted at finding that Miss Fitzherbert shone and sparkled at the breakfast table by the gaiety of her spirits and the brightness of her conversation. There was something frank and joyous, almost to childishness, in the actress's manner, which was full of fascination; and Lesbia felt herself at a disadvantage almost for the first time since she had been in London.

The editor, the wit, the poet, the actress, had a language of their own; and Lesbia felt herself out in the cold, unable to catch the ball as it glanced past her, not quick enough to follow the wit that evoked those ripples of silvery laughter from the two fair-haired, pale-faced girls in sea-green cashmere. She felt as an Englishman may feel who has made himself master of academical French, and who takes up one of Zola's novels, or goes into artistic society, and finds that there is another French, a complete and copious language, of which he knows not a word.

Lesbia began to think that she had a great deal to learn. She began to wonder even whether, in the event of her having made rather too free use of Lady Maulevrier's *carte blanche*, it might not be well to make a new departure in the art of dressing, and to wear untrimmed cashmere gowns, and rags of limp lace.

After breakfast they all went to look at Mr. Smithson's picture gallery. His pictures were, as he had told Lesbia, chiefly of the French school, and there may have been a remote period--say, in the time of good Queen Charlotte--when such pictures would hardly have been exhibited to young ladies. His pictures were Mr. Smithson's own unaided choice. Here the individual taste of the man stood revealed.

There were two or three Geromes; and in the place of honour at the end of the gallery there was a grand Delaroche, Anne Boleyn's last letter to the king, the hapless girl-queen sitting at a table in her gloomy cell in the Tower, a shaft of golden light from the narrow window streaming on the fair, disordered hair, the face bleached with unutterable woe, a sublime image of despair and self-abandonment.

The larger pictures were historical, classic, grand: but the smaller pictures--the lively little bits of colour dotted in here and there--were of that new school which Mr. Smithson affected. They were of that school which is called Impressionist, in which ballet dancers and jockeys, burlesque actresses, masked balls, and all the humours of the side scenes are represented with the sublime audacity of an art which disdains finish, and relies on **chic, fougue, chien, flou, v'lan**, the inspiration of the moment. Lesbia blushed as she looked at the ballet girls, the maskers in their scanty raiment, the **demi-mondaines** lolling out of their opera boxes, and half out of their gowns, with false smiles and frizzled hair. And then there came the works of that other school which lavishes the finish of a Meissonier on the most meretricious compositions. A woman in a velvet gown warming her dainty little feet on a gilded fender, in a boudoir all aglow with colour and lamplight; a cavalier in satin raiment buckling his sword-belt before a Venetian mirror; a pair of lovers kissing in a sunlit corridor; a girl in a hansom cab; a milliner's shop; and so on, and so on.

Then came the classical subjects of the last new school. Weak imitations of Alma Tadema. Nero admiring his mother's corpse; Claudius interrupting Messalina's marriage with her lover Silus; Clodius disguised among the women of Caesar's household; Pyrrha's grotto. Lady Kirkbank expatiated upon all the pictures, and generally made unlucky guesses at the subjects of them. Classical literature was not her strong point.

Mr. Meander, the poet, discovered that all the beautiful heads were like Miss Fitzherbert. 'It is the same line,' he exclaimed, 'the line of lilies and flowing waters--the gracious ineffable upward returning ripple of the true *retrousse* nose, the divine *flou*, the loveliness which has lain dormant for centuries--nay, was at one period of debased art scorned and trampled under foot by the porcine multitude, as akin to the pug and the turn-up, until discovered and enshrined on the altar of the Beautiful by the Boticelli Revivalists.'

Miss Fitzherbert simpered, and accepted these remarks as mere statements of obvious fact. She was accustomed to hear of Boticelli and the early Italian painters in connection with her own charms of face and figure.

Lesbia, whose faultless features were of the aquiline type, regarded the bard's rhapsody as insufferable twaddle, and began to think Mr. Smithson almost a wit when he made fun of the bard.

Smithson was enchanted when she laughed at his jokelets, even although she did not scruple to tell him that she thought his favourite pictures detestable, and looked with the eye of indifference on a collection of jade that was worth a small fortune.

Mr. Meander fell into another rhapsody over those classic cups and shallow little bowls of absinthe-coloured jade.

'Here if you like, are colour and beauty,' he murmured, caressing one of the little cups with the roseate tips of his supple fingers. 'These, dearest Smithson, are worth all the rest of your collection; worth vanloads of your cloisonne enamels, your dragon-jars in blood-colour and blue. This cloudy indefinable substance, not crudely transparent nor yet distinctly opaque, a something which touches the boundary line of two worlds--the real and the ideal. And then the colour! Great heaven, can anything be lovelier than this shadowy tint which is neither yellow nor green; faint, faint as the dawn of newly-awakened day? After the siege of blood-bedabbled Delhi, Baron Rothschild sent a special agent to India to buy him a little jade tea-pot which had been the joy of Eastern Kings. Only a tea-pot. Yet Rothschild deemed it worth a voyage from England to India. That is what the love of the beautiful means, in Jew or Gentile,' concluded the bard, smiling on the company, as they gathered round the Florentine table on which the jade specimens were set out, Lady Kirkbank looking at the little cups and basins as if she thought they were going to do something, after all this fuss had been made about them. It seemed hardly credible that any reasonable being could have given thirty guineas for one of those bits of greenish-yellow clouded glass, unless the thing had some peculiar property of expansion or contraction.

After this breakfast in Park Lane Lady Lesbia and her admirer met daily. He went to all her parties; he sat out waltzes with her, in conservatories, and on stair-cases; for Horace Smithson was much too shrewd a man too enter himself in the race for dancing men, handicapped by his forty years and his fourteen stone. He contrived to amuse Lesbia by his conversation, which was essentially mundane, depreciating people whom all the rest of the world admired, or pretended to ad-mire, telling her of the secret springs by which the society she saw around her was moved. He was judicious in his revelations of hidden evil, and careful to say nothing which should offend Lady Lesbia's modesty; yet he contrived in a very short time to teach her that the world in which she lived was an utterly corrupt world, whose high priest was Satan; that all lofty aspirations and noble sentiments were out of place in society; and that the worst among the people she met were the people who laid any claim to being better than their neighbours.

'That's why I adore Lady Kirkbank,' he said, confidentially. 'The dear soul nev-er pretends to be any better than the rest of us. She gambles, and we all know she gambles; she pegs, and we all know she pegs; and she makes rather a boast of being up to her eyes in debt. No humbug about dear old Georgie.'

Lesbia had seen enough, of her chaperon by this time to know that Mr. Smith-son's description of the lady was correct, and, this being so, she supposed that the facts and traits of character which he told her about in other people were also true. She thus adopted the Smithsonian, or fashionable-pessimist view of society in gen-eral, and resigned herself to the idea that the world was a very wicked world, as well as a very pleasant world, that the wickedest people were generally the pleas-antest, and that it did not much matter.

The fact that Mr. Smithson was at Lesbia Haselden's feet was obvious to every-body.

Lesbia, who had at first treated him with supreme hauteur, had grown more civil as she began to understand the place he held in the world, and how much social influence goes along with unlimited wealth. She was civil, but she had quite made up her mind that nothing could ever induce her to become Horace Smithson's wife. That offer which had hung fire in the case of poor Belle Trinder, was not too long delayed on this occasion. Mr. Smithson called in Arlington Street about ten days after the breakfast in Park Lane, before luncheon, and before Lady Kirkbank had left her room. He brought tickets for a *matinee d'invitation* in Belgrave Square, at which a new and wonderful Russian pianiste was to make a kind of semi-official *debut*, before an audience of critics and distinguished amateurs, and the elect of the musical world. They wore tickets which money could not buy, and were thus a meet offering for Lady Lesbia, and a plausible excuse for an early call.

Mr. Smithson succeeded in seeing Lesbia alone, and then and there, with very little circumlocution, asked her to be his wife.

Her social education had advanced considerably since that summer day in the pine-wood, when John Hammond had wooed her with passionate wooing. Mr. Smithson was a much less ardent suitor, and made his offer with the air of a man who expects to be accepted.

Lesbia's beautiful head bent a little, like a lily on its stalk, and a faint blush deepened the pale rose tint of her complexion. Her reply was courteous and conventional. She was flattered, she was grateful for Mr. Smithson's high opinion of her; but she was deeply grieved if anything in her manner had given him reason to think that he was more to her than a friend, an old friend of dear Lady Kirkbank's, whom she was naturally predisposed to like, as Lady Kirkbank's friend.

Horace Smithson turned pale as death, but if he was angry, he gave no utterance to his angry feelings. He only asked if Lady Lesbia's answer was final--and on being told that it was so, he dismissed the subject in the easiest manner, and with a gentlemanlike placidity which very much astonished the lady.

'You say that you regard me as your friend,' he said. 'Do not withdraw that privilege from me because I have asked for a higher place in your esteem. Forget all I have said this morning. Be assured I shall never offend you by repeating it.'

'You are more than good,' murmured Lesbia, who had expected a wild outbreak of despair or fury, rather than this friendly calm.

'I hope that you and Lady Kirkbank will go and hear Madame Metzikoff this afternoon,' pursued Mr. Smithson, returning to the subject of the *matinee*. 'The duchess's rooms are lovely; but no doubt you know them.'

Lesbia blushed, and confessed that the Duchess of Lostwithiel was one of those select few who were not on Lady Kirkbank's visiting list.

'There are people Lady Kirkbank cannot get on with,' she said. 'Perhaps she will hardly like to go to the duchess's, as she does not visit her.'

'Oh, but this affair counts for nothing. We go to hear Metzikoff, not to bow down to the duchess. All the people in town who care for music will be there, and you who play so divinely must enjoy fine professional playing.'

'I worship a really great player,' said Lesbia, 'and if I can drag Lady Kirkbank to the house of the enemy, we will be there.'

On this Mr. Smithson discreetly murmured '*au revoir*,' took up his hat and cane, and departed, without, in Sir George's parlance, having turned a hair.

'Refusal number one,' he said to himself, as he went downstairs, with his leisurely catlike pace, that velvet step by which he had gradually crept into society. 'We may have to go through refusal number two and number three; but she means to have me. She is a very clever girl for a countrybred one; and she knows that it is worth her while to be Lady Lesbia Smithson.'

This soliloquy may be taken to prove that Horace Smithson knew Lesbia Haselden better than she knew herself. She had refused him in all good faith; but even to-day, after he had left her, she fell into a day-dream in which Mr. Smithson's houses and yachts, drags and hunters, formed the shifting pictures in a dissolving view of society; and Lesbia wondered if there were any other young woman in London who would refuse such an offer as that which she had quietly rejected half-an-hour ago.

Lady Kirkbank surprised her while she was still absorbed in this dreamy review of the position. It is just possible that the fair Georgie may have had notice of Mr. Smithson's morning visit, and may have kept out of the way on purpose, for she was not a person of lazy habits, and was generally ready for her nine o'clock breakfast and her morning stroll in the park, however late she might have been out overnight.

'Mr. Smithson has been here, I understand,' said Lady Kirkbank, settling herself in an arm-chair by the open window, after she had kissed her *protegee*. 'Rilboche passed him on the stairs.'

'Rilboche is always passing people on the stairs,' answered Lesbia rather pettishly. 'I think she must spend her life on the landing, listening for arrivals and departures.'

'I had a kind of vague idea that Smithson would call to-day. He was so fussy about those tickets for the Metzikoff recital. I hate pianoforte recitals, and I detest that starched old duchess, but I suppose I shall have to take you there--or poor Smithson will be miserable,' said Lady Kirkbank, watching Lesbia keenly over the top of the newspaper.

She expected Lesbia to confide in her, to announce herself blushingly as the betrothed of one of the richest commoners in England. But Lesbia sat gazing dreamily across the flowers in the balcony at the house over the way, and said never a word; so Lady Kirkbank's curiosity burst into speech.

'Well, my dear, has he proposed? There was something in his manner last night when he put on your wraps that made me think the crisis was near.'

'The crisis is come and is past, and Mr. Smithson and I are just as good friends as ever.'

'What!' screamed Lady Kirkbank. 'Do you mean to tell me that you have refused him?'

'Certainly. You know I never meant to do anything else. Did you think I was like Miss Trinder, bent upon marrying town and country houses, stables and diamonds?'

'I did not think you were a fool,' cried Lady Kirkbank, almost beside herself with vexation, for it had been borne in upon her, as the Methodists sometimes say, that if Mr. Smithson should prosper in his wooing it would be better for her, Lady Kirkbank, who would have a claim upon his kindness ever after. 'What can be your motive in refusing one of the very best matches of the season--or of ever so many seasons? You think, perhaps, you will marry a duke, if you wait long enough for his Grace to appear: but the number of marrying dukes is rather small, Lady Lesbia, and I don't think any of those would care to marry Lord Maulevrier's granddaughter.'

Lesbia started to her feet, pale as ashes.

'Why do you fling my grandfather's name in my face--and with that diabolical sneer?' she exclaimed. 'When I have asked you about him you have always evaded my questions. Why should a man of the highest rank shrink from marrying Lord Maulevrier's granddaughter? My grandfather was a distinguished man--Governor of Madras. Such posts are not given to nobodies. How can you dare to speak as if it were a disgrace to me to belong to him?'

CHAPTER XXVIII.
'CLUBS, DIAMONDS, HEARTS, IN
WILD DISORDER SEEN.'

Lady Kirkbank had considerable difficulty in smoothing Lesbia's ruffled plumage. She did all in her power to undo the effect of her rash words--declared that she had been carried away by temper--she had spoken she knew not what--words of no meaning. Of course Lesbia's grandfather had been a great man--Governor of Madras; altogether an important and celebrated person--and Lady Kirkbank had meant nothing, could have meant nothing to his disparagement.

'My dearest girl, I was beside myself, and talked sheer nonsense,' said Georgie. 'But you know really now, dearest, any woman of the world would be provoked at your foolish refusal of that dear good Smithson. Only think of that too lovely house in Park Lane, a palace in the style of the Italian Renaissance--such a house is in itself equivalent to a peerage--and there is no doubt Smithson will be offered a peerage before he is much older. I have heard it confidently asserted that when the present Ministry retires Smithson will be made a Peer. You have no idea what a useful man he is, or what henchman's service he has done the Ministry in financial matters. And then there is his villa at Deauville--you don't know Deauville--a positively perfect place, the villa, I mean, built by the Duke de Morny in the golden days of the Empire--and another at Cowes, and his palace in Berkshire, a manor, my love, with a glorious old Tudor manor-house; and he has a ***pied a terre*** in Paris, in the Faubourg, a ground-floor furnished in the Pompeian style, half-a-dozen rooms opening one out of the other, and surrounding a small garden, with a fountain in the middle. Some of the greatest people in Paris occupy the upper part of the house, and their rooms of course are splendid; but Smithson's ground-floor is the gem of the Faubourg. However, I suppose there is no use in talking any more; for there is the gong for luncheon.'

Lesbia was in no humour for luncheon.

'I would rather have a cup of tea in my own room,' she said. 'This Smithson business has given me an abominable headache.'

'But you will go to hear Metzikoff?'

'No, thanks. You detest the Duchess of Lostwithiel, and you don't care for pi-anoforte recitals. Why should I drag you there?'

'But, my dearest Lesbia, I am not such a selfish wretch as to keep you at home, when I know you are passionately fond of good music. Forget all about your head-ache, and let me see how that lovely little Catherine of Aragon bonnet suits you. I'm so glad I happened to see it in Seraphine's hands yesterday, just as she was going to send it to Lady Fonvielle, who gives herself such intolerable airs on the strength of a pretty face, and always wants to get the *primeures* in bonnets and things.'

'Another new bonnet!' replied Lesbia. 'What an infinity of things I seem to be having from Seraphine. I'm afraid I must owe her a good deal of money.'

This was a vague way of speaking about actual facts. Lady Lesbia might have spoken with more certainty. Her wardrobes and old-fashioned hanging closets and chests of drawers in Arlington Street were crammed to overflowing with finery; and then there were all the things that she had grown tired of, or had thought un-becoming, and had given away to Kibble, her own maid, or to Rilboche, who had in a great measure superseded Kibble on all important occasions; for how could a Westmoreland girl know how to dress a young lady for London balls and drawing-rooms?

'If you had only accepted Mr. Smithson it would not matter how much money you owed people,' said Lady Kirkbank. 'You had better come down to lunch. A glass of Heidseck will bring you up to concert pitch.'

Champagne was Lady Kirkbank's idea of a universal panacea; and she had grad-ually succeeded in teaching Lesbia to believe in the sovereign power of Heidseck as a restorative for shattered nerves. At Fellside Lesbia had drunk only water; but then at Fellside she had never known that feeling of exhaustion and prostration which follows days and nights spent in society, the wear and tear of a mind forever on the alert, and brilliant spirits which are more often forced than real. For her chief stimulant Lesbia had recourse to the teapot; but there were occasions when she found that something more than tea was needed to maintain that indispensable vivacity of manner which Lady Kirkbank called concert pitch.

To-day she allowed herself to be persuaded. She went down to luncheon, and took a couple of glasses of dry champagne with her cutlet, and, thus restored, was equal to putting on the new bonnet, which was so becoming that her spirits revived as she contemplated the effect in her glass. So Lady Kirkbank carried her off to the musical *matinee*, beaming and radiant, having forgotten all about that dark hint of evil glancing at the name of her long dead grandfather.

The duchess was not on view when Lady Kirkbank and her *protegee* arrived, and a good many people belonging to Georgie's own particular set were scattered like flowers among those real music-lovers who had come solely to hear the new pianiste. The music-lovers were mostly dowdy in their attire, and seemed a race apart. Among them were several young women of the Blessed Damozel school, who wore flowing garments of sap-green or orche, or puffed raiment of Venetian red, and among whom the cartwheel hat, the Elizabethan sleeve, and the Toby frill were conspicuous.

There were very few men except the musical critics in this select assemblage, and Lesbia began to think that it was going to be very dreary. She had lived in such an atmosphere of masculine adulation while under Lady Kirkbank's wing that it was a new thing to find herself in a room where there were none to love and very few to praise her. She felt out in the cold, as it were. Those ungloved critics, with their shabby coats and dubious shirts, snuffy, smoky, everything they ought not to be, seemed to her a race of barbarians.

Finding herself thus cold and lonely in the midst of the duchess's splendour of peacock-blue velvet and peacock-feather decoration, Lesbia was almost glad when in the middle of Madame Metzikoff's opening gondolied--airy, fairy music, executed with surpassing delicacy--Mr. Smithson crept gently into the *fauteuil* just behind hers, and leant over the back of the chair to whisper an inquiry as to her opinion of the pianist's style.

'She is exquisite,' Lesbia murmured softly, but the whispered question and the murmured answer, low as they were, provoked indignant looks from a brace of damsels in Venetian red, who shook their Toby frills with an outraged air.

Lesbia felt that Mr. Smithson's presence was hardly correct. It would have been 'better form' if he had stayed away; and yet she was glad to have him here. At the worst he was some one--nay, according to Lady Kirkbank, he was the only one amongst all her admirers whose offer was worth having. All Lesbia's other conquests had counted as barren honour; but if she could have brought herself to accept Mr. Smithson she would have secured the very best match of the season.

To marry a plain Mr. Smithson--a man who had made his money in iron--in cochineal--on the Stock Exchange--had seemed to her absolute degradation, the surrender of all her lofty hopes, her golden dreams. But Lady Kirkbank had put the question in a new light when she said that Smithson would be offered a peerage. Smithson the peer would be altogether a different person from Smithson the commoner.

But was Lady Kirkbank sure of her facts, or truthful in her statement? Lesbia's experience of her chaperon's somewhat loose notions of truth and exactitude made her doubtful upon this point.

Be this it might she was inclined to be civil to Smithson, albeit she was inwardly surprised and offended at his taking her refusal so calmly.

'You see that I am determined not to lose the privilege of your society, because I have been foolish!' he said presently, in the pause after the first part of the recital. 'I hope you will consider me as much your friend to-day as I was yesterday.'

'Quite as much,' she answered sweetly, and then they talked of Raff, and Rubenstein, and Henselt, and all the composers about whom it is the correct thing to discourse nowadays.

Before they left Belgrave Square Lady Kirkbank had offered Mr. Smithson Sir George's place in her box at the Gaiety that evening, and had invited him to supper in Arlington Street afterwards.

It was Sarah Bernhardt's first season in London--the never-to-be-forgotten season of the Comedie Francaise.

'I should love of all things to be there,' said Mr. Smithson, meekly. He had a couple of stalls in the third row for the whole of the season. 'But how can I be sure that I shall not be turning Sir George out of doors?'

'Sir George can never sit out a serious play. He only cares for Chaumont or Judie. The Demi-monde is much too prosy for him.'

'The Demi-monde is one of the finest plays in the French language,' said Smithson. 'You know it, of course, Lady Lesbia?'

'Alas! no. At Fellside I was not allowed to read French plays or novels: or only a novel now and then, which my grandmother selected for me.'

'And now you read everything, I suppose,--including Zola?'

'The books are lying about, and I dip into them sometimes while I am having my hair brushed,' answered Lesbia, lightly.

'I believe that is the only time ladies devote to literature during the season,' said Mr. Smithson. 'Well, I envy you the delight of seeing the Demi-monde without knowing what it is all about beforehand.'

'I daresay there are a good many people who would not take their girls to see a play by Dumas,' said Lady Kirkbank, 'but I make a point of letting *my* girls see everything. It widens their minds and awakens their intelligence.'

'And does away with a good many silly prejudices,' replied Mr. Smithson.

Lady Kirkbank and Lesbia were due at a Kensington garden-party after the recital, and from the garden-party, for which any hour sufficed, they went to show themselves in the Park, then back to Arlington Street to dress for the play. Then a hurried dinner, and they were in their places at the theatre in time for the rising of the curtain.

'If it were an English play we would not care for being punctual,' said Lady Kirkbank; 'but I should hate to lose a word of Dumas. In his plays every speech tells.'

There were Royalties present, and the house was good; but not so full as it had been on some other nights, for the English public had been told that Sarah Bernhardt was the person to admire, and had been flocking sheep-like after that golden-haired enchantress, whereby many of these sheep--fighting greedily for Sarah's nights, and ignoring all other talent--lost some of the finest acting on the French stage, notably that of Croizette, Delaunay and Febvre, in this very Demi-monde. Lesbia, who, in spite of her affectations, was still fresh enough to be charmed with fine acting and a powerful play, was enthralled by the stage, so wrapt in the scene that she was quite unaware of her brother's presence in a stall just below Lady Kirkbank's box. He too had a stall at the Gaiety. He had come in very late, when the play was half over. Lesbia was surprised when he presented himself at the door of the box, after the fourth act.

Maulevrier and his sister had met very seldom since the young lady's *debut*. The young Earl did not go to many parties, and the society he cultivated was chiefly masculine; and as he neither played polo nor shot pigeons his masculine pursuits did not bring him in his sister's way. Lady Kirkbank had asked him to her house with that wide and general invitation which is so easily evaded. He had promised to go, and he had not gone. And thus Lesbia and he had pursued their several ways, only crossing each other's paths now and then at a race meeting or in a theatre.

'How d'ye do, Lady Kirkbank?--how d'ye do, Lesbia? Just caught sight of you from below as the curtain was going down,' said Maulevrier, shaking hands with the ladies and saluting Mr. Smithson with a somewhat supercilious nod. 'Rather surprised to see you and Lesbia here to-night, Lady Kirkbank. Isn't the Demi-monde rather strong meat for babes, eh? Not *exactly* the play one would take a young lady to see.'

'Why should a young lady be forbidden to see a fine play, because there are some hard and bitter truths told in it?' asked Lady Kirkbank. 'Lesbia sees Madame d'Ange and all her sisterhood in the Park and about London every day of her life. Why should not she see them on the stage, and hear their history, and understand how cruel their fate is, and learn to pity them, if she can? I really think this play is a lesson in Christian charity; and I should like to see that Oliver man strangled, though Delaunay plays the part divinely. What a voice! What a manner! How polished! How perfect! And they tell me he is going to leave the stage in a year or two. What will the world do without him?'

Maulevrier did not attempt to suggest a solution of this difficulty. He was watching Mr. Smithson as he leant against the back of Lesbia's chair and talked to her. The two seemed very familiar, laughingly discussing the play and the actors. Smithson knew, or pretended to know, all about the latter. He told Lesbia who made Croizette's gowns--the upholsterer who furnished that lovely house of hers in the Bois--the sums paid for her horses, her pictures, her diamonds. It seemed to Lesbia, when she had heard all, that Croizette was a much-to-be-envied person.

Mr. Smithson had unpublished *bon-mots* of Dumas at his finger ends; he knew Daudet, and Sarcey, and Sardou, and seemed to be thoroughly at home in Parisian artistic society. Lesbia began to think that he would hardly be so despicable a person as she had at first supposed. No wonder he and his wealth had turned poor Belle Trinder's head. How could a rural vicar's daughter, accustomed to poverty, help being dazzled by such magnificence?

Maulevrier stayed in the box only a short time, and refused Lady Kirkbank's invitation to supper. She did not urge the point, as she had surprised one or two very unfriendly glances at Mr. Smithson in Maulevrier's honest eyes. She did not want an antagonistic brother to interfere with her plans. She had made up her mind to 'run' Lesbia according to her own ideas, and any counter influence might be fatal. So, when Maulevrier said he was due at the Marlborough after the play she let him go.

'I might as well be at Fellside and you in London, for anything I see of you,' said Lesbia.

'You are up to your eyes in engagements, and I don't suppose you want to see any more of me.' Maulevrier answered, bluntly.

'But I'll call to-morrow morning, if I am likely to find you at home. I've some news for you.'

'Then I'll stay at home on purpose to see you. News is always delightful. Is it good news, by-the-bye?'

'Very good; at least, I think so.'

'What is it about?'

'Oh! that's a long story, and the curtain is just going up. The news is about Mary.'

'About Mary!' exclaimed Lesbia, elevating her eyebrows. 'What news can there possibly be about Mary?'

'Such news as there generally is about every nice jolly girl, at least once in her life.'

'You don't mean that she is engaged--to a curate?'

'No, not to a curate. There goes the curtain. "I'll see you later," as the Yankee President used to say when people bothered him, and he didn't like to say no.'

Engaged: Mary engaged! The idea of such an altogether unexpected event distracted Lesbia's mind all through the last act of the Demi-monde. She hardly knew what the actors were talking about. Mary, her younger sister! Mary, a good looking girl enough, but by no means a beauty, and with manners utterly unformed. That Mary should be engaged to be married, while she, Lesbia, was still free, seemed an obvious absurdity.

And yet the fact was, on reflection, easily to be accounted for. These unattractive girls are generally the first to bind themselves with the vows of betrothal.

Lady Kirkbank had told her of many such cases. The poor creatures know that their chances will be few, and therefore gratefully welcome the first wooer.

'But who can the man be?' thought Lesbia. 'Mary has been kept as secluded as a cloistered nun. There are so few families we have ever been allowed to mix with. The man must be a curate, who has taken advantage of grandmother's illness to force his way into the family circle at Fellside--and who has made love to Mary in some of her lonely rambles over the hills, I daresay. It is really very wrong to allow a girl to roam about in that way.'

Sir George and a couple of his horsey friends were waiting for supper when Lady Kirkbank and her party arrived in Arlington Street. The dining-room looked a picture of comfort. The oval table, the low lamps, the clusters of candles under coloured shades, the great Oriental bowl of wild flowers--eglantine, honeysuckle, foxglove, all the sweet hedge flowers of midsummer, made a central mass of colour and brightness against the subdued and even sombre tones of walls and curtains. The room was old, the furniture old. Nothing had been altered since the time of Sir George's great grandfather; and the whirligig of time had just now made the old things precious. Yes, those chairs and tables and sideboards and bookcases and wine-coolers against which Georgie's soul had revolted in the early years of her wedded life were now things of beauty, and Georgie's friends envied her the possession of indisputable Chippendale furniture.

Mr. Mostyn, a distinguished owner of race-horses, with his pretty wife, made up the party. The gentleman was full of his entries for Liverpool and Chester, and discoursed mysteriously with Sir George and the horsey bachelors all supper time. The lady had lately taken up science as a new form of excitement, not incompatible with frocks, bonnets, Hurlingham, the Ranelagh, and Sandown. She raved about Huxley and Tyndall, and was perpetually coming down upon her friends with awful facts about the sun, and startling propositions about latent heat, or spontaneous generation. She knew all about gases, and would hardly accept a glass of water without explaining what it was made of. Drawn by Mr. Smithson for Lesbia's amusement, the scientific matron was undoubtedly 'good fun.' The racing men were full of talk. Lesbia and Lady Kirkbank raved about the play they had just been seeing, and praised Delaunay with an enthusiasm which was calculated to make the rest of mankind burst with envy.

'Do you know you are making me positively wretched by your talk about that man?' said Colonel Delville, one of Sir George's racing friends, and an ancient adorer of the fair Georgie's. 'No, I tell you there was never anything offered higher than five to four on the mare,' interjectionally, to Sir George. 'There was a day when I thought I was your idea of an attractive man. Yes, George, a clear case of roping,' again interjectionally. 'And to hear you raving about this play-acting fellow--it is too humiliating.'

Lady Kirkbank simpered, and then sighed.

'We are getting old together,' she murmured. 'I have come to an age when one can only admire the charm of manner in the abstract--the Beautiful for the sake of the Beautiful. I think if I were lying in my grave, the music of Delaunay's voice would thrill me, under six feet of London clay. Will no one take any more wine? No. Then we may as well go into the next room and begin our little Nap.'

The adjoining room was Sir George's snuggery; and it was here that the cosy little round games after supper were always played. Sir George was not a studious person. He never read, and he never wrote, except an occasional cheque on account, for an importunate tradesman. His correspondence was conducted by the telegraph or telephone; and the room, therefore, was absorbed neither by books nor writing desks. It was furnished solely with a view to comfort. There was a round table in the centre, under a large moderator lamp which gave an exceptionally brilliant light. A divan covered with dark brown velvet occupied three sides of the room. A few choice pieces of old blue Oriental ware in the corners enlivened the dark brown walls. Three or four easy chairs stood about near the broad, old-fashioned fireplace, which had been improved with a modern-antique brass grate and a blue and white tiled hearth.

'There isn't a room in my house that looks half as comfortable as this den of yours, George,' said Mr. Smithson, as he seated himself by Lesbia's side at the card table.

They had agreed to be partners. 'Partners at cards, even if we are not to be partners for life,' Smithson had whispered, tenderly; and Lesbia's only reply had been a modest lowering of lovely eyelids, and a faint, faint blush. Lesbia's blushes were growing fainter every day.

'That is because everything in your house is so confoundedly handsome and expensive,' retorted Sir George, who did not very much care about being called George, *tout court*, by a person of Mr. Smithson's obscure antecedents, but who had to endure the familiarity for reasons known only to himself and Mr. Smithson. 'No man can expect to be comfortable in a house in which every room has cost a small fortune. My wife re-arranged this den half-a-dozen years ago when we took to sittin' here of an evenin'. She picked up the chairs and the blue pots at Bonham's, had everythin' covered with brown velvet--nice subdued tone, suit old people-- hung up that yaller curtain, just for a bit of colour, and here we are.'

'It's the cosiest room in town,' said Colonel Delville, whereupon Mrs. Mostyn, while counters were being distributed, explained to the company on scientific principles *why* the room was comfortable, expatiating upon the effect of yellow and brown upon the retina, and some curious facts relating to the optic machinery of water-fleas, as lately discovered by a great naturalist.

Unfortunately for science, the game had now begun, and the players were curiously indifferent as to the visual organs of water-fleas.

The game went on merrily till the pearly lights of dawn began to creep through the chinks of Lady Kirkbank's yellow curtain. Everybody seemed gay, yet everybody could not be winning. Fortune had not smiled upon Lesbia's cards, or on those of her partner. The Smithson and Haselden firm had come to grief. Lesbia's little ivory purse had been emptied of its three or four half-sovereigns, and Mr. Smithson had been capitalising a losing concern for the last two hours. And the play had been fast and furious, although nominally for small stakes.

'I am afraid to think of how much I must owe you,' said Lesbia, when Mr. Smithson bade her good night.

'Oh, nothing worth speaking of--sixteen or seventeen pounds, at most.'

Lesbia felt cold and creepy, and hardly knew whether it was the chill of new-born day, or the sense of owing money to Horace Smithson. Those three or four half-sovereigns to-night were the end of her last remittance from Lady Maulevrier. She had had a great many remittances from that generous grandmother; and the money had all gone, somehow. It was gone, and yet she had paid for hardly anything. She had accounts with all Lady Kirkbank's tradesmen. The money had melted away--it had oozed out of her pockets--at cards, on the race-course, in reckless gifts to servants and people, at fancy fairs, for trifles bought here and there by the way-side, as it were, for the sake of buying. If she had been suddenly asked for an account of her stewardship she could not have told what she had done with half of the money. And now she must ask for twenty pounds more, and immediately, to pay Mr. Smithson.

She went up to her room in the clear early light, and stood like a statue, with fixed thoughtful eyes, while Kibble took off her finery, the pretty pale yellow gown which set off her dark brown hair, her violet eyes. For the first time in her life she felt the keen pang of anxiety about money matters--the necessity to think of ways and means. She had no idea how much money she had received from her grand-mother since she had begun her career in Scotland last autumn. The cheques had been sent her as she asked for them; sometimes even before she asked for them; and she had kept no account. She thought her grandmother was so rich that expendi-ture could not matter. She supposed that she was drawing upon an inexhaustible supply. And now Lady Kirkbank had told her that Lady Maulevrier was not rich, as the world reckons nowadays. The savings of a dowager countess even in forty years of seclusion could be but a small fund to draw upon for the expenses of life at high pressure.

'The sums people spend nowadays are positively appalling,' said Lady Kirk-bank. 'A man with five or six thousand a year is an absolute pauper. I'm sure our existence is only genteel beggary, and yet we spend over ten thousand.'

Enlightened thus by the lips of the worldly-wise, Lesbia thought ruefully of the bills which her grandmother would have to pay for her at the end of the season, bills of the amount whereof she could not even make an approximate guess. Sera-phine's charges had never been discussed in her hearing--but Lady Kirkbank had admitted that the creature was dear.

CHAPTER XXIX.
'SWIFT SUBTLE POST, CARRIER OF GRISLY CARE.'

Maulevrier called in Arlington Street before twelve o'clock next day, and found Lesbia just returning from her early ride, looking as fresh and fair as if there had been no such thing as Nap or late hours in the story of her life. She was reposing in a large easy chair by the open window, in habit and hat, just as she had come from the Row, where she had been laughing and chatting with Mr. Smithson, who jogged demurely by her side on his short-legged hunter, dropping out envenomed little jokes about the passers by. People who saw him riding by her side upon this particular morning fancied there was something more than usual in the gentleman's manner, and made up their minds that Lady Lesbia Haselden was to be mistress of the fine house in Park Lane. Mr. Smithson had fluttered and fluttered for the last five seasons; but this time the flutterer was caught.

In her newly-awakened anxiety about money matters, Lesbia had forgotten Mary's engagement: but the sight of Maulevrier recalled the fact.

'Come over here and sit down,' she said, 'and tell me this nonsense about Mary. I am expiring with curiosity. The thing is too absurd.'

'Why absurd?' asked Maulevrier, sitting where she bade him, and studiously perusing the name in his hat, as if it were a revelation.

'Oh, for a thousand reasons,' answered Lesbia, switching the flowers in the balcony with her light little whip. 'First and foremost it is absurd to think of any one so buried alive as poor Mary is finding an admirer; and secondly--well--I don't want to be rude to my own sister--but Mary is not particularly attractive.'

'Mary is the dearest girl in the world.'

'Very likely. I only said that she is not particularly attractive.'

'And do you think there is no attraction in goodness, in freshness and innocence, candour, generosity--?'

'I don't know. But I think that if Mary's nose had been a thought longer, and if she had kept her skin free from freckles she would have been almost pretty.'

'Do you really? Luckily for Mary the man who is going to marry her thinks her lovely.'

'I suppose he likes freckles. I once heard a man say he did. He said they were so original--so much character about them. And, pray, who is the man?'

'Your old adorer, and my dear friend, John Hammond.'

Lesbia turned as pale as death--pale with rage and mortification. It was not jealousy, this pang which rent her shallow soul. She had ceased to care for John Hammond. The whirlpool of society had spun that first fancy out of her giddy brain. But that a man who had loved the highest, who had worshipped her, the peerless, the beautiful, should calmly transfer his affections to her younger sister, was to the last degree exasperating.

'Your friend Mr. Hammond must be a fickle fool,' she exclaimed, 'who does not know his own mind from day to day.'

'Oh, but it was more than a day after you rejected him that he engaged himself to Molly. It was all my doing, and I am proud of my work. I took the poor fellow back to Fellside last March, bruised and broken by your cruel treatment, heartsore and depressed. I gave him over to Molly, and Molly cured him. Unconsciously, innocently, she won that noble heart. Ah, Lesbia, you don't know what a heart it is which you so nearly broke.'

'Girls in our rank of life can't afford to marry noble hearts,' said Lesbia, scornfully. 'Do you mean to tell me that Lady Maulevrier consented to the engagement?'

'She cut up rather rough at first; but Molly held her own like a young lioness--and the grandmother gave way. You see she has a fixed idea that Molly is a very second-rate sort of person compared with you, and that a husband who was not nearly good enough for you might pass muster for Molly; and so she gave way, and there isn't a happier young woman in the three kingdoms than Mary Haselden.'

'What are they to live upon?' asked Lesbia, with an incredulous air.

'Mary will have her five hundred a year. And Hammond is a very clever fellow. You may be sure he will make his mark in the world.'

'And how are they to live while he is making his mark? Five hundred a year won't do more than pay for Mary's frocks, if she goes into society.'

'Perhaps they will live without society.'

'In some horrid little hovel in one of those narrow streets off Ecclestone Square,' suggested Lesbia, shudderingly. 'It is too dreadful to think of--a young woman dooming herself to life-long penury, just because she is so foolish as to fall in love.'

'Your days for falling in love are over, I suppose, Lesbia?' said Maulevrier, contemplating his sister with keen scrutiny.

The beautiful face, so perfect in line and colour, curiously recalled that other face at Fellside; the dowager's face, with its look of marble coldness, and the half-expressed pain under that, outward calm. Here was the face of one who had not yet known pain or passion. Here was the cold perfection of beauty with unawakened heart.

'I don't know; I am too busy to think of such things.'

'You have done with love; and you have begun to think of marriage, of establishing yourself properly. People tell me you are going to marry Mr. Smithson.'

'People tell you more about me than I know about myself.'

'Come now, Lesbia, I have a right to know the truth upon this point. Your brother--your only brother--should be the first person to be told.'

'When I am engaged, I have no doubt you will be the first person, or the second person,' answered Lesbia, lightly. 'Lady Kirkbank, living on the premises, is likely to be the first.'

'Then you are not engaged to Smithson?'

'Didn't I tell you so just now? Mr. Smithson did me the honour to make me an offer yesterday, at about this hour; and I did myself the honour to reject him.'

'And yet you were whispering together in the box last night, and you were riding in the Row with him this morning. I just met a fellow who saw you together. Do you think it is right, Lesbia, to play fast and loose with the man--to encourage him, if you don't mean to marry him?'

'How can you accuse me of encouraging a person whom I flatly refused yesterday morning? If Mr. Smithson likes my society as a friend, must I needs deny him my friendship, ask Lady Kirkbank to shut her door against him? Mr. Smithson is very pleasant as an acquaintance; and although I don't want to marry him, there's no reason I should snub him.'

'Smithson is not a man to be trifled with. You will find yourself entangled in a web which you won't easily break through.'

'I am not afraid of webs. By-the-bye, is it true that Mr. Smithson is likely to get a peerage?'

'I have heard people say as much. Smithson has spent no end of money on electioneering, and is a power in the House, though he very rarely speaks. His Berkshire estate gives him a good deal of influence in that county; at the last general election he subscribed twenty thou to the Conservative cause; for, like most men who have risen from nothing, your friend Smithson is a fine old Tory. He was specially elected at the Carlton six years ago, and has made himself uncommonly useful to his party. He is supposed to be great on financial questions, and comes out tremendously on colonial railways or drainage schemes, about which the House in general is in profound ignorance. On those occasions Smithson scores high. A man with immense wealth has always chances. No doubt, if you were to marry him, the peerage would be easily managed. Smithson's money, backed by the Maulevrier influence, would go a long way. My grandmother would move heaven and earth in a case of that kind. You had better take pity on Smithson.'

Lesbia laughed. That idea of a possible peerage elevated Smithson in her eyes. She knew nothing of his political career, as she lived in a set which ignored politics altogether. Mr. Smithson had never talked to her of his parliamentary duties; and it was a new thing for her to hear that he had some kind of influence in public affairs.

'Suppose I were inclined to accept him, would you like him as a brother-in-law?' she asked lightly. 'I thought from your manner last night that you rather disliked him.'

'I don't quite like him or any of his breed, the newly rich, who go about in society swelling with the sense of their own importance, perspiring gold, as it were. And one has always a faint suspicion of men who have got rich very quickly, an idea that there must be some kind of juggling. Not in the case of a great contractor, perhaps, who can point to a viaduct and docks and railways, and say, "I built that, and that, and that. These are the sources of my wealth." But a man who gets enormously rich by mere ciphering! Where can his money come from, except out of other people's pockets? I know nothing against your Mr. Smithson, but I always suspect that class of men,' concluded Maulevrier shaking his head significantly.

Lesbia was not much influenced by her brother's notions, she had never been taught to think him an oracle. On the contrary, she had been told that his life hitherto had been all foolishness.'

'When are Mary and Mr. Hammond to be married?' she asked, 'Grandmother says they must wait a year. Mary is much too young--and so on, and so forth. But I see no reason for waiting.'

'Surely there are reasons--financial reasons. Mr. Hammond cannot be in a position to begin housekeeping.'

'Oh, they will risk all that. Molly is a daring girl. He proposed to her on the top of Helvellyn, in a storm of wind and rain.'

'And she never wrote me a word about it. How very unsisterly!'

'She is as wild as a hawk, and I daresay she was too shy to tell you anything about it.'

'Pray when did it all occur?'

'Just before I came to London.'

'Two months ago. How absurd for me to be in ignorance all this time! Well, I hope Mary will be sensible, and not marry till Mr. Hammond is able to give her a decent home. It would be so dreadful to have a sister muddling in poverty, and clamouring for one's cast-off gowns.'

Maulevrier laughed at this gloomy suggestion.

'It is not easy to foretell the future,' he said, 'but I think I may venture to promise that Molly will never wear your cast-off gowns.'

'Oh, you think she would be too proud. You don't know, perhaps, how poverty--genteel poverty--lowers one's pride. I have heard stories from Lady Kirkbank that would make your hair stand on end. I am beginning to know the world.'

'I am glad of that. If you are to live in the world it is better that you should know what it is made of. But if I had a voice or a choice in the matter I had rather my sisters stayed at Grasmere, and remained ignorant of the world and all its ways.'

'While you enjoy your life in London. That is just like the selfishness of a man. Under the pretence of keeping his sisters or his wife secure from all possible contact with evil, he buries them alive in a country house, while he has all the wickedness for his own share in London. Oh, I am beginning to understand the creatures.'

'I am afraid you are beginning to be wise. Remember that knowledge of evil was the prelude to the Fall. Well, good-bye.'

'Won't you stay to lunch?'

'No, thanks, I never lunch--frightful waste of time. I shall drop in at the *Haute Gomme* and take a cup of tea later on.'

The *Haute Gomme* was a new club in Piccadilly, which Maulevrier and some of his friends affected.

Lesbia went towards the drawing-room door with her brother, and just as he reached the door she laid her hand caressingly upon his shoulder. He turned and stared at her, somewhat surprised, for he and she had never been given to demonstrations of affection.

'Maulevrier, I want you to do me a favour,' she said, in a low voice, blushing a little, for the thing she was going to ask was a new thing for her to ask, and she had a deep sense of shame in making her demand. 'I--I lost money at Nap last night. Only seventeen pounds. Mr. Smithson and I were partners, and he paid my losses. I want to pay him immediately, and----'

'And you are too hard up to do it. I'll write you a cheque this instant,' said Maulevrier goodnaturedly; but while he was writing the cheque he took occasion to remonstrate with Lesbia on the foolishness of card playing.

'I am obliged to do as Lady Kirkbank does,' she answered feebly. 'If I were to refuse to play it would be a kind of reproach to her.'

'I don't think that would kill Lady Kirkbank,' replied Maulevrier, with a touch of scorn. 'She has had to endure a good many implied reproaches in her day, and they don't seem to have hurt her very much. I wish to heaven my grandmother had chosen any one else in London for your chaperon.'

'I'm afraid Lady Kirkbank's is rather a rowdy set,' answered Lesbia, coolly; 'and I sometimes feel as if I had thrown myself away. We go almost everywhere--at least, there are only just a few houses to which we are not asked. But those few make all the difference. It is so humiliating to feel that one is not in quite the best society. However, Lady Kirkbank is a dear, good old thing, and I am not going to grumble about her.'

'I've made the cheque for five-and-twenty. You can cash it at your milliner's,' said Maulevrier. 'I should not like Smithson to know that you had been obliged to ask me for the money.'

'*Apropos* to Mr. Smithson, do you know if he is in quite the best society?' asked Lesbia.

'I don't know what you mean by quite the best. A man of Smithson's wealth can generally poke his nose in anywhere, if he knows how to behave himself. But of course there are people with whom money and fine houses have no weight. The Conservatives are all civil to Smithson because he comes down handsomely at General Elections, and is useful to them in other ways. I believe that Smithson's wife, if she were a thorough-bred one, could go into any society she liked, and make her house one of the most popular in London. Perhaps that is what you really wanted to ask.

'No, it wasn't,' answered Lesbia, carelessly; 'I was only talking for the sake of talking. A thousand thanks for the cheque, you best of brothers.'

'It is not worth talking about; but, Lesbia, don't play cards any more. Believe me, it is not good form.'

'Well, I'll try to keep out of it in future. It is horrid to see one's sovereigns melting away; but there's a delightful excitement in winning.'

'No doubt,' answered Maulevrier, with a remorseful sigh.

He spoke as a reformed plunger, and with many a bitter experience of the race-course and the card-room. Even now, though he had steadied himself wonderfully, he could not get on without a little mild gambling--half-crown pool, whist with half-guinea points--but when he condescended to such small stakes he felt that he had settled down into a respectable middle-aged player, and had a right to rebuke the follies of youth.

Lesbia flew to the piano and sang one of her little German ballads directly Maulevrier was gone. She felt as if a burden had been lifted from her soul, now that she was able to pay Mr. Smithson without waiting to ask Lady Maulevrier for the money. And as she sang she meditated upon Maulevrier's remarks about Smithson. He knew nothing to the man's discredit, except that he had grown rich in a short space of time. Surely no man ought to be blamed for that. And he thought that Mr. Smithson's wife might make her house the most popular in London. Lesbia, in her mind's eye, beheld an imaginary Lady Lesbia Smithson giving dances in that magnificent mansion, entertaining Royal personages. And the doorways would be festooned with roses, as she had seen them the other night at a ball in Grosvenor Square; but the house in Grosvenor Square was a hovel compared with the Smithsonian Palace.

Lesbia was beginning to be a little tired of Lady Kirkbank and her surroundings. Life taken *prestissimo* is apt to pall, Lesbia sighed as she finished her little song. She was beginning to look upon her existence as a problem which had been given to her to solve, and the solution just it present was all dark.

As she rose from the piano a footman came in with two letters on a salver--bulky letters, such packages as Lesbia had never seen before. She wondered what they could be. She opened the thickest envelope first. It was Seraphine's bill--such a bill, page after page on creamy Bath post, written in an elegant Italian hand by one of Seraphine's young women.

Lesbia looked at it aghast with horror. The total at the foot of the first page was appalling, ever so much more than she could have supposed the whole amount of her indebtedness; but the total went on increasing at the foot of every page, until at sight of the final figures Lesbia gave a wild shriek, like a wretched creature who has received a telegram announcing bitterest loss.

The final total was twelve hundred and ninety-three pounds seventeen and sixpence!

Thirteen hundred pounds for clothes in eight weeks!

No, the thing was a cheat, a mistake. They had sent her somebody else's bill. She had not had half these things.

She read the first page, her heart beating violently as she pored over the figures, her eyes dim and clouded with the trouble of her brain.

Yes, there was her court dress. The description was too minute to be mistaken; and the court dress, with feathers, and shoes, and gloves, and fan, came to a hundred and thirty pounds. Then followed innumerable items. The very simplest of her gowns cost five-and-twenty pounds--frocks about which Seraphine had talked so carelessly, as if two or three more or less could make no difference. Bonnets and hats, at five or seven guineas apiece, swelled the account. Parasols and fans were of fabulous price, as it seemed to Lesbia; and the shoes and stockings to match her various gowns occurred again and again between the more important items, like the refrain of an old ballad. All the useless and unnessary things which she had ordered, because she thought them pretty or because she was told they were fashionable, rose up against her in the figures of the bill, like the record of forgotten sins at the Day of Judgment.

She sank into a chair, pallid with consternation, and sat with the bill in her lap, turning the pages listlessly, and staring at the figures.

'It cannot be so much,' she cried to herself. 'It must be added up wrong;' and then she feebly tried to cast up a column; but arithmetic not being one of those accomplishments which Lady Maulevrier deemed necessary to a patrician beauty's success in life, Lesbia's education had been somewhat neglected upon this point, and she flung the bill from her in a rage, unable to hold the figures in her brain.

She opened the second envelope, her jeweller's account. At the very first item she gave another scream, fainter than the first, for her mind was getting hardened against such shocks.

'To re-setting a suite of amethysts, with forty-four finest Brazilian brilliants, three hundred and fifteen pounds.'

Then followed the trifles she had bought at different visits to the shop--casual purchases, bought on the impulse of the moment. These swelled the account to a little over eight hundred pounds. Lesbia sat like a statue, numbed by despair, appalled at the idea of owing over two thousand pounds.

CHAPTER XXX.
'ROSES CHOKED AMONG THORNS
AND THISTLES.'

Lady Lesbia ate no luncheon that day. She went to her own room and had a cup of tea to steady her nerves, and sent to ask Lady Kirkbank to go to her as soon as she had finished luncheon. Lady Kirkbank's luncheon was a serious business, a substantial leisurely meal with which she fortified herself for the day's work. It enabled her to endure all the fatigues of visits and park, and to be airily indifferent to the charms of dinner; for Lady Kirkbank was not one of those matrons who with advanced years take to *gourmandise* as a kind of fine art. She gave good dinners, because she knew people would not come to Arlington Street to eat bad ones; but she was not a person who lived only to dine. At luncheon she gave her healthy appetite full scope, and ate like a ploughman.

She found Lesbia in her white muslin dressing-gown, with cheeks as pale as the gown she wore. She was sitting in an easy chair, with a low tea-table at her side, and the two bills were in the tray among the tea-things.

'Have you any idea how much I owe Seraphine and Cabochon?' she asked, looking up despairingly at Lady Kirkbank.

'What, have they sent in their bills already?'

'Already! I wish they had sent them before. I should have known how deeply I was getting into debt.'

'Are they very heavy?'

'They are dreadful! I owe over two thousand pounds. How can I tell Lady Maulevrier that? Two thousand one hundred pounds! It is awful.'

'There are women in London who would think very little of owing twice as much,' said Lady Kirkbank, in a comforting tone, though the fact, seriously considered, could hardly afford comfort. 'Your grandmother said you were to have **carte blanche**. She may think that you have been just a little extravagant; but she can hardly be angry with you for having taken her at her word. Two thousand pounds! Yes, it certainly is rather stiff.'

'Seraphine is a cheat!' exclaimed Lesbia, angrily. 'Her prices are positively exorbitant!'

'My dear child, you must not say that. Seraphine is positively moderate in comparison with the new people.'

'And Mr. Cabochon, too. The idea of his charging me three hundred guineas for re-setting those stupid old amethysts.'

'My dear, you **would** have diamonds mixed with them,' said Lady Kirkbank, reproachfully.

Lesbia turned away her head with an impatient sigh. She remembered perfectly that it was Lady Kirkbank who had persuaded her to order the diamond setting; but there was no use in talking about it now. The thing was done. She was two thousand pounds in debt--two thousand pounds to these two people only--and there were ever so many shops at which she had accounts--glovers, bootmakers, habitmakers, the tailor who made her Newmarket coats and cloth gowns, the stationer who supplied her with note-paper of every variety, monogrammed, floral; sporting, illuminated with this or that device, the follies of the passing hour, hatched by penniless Invention in a garret, pandering to the vanities of the idle.

'I must write to my grandmother by this afternoon's post,' said Lesbia, with a heavy sigh.

'Impossible. We have to be at the Ranelagh by four o'clock. Smithson and some other men are to meet us there. I have promised to drive Mrs. Mostyn down. You had better begin to dress.'

'But I ought to write to-day. I had better ask for this money at once, and have done with it. Two thousand pounds! I feel as if I were a thief. You say my grandmother is not a rich woman?'

'Not rich as the world goes nowadays. Nobody is rich now, except your commercial magnates, like Smithson. Great peers, unless their money is in London ground-rents, are great paupers. To own land is to be destitute. I don't suppose two thousand pounds will break your grandmother's bank; but of course it is a large sum to ask for at the end of two months; especially as she sent you a good deal of money while we were at Cannes. If you were engaged--about to make a really good match--you could ask for the money as a matter of course; but as it is, although you have been tremendously admired, from a practical point of view you are a failure.'

A failure. It was a hard word, but Lesbia felt it was true. She, the reigning beauty, the cynosure of every eye, had made no conquest worth talking about, except Mr. Smithson.

'Don't tell your grandmother anything about the bills for a week or two,' said Lady Kirkbank, soothingly. 'The creatures can wait for their money. Give yourself time to think.'

'I will,' answered Lesbia, dolefully.

'And now make haste, and get ready for the Ranelagh. My love, your eyes are dreadfully heavy. You *must* use a little belladonna. I'll send Rilboche to you.'

And for the first time in her life, Lesbia, too depressed to argue the point, consented to have her eyes doctored by Rilboche.

She was gay enough at the Ranelagh, and looked her loveliest at a dinner party that evening, and went to three parties after the dinner, and went home in the faint light of early morning, after sitting out a late waltz in a balcony with Mr. Smithson, a balcony banked round with hot-house flowers which were beginning to droop a little in the chilly morning air, just as beauty drooped under the searching eye of day.

Lesbia put the bills in her desk, and gave herself time to think, as Lady Kirkbank advised her. But the thinking progress resulted in very little good. All the thought of which she was capable would not reduce the totals of those two dreadful accounts. And every day brought some fresh bill. The stationer, the bootmaker, the glover, the perfumer, people who had courted Lady Lesbia's custom with an air which implied that the honour of serving fashionable beauty was the first consideration, and the question of payment quite a minor point--these now began to ask for their money in the most prosaic way. Every straw added to Lesbia's burden; and her heart grew heavier with every post.

'One can see the season is waning when these people begin to pester with their accounts,' said Lady Kirkbank, who always talked of tradesmen as if they were her natural enemies.

Lesbia accepted this explanation of the avalanche of bills, and never suspected Lady Kirkbank's influence in the matter. It happened, however, that the chaperon, having her own reasons for wishing to bring Mr. Smithson's suit to a successful issue, had told Seraphine and the other people to send in their bills immediately. Lady Lesbia would be leaving London in a week or so, she informed these purveyors, and would like to settle everything before she went away.

Mr. Smithson appeared in Arlington Street almost every day, and was full of schemes for new pleasures--or pleasures as nearly new as the world of fashion can afford. He was particularly desirous that Sir George and Lady Kirkbank, with Lady Lesbia, should stay at his Berkshire place during the Henley week. He had a large steam launch, and the regatta was a kind of carnival for his intimate friends, who were not too proud to riot and batten upon the parvenu's luxurious hospitality, albeit they were apt to talk somewhat slightingly of his antecedents.

Lady Kirkbank felt that this invitation was a turning point, and that if Lesbia went to stay at Rood Hall, her acceptance of Mr. Smithson was a certainty. She would see him at his place in Berkshire in the most flattering aspect; his surroundings as lord of the manor, and owner of one of the finest old places in the county, would lend dignity to his insignificance. Lesbia at first expressed a strong disinclination to go to Rood Hall. There would be a most unpleasant feeling in stopping at the house of a man whom she had refused, she told Lady Kirkbank.

'My dear, Mr. Smithson has forgiven you,' answered her chaperon. 'He is the soul of good nature.'

'One would think he was accustomed to be refused,' said Lesbia. 'I don't want to go to Rood Hall, but I don't want to spoil your Henley week. Could not I run down to Grasmere for a week, with Kibble to take care of me, and see dear grandmother? I could tell her about those dreadful bills.'

'Bury yourself at Grasmere in the height of the season! Not to be thought of! Besides, Lady Maulevrier objected before to the idea of your travelling alone with

Kibble. No! if you can't make up your mind to go to Rood Hall, George and I must make up our minds to stay away. But it will be rather hard lines; for that Henley week is quite the jolliest thing in the summer.'

'Then I'll go,' said Lesbia, with a resigned air. 'Not for worlds would I deprive you and Sir George of a pleasure.'

In her heart of hearts she rather wished to see Rood Hall. She was curious to behold the extent and magnitude of Mr. Smithson's possessions. She had seen his Italian villa in Park Lane, the perfection of modern art, modern skill, modern taste, reviving the old eternally beautiful forms, recreating the Pitti Palace--the homes of the Medici--the halls of dead and gone Doges--and now she was told that Rood Hall--a genuine old English manor-house, in perfect preservation--was even more interesting than the villa in Park Lane. At Rood Hall there were ideal stables and farm, hot-houses without number, rose gardens, lawns, the river, and a deer park.

So the invitation was accepted, and Mr. Smithson immediately laid himself at Lesbia's feet, as it were, with regard to all other invitations for the Henley festival. Whom should he ask to meet her?--whom would she have?

'You are very good,' she said, 'but I have really no wish to be consulted. I am not a royal personage, remember. I could not presume to dictate.'

'But I wish you to dictate. I wish you to be imperious in the expression of your wishes.'

'Lady Kirkbank has a better right than I, if anybody is to be consulted,' said Lesbia, modestly.

'Lady Kirkbank is an old dear, who gets on delightfully with everybody. But you are more sensitive. Your comfort might be marred by an obnoxious presence. I will ask nobody whom you do not like--who is not thoroughly *simpatico*. Have you no particular friends of your own choosing whom you would like me to ask?'

Lesbia confessed that she had no such friends. She liked everybody tolerably; but she had not a talent for friendship. Perhaps it was because in the London season one was too busy to make friends.

'I can fancy two girls getting quite attached to each other, out of the season,' she said, 'but in May and June life is all a rush and a scramble----'

'And one has no time to gather wayside flowers of friendship,' interjected Mr. Smithson. 'Still, if there are no people for whom you have an especial liking, there **must** be people whom you detest.'

Lesbia owned that it was so. Detestation came of itself, naturally.

'Then let me be sure I do not ask any of your pet aversions,' said Mr. Smithson. 'You met Mr. Plantagenet Parsons, the theatrical critic, at my house. Shall we have him?'

'I like all amusing people.'

'And Horace Meander, the poet. Shall we have him? He is brimful of conceits and affectations, but he's a tremendous joke.'

'Mr. Meander is charming.'

'Suppose we ask Mostyn and his wife? Her scraps of science are rather good fun.'

'I haven't the faintest objection to the Mostyns,' replied Lesbia. 'But who are "we"?'

'We are you and I, for the nonce. The invitations will be issued ostensibly by me, but they will really emanate from you.'

'I am to be the shadow behind the throne,' said Lesbia. 'How delightful!'

'I would rather you were the sovereign ruler, on the throne,' answered Smithson, tenderly. 'That throne shall be empty till you fill it.'

'Please go on with your list of people,' said Lesbia, checking this gush of sentiment.

She began to feel somehow that she was drifting from all her moorings, that in accepting this invitation to Rood Hall she was allowing herself to be ensnared into an alliance about which she was still doubtful. If anything better had appeared in the prospect of her life--if any worthier suitor had come forward, she would have whistled Mr. Smithson down the wind; but no worthier suitor had offered himself. It was Smithson or nothing. If she did not accept Smithson, she would go back to Fellside heavily burdened with debt, and an obvious failure. She would have run the gauntlet of a London season without definite result; and this, to a young woman so impressed with her own transcendent merits, was a most humiliating state of things.

Other people's names were suggested by Mr. Smithson and approved by Lesbia, and a house party of about fourteen in all was made up. Mr. Smithson's steam launch would comfortably accommodate that number. He had a couple of barges for chance visitors, and kept an open table on board them during the regatta.

The visit arranged, the next question was gowns. Lesbia had gowns enough to have stocked a draper's shop; but then, as she and Lady Kirkbank deplored, the difficulty was that she had worn them all, some as many as three or four times. They were doubtless all marked and known. Some of them had been described in the society papers. At Henley she would be expected to wear something distinctly new, to introduce some new fashion of gown or hat or parasol. No matter how ugly the new thing might be, so long as it was startling; no matter how eccentric, provided it was original.

'What am I to do?' asked Lesbia, despairingly.

'There is only one thing that can be done. We must go instantly to Seraphine and insist upon her inventing something. If she has no idea ready she must telegraph Worth and get him to send something over. Your old things will do very well for Rood Hall. You have no end of pretty gowns for morning and evening; but you must be original on the race days. Your gowns will be in all the papers.'

'But I shall be only getting deeper into debt,' said Lesbia, with a sigh.

'That can't be helped. If you go into society you must be properly dressed. We'll go to Clanricarde Place directly after luncheon, and see what that old harpy has to show us.'

Lesbia had a rather uncomfortable feeling about facing the fair Seraphine, without being able to give her a cheque upon account of that dreadful bill. She had quite accepted Lady Kirkbank's idea that bills never need be discharged in full, and that the true system of finance was to give an occasional cheque on account, as a sop to Cerberus. True, that while Cerberus fattened on the sops the bill seemed always growing; and the final crash, when Cerberus grew savage and sops could be no more accepted, was too awful to be thought about.

Lesbia entered Seraphine's Louis-seize drawing-room with a faint expectation of unpleasantness; but after a little whispering between Lady Kirkbank and the dressmaker, the latter came to Lesbia smiling graciously, and seemingly full of eagerness for new orders.

'Miladi says you want something of the most original--*tant soit peu risque*--for 'Enley,' she said. 'Let us see now,' and she tapped her forehead with a gold thimble which nobody had ever seen her use, but which looked respectable. 'There is ze dresses that Chaumont wear in zis new play, ***Une Faute dans le Passe***. Yes, zere is the watare dress--a boating party at Bougival, a toilet of the most new, striking, ***ecrasant***, what you English call a "screamer."'

'What a genius you are, Fifine,' exclaimed Lady Kirkbank, rapturously. 'The ***Faute dans le Passe*** was only produced last week. No one will have thought of copying Chaumont's gowns yet awhile. The idea is an inspiration.'

'What is the boating costume like?' asked Lady Lesbia, faintly.

'An exquisite combination of simplicity with ***vlan***,' answered the dressmaker. 'A skin-tight indigo silk Jersey bodice, closely studded with dark blue beads, a flounced petticoat of indigo and amber foulard, an amber scarf drawn tightly round the hips, and a dark blue toque with a largo bunch of amber poppies. Tan-coloured mousquetaire gloves, and Hessian boots of tan-coloured kid.'

'Hessian boots!' ejaculated Lesbia.

'But, yes, Miladi. The petticoat is somewhat short, you comprehend, to escape the damp of the deck, and, after all, Hessians are much less indelicate than silk stockings, legs ***a cru***, as one may say.'

'Lesbia, you will look enchanting in yellow Hessians,' said Lady Kirkbank, 'Let the dress be put in hand instantly, Seraphine.'

Lesbia was inclined to remonstrate. She did not admire the description of the costume, she would rather have something less outrageous.

'Outrageous! It is only original,' exclaimed her chaperon. 'If Chaumont wears it you may be sure it is perfect.'

'But on the stage, by gaslight, in the midst of unrealities,' argued Lesbia. 'That makes such a difference.'

'My dear, there is no difference nowadays between the stage and the drawing-room. Whatever Chaumont wears you may wear. And now let us think of the second day. I think as your first costume is to be nautical, and rather masculine, your second should be somewhat languishing and ***vaporeux***. Creamy Indian muslin, wild flowers, a large Leghorn hat.'

'And what will Miladi herself wear?' asked the French woman of Lady Kirkbank. 'She must have something of new.'

'No, at my age, it doesn't matter. I shall wear one of my cotton frocks, and my Dunstable hat.'

Lesbia shuddered, for Lady Kirkbank in her cotton frock was a spectacle at which youth laughed and age blushed. But after all it did not matter to Lesbia. She would have liked a less rowdy chaperon; but as a foil to her own fresh young beauty Lady Kirkbank was admirable.

They drove down to Rood Hall early next week, Sir George conveying them in his drag, with a change of horses at Maidenhead. The weather was peerless; the country exquisite, approached from London. How different that river landscape looks to the eyes of the traveller returning from the wild West of England, the wooded gorges of Cornwall and Devon, the Tamar and the Dart. Then how small and poor and mean seems silvery Thames, gliding peacefully between his willowy bank, singing his lullaby to the whispering sedges; a poor little river, a flat common-place landscape, says the traveller, fresh from moorland and tor, from the rocky shore of the Atlantic, the deep clefts of the great, red hills.

To Lesbia's eyes the placid stream and the green pastures, breathing odours of meadow-sweet and clover, seemed passing lovely. She was pleased with her own hat and parasol too, which made her graciously disposed towards the landscape; and the last packet of gloves from North Audley Street fitted without a wrinkle. The glovemaker was beginning to understand her hand, which was a study for a sculptor, but which had its little peculiarities.

Nor was she ill-disposed to Mr. Smithson, who had come up to town by an early train, in order to lunch in Arlington Street and go back by coach, seated just behind Lady Lesbia, who had the box seat beside Sir George.

The drive was delightful. It was a few minutes after five when the coach drove past the picturesque old gate-house into Mr. Smithson's Park, and Rood Hall lay on the low ground in front of them, with its back to the river. It was an old red brick house in the Tudor style, with an advanced porch, and four projecting wings, three stories high, with picturesque spire roofs overtopping the main building. Around the house ran a boldly-carved stone parapet, bearing the herons and bulrushes which were the cognisance of the noble race for which the mansion was built. Numerous projecting mullioned windows broke up the line of the park front. Lesbia was fain to own that Rood Hall was even better than Park Lane. In London Mr. Smithson had created a palace; but it was a new palace, which still had a faint flavour of bricks and mortar, and which was apt to remind the spectator of that wonderful erection of Aladdin, the famous Parvenu of Eastern story. Here, in Berkshire, Mr. Smithson had dropped into a nest which had been kept warm for him for three centuries, aired and beautified by generations of a noble race which had obligingly decayed and dwindled in order to make room for Mr. Smithson. Here the Parvenu had bought a home mellowed by the slow growth of years, touched into poetic beauty by the chastening fingers of time. His artist friends told him that every brick in the red walls was 'precious,' a mystery of colour which only a painter could fitly understand and value. Here he had bought associations, he had bought history. He had bought the dust of Elizabeth's senators, the bones of her court beauties. The coffins in the Mausoleum yonder in the ferny depths of the Park, the village church just outside the gates--these had all gone with the property.

Lesbia went up the grand staircase, through the long corridors, in a dream of wonder. Brought up at Fellside, in that new part of the Westmoreland house which had been built by her grandmother and had no history, she felt thrilled by the so-ber splendour of this fine old manorial mansion. All was sound and substantial, as if created yesterday, so well preserved had been the goods and chattels of the noble race; and yet all wore such unmistakeable marks of age. The deep rich colouring of the wainscot, the faded hues of the tapestry, the draperies of costliest velvet and brocade, were all sobered by the passing of years.

Mr. Smithson had shown his good taste in having kept all things as Sir Hubert Heronville, the last of his race, had left them; and the Heronvilles had been one of those grand old Tory races which change nothing of the past.

Lady Lesbia's bedroom was the State chamber, which had been occupied by kings and queens in days of yore. That grandiose four-poster, with the carved ebony columns, cut velvet curtains, and plumes of ostrich feathers, had been built for Elizabeth, when she deigned to include Rood Hall in one of her royal progresses. Charles the First had rested his weary head upon those very pillows, before he went on to the Inn at Uxbridge, where he was to be lodged less luxuriously. James the Second had stayed there when Duke of York, with Mistress Anne Hyde, before he acknowledged his marriage to the multitude; and Anne's daughter had occupied the same room as Queen of England forty years later; and now the Royal Chamber, with adjacent dressing-room, and oratory, and spacious boudoir all in the same suite, was reserved for Lady Lesbia Haselden.

'I'm afraid you are spoiling me,' she told Mr. Smithson, when he asked if she approved of the rooms that had been allotted to her. 'I feel quite ashamed of myself among the ghosts of dead and gone queens.'

'Why so? Surely the Royalty of beauty has as divine a right as that of an anointed sovereign.'

'I hope the Royal personages don't walk,' exclaimed Lady Kirkbank, in her girlish tone; 'this is just the house in which one would expect ghosts.'

Whereupon Mrs. Mostyn hastened to enlighten the company upon the real causes of ghost-seeing, which she had lately studied in Carpenter's 'Mental Physiology,' and favoured them with a diluted version of the views of that authority.

This was at afternoon tea in the library, where the brass-wired bookcases, filled with mighty folios and handsome octavos in old bindings, looked as if they had not been opened for a century. The literature of past ages furnished the room, and made a delightful background. The literature of the present lay about on the tables, and testified that the highest intellectual flight of the inhabitants of Rood Hall was a dip into the **Contemporary** or the **Nineteenth Century**, or the perusal of the last new scandal in the shape of Reminiscences or Autobiography. One large round table was consecrated to Mudie, another to Rolandi. On the one side you had Mrs. Oliphant, on the other Zola, exemplifying the genius of the two nations.

After tea Mr. Smithson's visitors, most of whom had arrived in Sir George's drag, explored the grounds. These were lovely beyond expression in the low afternoon light. Cedars of Lebanon spread their broad shadows on the velvet lawn, yews and Wellingtonias of mighty growth made an atmosphere of gloom in some parts of the grounds. One great feature was the Ladies' Garden, a spot apart, a great square garden surrounded with a laurel wall, eight feet high, containing a rose garden, where the choicest specimens grew and flourished, while in the centre there was a circular fish-pond with a fountain. There was a Lavender Walk too, another feature of the grounds at Rood Hall, an avenue of tall lavender bushes, much affected by the stately dames of old.

Modern manners preferred the river terrace, as a pleasant place on which to loiter after dinner, to watch the boats flashing by in the evening light, or the sun going down behind a fringe of willows on the opposite bank. This Italian terrace, with its statues, and carved vases filled with roses, fuchsias, and geraniums, was the great point of rendezvous at Rood Hall--an ideal spot whereon to linger in the deepening twilight, from which to gaze upon the moonlit river later on in the night.

The windows of the drawing-room, and music-room, and ballroom opened on to this terrace, and the royal wing--the tower-shaped wing now devoted to Lady Lesbia, looked upon the terrace and the river.

'Lovely, as your house is altogether, I think this river view is the best part of it,' said Lady Lesbia, as she strolled with Mr. Smithson on the terrace after dinner, dressed in Indian muslin which was almost as poetical as a vapour, and with a cloud of delicate lace wrapped round her head. 'I think I shall spend half of my life at my boudoir window, gloating over that delicious landscape.'

Horace Meander, the poet, was discoursing to a select group upon that peculiar quality of willows which causes them to shiver, and quiver, and throw little lights and shadows on the river, and on the subtle, ineffable beauty of twilight, which perhaps, however utterly beautiful in the abstract, would have been more agreeable to him personally if he had not been surrounded by a cloud of gnats, which refused to be buffeted off his laurel-crowned head.

While Mr. Meander poetised in his usual eloquent style, Mrs. Mostyn, as a still newer light, discoursed as eloquently to little a knot of women, imparting valu- able information upon the anatomical structure and individual peculiarities of those various insects which are the pests of a summer evening.

'You don't like gnats!' exclaimed the lady; 'how very extraordinary. Do you know I have spent days and weeks upon the study of their habits and dear little ways. They are the most interesting creatures--far superior to *us* in intellect. Do you know that they fight, and that they have tribes which are life-long enemies- -like those dreadful Corsicans--and that they make little sepulchres in the bark of trees, and bury each other--alive, if they can; and they hold vestries, and have burial boards. They are most absorbing creatures, if you only give yourself up to the study of them; but it is no use to be half-hearted in a study of that kind. I went without so much as a cup of tea for twenty-four hours, watching my gnats, for fear the opening of the door should startle them. Another time I shall make the nursery governess watch for me.'

'How interesting, how noble of you,' exclaimed the other ladies; and then they began to talk about bonnets, and about Mr. Smithson, to speculate how much money this house and all his other houses had cost him, and to wonder if he was really rich, or if he were only one of those great financial windbags which so often explode and leave the world aghast, marvelling at the ease with which it has been deluded.

They wondered, too, whether Lady Lesbia Haselden meant to marry him.

'Of course she does, my dear,' answered Mrs. Mostyn, decisively.

'You don't suppose that after having studied the habits of **gnats** I cannot read such a poor shallow creature as a silly vain girl. Of course Lady Lesbia means to marry Mr. Smithson's fine houses; and she is only amusing herself and swelling her own importance by letting him dangle in a kind of suspense which is not suspense; for he knows as well as she does that she means to have him.'

The next day was given up, first to seeing the house, an amusement which lasted very well for an hour or so after breakfast, and then to wandering in a desultory manner, to rowing and canoeing, and a little sailing, and a good deal of screaming and pretty timidity upon the blue bright river; to gathering wild flowers and ferns in rustic lanes, and to an *al fresco* luncheon in the wood at Medmenham, and then dinner, and then music, an evening spent half within and half without the music-room, cigarettes sparkling, like glowworms on the terrace, tall talk from Mr. Meander, long quotations from his own muse and that of Rossetti, a little Shelley, a little Keats, a good deal of Swinburne. The festivities were late on this second evening, as Mr. Smithson had invited a good many people from the neighbourhood, but the house party were not the less early on the following morning, which was the first Henley day.

It was a peerless morning, and all the brasswork of Mr. Smithson's launch sparkled and shone in the sun, as she lay in front of the terrace. A wooden pier, a portable construction, was thrown out from the terrace steps, to enable the company to go on board the launch without the possibility of wet feet or damaged raiment.

Lesbia's Chaumount costume was a success. The women praised it, the men stared and admired. The dark-blue silken jersey, sparkling with closely studded indigo beads, fitted the slim graceful figure as a serpent's scales fit the serpent. The coquettish little blue silk toque, the careless cluster of gold-coloured poppies, against the glossy brown hair, the large sunshade of old gold satin lined with indigo, the flounced petticoat of softest Indian silk, the dainty little tan-coloured boots with high heels and pointed toes, were all perfect after their fashion; and Mr. Smithson felt that the liege lady of his life, the woman he meant to marry willy nilly, would be the belle of the race-course. Nor was he disappointed. Everybody in London had heard of Lady Lesbia Haselden. Her photograph was in all the West-End windows, was enshrined in the albums of South Kensington and Clapham, Maida Vale and Haverstock Hill. People whose circles were far remote from Lady Lesbia's circle, were as familiar with her beauty as if they had known her from her cradle. And all these outsiders wanted to see her in the flesh, just as they always thirst to behold Royal personages. So when it became known that the beautiful Lady Lesbia Haselden was on board Mr. Smithson's launch, all the people in the small boats, or on neighbouring barges, made it their business if have a good look at her. The launch was almost mobbed by those inquisitive little boats in the intervals between the races.

'What are the people all staring and hustling one another for?' asked Lesbia, innocently. She had seen the same hustling and whispering and staring in the hall at the opera, when she was waiting for her carriage; but she chose to affect unconsciousness. 'What do they all want?'

'I think they want to see you,' said Mr. Smithson, who was sitting by her side. 'A very natural desire.'

Lesbia laughed, and lowered the big yellow sunshade, so as to hide herself altogether from the starers.

'How silly!' she exclaimed. 'It is all the fault of those horrid photographers: they vulgarise everything and everybody. I will never be photographed again.'

'Oh yes, you will, and in that frock. It's the prettiest thing I've seen for a long time. Why do you hide yourself from those poor wretches, who keep rowing backwards and forwards in an obviously aimless way, just to get a peep at you *en passant*? What happiness for us who live near you, and can gaze when we will, without all those absurd manoeuvres. There goes the signal--and now for a hard-fought race.'

Lesbia pretended to be interested in the racing--she pretended to be gay, but her heart was as heavy as lead. The burden of debt, which had been growing ever since Seraphine sent in her bill, was weighing her down to the dust.

She owed three thousand pounds. It seemed incredible that she should owe so much, that a girl's frivolous fancies and extravagances could amount to such a sum within so short a span. But thoughtless purchases, ignorant orders, had run on from week to week, and the main result was an indebtedness of close upon three thousand pounds.

Three thousand pounds! The sum was continually sounding in her ears like the cry of a screech owl. The very ripple of the river flowing so peacefully under the blue summer sky seemed to repeat the words. Three thousand pounds! 'Is it much?' she wondered, having no standard of comparison. 'Is it very much more than my grandmother will expect me to have spent in the time? Will it trouble her to have to pay those bills? Will she be very angry?'

These were questions which Lesbia kept asking herself, in every pause of her frivolous existence; in such a pause as this, for instance, while the people round her were standing breathless, open-mouthed, gazing after the boats. She did not care a straw for the boats, who won, or who lost the race. It was all a hollow mockery. Indeed it seemed just now that the only real thing in life was those accursed bills, which would have to be paid somehow.

She had told Lady Maulevrier nothing about them as yet. She had allowed herself to be advised by Lady Kirkbank, and she had taken time to think. But thought had given her no help. The days were gliding onward, and Lady Maulevrier would have to be told.

She meditated perplexedly about her grandmother's income. She had never heard the extent of it, but had taken for granted that Lady Maulevrier was rich. Would three thousand pounds make a great inroad on that income? Would it be a year's income?--half a year's? Lesbia had no idea. Life at Fellside was carried on in an elegant manner--with considerable luxury in house and garden--a luxury of flowers, a lavish expenditure of labour. Yet the expenditure of Lady Maulevrier's existence, spent always on the same spot, must be as nothing to the money spent in such a life as Lady Kirkbank's, which involved the keeping up of three or four houses, and costly journeys to and fro, and incessant change of attire.

No doubt Lady Maulevrier had saved money; yes, she must have saved thousands during her long seclusion, Lesbia argued. Her grandmother had told her that she was to look upon herself as an heiress. This could only mean that Lady Maulevrier had a fortune to leave her; and this being so, what could it matter if she had anticipated some of her portion? And yet there was in her heart of hearts a terrible fear of that stern dowager, of the cold scorn in those splendid eyes when she should stand revealed in all her foolishness, her selfish, mindless, vain extravagances. She, who had never been reproved, shrank with a sickly dread from the idea of reproof. And to be told that her career as a fashionable beauty had been a failure! That would be the bitterest pang of all.

Soon came luncheon, and Heidseck, and then an afternoon which was gayer than the morning had been, inasmuch as every one babbled and laughed more after luncheon. And then there was five o'clock tea on deck, under the striped Japanese awning, to the jingle of banjos, enlivened by the wit of black-faced minstrels, amidst wherries and canoes and gondolas, and ponderous houseboats, and snorting launches, crowding the sides of the sunlit river, in full view of the crowd yonder in front of the Red Lion, and here on this nearer bank, and all along either shore, fringing the green meadows with a gaudy border of smartly-dressed humanity.

It was a gay scene, and Lesbia gave herself up to the amusement of the hour, and talked and chaffed as she had learned to talk and chaff in one brief season, holding her own against all comers.

Rood Hall looked lovely when they went back to it in the gloaming, an Elizabethan pile crowned with towers. The four wings with their conical roofs, the massive projecting windows, grey stone, ruddy brickwork, lattices reflecting the sunlight, Italian terrace and blue river in the foreground, cedars and yews at the back, all made a splendid picture of an English ancestral home.

'Nice old place, isn't it?' asked Mr. Smithson, seeing Lesbia's admiring gaze as the launch neared the terrace. They two were standing in the bows, apart from all the rest.

'Nice! it is simply perfect.'

'Oh no, it isn't. There is one thing wanted yet.'

'What is that?'

'A wife. You are the only person who can make any house of mine perfect. Will you?' He took her hand, which she did not withdraw from his grasp. He bent his head and kissed the little hand in its soft Swedish glove.

'Will you, Lesbia?' he repeated earnestly; and she answered softly, 'Yes.'

That one brief syllable was more like a sigh than a spoken word, and it seemed to her as if in the utterance of that syllable the three thousand pounds had been paid.

CHAPTER XXXI.
'KIND IS MY LOVE TO-DAY, TO-MORROW KIND.'

While Lady Lesbia was draining the cup of London folly and London care to the dregs, Lady Mary was leading her usual quiet life beside the glassy lake, where the green hill-sides and sheep walks were reflected in all their summer verdure under the cloudless azure of a summer sky. A monotonous life--passing dull as seen from the outside--and yet Mary was very happy, happy even in her solitude, with the grave deep joy of a satisfied heart, a mind at rest. All life had taken a new colour since her engagement to John Hammond. A sense of new duties, an awakening earnestness had given a graver tone to her character. Her spirits were less wild, yet not less joyous than of old. The joy was holier, deeper.

Her lover's letters were the chief delight of her lonely days. To read them again and again, and ponder upon them, and then to pour out all her heart and mind in answering them. These were pleasures enough for her young like. Hammond's letters were such as any woman might be proud to receive. They were not love-letters only. He wrote as friend to friend; not descending from the proud pinnacle of masculine intelligence to the lower level of feminine silliness; not writing down to a simple country girl's capacity; but writing-fully and fervently, as if there were no subject too lofty or too grave for the understanding of his betrothed. He wrote as one sure of being sympathised with, wrote as to his second self: and Mary showed herself not unworthy of the honour thus rendered to her intellect.

There was one world which had newly opened to Mary since her engagement, and that was the world of politics. Hammond had told her that his ambition was to succeed as a politician--to do some good in his day as one of the governing body; and of late she had made it her business to learn how England and the world outside England were governed.

She had no natural leaning to the study of political economy. Instead, she had always imagined any question relating to the government of her country to be inherently dry-as-dust and uninviting. But had John Hammond devoted his days to the study of Coptic manuscripts, or the arrow headed inscriptions upon Assyrian tablets, she would have toiled her hardest in the endeavour to make herself a Coptic scholar, or an adept in the cuneiform characters. If he had been a student of Chinese, she would not have been discomfited by such a trifle as the fifty thousand characters in the Chinese alphabet.

And so, as he was to make his name in the arena of public life, she set herself to acquire a proper understanding of the science of politics; and to this end she gorged herself with English history,--Hume, Hallam, Green, Justin McCarthy, Palgrave, Lecky, from the days of Witenagemote to the Reform Bill; the Repeal of the Corn Laws, the Disestablishment of the Irish Church, Ballot, Trade Unionism, and unreciprocated Free Trade. No question was deep enough to repel her; for was not her lover interested in the dryest thereof; and what concerned him and his welfare must needs be full of interest for her.

To this end she read the debates religiously day by day; and she one day ventured shyly to suggest that she should read them aloud to Lady Maulevrier.

'Would it not be a little rest for you if I were to read your Times aloud to you every afternoon, grandmother?' she asked. 'You read so many books, French, English, and German, and I think your eyes must get a little tired sometimes.'

Mary ventured the remark with some timidity, for those falcon eyes were fixed upon her all the time, bright and clear and steady as the eyes of youth. It seemed almost an impertinence to suggest that such eyes could know weariness.

'No, Mary, my sight, holds out wonderfully for an old woman,' replied her ladyship, gently. 'The new theory of the last oculist whose book I dipped into--a very amusing and interesting book, by-the-bye--is that the sight improves and strengthens by constant use, and that an agricultural labourer, who hardly uses his eyes at all, has rarely in the decline of life so good a sight as the watchmaker or the student. I have read immensely all my life, and find myself no worse for that indulgence. But you may read the debates to me if you like, my dear, for if my eyes are strong, I myself am very tired. Sick to death, Mary, sick to death.'

The splendid eyes turned from Mary, and looked away to the blue sky, to the hills in their ineffable beauty of colour and light--shifting, changing with every moment of the summer day. Intense weariness, a settled despair, were expressed in that look--tearless, yet sadder than all tears.

'It must be very monotonous, very sad for you,' murmured Mary, her own eyes brimming over with tears. 'But it will not be always so, dear grandmother. I hope a time will come when you will be able to go about again, to resume your old life.'

'I do not hope, Mary. No, child, I feel and know that time will never come. My strength is ebbing slowly day by day. If I live for another year, live to see Lesbia married, and you, too, perhaps--well, I shall die at peace. At peace, no; not----' she faltered, and the thin, semi-transparent hand was pressed upon her brow. 'What will be said of me when I am dead?'

Mary feared that her grandmother's mind was wandering. She came and knelt beside the couch, laid and her head against the satin pillows, tenderly, caressingly.

'Dear grandmother, pray be calm,' she murmured.

'Mary, do not look at me like that, as if you would read my heart. There are hearts that must not be looked into. Mine is like a charnel-house. Monotonous, yes; my life has been monotonous. No conventual gloom was ever deeper than the gloom of Fellside. My boy did nothing to lighten it for me, and his son followed in his father's footsteps. You and Lesbia have been my only consolation. Lesbia! I was so proud of her beauty, so proud and fond of her, because she was like me, and re-called my own youth. And see how easily she forgets me. She has gone into a new world, in which my age and my infirmities have no part; and I am as nothing to her.'

Mary changed from red to pale, so painful was her embarrassment. What could she say in defence of her sister? How could she deny that Lesbia was an ingrate, when those rare and hurried letters, so careless in their tone, expressing the selfish-ness of the writer in every syllable, told but too plainly of forgetfulness and ingrati-tude?

'Dear grandmother, Lesbia has so much to do--her life is so full of engage-ments,' she faltered feebly.

'Yes, she goes from party to party--she gives herself up heart and mind and soul to pleasures which she ought to consider only as the trivial means to great ends; and she forgets the woman who reared her, and cared for her, and watched over her from her infancy, and who tried to inspire her with a noble ambition.--Yes, read to me, child, read. Give me new thoughts, if you can, for my brain is weary with grinding the old ones. There was a grand debate in the Lords last night, and Lord Hartfield spoke. Let me hear his speech. You can read what was said by the man before him; never mind the rest.'

Mary read Lord Somebody's speech, which was passing dull, but which pre-pared the ground for a magnificent and exhaustive reply from Lord Hartfield. The question was an important one, affecting the well-being of the masses, and Lord Hartfield spoke with an eloquence which rose in force and fire as he wound him-self like a serpent into the heart of his subject--beginning quietly, soberly, with no opening flashes of rhetoric, but rising gradually to the topmost heights of oratory.

'What a speech!' cried Lady Maulevrier, delighted, her cheeks glowing, her eyes kindling; 'what a noble fellow the speaker must be! Oh, Mary, I must tell you a secret. I loved that man's father. Yes, my dear, I loved him fondly, dearly, truly, as you love that young man of yours; and he was the only man I ever really loved. Fate parted us. But I have never forgotten him--never, Mary, never. At this mo-ment I have but to close my eyes and I can see his face--see him looking at me as he looked the last time we met. He was a younger son, poor, his future quite hopeless in those days; but it was not my fault we were parted. I would have married him--yes, wedded poverty, just as you are going to marry this Mr. Hammond; but my people would not let me; and I was too young, too helpless, to make a good fight. Oh, Mary, if I had only fought hard enough, what a happy woman I might have been, and how good a wife.'

'You were a good wife to my grandfather, I am sure,' faltered Mary, by way of saying something consolatory.

A dark frown came over Lady Maulevrier's face, which had softened to deepest tenderness just before.

'A good wife to Maulevrier,' she said, in a mocking tone. Well, yes, as good a wife as such a husband deserved. 'I was better than Caesar's wife, Mary, for no breath of suspicion ever rested upon my name. But if I had married Ronald Hollis-ter, I should have been a happy woman; and that I have never been since I parted from him.'

'You have never seen the present Lord Hartfield, I think?'

'Never; but I have watched his career, I have thought of him. His father died while he was an infant, and he was brought up in seclusion by a widowed mother, who kept him tied to her apron-strings till he went to Oxford. She idolised him, and I am told she taught herself Latin and Greek, mathematics even, in order to help him in his boyish, studies, and, later on, read Greek plays and Latin poetry with him, till she became an exceptional classic for a woman. She was her son's companion and friend, sympathised with his tastes, his pleasures, his friendships; devoted every hour of her life, every thought of her mind to his welfare, his interests, walked with him, rode with him, travelled half over Europe, yachted with him. Her friends all declared that the lad would grow up an odious milksop; but I am told that there never was a manlier man than Lord Hartfield. From his boyhood he was his mother's protector, helped to administer her affairs, acquired a premature sense of responsibility, and escaped almost all those vices which make young men detestable. His mother died within a few months of his majority. He was broken-hearted at losing her, and left Europe immediately after her death. From that time he has been a great traveller. But I suppose now that he has taken his seat in the House of Lords, and has spoken a good many times, he means to settle down and take his place among the foremost men of his day. I am told that he is worthy to take such a place.'

'You must feel warmly interested in watching his career,' said Mary, sympathetically.

'I am interested in everything that concerns him. I will tell you another secret, Mary. I think I am getting into my dotage, my dear, or I should hardly talk to you like this,' said Lady Maulevrier, with a touch of bitterness.

Mary was sitting on a stool by the sofa, close to the invalid's pillow. She clasped her grandmother's hand and kissed it fondly.

'Dear grandmother, I think you are talking to me like this to-day because you are beginning to care for me a little,' she said, tenderly.

'Oh, my dear, you are very good, very sweet and forgiving to care for me at all, after my neglect of you,' answered Lady Maulevrier, with a sigh. 'I have kept you out in the cold so long, Mary. Lesbia--well, Lesbia has been a kind of infatuation for me, and like all infatuations mine has ended in disappointment and bitterness. Ambition has been the bane of my life, Mary; and when I could no longer be ambitious for myself--when my own existence had become a mere death in life, I began to dream and to scheme for the aggrandisement of my granddaughter. Lesbia's beauty, Lesbia's elegance seemed to make success certain--and so I dreamt my dream--which may never be fulfilled.'

'What was your dream, grandmother? May I know all about it?'

'That was the secret I spoke of just now. Yes, Mary, you may know, for I fear the dream will never be realised. I wanted my Lesbia to become Lord Hartfield's wife. I would have brought them together myself, could I have but gone to London; but, failing that, I fancied Lady Kirkbank would have divined my wishes without being told them, and would have introduced Hartfield to Lesbia; and now the London season is drawing to a close, and Hartfield and Lesbia have never met. He hardly goes anywhere, I am told. He devotes himself exclusively to politics; and he is not in Lady Kirkbank's set. A terrible disappointment to me, Mary!'

'It is a pity,' said Mary. 'Lesbia is so lovely. If Lord Hartfield were fancy-free he ought to fall in love with her, could they but meet. I thought that in London all fashionable people knew each other, and were continually meeting.'

'It used to be so in my day, Mary. Almack's was a common ground, even if there had been no other. But now there are circles and circles, I believe, rings that touch occasionally, but never break and mingle. I am afraid poor Georgie's set is not quite so nice as I could have wished. Yet Lesbia writes as if she were in raptures with her chaperon, and with all the people she meets. And then Georgie tells me that this Mr. Smithson whom Lesbia has refused is a very important personage, a millionaire, and very likely to be made a peer.'

'A new peer,' said Mary, making a wry face. 'One would rather have an old commoner. I always fancy a newly-made peer must be like a newly-built house, glaring, and staring, and arid and uncongenial.'

'*C'est selon*,' said Lady Maulevrier. 'One would not despise a Chatham or a Wellington because of the newness of his title; but a man who has only money to recommend him----'

Lady Maulevrier left her sentence unfinished, save by a shrug; while Mary made another wry face. She had that grand contempt for sordid wealth which is common to young people who have never known the want of money.

'I hope Lesbia will marry some one better than Mr. Smithson,' she said.

'I hope so too, dear; and yet do you know I have an idea that Lesbia means to accept Mr. Smithson, or she would hardly have consented to go to his house for the Henley week. Here is a letter from Georgie Kirkbank which you will have to answer for me to-morrow--a letter full of raptures about Mr. Smithson's place in Berkshire, Rood Hall. I remember the house well. I was there nearly fifty years ago, when the Heronvilles owned it; and now the Heronvilles are all dead or ruined, and this city person is master of the fine old mansion. It is a strange world, Mary.'

From that time forward Mary and her grandmother were on more confidential terms, and when, two days later, Fellside was startled into life by the unexpected arrival of Lord Maulevrier and Mr. Hammond, the dowager seemed almost as pleased as her granddaughter at the arrival of the young men.

As for Mary, she was almost beside herself with joy when she heard their voices from the lawn, and, rushing to the shrubbery, saw them walk up the hill, as she had seen them on that first evening nearly a year ago, when John Hammond came as a stranger to Fellside.

She tried to take her joy soberly, though her eyes were dancing with delight, as she went to the porch to meet them.

'What extraordinary young men you are,' she said, as she emerged breathless from her lover's embrace. 'The idea of your descending upon us without a moment's notice. Why did you not write or telegraph, that your rooms might be ready?'

'Am I to understand that all the spare rooms at Fellside are kept as damp as at the bottom of the lake?' asked Maulevrier.

'I did not think any preparation was necessary; but we can go back if we're not wanted, can't we, Jack?'

'You darling,' cried Mary, hanging affectionately upon her brother's arm. 'You *know* I was only joking, you *know* how enraptured I am to have you.'

'To have *me*, only me,' said Maulevrier. 'Jack doesn't count, I suppose?'

'You know how glad I am, and that I want to hide my gladness,' answered Mary, radiant and blushing like the rich red roses in the porch. 'You men are so vain. And now come and see grandmother, she will be cheered by your arrival. She has been so good to me just lately, so sweet.'

'She might have been good and sweet to you all your life,' said Hammond. 'I am not prepared to be grateful to her at a moment's notice for any crumbs of affection she may throw you.'

'Oh but you must be grateful, sir; and you must love her and pity her,' retorted

Mary. 'Think how sadly she has suffered. We cannot be too kind to her, or too fond of her, poor dear.'

'Mary is right,' said Hammond, half in jest and half in earnest. 'What wonderful instincts these young women have.'

'Come and see her ladyship; and then you must have dinner, just as you had that first evening,' said Mary. 'We'll act that first evening over again, Jack; only you can't fall in love with Lesbia, as she isn't here.'

'I don't think I surrendered that first evening, Mary. Though I thought your sister the loveliest girl I had ever seen.'

'And what did you think of me, sir? Tell me that,' said Mary.

'Shall I tell you the truth, the whole truth, and nothing but the truth?'

'Of course.'

'Then I freely confess that I did not think about you at all. You were there--a pretty, innocent, bright young maiden, with big brown eyes and auburn hair; but I thought no more about you than I did about the Gainsborough on the wall, which you very much resemble.'

'That is most humiliating,' said Mary, pouting a little in the midst of her bliss.

'No, dearest, it is only natural,' answered Hammond. 'I believe if all the happy lovers in this world could be questioned, at least half of them would confess to having thought very little about each other at first meeting. They meet, and touch hands, and part again, and never guess the mystery of the future, which wraps them round like a cloud, never say of each other, There is my fate; and then they meet again, and again, as hazard wills, and never know that they are drifting to their doom.'

Mary rang bells and gave orders, just as she had done in that summer gloaming a year ago. The young men had arrived just at the same hour, on the stroke of nine, when the eight o'clock dinner was over and done with; for a ***tete-a-tete*** meal with Fraeulein Mueller was not a feast to be prolonged on account of its felicity. Perhaps they had so contrived as to arrive exactly at this hour.

Lady Maulevrier received them both with extreme cordiality. But the young men saw a change for the worse in the invalid since the spring. The face was thinner, the eyes too bright, the flush upon the hollow cheek had a hectic tinge, the voice was feebler. Hammond was reminded of a falcon or an eagle pining and wasting in a cage.

'I am very glad to see you, Mr. Hammond,' said Lady Maulevrier, giving him her hand, and addressing him with unwonted cordiality. 'It was a happy thought that brought you and Maulevrier here. When an old woman is as near the grave as I am her relatives ought to look after her. I shall be glad to have a little private conversation with you to-morrow, Mr. Hammond, if you can spare me a few minutes.'

'As many hours, if your ladyship pleases,' said Hammond. 'My time is entirely at your service.'

'Oh, no, you will want to be roaming about the hills with Mary, discussing your plans for the future. I shall not encroach too much on your time. But I am very glad you are here.'

'We shall only trespass on you for a few days,' said Maulevrier, 'just a flying visit.'

'How is it that you are not both at Henley?' asked Mary. 'I thought all the world was at Henley.'

'Who is Henley? what is Henley?' demanded Maulevrier, pretending ignorance.

'I believe Maulevrier has lost so much money backing, his college boat on previous occasions that he is glad to run away from the regatta this year,' said Hammond.

'I have a sister there,' replied his friend. 'That's an all-sufficient explanation. When a fellow's women-kind take to going to races and regattas it is high time for *him* to stop away.'

'Have you seen Lesbia lately?' asked his grandmother.

'About ten days ago.'

'And did she seem happy?'

Maulevrier shrugged his shoulders.

'She was vacillating between the refusal or the acceptance of a million of money and four or five fine houses. I don't know whether that condition of mind means happiness. I should call it an intermediate state.'

'Why do you make silly jokes about serious questions? Do you think Lesbia means to accept this Mr. Smithson?'

'All London thinks so.'

'And is he a good man?'

'Good for a hundred thousand pounds at half an hour's notice.'

'Is he worthy of your sister?'

Maulevrier paused, looked at his grandmother with a curious expression, and then replied--

'I think he is--quite.'

'Then I am content that she should marry him,' said Lady Maulevrier, 'although he is a nobody.'

'Oh, but he is a very important nobody, a nobody who can get a peerage next year, backed by the Maulevrier influence, which I suppose would count for something.'

'Most of my friends are dead,' said Lady Maulevrier, 'but there are a few survivors of the past who might help me.'

'I don't think there'll be any difficulty or doubt about the peerage. Smithson stumped up very handsomely at the last General Election, and the Conservatives are not strong enough to be ungrateful. "These have, no master."'

CHAPTER XXXII.
WAYS AND MEANS.

The three days that followed were among the happiest days of Mary Haselden's young life. Lady Maulevrier had become strangely indulgent. A softening influence of some kind had worked upon that haughty spirit, and it seemed as if her whole nature was changed--or it might be, Mary thought, that this softer side of her character had always been turned to Lesbia, while to Mary herself it was altogether new. Lesbia had been the peach on the sunny southern wall, ripening and reddening in a flood of sunshine; Mary had been the stunted fruit growing in a north-east corner, hidden among leaves, blown upon by cold winds green and hard and sour for lack of the warm bright light. And now Mary felt the sunshine, and grew glad and gay in those glowing beams.

'Dear grandmother, I believe you are beginning to love me,' she said, bending over to arrange the invalid's pillows in the July morning, the fresh mountain air blowing in upon old and young from the great open window, like a caress.

'I am beginning to know you,' answered Lady Maulevrier, gently.

'I think it is the magic of love, Mary, that has sweetened and softened your nature, and endeared you to me. I think you have grown ever so much sweeter a girl since your engagement. Or it may be that you were the same always, and it was I who was blind. Lesbia was all in all to me. All in all--and now I am nothing to her,' she murmured, to herself rather than to Mary.

'I am so proud to think that you see an improvement in me since my engagement,' said Mary, modestly. 'I have tried very hard to improve myself, so that I might be more worthy of him.'

'You are worthy, Mary, worthy of the best and the highest: and I believe that, although you are making what the world calls a very bad match, you are marrying wisely. You are wedding yourself to a life of obscurity; but what does that matter, if it be a happy life? I have known what it is to pursue the phantom fortune, and to find youth and hope and happiness vanish from the pathway which I followed.'

'Dear grandmother, I wish you had been able to marry the man of your choice,' answered Mary, tenderly.

She was ready to weep over that wasted life of her grandmother's; to weep for that forced parting of true lovers, albeit the tragedy was half a century old.

'I should have been a happier woman and a better woman if fate had been kind to me, Mary,' answered Lady Maulevrier, gravely; 'and now that I am daily drawing nearer the land of shadows, I will not stand in the way of faithful lovers. I have a fancy, Mary, that I have not many months to live.'

'Only an invalid's fancy,' said Mary, stooping down to kiss the pale forehead, so full of thought and care; 'only a morbid fancy, nursed in the monotony of this quiet room. Maulevrier and Jack and I must find some way of amusing you.'

'You will never amuse me out of that conviction, my dear. I can see the shadows lengthening and the sands running out. There are but a few grains left in the glass, Mary; and while those last I should like to see you and Mr. Hammond married. I should like to feel that your fate is settled before I go. God knows what confusion and trouble may follow my death.'

This was said with a sharp ring of despair.

'I am not going to leave you, grandmother,' said Mary.

'Not even for the man you love? You are a good girl, Mary. Lesbia has forsaken me for a lesser temptation.'

'Grandmother, that is hardly fair. It was your own wish to have Lesbia presented this season,' remonstrated Mary, loyal to the absent.

'True, my dear. I saw she was very tired of her life here, and I thought it was better. But I'm sorely afraid London has spoiled her. No, Mary, you can stay with me to the end, if you like. There is room enough for you and your husband under this roof. I like this Mr. Hammond. His is the only face that ever recalled the face of the dead. Yes, I like him; and although I know nothing about him except what Maulevrier tells me--and that is of the scantiest--still I feel, somehow, that I can trust him. Send your lover to me, Mary. I want to have a serious talk with him.'

Mary ran off to obey, fluttered, blushing, and trembling. This idea of marriage in the immediate future was to be the last degree startling. A year had seemed a very long time; and she had been told that she and her lover must wait a year at the very least; so that vision of marriage had seemed afar off in the dim shadowland of the future. She had been told nothing by her lover of where she was to live, or what her life was to be like when she was his wife. And now she was told that they were to be married almost immediately, that they were to live in the house where she had been reared, in that familiar land of hills and waters, that they were to roam about the dales and mountains together, they two, as man and wife. The whole thing was wonderful, bewildering, impossible almost.

This was on the first morning after Mr. Hammond's arrival. Maulevrier had gone off to hunt the Rotha for otters, and was up to his waist in the water, no doubt, by this time. Hammond was strolling up and down the terrace in front of the house, looking at the green expanse of Fairfield, the dark bulk of Seat Sandal, the nearer crests of Helm Crag and Silver Howe.

'You are to come to her ladyship directly, please,' said Mary, going up to him.

He took both her hands, drew her nearer to him, smiling down at her. They had been sitting side by side at the breakfast table half-an-hour ago, he waiting upon her as she poured out the tea; yet by his tender greeting and the delight in his face it might have been supposed they had not met for weeks. Such are the sweet inanities of love.

'What does her ladyship want with me, darling? and why are you blushing?' he asked.

'I--I think she is going to talk about--our--marriage,' faltered Mary.

'"Why, I will talk to her upon this theme until mine eyelids can no longer wag,"' quoted Hammond. 'Take me to her, Mary. I hope her ladyship is growing sensible.'

'She is very kind, very sweet. She has changed so much of late.'

Mary went with him to the door of her ladyship's sitting-room, and there left him to go in alone. She went to the library--that room over which a gloomy shadow seemed to have hung ever since that awful winter afternoon when Mary found Lady Maulevrier lying on the floor in the twilight. But it was a noble room, and in her studious hours Mary loved to sit here, walled round with books, and able to consult or dip into as many volumes as she liked. To-day, however, her mind was not attuned to study. She sat with a volume of Macaulay open before her: but her thoughts were not with the author. She was wondering what those two were saying in the room overhead, and finding all attempts at reading futile, she let her head sink back upon the cushion of her deep luxurious chair, and sat with her dreamy eyes fixed on the summer landscape and her thoughts with her lover.

Lady Maulevrier looked very wan and tired in the bright morning light, when Mr. Hammond seated himself beside her sofa. The change in her appearance since the spring was more marked to-day than it had seemed to him last night in the dim lamplight. Yes, there was need hero for a speedy settlement of air earthly matters. The traveller was nearing the mysterious end of the journey. The summons might come at any hour.

'Mr. Hammond, I feel a confidence in your integrity, your goodness of heart, and high principle which I never thought I could feel for a man of whom I know so little,' began Lady Maulevrier, gravely. 'All I know of you or your antecedents is what my grandson has told me--and I must say that the information so given has been very meagre. And yet I believe in you--and yet I am going to trust you, wholly, blindly, implicitly--and I am going to give you my granddaughter, ever so much sooner than I intended to give her to you. Soon, very soon, if you will have her!'

'I will have her to-morrow, if there is time to get a special licence,' exclaimed Hammond, bending down to kiss the dowager's hand, radiant with delight.

'You shall marry her very soon, if you like, marry her by special licence, in this room. I should like to see your wedding. I have a strange impatience to behold one of my granddaughters happily married, to know that her future is secure, that come weal, come woe, she is safe in the protection of a brave true man. I am not scared by the idea of a little poverty. That is often the best education for youth. But while you and I are alone we may as well talk about ways and means. Perhaps you may hardly feel prepared to take upon yourself the burden of a wife this year.'

'As well this year as next. I am not afraid.'

'Young men are so rash. However, as long as I live your responsibilities will be only nominal. This house will be Mary's home, and yours whenever you are able to occupy it. Of course I should not like to interfere with your professional efforts--but if you are cultivating literature,--why books can be written at Fellside better than in London. This lakeland of ours has been the nursery of deathless writers. But I feel that my days are numbered--and when I am dead--well death is always a cause of change and trouble of some kind, and Mary will profit very little by my death. The bulk of my fortune is left to Lesbia. I have taught her to consider herself my heiress; and it would be unjust to alter my will.'

'Pray do not dream of such a thing--there is no need--Mary will be rich enough,' exclaimed Hammond, hastily.

'With five hundred a year and the fruits of your industry,' said Lady Maulevrier. 'Yes, yes, with modest aspirations and simple habits, people can live happily, honourably, on a few hundreds a year. And if you really mean to devote yourself to literature, and do not mind burying yourself alive in this lake district until you have made your name as a writer, why the problem of ways and means will be easily solved.'

'Dear Lady Maulevrier, I am not afraid of ways and means. That is the last question which need trouble you. I told Lesbia when I offered myself to her nearly a year ago, that if she would trust me, if she would cleave to me, poverty should never touch her, sordid care should never come near her dwelling. But she could not believe me. She was like Thomas the twin. I could show her no palpable security for my promise--and she would not believe for the promise' sake. Mary trusted me; and Mary shall not regret her confidence.'

'Ah! it was different with Lesbia,' sighed Lady Maulevrier. 'I taught her to be ambitious. She had been schooled to set a high price upon herself. I know she cared for you--very much, even. But she could not face poverty; or, if you like, I will say that she could not face an obscure existence--sacrifice her ambition, a justifiable ambition in one so lovely, at the bidding of her first wooer. And then, again, she was told that if she married you, she would for ever forfeit my regard. You must not blame her for obeying me.'

'I do not blame her; for I have won the peerless pearl--the jewel above all price--a perfect woman. And now, dear Lady Maulevrier, give me but your consent, and I am off to York this afternoon, to interview the Archbishop, and get the special licence, which will allow me to wed my darling here by your couch to-morrow afternoon.'

'I have no objection to your getting the licence immediately; but you must let me write a cheque before you go. A special licence is expensive--I believe it costs fifty pounds.'

'If it cost a thousand I should not think it dear. But I have a notion that I shall be able to get the licence--cheap. You have made me wild with happiness.'

'But you must not refuse my cheque.'

'Indeed I must, Lady Maulevrier. I am not quite such a pauper as you think me.'

'But fifty pounds and the expenses of the journey; an outlay altogether unexpected on your part. I begin to fear that you are very reckless. A spendthrift shall never marry my granddaughter, with my consent.'

'I have never yet spent above half my income.'

Lady Maulevrier looked at him in wonderment and perplexity. Had the young man gone suddenly out of his mind, overwhelmed by the greatness of his bliss?

'But I thought you were poor,' she faltered.

'It has pleased you to think so, dear Lady Maulevrier; but I have more than enough for all my wants, and I shall be able to provide a fitting home for my Mary, when you can spare her to preside over her own establishment.'

'Establishment' seemed rather a big word, but Lady Maulevrier supposed that in this case it meant a cook and housemaid, with perhaps later on a boy in buttons, to break windows and block the pantry sink with missing teaspoons.

'Well, Mr. Hammond, this is quite an agreeable surprise,' she said, after a brief silence. 'I really thought you were poor--as poor as a young man of gentleman-like habits could be, and yet exist. Perhaps you will wonder why, thinking this, I brought myself to consent to your marriage with my granddaughter.'

'It was a great proof of your confidence in me, or in Providence,' replied Hammond, smiling.

'It was no such thing. I was governed by a sentiment--a memory. It was my love for the dead which softened my heart towards you, John Hammond.'

'Indeed!' he murmured, softly.

'There was but one man in this world I ever fondly loved--the love of my youth--my dearest and best, in the days when my heart was fresh and innocent and unambitious. That man was Ronald Hollister, afterwards Lord Hartfield. And yours is the only face that ever recalled his to my mind. It is but a vague likeness--a look now and then; but slight as that likeness is it has been enough to make my heart yearn towards you, as the heart of a mother to her son.'

John Hammond knelt beside the sofa, and bent his handsome face over the pale face on the pillow, imprinting such a kiss as a son might have given. His eyes were full of tears.

'Dear Lady Maulevrier, think that it is the spirit of the dead which blesses you for your fidelity to old memories,' he said, tenderly.

CHAPTER XXXIII.
BY SPECIAL LICENCE.

After that interview with John Hammond all the arrangements for the marriage were planned by Lady Maulevrier with a calm and business-like capacity which seemed extraordinary in one so frail and helpless. For a little while after Hammond left her she remained lost in a reverie, deeply affected by the speech and manner of her granddaughter's lover, as he gave her that first kiss of duty and affection, the affection of one who in that act declared the allegiance of a close and holy bond.

Yes, she told herself, this marriage, humble as it might be, was altogether satisfactory. Her own feeling towards the man of her granddaughter's choice was one of instinctive affection. Her heart had yearned to him from the beginning of their acquaintance; but she had schooled herself to hide all indications of her liking for him, she had made every effort to keep him at a distance, deeming his very merits a source of danger in a household where there were two fresh impressionable girls.

And despite all her caution and care he had succeeded in winning one of those girls: and she was glad, very glad, that he had so succeeded in baffling her prudence. And now it was agreeable to discover that he was not quite such a pauper as she had supposed him to be.

Her heart felt lighter than it had been for some time when she set about planning the wedding.

The first step in the business was to send for James Steadman. He came immediately, grave and quiet as of old, and stood with his serious eyes bent upon the face of his mistress, awaiting her instructions.

'Lady Mary is going to be married to Mr. Hammond, by special licence, in this room, to-morrow afternoon, if it can be managed so soon,' said Lady Maulevrier.

'I am very glad to hear it, my lady,' answered Steadman, without the faintest indication of surprise.

'Why are you so--particularly glad?' asked his mistress, looking at him sharply.

'Because Lady Mary's presence in this house is a source of danger to--your arrangements. She is very energetic and enterprising--very shrewd--and--well, she is a woman--so I suppose there can be no harm in saying she is somewhat inquisitive. Things will be much safer here when Lady Mary is gone!'

'But she will not be gone--she is not going away--except for a very brief honeymoon. I cannot possibly do without her. She has become necessary to my life, Steadman; and there is so little left of that life now, that there is no need for me to sacrifice the last gleams of sunshine. The girl is very sweet, and loving, and true. I was not half fond enough of her in the past; but she has made herself very dear to me of late. There are many things in this life, Steadman, which we only find out too late.'

'But, surely, my lady, Lady Mary will leave Fellside to go to a home of her own after her marriage.'

'No, I tell you, Steadman,' his mistress answered, with a touch of impatience; 'Lady Mary and her husband will make this house their home so long as I am here.

It will not be long.'

'God grant it may be very long before you cease to be mistress here,' answered Steadman, with real feeling; and then in a lower tone he went on: 'Pardon me, my lady, for the suggestion, but do you think it wise to have Mr. Hammond here as a resident?'

'Why should it not be wise? Mr. Hammond is a gentleman.'

'True, my lady; but any accident, such as that which brought Lady Mary into the old garden----'

'No such accident need occur--it must not occur, Steadman,' exclaimed Lady Maulevrier, with kindling eyes. She who had so long ruled supreme was not inclined to have any desire of hers questioned. 'There must have been gross carelessness that day--carelessness on your part, or that stable door would never have been left open. The key ought to have been in your possession It ought not to have been in the power of the stableman to open that door. As to Mr. Hammond's presence at Fellside, I cannot see any danger--any reason why harm should come of it, more than of Lord Maulevrier's presence here in the past.'

'The two gentlemen are so different, my lady,' said Steadman, with a gloomy brow. 'His lordship is so light-hearted and careless, his mind taken up with his horses, guns, dogs, fishing, shooting, and all kinds of sport. He is not a gentleman to take much notice of anything out of his own line. But this Mr. Hammond is different--a very thoughtful gentleman, an inquiring mind, as one would say.'

'Steadman, you are getting cowardly in your old age. The danger--such a risk as you hint at, must be growing less and less every day. After forty years of security----'

'Security' echoed Steadman, with a monosyllabic laugh which expressed intense bitterness. 'Say forty years during which I have felt myself upon the edge of a precipice every day and every hour. Security! But perhaps you are right, my lady, I am growing old and nervous, a feebler man than I was a few years ago, feebler in body and mind. Let Mr. Hammond make his home here, if it pleases your ladyship to have him. So long as I am well and able to get about there can be no danger of anything awkward happening.'

Lady Maulevrier looked alarmed.

'But you have no expectation of falling ill, I hope, Steadman; you have no premonition of any malady?'

'No, my lady, none--except the malady of old age. I feel that I am not the man I once was, that is all. My brain is getting woolly, and my sight is clouded now and then. And if I were to fall ill suddenly----'

'Oh, it would be terrible, it would be a dire calamity! There is your wife, certainly, to look after things, but----'

'My wife would do her best, my lady. She is a faithful creature, but she is not-- yes, without any unkindness I must say that Mrs. Steadman is not a genius!'

'Oh, Steadman, you must not fail me! I am horror-stricken at the mere idea,' exclaimed Lady Maulevrier. 'After forty years--great God! it would be terrible. Lesbia, Mary, Maulevrier! the great, malignant, babbling world outside these doors. I am hemmed round with perils. For God's sake preserve your strength. Take care of your health. You are my strong rock. If you feel that there is anything amiss with you, or that your strength is failing, consult Mr. Horton--neglect no precaution. The safety of this house, of the family honour, hangs upon you.'

'Pray do not agitate yourself, my lady,' entreated Steadman. 'I was wrong to trouble you with my fears. I shall not fail you, be sure. Although I am getting old, I shall hold out to the end.'

'The end cannot be very far off,' said Lady Maulevrier, gloomily.

'I thought that forty years ago, my lady. But you are right--the end must be near now. Yes, it must be near. And now, my lady, your orders about the wedding.'

'It will take place to-morrow, as I told you, in this room. You will go to the Vicar and ask him to officiate. His two daughters will no doubt consent to be Lady Mary's bridesmaids. You will make the request in my name. Perhaps the Vicar will call this afternoon and talk matters over with me. Lady Mary and her husband will go to Cumberland for a brief honeymoon--a week at most--and then they will come back to Fellside. Tell Mrs. Power to prepare the east wing for them. She will make one of the rooms into a boudoir for Lady Mary; and let everything be as bright and pretty as good taste can make it. She can telegraph to London for any new furniture that may be wanted to complete her arrangements. And now send Lady Mary to me.'

Mary came, fresh from the pine-wood, where she had been walking with her lover; her lover of to-day, her husband to-morrow. He had told her how he was to start for York directly after luncheon, and to come back by the earliest train next day, and how they two were to be married to-morrow afternoon.

'It is more wonderful than any dream that I ever dreamt.' exclaimed Mary. 'But how can it be? I have not even a wedding gown.'

'A fig for wedding gowns! It is Mary I am to wed, not her gown. Were you clad like patient Grisel I should be content. Besides you have no end of pretty gowns. And you are to be dressed for travelling, remember; for I am going to carry you off to Lodore directly we are married, and you will have to clamber up the rocky bed of the waterfall to see the sun set behind the Borrowdale hills in your wedding gown. It had better be one of those neat little tailor gowns which become you so well.'

'I will wear whatever you tell me,' answered Mary. 'I shall always dress to please you, and not the outside world.'

'Will you, my Griselda. Some day you shall be dressed as Grisel was--

"In a cloth of gold that brighte shone,   With a coroune of many a riche stone."

'Yes, you darling, when you are Lord Chancellor: and till that day comes I will wear tailor gowns, linsey-wolsey, anything you like,' cried Mary, laughing.

She ran to her grandmother's room, ineffably content, without a thought of trousseau or finery; but then Mary Haselden was one of those few young women for whom life is not a question of fashionable raiment.

'Mary, I am going to send you off upon your honeymoon to-morrow afternoon,' said Lady Maulevrier, smiling at the bright, happy face which was bent over her. 'Will you come back and nurse a fretful old woman when the honeymoon is over?'

'The honeymoon will never be over,' answered Mary, joyously 'Our wedded life is to be one long honeymoon. But I will come back in a very few days, and take care of you. I am not going to let you do without me, now that you have learnt to love me.'

'And will you be content to stay with me when your husband has gone to London?'

'Yes, but I shall try to prevent his going very often, or staying very long. I shall try to wind myself into his heart, so that there will be an aching void there when we are parted.'

Lady Maulevrier proceeded to tell Mary all her arrangements. Three handsome rooms in the east wing, a bedroom, dressing-room, and boudoir, were to be made ready for the newly-married, couple. Fraeulein Mueller was to be dismissed with a retiring pension, in order that Lady Mary and her husband might feel themselves master and mistress in the lower part of the house.

'And if your husband really means to devote himself to literature, he can have no better workshop than the library I have put together,' said Lady Maulevrier.

'And no better adviser and guide than you, dear grandmother, you who have read everything that has been written worth reading during the last half century.'

'I have read a great deal, Mary, but I hardly know if I am any wiser on that account,' answered Lady Maulevrier. 'After all, however much of other people's wisdom we may devour, it is in ourselves that we are thus, or thus. Our past follies rise up against us at the end of life; and we see how little our book-learning has helped us to stand against foolish impulses, against evil passions. "Be good," Mary, "and let who will be wise," as the poet says. A faithful heart is your only anchor in the stormy seas of life. My dear, I am so glad you are going to be married.'

'It is very sudden,' said Mary.

'Very sudden; yet in your case that does not much matter. You have quite made up your mind about Mr. Hammond, I believe.'

'Made up my mind! I began to worship him the first night he came here.'

'Foolish child. Well, there is no deed to wait for settlements. You have only your allowance as Lord Maulevrier's daughter--a first charge on the estate, which cannot be made away with or anticipated, and of which no husband can deprive you.'

'He shall have every sixpence of it,' murmured Mary.

'And Mr. Hammond, though he tells me he is better off than I supposed, can have nothing to settle. So there will be nothing forfeited by a marriage without settlements.'

Mary could not enter upon the question. It was even of less importance than the wedding gown.

The gong sounded for luncheon.

'Steadman's dogcart is to take Mr. Hammond to the station at half-past two,' said Lady Maulevrier, 'so you had better go and give him his luncheon.'

Mary needed no second bidding. She flew downstairs, and met her lover in the hall.

What a happy luncheon it was! Fraeulein 'mounched, and mounched, and mounched,' like the sailor's wife eating chestnuts: but those two lovers lunched upon moonshine, upon each other's little words and little looks, upon their own ineffable bliss. They sat side by side, and helped each other to the nicest thing's on the table, but neither could eat, and they got considerably mixed in their way of eating, taking chutnee with strawberry cream, and currant jelly with asparagus. What did it matter? Everything tasted of bliss.

'You have had absolutely nothing to eat,' said Mary, piteously, as the dogcart came grinding round upon the dry gravel.

'Oh, I have done splendidly--thanks. I have just had a macaroon and some of that capital gorgonzola. God bless you, dearest, and *a revoir, a revoir* to-morrow.'

'And to-morrow I shall be Mary Hammond,' cried Mary, clasping her hands. 'Isn't it capital fun?'

They were in the porch alone. The servants were all at dinner, save the groom with the cart, Miss Mueller was still munching at the well-spread table in the dining-room.

John Hammond folded his sweetheart in his arms for one brief embrace; there was no time for loitering. In another moment he was springing into the cart. A shake of the reins, and he was driving slowly down the steep avenue.

'Life is full of partings,' Mary said to herself, as she watched the last glimpse of the dogcart between the trees down in the road below, 'but this one is to be very short, thank God.'

She wondered what she should do with herself for the rest of the afternoon, and finally, finding that she was not wanted by her grandmother until afternoon tea, she set out upon a round of visits to her favourite cottagers, to bid them a long farewell as a spinster.

'You'll be away a long time, I suppose, Lady Mary?' said one of her humble friends; 'you'll be going to Switzerland or Italy, or some of those foreign parts where great ladies and gentlemen travel for their honeymoons?'

But Mary declared that she would be absent a week at longest She was coming back to take care of her invalid grandmother; and she was not going to marry a great gentleman, but a man who would have to work for his living.

She went back to Fellside, and read the **Times**, and poured out Lady Maulevrier's tea, and sat on her low stool by the sofa, and the old and the young woman were as happy and confidential together as if they had been always the nearest and dearest to each other. Her ladyship had seen Miss Mueller, and had informed that excellent person that her services at Fellside would no longer be required after Lady Mary's marriage; but that her devotion to her duties during the last fourteen years should be rewarded by a pension which, together with her savings, would enable her to spend the rest of her days in repose. Miss Mueller was duly grateful, and owned to a tender longing for the **Heimath**, and declared herself ready to retire from her post whenever her ladyship pleased.

'I shall go back to Germany directly I leave you, and I shall live and die there, unless I am wanted by one of my old pupils. But should Lady Lesbia or Lady Mary need my services for their daughters, in days to come, they can command me. For no one else will I abandon the Fatherland.'

The Fraeulein thus easily disposed of, Lady Mary felt that matrimony would verily mean independence. And yet she was prepared to regard her husband as her master. She meant to obey him in all meekness and reverence of spirit.

She spent the rest of the afternoon and the whole of the evening in her grandmother's sitting-room, dining **tete-a-tete** with the invalid for the first time since her illness. Lady Maulevrier talked much of Mary's future, and of Lesbia's; but it was evident that she was full of uneasiness upon the latter subject.

'I don't know what Lesbia is going to do with her life,' she said, with a sigh. 'Her letters tell me of nothing but gowns and parties; and Georgina Kirkbank can only expatiate upon Mr. Smithson's wealth, and the grand position he is going to occupy by-and-by. I should like to see both my granddaughters married before I die--yes, I should like to see Lesbia's fate secure, if she were to be only Lady Lesbia Smithson.'

'She cannot fail to make a good match, grandmother,' said Mary.

'I am beginning to lose faith in her future,' answered Lady Maulevrier. 'There seems to be a fatality about the career of particularly attractive girls. They are too confident of their power to succeed in life. They trifle with fortune, fascinate the wrong people, and keep the right people at arm's length. I think if I had been Lesbia's guide in society her first season would have counted for more than it is likely to count for under Lady Kirkbank's management. I should have awakened Lesbia from the dream of dress and dancing--the mere butterfly life of a girl who never looks beyond the present moment. But now go and give orders about your packing, Mary. It is past ten, and Clara had better pack your trunks early to-morrow morning.'

Clara was a modest Easedale damsel, who had been promoted to be Lady Mary's personal attendant, when the more mature Kibble had gone away with Lady Lesbia. Mary required very little waiting upon, but she was not the less glad to have a neat little smiling maiden devoted to her service, ready to keep her rooms neat and trim, to go on errands to the cottagers, to arrange the flowers in the old china bowls, and to make herself generally useful.

It seemed a strange thing to have to furnish a trousseau from the wardrobe of everyday life--a trousseau in which nothing, except half-a-dozen pairs of gloves, a pair of boots, and a few odds and ends of lace and ribbons would be actually new. Mary thought very little of the matter, but the position of things struck her maid as altogether extraordinary and unnatural.

'You should have seen the things Miss Freeman had, Lady Mary,' exclaimed the damsel, 'the daughter of that cotton-spinning gentleman from Manchester, who lives at The Gables--you should have seen her new gowns and things when she was married. Mrs. Freeman's maid keeps company with my brother James--he's in the stables at Freeman's, you know, Lady Mary--and she asked me in to look at the trousseau two days before the wedding. I never saw such beautiful dresses--such hats--such bonnets--such jackets and mantles. It was like going into one of those grand shops at York, and having all the things in the shop pulled out for one to look at--such silks and satins--and trimmed--ah! how those dresses was trimmed. The mystery was how the young lady could ever get herself into them, or sit down when she'd got one of them on.'

'Instruments of torture, Clara. I should hate such gowns, even if I were going to marry a rich man, as I suppose Miss Freeman was.'

'Not a bit of it, Lady Mary. She was only going to marry a Bolton doctor with a small practice; but her maid told me she was determined she'd get all she could out of her pa, in case he should lose all his money and go bankrupt. They said that trousseau cost two thousand pounds.'

'Well, Clara, I'd rather have my tailor gowns, in which I can scramble about the ghylls and crags just as I like.' There was a pale yellow Indian silk, smothered with soft yellow lace, which would serve for a wedding gown; for indifferent as Mary was to the great clothes question, she wanted to look in some wise as a bride. A neat chocolate-coloured cloth, almost new from the tailor's hands, with a little cloth toque to match, would do for the wedding journey. All the details of Mary's wardrobe were the perfection of neatness. She had grown very neat and careful in her habits since her engagement, anxious to be industrious and frugal in all things- -a really handy housewife for a hard-worked bread-winner. And now she was told that Mr. Hammond was not so poor as she had thought. She would not be obliged to stint herself, and manage, as she had supposed when she went about among the cottagers, taking lessons in household economy. It was almost a disappointment.

She and Clara finished the packing that night, Mary being much too excited for the possibility of sleep. There was not much to pack, only one roomy American trunk--a trunk which held everything--a Gladstone bag for things that might possibly be wanted in a hurry, and a handsome dressing-bag, Maulevrier's last birthday gift to his sister.

Mary had received no gifts from her lover, save the plain gold engagement ring, and a few new books sent straight from the publishers. Clara took care to inform her young mistress that Miss Freeman's sweetheart had sent her all manner of splendid presents, scent bottles, photograph albums, glove boxes, and other things of beauty, albeit his means were supposed to be *nil*. It was evident that Clara disapproved of Mr. Hammond's conduct in this matter, and even suspected him of meanness.

'He did ought to have sent you his photograph, Lady Mary,' said Clara, with a reproachful air.

'I daresay he would have done so, Clara, but he has been photographed only once in his life.'

'Lawk a mercy, Lady Mary! Why most young gentlemen have themselves photographed in every new place they go to; and as Mr. Hammond has been a traveller, like his lordship, I made sure he'd have been photographed in knickerbockers and every other kind of attitude.'

Mary had not refrained from asking for her lover's portrait; and he had told

Phantom Fortune, A Novel

her that he had carefully abstained from having his countenance reproduced in any manner since his fifteenth year, when he had been photographed at his mother's desire.

'The present fashion of photographs staring out of every stationer's window makes a man's face public property,' he told Mary. 'I don't want every street Arab in London to recognise me.'

'But you are not a public man,' said Mary. 'Your photograph would not be in all the windows; although, in my humble opinion, you are a very handsome man.'

Hammond blushed, laughed, and turned the conversation, and Mary had to exist without any picture of her lover.

'Millais shall paint me in his grand Reynolds manner by-and-by,' he told Mary.

'Millais! Oh, Jack! When will you and I be able to give a thousand or so for a portrait?'

'Ah, when, indeed? But we may as well enjoy our day-dreams, like Alnaschar, without smashing our basket of crockery.'

And now Mary, who had managed to exist without the picture, was to have the original. He was to be all her own--her master, her lord, her love, after to-morrow--unto eternity, in life, and in the grave, and in the dim hereafter beyond the grave, they two were to be one. In heaven there was to be no marrying or giving in marriage, Mary was told; but her own heart cried aloud to her that the happily wedded must remain linked in heaven. God would not part the blessed souls of true lovers.

A short sleep, broken by happy dreams, and it was morning, Mary's wedding morning, fairest of summer days, July in all her beauty. Mary went to her grandmother's room, and waited upon her at breakfast.

Lady Maulevrier was in excellent spirits.

'Everything is arranged, Mary, I have had a telegram from Hammond, who has got the licence, and will come at half-past one. At three the Vicar will come to marry you, his daughters, Katie and Laura, acting as your bridesmaids.'

'Bridesmaids!' exclaimed Mary. 'I forgot all about bridesmaids. Am I really to have any?'

'You will have two girls of your own age to bear you company, at any rate. I have asked dear old Horton to be present; and he, Fraeulein, and Maulevrier will complete the party. It will not be a brilliant wedding, Mary, or a costly ceremonial, except for the licence.'

'And poor Jack will have to pay for that,' said Mary, with a long face.

'Poor Jack refused to let me pay for it,' answered Lady Maulevrier. 'He is vastly independent, and I fear somewhat reckless.'

'I like him for his independence; but he mustn't be reckless,' said Mary, severely.

He was to be the master in all things! and yet she was to exercise a restraining influence, she was to guard him against his own weaknesses, his too generous impulses. Her voice was to be the voice of prudence. This is how Mary understood the marriage tie.

Under ordinary conditions Mary would have been in the avenue, lying in wait for her lover, eager to get the very first glimpse of him when he arrived, to see him before he had brushed the dust of the journey from his raiment. But to-day she hung back. She stayed in her grandmother's room and sat beside the sofa, shy, and even a little downcast. This lover who was so soon to be transformed into a husband was a formidable personage. She dare not rush forth to greet him. Perhaps he had changed his mind by this time, and was sorry he had ever asked her to marry him. Perhaps he thought he was being hustled into a marriage. He had been told that he was to wait at least a year. And now, all in a moment, he was sent off to get a special licence. How could she be quite sure that he liked this kind of treatment?

If there is any faith to be placed in the human countenance, Mr. Hammond was in no wise an unwilling bridegroom; for his face teamed with happy light as he came into the room presently, followed by an elderly man with grey hair and whiskers, and in a strictly professional frock coat, whom the butler announced as Mr. Dorncliffe. Lady Maulevrier looked startled, somewhat offended even at this intrusion, and she gave Mr. Dorncliffe a very haughty salutation, which was almost more crushing than no salutation at all.

Mary stood up by her grandmother's sofa, and looked rather frightened.

'Dear Lady Maulevrier,' said Hammond, 'I ventured to telegraph to my lawyer to meet me at York last night, and come on here with me this morning. He has prepared a settlement, which I should like you to hear him read, and which he will explain to you, if necessary, while Molly and I go for a stroll in the grounds.'

He had never called her Molly before. He put his arm round her with a proud air of possession, even under her grandmother's eyes. And she nestled close up to his side, forgetting everything but the delight of belonging to him.

They went downstairs, and through the billiard room to the terrace, and from the terrace to the tennis lawn, where John Hammond sat reading Heine nearly a year ago, just before he proposed to Lesbia.

'Do you remember that day?' asked Mary, looking at him, solemnly.

'I remember every day and every hour we have spent together since I began to love you,' answered Hammond.

'Ah, but this was before you began to love me,' said Mary, with a piteous little grimace. 'This was while you were loving Lesbia as hard as ever you could. Don't you remember the day you proposed to her--a lovely summer day like this, the lake just as blue, the sun shining upon Fairfield just as it is shining now, and you sat there reading Heine--those sweet, sweet verses, that seemed made of sighs and tears; and every now and then you paused and looked up at Lesbia, and there was more love in your eyes than in all Heine's poetry, though that brims over with love.'

'But how did you know all this, Molly? You were not here.'

'I was not very far off. I was behind those bushes, watching and listening. I knew you were in love with Lesbia, and I thought you despised me, and I was very, very wretched; and I listened afterwards when you proposed to her there--behind the pine trees--and I hated her for refusing you, and I am afraid I hated you for proposing to her.'

'When I ought to have been proposing to my Molly, blind fool that I was,' said Hammond, smiling tenderly at her, smiling, though his eyes were dim with tears. 'My own sweet love, it was a terrible mistake, a mistake that might have cost me the happiness of a lifetime. But Fate was very good to me, and let me have my Mary after all. And now let us sit down under the old red beech and talk till it is time to go and get ready for our wedding. I suppose one ought to brush one's hair and wash one's hands for that kind of thing, even when the function is not on a ceremonious scale.'

Mary laughed.

'I have a prettier gown than this to be married in, although it isn't a wedding gown,' she said.

'Oh, by-the-by, I have something for you,' said her lover, 'something in the way of ornaments, but I don't suppose you'd care to wear them to-day. I'll run and get them.'

He went back to the house, leaving Mary sitting on the rustic bench under the fine old copper beech, a tree that had been standing long before Lady Maulevrier enlarged the old stone house into a stately villa. He returned in a few minutes, bringing a morocco bag about the size of those usually carried by lawyers or lawyers' clerks.

'I don't think I have given you anything since we were engaged, Mary,' he said, as he seated himself by her side.

Mary blushed, remembering how Clara, the maid, had remarked upon this fact.

'You gave me my ring,' she said, looking down at the massive band of gold, 'and you have given me ever so many delightful books.'

'Those were very humble gifts, Molly: but to-day I have brought you a wedding present.'

He opened the bag and took out a red morocco case, and then half-a-dozen more red morocco cases of various shapes and sizes. The first looked new, but the others were old-fashioned and passing shabby, as if they had been knocking about brokers' shops for the last quarter of a century.

'There is my wedding gift, Mary,' he said, handing her the new case.

It contained an exquisitely painted miniature of a very beautiful woman, in a large oval locket set with sapphires.

'You have asked me for my portrait, dearest,' he said. 'I give you my mother's rather than my own, because I loved her as I never thought to love again, till I knew you. I should like you to wear that locket sometimes, Mary, as a kind of link between the love of the past and the love of the present. Were my mother living, she would welcome and cherish my bride and my wife. She is dead, and you and she can never meet on earth: but I should like you to be familiar with the face which was once the light of my life.'

Mary's eyes filled with tears as she gazed at the face in the miniature. It was the portrait of a woman of about thirty--a face of exquisite refinement, of calm and pensive beauty.

'I shall treasure this picture always, above all things,' she said: but 'why did you have it set so splendidly, Jack? No gems were needed to give your mother's portrait value in my eyes.'

'I know that, dearest, but I wanted to make the locket worth wearing. And now for the other cases. The locket is your lover's free gift, and is yours to keep and to bequeath to your children. These are heirlooms, and yours only during your husband's lifetime.'

He opened one of the largest cases, and on a bed of black velvet Mary beheld a magnificent diamond necklace, with a large pendant. He opened another and displayed a set of sprays for the hair. Another contained earrings, another bracelets, the last a tiara.

'What are they for?' gasped Mary.

'For my wife to wear.'

'Oh, but I could never wear such things,' she exclaimed, with an idea that these must be stage jewellery. 'They are paste, of course--very beautiful for people who like that kind of thing--but I don't.'

She felt deeply shocked at this evidence of bad taste on the part of her lover. How the things flashed in the sunshine--but so did the crystal drops in the old Venetian girondoles.

'No, Molly, they are not paste; they are Brazilian diamonds, and, as Maulevrier would say, they are as good as they make them. They are heirlooms, Molly. My dear mother wore them in her summer-tide of wedded happiness. My grandmother wore them for thirty years before her; my great grandmother wore them at the Court of Queen Charlotte, and they were worn at the Court of Queen Anne. They are nearly two hundred years old; and those central stones in the tiara came out of a cap worn by the Great Mogul, and are the largest table diamonds known. They are historic, Mary.'

'Why, they must be worth a fortune.'

'They are valued at something over seventy thousand pounds.'

'But why don't you sell them?' exclaimed Mary, opening her eyes wide with surprise, 'they would give you a handsome income.'

'They are not mine to sell, Molly. Did not I tell you that they are heirlooms? They are the family jewels of the Countesses of Hartfield.'

'Then what are you?'

'Ronald Hollister, Earl of Hartfield, and your adoring lover!'

Mary gave a cry of surprise, a cry of distress even.

'Oh, that is too dreadful!' she exclaimed; 'grandmother will be so unhappy. She had set her heart upon Lesbia marrying Lord Hartfield, the son of the man *she* loved.'

'I got wind of her wish more than a year ago,' said Hartfield, 'from your brother; and he and I hatched a little plot between us. He told me Lesbia was not worthy of his friend's devotion--told me that she was vain and ambitious--that she had been educated to be so. I determined to come and try my fate. I would try to win her as plain John Hammond. If she was a true woman, I told myself, vanity and ambition would be blown to the four winds, provided I could win her love. I came, I saw her; and to see was to love her. God knows I tried honestly to win her; but I had sworn to myself that I would woo her as John Hammond, and I did not waver in my resolution--no, not when a word would have turned the scale. She liked me, I think, a little; but she did not like the notion of an obscure life as the wife of a hard-working professional man. The pomps and vanities of this world had it against love or liking, and she gave me up. I thank God that the pomps and vanities prevailed; for this happy chance gave me Mary, my sweet Wordsworthian damsel, found, like the violet or the celandine, by the wayside, in Wordsworth's own country.'

'And you are Lord Hartfield!' exclaimed Mary, still lost in wonder, and with no elation at this change in the aspect of her life. 'I always knew you were a great man. But poor grandmother! It will be a dreadful disappointment to her.'

'I think not. I think she has learned my Molly's value; rather late, as I learned it; and I believe she will be glad that one of her granddaughters should marry the son of her first lover. Let us go to her, love, and see if she is reconciled to the idea, and whether the settlement is ready for execution. Dorncliffe and his clerk were working at it half through the night.'

'What is the good of a settlement?' asked Mary. 'I'm sure I don't want one.'

'Lady Hartfield must not be dependent upon her husband's whim or pleasure for her milliner's bill or her private charities,' answered her lover, smiling at her eagerness to repudiate anything business-like.

'But I would rather be dependent on your pleasure. I shall never have any milliner's bills; and I am sure you would never deny me money for charity.'

'You shall not have to ask me for it, except when you have exceeded your pin-money I hope you will do that now and then, just to afford me the pleasure of doing you a favour.'

'Hartfield,' repeated Mary, to herself, as they went towards the house; 'shall I have to call you Hartfield? I don't like the name nearly so well as Jack.'

'You shall call me Jack for old sake's sake,' said Hartfield, tenderly.

'How did you think of such a name as Jack?'

'Rather an effort of genius, wasn't it. Well, first and foremost I was christened Ronald John--all the Hollisters are christened John--name of the founder of the race; and, secondly, Maulevrier and I were always plain Mr. Morland and Mr. Hammond in our travels, and always called each other Jack and Jim.'

'How nice!' said Mary; 'would you very much mind our being plain Mr. and Mrs. Hammond, while we are on our honeymoon trip?'

'I should like it of all things.'

'So should I. People will not take so much notice of us, and we can do what we like, and go where we like.'

'Delightful! We'll even disguise ourselves as Cook's tourists, if you like. I would not mind.'

They were at the door of Lady Maulevrier's sitting room by this time. They went in, and were greeted with smiles.

'Let me look at the Countess of Hartfield that is to be in half an hour,' said her ladyship. 'Oh, Mary, Mary, what a blind idiot I have been, and what a lucky girl you are! I told you once that you were wiser than Lesbia, but I little thought how much wiser you had been.'

CHAPTER XXXIV.
'OUR LOVE WAS NEW, AND THEN BUT IN THE SPRING.'

Henley Regatta was over. It had passed like a tale that is told; like Epsom and

Ascot, and all the other glories of the London season. Happy those for whom the glory of Henley, the grace of Ascot, the fever of Epsom, are not as weary as a twice-told tale, bringing with them only bitterest memories of youth that has fled, of hopes that have withered, of day-dreams that have never been realised. There are some to whom that mad hastening from pleasure to pleasure, that rush from scene to scene of excitement, that eager crowding into one day and night of gaieties which might fairly relieve the placid monotony of a month's domesticity, a month's professional work--some there are to whom this Vanity Fair is as a treadmill or the turning of a crank, the felon's deepest humiliation, purposeless, unprofitable, labour.

The regatta was over, and Lady Kirkbank and her charge hastened back to Arlington Street. Theirs was the very first departure; albeit Mr. Smithson pleaded hard for a prolongation of their visit. The weather was exceptionally lovely, he urged. Water picnics were delightful just now--the banks were alive with the colour of innumerable wild flowers, as beautiful and more poetical than the gorgeous flora of the Amazon or the Paraguay river. And Lady Lesbia had developed a genius for punting; and leaning against her pole, with her hair flying loose and sleeves rolled up above the elbow, she was a subject for canvas or marble, Millais or Adams Acton.

'When we are in Italy I will have her modelled, just in that attitude, and that dress,' said Mr. Smithson. 'She will make a lovely companion for my Reading Girl: one all repose and reverie, the other all life and action. Dear Lady Kirkbank, you really must stay for another week at least. Why go back to the smoke and sultriness of town? Here we can almost live on the water; and I will send to London for some people to make music for us in the evenings, or if you miss your little game at "Nap," we will play for an hour or so every night. It shall not be my fault if my house is not pleasant for you.'

'Your house is charming, and I shall be here only too often in the days to come; you will have more than enough of me *then*, I promise you,' replied Georgie, with her girlish laugh, 'but we must not stop a day longer now. People would begin to talk. Besides, we have engagements for every hour of the week that is coming, and for a fortnight after: and then I suppose I ought to take Lesbia to the North to see her grandmother, and to discuss all the preparations and arrangements for this very serious event in which you and Lesbia are to be the chief performers.'

'I shall be very glad to go to Grasmere myself, and to make the acquaintance of my future grandmother-in-law,' said Mr. Smithson.

'You will be charmed with her. She belongs to the old school--something of a fossil, perhaps, but a very dignified fossil. She has grown old in a rustic seclusion, and knows less of *our* world than a mother abbess; but she has read immensely, and is wonderfully clever. I am bound to tell you that she has very lofty ideas about her granddaughter; and I believe she will only be reconciled to Lesbia's marriage with a commoner by the notion that you are sure of a peerage. I ventured to hint as much in my letter to Lady Maulevrier yesterday.'

A shade of sullenness crept over Horace Smithson's visage.

'I should hope that such settlements as I am in a position to make will convince Lady Maulevrier that I am a respectable suitor for her granddaughter, ex peerage,' he said, somewhat haughtily.

'My dear Smithson, did I not tell you that poor Lady Maulevrier is a century behind the times,' exclaimed Lady Kirkbank, with an aggrieved look. 'If she were one of *us*, of course she would know that wealth is the paramount consideration, and that you are quite the best match of the season. But she is dreadfully *arrieree*, poor dear thing; and she must have amused herself with the day-dream of seeing Lesbia a duchess, or something of that kind. I shall tell her that Lesbia can be one of the queens of society without having strawberry leaves on her coach panels, and that my dear friend Horace Smithson is a much better match than a seedy duke. So don't look cross, my dear fellow; in me you have a friend who will never desert you.'

'Thanks,' said Smithson, inwardly resolving that, so soon as this little transaction of his marriage were over, he would see as little of Georgie Kirkbank and her cotton frocks and schoolgirl hats as bare civility would allow.

He had promised her that she should be the richer by a neat little bundle of fat and flourishing railway stock when his happiness was secured, and he was not going to break his promise. But he did not mean to give George and Georgie free quarters at Rood Hall, or at Cowes, or Deauville; and he meant to withdraw his wife altogether from Lady Kirkbank's pinchbeck set.

What were Lesbia's feelings in the early morning after the last day of the regatta, as she slowly paced the lavender walk in the Ladies' Garden, alone?--for happily

Mr. Smithson was not so early a riser as the Grasmere-bred damsel, and she had this fresh morning hour to herself. Of what was she thinking as she paced slowly up and down the broad gravel walk, between two rows of tall old bushes, on which masses of purple blossom stood up from the pale grey foliage, silvery where the summer breeze touched it?

Well, she was thinking first what a grand old place Rood Hall was, and that it was in a manner hers henceforward. She was to be mistress of this house, and of other houses, each after its fashion as perfect as Rood Hall. She was to have illimitable money at her command, to spend and give away as she liked. She, who yesterday had been tortured by the idea of owing a paltry three thousand pounds, was henceforward to count her thousands by the hundred. Her senses reeled before that dazzling vision of figures with rows of ciphers after them, one cipher more or less meaning the difference between thousands and millions. Everybody had agreed in assuring her that Mr. Smithson was inordinately rich. Everybody had considered it his or her business to give her information about the gentleman's income; clearly implying thereby that in the opinion of society Mr. Smithson's merits as a suitor were a question of so much bullion.

Could she doubt--she who had learned in one short season to know what the world was made of and what it most valued--could she, steeped to the lips in the wisdom of Lady Kirkbank's set, doubt for an instant that she was making a better match in the eye of society, than if she had married a man of the highest lineage in all England, a peer of the highest rank, without large means? She knew that money was power, that a man might begin life as a pot-boy or a greengrocer, a knacker or a dust contractor, and climb to the topmost pinnacles, were he only rich enough. She knew that society would eat such a man's dinners and dance at his wife's balls, and pretend to think him an altogether exceptional man, make believe to admire him for his own sake, to think his wife most brilliant among women, if he were only rich enough. And could she doubt that society would bow down to her as Lady Lesbia Smithson? She had learned a great deal in her single season, and she knew how society was influenced and governed, almost as well as Sir Robert Walpole knew how human nature could be moulded and directed at the will of a shrewd diplomatist. She knew that in the fashionable world every man and every woman, every child even, has his or her price, and may be bought and sold at pleasure. She had her price, she, Lesbia, the pearl of Grasmere; and the price having been fairly bidden she had surrendered to the bidder.

'I suppose I always meant to marry him,' she thought, pausing in her promenade to gaze across the verdant landscape, a fertile vale, against a background of low hills. All the landscape, to the edge of those hills, belonged to Mr. Smithson. 'Yes, I must have meant to give way at last, or I should hardly have tolerated his attentions. It would have been a pity to refuse such a place as this; and, he is quite gentlemanlike; and as I have done with all romantic ideas, I do not see why I should not learn to like him very much.'

She dismissed the idea of Smithson lightly, with this conclusion, which she believed very virtuous; and then as she resumed her walk her thoughts reverted to the Park Lane Palace.

'I hardly know whether I like it,' she mused languidly; 'beautiful as it is, it is only a reproduction of bygone splendour, and it is painfully excruciating now. For my own part I would much rather have the shabbiest old house which had belonged to one's ancestors, which had come to one as a heritage, by divine right as it were, instead of being bought with newly made money. To my mind it would rank higher. Yet I doubt if anybody nowadays sets a pin's value upon ancestors. People ask, Who is he? but they only mean, How much has he? And provided a person is not absolutely in trade, not actually engaged in selling soap, or matches, or mustard, society doesn't care a straw how his money has been made. The only secondary question is, How long will it last? And that is of course important.'

Musing thus, wordly wisdom personified, the maiden looked up and saw her lover entering at the light little iron gate which gave entrance to this feminine Eden. She went to meet him, looking all simplicity and freshness in her white morning gown and neat little Dunstable hat. It seemed to him as he gazed at her almost as if this delicate, sylph-like beauty were some wild white flower of the woods personified.

She gave him her hand graciously, but he drew her to his breast and kissed her, with the air of a man who was exercising an indisputable right. She supposed that it was his right, and she submitted, but released herself as quickly as possible.

'My dearest, how lovely you look in this morning light,' he exclaimed, 'while all the other women are upstairs making up their faces to meet the sun, and we shall see every shade of bismuth by-and-by, from pale mauve to purple.'

'It is very uncivil of you to say such a thing of your guests,' exclaimed Lesbia.

'But they all indulge in bismuth--you must be quite aware of that. They call the stuff by different names--Blanc Rosati, Creme de l'Imperatrice, Milk of Beauty, Perline, Opaline, Ivorine--but it means bismuth all the same. Expose your fashionable beauty to the fumes of sewer-gas, and that dazzling whiteness would turn to a dull brown hue, or even black. Thank heaven, my Lesbia wears real lilies and roses. Have you been here long?'

'About half an hour'

'I only wish I had known. I should not have dawdled so long over my dressing.'

'I am very glad you did not know,' Lesbia answered coolly.

'Do you suppose I never want to be alone? Life in London is perpetual turmoil; one's eyes grow weary with ever-moving crowds, one's ears ache with trying to distinguish one voice among the buzz of voices.'

'Then why go back to town? Why go back to the turmoil and the treadmill? It is only a kind of treadmill, after all, though we choose to call it pleasure. Stay here, Lesbia, and let us live upon the river, and among the flowers,' urged Smithson, with as romantic an air as if he had never heard of contango, or bulling and bearing; and yet only half an hour ago, while his valet was shaving him, he was debating within himself whether he should be bear or bull in his influence upon certain stock.

It was supposed that he never went near the city, that he had shaken the dust of Lombard Street and the House off his shoes, that his fortune was made, and he had no further need of speculation. Yet the proverb holds good with the stock-jobber. 'He who has once drunk will drink again.' Of that fountain there is no satiety.

'Stay and hear the last of the nightingales,' he murmured; 'we are famous for our nightingales.'

'I wonder you don't order a *fricassee* of their tongues, like that loathsome person in Roman history.'

'I hope I shall never resemble any loathsome person. Why can you not stay?'

'Why, because it is not etiquette, Lady Kirkbank says.'

'Lady Kirkbank, eh? *la belle farce*, Lady Kirkbank standing out for etiquette.'

'Don't laugh at my chaperon, sir. Upon what rock can a poor girl lean if you undermine her faith in her chaperon, sir.'

'I hope you will have a better guardian before you are a month older. I mean to be a very strong rock, Lesbia. You do not know how firmly I shall stand between you and all the perils of society. You have been but poorly guarded hitherto.'

'You talk as if you mean to be an abominable tyrant,' said Lesbia. 'If you don't take care I shall change my mind, and recall my promise.'

'Not on that account, Lesbia: every woman likes a man who stands up for his own. It is only your invertebrate husband whose wife drifts into the divorce court. I mean to keep and hold the prize I have won. When is it to be, dearest--our wedding day?'

'Not for ages, I hope--some time next summer, at the earliest.'

'You would not be so cruel as to keep me waiting a year?'

'Why not?'

'You would not ask that if you loved me.'

'You are asking too much,' said Lesbia, with a flash of defiance. 'There has been nothing said about love yet. You asked me to be your wife, and I said yes--meaning that at some remote period such a thing might be.'

She knew that the man was her slave--slave to her beauty, slave to her superior rank--and she was determined not to lessen the weight of his chain by so much as a feather.

'Did not that promise imply something like love?' he asked, earnestly.

'Perhaps it implied a little gratitude for your devotion, which I have neither courted nor encouraged a little respect for your talents, your perseverance--a little admiration for your wonderful success in life. Perhaps love may follow these sentiments, naturally, easily, if you are very patient; but if you talk about our being married before next year, you will simply make me hate you.'

'Then I will say very little, except to remind you that there is no earthly reason why we should not be married next month. October and November are the best months for Rome, and I heard you say last night you were pining to see Rome.'

'What then--cannot Lady Kirkbank take me to Rome?'

'And introduce you to the rowdiest people in the city,' cried Mr. Smithson. 'Lesbia, I adore you. It is the dream of my life to be your husband: but if you are going to spend a winter in Italy with Lady Kirkbank, I renounce my right, I surrender my hope. You will not be the wife of my dreams after that.'

'Do you assert a right to control my life during our engagement?'

'Some little right; above all, the privilege of choosing your friends. And that is one reason why I most fervently desire our marriage should not be delayed. You would find it difficult, impossible perhaps, to get out of Lady Kirkbank's claws while you are single; but once my wife, that amiable old person can be made to keep her distance.'

'Lady Kirkbank's claws! What a horrible way in which to speak of a friend. I thought you adored Lady Kirkbank.'

'So I do. We all adore her, but not as a guide for youth. As a specimen of the elderly female of the latter half of the nineteenth century, she is perfect. Such gush, such juvenility, such broad views, such an utter absence of starch; but as a lamp for the footsteps of girlhood--no *there* we must pause.'

'You are very ungrateful. Do you know that poor Lady Kirkbank has been most strenuous in your behalf?'

'Oh, yes, I know that.'

'And you are not grateful?'

'I intend to be very grateful, so grateful as to entirely satisfy Lady Kirkbank.'

'You are horribly cynical. That reminds me, there was a poor girl whom Lady Kirkbank had under her wing one season--a Miss Trinder, to whom I am told you behaved shamefully.'

'There was a parson's daughter who threw herself at my head in a most audacious way, and who behaved so badly, egged on by Lady Kirkbank, that I had to take refuge in flight. Do you suppose I am the kind of man to marry the first adventurous damsel who takes a fancy to my town house, and thinks it would be a happy hunting ground for a herd of brothers and sisters? Miss Trinder was shocking bad style, and her designs were transparent from the very beginning! I let her flirt as much as she liked; and when she began to be seriously sentimental I took wing for the East?'

'Was she pretty?' asked Lesbia, not displeased at this contemptuous summing up of poor Belle Trinder's story.

'If you admire the Flemish type, as illustrated by Rubens, she was lovely. A complexion of lilies and roses--cabbage roses, *bien entendu*, which were apt to deepen into peonies after champagne and mayonaise at Ascot or Sandown--a figure---oh--well--a tremendous figure--hair of an auburn that touched perilously on the confines of red--large, serviceable feet, and an appetite--the appetite of a ploughman's daughter reared upon short commons.'

'You are very cruel to a girl who evidently admired you.'

'A fig for her admiration! She wanted to live in my house and spend my money.'

'There goes the gong,' exclaimed Lesbia; 'pray let us go to breakfast. You are hideously cynical, and I am wofully tired of you.'

And as they strolled back to the house, by lavender walk and rose garden, and across the dewy lawn, Lesbia questioned herself as to whether she was one whit better or more dignified than Isabella Trinder. She wore her rue with a difference, that was all.

CHAPTER XXXV.
'ALL FANCY, PRIDE, AND FICKLE MAIDENHOOD.'

The return to Arlington Street meant a return to the ceaseless whirl of gaiety. Even at Rood Hall life had been as near an approach to perpetual motion as one could hope for in this world; but the excitement and the hurrying and scampering in Berkshire had a rustic flavour; there were moments that were almost repose, a breathing space between the blue river and the blue sky, in a world that seemed made of green fields and hanging woods, the plashing of waters, and the song of the lark. But in London the very atmosphere was charged with hurry and agitation; the freshness was gone from the verdure of the parks; the glory of the rhododendrons had faded; the Green Park below Lady Kirkbank's mansion was baked and rusty; the towers of the Houses of Parliament yonder were dimly seen in a mist of heat. London air tasted of smoke and dust, vibrated with the incessant roll of carriages, and the trampling of multitudinous feet.

There are women of rank who can take the London season quietly, and live their own lives in the midst of the whirl and the riot--women for whom that squirrel-like circulation round and round the fashionable wheel has no charm--women who only receive people they like, only go into society that is congenial. But Lady Kirkbank was not one of these. The advance of age made her only more keen in the pursuit of pleasure. She would have abandoned herself to despair had the glass over the mantelpiece in her boudoir ceased to be choked and littered with cards--had her book of engagements shown a blank page. Happily there were plenty of people--if not all of them the best people--who wanted Sir George and Lady Kirkbank at their parties. The gentleman was sporting and harmless, the lady was good-natured, and just sufficiently eccentric to be amusing without degenerating into a bore. And this year she was asked almost everywhere, for the sake of the beauty who went under her wing. Lesbia had been as a pearl of price to her chaperon, from a social point of view; and now that she was engaged to Horace Smithson she was likely to be even more valuable.

Mr. Smithson had promised Lady Kirkbank, sportively as it were, and upon the impulse of the moment, as he would have offered to wager a dozen of gloves, that were he so happy as to win her *protegee's* hand he would find her an invest-ment for, say, a thousand, which would bring her in twenty per cent.; nay, more, he would also find the thousand, which would have been the initial difficulty on poor Georgie's part. But this little matter was in Georgie's mind a detail, compared with the advantages to accrue to her indirectly from Lesbia's union with one of the richest men in London.

Lady Kirkbank had brought about many good matches, and had been too often rewarded with base ingratitude upon the part of her *protegees*, after marriage; but there was a touch of Arcady in the good soul's nature, and she was always trust-ful. She told herself that Lesbia would not be ungrateful, would not basely kick down the ladder by which she had mounted to heights empyrean, would not cru-elly shelve the friend who had pioneered her to high fortune. She counted upon making the house in Park Lane as her own house, upon being the prime mover of all Lesbia's hospitalities, the supervisor of her visiting list, the shadow behind the throne.

There were balls and parties nightly, dinners, luncheons, garden-parties; and yet there was a sense of waning in the glory of the world--everybody felt that the fag-end of the season was approaching. All the really great entertainments were over--the Cabinet dinners, the Reception at the Foreign Office, the last of the State balls and concerts. Some of the best people had already left town; and senators were beginning to complain that they saw no prospect of early deliverance. There was Goodwood still to look forward to; and after Goodwood the Deluge--or rather Cowes Regatta, about which Lady Kirkbank's set were already talking.

Lady Lesbia was to be at Cowes for the Regatta week. That was a settled thing. Mr. Smithson's schooner-yacht, the Cayman, was to be her hotel. It was to be Lady Kirkbank and Lady Lesbia's yacht for the nonce; and Mr. Smithson was to live on shore at his villa, and at that aristocratic club to which, by Maulevrier's influence, and on the score of his approaching marriage with an earl's daughter, he had been just selected. He would be only Lady Kirkbank's visitor on board the Cayman. The severe etiquette of the situation would therefore not be infringed; and yet Mr. Smithson would have the happiness of seeing his betrothed sole and sovereign mistress of his yacht, and of spending the long summer days at her feet. Even to Lady Lesbia this idea of the yacht was not without its charm. She had never been on board such a yacht as the Cayman; she was a good sailor, as testified by many an excursion, in hired sailing boats, at Tynemouth, and St. Bees; and she knew that she would be the queen of the hour. She accepted Mr. Smithson's invitation for the Cowes week more graciously than she was wont to receive his attentions, and was pleased to say that the whole thing would be rather enjoyable.

'It will be simple enchantment,' exclaimed the more enthusiastic Georgie Kirkbank. 'There is nothing so rapturous as life on board a yacht; there is a flavour of adventure, a **sansgene**, a--in short everything in the world that I like. I shall wear my cotton frocks, and give myself up to enjoyment, lie on the deck and look up at the blue sky, too deliciously idle even to read the last horrid thing of Zola's.'

But the Cowes Regatta was nearly three weeks ahead; and in the meantime there was Goodwood, and the ravelled threads of the London season had to be wound up. And by this time it was known everywhere that the affair between Mr. Smithson and Maulevrier's sister was really on. 'It's as settled a business as the entries and bets for next year's Derby,' said one lounger to another in the smoking-room of the Haute Gomme. 'Play or pay, don't you know.'

Lady Kirkbank and Lesbia had both written to Lady Maulevrier, Lesbia writing somewhat coldly, very briefly, and in a half defiant tone, to the effect that she had accepted Mr. Smithson's offer, and that she hoped her grandmother would be pleased with a match which everybody supposed to be extremely advantageous. She was going to Grasmere immediately after the Cowes week to see her dear grandmother, and to be assured of her approval. In the meanwhile she was awfully busy; there were callers driving up to the door at that very moment, and her brain was racked by the apprehension that she might not get her new gown in time for the Bachelor's Ball, which was to be quite one of the nicest things of the year, so dearest grandmother must excuse a hurried letter, etc., etc., etc.

Georgie Kirkbank was more effusive, more lengthy. She expatiated upon the stupendous alliance which her sweetest Lesbia was about to make; and took credit to herself for having guided Lesbia's footsteps in the right way.

'Smithson is a most difficult person,' she wrote. 'The least error of taste on your dear girl's part would have *froissed* him. Men with that immense wealth are always suspicious, ready to imagine mercenary motives, on their guard against being trapped. But Lesbia had *me* at her back, and she managed him perfectly. He is positively her slave; and you will be able to twist him round your little finger in the matter of settlements. You may do what you like with him, for the ground has been thoroughly prepared by *me*.'

Lady Maulevrier's reply was not enthusiastic. She had no doubt Mr. Smithson was a very good match, according to the modern estimate of matrimonial alliances, in which money seemed to be the Alpha and Omega. But she had cherished views of another kind. She had hoped to see her dear granddaughter wear one of those noble and historic names which are a badge of distinction for all time. She had hoped to see her enter one of those grand old families which are a kind of royalty. And that Lesbia should marry a man whose sole distinction consisted of an immense fortune amassed heaven knows how, was a terrible blow to her pride.

'But it is not the first,' wrote Lady Maulevrier. 'My pride has received crushing blows in days past, and I ought to be humbled to the dust. But there is a stubborn resistance in some natures which stands firm against every shock. You and Lesbia will both be surprised to hear that Mary, from whom I expected so little, has made a really great match. She was married yesterday afternoon in my morning room, by special licence, to the Earl of Hartfield, the lover of her choice, whom we at Fellside have all known as plain John Hammond. He is an admirable young man, and sure to make a great figure in the world, as no doubt you know better than I do, for you are in the way of hearing all about him. His courtship of Mary is quite an idyll; and the happy issue of this romantic love-affair has cheered and comforted me more than anything that has happened since Lesbia left me.'

This letter, written in Fraeulein's niggling little hand, Lady Kirkbank handed to Lesbia, who read it through in silence; but when she came to that part of the letter which told of her sister's marriage, her cheek grew ashy pale, her brow contracted, and she started to her feet and stared at Lady Kirkbank with wild, dilated eyes, as if she had been stung by an adder.

'A strange mystification, wasn't it?' said Lady Kirkbank, almost frightened at the awful look in Lesbia's face, which was even worse than Belle Trinder's expression when she read the announcement of Mr. Smithson's flight.

'Strange mystification! It was base treachery--a vile and wicked lie!' cried Lesbia, furiously. 'What right had he to come to us under false colours, to pretend to be poor, a nobody--with only the vaguest hope of making a decent position in the future?--and to offer himself under such impossible conditions to a girl brought up as I had been--a girl educated by one of the proudest and most ambitious of women--to force me to renounce everything except him? How could he suppose that any girl, so placed, could decide in his favour? If he had loved me he would have told me the truth--he would not have made it impossible for me to accept him.'

'I believe he is a very high flown young man,' said Lady Kirkbank, soothingly; 'he was never in *my* set, you know, dear. And I suppose he had some old Minerva-press idea that he would find a girl who would marry him for his own sake. And your sister, no doubt, eager to marry *anybody*, poor child, for the sake of getting away from that very lovely dungeon of Lady Maulevrier's, snapped at the chance; and by a mere fluke she becomes a countess.'

Lesbia ignored these consolatory remarks. She was pacing the room like a tigress, her delicate cambric handkerchief grasped between her two hands, and torn and rent by the convulsive action of her fingers. She could have thrown herself from the balcony on to the spikes of the area railings, she could have dashed herself against yonder big plate-glass window looking towards the Green Park, like a bird which shatters his little life against the glass barrier which he mistakes for the open sky. She could have flung herself down on the floor and grovelled, and torn her hair--she could have done anything mad, wicked, desperate, in the wild rage of this moment.

'Loved me!' she exclaimed; 'he never loved me. If he had he would have told me the truth. What, when I was in his arms, my head upon his breast, my whole being surrendered to him, adoring him, what more could he want? He must have known that this meant real love. And why should he put it upon me to fight so hard a fight--to brave my grandmother's anger--to be cursed by her--to face poverty for his sake? I never professed to be a heroine. He knew that I was a woman, with all a woman's weakness, a woman's fear of trial and difficulty in the future. It was a cowardly thing to use me so.'

'It was,' said Lady Kirkbank, in the same soothing tone; 'but if you liked this Hammond-Hartfield creature--a little in those old days, I know you have outlived that liking long ago.'

'Of course; but it is a hard thing to know one has been fooled, cheated, weighed in the balance and found wanting,' said Lesbia, scornfully.

She was taming down a little by this time, ashamed of that outbreak of violent passion, feeling that she had revealed too much to Lady Kirkbank.

'It was a caddish thing to do,' said Georgie; 'and this Hartfield is just what I always thought him--an insufferable prig. However, my sweetest girl, there is really nothing to lament in the matter. Your sister has made a good alliance, which will score high in your favour by-and-by, and you are going to marry a man who is three times as rich as Lord Hartfield.'

'Rich, yes; and nothing but rich; while Lord Hartfield is a man of the very highest standing, belongs to the flower of English nobility. Rich, yes; Mr. Smithson is rich; but, as Lady Maulevrier says, He has made his money heaven knows how.'

'Mr. Smithson has not made his money heaven knows how,' answered Lady Kirkbank, indignantly. 'He has made it in cochineal, in iron, in gunpowder, in coal, in all kinds of commodities. Everybody in the City knows how he has made his money, and that he has a genius for turning everything into gold. If the gold changes back into one of the baser metals, it is only when Mr. Smithson has made all he wanted to make. And now he has quite done with the City. The House is the only business of his life; and he is becoming a power in the House. You have every reason to be proud of your choice, Lesbia.'

'I will try to be proud of it,' said Lesbia, resolutely. 'I will not be scorned and trampled upon by Mary.'

'She seemed a harmless kind of girl,' said Lady Kirkbank, as if she had been talking of a housemaid.

'She is a designing minx,' exclaimed Lesbia, 'and has set her cap at that man from the very beginning.'

'But she could not have known that he was Lord Hartfield.'

'No; but he was a man; and that was enough for her.'

From this time forward there was a change in Lady Lesbia's style and manner--a change very much for the worse, as old-fashioned people thought; but to the taste of some among Lady Kirkbank's set, the change was an improvement. She was gayer than of old, gay with a reckless vivacity, intensely eager for action and excitement, for cards and racing, and all the strongest stimulants of fashionable life. Most people ascribed this increased vivacity, this electric manner, to the fact of her engagement to Horace Smithson. She was giddy with her triumph, dazzled by a vision of the gold which was soon to be hers.

'Egad, if I saw myself in a fair way of being able to write cheques upon such an account as Smithson's I should be as wild as Lady Lesbia,' said one of the damsel's military admirers at the Rag. 'And I believe the young lady was slightly dipped.'

'Who told you that?' asked his friend.

'A mother of mine,' answered the youth, with an apologetic air, as if he hardly cared to own such a humdrum relationship. 'Seraphine, the dressmaker, was complaining--wanted to see the colour of Lady Lesbia Haselden's money--vulgar curiosity--asked my old mother if she thought the account was safe, and so on. That's how I came to know all about it.'

'Well, she'll be able to pay Seraphine next season.'

Lord Maulevrier came back to London directly after his sister's wedding. The event, which came off so quietly, so happily, filled him with unqualified joy. He had hoped from the very first that his Molly would win the cup, even while Lesbia was making all the running, as he said afterwards. And Molly had won, and was the wife of one of the best young men in England. Maulevrier, albeit unused to the melting-mood, shed a tear or two for very joy as the sister he loved and the friend of his boyhood and youth stood side by side in the quiet room at Grasmere, and spoke the solemn words that made them one for ever.

The first news he heard after his return to town was of Lesbia's engagement, which was common talk at the clubs. The visitors at Rood Hall had come back to London full of the event, and were proud of giving a detailed account of the affair to outsiders.

They all talked patronisingly of Smithson, and seemed to think it rather a wonderful fact that he did not drop his aspirates or eat peas with a knife.

'A man of stirling metal,' said the gossips, 'who can hold his own with many a fellow born in the purple.'

Maulevrier called in Arlington Street, but Lady Kirkbank and her *protegee* were out; and it was at a cricket match at the Orleans Club that the brother and sister met for the first time after Lord Hartfield's wedding, which by this time had been in all the papers; a very simple announcement:

'On the 29th inst., at Grasmere, by the Reverend Douglass Brooke, the Earl of Hartfield to Mary, younger daughter of the ninth Earl of Maulevrier.'

Lesbia was the centre of a rather noisy little court, in which Mr. Smithson was conspicuous by his superior reserve.

He did not exert himself as a lover, paid no compliments, was not sentimental. The pearl was won, and he wore it very quietly; but wherever Lesbia went he went; she was hardly ever out of his sight.

Maulevrier received the coolest possible greeting. Lesbia turned pale with anger at sight of him, for his presence reminded her of the most humiliating passage in her life; but the big red satin sunshade concealed that pale angry look, and nothing in Lesbia's manner betrayed emotion.

'Where have you been hiding yourself all this time, and why were you not at Henley?' she asked.

'I have been at Grasmere.'

'Oh, you were a witness of that most romantic marriage. The Lady of Lyons reversed, the gardener's son turning out to be an earl. Was it excruciatingly funny?'

'It was one of the most solemn weddings I ever saw.'

'Solemn! what, with my Tomboy sister as bride! Impossible!'

'Your sister ceased to be a Tomboy when she fell in love. She is a sweet and womanly woman, and will make an adorable wife to the finest fellow I know. I hear I am to congratulate you, Lesbia, upon your engagement with Mr. Smithson.'

'If you think *I* am the person to be congratulated, you are at liberty to do so. My engagement is a fact.'

'Oh, of course, Mr. Smithson is the winner. But as I hope you intend to be happy, I wish you joy. I am told Smithson is a really excellent fellow when one gets to know him; and I shall make it my business to be better acquainted with him.'

Smithson was standing just out of hearing, watching the bowling. Maulevrier went over to him and shook hands, their acquaintance hitherto having been of the slightest, and very shy upon his lordship's part; but now Smithson could see that Maulevrier meant to be cordial.

CHAPTER XXXVI.
A RASTAQUOUERE.

There was a dinner party in one of the new houses in Grosvenor Place that evening, to which Lady Kirkbank and Lesbia had been bidden. The new house belonged to a new man, who was supposed to have made millions out of railways, and other gigantic achievements in the engineering line; and the new man and his wife were friends of Mr. Smithson, and had made the simple Georgie's acquaintance only within the last three weeks.

'Of course they are stupid, my dear,' she remarked, in response to some slighting remark of Lesbia's, 'but I am always willing to know rich people. One drops in for so many good things; and they never want any return in kind. It is quite enough for them to be allowed to spend their money *upon us.*'

The house was gorgeous in all the glory of the very latest fashions in upholstery; hall Algerian; dining-room Pompeian; drawing-room Early Italian; music-room Louis Quatorze; billiard-room mediaeval English. The dinner was as magnificent as dinner can be made. Three-fourths of the guests were the *haute gomme* of the financial world, and perspired gold. The other third belonged to a class which Mr. Smithson described somewhat contemptuously as the shake-back nobility. An Irish peer, a younger son of a ducal house that had run to seed, a political agitator, a grass widow whose titled husband was governor of an obscure colony, an ancient dowager with hair which was too luxuriant to be anything but a wig, and diamonds which were so large as to suggest paste.

Lesbia sat by her affianced at the glittering table, lighted with clusters of wax candles, which shone upon a level *parterre* of tea roses, gardenias, and gloire de Malmaison carnations; from which rose at intervals groups of silver-gilt dolphins, supporting shallow golden dishes piled with peaches, grapes, and all the costliest produce of Covent Garden.

Conversation was not particularly brilliant, nor had the guests an elated air. The thermometer was near eighty, and at this period of the season everybody was tired of this kind of dinner, and would gladly have foregone the greatest achievements of culinary art, in favour of a chicken and a salad, eaten under green leaves, in a garden at Wargrave or Henley, within sound of the rippling river.

On Lesbia's right hand there was a portly personage of Jewish type, dark to swarthiness, and somewhat oily, whose every word suggested bullion. He and Mr. Smithson were evidently acquaintances of long standing, and Mr. Smithson presented him to Lesbia, whereupon he joined in their conversation now and then.

His talk was of the usual standard. He had seen everything worth seeing in London and in Paris, between which cities he seemed to oscillate with such frequency that he might be said to live in both places at once. He had his stall at Covent Garden, and his stall at the Grand Opera. He was a subscriber at the Theatre Francais. He had seen all the races at Longchamps and Chantilly, as well as at Sandown and Ascot. But every now and then he and Mr. Smithson drifted from the customary talk about operas and races, pictures and French novels, to the wider world of commerce and speculation, mines, waterworks, and foreign loans--and Lesbia leant back in her chair, and fanned herself languidly, with half-closed eyelids, while two or three courses went round, she giving the little supercilious look at each entree offered to her, to be observed on such occasions, as if the thing offered were particularly nasty.

She wondered how long the two men were going to prose about mines and shares, in those subdued half-mysterious voices, telling each other occult facts in half-expressed phrases, utterly dark to the outside world; but, while she was languidly wondering, a change in her lover's manner startled her into keenest curiosity.

'Montesma is in Paris,' said Mr. Sampayo, the dark gentleman; 'I dined last week with him at the Continental.'

Mr. Smithson's complexion faded curiously, and a leaden darkness came over his countenance, as of a man whose heart and lungs suddenly refuse their office. But in a few moments he was smiling feebly.

'Indeed! I thought he was played out years ago.'

'A man of that kind is never played out. Don Gomez de Montesma is as clever as Satan, as handsome as Apollo, and he bears one of the oldest names in Castile. Such a man will always come to the front. ***C'est un rastaquouere mais rastaquouere de bon genre***. You knew him intimately ***la bas***, I believe?'

'In Cuba; yes, we were pretty good friends once.'

'And were useful to each other, no doubt,' said Mr. Sampayo, pleasantly. 'Was that Argentiferous Copper Company in sixty-four yours or his?'

'There were a good many people concerned in it.'

'No doubt; it takes a good many people to work that kind of thing, but I fancy you and Montesma were about the only two who came out of it pleasantly. And he and you did a little in the shipping line, didn't you--African produce? However, that's an old song. You have had so many good things since then.'

'Did Montesma talk of coming to London?'

'He did not talk about it; but he would hardly go back to the tropics without having a look round on both sides of the Channel. He was always fond of society, pretty women, dancing, and amusements of all kinds. I have no doubt we shall see him here before the end of the season.'

Mr. Smithson pursued the subject no further He turned to Lesbia, who had been curiously interested in this little bit of conversation--interested first because Smithson had seemed agitated by the mention of the Spaniard's name; secondly, because of the description of the man, which had a romantic sound. The very word tropic suggested a romance. And Lesbia, whose mind was jaded by the monotony of a London season, the threadbare fabric of society conversation, kindled at any image which appealed to her fancy.

Clever as Satan, handsome as Apollo, scion of an old Castilian family, fresh from the tropics. Her imagination dwelt upon the ideas which these words had conjured up.

Three days after this she was at the opera with her chaperon, her lover in attendance as usual. The opera was "Faust," with Nillson as Marguerite. After the performance they were to drive down to Twickenham on Mr. Smithson's drag, and to dance and sup at the Orleans. The last ball of the season was on this evening; and Lesbia had been persuaded that it was to be a particular *recherche* ball, and that only the very nicest people were to be present. At any rate, the drive under the light of a July moon would be delicious; and if they did not like the people they found there they could eat their supper and come away immediately after, as Lady Kirkbank remarked philosophically.

The opera was nearly over--that grand scene of Valentine's death was on--and Lesbia was listening breathlessly to every note, watching every look of the actors, when there came a modest little knock at the door of her box. She darted an angry glance round, and shrugged her shoulders vexatiously. What Goth had dared to knock during that thrilling scene?

Mr. Smithson rose and crept to the door and quietly opened it.

A dark, handsome man, who was a total stranger to Lesbia, glided in, shaking hands with Smithson as he entered.

Till this moment Lesbia's whole being had been absorbed in the scene--that bitter anathema of the brother, the sister's cry of anguish and shame. Where else is there tragedy so human, so enthralling--grief that so wrings the spectator's heart? It needed a Goethe and a Gounod to produce this masterpiece.

In an instant, in a flash, Lesbia's interest in the stage was gone. Her first glance at the stranger told, her who he was. The olive tint, the eyes of deepest black, the grand form of the head and perfect chiselling of the features could belong only to that scion of an old Castilian race whom she had heard described the other evening--'clever as Satan, handsome as Apollo.'

Yes, this must be the man, Don Gomez de Montesma. There was nothing in Mr. Smithson's manner to indicate that the Spaniard was an unwelcome guest. On the contrary, Smithson received him with a cordiality which in a man of naturally reserved manner seemed almost rapture. The curtain fell, and he presented Don Gomez to Lady Kirkbank and Lady Lesbia; whereupon dear Georgie began to gush, after her wont, and to ask a good many questions in a manner that was too girlish to seem impertinent.

'How perfectly you speak English!' she exclaimed. 'You must have lived in England a good deal.'

'On the contrary, it is my misfortune to have, lived here very little, but I have known a good many English and Americans in Cuba and in Paris.'

'In Cuba! Do you really come from Cuba? I have always fancied that Cuba must be an altogether charming place to live in--like Biarritz or Pau, don't you know, only further away. Do please tell me where it is, and what kind of a place.'

Geographically, Lady Kirkbank's mind was a blank. It was quite a revelation to her to find that Cuba was an island.

'It must be a lovely spot!' exclaimed the fervid creature. 'Let me see, now, what do we get from Cuba?--cigars--and--and tobacco. I suppose in Cuba everybody smokes?'

'Men, women, and children.'

'How delicious! Would that I were a Cuban! And the natives, are they nice?'

'There are no aborigines. The Indians whom Columbus found soon perished off the face of the island. European civilisation generally has that effect. But one of our most benevolent captain-generals provided us with an imported population of niggers.'

'How delightful. I have always longed to live among a slave population, dear submissive black things dressed in coral necklaces and feathers, instead of the horrid over-fed wretches we have to wait upon us. And if the aborigines were not wanted it was just as well for them to die out, don't you know,' prattled Lady Kirkbank.

'It was very accommodating of them, no doubt. Yet we could employ half a million of them, if we had them, in draining our swamps. Agriculture suffered by the loss of Indian labour.'

'I suppose they were like the creatures in Pizarro, poor dear yellow things with brass bracelets,' said Lady Kirkbank. 'I remember seeing Macready as Rolla when I was quite a little thing.'

And now the curtain rose for the last act.

'Do you care about staying for the end?' asked Mr. Smithson of Lesbia. 'It will make us rather late at the Orleans.'

'Never mind how late we are,' said Lesbia, imperiously. 'I have always been cheated out of this last act for some stupid party. Imagine losing Gounod and Nillson for the sake of struggling through the mob on a stifling staircase, and being elbowed by inane young men, with gardenias in their coats.'

Lady Lesbia had a pretty little way of always opposing any suggestion of her sweetheart. She was resolved to treat him as badly as a future husband could be treated. In consenting to marry him she had done him a favour which was a great deal more than such a person had any right to expect.

She leant forward to watch and listen, with her elbow resting on the velvet cushion--her head upon her hand, and she seemed absorbed in the scene. But this was mere outward seeming. All the enchantment of music and acting was over. She only heard and saw vaguely, as if it were a shadowy scene enacted ever so far away. Every now and then her eyes glanced involuntarily toward Don Gomez, who stood leaning against the back of the box, pale, languid, graceful, poetic, an altogether different type of manhood from that with which she had of late been satiated.

Those deep dark eyes of his had a dreamy look. They gazed across the dazzling house, into space, above Lady Lesbia's head. They seemed to see nothing; and they certainly were not looking at her.

Don Gomez was the first man she ever remembered to have been presented to her who did not favour her with a good deal of hard staring, more or less discreetly managed, during the first ten minutes of their acquaintance. On him her beauty fell flat. He evidently failed to recognise her supreme loveliness. It might be that she was the wrong type for Cuba. Every nation has its own Venus; and that far away spot beyond the torrid zone might have a somewhat barbarous idea of beauty. At any rate, Don Gomez was apparently unimpressed. And yet Lesbia flattered herself that she was looking her best to-night, and that her costume was a success. She wore a white satin gown, short in the skirt, for the luxury of freedom in waltzing, and made with Quaker-like simplicity, the bodice high to the throat, fitting her like a sheath.

Her only ornaments were a garland of scarlet poppies wreathed from throat to shoulder, and a large diamond heart which Mr. Smithson had lately given her; 'a bullock's heart,' as Lady Kirkbank called it.

When the curtain fell, and not till then, she rose and allowed herself to be clad in a brown velvet Newmarket, which completely covered her short satin gown. She had a little brown velvet toque to match the Newmarket, and thus attired she would be able to take her seat on the drag which was waiting on the quietest side of Covent Garden.

'Why should not you go with us, Don Gomez?' exclaimed Lady Kirkbank, in a gush of hospitality. 'The drive will be charming--not equal to your tropical Cuba--but intensely nice. And the gardens will be something too sweet on such a night as this. I knew them when the dear Duc d'Aumale was there. Ay de mi, such a man!'

Lady Kirkbank sighed, with the air of having known his Altesse Royale intimately.

'I should be charmed,' said Don Gomez, 'if I thought my friend Smithson wanted me. Would you really like to have me, Smithson?'

'I should be enchanted.'

'And there is room on the drag?'

'Room enough for half-a-dozen. I am only taking Sir George Kirkbank and Colonel Delville--whom we are to pick up at the Haute Gomme--and Mr. and Mrs. Mostyn, who are in the stalls.'

'A nice snug little party,' exclaimed that charming optimist, Lady Kirkbank. 'I hate a crowd on a drag. The way some of the members of the Four-in-hand Club load their coaches on parade reminds me of a Beanfeast!'

They found Lady Kirkbank's footman and one of Mr. Smithson's grooms waiting in the hall of the opera house. The groom to conduct them to the spot where the drag was waiting; the footman to carry wraps and take his mistress's final orders. There was a Bohemian flavour in the little walk to the great fruit garden, which was odorous of bruised peaches and stale salads as they passed it. Waggon-loads of cabbages and other garden stuff were standing about by the old church; the roadway was littered with the refuse of the market; and the air was faint and heavy with the scent of herbs and flowers.

Lesbia mounted lightly to her place of honour on the box-seat; and Lady Kirkbank was hoisted up after her. Mr. and Mrs. Mostyn followed; and then Don Gomez took his seat by Lady Kirkbank's side and behind Lesbia, a vantage point from which he could talk to her as much as he liked. Mr. Smithson seated himself a minute afterwards, and drove off by King Street and Leicester Square and on to Piccadilly, steering cleverly through the traffic of cabs and carriages, which was at its apogee just now, when all the theatres were disgorging their crowds. Piccadilly was quieter, yet there were plenty of carriages, late people going to parties and early people going home, horses slipping and sliding on stones or wood, half the road-way up, and luminous with lanterns. They stopped in front of the Haute Gomme, where they picked up Sir George Kirkbank and Colonel Delville, a big man with a patriarchal head, supposed to be one of the finest whist players in London, and to make a handsome income by his play. He had ridden in the Balaclava charge, was a favourite everywhere, and, albeit no genius, was much cleverer than his friend and school-fellow, George Kirkbank. They had been at Eton together, had both made love to the lively Georgie, and had been inseparables for the last thirty years.

'Couldn't get on without Delville,' said Sir George; 'dooced smart fellow, sir. Knows the ropes; and does all the thinking for both of us.'

And now they were fairly started, and the team fell into a rattling pace, with the road pretty clear before them. Hyde Park was one umbrageous darkness, edged by long lines of golden light. Coolness and silence enfolded all things in the summer midnight, and Lesbia, not prone to romance, sank into a dreamy state of mind, as she leaned back in her seat and watched the shadowy trees glide by, the long vista of lamps and verdure in front of her. She was glad that no one talked to her, for talk of any kind must have broken the spell. Don Gomez sat like a statue in his place behind her. From Lady Kirkbank, the loquacious, came a gentle sound of snoring, a subdued, ladylike snore, breathed softly at intervals, like a sigh. Mr. Smithson had his team, and his own thoughts, too, for occupation,--thoughts which to-night were not altogether pleasant.

At the back of the coach Mrs. Mostyn was descanting on the evolution of the nautilus, and the relationship of protoplasm and humanity, to Colonel Delville, who sat smiling placidly behind an immense cigar, and accepted the most stupendous facts and the most appalling theories with a friendly little nod of his handsome head.

Mr. Mostyn frankly slept, as it was his custom to do upon all convenient occasions. He called it recuperating.

'Frank ought to be delightfully fresh, for he recuperated all the way down,' said his wife, when they alighted in the dewy garden at Twickenham, in front of the lamp-lit portico.

'I wouldn't have minded his recuperating if he hadn't snored so abominably,' remarked Colonel Delville.

It was nearly one o'clock, and the ball had thinned a little, which made it all the better for those who remained. Mr. Smithson's orders had been given two days ago, and the very best of the waiters had been told off for his especial service. The ladies went upstairs to take off their wrappings and mufflings, and Lesbia emerged dazzling from her brown velvet Newmarket, while Lady Kirkbank, bending closely over the looking-glass, like a witch over a caldron, repaired her complexion with cotton wool.

They went through the conservatory to the octagon dining-room, where the supper was ready, a special supper, on a table by a window, a table laden with exotics and brilliant with glass and silver. The supper was, of course, perfect in its way. Mr. Smithson's *chef* had been down to see about it, and Mr. Smithson's own particular champagne and the claret grown in his own particular *clos* in the Gironde, had been sent down for the feast. No common cuisine, no common wine could be good enough; and yet there was a day when the cheapest gargote in Belleville or Montmartre was good enough for Mr. Smithson. There had been days on which he did not dine at all, and when the fumes of a *gibelotte* steaming from a workman's restaurant made his mouth water.

The supper was all life and gaiety. Everyone was hungry and thirsty, and freshioned by the drive, except Lesbia. She was singularly silent, ate hardly anything, but drank three or four glasses of champagne.

Don Gomez was not a great talker. He had the air of a prince of the blood royal, who expects other people to talk and to keep him amused, But the little he said was to the point. He had a fine baritone, very low and subdued, and had a languor which was almost insolent, but not without its charm. There was an air of originality about the manner and the man.

He was the typical *rastaquouere*, a man of finished manners, and unknown antecedents, a foreigner, apparently rich, obviously accomplished, but with that indefinable air which bespeaks the adventurer; and which gives society as fair a warning as if the man wore a placard on his shoulder with the word *cave*.

But to Lesbia this Spaniard was the first really interesting man she had met since she saw John Hammond; and her interest in him was much more vivid than her interest in Hammond had been at the beginning of their acquaintance. That pale face, with its tint of old ivory, those thin, finely-cut lips, indicative of diabolical craft, could she but read aright, those unfathomable eyes, touched her fancy as it had never yet been touched, awoke within her that latent vein of romance, self-abnegation, supreme foolishness, which lurks in the nature of every woman, be she chaste as ice and pure as snow.

The supper was long. It was past two o'clock, and the ballroom was thinly occupied, when Mr. Smithson's party went there.

'You won't dance to-night, I suppose?' said Smithson, as Lesbia and he went slowly down the room arm in arm. It was in a pause between two waltzes. The wide window at the end was opened to the summer night, and the room was delightfully cool. 'You must be horribly tired?'

'I am not in the least tired, and I mean to waltz, if anyone will ask me,' replied Lesbia, decisively.

'I ought to have asked you to dance, and then it would have been the other way,' said Smithson, with a touch of acrimony. 'Surely you have dancing enough in town, and you might be obliging for once in a way, and come and sit with me in the garden, and listen to the nightingales.'

'There are no nightingales after June. There is the Manola,' as the band struck up, 'my very favourite waltz.'

Don Gomez was at her elbow at this moment

'May I have the honour of this waltz with you, Lady Lesbia?' he asked; and then with a serio-comic glance at his stoutish friend, 'I don't think Smithson waltzes?'

'I have been told that nobody can waltz who has been born on this side of the Pyrenees,' answered Lesbia, withdrawing her arm from her lover's, and slipping, it through the Spaniard's, with the air of a slave who obeys a master.

Smithson looked daggers, and retired to a corner of the room glowering. Were a man twenty-two times millionaire, like the Parisian Rothschild, he could not find armour against the poisoned arrows of jealousy. Don Gomez possessed many of those accomplishments which make men dangerous, but as a dancer he was *hors ligne*; and Horace Smithson knew that there is no surer road to a girl's fancy than the magic circle of a waltz.

Those two were floating round the room in the old slow legato step, which recalled to Smithson the picture of a still more spacious room in an island under the

Southern Cross--the blue water of the bay shining yonder under the starlight of the tropics, fire-flies gleaming and flashing in the foliage beyond the open windows, fire-flies flashing amidst the gauzy draperies of the dancers, and this same Gomez revolving with the same slow languid grace, his arm encircling the *svelte* figure of a woman whose southern beauty outshone Lesbia's blonde English loveliness as the tropical stars outshine the lamps that light our colder skies. Yes, every detail of the scene flashed back into his mind, as if a curtain had been suddenly plucked back from a long-hidden picture. The Cuban's tall slim figure, the head gently bent towards his partner's head, as at this moment, and those dark eyes looking up at him, intoxicated with that nameless, indefinable fascination which it is the lot of some men to exercise.

'He robbed me of *her*!' thought Smithson, gloomily. 'Will he rob me of this one too? Surely not! Havana is Havana--and this one is not a Creole. If I cannot trust that lovely piece of marble, there is no woman on earth to be trusted.'

He turned his back upon the dancers, and went out into the garden. His soul was wrung with jealousy, yet he could watch no longer. There was too much pain--there were too many bitter memories of shame, and loss, and ignominy evoked by that infernal picture. If he had been free he would have asserted his authority as Lesbia's future husband; he would have taken her away from the Orleans; he would have told her plainly and frankly that Don Gomez was no fit person for her to know; and he would have so planned that they two should never meet again. But Horace Smithson was not free. He was bound hand and foot by those fetters which the chain of past events had forged--stern facts which the man himself may forget, or try to forget, but which other people never forget. There is generally some dark spot in the history of such men as Smithson--men who climb the giddiest heights of this world with that desperate rapidity which implies many a perilous leap from crag to crag, many a moraine skimmed over, and many an awful gulf spanned by a hair-breadth bridge. Mr. Smithson's history was not without such spots; and the darkest of all had relation to his career in Cuba. The story had been known by very few--perhaps completely known only by one man; and that man was Gomez de Montesma.

For the last fifteen years the most fervent desire of Horace Smithson's heart had been the hope that tropical nature, in any one of her various disagreeable forms, would be obliging enough to make an end of Gomez. But the forces of nature had not worked on Mr. Smithson's side. No loathsome leprosy had eaten his enemy's flesh; neither cayman nor crocodile, neither Juba snake nor poisonous spider had marked him for its prey. The tropical sun had left him unsmitten. He had lived and he had prospered; and he was here, like a guilty conscience incarnate, to spoil Horace Smithson's peace.

'I must be diplomatic,' Smithson said to himself, as he walked up and down an avenue of Irish yews, in a solitary part of the grounds, smoking his cigarette, and hearing the music swell and sink in the distance. 'I will give her a hint as to that man's character, and I will keep them apart as much as I can. But if he forces himself upon me there is no help for it. I cannot afford to be uncivil to him.'

'Cannot afford' in this instance meant 'dare not,' and Horace Smithson's thoughts as he paced the yew-tree walk were full of gloom.

During that long meditation he made up his mind on one point, namely, that, let him suffer what pangs he might, he must not betray his jealousy. To do that would be to lower himself in Lesbia's eyes, and to play into his rival's hand; for a jealous man is almost always contemptible in the sight of his mistress. He would carry himself as if he were sure of her fidelity; and this very confidence, with a woman of honour, a girl reared as Lesbia had been reared, would render it impossible for her to betray him. He would show himself high-minded, confident, generous, chivalrous, even; and he would trust to chance for the issue. Chance were Mr. Smithson's only idea of Divinity; and Chance had hitherto been kind to him. There had been dark hours in his life, but the darkness had not lasted long; and the lucky accidents of his career had been of a nature to beguile him into the belief that among the favourites of Destiny he stood first and foremost.

While Mr. Smithson mused thus, alone and in the darkness, Montesma and Lady Lesbia were wandering arm in arm in another and lovelier part of the grounds, where golden lights were scattered like Cuban fire-flies among the foliage of seringa and magnolia, arbutus and rhododendron, while at intervals a sudden flush of rosier light was shed over garden and river, as if by enchantment, surprising a couple here and there in the midst of a flirtation which had begun in darkness.

The grounds were lovely in the balmy atmosphere of a July night, the river gliding with mysterious motion under the stars, great masses of gloom darkening the stream with an almost awful look where the woods of Petersham and Ham House cast their dense shadows on the water. Don Gomez and his companion wandered by the river side to a spot where a group of magnolias sheltered them from the open lawn, and where there were some rustic chairs close to the balustrade which protected the parapet. In this spot, which was a kind of island, divided from the rest of the grounds by the intervening road, they found themselves quite alone, and in the midst of a summer stillness which was broken only by the low, lazy ripple of the tide running seawards. The lights of Richmond looked far away, and the little town with its variety of levels had an Italian air in the distance.

From the ballroom, faint and fitful, came the music of a waltz.

'I'm afraid I've brought you too far,' said Don Gomez.

'On the contrary, it is a relief to get away from the lights and the people. How delicious this river is! I was brought up on the shores of a lake; but after all a lake is horribly tame. Its limits are always staring one in the face. There is no room for one's imagination to wander. Now a river like this suggests an infinity of possibilities, drifting on and on and on into undiscovered regions, by ever-varying shores. I feel to-night as if I should like to step into that little boat yonder,' pointing to a light skiff bobbing gently up and down with the tide, at the bottom of a flight of steps, 'and let the stream take me wherever it chose.'

'If I could but go with you,' said Gomez, in that deep and musical tone which made the commonest words seem melody, 'I would ask for neither compass nor rudder. What could it matter whither the boat took me? There is no place under the stars which would not be a paradise--with you.'

'Please don't make a dreamy aspiration the occasion for a compliment,' exclaimed Lesbia, lightly. 'What I said was so silly that I don't wonder you thought it right to say something just a little sillier. But moonlight and running water have a curious effect upon me; and I, who am the most prosaic among women, become ridiculously sentimental.'

'I cannot believe that you are prosaic.'

'I assure you it is perfectly true. I am of the earth, earthy; a woman of the world, in my first season, ambitious, fond of pleasure, vain, proud, exacting, all those things which I am told a woman ought not to be.'

'You pain me when you so slander yourself; and I shall make it the business of my life to find out how much truth there is in that self-slander. For my own part I do not believe a word of it; but as it is rude to contradict a lady I will only say that I reserve my opinion.'

'Are you to stay long in England?' asked Lesbia.

She was leaning against the stone balustrade in a careless attitude, as of one who was weary, her elbow on the stone slab, and her head thrown hack against her arm. The white satin gown, moulded to her figure, had a statuesque air, and she looked like a marble statue in the dim light, every line of the graceful form expressive of repose.

'That will depend. I am not particularly fond of London. A very little of your English Babylon satisfies me, in a general way; but there are conditions which might make England enchanting. Where do you go at the end of the season?'

'First to Goodwood, and then to Cowes. Mr. Smithson is so kind as to place his yacht at Lady Kirkbank's disposal, and I am to be her guest on board the Cayman, just as I am in Arlington Street.'

'The Cayman! That name is a reminiscence of Mr. Smithson's South American travels.'

'No doubt! Was he long in South America?'

'Three or four years.'

'But not in Cuba all that time, I suppose?'

'He had business relations with Cuba all that time, and oscillated between our island and the main. He was rather fortunate in his little adventures with us--made almost as much money as General Tacon, of blessed memory. But I dare say Smithson has told you all his adventures in that part of the world.'

'No, he very rarely talks about his travels: and I am not particularly interested in commercial speculations. There is always so much to think of and talk about in the business of the moment. Are you fond of Cuba?'

'Not passionately. I always feel as if I were an exile there, and yet one of my ancestors was with Columbus when be discovered the island, and my race were among the earliest settlers. My family has given three Captain-generals to Cuba: but I cannot forget that I belong to an older world, and have forfeited that which ought to have been a brilliant place in Europe for the luxurious obscurity of a colony.'

'But you must be attached to a place in which your family have lived for so many generations?'

'I like the stars and the sea, the mountains and savannas, the tropical vegetation, and the dreamy, half-oriental life; but at best it is a kind of stagnation, and after a residence of a few months in the island of my birth I generally spread my wings for the wider world of the old continent or the new.'

'You must have travelled so much,' said Lesbia, with a sigh. 'I have been nowhere and seen nothing. I feel like a child who has been shut up in a nursery all its life, and knows of no world beyond four walls.'

'Not to travel is not to live,' said Don Gomez.

'I am to be in Italy next November, I believe,' said Lesbia, not caring to own that this Italian trip was to be her honeymoon.

'Italy!' exclaimed the Spaniard, contemptuously. 'Once the finishing school of the English nobility; now the happy hunting-ground of the Cockney tourist and the prosperous Yankee. All the poetry of Italy has been dried up, and the whole country vulgarised. If you want romance in the old world go to Spain; in the new, try Peru or Brazil, Mexico or California.'

'I am afraid I am not adventurous enough to go so far.'

'No: women cling to beaten tracks.'

'We obey our masters,' answered Lesbia, meekly.

'Ah, I forgot. You are to have a master--and soon. I heard as much before I saw you to-night.'

Lesbia half rose, as if to leave this cool retreat above the rippling tide.

'Yes, it is all settled,' she said; 'and now I think I must go back. Lady Kirkbank will be wondering what has become of me.'

'Let her wonder a little longer,' said Don Gomez. 'Why should we hurry away from this delightful spot? Why break the spell of--the river? Life has so few moments of perfect contentment. If this is one with you--as it is with me--let us make the most of it. Lady Lesbia, do you see those weeds yonder, drifting with the tide, drifting side by side, touching as they drift? They have met heaven knows how, and will part heaven knows where, on their way to the sea; but they let themselves go with the tide. We have met like those poor weeds. Don't let us part till the tide parts us.'

Lesbia gave a little sigh, and submitted. She had talked of women obeying their masters; and the implication was that she meant to obey Mr. Smithson. But there is a fate in these things; and the man who was to be her master, whose lightest breath was to sway her, whose lightest look was to rule her, was here at her side in the silence of the summer night.

They talked long, but of indifferent subjects; and their talk might have been heard by every member of the Orleans Club, and no harm done. Yet words and phrases count for very little in such a case. It is the tone, it is the melody of a voice, it is the magic of the hour that tells.

The tide came, in the person of Mr. Smithson, and parted these two weeds that were drifting towards the great mysterious ocean of fate.

'I have been hunting for you everywhere,' he said, cheerfully. 'If you want another waltz, Lady Lesbia, you had better take the next. I believe it is to be the last. At any rate our party are clamouring to be driven home. I found poor Lady Kirkbank fast asleep in a corner of the drawing-room.'

'Will you give me that last waltz?' asked Don Gomez.

Lady Lesbia felt that the long-suffering Smithson had endured enough. Womanly instinct constrained her to refuse that final waltz: but it seemed to her as if she were making a tremendous sacrifice in so doing. And yet she had waltzed to her heart's content during the season that was waning, and knew all the waltzes played by all the fashionable bands. She gave a little sigh, as she said--

'No, I must not indulge myself. I must go and take care of Lady Kirkbank.'

Mr. Smithson offered his arm, and she took it and went away with him, leaving Don Gomez to follow at his leisure. There would be some delay no doubt before the drag started. The lamps had gone out among the foliage, and the stars were waning a little, and there was a faint cold light creeping over the garden which meant the advent of morning. Don Gomez strolled towards the lighted house, smoking a cigarette.

'She is very lovely, and she is--well--not quite spoiled by her *entourage*, and they tell me she is an heiress--sure to inherit a fine fortune from some ancient grandmother, buried alive in Westmoreland,' he mused. 'What a splendid opportunity it would be if--if the business could be arranged on the square. But as it is--well--as it is there is the chance of an adventure; and when did a Montesma ever avoid an adventure, although there were dagger or poison lurking in the background?

And here there is neither poison nor steel, only a lovely woman, and an infatuated stockbroker, about whom I know enough to disgrace and ruin an archbishop. Poor Smithson! How very unlucky that I should happen to come across your pathway in the heyday of your latest love affair. We have had our little adventures in that line already, and we have measured swords together, metaphorically, before to-night. When it comes to a question of actual swords my Smithson declines. ***Pas si bete.***'

CHAPTER XXXVII.
LORD HARTFIELD REFUSES A FORTUNE.

A honeymoon among lakes and mountains, amidst the gorgeous confusion of Borrowdale, in a little world of wild, strange loveliness, shut in and isolated from the prosaic outer world by the vast and towering masses of Skiddaw and Blenca-thara--a world of one's own, as it were, a world steeped in romance and poetry, dear to the souls of poets. There are many such honeymoons every summer; indeed, the mountain paths, the waterfalls and lakes swarm with happy lovers; and this land of hills and waters seems to have been made expressly for honeymoon travellers; yet never went truer lovers wandering by lake and torrent, by hill and valley, than those two whose brief honeymoon was now drawing to a close.

It was altogether a magical time for Mary, this dawn of a new life. The immensity of her happiness almost frightened her. She could hardly believe in it, or trust in its continuance.

'Am I really, really, really your wife?' she asked on their last day, bending down to speak to her husband, as he led her pony up the rough ways of Skiddaw. 'It is all so dreadfully like a dream.'

'Thank God, it is the very truth,' answered Lord Hartfield, looking fondly at the fresh young face, brightened by the summer wind, which faintly stirred the auburn hair under the neat little hat.

'And am I actually a Countess? I don't care about it one little bit, you know, except as a stupendous joke. If you were to tell me that you had been only making fun of poor grandmother and me, and that those diamonds are glass, and you only plain John Hammond, it wouldn't make the faintest difference. Indeed, it would be a weight off my mind. It is an awfully oppressive thing to be a Countess.'

'I'm sorry I cannot relieve you of the burden. The law of the land has made you Lady Hartfield; and I hope you are preparing your mind for the duties of your position.'

'It is very dreadful,' sighed Mary. 'If her ladyship were as well and as active as she was when first you came to Fellside, she could have helped me; but now there will be no one, except you. And you will help me, won't you Jack?'

'With all my heart.'

'My own true Jack,' with a little fervent squeeze of his sunburnt hand. 'In society I suppose I shall have to call you Hartfield. "Hartfield, please ring the bell." "Give me a footstool, Hartfield." How odd it sounds. I shall be blurting out the old dear name.'

'I don't think it will much matter. It will pass for one of Lady Hartfield's little ways. Every woman is supposed to have little ways, don't you know. One has a little way of dropping her friends; another has a little way of not paying her dressmaker; another's little way is to take too much champagne. I hope Lady Hartfield's little way will be her devotion to her husband.'

'I'm afraid I shall end by being a nuisance to you, for I shall love you ridiculously,' answered Mary, gaily; 'and from what you have told me about society, it seems to me that there can be nothing so unfashionable as an affectionate wife. Will you mind my being quite out of fashion, Jack?'

'I should very much object to your being in the fashion.'

'Then I am happy. I don't think it is in my nature to become a woman of fashion; although I have cured myself, for your sake, of being a hoyden. I had so schooled myself for what I thought our new life was to be; so trained myself to be a managing economical wife, that I feel quite at sea now that I am to be mistress of a house in Grosvenor Square and a place in Kent. Still, I will bear with it all; yes, even endure the weight of those diamonds for your sake.'

She laughed, and he laughed. They were quite alone among the hills--hardy mountaineers both--and they could be as foolish as they liked. She rested her head upon his shoulder, and he and she and the pony made one as they climbed the hill, close together.

'Our last day,' sighed Mary, as they went down again, after a couple of blissful hours in that wild world between earth and sky. 'I shall be glad to go back to poor grandmother, who must be sadly lonely; but it is so sweet to be quite alone with you.'

They left the Lodore Hotel in an open carriage, after luncheon next day, and posted to Fellside, where they arrived just in time to assist at Lady Maulevrier's afternoon tea. She received them both with warm affection, and made Hartfield sit close beside her sofa; and every now and then, in the pauses of their talk, she laid her wasted and too delicate fingers upon the young man's strong brown hand, with a caressing gesture.

'You can never know how sweet it is to me to be able to love you,' she said tenderly. 'You can never know how my heart yearned to you from the very first, and how hard it was to keep myself in check and not be too kind to you. Oh, Hartfield, you should have told me the truth. You should not have come here under false colours.'

'Should I not, Lady Maulevrier? It was my only chance of being loved for my own sake; or, at least of knowing that I was so loved. If I had come with my rank and my fortune in my hand, as it were--one of the good matches of the year--what security could I ever have felt in the disinterested love of the girl who chose me? As plain John Hammond I wooed and was rejected; as plain John Hammond I wooed and won; and the prize which I so won is a pearl above price. Not for worlds, were the last year to be lived over again, would I have one day of my life altered.'

'Well, I suppose I ought to be satisfied, I wanted you for Lesbia, and I have got you for Mary. Best of all, I have got you for myself. Ronald Hollister's son is mine; he is of my kin; he belongs to me; he will not forsake me in life; he will be near me, God grant, when I die.'

'Dear Lady Maulevrier, as far as in me lies, I will be to you as a son,' said Lord Hartfield, very solemnly, stooping to kiss her hand.

Mary came away from her tea-table to embrace her grandmother.

'It makes me so happy to have won a little of your regard,' she murmured, 'and to know that I have married a man whom you can love.'

'Of course you have heard of Lesbia's engagement?' Lady Maulevrier said presently, when they were taking their tea.

'Maulevrier wrote to us about it.'

'To us.' How nice it sounded, thought Mary, as if they were a firm, and a letter written to one was written to both.

'And do you know this Mr. Smithson?'

'Not intimately. I have met him at the Carlton.'

'I am told that he is very much esteemed by your party, and that he is very likely to get a peerage when this Ministry goes out of office.'

'That is not improbable. Peerages are to be had if a man is rich enough; and Smithson is supposed to be inordinately rich.'

'I hope he has character as well as money,' said Lady Maulevrier, gravely. 'But do you think a man can become inordinately rich in a short time, with unblemished honour?'

'We are told that nothing is impossible,' answered Hartfield. 'Faith can remove a mountain; only one does not often see it done. However, I believe Mr. Smithson's character is fairly good as millionaires go. We do not inquire too closely into these things nowadays.'

Lady Maulevrier sighed and held her peace. She remembered the day when she had protested vehemently, passionately, against Lesbia's marriage with a poor man. And now she had an unhappy feeling about Mr. Smithson's wealth, a doubt, a dread that all might not be well with those millions, that some portion of that golden tide might flow from impure sources. She had lived remote from the world, but she had read the papers diligently, and she knew how often the splendour of commercial wealth has been suddenly obscured behind a black cloud of obloquy. She could not rejoice heartily at the idea of Lesbia's engagement.

'I am to see the man early in August,' she said, as if she were talking of a butler. 'I hope I may like him. Lady Kirkbank tells me it is a brilliant marriage, and I must take her word. What can *I* do for my granddaughter--a useless log--a prisoner in two rooms?'

'It is very hard,' murmured Mary, tenderly, 'but I do not see any reason why Lesbia should not be happy. She likes a brilliant life; and Mr. Smithson can give her as much gaiety and variety as she can possibly desire. And, after all, yachts, and horses, and villas, and diamonds *are* nice things.'

'They are the things for which half the world is ready to cheat or murder the other half,' said Lady Maulevrier, bitterly. She had told herself long ago that wealth was power, and she had sacrificed many things, her own peace, her own conscience among them, in order that her children and grandchildren should be rich; and, knowing this, she felt it ill became her to be scrupulous, and to inquire too, closely as to the sources of Mr. Smithson's wealth. He was rich, and the world had no fault to find with him. He had attended the last *levee*. He went into reputable society. And he could give Lesbia all those things which the world calls good.

Fraeulein Mueller had packed her heavy old German trunks, and had gone back to the **Heimath**, laden with presents of all kinds from Lady Maulevrier; so Mary and her husband felt as if Fellside was really their own. They dined with her ladyship, and left her for the night an hour after dinner; and then they went down to the gardens, and roamed about in the twilight, and talked, and talked, and talked, as only true lovers can talk, be they Strephon and Daphne in life's glad morning, or grey-haired Darby and Joan; and lastly they went down to the hike, and rowed about in the moonlight, and talked of King Arthur's death, and of that mystic sword, Excalibur, 'wrought by the lonely maiden of the lake.'

They spent three happy days in wandering about the neighbourhood, revisiting in the delicious freedom of their wedded life those spots which they had seen together, when Mary was still in bondage, and the eye of propriety, as represented by Miss Mueller, was always upon her. Now they were free to go where they pleased--to linger where they liked--they belonged to each other, and were under no other dominion.

The dogcart, James Steadman's dogcart, which he had rarely used during the last six months, was put in requisition and Lord Hartfield drove his wife about the country. They went to the Langdale Pikes, and to Dungeon Ghyll; and, standing beside the waterfall, Mary told her husband how miserable she had felt on that very spot a little less than a year ago, when she believed that he thought her plain and altogether horrid. Whereupon he had to console her with many kisses and sweet words, for the bygone pain on her part, the neglect of his.

'I was a wretch,' he said, 'blind, besotted, imbecile.'

'No, no, no. Lesbia is very lovely--and I could not expect you would care for me till she was gone away. How glad I am that she went,' added Mary, naively.

The sky, which had been cloudless all day, began to darken as Lord Hartfield drove back to Fellside, and Mary drew a little closer to the driver's elbow, as if for shelter from an impending tempest.

'You have no waterproof, of course,' he said, looking down at her, as the first big drops of a thunder shower dashed upon the splash-board. 'No young woman in the Lake country would think of being without a waterproof.'

Mary was duly provided, and with the help of the groom put herself into a snug little tartan Inverness, while Hartfield sent the cart spinning along twelve miles an hour.

They were at Fellside before the storm developed its full power, but the sky was leaden, the landscape dull and blotted, the atmosphere heavy and stifling. The thunder grumbled hoarsely, far away yonder in the wild gorges of Borrowdale; and Mary and her husband made up their minds that the tempest would come before midnight.

Lady Maulevrier was suffering from the condition of the atmosphere. She had gone to bed, prostrate with a neuralgic headache, and had given orders that no one but her maid should go near her. So Lord Hartfield and his wife dined by themselves, in the room where Mary had eaten so many uninteresting dinners *tete-a-tete* with Fraeulein; and in spite of the storm which howled, pelted, and lightened every now and then, Mary felt as if she were in Paradise.

There was no chance of going out after dinner. The lake looked like a pool of ink, the mountains were monsters of dark and threatening aspect, the rain rattled against the windows, and ran from the verandah in miniature water-spouts. There was nothing to do but stay in doors, in the sultry, dusky house.

'Let us go to my boudoir,' said Mary. 'Let me enjoy the full privilege of having a boudoir--my very own room. Wasn't it too good of grandmother to have it made so smart for me?'

'Nothing can be too good for my Mary,' answered her husband, still in the doting stage, 'but it was very nice of her ladyship--and the room is charming.'

Delightful as the new boudoir might be, they dawdled in the picture gallery, that long corridor on which all the upper rooms opened, and at one end of which was the door of Lady Maulevrier's bedroom, at right angles with that red-cloth door, which was never opened, except to give egress or ingress to James Steadman, who kept the key of it, as if the old part of Fellside House had been an enchanted castle. Lord Hartfield had not forgotten that summer midnight last year, when his

meditations were disturbed by a woman's piercing cry. He thought of it this evening, as Mary and he lowered their voices on drawing near Lady Maulevrier's door.
She was asleep within there now, perhaps, that strange old woman; and at any moment an awful shriek, as of a soul in mortal agony, might startle them in the midst
of their bliss.

The lamps were lighted below; but this upper part of the house was wrapped
in the dull grey twilight of a stormy evening. A single lamp burned dimly at the
further end of the corridor, and all the rest was shadow.

Mary and her husband walked up and down, talking in subdued tones. He was
explaining the necessity of his being in London next week, and promising to come
back to Fellside directly his business at the House was over.

'It will be delightful to read your speeches,' said Mary; 'but I am silly and selfish
enough to wish you were a country squire, with no business in London. And yet I
don't wish that either, for I am intensely proud of you.'

'And some day, before we are much older, you will sit in your robes in the
peeress's gallery.'

'Oh, I couldn't,' cried Mary. 'I should make a fool of myself, somehow. I should
look like a housemaid in borrowed plumes. Remember, I have no *Anstand*--I have
been told so all my life.'

'You will be one of the prettiest peeresses who ever sat in that gallery, and the
purest, and truest, and dearest,' protested her lover-husband.

'Oh, if I am good enough for you, I am satisfied. I married *you*, and not the
House of Lords. But I am afraid your friends will all say, "Hartfield, why in heaven's
name did you marry that uncultivated person?" Look!'

She stopped suddenly, with her hand on her husband's arm. It was growing
momentarily darker in the corridor. They were at the end near the lamp, and that
other end by Lady Maulevrier's door was in deeper darkness, yet not too dark for
Lord Hartfield to see what it was to which Mary pointed.

The red-cloth door was open, and a faint glimmer of light showed within. A
man was standing in the corridor, a small, shrunken figure, bent and old.

'It is Steadman's uncle,' said Mary 'Do let me go and speak to him, poor, poor
old man.'

'The madman!' exclaimed Hartfield. 'No, Mary; go to your room at once. I'll get him back to his own den.'

'But he is not mad--at any rate, he is quite harmless. Let me just say a few words to him. Surely I am safe with you.'

Lord Hartfield was not inclined to dispute that argument; indeed, he felt himself strong enough to protect his wife from all the lunatics in Bedlam. He went towards the end of the corridor, keeping Mary well behind him; but Mary did not mean to lose the opportunity of renewing her acquaintance with Steadman's uncle.

'I hope you are better, poor old soul,' she murmured, gently, lovingly almost, nestling at her husband's side.

'What, is it you?' cried the old man, tremulous with joy.

'Oh, I have been looking for you--looking--looking--waiting, waiting for you. I have been hoping for you every hour and every minute. Why didn't you come to me, cruel girl?'

'I tried with all my might,' said Mary, 'but people blocked up the door in the stables, and they wouldn't let me go to you; and I have been rather busy for the last fortnight,' added Mary, blushing in the darkness, 'I--I--am married to this gentle-man.'

'Married! Ah, that is a good thing. He will take care of you, if he is an honest man.'

'I thought he was an honest man, but he has turned out to be an earl,' answered Mary, proudly. 'My husband is Lord Hartfield.' 'Hartfield--Hartfield,' the old man repeated, feebly. 'Surely I have heard that name before.'

There was no violence in his manner, nothing but imbecility: so Lord Hartfield made up his mind that Mary was right, and that the old man was quite harmless, worthy of all compassion and kindly treatment.

This was the same old man whom he had met on the Fell in the bleak March morning. There was no doubt in his mind about that, although he could hardly see the man's face in the shadowy corridor.

'Come,' said the man, 'come with me, my dear. You forgot me, but I have not forgotten you. I mean to leave you my fortune. Come with me, and I'll show you your legacy. It is all for you--every rupee--every jewel.'

This word rupee startled Lord Hartfield. It had a strange sound from the lips of a Westmoreland peasant.

'Come, child, come!' said the man impatiently. 'Come and see what I have left you in my will. I make a new will every day, but I leave everything to you--every will is in your favour; But if you are married you had better have your legacy at once. Your husband is strong enough to take care of you and your fortune.'

'Poor old man,' whispered Mary; 'pray let us humour him.'

It was the usual madman's fancy, no doubt. Boundless wealth, exalted rank, sanctity, power--these things all belong to the lunatic. He is the lord of creation, and, fed by such fancies, he enjoys flashes of wild happiness in the midst of his woe.

'Come, come, both of you,' said the old man, eagerly, breathless with impatience.

He led the way across the sacred threshold, looking back, beckoning to them with his wasted old hand, and Mary for the first time in her life entered that house which had seemed to her from her very childhood as a temple of silence and mystery. The passage was dimly lighted by a little lamp on a bracket. The old man crept along stealthily, looking back, with a face full of cunning, till he came to a broad landing, from which an old staircase, with massive oak banisters, led down to the square hall below. The ceilings were low, the passages were narrow. All things in the house were curiously different from that spacious mansion which Lady Maulevrier had built for herself.

A door on the landing stood ajar. The old man pushed it open and went in, followed by Mary and her husband.

They both expected to see a room humble almost to poverty--an iron bedstead, perhaps, and such furniture as the under servants in a nobleman's household are privileged to enjoy. Both were alike surprised at the luxury of the apartment they entered, and which was evidently reserved exclusively for Steadman's uncle.

It was a sitting-room. The furniture was old-fashioned, but almost as handsome as any in Lady Maulevrier's apartments. There was a large sofa of most comfortable shape, covered with dark red velvet, and furnished with pillows and foot rugs, which would have satisfied a Sybarite of the first water. Beside the sofa stood a hookah, with all appliances in the Oriental fashion; and half a dozen long cherry-wood pipes neatly arranged above the mantelpiece showed that Mr. Steadman's uncle was a smoker of a luxurious type.

In the centre of the room stood a large writing table, with a case of pigeon-holes at the back, a table which would not have disgraced a Prime Minister's study. A pair of wax candles, in tall silver candlesticks, lighted this table, which was littered with papers, in a wild confusion that too plainly indicated the condition of the owner's mind. The oak floor was covered with Persian prayer rugs, old and faded, but of the richest quality. The window curtains were dark red velvet; and through an open doorway Mary and her husband saw a corresponding luxury in the arrangements of the adjoining bedroom.

The whole thing seemed wild and strange as a fairy tale. The weird and wizened old man, grinning and nodding his head at them. The handsome room, rich with dark, subdued colour, in the dim light of four wax candles, two on the table, two on the mantelpiece. The perfume of stephanotis and tea-roses, blended faintly with the all-pervading odour of latakia and Turkish attar. All was alike strange, bearing in mind that this old man was a recipient of Lady Maulevrier's charity, a hanger-on upon a confidential servant, who might be supposed to be generously treated if he had the run of his teeth and the shelter of a decent garret. Verily, there was something regal in such hospitality as this, accorded to a pauper lunatic.

Where was Steadman, the alert, the watchful, all this time? Mary wondered. They had met no one. The house was as mute as if it were under the spell of a magician. It was like that awful chamber in the Arabian story, where the young man found the magic horse, and started on his fatal journey. Mary felt as if here, too, there must be peril; here, too, fate was working.

The old man went to the writing table, pushed aside the papers, and then stooped down and turned a mysterious handle or winch under the knee-hole, and the writing-desk moved slowly on one side, while the pigeon-holes sank, and a deep well full of secret drawers was laid open.

From one of these secret drawers the old man took a bunch of keys, nodding, chuckling, muttering to himself as he groped for them with tremulous hand.

'Steadman is uncommonly clever--thinks he knows everything--but he doesn't know the trick of this table. I could hide a regiment of Sepoys in this table, my dear. Well, well, perhaps not Sepoys--too big, too big--but I could hide all the State papers of the Presidency. There are drawers enough for that.'

Hartfield watched him intently, with thoughtful brow. There was a mystery here, a mystery of the deepest dye; and it was for him--it must needs be his task, welcome or unwelcome, to unravel it.

This was the Maulevrier skeleton.

'Now, come with me,' said the old man, clutching Mary's wrist, and drawing her towards the half-open door leading into the bedroom.

She had a feeling of shrinking, for there was something uncanny about the old man, something that might be life or death, might belong to this world or the next; but she had no fear. In the first place, she was courageous by nature, and in the second her husband was with her, a tower of strength, and she could know no fear while he was at her side.

The strange old man led the way across his bedroom to an inner chamber, oak pannelled, with very little furniture, but holding much treasure in the shape of trunks, portmanteaux--all very old and dusty--and two large wooden cases, banded with iron.

Before one of these cases the man knelt down, and applied a key to the padlock which fastened it. He gave the candle to Lord Hartfield to hold, and then opened the box. It seemed to be full of books, which he began to remove, heaping them on the floor beside him; and it was not till he had cleared away a layer of dingy volumes that he came to a large metal strong box, so heavy that he could not lift it out of the chest.

Slowly, tremulously, and with quickened breathing, he unlocked the box where it was, and raised the lid.

'Look,' he said eagerly, 'this is her legacy--this is my little girl's legacy.'

Lord Hartfield bent down and looked at the old man's treasure, by the wavering light of the candle; Mary looking over his shoulder, breathless with wonder.

The strong box was divided into compartments. One, and the largest, was filled with rouleaux of coin, packed as closely as possible. The others contained jewels, set and unset--diamonds, emeralds, rubies, sapphires--which flashed back the flickering flame of the candle with glintings of rainbow light.

'These are all for her--all--all,' exclaimed the old man. 'They are worth a prince's ransom. Those rouleaux are all gold; those gems are priceless. They were the dowry of a princess. But they are hers now--yes, my dear, they are yours--because you spoke sweetly, and smiled prettily, and were very good to a lonely old man--and because you have my mother's face, dear, a smile that recalls the days of my youth. Lift out the box and take it away with you, if you are strong enough,--you, you,' he said, touching Lord Hartfield. 'Hide it somewhere--keep it from *her*. Let no one know--no one except your wife and you must be in the secret.'

'My dear sir, it is out of the question--impossible that my wife or I should accept one of those coins--or the smallest of those jewels.'

'Why not, in the devil's name?'

'First and foremost, we do not know how you came in possession of them; secondly, we do not know who you are.'

'They came to me fairly enough--bequeathed to me by one who had the right to leave them. Would you have had all that gold left for an adventurer to wallow in?'

'You must keep your treasure, sir, however it may have come to you,' answered Lord Hartfield firmly. 'My wife cannot take upon herself the burden of a single gold coin--least of all from a stranger. Remember, sir, to us your possession of this wealth--nay, your whole existence--is a mystery.'

'You want to know who I am?' said the old man drawing himself up, with a sudden *hauteur* which was not without dignity, despite his shrunken form and grotesque appearence. 'Well, sir. I am----'

He checked himself abruptly, and looked round the room with a scared expression.

'No, no, no,' he muttered; 'caution, caution! They have not done with me yet; she warned me--they are lying in wait; I mustn't walk into their trap.' And then turning to Lord Hartfield, he said, haughtily, 'I shall not condescend to tell you who I am, sir. You must know that I am a gentleman, and that is enough for you. There is my gift to your wife'--pointing to the chest--'take it or leave it.'

'I shall leave it, sir, with all due respect.'

A frightful change came over the old man's face at this determined refusal. His eyes glowered at Lord Hartfield under the heavy scowling brows; his bloodless lips worked convulsively.

'Do you take me for a thief?' he exclaimed. 'Are you afraid to touch my gold--that gold for which men and women sell their souls, blast their lives with shame, and pain, and dishonour, all the world over? Do you stand aloof from it--refuse to touch it, as if it were infected? And you, too, girl! Have you no sense? Are you an idiot?'

'I can do nothing against my husband's wish,' Mary answered, quietly; 'and, indeed, there is no need for us to take your money. We are rich without it. Please leave that chest to a hospital. It will be ever so much better than giving it to us.'

'You told me you were going to marry a poor man?'

'I know. But he cheated me, and turned out to be a rich man. He was a horrid impostor,' said Mary, drawing closer to her husband, and smiling up at him.

The old man flung down the lid of his strong box, which shut with a sonorous clang. He locked it, and put the key in his pocket.

'I have done with you.' he said. 'You can go your ways, both of you. Fools, fools, fools! The world is peopled with rogues and fools; and, by heaven, I would rather have to do with the rogues!'

He flung himself into an arm-chair, one of the few objects of furniture in the room, and left them to find their way back alone.

'Good-night, sir,' said Lord Hartfield; but the old man made no reply. He sat frowning sullenly.

'Good-night, sir,' said Mary, in her gentle voice, breathing infinite pity.

'Good-night, child,' he growled. 'I am sorry you have married an ass.'

This was more than Mary could stand, and she was about to reply with some acrimony, when her husband put his hand upon her lips and hurried her away.

On the landing they met Mrs. Steadman, a stout, commonplace person, who always had the same half-frightened look, as of one who lived in the shadow of an abiding terror, obviously cowed and brow beaten by her husband, according to the Fellside household.

At sight of Lord Hartfield and his wife she looked a little more frightened than usual.

'Goodness gracious, Lady Mary! how ever did you come here?' she gasped, not yet having quite realised the fact that Mary had been promoted.

'We came to please Steadman's uncle--he brought us in here,' Mary answered, quietly.

'But where did you find him?'

'In the corridor--just by her ladyship's room.'

'Then he must have taken the key out of Steadman's pocket, or Steadman must have left it about somewhere,' muttered Mrs. Steadman, as if explaining the matter to herself, rather than to Mary. 'My poor husband is not the man he was. And so you met him in the corridor, and he brought you in here. Poor old gentleman! He gets madder and madder every day.'

'There is method in his madness,' said Lord Hartfield. 'He talked very much like sanity just now. Has your husband had the charge of him long?'

Mrs. Steadman answered somewhat confusedly.

'A goodish time, sir. I can't quite exactly say--time passes so quiet in a place like this. One hardly keeps count of the years.'

'Forty years, perhaps?'

Mrs. Steadman blenched under Lord Hartfield's steadfast look--a look which questioned more searchingly than his words.

'Forty years,' she repeated, with a faint laugh. 'Oh, dear no, sir, not a quarter as long. It isn't so many years, after all, since Steadman's poor old uncle went a little queer in his head; and Steadman, having such a quiet home here, and plenty of spare room, made bold to ask her ladyship if he might give the poor old man a home, where he would be in nobody's way.'

'And the poor old man seems to have a very luxurious home,' answered Lord Hartfield. 'Pray when and where did Mr. Steadman's uncle learn to smoke a hookah?'

Simple as the question was, it proved too much for Mrs. Steadman. She only shook her head, and faltered some unintelligible reply.

'Where is your husband?' asked Lord Hartfield: 'I should like to have a little talk with him, if he is disengaged.'

'He is not very well, my lord,' answered Mrs. Steadman. 'He has been ailing off and on for the last six months, but I couldn't get him to see the doctor, or to tell her ladyship that he was in bad health. And about a week ago he broke down altogether, and fell into a kind of drowsy state. He keeps about, and he does his work pretty much the same as usual, but I can see that it's too much for him. If you like to come downstairs I can let you through the lower door into the hall; and if he should have woke up since I have left him he'll be at your lordship's service. But I'd rather not wake him out of his sleep.'

'There is no occasion. What I have to say will keep till to-morrow.'

Lord Hartfield and his wife followed Mrs. Steadman downstairs to the low dark hall, where an old eight-day clock ticked with hoarse and solemn heat, and a fine stag's head over each doorway gave evidence of some former Haselden's sporting tastes. The door of a small panelled parlour stood half-way open; and within the room Lord Hartfield saw James Steadman asleep in an arm-chair by the fire, which burned as brightly as if it had been Christmas time.

'He was so chilly and shivery this afternoon that I was obliged to light a fire,' said Mrs. Steadman.

'He seems to be sleeping heavily,' said Hartfield. 'Don't awaken him. I'll see him to-morrow morning before I go to London.'

'He sleeps half the day just as heavy as that, my lord,' said the wife, with a troubled air. 'I don't think it can be right.'

'I don't think so either,' answered Lord Hartfield. 'You had better call in the doctor.'

'I will, my lord, to-morrow morning. James will be angry with me, I daresay; but I must take upon myself to do it without his leave.'

She led the way along a passage corresponding with the one above, and un-locked a door opening into a lobby near the billiard-room.

'Come, Molly, see if you can beat me at a fifty game,' said Lord Hartfield, with the air of a man who wants to shake off the impression of some dominant idea.

'Of course you will annihilate me, but it will be a relief to play,' answered Mary. 'That strange old man has given me a shock. Everything about his surroundings is so different from what I expected. And how could an uncle of Steadman's come by all that money--and those jewels--if they were jewels, and not bits of glass which the poor old thing has chopped up, in order to delude himself with an imaginary treasure?'

'I do not think they are bits of glass, Molly.'

'They sparkled tremendously--almost as much as my--our--the family dia-monds,' said Mary, puzzled how to describe that property which she held in right of her position as countess regnant; 'but if they are real jewels, and all those rouleaux real money, how could Steadman's uncle become possessed of such wealth?'

'How, indeed?' said Lord Hartfield, choosing his cue

CHAPTER XXXVIII.
ON BOARD THE 'CAYMAN.'

Goodwood had come and gone, a brief bright season of loss and gain, fine gowns, flirtation, lobster en mayonaise, champagne, sunshine, dust, glare, babble of many voices, successes, failures, triumphs, humiliations. A very pretty picture to contemplate from the outside, this little world in holiday clothes, framed in greenery! but just on the Brocken, where the nicest girl among the dancers had the unpleasant peculiarity of dropping a little red mouse out of her mouth--so too here under different forms there were red mice dropping about among the company. Here a hint of coming insolvency; there a whisper of a threatened divorce suit, staved off for awhile, compromises, family secrets, little difficulties everywhere; betrothed couples smilingly accepting congratulations, who should never have been affianced were truth and honour the rule of life; forsaken wives pretending to think their husbands models of fidelity; jovial creatures with ruin staring in their faces; households divided and shamming union; almost everybody living above his or her means; and the knowledge that nobody is any better or any happier than his neighbour society's only fountain of consolation.

Lady Lesbia's gowns and parasols had been admired, her engagement had furnished an infinity of gossip, and the fact of Montesma's constant attendance upon her had given zest to the situation, just that flavour of peril and fatality which the soul of society loveth.

'Is she going to marry them both?' asked an ancient dowager of the ever-young type.

'No, dear Lady Sevenoaks, she can only marry one, don't you know; but the other is nice to go about with; and I believe it is the other she really likes.'

'It is always the other that a woman likes,' answered the dowager; 'I am madly in love with this Peruvian--no, I think you said Cuban--myself. I wish some good-natured creature would present him to me. If you know anybody who knows him, tell them to bring him to my next afternoon--Saturday. But why does--*chose*--*machin*--Smithson allow such a handsome hanger-on? After marriage I could understand that he might not be able to help himself; but before marriage a man generally has some kind of authority.'

The world wondered a little, just as Lady Sevenoaks wondered, at Smithson's complacency in allowing a man so attractive as Montesma to be so much in the society of his future wife, yet even the censorious could but admit that the Cuban's manner offered no ground for offence. He came to Goodwood 'on his own hook,' as society put it: and every man who wears a decent coat and is not a welsher has a right to enjoy the prettiest race-course in England. He spent a considerable part of the day in Lesbia's company; but since she was the centre of a little crowd all the time, there could be no offence in this. He was a stranger, knowing very few people, and having nothing to do but to amuse himself. Smithson was an old and familiar friend, and was in a measure bound to give him hospitality.

Mr. Smithson had recognised that obligation, but in a somewhat sparing manner. There were a dozen unoccupied bedchambers in the Park Lane Renaissance villa; but Smithson did not invite his Cuban acquaintance to shift his quarters from the Bristol to Park Lane. He was civil to Don Gomez: but anyone who had taken the trouble to watch and study the conduct and social relations of these two men would have seen that his civility was a forced civility, and that he endured the Spaniard's society under constraint of some kind.

And now all the world was flocking to Cowes for the regatta, and Lesbia and her chaperon were established on board Mr. Smithson's yacht, the *Cayman*; and the captain of the *Cayman* and all her crew were delivered over to Lesbia to be her slaves and to obey her lightest breath. The *Cayman* was to lie at anchor off Cowes for the regatta week; and then she was to sail for Hyde, and lie at anchor there for another regatta week; and she was to be a floating-hotel for Lady Lesbia so long as the young lady would condescend to occupy her.

The captain was an altogether exceptional captain, and the crew were a picked crew, ruddy faced, sandy whiskered for the most part, Englishmen all, honest, hardy fellows from between the Nore and the Wash, talking in an honest provincial patois, dashed with sea slang. They were the very pink and pattern of cleanliness, and the *Cayman* herself from stem to stern was dazzling and spotless to an almost painful degree.

Not content with the existing arrangements of the yacht, which were at once elegant and luxurious, Mr. Smithson had sent down a Bond Street upholsterer to re-fit the saloon and Lady Lesbia's cabin. The dark velvet and morocco which suited a masculine occupant would not have harmonised with girlhood and beauty; and Mr. Smithson's saloon, as originally designed, had something of the air of a *tabagie*. The Bond Street man stripped away all the velvet and morocco, plucked up the Turkey carpet, draped the scuttle-ports with pale yellow cretonne garnished with orange pompons, subdued the glare of the skylight by a blind of oriental silk, covered the divans with Persian saddlebags, the floor with a delicate Indian matting, and fur-nished the saloon with all that was most feminine in the way of bamboo chairs and tea-tables, Japanese screens and fans of gorgeous colouring. Here and there against the fluted yellow drapery he fastened a large Rhodes plate; and the thing was done. Lady Lesbia's cabin was all bamboo and embroidered India muslin. An oval glass, framed in Dresden biscuit, adorned the side, a large white bearskin covered the floor. The berth was pretty enough for the cradle of a duchess's first baby. Even Les-bia, spoiled by much indulgence and unlimited credit, gave a little cry of pleasure at sight of the nest that had been made ready for her.

'Really, Mr. Smithson is immensely kind!' she exclaimed.

'Smithson is always kind,' answered Lady Kirkbank, 'and you don't half enough appreciate him. He has given me his very own cabin--such a dear little den! There are his cigar boxes and everything lovely on the shelves, and his own particular dressing-case put open for me to use--all the backs of all the brushes *repousse* sil-ver, and all the scent-bottles filled expressly for me. If the yacht would only stand quite still, I should think it more delicious than the best house I ever stayed in: only I don't altogether enjoy that little way it has of gurgling up and down perpetually.'

Mr. Smithson's chief butler, a German Swiss, and a treasure of intelligence, had come down to take the domestic arrangements of the yacht into his control. The Park Lane *chef* was also on board, Mr. Smithson's steward acting as his subordinate. This great man grumbled sorely at the smallness of his surroundings; for the most luxurious yacht was a poor substitute for the spacious kitchens and storerooms and stillrooms of the London mansion. There was a cabin for Lady Kirkbank's Rilboche and Lady Lesbia's Kibble, where the two might squabble at their leisure; in a word, everything had been done that forethought could do to make the yacht as perfect a place of sojourn as any floating habitation, from Noah's Ark to the Orient steamers, had ever been made.

It was between four and five upon a delicious July afternoon that Lady Kirkbank and her charge came on board. The maids and the luggage had been sent a day in advance, so that everything might be in its place, and the empty boxes all stowed away, before the ladies arrived. They had nothing to do but walk on board and fling themselves into the low luxurious chairs ready for them on the deck, a little wearied by the heat and dust of a railway journey, and with that delicious sense of languid indifference to all the cares of life which seems to be in the very atmosphere of a perfect summer afternoon.

A striped awning covered the deck, and great baskets of roses--pink, and red, and yellow--were placed about here and there. Tea was ready on a low table, a swinging brass kettle hissing merrily, with an air of supreme homeliness.

Mr. Smithson had accompanied his *fiancee* from town, and now sat reading the *Globe*, and meekly waiting for his tea, while Lesbia took a languid survey of the shore and the flotilla of boats, little and big, and while Lady Kirkbank rhapsodised about the yacht, praising everything, and calling everything by a wrong name. He was to be their guest all day, and every day. They were to have enough of him, as Lesbia had observed to her chaperon, with a spice of discontent, not quite so delighted with the arrangement as her faithful swain. To him the idea was rapture.

'You have contrived somehow to keep me very much at a distance hitherto,' he told Lesbia, 'and I feel sometimes as if we were almost strangers; but a yacht is the best place in the world to bring two people together, and a week at Cowes will make us nearer to each other and more to each other than three months in London;' and Lesbia had said nothing, inwardly revolting at the idea of becoming any nearer and dearer to this man whom she had pledged herself to marry. She was to be his wife--yes, some day--and it was his desire the some day should be soon: but in the interval her dearest privilege was the power to keep him at a distance.

And yet she could not make up her mind to break with him, to say honestly, 'I never liked you much, and now we are engaged I find myself liking you less and less every day. Save me from the irrevocable wickedness of a loveless marriage. Forgive me, and let me go.' No, this she could not bring herself to say. She did not like Mr. Smithson, but she valued the position he was able to give her. She wanted to be mistress of that infinite wealth--she could not renounce that right to which she fancied she had been born, her right to be one of the Queens of Society: and the only man who had offered to crown her as queen, to find her a palace and a court, was Horace Smithson. Without Mr. Smithson her first season would have resulted in dire failure. She might perhaps have endured that failure, and been content to abide the chances of a second season, had it not been for Mary's triumph. But for Mary to be a Countess, and for Lesbia to remain Lesbia Haselden, a nobody, dependent upon the caprices of a grandmother whose means might after all be but limited--no, such a concatenation as that was not to be endured. Lesbia told herself that she could not go back to Fellside to remain there indefinitely, a spinster and a dependent. She had learnt the true value of money; she had found out what the world was like; and it seemed to her that some such person as Mr. Smithson was essential to her existence, just as a butler is a necessity in a house. One may not like the man, but the post must be filled.

Again, if she were to throw over Mr. Smithson, and speculate upon her chances of next year, what hope had she of doing better in her second season than in her first? The horizon was blank. There was no great *parti* likely to offer himself for competition. She had seen all that the market could produce. Wealthy bachelors, high-born lovers, could not drop from the moon. Lesbia, schooled by Lady Kirkbank, knew her peerage by heart; and she knew that, having missed Lord Hartfield, there was really no one in the Blue Book worth waiting for. Thus, caring only for those things which wealth can buy, she had made up her mind that she could not do without Horace Smithson's money; and she must therefore needs resign herself to the disagreeable necessity of taking Smithson and his money together. The great auctioneer Fate would not divide the lot.

She told herself that for her a loveless marriage was, after all, no prodigious sacrifice. She had found out that heart made but a small figure in the sum of her life. She could do without love. A year ago she had fancied herself in love with John Hammond. In her seclusion at St. Bees, in the long, dull August days, sauntering up and down by the edge of the sea, in the melancholy sunset hour, she thought that her heart was broken, that life was worthless without the man she loved. She had thought and felt all this, but not strongly enough to urge her to any great effort, not keenly enough to make her burst her chains. She had preferred to suffer this loss than to sacrifice her chances of future aggrandisement. And now she looked back and remembered those sunset walks by the sea, and all her thoughts and feelings in those silent summer hours; and she smiled at herself, half in scorn, half in pity, for her own weakness. How easily she had learned to do without him who at that hour seemed the better part of her existence. A good deal of gaiety and praise, a little mild flirtation at Kirkbank Castle, and lo! the image of her first lover began to grow dim and blurred, like a faded photograph. A season at Cannes, and she was cured. A week in London, and that first love was a thing of the past, a dream from which the dreamer awaketh, forgetting the things that he has dreamt.

Remembering all this she told herself that she had no heart, that love or no love was a question of very little moment, and that the personal qualities of the man whom she chose for a husband mattered nothing to her, provided that his lands and houses and social status came up to her standard of merit. She had seen Mr. Smithson's houses and lands; and she was distinctly assured that he would in due course be raised to the peerage. She had, therefore, every reason to be satisfied.

Having thus reasoned out the circumstances of her new life, she accepted her fate with a languid grace, which harmonised with her delicate and patrician beauty. Nobody could have for a moment supposed from her manner that she loved Horace Smithson; but nobody had the right to think that she detested him. She accepted all his attentions as a thing of course. The flowers which he strewed beneath her footsteps, the pearls which he melted in her wine--metaphorically speaking--were just 'good enough' and no more. This afternoon, when Mr. Smithson asked her how she liked the arrangements of the saloon and cabin, she said she thought they would do very nicely. 'They would do.' Nothing more.

'It is dreadfully small, of course,' she said, 'when one is accustomed to rooms: but it is rather amusing to be in a sort of doll's house, and on deck it is really very nice.'

This was the most Mr. Smithson had for his pains, and he seemed to be content therewith. If a man will marry the prettiest girl of the year he must be satisfied with such scant civility as conscious perfection may give him. We know that Aphrodite was not altogether the most comfortable wife, and that Helen was a cause of trouble.

Mr. Smithson sat in a bamboo chair beside his mistress, and looked ineffably happy when she handed him a cup of tea. Sky and sea were one exquisite azure--

the colours of the boats glancing in the sunshine as if they had been jewels; here an emerald rudder, there a gunwale painted with liquid rubies. White sails, white frocks, white ducks made vivid patches of light against the blue. The landscape yonder shone and sparkled as if it had been incandescent. All the world of land and sky and sea was steeped in sunshine. A day on which to do nothing, read nothing, think nothing, only to exist.

While they sat basking in the balmy atmosphere, looking lazily at that bright, almost insupportable picture of blue sea under blue sky, there came the dip of oars, making music, and a sound of coolness with every plash of water.

'How good it is of somebody to row about, just to give us that nice soothing sound,' murmured Lesbia.

Lady Kirkbank, with her dear old head thrown back upon the cushion of her luxurious chair, and her dear little cornflower hat just a thought on one side, was sleeping the sleep of the just, and unconsciously revealing the little golden arrangements which gave variety to her front teeth.

The soothing sound came nearer and nearer, close under the *Cayman's* quarter, and then a brown hand clasped the man-ropes, and a light slim figure swung itself upon deck, while the boat bobbed and splashed below.

It was Montesma, who had not been expected till the racing, which was not to begin for two days. A faint, faint rose bloom flushed Lady Lesbia's cheek at sight of him; and Mr. Smithson gave a little look of vexation, just one rapid contraction of the eyebrows, which resumed their conventional placidity the next instant.

'So good of you,' he murmured. 'I really did not expect you till the beginning of the week.'

'London is simply insupportable in this weather--most of all for a man born in the Havanas. My soul thirsted for blue water. So I said to myself, This good Smithson is at Cowes; he will give me the run of his yacht and a room at his villa. Why not go to Cowes at once?'

'The room is at your service. I have only two or three of my people at Formosa, but just enough to look after a bachelor friend.'

'I want very little service, my dear fellow,' answered Montesma, pleasantly. 'A man who has crossed the Cordilleras and camped in the primeval forest on the shores of the Amazon, learns to help himself. So this is the *Cayman*? *Muy deleito-*

so, mi amigo. A floating Paradise in little. If the ark had been like this, I don't think any of the passengers would have wanted the flood to dry up.'

He shook hands with Lady Lesbia as he spoke, and with Lady Kirkbank, who looked at him as if he were part of her dream, and then he sank into the chair on Lesbia's left hand, with the air of being established for the rest of the day.

'I have left my portmanteaux at the end of the pier,' he said lazily. 'I dare say one of your fellows will be good enough to take them to Formosa for me?'

Mr. Smithson gave the necessary order. All the beauty had gone out of the sea and the sky for him, all the contentment from his mind; and yet he was in no position to rebel against Fate--in no position to say directly or indirectly, 'Don Gomez de Montesma, I don't want you here, and I must request you to transfer yourself elsewhither.'

Lesbia's feelings were curiously different. The very sight of that nervous brown hand upon the rope just now had sent a strange thrill through her veins. She who believed herself heartless could scarce trust herself to speak for the vehement throbbing of her heart. A sense of joy too deep for words possessed her as she reclined in her low chair, with drooping eyelids, yet feeling the fire of those dark southern eyes upon her face, scorching her like an actual flame.

'Lady Lesbia, may I have a cup of tea?' he asked; not because he wanted the tea, but only for the cruel delight of seeing if she were able to give it to him calmly.

Her hands shook, fluttered, wandered helplessly, as she poured out that cup of tea and handed it to Montesma, a feminine office which she had performed placidly enough for Mr. Smithson. The Spaniard took the cup from her with a quiet smile, a subtle look which seemed to explore the inmost depth of her consciousness.

Yes, this man was verily her master. She knew it, and he know it, as that look of his told her. Vain to play her part of languid indifference--vain to struggle against her bondage. In heart and spirit she was at his feet, an odalisque, recognising and bowing down to her sultan.

Happily for the general peace, Mr. Smithson had been looking away seaward, with a somewhat troubled brow, while that little cap and saucer episode was being enacted. And in the next minute Lesbia had recovered her self-command, and resumed that graceful languor which was one of her charms. She was weak, but she was not altogether foolish; and she had no idea of succumbing to this new influence--of yielding herself up to this conqueror, who seemed to take her life into his hand as if it were a bit of thistledown. Her agitation of those first few minutes was due to the suddenness of his appearance--the reaction from dulness to delight. She had been told that he was not to be at Cowes till Monday, and lo! he was here at her side, just as she was thinking how empty and dreary life was without him.

He dropped into his place so naturally and easily, made himself so thoroughly at home and so agreeable to every one, that it was almost impossible for Horace Smithson to resent his audacity! Mr. Smithson's vitals might be devoured by the gnawing of the green-eyed monster, but however fierce that gnawing were, he did not want to seem jealous. Montesma was there as the very incarnation of some experiences in Mr. Smithson's past career, and he dared not object to the man's presence.

And so the summer day wore on. They had the yacht all to themselves that evening, for the racing yachts were fulfilling engagements in other waters, and the gay company of pleasure-seekers had not yet fully assembled. They were dropping in one by one, all the evening, and Cowes roads grew fuller of life with every hour of the summer night.

Mr. Smithson and his guests dined in the saloon, a snug little party of four, and sat long over dessert, deep into the dusk; and they talked of all things under heaven, things frivolous, things grave, but most of all about that fair, strange world in far-off southern waters, the sunny islands of the Caribbean Sea, and the dreamy, luxurious life of that tropical clime, half Spanish, half Oriental, wholly independent of European conventionalities. Lesbia listened, enchanted by the picture. What were Park Lane palaces, and Berkshire manors, the petty splendours of the architect and the upholsterer, weighed against a world in which all nature is on a grander scale? Mr. Smithson might give her fine houses and costly upholstery; but only the Tropic of Cancer could give her larger and brighter stars, a world of richer colouring, a land of perpetual summer, nights luminous with fire-flies, gardens in which the fern and the cactus were as forest trees, and where humming-birds flashed among the foliage like living flowers; nay, where the flowers themselves took the forms of the animal world and seemed instinct with life and motion.

'Yes,' said Mr. Smithson, with his gentlemanlike drawl, 'Spanish America and the West Indies are delightful places to talk about. There are so many things one leaves out of the picture--thieves, niggers, jiggers, snakes, mosquitoes, yellow Jack, creeping, crawling creatures of all kinds. I always feel very glad I have been to South America.'

'Why?'

'In order that I may never go there again,' replied Mr. Smithson.

'I was beginning to hope you would take me there some day,' said Lesbia.

'Never again, no, not even for your sake. No man should ever leave Europe after he is five-and-thirty; indeed, I doubt if after that age he should venture beyond the Mediterranean. That is the sea of civilisation. Anything outside it means barbarism.'

'I hope we are going to travel by-and-by,' said Lesbia; 'I have been mewed up in Grasmere half my life, and if you are going to confine me to the shores of the Mediterranean, which is, after all, only a larger lake, for the other half of my life, my existence will be a dull piece of work after all. I agree with what Don Gomez said the other night: "Not to travel is not to live."'

They went on deck presently and sat in the summer darkness, lighted only by the stars, and by the lights of the yachts, and the faintly gleaming windows of the lighted town, sat long and late, in a state of ineffable repose. Lady Kirkbank. fortified by the produce of Mr. Smithson's particular *clos*, and by a couple of glasses of green Chartreuse, slept profoundly. She had not enjoyed herself so much for the last three months. She had been stretched on Society's rack, and she had been ground in Society's mill; and neither mind nor body had been her own to do what she liked withal. She had toiled early and late, and had spared herself in no wise. And now the trouble was over for a space. Here were rest and respite. She had done her duty as a chaperon, had provided her charge with the very best thing the matrimonial market offered. She had paid her creditors something on account all round, and had left them appeased and trustful, if not content. Sir George had gone oft alone to drink the waters at Spa, and to fortify himself for Scotland and the grouse season. She was her own mistress, and she could fold her hands and take her rest, eat and drink and sleep and be merry, all at Mr. Smithson's expense.

The yachts came flocking in next day, like a flight of white-winged sea birds, and Mr. Smithson had enough to do receiving visitors upon the *Cayman*. He was fully occupied; but Montesma had nothing to do, except to amuse Lady Lesbia and her chaperon, and in this onerous task he succeeded admirably. Lesbia found that it was too warm to be on the deck when there were perspiring people, whose breath must be ninety by the thermometer, perpetually coming on board; so she and Lady Kirkbank sat in the saloon, and had the more distinguished guests brought down to them as to a Court; and the shrewder of the guests were quick to divine that no company beyond that of Don Gomez de Montesma was really wanted in that rose-scented saloon.

The Spaniard taught Lady Kirkbank *monte*, which delighted her, and which she vowed she would introduce at her supper parties in the half season of November, when she should be in London for a week or two, as a bird of passage, flitting southwards. He began to teach Lesbia Spanish, a language for which she had taken a sudden fancy; and it is curious what tender accents, what hidden meanings even a grammar can take from such a teacher. Spanish came easily enough to a learner who had been thoroughly drilled in French and Italian, and who had been taught the rudiments of Latin; so by the end of a lesson, which went on at intervals all day, the pupil was able to lisp a passage of Don Quixote in the sweetest Castilian, very sweet to the ear of Don Gomez--a kind of baby language, precious as the first half-formed syllables of infancy to mothers.

Montesma had nothing to do but to amuse himself and his companions all day in the saloon, amidst odours of roses and peaches, in a shadowy coolness made by striped silken blinds; but Mr. Smithson was not so much his own master. That innumerable company of friends which are the portion of the rich man given to hospitality would not let the owner of the *Cayman* go scot-free.

At a place like Cowes, on the eve of the regatta week, the freelances of society expect to find entertainment; and Mr. Smithson had to maintain his character for princely hospitalities at the sacrifice of his feelings as a lover. Every ripple of Lesbia's silvery laughter, every deep tone of Montesma's voice, from the cabin below, sent a pang to his jealous soul; and yet he had to smile, and to order more champagne cup, and to be lavish of his best cigars, albeit insisting that his friends should smoke their cigars in the bows well to leeward, so that no foul breathings of tobacco should pollute his Cleopatra galley.

Cleopatra was very happy meanwhile, sublimely indifferent even to the odours of tobacco. She had her Antony at her feet, looking up at her, as she recited her lesson, with darkly luminous eyes, obviously worshipping her, obviously intent on winning her without counting the cost. When had a Montesma ever counted the cost to himself or others--the cost in gold, in honour, in human life? The records of Cuba in the palmy days of the slave trade would tell how lightly they held the last; and for honour, well, the private hells of island and main could tell their tale of specially printed playing cards, in which the swords or stars on the back of each card had a secret language of their own, and were as finger-posts for the initiated player.

Mr. Smithson had business on shore, and was fain to leave the yacht for an hour or two before dinner. He invited Don Gomez to go with him, but the offer was graciously declined.

'Amigo, I don't care even to look at land in such weather. It is so detestably dry,' he pleaded. 'It is only the sound of the sea gurgling against the hull that reconciles one to existence. Go, and be happy at your club, and send off those occult telegrams of yours, dearest. I shall not leave the *Cayman* till bed-time.'

He looked as fresh and cool as if utterly unaffected by the heat, which to a Cuban must have been a merely lukewarm condition of the atmosphere. But he affected to be prostrate, and Smithson could not insist. He had his cards to play in a game which required extremest caution, and there were no friendly indicators on the backs of his kings and aces. He was feeling his way in the dark, and did not know how much mischief Montesma was prepared to do.

When the owner of the yacht was gone Don Gomez proposed an adjournment to the deck for afternoon tea, and the trio sat under the awning, tea-drinking and gossiping for the next hour. Lady Kirkbank told the steward to say not at home to everybody, just as if she had a street door.

'There is a good deal of the ***dolce far niente*** about this,' said Montesma, presently; 'but don't you think we have been anchored in sight of that shabby little town quite long enough, and that it would be rather nice to spread our wings and sail round the island before the racing begins?'

'It would be exquisite,' said Lesbia. 'I am very tired of inaction, though I dearly love learning Spanish,' she added, with a lovely smile, and a look that was half submissive, half mutinous. 'But I have really been beginning to wonder whether this boat can move.'

'You will see that she can, and at a smart pace, too, if I sail her. Shall we circumnavigate the island? We can set sail after dinner.'

'Will Mr. Smithson consent, do you think?'

'Why does Smithson exist, except to obey you?'

'I don't know if Lady Kirkbank would quite like it,' said Lesbia, looking at her chaperon, who was waving a big Japanese fan, slowly, unsteadily, and with a somewhat drunken air, the while she slid into dreamland.

'Quite like what?' she murmured, drowsily.

'A little sail.'

'I should dearly love it, if it didn't make me sea-sick.'

'Sea-sick on a glassy lake like this! Impossible,' said Montesma. 'I consider the thing settled. We set sail after dinner.'

Mr. Smithson came back to the yacht just in time to dress for dinner. Don Gomez excused himself from putting on his dress suit. He was going to sail the yacht himself, and he was dressed for his work, picturesquely, in white duck trousers, white silk shirt, and black velvet shooting jacket. He dined with the permission of the ladies, in this costume, in which he looked so much handsomer than in the livery of polite life. He had a red scarf tied round his waist, and when at his work by-and-by, he wore a little red silk cap, just stuck lightly on his dark hair. The dinner to-day was all animation and even excitement, very different from the languorous calm of yesterday. Lesbia seemed a new creature. She talked and laughed and flashed and sparkled as she had never yet done within Mr. Smithson's experience. He contemplated the transformation with wonder not unmixed with suspicion. Never for him had she been so brilliant--never in response to his glances had her violet eyes thus kindled, had her smile been so entrancingly sweet. He watched Montesma, but in him he could find no fault. Even jealousy could hardly take objection to the Spaniard's manner to Lady Lesbia. There was not a look, not a word that hinted at a private understanding between them, or which seemed to convey deeper meanings than the common language of society. No, there was no ground for fault-finding; and yet Smithson was miserable. He knew this man of old, and knew his influence over women.

Mr. Smithson handed over the management of the yacht without a murmur, albeit he pretended to be able to sail her himself, and was in the habit of taking the command for a couple of hours on a sunny afternoon, much to the amusement of skipper and crew. But Montesma was a sailor born and bred--the salt keen breath of the sea had been the first breath in his nostrils--he had managed his light felucca before he was twelve years old, had sailed every inch of the Caribbean Sea, and northward to the furthermost of the Bahamas before he was fifteen. He had lived more on the water than on the land in that wild boyhood of his; a boyhood in which books and professors had played but small part. Montesma's school had been the world, and beautiful women his only professors. He had learnt arithmetic from the transactions of bubble companies; modern languages from the lips of the women who loved him. He was a crack shot, a perfect swordsman, a reckless horseman, and a dancer in whom dancing almost rose to genius. Beyond these limits he was as ignorant as dirt; but he had a cleverness which served as a substitute for book learning, and he seldom failed in impressing the people he met with the idea that he, Gomez de Montesma, was no ordinary man.

Directly after dinner the preparations for an immediate start began; very much to the disgust of skipper and crew, who were not in the habit of working after dinner; but Montesma cared nothing for the short answers of the captain, or the black look of the men.

Lesbia wanted to learn all about everything--the name of every sail, of every rope. She stood near the helmsman, a slim graceful figure in a white gown of some soft material, with never a jewel or a flower to relieve that statuesque simplicity. She wore no hat, and the rich chesnut hair was rolled in a loose knot at the back of the small Greek-looking head. Montesma came to her every now and then to explain what was being done; and by-and-by, when the canvas was all up, and the yacht was skimming over the water, like a giant swan borne by the current of some vast strong river, he came and stayed by her side, and they two sat making little baby sentences in Spanish, he as teacher and she as pupil, with no one near them but the sailors.

The owner of the *Cayman* had disappeared mysteriously a quarter of an hour after the sails were unfurled, and Lady Kirkbank had tottered down to the saloon.

'I am not going--cabin,' she faltered, when Lesbia remonstrated with her, 'only--going--saloon--sofa--lie down--little--Smithson take care--you,' not perceiving that Smithson had vanished, 'shall be--quite close.'

So Lesbia and Don Gomez were alone under the summer stars, murmuring little bits of Spanish.

'It is the only true way of learning a language,' he said; 'grammars are a delusion.'

It was a very delightful and easy way of learning, at any rate. Lesbia reclined in her bamboo chair, and fanned herself indolently, and watched the shadowy shores of the island, cliff and hill, down and wooded crest, flitting past her like dream-pictures, and her lips slowly shaped the words of that soft lisping language--so simple, so musical--a language made for lovers and for song, one would think. It was wonderful what rapid progress Lesbia made.

She heard a church clock on the island striking, and asked Don Gomez the hour.

'Ten,' he said.

'Ten! Surely it must be later. It was past eight before we began dinner, and we have been sailing for ever so long. Captain, kindly tell me the time,' she called to the skipper, who was lolling over the gunwale near the foremast smoking a meditative pipe.

'Twelve o'clock, my lady.'

'Heavens, can I possibly have been sitting here so long. I should like to stay on deck all night and watch the sailing; but I must really go and take care of poor Lady Kirkbank. I am afraid she is not very well.'

'She had a somewhat distracted air when she went below, but I daresay she will sleep off her troubles. If I were you I should leave her to herself.'

'Impossible! What can have become of Mr. Smithson?'

'I have a shrewd suspicion that it is with Smithson as with poor Lady Kirkbank.'

'Do you mean that he is ill?'

'Precisely.'

'What, on a calm summer night, sailing over a sea of glass. The owner of a yacht!'

'Rather ignominious for poor Smithson, isn't it? But men who own yachts are only mortal, and are sometimes wretched sailors. Smithson is feeble on that point, as I know of old.'

'Then wasn't it rather cruel of us to sail his yacht?'

'Yachts are meant for sailing, and again, sea-sickness is supposed to be a wholesome exercise.'

'Good-night.'

'Good-night,' both good nights in Spanish, and with a touch of tenderness which the words could hardly have expressed in English.

'Must you really go?' pleaded Montesma, holding her hand just a thought longer than he had ever held it before.

'Ah, the little more, and how much it is,' says the poet.

'Really and truly.'

'I am so sorry. I wish you could have stayed on deck all night.'

'So do I, with all my heart. This calm sea under the starlit sky is like a dream of heaven.'

'It is very nice, but if you stayed I think I could promise you considerable variety. We shall have a tempest before morning.'

'Of all things in the world I should love to see a thunderstorm at sea.'

'Be on the alert then, and Captain Parkes and I will try to oblige you.'

'At any rate you have made it impossible for me to sleep. I shall stay with Lady Kirkbank in the saloon. Good-night, again.'

'Good-night.'

CHAPTER XXXIX.
IN STORM AND DARKNESS.

Lesbia found Lady Kirkbank prostrate on a low divan in the saloon, sleepless, and very cross. The atmosphere reeked with red lavender, sal-volatile, eau de Cologne, and brandy, which latter remedy poor Georgie had taken freely in her agonies. Kibble, the faithful Grasmere girl, sat by the divan, fanning the sufferer with a large Japanese fan. Rilboche had naturally, as a Frenchwoman, succumbed utterly to her own feelings, and was moaning in her berth, wailing out every now and then that she would never have taken service with Miladi had she suspected her to be capable of such cruelty as to take her to live for weeks upon the sea.

If this was the state of affairs now while the ocean was only gently stirred, what would it be by-and-by if the tempest should really come?

'What can you be thinking of, staying on deck all night with those men?' exclaimed Lady Kirkbank, peevishly. 'It is hardly respectable.'

She would have been still more inclined to object had she known that Lesbia's companion had been 'that man' rather than 'those men.'

'What do you mean by all night?' Lesbia retorted, contemptuously; 'it is only just twelve.'

'Only twelve. I thought we were close upon daylight. I have suffered an eternity of agony.'

'I am very sorry you should be ill; but really the sea has been so deliciously calm.'

'I believe I should have suffered less if it had been diabolically rough. Oh, that monotonous flip-flap of the water, that slow heaving of the boat! Nothing could be worse.'

'I am glad to hear you say that, for Don Gomez says we are likely to have a tempest.'

'A tempest!' shrieked Georgie. 'Then let him stop the boat this instant and put me on shore. Tell him to land me anywhere--on the Needles even. I could stop at the lighthouse till morning. A storm at sea will be simply my death.'

'Dear Lady Kirkbank, I was only joking,' said Lesbia, who did not want to be worried by her chaperon's nervous apprehensions: 'so far the night is lovely.'

'Give me a spoonful more brandy, my good creature,'--to Kibble. 'Lesbia, you ought never to have brought me into this miserable state. I consented to staying on board the yacht; but I never consented to sailing on her.'

'You will soon be well, dear Lady Kirkbank; and you will have such an appetite for breakfast to-morrow morning.'

'Where shall we be at breakfast time?'

'Off St. Catherine's Point, I believe--just half way round the island.'

'If we are not at the bottom of the sea,' groaned Georgie.

They were now in the open Channel, and the boat dipped and rose to larger billows than had encountered her course before. Lady Kirkbank lay in a state of collapse, in which life seemed only sustainable by occasional teaspoonfuls of cognac gently tilted down her throat by the patient Kibble.

Lesbia went to her cabin, but with no intention of remaining there. She was firmly convinced that the storm would come, and she meant to be on deck while it was raging. What harm could thunder or lightning, hail or rain, do to her while he was by to protect her? He would be busy sailing the boat, perhaps, but still he would have a moment now and then in which to think of her and care for her.

Yes, the storm was coming. There was a livid look upon the waters, and the atmosphere was heavy with heat; the sky to windward black as a funeral pall. Lesbia was almost fearless, yet she felt a thrill of awe as she looked into that dense blackness. To leeward the stars were still visible; but that gigantic mass of cloud came creeping slowly, solemnly over the sky, while the shadow flitted fast across the water, swallowing up that ghastly electric glare.

Lesbia wrapped herself in a white cashmere *sortie de bal* and stole up the companion. Montesma was working at the ropes with his own hands, calling directions to the sailors to shorten and take in the canvas, urging them to increased efforts by working at the ropes with his own hands, springing up the rigging and on deck, flashing backwards and forwards amidst the rigging like a being of supernatural power. He had taken off his jacket, and was clad from top to toe in white, save for that streak of scarlet which tightly girdled his waist. His tall flexible form, perfect in line as a Greek statue of Hermes, stood out against the background of black night. His voice, with its tones of brief imperious command, the proud carriage of his head, the easy grace of his rapid movements, all proclaimed the man born to rule over his fellow-men. And it is these master spirits, these born rulers, whom women instinctively recognise as their sovereign lords, and for whom women count no sacrifice too costly.

In the midst of his activity Montesma suddenly saw that white-robed figure standing at the top of the companion, and flew to her side. The boat was pitching heavily, dipping into the trough of the sea at an angle of forty-five degrees, as it seemed to Lesbia.

'You ought not to be here,' said Montesma; 'it is much rougher than I expected.'

'I am not afraid,' she answered; 'but I will go back to my cabin if I am in your way.'

'In my way' (with deepest tenderness): 'yes, you are in my way, for I shall think of nothing else now you are here. But I believe we have done all that need be done to the yacht, and I can take care of you till the storm is over.'

He put his arm round her as the stem dipped, and led her towards the stern, guiding her footsteps, supporting her as her light figure swayed against him with the motion of the boat. A vivid flash of lightning showed him her face as they stood for an instant leaning against each other, his arm encircling her. Ah, what deep feeling in that countenance, once so passionless; what a new light in those eyes. It was like the awakening of a long dormant soul.

He took the helm from the captain and stood steering the vessel, and calling out his orders, with Lesbia close beside him, holding her with his disengaged arm, drawing her near him as the vessel pitched violently, drawing her nearer still when they shipped a sea, and a great fountain of spray enfolded them both in a dense cloud of salt water.

The thunder roared and rattled, as if it began and ended close beside them. Forked lightnings zigzagged amidst the rigging. Sheet lightning enwrapped those two in a luminous atmosphere, revealing faces that were pale with passion, lips that trembled with emotion. There were but scant opportunity for speech, and neither of these two felt the need of words. To be together, bound nearer to each other than they had ever been yet, than they might ever be again, in the midst of thunder and lightning and dense clouds of spray. This was enough. Once when the *Cayman* pitched with exceptional fury, when the thunder crashed and roared loudest, Lesbia found her head lying on Montesma's breast and his arms round her, his lips upon her face. She did not wrench herself from that forbidden embrace. She let those lips kiss hers as never mortal man had kissed her before. But an instant later, when Montesma's attention was distracted by his duties as steersman, and he let her go, she slipped away in the darkness, and melted from his sight and touch like a modern Undine. He dared not leave the helm and follow her then. He sent one of the sailors below a little later, to make sure that she was safe in her cabin; but he saw her no more that night.

The storm abated soon after daybreak, and the morning was lovely; but Don Gomez and Lady Lesbia did not meet again till the church bells on the island were ringing for morning service, and then the lady was safe under the wing of her chaperon, with her affianced husband in attendance upon her at the breakfast table in the saloon.

She received Montesma with the faintest inclination of the head, and she carefully avoided all occasion of speech with him during the leisurely, long spun-out meal. She was as white as her muslin gown, and her eyes told of a sleepless night. She talked a little, very little to Lady Kirkbank and Mr. Smithson; to the Spaniard not at all. And yet Montesma was in no manner dashed by this appearance of deep offence. So might Francesca have looked the morning after that little scene over the book; yet she sacrificed her salvation for her lover all the same. It was a familiar stage upon the journey which Montesma knew by heart. Here the inclination of the road was so many degrees more or less; for this hill you are commanded to put on an extra horse; at this stage it is forbidden to go more than eight miles an hour, and so on, and so on. Montesma knew every inch of the ground. He put on a melancholy look, and talked very little. He had been on deck all night, and so there was an excuse for his being quiet.

Lady Kirkbank related her impressions of the storm, and talked enough for four. She had suffered the pangs of purgatory, but her natural cheeriness asserted itself, and she made no moaning about past agonies which had exercised a really delightful influence on her appetite. Mr. Smithson also was cheerful. He had paid his annual tribute to Neptune, and might hope to go scot-free for the rest of the season.

'If I had stayed on deck I must have had my finger in the pie; so I thought it better to go below and get a good night's rest in the steward's cabin,' he said, not caring to confess his sufferings as frankly as Lady Kirkbank admitted hers.

After breakfast, which was prolonged till noon, Montesma asked Smithson to smoke a cigarette on deck with him.

'I want to talk to you on a rather serious matter,' he said.

Lesbia heard the words, and looked up with a frightened glance. Could he mean to attempt anything desperate? Was he going to confess the fatal truth to Horace Smithson, to tell her affianced lover that she was untrue to her bond, that she loved him, Montesma, as fondly as he loved her, that their two souls had mingled like two flames fanned by the same current, and thence had risen to a conflagration which must end in ruin, if she were not set free to follow where her heart had gone, free to belong to that man whom her spirit chose for lord and master. Her heart leapt at the hope that Montesma was going to do this, that he was strong enough to break her bonds for her, powerful and rich enough to secure her a brilliant future. Yet this last consideration, which hitherto had been paramount, seemed now of but little moment. To be with *him*, to belong to *him*, would be enough for bliss. Albeit that in such a choice she forfeited all that she had ever possessed or hoped for of earthly prosperity. Adventurer, beggar, whatever he might be, she chose him, and loved him with all the strength of a weak soul newly awakened to passionate feeling.

Unhappily for Lesbia Haselden, Montesma was not at all the kind of man to take so direct and open a course as that which she imagined possible.

His business with Mr. Smithson was of quite a different kind.

'Smithson, do you know that you have an utterly incompetent crew?' he said, gravely, when they two were standing aft, lighting their cigarettes.

'Indeed I do not. The men are all experienced sailors, and the captain ranks high among yachtsmen.'

'English yachtsmen are not particularly good judges of sailors. I tell you your skipper is no sailor, and his men are fools. If it had not been for me the *Cayman* would have gone to pieces on the rocks last night, and if you are to cross to St. Malo, as you talked of doing, for the regatta there, you had better sack these men and let me get you a South American crew. I know of a fellow who is in London just now--the captain of a Rio steamer, who'll send you a crew of picked men, if you give me authority to telegraph to him.'

'I don't like foreign sailors,' said Smithson, looking perplexed and worried; 'and I have perfect confidence in Wilkinson.'

'Which is as much as to say that you consider me a liar! Go to the bottom your own way, *mon ami: ce n'est pas mon affaire,*' said Montesma, turning on his heel, and leaving his friend to his own devices.

Had he pressed the point, Smithson would have suspected him of some evil motive, and would have been resolute in his resistance; but as he said no more about it, Smithson began to feel uncomfortable.

He was no sailor himself, knew absolutely nothing about the navigation of his yacht, though he sometimes pretended to sail her; and he had no power to judge of his skipper's capacity or his men's seamanship. He had engaged the captain wholly on the strength of the man's reputation, guaranteed by certain certificates which seemed to mean a great deal. But after all such certificates might mean very little--such a reputation might be no real guarantee. The sailors had been engaged by the captain, and their ruddy faces and thoroughly British appearence, the exquisite cleanliness which they maintained in every detail of the yacht, had seemed to Mr. Smithson the perfection of seamanship.

But it was not the less true that the cleanest of yachts, with deck of spotless whiteness, sails of unsullied purity, brasses shining and sparkling like gold fresh from the goldsmith's, might be spiked upon a rock, or might founder on a sand-bank, or heel over under too much canvas. Mr. Smithson was inclined to suspect any proposition of Montesma's; yet he was not the less disturbed in mind by the assertion.

The day wore on, and the yacht sailed merrily over a summer sea. Mr. Smithson fidgeted about the deck uneasily, watching every movement of the sailors. No boat could be sailing better, as it seemed to him; but in such weather and over such waters any boat must needs go easily. It was in the blackness of night, amidst the fury of the storm, that Montesma's opinion had been formed. Smithson began to think that his friend was right. The sailors had honest countenances, but they looked horribly stupid. Could men with such vacuous grins, such an air of imbecile good-nature, be capable of acting wisely in any terrible crisis?--could they have nerve and readiness, quickness, decision, all those grand qualites which are needed by the seaman who has to contend with the fury of the elements?

Mr. Smithson and his guests had breakfasted too late for the possibility of lun-cheon. They were in Cowes Roads by one o'clock. A fleet of yachts had arrived during their absence, and the scene was full of life and gaiety. Lady Lesbia held a *levee* at the afternoon tea, and had a crowd of her old admirers around her--ador-ers whose presence in no wise disturbed Horace Smithson's peace. He would have been content that his wife should go through life with a herd of such worshippers following in her footsteps. He knew the aimless innocence, the almost infantine simplicity of the typical Johnnie, Chappie, ***Muscadin, Petit Creve, Gommeux***--call him by what name you will. From these he feared no evil. But in that one follower who gave no outward token of his worship he dreaded peril. It was Montesma he watched, while dragoons with close-cropped hair, and imbecile youths with heads rigid in four-inch collars, were hanging about Lady Lesbia's low bamboo chair, and administering obsequiously to the small necessities of the tea-table.

It was while this tea-table business was going on that Mr. Smithson took the opportunity of setting his mind at rest, were it possible, as to the merits of Captain Wilkinson. Among his visitors this afternoon there was the owner of three or four racing yachts--a man renowned for his victories, at home and abroad.

'I think you knew something of my captain, Wilkinson, before I engaged him,' said Smithson, with assumed carelessness.

'I know every skipper on board every boat in the squadron,' answered his friend. 'A good fellow, Wilkinson--thoroughly honest fellow.'

'Honest; oh yes, I know all about that. But how about his seamanship? His certificates were wonderfully good, but they are not everything.'

'Everything, my dear fellow,' cried the other; 'they are next to nothing. But I believe Wilkinson is a tolerable sailor.'

This was not encouraging.

'He has never been unlucky, I believe.'

'My dear Smithson, you are a great authority in the City, but you are not very well up in the records of the yachting world, or you would know that your Captain Wilkinson was skipper on the *Orinoco* when she ran aground on the Chesil Bank, coming home from Cherbourg Regatta, fifteen lives lost, and the yacht, in less than half an hour, ground to powder. That was rather a bad case, I remember; for though it was a tempestuous night, the accident would never have happened if Wilkinson had not mistaken the lights. So you see his Trinity House papers didn't prevent his going wrong.'

Good heavens! This was the strongest confirmation of Montesma's charge. The man was a stupid man, an incapable man, a man to whose intelligence and care human life should never be trusted. A fig for his honesty! What would honesty be worth in a hurricane off the Chesil Beach? What would honesty serve a ship spitted on the Jailors off Jersey? Montesma was right. If the *Cayman* was to make a trip to St. Malo she must be navigated by competent men. Horace Smithson hated foreign sailors, copper-faced ruffians, with flashing black eyes which seemed to threaten murder, did you but say a rough word to them; sleek, raven-haired scoundrels, with bowie-knives in their girdles, ready for mutiny. But, after all, life is worth too much to be risked for a prejudice, a sentiment.

Perhaps that St. Malo business might be avoided; and then there need be no change in captain or crew. The yacht must be safe enough lying at anchor in the roadstead. By-and-by, when the visitors had departed, and Mr. Smithson was re-posefully enjoying his tea by Lady Lesbia's side, he approached the subject.

'Do you really care about crossing to St. Malo after this--really prefer the idea to Ryde?'

'Infinitely,' exclaimed Lesbia, quickly. 'Ryde would only be Cowes ever again--a lesser Cowes; and I thought when you first proposed it that the plan was rather stupid, though I did not want to be uncivil and say so. But I was delighted with Don Gomez de Montesma's amendment, substituting St. Malo for Ryde. In the first place the trip across will be delicious'--Lady Kirkbank gave a faint groan--'and in the second place I am dying to see Brittany.'

'I doubt if you will highly appreciate St. Malo. It is a town of many and various smells.'

'But I want to smell those foreign smells of which one hears much. At least it is an experience. We need not be on shore any longer than we like. And I want to see that fine rocky coast, and Chateaubriand's tomb on the what's-its-name. So nice to be buried in that way.'

'Then you have set your heart on going to St. Malo, and would not like any change in our plan?'

'Any change will be simply detestable,' answered Lesbia, all the more decid-edly since she suspected a desire for change on the part of Mr. Smithson.

She was in no amiable humour this afternoon. All her nerves seemed strained to their utmost tension. She was irritated, tremulous with nervous excitement, in-clined to hate everybody, Horace Smithson most of all. In her cabin a little later on, when she was changing her gown for dinner, and Kibble was somewhat slow and clumsy in the lacing of the bodice, she wrenched herself from the girl's hands, flung herself into a chair, and burst into a flood of passionate tears.

'O God! that I were on one of those islands in the Caribbean Sea--an island where Europeans never come--where I might lie down among the poisonous tropi-cal flowers, and sleep the rest of my days away. I am sick to death of my life here; of the yacht, the people--everything.'

'This air is too relaxing, Lady Lesbia,' the girl murmured, soothingly; 'and you didn't have your natural rest last night. Shall I get you a nice strong cup of tea?'

'Tea! no. I have been living upon tea for the last twenty-four hours. I have eaten nothing. My mouth is parched and burning. Oh, Kibble!' flinging her head upon the girl's buxom arm, and letting it rest there, 'what a happy creature you are--not a care--not a care.'

'I'm sure you can't have any cares, Lady Lesbia,' said Kibble, with an incredulous smile, trying to smooth the disordered hair, anxious to make haste with the unfinished toilet, for it was within a few minutes of eight.

'I am full of care. I am in debt--horribly in debt--getting deeper and deeper every day--and I am going to sell myself to the only man who can pay my debts and give me fine houses, and finery like this,' plucking at the *crepe de chine* gown, with its flossy fringe, its delicate lace, a marvel of artistic expenditure; a garment which looked simplicity itself, and yet was so cleverly contrived as to cost five-and-thirty guineas. The greatest effects in it required to be studied with a microscope.

'But surely, dear Lady Lesbia, you won't marry Mr. Smithson, if you don't love him?'

'Do you suppose love has anything to do with marriages in society?'

'Oh, Lady Lesbia, it would be so unkind to him, so cruel to yourself.'

'Cruel to myself. Yes, I am cruel to myself. I had the chance of happiness a year ago, and I lost it. I have the chance of happiness now--yes, of consummate bliss--and haven't the courage to snatch at it. Take off this horrid gown, Kibble; my head is splitting: I shan't go to dinner.'

'Oh, Lady Lesbia, you are treading on the pearl embroidery,' remonstrated poor Kibble, as Lesbia kicked the new gown from under her feet.

'What does it matter!' she exclaimed with a bitter little laugh. 'It has not been paid for--perhaps it never will be.'

The dinner was silent and gloomy. It was as if a star had been suddenly blotted out of the sky. Smithson, ordinarily so hospitable, had been too much disturbed in mind to ask any of his friends to stay to dinner; so there were only Lady Kirkbank, who was too tired to be lively, and Montesma, who was inclined to be thoughtful. Lesbia's absence, and the idea that she was ill, gave the feast almost a funereal air.

After dinner Smithson and Montesma sat on deck, smoking their cigars, and lazily watching the lights on sea, and the lights on shore; these brilliant in the foreground, those dim in the distance.

'You can telegraph to your Rio Janeiro friend to-morrow morning, if you like,' said Smithson, presently, 'and tell him to send a first-rate skipper and crew. Lady Lesbia has made up her mind to see St. Malo Regatta, and with such a sacred charge I can't be too careful.'

'I'll wire before eight o'clock to-morrow,' answered Montesma, 'You have decided wisely. Your respectable English Wilkinson is an excellent man--but nothing would surprise me less than his reducing your *Cayman* to matchwood in the next gale.'

CHAPTER XL.
A NOTE OF ALARM.

That strange scene in the old house at Fellside made a profound impression upon Lord Hartfield. He tried to disguise his trouble, and did all in his power to seem gay and at perfect ease in his wife's company; but his mind was full of anxiety, and Mary loved him too well to be for a moment in doubt as to his feelings.

'There is something wrong, Jack,' she said, while they were breakfasting at a table in the verandah, with the lake and the bills in front of them and the sweet morning air around them. 'You try to talk and to be lively, but there is a little perpendicular wrinkle in your forehead which I know as well as the letters of the alphabet, and that little line means worry. I used to see it in the old days, when you were breaking your heart for Lesbia. Why cannot you be frank and confide in me. It is your duty, sir, as my husband.'

'Is it my duty to halve my burdens as well as my joys? How do I know if those girlish shoulders are strong enough to bear the weight of them?'

'I can bear anything you can bear, and I won't be cheated out of my share in your worries. If you were obliged to have a tooth out, I would have one out too, for company.'

'I hope the dentist would be too conscientious to allow that.'

'Tell me your trouble, Hartfield,' she said, earnestly, leaning across the table, bringing her grave intelligent face near to him.

They were quite alone, he and she. The servants had done their ministering. Behind them there was the empty dining-room, in front of them the sunlit panorama of lake and hill. There could not be a safer place for telling secrets.

'Tell me what it is that worries you,' Mary pleaded again.

'I will, dear. After all perfect trust is the best; nay, it is your due, for you are brave enough and true enough to be trusted with secrets that mean life and death. In a word, then, Mary, the cause of my trouble is that old man we saw the other night.'

'Steadman's uncle?'

'Do you really believe that he is Steadman's uncle?'

'My grandmother told me so,' answered Mary, reddening to the roots of her hair.

To this girl, who was the soul of truth, there was deepest shame in the idea that her kinswoman, the woman whom of all the world she most owed reverence and honour, could be deemed capable of falsehood.

'Do you think my grandmother would tell me an untruth?'

'I do not believe that man is a poor dependent, an old servant's kinsman, sheltered and cared for in this house for charity's sake. Forgive me, Mary, if I doubt the word of one you love; but there are positions in life in which a man must judge for himself. Would Mr. Steadman's kinsman be lodged as that old man is lodged; would he talk as that old man talks; and last and greatest perplexity of all, would he possess a treasure of gold and jewels which must be worth many thousands?'

'But you cannot know for certain that those things are valuable; they may be rubbish that this poor old man has scraped together and hoarded for years, glass jewels bought at country fairs. Those rouleaux may contain lead or coppers.'

'I do not think so, Mary. The stones had all the brilliancy of valuable gems, and then there were others in the finest filagree settings--goldsmith's work which bore the stamp of an Eastern world. Take my word for it, that treasure came from India; and it must have been brought to England by Lord Maulevrier. It may have existed all these years without your grandmother's knowledge. That is quite possible; but it seems to me impossible that such wealth should be within the knowledge and the power of a pauper lunatic.'

'But if that unhappy old man is not a relation of Steadman's supported here by my grandmother's benevolence, who can he be, and why is he here?' asked Mary.

'Oh, Molly dear, these are two questions which I cannot answer, and which yet ought to be answered somehow. Since that night I have felt as if there were a dark cloud lowering over this house--a cloud almost as terrible in its menace of danger as the forshadowing of fate in a Greek legend. For your sake, for the honour of your race, for my own self-respect as your husband, I feel that this mystery ought to be solved, and all dark things made light before your grandmother's death. When she is gone the master-key to the past will be lost.'

'But she will be spared for many years, I hope, spared to sympathise with my happiness, and with Lesbia's.'

My dearest girl, we cannot hope that. The thread of her life is worn very thin. It may snap at any moment. You cannot look seriously in your grandmother's face, and yet delude yourself with the hope that she has years of life before her.'

'It will be very hard to part, just as she has begun to care for me,' said Mary, with her eyes full of tears.

'All such partings are hard, and your grandmother's life has been so lonely and joyless that the memory of it must always have a touch of pain. One cannot say of her as we can of the happy; she has lived her life--all things have been given to her, and she falls asleep at the close of a long and glorious day. For some reason which I cannot understand, Lady Maulevrier's life has been a prolonged sacrifice.'

'She has always given us to understand that she was fond of Fellside, and that this secluded life suited her,' said Mary, meditatively.

'I cannot help doubting her sincerity on that point. Lady Maulevrier is too clever a woman, and forgive me, dear, if I add too worldly a woman, to be content to live out of the world. The bird must have chafed its breast against the bars of the cage many and many a time when you thought that all was peace. Be sure, Mary, that your grandmother had a powerful motive for spending all her days in this place, and I can but think that the old man we saw the other night had some part in that motive. Do you remember telling me of her ladyship's vehement anger when she heard you had made the acquaintance of her pensioner?'

'Yes, she was very angry,' Mary answered, with a troubled look. 'I never saw her so angry--she was almost beside herself--said the harshest things to me--talked as if I had done some dreadful mischief.'

'Would she have been so moved, do you think, unless there was some fatal secret involved in that man's presence here?'

'I hardly know what to think. Tell me everything. What is it that you fear?-- what is it that you suspect?'

'To tell you my fears and suspicions is to tell you a family secret that has been kept from you out of kindness all the years of your life--and I hardly think I could bring myself to that if I did not know what the world is, and how many good-natured friends Lady Hartfield will meet in society, by-and-by, ready to tell her, by hints and inuendoes, that her grandfather, the Governor of Madras, came back to England under a cloud of disgrace.'

'My poor grandfather! How dreadful!' exclaimed Mary, pale with pity and shame. 'Did he deserve his disgrace, poor unhappy creature--or was he the victim of false accusation?'

'I can hardly tell you that, Mary, any more than I can tell whether Warren Hastings deserved the abuse that was wreaked upon him at one time, or the acquittal that gave the lie to his slanderers in after years. The events occurred forty years ago--the story was only half known then, and like all such stories formed the basis for every kind of exaggeration and perversion.'

'Does Maulevrier know?' faltered Mary.

'Maulevrier knows all that is known by the general public, and no more.'

'And you have married the granddaughter of a disgraced man,' said Mary, with a piteous look. 'Did you know--when you married me?'

'As much as I know now, dear love. If you had been Jonathan Wild's granddaughter you would have been just as dear to me. I married *you*, dearest; I love *you*; I believe in *you*. All the grandfathers in Christendom would not shake my faith by one tittle.'

She threw herself into his arms, and sobbed upon his breast. But sweet as this assurance of his love was to her, she was not the less stricken by shame at the thought of possible infamy in the past, a shameful memory for ever brooding over her name in the present.

'Society never forgets a scandal,' she said: 'I have heard Maulevrier say that.'

'Society has a long memory for other people's sins, but it only avenges its own wrongs. Give the wicked fairy Society a bad dinner, or leave her out of your invitation list for a ball, and she will twit you with the crimes or the misfortunes of a remote ancestor--she will go about talking of your grandfather the leper, or your great aunt who ran away with her footman. But so long as the wicked fairy gets all she wants out of you, she cares not a straw for the misdeeds of past generations.'

He spoke lightly, laughingly almost, and then he ordered the dogcart to be brought round immediately, and he drove Mary across the hills towards Langdale, to bring the colour back to her blanched cheeks. He brought her home in time to give her grandmother an hour for letter-writing before luncheon, while he walked up and down the terrace below Lady Maulevrier's windows, meditating the course he was to take.

He was to leave Westmoreland next day to take his place in the House of Lords during the last important debate of the session. He made up his mind that before he left he would seek an interview with Lady Maulevrier, and boldly ask her to explain the mystery of that old man's presence at Fellside. He was her kinsman by marriage, and he had sworn to honour her and to care for her as a son; and as a son he would urge her to confide in him, to unburden her conscience of any dark secret, and to make the crooked things straight, before she was called away.

While he was forecasting this interview, meeting imaginary objections, arguing points which might have to be argued, a servant came out to him with an ochre envelope on a little silver tray--that unpleasant-looking envelope which seems always a presage of trouble, great or small.

'Lord Maulevrier, Albany, to Lord Hartfield, Fellside, Grasmere.

'For God's sake come to me at once. I am in great trouble; not on my own account, but about a relation.'

A relation--except his grandmother and his two sisters Maulevrier had no relations for whom he cared a straw. This message must have relation to Lesbia. Was she ill--dying, the victim of some fatal accident, runaway horses, boat upset, train smashed? There was something; and Maulevrier appealed to his nearest and best friend. There was no withstanding such an appeal. It must be answered, and immediately.

Lord Hartfield went into the library and wrote his reply message, which consisted of six words.

'Going to you by first train.'

The next train left Windermere at three. There was just time to get a fresh horse put in the dogcart, and a Gladstone bag packed.

CHAPTER XLI.
PRIVILEGED INFORMATION.

Lord Hartfield did not arrive at Euston Square until near eleven o'clock at night. A hansom deposited him at the entrance to the Albany just as the clock of St. James's Church chimed the hour. He found only Maulevrier's valet. His lordship had waited indoors all the evening, and had only gone out a quarter of an hour ago. He had gone to the Cerberus, and begged that Lord Hartfield would be kind enough to follow him there.

Lord Hartfield was not fond of the Cerberus, and indeed deemed that lively place of rendezvous a very dangerous sphere for his friend Maulevrier; but in the face of Maulevrier's telegram there was no time to be lost, so he walked across Piccadilly and down St. James's Street to the fashionable little club, where the men were dropping in after the theatres and dinners, and where sheaves of bank notes were being exchanged for those various coloured counters which represented divers values, from the respectable 'pony' to the modest 'chip.'

Maulevrier was in the first room Hartfield looked into, standing behind some men who were playing.

'That's something like friendship,' he exclaimed, when he saw Lord Hartfield, and then he hooked his arm through his friend's, and led him off to the dining room.

'Come and have some supper, old fellow,' he said, 'and I can tell you my troubles while you are eating it. James, bring us a grill, and a lobster, and a bottle of Mumms, number 27, you know.'

'Yes, my lord.'

'Sorry to find you in this den, Maulevrier,' said Lord Hartfield.

'Haven't touched a card. Haven't done half an hour's punting this season. But it's a kind of habit with me to wander in here now and then. I know so many of the members. One poor devil lost nine thousand one night last week. Bather rough upon him, wasn't it? All ready money at this shop, don't you know.'

'Thank God, I know nothing about it. And now, Maulevrier, what is wrong, and with whom?'

'Everything is wrong, and with my sister Lesbia.'

'Good heavens! what do you mean?'

'Only this, that there is a fellow after her whose very name means ruin to women--a Spanish-American adventurer--reckless, handsome, a gambler, seducer, duellest, dare-devil. The man she is to marry seems to have neither nous nor spunk to defend her. Everybody at Goodwood saw the game that was being played, everybody at Cowes is watching the cards, betting on the result. Yes, great God, the men at the Squadron Club are staking their money upon my sister's character--even monkeys that she bolts with Montesma--five to three against the marriage with Smithson ever coming off.'

'Is this true.'

'It is as true as your marriage with Molly, as true as your loyalty to me. I was told of it all this morning at the Haute Gomme by a man I can rely upon, a really good fellow, who would not leave me in the dark about my sister's danger when all the smoking-rooms in Pall Mall were sniggering about it. My first impulse was to take the train for Cowes; but then I knew if I went alone I should let my temper get the better of me. I should knock somebody down--throw somebody out of the window--make a devil of a scene. And this would be fatal for Lesbia. I wanted your counsel, your cool head, your steady common-sense. "Not a step forward without Jack," I said to myself, so I bolted off and sent that telegram. It relieved my feeling a little, but I've had a wretched day.'

'Waiter, bring me a Bradshaw, or an A B C,' said Lord Hartfield.

He had eaten nothing but a biscuit since breakfast, but he was ready to go off at once, supperless, if there were a train to carry him. Unluckily there was no train. The mail had started. Nothing till seven o'clock next morning.

'Eat your supper, old fellow,' said Maulevrier. 'After all, the danger may not be so desperate as I fancied this morning. Slander is the favourite amusement of the age we live in. We must allow a margin for exaggeration.'

'A very liberal margin,' answered Hartfield. 'No doubt the man who warned you meant honestly, but this scandal may have grown out of the merest trifles. The feebleness of the Masher's brain is only exceeded by the foulness of the Masher's tongue. I daresay this rumour about Lady Lesbia has its beginning and end among the Masher species.'

'I hope so, but--I have seen those two together--I met them at Victoria one evening after Goodwood. Old Kirkbank was shuffling on ahead, carrying Smithson with her, absorbing his attention by fussification about her carriage. Lesbia and that Cuban devil were in the rear. They looked as if they had all the world to themselves. Faust and Marguerite in the garden were not in it for the expression of intense absorbing feeling compared with those two. I'm not an intellectual party, but I know something of human nature, and I know when a man and woman are in love with each other. It is one of the things that never has been, that never can be hidden.'

'And you say this Montesma is a dangerous man?'

'Deadly.'

'Well, we must lose no time. When we are on the spot it will be easy to find out the truth; and it will be your duty, if there be danger, to warn Lesbia and her future husband.'

'I would much rather shoot the Cuban,' said Maulevrier. 'I never knew much good come of a warning in such a case: it generally precipitates matters. If I could play *ecarte* with him at the club, find him sporting an extra king, throw my cards in his face, and accept his challenge for an exchange of shots on the sands beyond Cherbourg--there would be something like satisfaction'

'You say the man is a gambler?'

'Report says something worse of him. Report says he is a cheat.'

'We must not be dependent upon society gossip,' replied Lord Hartfield. 'I have an idea, Maulevrier. The more we know about this man--Montesma, I think you called him----'

'Gomez de Montesma.'

'The more fully we are acquainted with Don Gomez de Montesma's antecedents the better we shall be able to cope with him, if we come to handy-grips. It's too late to start for Cowes, but it is not too late to do something. Fitzpatrick, the political-economist, spent a quarter of a century in South America. He is a very old friend--knew my father--and I can venture to knock at his door after midnight--all the more as I know he is a night-worker. He is very likely to enlighten us about your Cuban hidalgo.'

'You shall finish your supper before I let you stir. After that you may do what you like. I was always a child in your hands, Jack, whether it was climbing a mountain or crossing the Horse-shoe Fall. I consider the business in your hands now. I'll go with you wherever you like, and do what you tell me. When you want me to kick anybody, or fight anybody, you can give me the office and I'll do it. I know that Lesbia's interests are safe in your hands. You once cared very much for her. You are her brother-in-law now, and, next to me, you are her natural protector, taking into account that her future husband is a cad and doesn't score.'

'Meet me at Waterloo at ten minutes to seven to-morrow morning, and we'll go down to Cowes together. I'm off to find Fitzpatrick. Good night.'

So they parted. Lord Hartfield walked across the Park to Great George Street, where Mr. Fitzpatrick had chambers of a semi-official character, on the first floor of a solemn-looking old house, spacious, gloomy without and within, walls sombre with the subdued colouring of decorations half a century old.

The lighted windows of those first-floor rooms told Lord Hartfield that he was not too late. He rang the bell, which was answered with the briefest delay by a sleepy-looking clerk, who had been taking shorthand notes for Mr. Fitzpatrick's great book upon 'Protection *versus* Free Trade.' The clerk looked sleepy, but his employer had as brisk an air as if he were just beginning the day; although he had been working without intermission since nine o'clock that evening, and had done a long day's work before dinner. He was walking up and down the spacious unluxurious room, half office, half library, smoking a cigar. Upon a large table in the centre of the room stood two powerful reading lamps with green shades, illuminating a chaotic mass of books and pamphlets, heaped and scattered all over the table, save just on that spot between the two lamps, which accommodated Mr. Fitzpatrick's blotting pad and inkpot, a pewter inkpot which held about a pint.

'How d'ye do, Hartfield? Glad you've looked me up at last,' said the Irishman, as if a midnight call were the most natural thing in the world. 'Just come from the House?'

'No; I've just come from Westmoreland. I thought I should find you among those everlasting books of yours, late as it is. Can I have a few words alone with you?'

'Certainly. Morgan, you can go away for a bit.'

'Home, sir?'

'Home--well--yes, I suppose it's late. You look sleepy. I should have been glad to finish the chapter on Beetroot Sugar to-night--but it may stand over for the morning. Be sure you're early.'

'Yes, sir,' the clerk responded with a faint sigh.

He was paid handsomely for late hours, liberally rewarded for his shorthand services; and yet he wished the great Fitzpatrick had not been quite so industrious.

'Now, my dear Hartfield, what can I do for you?' asked Fitzpatrick, when the clerk had gone. 'I can see by your face that you've something serious in hand. Can I help you?'

'You can, I believe, in a very material way. You were five-and-twenty years in Spanish America?'

'Rather more than less.'

'Here, there, and everywhere?'

'Yes; there is *not* a city in South America that I have not lived in--for something between a day and a year.'

'You know something about most men of any mark in that part of the world, I conclude?'

'It was my business to know men of all kinds. I had my mission from the Spanish Government. I was engaged to examine the condition of commerce throughout the colony, the working of protection as against free trade, and so on. Strange, by-the-bye, that Cuba, the last place to foster the slave trade, was of all spots of the earth the first to carry free-trade principles into practical effect, long before they were recognised in any European country.'

'Strange to me that you should speak of Cuba so soon after my coming in,' answered Lord Hartfield. 'I am here to ask you to help me to find out the antecedents of a man who hails from that island.'

'I ought to know something about him, whoever he is,' replied Mr. Fitzpatrick, briskly. 'I spent six months in Cuba not very long before my return to England. Cuba is one of my freshest memories; and I have a pretty tight memory for facts, names and figures. Never could remember two lines of poetry in my life.'

'Did you ever hear of, or meet with, a man called Montesma--Gomez de Montesma?'

'Couldn't have stopped a month in Havana without hearing something about that gentleman,' answered Fitzpatrick, 'I hope he isn't a friend of yours, and that you have not lent him money?'

'Neither; but I want to know all you can tell me about him.'

'You shall have it in black and white, out of my Cuban note-book,' replied the other, unlocking a drawer in the official table; 'I always take notes of anything worth recording, on the spot. A man is a fool who trusts to memory, where personal character is at stake. Montesma is as well known at Havana as the Morro Fort or the Tacon Theatre. I have heard stories enough about him to fill a big volume; but all the facts recorded there'--striking the morocco cover of the note-book--'have been thoroughly sifted; I can vouch for them.'

He looked at the index, found the page, and handed the book to Lord Hartfield.

'Read for yourself,' he said, quietly.

Lord Hartfield read three or four pages of plain statement as to various adventures by sea and land in which Gomez de Montesma had figured, and the reputation which he bore in Cuba and on the Main.

'You can vouch for this?' he said at last, after a long silence.

'For every syllable.'

'The story of his marriage?'

'Gospel truth: I knew the lady.'

'And the rest?'

'All true.'

'A thousand thanks. I know now upon what ground I stand. I have to save an innocent, high-bred girl from the clutches of a consummate scoundrel.'

'Shoot him, and shoot her, too, if there's no better way of saving her. It will be an act of mercy,' said Mr. Fitzpatrick, without hesitation.

CHAPTER XLII.
'SHALL IT BE?'

While Lord Hartfield sat in his friend's office in Great George Street reading the life story of Gomez de Montesma, told with the cruel precision and the unvarnished language of a criminal indictment, the hero of that history was gliding round the spacious ballroom of the Cowes Club, with Lady Lesbia Haselden's dark-brown head almost reclining on his shoulder, her violet eyes looking up at his every now and then, shyly, entrancingly, as he bent his head to talk to her.

The Squadron Ball was in full swing between midnight and the first hour of morning. The flowers had not lost their freshness, the odours of dust and feverish human breath had not yet polluted the atmosphere. The windows were open to the purple night, the purple sea. The stars seemed to be close outside the verandah, shining on purpose for the dancers; and these two--the man tall, pale, dark, with flashing eyes and short, sleek raven hair, small head, noble bearing; the girl divinely lovely in her marble purity of complexion, her classical grace of form--these two were, as every one avowed and acknowledged, the handsomest couple in the room.

'We're none of us in it compared with them,' said a young naval commander to his partner, whereupon the young lady looked somewhat sourly, and replied that Lady Lesbia's features were undeniably regular and her complexion good, but that she was wanting in soul.

'Is she?' asked the sailor, incredulously, 'Look at her now. What do you call that, if it isn't soul?'

'I call it simply disgraceful,' answered his partner, sharply turning away her head.

Lesbia was looking up at the Spaniard, her lips faintly parted, all her face listening eagerly as she caught some whispered word, breathed among the soft ripples of her hair, from lips that almost touched her brow. People cannot go on waltzing for ten minutes in a dead silence, like automatic dancers. There must be conversation. Only it is better that the lips should do most of the talking. When the eyes have so much to say society is apt to be censorious.

Mr. Smithson was smoking a cigarette on the lawn with a sporting peer. A man to whom tobacco is a necessity cannot be always on guard; but it is quite possible that in the present state of Lady Lesbia's feelings Smithson would have had no restraining influence had he been ever so watchful. To what act in the passion drama had her love come to-night as she floated round the room, with her head inclined towards her lover's breast, the strong pulsation of his heart sounding in her ear, like the rhythmical beat of the basses yonder in Waldteufel's last waltz? Was there still the uncertainty as to the **denouement** which marks the third act of a good play? or was there the dread foreboding, the sense of impending doom which should stir the spectators with pity and terror as the fourth act hurries to its passionate close? Who could tell? She had been full of life and energy to-day on board the yacht during the racing, in which she seemed to take an ardent interest. The **Cayman** had followed the racers for three hours through a freshening sea, much to Lady Kirkbank's disgust, and Lesbia had been the soul of the party. The same yesterday. The yacht had only got back to Cowes in time for the ball, and all had been hurry and excitement while the ladies dressed and crossed to the club, the spray dashing over their opera mantles, poor Lady Kirkbank's complexion yellow with **mal de mer**, in spite of a double coating of **Blanc de Fedora**, the last fashionable cosmetic.

To-night Lesbia was curiously silent, depressed even, as it seemed to those who were interested in observing her; and all the world is interested in a famous beauty. She was very pale, even her lips were colourless, and the large violet eyes and firmly pencilled brows alone gave colour to her face. She looked like a marble statue, the eyes and eyebrows accentuated with touches of colour. Those lovely eyes had a heavy look, as of trouble, weariness; nay, absolute distress.

Never had she looked less brilliant than to-night; never had she looked more beautiful. It was the loveliness of a newly-awakened soul. The wonderful Pandora-casket of life, with its infinite evil, its little good, had given up its secret. She knew what passionate love really means. She knew what such love mostly means--self-sacrifice, surrender of the world's wealth, severance from friends, the breaking of all old ties. To love as she loved means the crossing of a river more fatal than the Rubicon, the casting of a die more desperate than that which Caesar flung upon the board when he took up arms against the Republic.

The river was not yet crossed, but her feet were on the margin, wet with the ripple of the stream. The fatal die was not yet cast, but the dice-box was in her hand ready for the throw. Lesbia and Montesma danced together--not too often, three waltzes out of sixteen--but when they were so waltzing they were the cynosure of the room. That betting of which Maulevrier had heard was rife to-night, and the odds upon the Cuban had gone up. It was nine to four now that those two would be over the border before the week was out.

Mr. Smithson was not neglectful of his affianced. He took her into the supper-room, where she drank some Moselle cup, but ate nothing. He sat out three or four waltzes with her on the lawn, listening to the murmer of the sea, and talking very little.

'You are looking wretchedly ill to-night, Lesbia,' he said, after a dismal silence.

'I am sorry that I should put you to shame by my bad looks,' she answered, with that keen acidity of tone which indicates irritated nerves.

'You know that I don't mean anything of the kind; you are always lovely, always the loveliest everywhere; but I don't like to see you so ghastly pale.'

'I suppose I am over-fatigued: that I have done too much in London and here. Life in Westmoreland was very different,' she added, with a sigh, and a touch of wonder that the Lesbia Haselden, whose methodical life had never been stirred by a ruffle of passion, could have been the same flesh and blood--yes, verily, the same woman, whose heart throbbed so vehemently to-night, whose brain seemed on fire.

'Are you sure there is nothing the matter?' he asked, with a faint quiver in his voice.

'What should there be the matter?'

'Who can say? God knows that I know no cause for evil. I am honest enough, and faithful enough, Lesbia. But your face to-night is like a presage of calamity, like the dull, livid sky that goes before a thunderstorm.'

'I hope there is no thunderbolt coming,' she answered, lightly. 'What very tall talk about a headache, for really that is all that ails me. Hark, they have begun "My Queen." I am engaged for this waltz.'

'I am sorry for that.'

'So am I. I would ever so much rather have stayed out here.'

Two hours later, in the steely morning light, when sea and land and sky had a metallic look as if lit by electricity, Lady Lesbia stood with her chaperon and her affianced husband on the landing stage belonging to the club, ready to step into the boat in which six swarthy seamen in red shirts and caps were to row them back to the yacht. Mr. Smithson drew the warm *sortie de bal*, with its gold-coloured satin lining and white fox border, closer round Lesbia's slender form.

'You are shivering,' he said; 'you ought to have warmer wraps.

'This is warm enough for St. Petersburg. I am only tired--very tired.'

'The *Cayman* will rock you to sleep.'

Don Gomez was standing close by, waiting for his host. The two men were to walk up the hill to Formosa, a village with a classic portico, delightfully situated above the town.

'What time are we to come to breakfast? asked Mr. Smithson.

'Not too early, in mercy's name. Two o'clock in the afternoon, three, four;--why not make it five--combine breakfast with afternoon tea,' exclaimed Lady Kirkbank, with a tremendous yawn. 'I never was so thoroughly fagged; I feel as if I had been beaten with sticks, basti--what's its name.'

She was leaning all her weight upon Mr. Smithson, as he handed her down the steps and into the boat. Her normal weight was not a trifle, and this morning she was heavy with champagne and sleep. Carefully as Smithson supported her she gave a lurch at the bottom of the steps, and plunged ponderously into the boat, which dipped and careened under her, whereat she shrieked, and implored Mr. Smithson to save her.

All this, occupied some minutes, and gave Lesbia and the Cuban just time for a few words that had to be said somehow.

'Good-night,' said Montesma, as they clasped hands; 'good-night;' and then in a lower voice he said, 'Well, have you decided at last? Shall it be?'

She looked at him for a moment or so, pale in the starlight, and then murmured an almost inaudible syllable.

'Yes.'

He bent quickly and pressed his lips upon her gloved hand, and when Mr. Smithson looked round they two were standing apart, Montesma in a listless attitude, as if tired of waiting for his host.

It was Smithson who handed Lesbia into the boat and arranged her wraps, and hung over her tenderly as he performed those small offices.

'Now really,' he asked, just before the boat put off, 'when are we to be with you to-morrow?'

'Lady Kirkbank says not till afternoon tea, but I think you may come a few hours earlier. I am not at all sleepy.'

'You look as if you needed sleep badly,' answered Smithson. 'I'm afraid you are not half careful enough of yourself. Good-night.'

The boat was gliding off, the oars dipping, as he spoke. How swiftly it shot from his ken, flashing in and out among the yachts, where the lamps were burning dimly in that clear radiance of new-born day.

Montesma gave a tremendous yawn as he took out his cigar-case, and he and Mr. Smithson did not say twenty words between them during the walk to Formosa, where servants were sitting up, lamps burning, a great silver tray, with brandy, soda, liqueurs, coffee, in readiness.

CHAPTER XLIII.
'ALAS, FOR SORROW IS ALL THE END OF THIS'

Lady Kirkbank retired to her cabin directly she got on board the *Cayman*.

'Good-night, child! I am more than half asleep,' she said; 'and I think if there were to be an earthquake an hour hence I should hardly hear it. Go to your berth directly, Lesbia; you look positively awful. I have seen girls look bad after balls before now, but I never saw such a spectre as you look this morning.'

Poor Georgie's own complexion left something to be desired. The *Blanc de Fedora* had been a brilliant success for the first two hours: after that the warm room began to tell upon it, and there came a greasiness, then a streakiness, and now all that was left of an alabaster skin was a livid patch of purplish paint here and there, upon a crow's-foot ground. The eyebrows, too, had given in, and narrow lines of Vandyke brown meandered down Lady Kirkbank's cheeks. The frizzy hair had gone altogether wrong, and had a wild look, suggestive of the witches in Macbeth, and the scraggy neck and poor old shoulders showed every year of their age in the ghastly morning light.

Lesbia waited in the saloon till Lady Kirkbank had bolted herself into her cabin, and then she went up to the deck wrapped in her satin-lined, fur-bordered cloak, and coiled herself in a bamboo arm-chair, and nestled her bare head into a Turkish pillow, and tried to sleep, there with the cool morning breeze blowing upon her burning forehead, and the plish-plash of seawater soothing her ear.

There were only three or four sailors on deck, weird, almost diabolical-looking creatures, Lesbia thought, in striped shirts, with bare arms, of a shining bronze complexion, flashing black eyes, sleek raven hair, a sinister look. What species of men they were--Mestizoes, Coolies, Yucatekes--she knew not, but she felt that they were something wild and strange, and their presence filled her with a vague fear. *He*, whose influence now ruled her life, had told her that these men were born mariners, and that she was twenty times safer with them than when the yacht had been under the control of those honest, grinning red-whiskered English Jack Tars. But she liked the English sailors best, all the same; and she shrank from the faintest contact with these tawny-visaged strangers, plucking away the train of her gown as they passed her chair, lest they should brush against her drapery.

On deck this morning, with only those dark faces near, she had a sense of loneliness, of helplessness, of abandonment even. Unbidden the image of her home at Grasmere flashed into her mind--all things so calm, so perfectly ordered, such a sense of safety, of home--no peril, no temptation, no fever--only peace: and she had grown sick to death of peace. She had prayed for tempest: and the tempest had come.

There was a heavenly quiet in the air in the early summer morning, only the creaking of a spar, the scream of a seagull now and then. How pale the lamps were growing on board the yachts. Paler still, yellow, and dim, and blurred yonder in the town. The eastward facing windows were golden with the rising sun. Yes, this was morning. The yachts were moving away yonder, majestical, swan-like, white sails shining against the blue.

She closed her eyes, and tried to sleep; but sleep would not come. She was always listening--listening for the dip of oars, listening for a snatch of melody from a mellow baritone whose every accent she knew so well.

It came at last, the sound her soul longed for. She lay among her cushions with closed eyes, listening, drinking in those rich ripe notes as they came nearer and nearer, to the measure of dipping oars, *'La donna e mobile--'*

Nearer and nearer, until the little boat ground against the hull. She lifted her heavy eyelids as Montesma leapt over the gunwale, almost into her arms. He was at her side, kneeling by her low chair, kissing the little hands, chill with the freshness of morning.

'My own, my very own,' he murmured, passionately.

He cared no more for those copper-faced Helots yonder than if they had been made of wood. He had fate in his own hands now, as it seemed to him. He went to the skipper and gave him some orders in Spanish, and then the sails were unfurled, the **Cayman** spread her broad white wings, and moved off among those other yachts which were gliding, gliding, gliding out to sea, melting from Cowes Roads like a vision that fadeth with the broad light of morning.

When the sails were up and the yacht was running merrily through the water, Montesma went back to Lady Lesbia, and they two sat side by side, gilded and glorified in the vivid lights of sunrise, talking as they had never talked before, her head upon his shoulder, a smile of ineffable peace upon her lips, as of a weary child that has found rest.

They were sailing for Havre, and at Havre they were to be married by the English chaplain, and from Havre they were to sail for the Havana, and to live there ever afterwards in a fairy-tale dream of bliss, broken only by an annual visit to Paris, just to buy gowns and bonnets. Surrendered were all Lesbia's ambitious hopes--forgotten--gone; her desire to reign princess paramount in the kingdom of fashion--her thirst to be wealthiest among the wealthy--gone--forgotten. Her dreams now were of the **dolce far niente** of a tropical climate, a boudoir giving on the Caribbean sea, cigarettes, coffee, nights spent in a foreign opera house, the languid, reposeful existence of a Spanish dama--with him, with him. It was for his sake that she had modified all her ideas of life. To be with him she would have been content to dwell in the tents of the Patagonians, on the wild and snow-clad Pampas. A love which was strong enough to make her sacrifice duty, the world, her fair fame as a well-bred woman, was a love that recked but little of the paths along which her lover's hand was to lead. For him, to be with him, she renounced the world. The rest did not count.

The summer hours glided past them. The **Cayman** was far out at sea; all the other yachts had vanished, and they were alone amidst the blue, with only a solitary three-master yonder, on the edge of the horizon. More than once Lesbia had talked of going below to change her ball gown for the attire of everyday life; but each time her lover had detained her a little longer, had pleaded for a few more words. Lady Kirkbank would be astir presently, and there would be no more solitude for them till they were married, and could shake her off altogether. So Lesbia stayed, and those two drank the cup of bliss, hushed by the monotonous sing-song of the sea, the rhythm of the swinging sails. But now it was broad morning. The hour when society, however late it may keep its revels overnight, is apt to awaken, were it only to call for a cup of strong tea and to turn again on the pillow of lassitude, after that refreshment, like the sluggard of Holy Writ. At ten o'clock the sun sent his golden arrows across the silken coverlet of her berth and awakened Lady Kirkbank, who opened her eyes and looked about languidly. The little cabin was heaving itself up and down in a curious way; Mr. Smithson's cigar-cases were sloping as if they were going to fall upon Lady Kirkbank's couch, and the looking-glass, with all its dainty appliances, was making an angle of forty-five degrees. There was more swirling and washing of water against the hull than ever Georgie Kirkbank had heard in Cowes Roads.

'Mercy on me! this horrid thing must be moving,' she exclaimed to the empty air. 'It must have broken loose in the night.'

She had no confidence in those savage-looking sailors, and she had a vision of the yacht drifting at the mercy of winds and waves, drifting for days, weeks, and months; drifting to the German Ocean, drifting to the North Pole. Mr. Smithson and Montesma on shore--no one on board to exercise authority over those fearful men.

Perhaps they had mutinied, and were carrying off the yacht as their booty, with Lesbia and her chaperon, and all their gowns.

'I am almost glad that harpy Seraphine has my diamonds,' thought poor Georgie, 'or I should have had them with me on board this hateful boat.'

And then she rapped vehemently against the panel of the cabin, and screamed for Rilboche, whose den was adjacent.

Rilboche, who detested the sea, made her appearance after some delay, looking even greener than her mistress, who, in rising from her berth, already began to suffer the agonies of sea-sickness.

'What does this mean?' exclaimed Lady Kirkbank; 'and where are we going?'

'That's what I should like to know, my lady. But I daresay Lady Lesbia and Mr. Montesma can tell you. They are both on deck.'

'Montesma! Why, we left him on shore!'

'Yes, my lady, but he came on board at five o'clock this morning. I looked at my watch when I heard him land, and he and Lady Lesbia have been sitting on deck ever since.'

'And now it is ten. Five hours on deck--impossible!'

'Time doesn't seem long when one is happy, my lady,' murmured Rilboche, in her own language.

'Help me to dress this instant,' screamed her mistress: 'that dreadful Spaniard is eloping with us.'

Despite the hideous depression of that malady which strikes down Kaiser and beggar with the same rough hand, Lady Kirkbank contrived to get herself dressed decently, and to stagger up the companion to that part of the deck where the Persian carpet was spread, and the bamboo chairs and tables were set out under the striped awning. Lesbia and her lover were sitting together, he giving her a first lesson in the art of smoking a cigarette. He had told her playfully that every man, woman, and child in Cuba was a smoker, and she had besought him to let her begin, and now, with infinite coquetry, was taking her first lesson.

'You shameless minx!' exclaimed Georgie, pale with anger.

'Where is Smithson--my poor, good Smithson?'

'Fast asleep in his bed at Formosa, I hope, dear Lady Kirkbank,' the Cuban answered, with perfect *sang froid*. 'Smithson is out of it, as you idiomatic English say. I hope, Lady Kirkbank, you will be as kind to me as you have been to Smithson; and depend upon it I shall make Lady Lesbia as good a husband as ever Smithson could have done.'

'You!' exclaimed the matron, contemptuously. 'You!--a foreigner, an adventurer, who may be as poor as Job, for anything I know about you.'

'Job was once rather comfortably off, Lady Kirkbank; and I can answer for it that Montesma's wife will know none of the pangs of poverty.'

'If you were a beggar I would not care,' said Lesbia, drawing nearer to him.

They had both risen at Lady Kirkbank's approach, and were standing side by side, confronting her. Lesbia had shrunk from the idea of poverty with John Hammond; yet, for this man's sake, she was ready to face penury, ruin, disgrace, anything.

'Do you mean to tell me that Lord Maulevrier's sister, a young lady under my charge, answerable to me for her conduct, is capable of jilting the man to whom she has solemnly bound herself, in order to marry you?' demanded Lady Kirkbank, turning to Montesma.

'Yes; that is what I am going to do,' answered Lesbia, boldly. 'It would be a greater sin to keep my promise than to break it. I never liked that man, and you know it. You badgered me into accepting him, against my own better judgment. You drifted me so deeply into debt that I was willing to marry a man I loathed in order to get my debts paid. *This* is what you did for the girl placed under your charge. But, thank God, I have released myself from your clutches. I am going far away to a new world, where the memory of my old life cannot follow me. People may be angry or pleased! I do not care. I shall be the wife of the man I have chosen out of all the world for my husband--the man God made to be my master.'

'You are----' gasped Lady Kirkbank. 'I can't say what you are. I never in my life felt so tempted to use improper language.'

'Dear Lady Kirkbank, be reasonable,' pleaded Montesma; 'you can have no interest in seeing Lesbia married to a man she dislikes.'

Georgia reddened a little, remembering that she was interested to the amount of some thousands in the Smithson and Haselden alliance; but she took a higher ground than mercenary considerations.

'I am interested in doing the very best for a young lady who has been entrusted to my care, the granddaughter of an old friend,' she answered, with dignity. 'I have no objection to you in the abstract, Don Gomez. You have always been vastly civil, I am sure----'

'Stand by us in our day of need, Lady Kirkbank, and you will find me the staunchest friend you ever had.'

'I am bound in honour to consider Mr. Smithson, Lesbia,' said Lady Kirkbank.

'I wonder that a decently-brought up girl can behave so abominably.'

'It would be more abominable to marry a man I detest. I have made up my mind, Lady Kirkbank. We shall be at Havre to-morrow morning, and we shall be married to-morrow--shall we not, Gomez?'

She let her head sink upon his breast, and his arm enfold her. Thus sheltered, she felt safe, thus and thus only. She had thrown her cap over the mills; snapped her fingers at society; cared not a jot what the world might think or say of her. This man would she marry and no other; this man's fortune would she follow for good or evil. He had that kind of influence with women which is almost 'possession.' It smells of brimstone.

'Come, my dear good soul,' said Montesma, smiling at the angry matron, 'why not take things quietly? You have had a good many girls under your wing; and you must know that youth and maturity see life from a different standpoint. In your eyes my old friend Smithson is an admirable match. You measure him by his houses, his stable, his banker's book; but Lesbia would rather marry the man she loves, and take the risks of his fate. I am not a pauper, Lady Kirkbank, and the home to which I shall take my love is pretty enough for a princess of the blood royal, and for her sake I shall grow richer yet,' he added, with his eyes kindling; 'and if you care to pay us a visit next February in our Parisian apartment I will promise you as pleasant a nest as you can wish to occupy.'

'How do I know that you will ever bring her back to Europe?' said Lady Kirkbank, piteously. 'How do I know that you will not bury her alive in your savage country, among blackamoors, like those horrid sailors, over there--kill her, perhaps, when you are tired of her?'

At these words of Lady Kirkbank's, flung out at random, Montesma blanched, and his deep black eye met hers with a strangely sinister look.

'Yes,' she cried, hysterically--'kill her, kill her! You look as if you could do it.'

Lesbia nestled closer to her lover's heart.

'How dare you say such things to him,' she cried, angrily. '*I* trust him, don't you see; trust him with my whole heart, with all my soul. I shall be his wife to-morrow, for good or evil.'

'Very much for evil, I'm afraid,' said Lady Kirkbank. 'Perhaps you will be kind enough to come to your cabin and take off that ball gown, and make yourself just a little less disreputable in outward appearance, while I get a cup of tea.'

Lesbia obeyed, and went down to her cabin, where Kibble was waiting with a fresh white muslin frock and all its belongings, laid out ready for her mistress, sorely perplexed at the turn which affairs were taking. She had never liked Horace Smithson, although he had given her tips which were almost a provision for her old age; but she had thought it a good thing that her mistress, who was frightfully extravagant, should marry a millionaire; and now they were sailing over the sea with a lot of coloured sailors, and the millionaire was left on shore.

Lady Kirkbank went into the saloon, where breakfast was laid ready, and where the steward was in attendance with that air of being absolutely unconscious of any domestic disturbance, which is the mark of a well-trained servant.

Lesbia appeared in something less than an hour, newly dressed and fresh looking, in her pure white gown, her brown hair bound in a coronet round her small Greek head. She sat down by Lady Kirkbank's side, and tried to coax her into good humour.

'Why can't you take things pleasantly, dear?' she pleaded. 'Do now, like a good soul. You heard him say he was well off, and that he will take me to Paris next winter, and you can come to us there on your way from Cannes, and stay with us till Easter. It will be so nice when the Prince and all the best people are in Paris. We shall only stay in Cuba till the fuss about my running away is all over, and people have forgotten, don't you know. As for Mr. Smithson, why should I have any more compunction about jilting him than he had about that poor Miss Trinder? By-the-bye, I want you to send him back all his presents for me. They are almost all in Arlington Street. I brought nothing with me except my engagement ring,' looking down at the half-hoop of diamonds, and pulling it off her fingers as she talked. 'I had a kind of presentiment----'

'You mean that you had made up your mind to throw him over.'

'No. But I felt there were breakers ahead. It might have come to throwing myself into the sea. Perhaps you would have liked that better than what has happened.'

'I don't know, I'm sure. The whole thing is disgraceful. London will ring with the scandal. What am I to say to Lady Maulevrier, to your brother? And pray how do you propose to get married at Havre? You cannot be married in a French town by merely holding up your finger. There are no registry offices. I am sure I have no idea how the thing is done.'

'Don Gomez has arranged all that--everything has been thought of--everything has been planned. A steamer will take us to St. Thomas, and another steamer will take us on to Cuba.'

'But the marriage--the licence?'

'I tell you everything has been provided for. Please take this ring and send it to Mr. Smithson when you go back to England.'

'Send it to him yourself. I will have nothing to do with it.'

'How dreadfully disagreeable you are,' said Lesbia, pouting, 'just because I am marrying to please myself, instead of to please you. It is frightfully selfish of you.'

Montesma came in at this moment. He, too, had dressed himself freshly, and was looking his handsomest, in that buccaneer style of costume which he wore when he sailed the yacht. He and Lesbia breakfasted at their ease, while Lady Kirkbank reclined in her bamboo arm-chair, feeling very unhappy in her mind and far from well. Neptune and she could not accommodate themselves.

After a leisurely breakfast, enlivened by talk and laughter, the cabin windows open, the sun shining, the freshening breeze blowing in, Lesbia and Don Gomez went on deck, and he reclined at her feet while she read to him from the pages of her favourite Keats, read languidly, lazily, yet exquisitely, for she had been taught to read as well as to sing. The poetry seemed to have been written on purpose for them; and the sky and the atmosphere around them seemed to have been made for the poetry. And so, with intervals of strolling on the deck, and an hour or so dawdled away at luncheon, and a leisurely afternoon tea, the day wore on to sunset, and they went back to Keats, while Lady Kirkbank sulked and slept in a corner of the saloon.

'This is the happiest day of my life,' Lesbia murmured, in a pause of their reading, when they had dropped Endymion's love to talk of their own.

'But not of mine, my angel. I shall be happier still when we are far away on broader waters, beyond the reach of all who can part us.'

'Can any one part us, Gomez, now that we have pledged ourselves to each other?' she asked, incredulously.

'Ah, love, such pledges are sometimes broken. All women are not lion-hearted.

While the sea is smooth and the ship runs fair, all is easy enough; but when tempest and peril come--that is the test, Lesbia. Will you stand by me in the tempest, love?'

'You know that I will,' she answered, with her hand locked in his two hands, clasped as with a life-long clasp.

She could not imagine any severe ordeal to be gone through. If Maulevrier heard of her elopement in time for pursuit, there would be a fuss, perhaps--an angry bother raging and fuming. But what of that? She was her own mistress. Maulevrier could not prevent her marrying whomsoever she pleased.

'Swear that you will hold to me against all the world,' he said, passionately, turning his head to look across the stern of the vessel.

'Against all the world,' she answered, softly.

'I believe your courage will be tested before long,' he said; and then he cried to the skipper, 'Crowd on all sail, Tomaso. That boat is chasing us.'

Lesbia sprang to her feet, looking as he looked to a spot of vivid white on the horizon. Montesma had snatched up a glass and was watching that distant spot.

'It is a steam-yacht,' he said. 'They will catch us.'

He was right. Although the *Cayman* strained every timber so that her keel cut through the water like a boomerang, wind and steam beat wind without steam. In less than an hour the steam-yacht was beside the *Cayman*, and Lord Maulevrier and Lord Hartfield had boarded Mr. Smithson's deck.

'I have come to take you and Lady Kirkbank back to Cowes, Lesbia,' said Maulevrier. 'I'm not going to make any undue fuss about this little escapade of yours, provided you go back with Hartfield and me at once, and pledge yourself never to hold any further communication with Don Gomez de Montesma.'

The Spaniard was standing close by, silent, white as death, but ready to make a good fight. That pallor of the clear olive skin was not from want of pluck; but there was the deadly knowledge of the ground he stood upon, the doubt that any woman, least of all such a woman as Lady Lesbia Haselden, could be true to him if his character and antecedents were revealed to her. And how much or how little these two men could tell her about himself or his past life was the question which the next few minutes would solve.

'I am not going back with you,' answered Lesbia. 'I am going to Havre with

Don Gomez de Montesma. We are to be married there as soon as we arrive.'

'To be married--at Havre,' cried Maulevrier. 'An appropriate place. A sailor has a wife in every port, don't you know.'

'We had better go down to the cabin,' said Hartfield, laying his hand upon his friend's shoulder. 'If Lady Lesbia will be good enough to come with us we can tell her all that we have to tell quietly there.'

Lord Hartfield's tone was unmistakeable. Everything was known.

'You can talk at your ease here,' said Montesma, facing the two men with a diabolical recklessness and insolence of manner. 'Not one of these fellows on board knows a dozen sentences of English.'

'I would rather talk below, if it is all the same to you, Senor; and I should be glad to speak to Lady Lesbia alone.'

'That you shall not do unless she desires it,' answered Montesma.

'No, he shall hear all that you have to say. He shall hear how I answer you,' said Lesbia.

Lord Hartfield shrugged his shoulders.

'As you please,' he said. 'It will make the disclosure a little more painful than it need have been; but that cannot be helped.'

CHAPTER XLIV.
'OH, SAD KISSED MOUTH, HOW SORROWFUL IT IS!'

They all went down to the saloon, where Lady Kirkbank sat, looking the image of despair, which changed to delighted surprise at sight of Lord Hartfield and his friend.

'Did you give your consent to my sister's elopement with this man, Lady Kirkbank?' Maulevrier asked, brusquely.

'I give my consent! Good gracious! no. He has eloped with me ever so much more than with your sister. She knew all about it, I've no doubt: but the wretch ran away with me in my sleep.'

'I am glad, for your own self-respect, that you had no hand in this disgraceful business,' replied Maulevrier; and then turning to Lord Hartfield, he said, 'Hartfield, will you tell my sister who and what this man is? Will you make her understand what kind of pitfall she has escaped? Upon my soul, I cannot speak of it.'

'I recognise no right of Lord Hartfield's to interfere with my actions, and I will hear nothing that he may have to say,' said Lesbia, standing by her lover's side, with head erect and eyes dark with anger.

'Your sister's husband has the strongest right to control your actions, Lady Lesbia, when the family honour is at stake,' answered Hartfield, with grave authority. 'Accept me at least as a member of your family, if you will not accept me as your disinterested and devoted friend.'

'Friend!' echoed Lesbia, scornfully. 'You might have been my friend once. Your friendship then would have been of some value to me, if you had told me the truth, instead of approaching me with a lie upon your lips. You talk of honour, Lord Hartfield; you, who came to my grandmother's house as an impostor, under a false name!'

'I went there as a man standing on his own merits, assuming no rank save that which God gave him among his fellow-men, claiming to be possessed of no fortune except intellect and industry. If I could not win a wife with such credentials, it were better for me never to marry at all, Lady Lesbia. But we have no time to speak of the past. I am here as your brother's friend, here to save you.'

'To part me from the man to whom I have given my heart. That you cannot do. Gomez, why do you not speak? Tell him, tell him!' cried Lesbia, with a voice strangled by sobs; 'tell him that I am to be your wife to-morrow, at Havre. Your wife!'

'Dear Lady Lesbia, that cannot be,' said Lord Hartfield, sorrowfully, pitying her in her helplessness, as he might have pitied a young bird in the fowler's net. 'I am assured upon undeniable authority that Senor Montesma has a wife living at Cuba; and even were this not so--were he free to marry you--his character and antecedents would for ever forbid such a marriage.'

'A wife! No, no, no!' shrieked Lesbia, looking wildly from one to the other. 'It is a lie--a lie, invented by my brother, who always hated me--by you, who fooled and deceived me! It is a lie, an infamous invention! Don Gomez, speak to them: for pity's sake answer them! Don't you see that they are driving me mad?'

She flung herself into his arms, she buried her dishevelled head upon his breast; she clung to him with hands that writhed convulsively in her agony.

Maulevrier sprang across the cabin and wrenched her from her lover's grasp.

'You shall not pollute her with your touch,' he cried; 'you have poisoned her mind already. Scoundrel, seducer, slave-dealer! Do you hear, Lesbia? Shall I tell you what this man is--what trade he followed yonder, on his native island--this Spanish hidalgo--this all-accomplished gentleman--lineal descendant of the Cid--fine flower of Andalusian chivalry? It was not enough for him to cheat at cards, to float bubble companies, bogus lotteries. His profligate extravagance, his love of sybarite luxury, required a larger resource than the petty schemes which enrich smaller men. A slave ship, which could earn nearly twenty thousand pounds on every voyage, and which could make two runs in a year--that was the trade for Don Gomez de Montesma, and he carried it on merrily for six or seven years, till the British cruisers got too keen for him, and the good old game was played out. You see that scar upon the hilalgo's forehead, Lesbia--a token of knightly prowess, you think, perhaps. No, my girl, that is the mark of an English cutlass in a scuffle on board a slaver. A merry trade, Lesbia--the living cargo stowed close under hatches have rather a bad time of it now and then--short rations of food and water, yellow Jack. They die like rotten sheep sometimes--bad then for the dealer. But if he can land the bulk of his human wares safe and sound the profits are enormous. The Captain-General takes his capitation fee, the blackies are drafted off to the sugar plantations, and everybody is satisfied; but I think, Lesbia, that your British prejudices would go against marriage with a slave-trader, were he ever so free to make you his wife, which this particular dealer in blackamoors is not.'

'Is this true, this part of their vile story?' demanded Lesbia, looking at her lover, who stood apart from them all now, his arms folded, his face deadly pale, the lower lip quivering under the grinding of his strong white teeth.

'There is some truth in it,' he answered, hoarsely. 'Everybody in Cuba had a finger in the African trade, before your British philanthropy spoiled it. Mr. Smithson made sixty thousand pounds in that line. It was the foundation of his fortune. And yet he had his misfortunes in running his cargo--a ship burnt, a freight roasted alive. There are some very black stories in Cuba against poor Smithson. He will never go there again.'

'Mr. Smithson may be a scoundrel; indeed, I believe he is a pretty bad specimen in that line,' said Lord Hartfield. 'But I doubt if there is any story that can be told of him quite so bad as the history of your marriage, and the events that went before it. I have been told the story of the beautiful Octoroon, who loved and trusted you, who shared your good and evil fortunes for the most desperate years of your life, was almost accepted as your wife, and whose strangled corpse was found in the harbour while the bells were ringing for your marriage with a rich planter's heiress--the lady who, no doubt, now patiently awaits your return to her native island.'

'She will wait a long time,' said Montesma, 'or fare ill if I go back to her. Lesbia, his lordship's story of the Octoroon is a fable--an invention of my Cuban enemies, who hate us old Spaniards with a poisonous hatred. But this much is true. I am a married man--bound, fettered by a tie which I abhor. Our Havre marriage would have been bigamy on my part, a delusion on yours. I could not have taken you to Cuba. I had planned our life in a fairer, more civilised world. I am rich enough to have surrounded you with all that makes life worth living. I would have given you love as true and as deep as ever man gave to woman. All that would have been wanting would have been the legality of the tie: and as law never yet made a marriage happy which lacked the elements of bliss, our lawless union need not have missed happiness. Lesbia, you said that you would hold by me, come what might. The worst has come, love; but it leaves me not the less your true lover.'

She looked at him with wild despairing eyes, and then, with a hoarse strange cry, rushed from the cabin, and up the companion, with a desperate swiftness which seemed like the flight of a bird. Montesma, Hartfield, Maulevrier, all followed her, heedless of everything except the dire necessity of arresting her flight. Each in his own mind had divined her purpose.

They were not too late. It was Hartfield's strong arm that caught her, held her as in a vice, dragged her away from the edge of the deck, just where there was a space open to the waves. Another instant and she would have flung herself overboard. She fell back into Lord Hartfield's arms, with a wild choking cry: 'Let me go! Let me go!' Another moment, and a flood of crimson stained his shirt-front, as she lay upon his breast, with closed eyelids and blood-bedabbled lips, in blessed unconsciousness.

They carried her on to the steam-yacht, and down to the cabin, where there was ample accommodation and some luxury, although not the elegance of Bond Street upholstery. Rilboche, Lady Kirkbank, Kibble, luggage of all kinds were transferred from one yacht to the other, even to the vellum bound Keats which lay face downwards on the deck, just where Lesbia had flung it when the *Cayman* was boarded. The crew of the steam-yacht *Philomel* helped in the transfer: there were plenty of hands, and the work was done quickly; while the Meztizoes, Yucatekes, Caribs, or whatever they were, looked on and grinned; and while Montesma stood leaning against the mast, with folded arms and sombre brow, a cigarette between his lips.

When the women and all their belongings were on board the *Philomel*, Lord Hartfield addressed himself to Montesma.

'If you consider yourself entitled to call me to account for this evening's work you know where to find me,' he said.

Montesma shrugged his shoulders, and threw away his cigarette with a contemptuous gesture.

'*Ce n'est pas la peine,*' he said; 'I am a dead shot, and should be pretty sure to send a bullet through you if you gave me the chance; but I should not be any nearer winning her if I killed you: and it is she and she only that I want. You may think me an adventurer--swindler--gambler--slave-dealer--what you will--but I love her as I never thought to love a woman, and I should have been true as steel, if she had been plucky enough to trust me. But, as I told her an hour ago, women have not lion hearts. They can talk tall while the sky is clear and the sun shines, but at the first crack of thunder--*va te promener.*'

'If you have killed her--' began Hartfield.

'Killed her! No. Some small bloodvessel burst in the agitation of that terrible scene. She will be well in a week, and she will forget me. But I shall not forget her. She is the one flower that has sprung on the barren plain of my life. She was my Picciola.'

He turned his back on Lord Hartfield and walked to the other end of the deck. Something in his face, in the vibration of his deep voice, convinced Hartfield of his truth. A bad man undoubtedly--steeped to the lips in evil--and yet so far true that he had passionately, deeply, devotedly loved this one woman.

It was the dead of night when Lesbia recovered consciousness, and even then she lay silent, taking no heed of those around her, in a state of utter prostration. Kibble nursed her carefully, tenderly, all through the night; Maulevrier hardly left the cabin, and Lady Kirkbank, always more or less a victim to the agonies of sea-sickness, still found time to utter lamentations and wailings over the ruin of her protegee's fortune.

'Never had a girl such a chance,' she moaned. 'Quite the best match in society. The house in Park Lane alone cost a fortune. Her diamonds would have been the finest in London.'

'They would have been stained with the blood of the niggers he traded in out yonder,' answered Maulevrier. 'Do you think I would have let my sister marry a slave-dealer?'

'I don't believe a syllable of it,' protested Lady Kirkbank, dabbing her brow with a handkerchief steeped in eau de Cologne. 'A vile fabrication of Montesma's, who wanted to blacken poor Smithson's character in order to extenuate his own crimes.'

'Well, we won't go into that question,' said Maulevrier wearily. 'The Smithson match is off, anyhow; and it matters very little to us whether he made most money out of niggers or bubble companies, or lotteries or gaming hells.'

'I am convinced that Smithson made his fortune in a thoroughly gentlemanlike manner,' argued Lady Kirkbank. 'Look at the people who visit him, and the houses he goes to. And I don't see why the match need be off. I'm sure, if Lesbia plays her cards properly, he will look over this--this--little escapade.'

Maulevrier contemplated the worldly old face with infinite scorn.

'Does she look like a girl who will play her cards in your fashion?' he asked, pointing to his sister, whose white face upon the pillow seemed like a mask cut out of marble. 'Upon my soul, Lady Kirkbank, I consider my sister's elopement with this Spanish adventurer, with whom she was over head and ears in love, a far more respectable act than her engagement to Smithson, for whom she cared not a straw.'

'Well, I hope if you so approve of her conduct you will help her to pay her dressmaker, and the rest of them,' retorted Lady Kirkbank. 'She has been plunging rather deeply, I believe, under the impression that Smithson would pay all her bills when she was married. Your grandmother may not quite like the budget.'

'I will do all I can for her,' answered Maulevrier. 'I would do a great deal to save her from the degradation to which your teaching has brought her.'

Lady Kirkbank looked at him for a moment or so with reproachful eyes, and then shrugged her shoulders contemptuously.

'If I ever expected gratitude from people I might feel the injustice--the insolence--of your last remark,' she said; 'but as I never do expect gratitude, I am not disappointed in this case. And now I think if there is a cabin which I can have to myself I should like to retire to it,' she added. 'My cares are thrown away here.'

There was a cabin at Lady Kirkbank's disposal. It had been already appropriated by Rilboche, and smelt of cognac; but Rilboche resigned her berth to her mistress, and laid herself meekly on the floor for the rest of the voyage.

They were in Cowes Roads at eight o'clock next morning, and Lord Hartfield went on shore for a doctor, whom he brought back before nine, and who pronounced Lady Lesbia to be in a very weak and prostrate condition, and forbade her being moved within the next two days. Happily Lord Hartfield had borrowed the **Philomel** and her crew from a friend who had given him **carte blanche** as to the use he made of her, and who freely left her at his disposal so long as he and his party should need the accommodation. Lesbia could nowhere be better off than on the yacht, where she was away from the gossip and tittle-tattle of the town.

The roadstead was quiet enough now. All the racing yachts had melted away like a dream, and most of the pleasure yachts were off to Ryde. Lady Lesbia lay in her curtained cabin, with Kibble keeping watch beside her bed, while Maulevrier came in every half-hour to see how she was--sitting by her a little now and then, and talking of indifferent things in a low kind voice, which was full of comfort.

She seemed grateful for his kindness, and smiled at him once in a way, with a piteous little smile; but she had the air of one in whom the mainspring of life is broken. The pallid face and heavy violet eyes, the semi-transparent hands which lay so listlessly upon the crimson coverlet, conveyed an impression of supreme despair. Hartfield, looking down at her for the last time when he came to say good-bye before leaving for London, was reminded of the story of one whose life had been thus rudely broken, who had loved as foolishly and even more fondly, and for whom the world held nothing when that tie was severed.

'She looked on many a face with vacant eye,
    On many a token without knowing what;
She saw them watch her, without asking why,
    And recked not who around her pillow sat.'

But Lesbia Haselden belonged to a wider and more sophisticated world than that of the daughter of the Grecian Isle, and for her existence offered wider horizons. It might be prophesied that for her the dark ending of a girlish dream would not be a life-long despair. The passionate love had been at fever point; the passionate grief must have its fever too, and burn itself out.

'Do all you can to cheer her,' said Lord Hartfield to Maulevrier, 'and bring her to Fellside as soon as ever she is strong enough to bear the journey. You and Kibble, with your own man, will be able to do all that is necessary.'

'Quite able.'

'That's right. I must be in the House for the expected division to-night, and I shall go back to Grasmere to-morrow morning. Poor Mary is horribly lonely.'

Lord Hartfield went off in the boat to catch the Southampton steamer; and Maulevrier was now sole custodian of the yacht and of his sister. He and the doctor had agreed to keep her on board, in the fresh sea air, till she was equal to the fatigue of the journey to Grasmere. There was nothing to be gained by taking her on to the island or by carrying her to London. The yacht was well found, provided with all things needful for comfort, and Lesbia could be nowhere better off until she was safe in her old home:--that home she had left so gaily, in the freshness of her youthful inexperience, nearly a year ago, and to which she would return so battered and broken, so deeply degraded by the knowledge of evil.

Lady Kirkbank had started for London on the previous day.

'I am evidently not wanted *here*,' she said, with an offended air; 'and I must have everything at Kirkbank ready for a house full of people before the twelfth of August, so the sooner I get to Scotland the better. I shall make a *detour* in order to go and see Lady Maulevrier on my way down. It is due to myself that I should let her know that *I* am entirely blameless in this most uncomfortable business.'

'You can tell her ladyship what you please,' answered Maulevrier, bluntly. 'I shall not gainsay you, so long as you do not slander my sister; but as long as I live I shall regret that I, knowing something of London society, did not interfere to prevent Lesbia being given over to your keeping.'

'If I had known the kind of girl she is I would have had nothing to do with her,' retorted Lady Kirkbank with exasperation; and so they parted.

The *Philomel* had been lying off Cowes three days before Mr. Smithson appeared upon the scene. He had got wind somehow from a sailor, who had talked with one of the foreign crew, of the destination of the *Cayman*, and he had crossed from Southampton to Havre on the steamer *Wolf* during that night in which Lesbia had been carried back to Cowes on the *Philomel*.

He was at Havre when the *Cayman* arrived, with Montesma and his tawny-visaged crew on board, no one else.

'You may examine every corner of your ship,' Montesma cried, scornfully, when Smithson came on board and swore that Lesbia must be hidden somewhere in the vessel. 'The bird has flown: she will shelter in neither your nest nor in mine, Smithson. You have lost her--and so have I. We may as well be friends in misfortune.'

He was haggard, livid with grief and anger. He looked ten years older than he had looked the other night at the ball, when his dash and swagger, and handsome Spanish head had been the admiration of the room.

Smithson was very angry, but he was not a fighting man. He had enjoyed various opportunities for distinguishing himself in that line in the island of Cuba; but he had always avoided such opportunities. So now, after a good deal of bluster and violent language, which Montesma took as lightly as if it had been the whistling of the wind in the shrouds, poor Smithson calmed down, and allowed Gomez de Montesma to leave the yacht, with his portmanteaux, unharmed. He meant to take the first steamer for the Spanish Main, he told Smithson. He had had quite enough of Europe.

'I daresay it will end in your marrying her,' he said, at the last moment. 'If you do, be kind to her.'

His voice faltered, choked by a sob, at those last words. After all, it is possible for a man without principle, without morality, to begin to make love to a woman in a mere spirit of adventure, in sheer devilry, and to be rather hard hit at the last.

Horace Smithson sailed his yacht back to Cowes without loss of time, and sent his card to Lord Maulevrier on board the ***Philomel***. His lordship replied that he would wait upon Mr. Smithson that afternoon at four o'clock, and at that hour Maulevrier again boarded the ***Cayman***; but this time very quietly, as an expected guest.

The interview that followed was very painful. Mr. Smithson was willing that this unhappy episode in the life of his betrothed, this folly into which she had been beguiled by a man of infinite treachery, a man of all other men fatal to women, should be forgotten, should be as if it had never been.

'It was her very innocence which made her a victim to that scoundrel,' said Smithson, 'her girlish simplicity and Lady Kirkbank's folly. But I love your sister too well to sacrifice her lightly, Lord Maulevrier; and if she can forget this midsummer madness, why, so can I.'

'She cannot forget, Mr. Smithson,' answered Maulevrier, gravely. 'She has done you a great wrong by listening to your false friend's addresses; but she did you a still greater wrong when she accepted you as her husband without one spark of love for you. She and you are both happy in having escaped the degradation, the deep misery of a loveless union. I am glad--yes, glad even of this shameful escapade with Montesma--though it has dragged her good name through the gutter,--glad of the catastrophe that has saved her from such a marriage. You are very generous in your willingness to forget my sister's folly. Let your forgetfulness go a step further, and forget that you ever met her.'

'That cannot be, Lord Maulevrier. She has ruined my life.'

'Not at all. An affair of a season,' answered Maulevrier, lightly. 'Next year I shall hear of you as the accepted husband of some new beauty. A man of Mr. Smithson's wealth--and good nature--need not languish in single blessedness.'

With this civil speech Lord Maulevrier went back to the ***Philomel's*** gig, and this was his last meeting with Mr. Smithson, until they met a year later in the beaten tracks of society.

CHAPTER XLV.
'THAT FELL ARREST, WITHOUT ALL BAIL.'

It was the beginning of August before Lesbia was pronounced equal to the fatigue of a long journey; and even then it was but the shadow of her former self which returned to Fellside, the pale spectre of joys departed, of trust deceived.

Maulevrier had been very good to her, patient, unselfish as a woman, in his ministering to the broken-hearted girl. That broken heart would be whole again, no doubt, in the future, as many other broken hearts have been; but the grief, the despair, the sense of hopelessness and aimlessness in life were very real in the present. If the picturesque seclusion of Fellside had seemed dull and joyless to Lesbia in days gone by, it was much duller to her now. She was shocked at the change in her grandmother, and she showed a good deal of feeling and affection in her intercourse with the invalid; but once out of her presence Lady Maulevrier was forgotten, and Lesbia's thoughts drifted back into the old current. They dwelt obstinately, unceasingly upon Montesma, the man whose influence had awakened the slumbering soul from its torpor, had stirred the deeps of a passionate nature.

Slave-dealer, gambler, adventurer, liar--his name blackened by the suspicion of a still darker crime. She shuddered at the thought of the villain from whose snare she had been rescued: and yet, his image as he had been to her in the brief golden time when she believed him noble, and chivalrous, and true, haunted her lonely days, mixed itself with her troubled dreams, came between her and every other thought.

Everybody was good to her. That pale and joyless face, that look of patient, hopeless suffering which she tried to disguise every now and then with a faint forced smile; and silvery little ripple of society laughter, seemed unconsciously to implore pity and pardon. Lady Maulevrier uttered no word of reproach. 'My dearest, Fate has not been kind to you,' she said, gently, after telling Lesbia of Lady Kirkbank's visit. 'The handsomest women are seldom the happiest. Destiny seems to have a grudge against them. And if things have gone amiss it is I who am most to blame. I ought never to have entrusted you with such a woman as Georgina Kirkbank. But you will be happier next season, I hope, dearest. You can live with Mary and Hartfield. They will take care of you.'

Lesbia shuddered.

'Do you think I am going back to the society treadmill?' she exclaimed. 'No, I have done with the world. I shall end my days here, or in a convent.'

'You think so now, dear, but you will change your mind by-and-by. A fancy that has lasted only a few weeks cannot alter your life. It will pass as other dreams have passed. At your age you have the future before you.'

'No, it is the past that is always before me,' answered Lesbia. 'My future is a blank.'

The bills came pouring in; dressmaker, milliner, glover, bootmaker, tailor, stationer, perfumer; awful bills which made Lady Maulevrier's blood run cold, so degrading was their story of selfish self-indulgence, of senseless extravagance. But she paid them all without a word. She took upon her shoulders the chief burden of Lesbia's wrongdoing. It was her indulgence, her weak preference which had fostered her granddaughter's selfishness, trained her to vanity and worldly pride. The result was ignominious, humiliating, bitter beyond all common bitterness; but the cup was of her own brewing, and she drank it without a murmur.

Parliament was prorogued; the season was over; and Lord Hartfield was established at Fellside for the autumn--he and his wife utterly happy in their affection for each other, but not without care as to their surroundings, which were full of trouble. First there was Lesbia's sorrow. Granted that it was a grief which would inevitably wear itself out, as other such griefs have done from time immemorial; but still the sorrow was there, at their doors. Next, there was the state of Lady Maulevrier's health, which gave her old medical adviser the gravest fears. At Lord Hartfield's earnest desire a famous doctor was summoned from London; but the great man could only confirm Mr. Horton's verdict. The thread of life was wearing thinner every day. It might snap at any hour. In the meantime the only regime was repose of body and mind, an all-pervading calm, the avoidance of all exciting topics. One moment of violent agitation might prove fatal.

Knowing this, how could Lord Hartfield call her ladyship to account for the presence of that mysterious old man under Steadman's charge?--how venture to touch upon a topic which, by Mary's showing, had exercised a most disturbing influence upon her ladyship's mind on that solitary occasion when the girl ventured to approach the subject?

He felt that any attempt at an explanation was impossible. It was not for him to precipitate Lady Maulevrier's end by prying into her secrets. Granted that shame and dishonour of some kind were involved in the existence of that strange old man, he, Lord Hartfield, must endure his portion in that shame--must be content to leave the dark riddle unsolved.

He resigned himself to this state of things, and tried to forget the cloud that hung over the house of Haselden; but the sense of a mystery, a fatal family secret, which must come to light sooner or later--since all such secrets are known at last--known, sifted, and bandied about from lip to lip, and published in a thousand different newspapers, and cried aloud in the streets--the sense of such a secret, the dread of such a revelation weighed upon him heavily.

Maulevrier, the restless, was off to Argyleshire for the grouse shooting as soon as he had deposited Lady Lesbia comfortably at Fellside.

'I should only be in your way if I stopped,' he said, 'for you and Molly have hardly got over the honeymoon stage yet, though you put on the airs of Darby and Joan. I shall be back in a week or ten days.'

'In Lady Maulevrier's state of health I don't think you ought to stay away very long,' said Hartfield.

'Poor Lady Maulevrier! She never cared much for me, don't you know. But I suppose it would seem unkind if I were to be out of the way when the end comes. The end! Good heavens! how coolly I talk of it; and a year ago I thought she was as immortal as Fairfield yonder.'

He went away, his spirits dashed by that awful thought of death, and Lord and Lady Hartfield had the house to themselves, since Lesbia hardly counted. She seldom left her own rooms, except to sit with her grandmother for an hour. She lay on her sofa--or sat in a low arm-chair by the window, reading Keats or Shelley--or only dreaming--dreaming over the brief golden time of her life, with its fond delusions, its false brightness. Mr. Horton went to see her every day--felt the feeble little pulse which seemed hardly to have force enough to beat--urged her to struggle against apathy and inertia, to walk a little, to go for a long drive every day, to live in the open air--to which instructions she paid not the slightest attention. The desire for life was gone. Disappointed in her ambition, betrayed in her love, humiliated, duped, degraded--a social failure. What had she to live for? She felt as if it would have been a good thing, quite the best thing that could happen, if she could turn her face to the wall and die. All that past season, its triumphs, its pleasures, its varieties, was like a garish dream, a horror to look back upon, hateful to remember.

In vain did Mary and Hartfield urge Lesbia to join in their simple pleasures, their walks and rides and drives, and boating excursions. She always refused.

'You know I never cared much for roaming about these everlasting hills,' she told Mary. 'I never had your passion for Lakeland. It is very good of you to wish to have me, but it is quite impossible. I have hardly strength enough for a little walk in the garden.'

'You would have more strength if you went out more,' pleaded Mary, almost with tears. 'Mr. Horton says sun and wind are the best doctors for you. Lesbia, you frighten me sometimes. You are just letting yourself fade away.'

'If you knew how I hate the world and the sky, Mary, you wouldn't urge me to go out of doors,' Lesbia answered, moodily. 'Indoors I can read, and get away from my own thoughts somehow, for a little while. But out yonder, face to face with the hills and the lake--the scenes I have known all my life--I feel a heart-sickness that is worse than death. It maddens me to see that old, old picture of mountain and water, the same for ever and ever, no matter what hearts are breaking.'

Mary crept close beside her sister's couch, put her arm round her neck, laid her cheek--rich in the ruddy bloom of health--against Lesbia's pallid and sunken cheek, and comforted her as much as she could with tender murmurs and loving kisses. Other comfort, she could give none. All the wisdom in the world will not cure a girl's heart-sickness when she has flung away the treasures of her love upon a worthless object.

And so the days went by, peacefully, but sadly; for the shadow of doom hung heavily over the house upon the Fell. Nobody who looked upon Lady Maulevrier could doubt that her days were numbered, that the oil was waxing low in the lamp of life. The end, the awful, mysterious end, was drawing near; and she who was called was making no such preparations as the Christian makes to answer the dread summons. As she had lived, she meant to die--an avowed unbeliever. More than once Mary had taken courage, and had talked to her grandmother of the world beyond, the blessed hope of re-union with the friends we have lost, in a new and brighter life, only to be met by the sceptic's cynical smile, the materialist's barren creed.

'My dearest, we know nothing except the immutable laws of material life. All the rest is a dream--a beautiful dream, if you like--a consolation to that kind of temperament which can take comfort from dreams; but for anyone who has read much, and thought much, and kept as far as possible on a level with the scientific intellect of the age--for such an one, Mary, these old fables are too idle. I shall die as I have lived, the victim of an inscrutable destiny, working blindly, evil to some, good to others. Ah! love, life has begun very fairly for you. May the fates be kind always to my gentle and loving girl!'

There was more talk between them on this dark mystery of life and death. Mary brought out her poor little arguments, glorified by the light of perfect faith; but they were of no avail against opinions which had been the gradual growth of a long and joyless life. Time had attuned Lady Maulevrier's mind to the gospel of Schopenhauer and the Pessimists, and she was contented to see the mystery of life as they had seen it. She had no fear, but she had some anxiety as to the things that were to happen after she was gone. She had taken upon herself a heavy burden, and she had not yet come to the end of the road where her burden might be laid quietly down, her task accomplished. If she fell by the wayside under her load the consequences for the survivors might be full of trouble.

Her anxieties were increased by the fact that her faithful servant and adviser, James Steadman, was no longer the man he had been. The change in him was painfully evident--memory failing, energy gone. He came to his mistress's room every morning, received her orders, answered her questions; but Lady Maulevrier felt that he went through the old duties in a mechanical way, and that his dull brain but half understood their importance.

One evening at dusk, just as Hartfield and Mary were leaving Lady Maulevrier's room, after dinner, an appalling shriek ran through the house--a cry almost as terrible as that which Lord Hartfield heard in the summer midnight just a year ago. But this time the sound came from the old part of the house.

'Something has happened,' exclaimed Hartfield, rushing to the door of communication.

It was bolted inside. He knocked vehemently; but there was no answer. He ran downstairs, followed by Mary, breathless, in an agony of fear. Just as they approached the lower door, leading to the old house, it was flung open, and Steadman's wife stood before them pale with terror.

'The doctor,' she cried; 'send for Mr. Horton, somebody, for God's sake. Oh, my lord,' with a sudden burst of sobbing, 'I'm afraid he's dead.'

'Mary, despatch some one for Horton,' said Lord Hartfield. Keeping his wife back with one hand, he closed the door against her, and then followed Mrs. Steadman through the long low corridor to her husband's sitting-room.

James Steadman was lying upon his back upon the hearth, near the spot were Lord Hartfield had seen him sleeping in his arm-chair a month ago.

One look at the distorted face, dark with injected blood, the dreadful glassy glare of the eyes, the foam-stained lips, told that all was over. The faithful servant had died at his post. Whatever his charge had been, his term of service was ended. There was a vacancy in Lady Maulevrier's household.

CHAPTER XLVI.
THE DAY OF RECKONING.

Lord Hartfield stayed with the frightened wife while she knelt beside that awful figure on the hearth, wringing her hands with piteous bewailings and lamentations over the unconscious clay. He had always been a good husband to her, she murmured; hard and stern perhaps, but a good man. And she had obeyed him without a question. Whatever he did or said she had counted right.

'We have not had a happy life, though there are many who have envied us her ladyship's favour,' she said in the midst of her lamentations. 'No one knows where the shoe pinches but those who have to wear it. Poor James! Early and late, early and late, studying her ladyship's interests, caring and thinking, in order to keep trouble away from her. Always on the watch always on the listen. That's what wore him out, poor fellow!'

'My good soul, your husband was an old man,' argued Lord Hartfield, in a consolatory tone, 'and the end must come to all of us somehow.'

'He might have lived to be a much older man if he had had less worry,' said the wife, bending her face to kiss the cold dead brow. 'His days were full of care. We should have been happier in the poorest cottage in Grasmere than we ever were in this big grand house.'

Thus, in broken fragments of speech, Mrs. Steadman lamented over her dead, while the heavy pendulum of the eight-day clock in the hall sounded the slowly-passing moments, until the coming of the doctor broke upon the quiet of the house, with the noise of opening doors and approaching footsteps.

James Steadman was dead. Medicine could do nothing for that lifeless clay, lying on the hearth by which he had sat on so many winter nights, for so many years of faithful unquestioning service. There was nothing to be done for that stiffening form, save the last offices for the dead; and Lord Hartfield left Mr. Horton to arrange with the weeping woman as to the doing of these. He was anxious to go to Lady Maulevrier, to break to her, as gently as might be, the news of her servant's death.

And what of that strange old man in the upper rooms? Who was to attend upon him, now that the caretaker was laid low?

While Lord Hartfield lingered on the threshold of the door that led from the old house to the new, pondering this question, there came the sound of wheels on the carriage drive, and then a loud ring at the hall door.

It was Maulevrier, just arrived from Scotland, smelling of autumn rain and cool fresh air.

'Dreadfully bored on the moors,' he said, as they shook hands. 'No birds--nobody to talk to--couldn't stand it any longer. How are the sisters? Lesbia better? Why, man alive, how queer you look! Nothing amiss, I hope?'

'Yes, there is something very much amiss. Steadman is dead.'

'Steadman! Her ladyship's right hand. That's rather bad. But you will drop into his stewardship. She'll trust your long head, I know. Much better that she should look to her granddaughter's husband for advice in all business matters than to a servant When did it happen?'

'Half an hour ago. I was just going to Lady Maulevrier's room when you rang the bell. Take off your Inverness, and come with me.'

'The poor grandmother,' muttered Maulevrier. 'I'm afraid it will be a blow.'

He had much less cause for fear than Lord Hartfield, who knew of deep and secret reasons why Steadman's death should be a calamity of dire import for his mistress, Maulevrier had been told nothing of that scene with the strange old man--the hidden treasures--the Anglo-Indian phrases--which had filled Lord Hartfield's mind with the darkest doubts.

If that half-lunatic old man, described by Lady Maulevrier as a kinsman of Steadman's, were verily the person Lord Hartfield believed, his presence under that roof, unguarded by a trust-worthy attendant, was fraught with danger. It would be for Lady Maulevrier, helpless, a prisoner to her sofa, at death's door, to face that danger. The very thought of it might kill her. And yet it was imperative that the truth should be told her without delay.

The two young men went to her ladyship's sitting room. She was alone, a volume of her favourite Schopenhauer open before her, under the light of the shaded reading-lamp. Sorry comfort in the hour of trouble!

Maulevrier went over to her and kissed her; and then dropped silently into a chair near at hand, his face in shadow. Hartfield seated himself nearer the sofa, and nearer the lamp.

'Dear Lady Maulevrier, I have come to tell you some very bad news--'

'Lesbia?' exclaimed her ladyship, with a frightened look.

'No, there is nothing wrong with Lesbia. It is about your old servant Steadman.'

'Dead?' faltered Lady Maulevrier, ashy pale, as she looked at him in the lamplight.

He bent his head affirmatively.

'Yes. He was seized with apoplexy--fell from his chair to the hearth, and never spoke or stirred again.'

Lady Maulevrier uttered no word of sorrow or surprise. She lay, looking straight before her into vacancy, the pale attenuated features rigid as if they had been marble. What was to be done--what must be told--whom could she trust? Those were the questions repeating themselves in her mind as she stared into space. And no answer came to them.

No answer came, except the opening of the door opposite her couch. The handle turned slowly, hesitatingly, as if moved by feeble fingers; and then the door was pushed slowly open, and an old man came with shuffling footsteps towards the one lighted spot in the middle of the room.

It was the old man Lord Hartfield had last seen gloating over his treasury of gold and jewels--the man whom Maulevrier had never seen--whose existence for forty years had been hidden from every creature in that house, except Lady Maulevrier and the Steadmans, until Mary found her way into the old garden.

He came close up to the little table in front of Lady Maulevrier's couch, and looked down at her, a strange, uncanny being, withered and bent, with pale, faded eyes in which there was a glimmer of unholy light.

'Good-evening to you, Lady Maulevrier,' he said in a mocking voice. 'I shouldn't have known you if we had met anywhere else. I think, of the two of us, you are more changed than I.'

She looked up at him, her features quivering, her haughty head drawn back; as a bird shrinks from the gaze of a snake, recoiling, but too fascinated to fly. Her eyes met his with a look of unutterable horror. For some moments she was speechless, and then, looking at Lord Hartfield, she said, piteously--

'Why did you let him come here? He ought to be taken care of--shut up. It is Steadman's old uncle--a lunatic--I sheltered. Why is he allowed to come to my room?'

'I am Lord Maulevrier,' said the old man, drawing himself up and planting his crutch stick upon the floor; 'I am Lord Maulevrier, and this woman is my wife. Yes, I am mad sometimes, but not always, I have my bad fits, but not often. But I never forget who and what I am, Algernon, Earl of Maulevrier, Governor of Madras.'

'Lady Maulevrier, is this horrible thing true?' cried her grandson, vehemently.

'He is mad, Maulevrier. Don't you see that he is mad?' she exclaimed, looking from Hartfield to her grandson, and then with a look of loathing and horror at her accuser.

'I tell you, young man, I am Maulevrier,' said the accuser; 'there is no one else who has a right to be called by that name, while I live. They have shut me up--she and her accomplice--denied my name--hidden me from the world. He is dead, and she lies there--stricken for her sins.'

'My grandfather died at the inn at Great Langdale, faltered Maulevrier.

'Your grandfather was brought to this house--ill--out of his wits. All cloud and darkness here,' said the old man, touching his forehead. 'How long has it been?

Who can tell? A weary time--long, dark nights, full of ghosts. Yes, I have seen him--the Rajah, that copper-faced scoundrel, seen him as she told me he looked when she gave the signal to her slaves to strangle him, there in the hall, where the grave was dug ready for the traitor's carcass. She too--yes, she has haunted me, calling upon me to give up her treasure, to restore her son.'

'Yes,' cried the paralytic woman, suddenly lifted out of herself, as it were, in a paroxysm of fury, every feature convulsed, every nerve strained to its utmost tension; 'yes, this is Lord Maulevrier. You have heard the truth, and from his own lips. You, his only son's only son. You his granddaughter's husband. You hear him avow himself the instigator of a diabolical murder; you hear him confess how his paramour's husband was strangled at his false wife's bidding, in his own palace, buried under the Moorish pavement in the hall of many arches. You hear how he inherited the Rajah's treasures from a mistress who died strangely, swiftly, conveniently, as soon so he had wearied of her, and a new favourite had begun to exercise her influence. Such things are done in the East--dynasties annihilated, kingdoms overthrown, poison or bowstring used at will, to gratify a profligate's passion, or pay for a spendthrift's extravagances. Such things were done when that man was Governor of Madras as were never done by an Englishman in India before his time. He went there fettered by no prejudices--he was more Mussulman than the Mussulmen themselves--a deeper, darker traitor. And it was to hide such crimes as these--to interpose the great peacemaker Death between him and the Government which was resolved upon punishing him--to save the honour, the fortune of my son, and the children who were to come after him, the name of a noble race, a name that was ever stainless until he defiled it--it was for this great end I took steps to hide that feeble, useless life of his from the world he had offended; it was for this end that I caused a peasant to be buried in the vault of the Maulevriers, with all the pomp and ceremony that befits the funeral of one of England's oldest earls. I screened him from his enemies--I saved him from the ignominy of a public trial--from the execration of his countrymen. His only punishment was to eat his heart under this roof, in luxurious seclusion, his comfort studied, his whims gratified so far as they could be by the most faithful of servants. A light penance for the dark infamies of his life in India, I think. His mind was all but gone when he came here, but he had his rational intervals, and in these the burden of his lonely life may have weighed heavily upon him. But it was not such a heavy burden as I have borne--I, his gaoler, I who have devoted my existence to the one task of guarding the family honour.'

He, whom she thus acknowledged as her husband, had sunk exhausted into a chair near her. He took out his gold snuff-box, and refreshed himself with a lei-surely pinch of snuff, looking about him curiously all the while, with a senile grin. That flash of passion which for a few minutes had restored him to the full possession of his reason had burnt itself out, and his mind had relapsed into the condition in which it had been when he talked to Mary in the garden.

'My pipe, Steadman,' he said, looking towards the door; 'bring me my pipe,' and then, impatiently, 'What has become of Steadman? He has been getting inattentive--very inattentive.'

He got up, and moved slowly to the door, leaning on his crutch-stick, his head sunk upon his breast, muttering to himself as he went; and thus he vanished from them, like the spectre of some terrible ancestor which had returned from the grave to announce the coming of calamity to a doomed race. His grandson looked after him, with an expression of intense displeasure.

'And so, Lady Maulevrier,' he exclaimed, turning to his grandmother, 'I have borne a title that never belonged to me, and enjoyed the possession of another man's estates all this time, thanks to your pretty little plot. A very respectable posi-tion for your grandson to occupy, upon my life!'

Lord Hartfield lifted his hand with a warning gesture. 'Spare her,' he said. 'She is in no condition to endure your reproaches.' Spare her--yes. Fate had not spared her. The beautiful face--beautiful even in age and decay--changed suddenly as she looked at them--the mouth became distorted, the eyes fixed: and then the heavy head fell back upon the pillow--the paralysed form, wholly paralysed now, lay like a thing of stone. It never moved again. Consciousness was blotted out for ever in that moment. The feeble pulses of heart and brain throbbed with gradually dimin-ishing power for a night and a day; and in the twilight of that dreadful day of noth-ingness the last glimmer of the light died in the lamp, and Lady Maulevrier and the burden of her sin were beyond the veil. Viscount Haselden, *alias* Lord Maulevrier, held a long consultation with Lord Hartfield on the night of his grandmother's death, as to what steps ought to be taken in relation to the real Earl of Maulevrier: and it was only at the end of a serious and earnest discussion that both young men came to the decision that Lady Maulevrier's secret ought to be kept faithfully to the end. Assuredly no good purpose could be achieved by letting the world know of old Lord Maulevrier's existence. A half-lunatic octogenarian could gain nothing by being restored to rights and possessions which he had most justly forfeited. All that justice demanded was that the closing years of his life should be made as comfortable as care and wealth could make them; and Hartfield and Haselden took immediate steps to this end. But their first act was to send the old earl's treasure chest under safe convoy to the India House, with a letter explaining how this long-hidden wealth, brought from India by Lord Maulevrier, had been discovered among other effects in a lumber-room at Lady Maulevrier's country house. The money so delivered up might possibly have formed part of his lordship's private fortune; but, in the absence of any knowledge as to its origin, his grandson, the present Lord Maulevrier, preferred to deliver it up to the authorities of the India House, to be dealt with as they might think fit. The old earl made no further attempt to assert himself. He seemed content to remain in his own rooms as of old, to potter about the garden, where his solitude was as complete as that of a hermit's cell. The only moan be made was for James Steadman, whose services he missed sorely. Lord Hartfield replaced that devoted servant by a clever Austrian valet, a new importation from Vienna, who understood very little English, a trained attendant upon mental invalids, and who was quite capable of dealing with old Lord Maulevrier. Lord Hartfield went a step farther; and within a week of those two funerals of servant and mistress, which cast a gloom over the peaceful valley of Grasmere, he brought down a famous mad-doctor to diagnose his lordship's case. There was but little risk in so doing, he argued with his friend, and it was their duty so to do. If the old man should assert himself to the doctor as Lord Maulevrier, the declaration would pass as a symptom of his lunacy. But it happened that the physician arrived at Fellside on one of Lord Maulevrier's bad days, and the patient never emerged from the feeblest phase of imbecility. 'Brain quite gone,' pronounced the doctor, 'bodily health very poor. Take him to the South of France for the winter--Hyeres, or any quiet place. He can't last long.'

To Hyeres the old man was taken, with Mrs. Steadman as nurse, and the Austrian valet as body-servant and keeper. Mary, for whom, in his brighter hours he showed a warm affection, went with him under her husband's wing.

Lord Hartfield rented a chateau on the slope of an olive-clad hill, where he and his young wife, whose health was somewhat delicate at this time, spent a winter in peaceful seclusion; while Lesbia and her brother travelled together in Italy. The old man's strength improved in that lovely climate. He lived to see the roses and orange blossoms of the early spring, and died in his arm-chair suddenly, without a pang, while Mary sat at his feet reading to him: a quiet end of an evil and troubled life. And now he whom the world had known as Lord Maulevrier was verily the earl, and could hear himself called by his title once more without a touch of shame.

The secret of Lady Maulevrier's sin had been so faithfully kept by the two young men that neither of her granddaughters knew the true story of that mysterious person whom Mary had first heard of as James Steadman's uncle. She and Lesbia both knew that there were painful circumstances of some kind connected with this man's existence, his hidden life in the old house at Fellside; but they were both content to learn no more. Respect for their grandmother's memory, sorrowful affection for the dead, prevailed over natural curiosity. Early in February Maulevrier sent decorators and upholsterers into the old house in Curzon Street, which was ready before the middle of May to receive his lordship and his young wife, the girlish daughter of a Florentine nobleman, a gazelle-eyed Italian, with a voice whose every tone was music, and with the gentlest, shyest, most engaging manners of any girl in Florence. Lady Lesbia, strangely subdued and changed by the griefs and humiliations of her last campaign, had been her brother's counsellor and confidante throughout his wooing of his fair Italian bride. She was to spend the season under her brother's roof, to help to initiate young Lady Maulevrier in the mysterious rites of London society, and to warn her of those rocks and shoals which had wrecked her own fortunes.

The month of May brought a son and heir to Lord Hartfield; and it was not till after his birth that Mary, Countess of Hartfield, was presented to her sovereign, and began her career as a matron of rank and standing, very much overpowered by the weight of her honours, and looking forward with delight to the end of the season and a flight to Argyleshire with her husband and baby.

THE END.

The Codes Of Hammurabi And Moses
W. W. Davies

QTY

The discovery of the Hammurabi Code is one of the greatest achievements of archaeology, and is of paramount interest, not only to the student of the Bible, but also to all those interested in ancient history...

Religion   ISBN: *1-59462-338-4*   Pages:132
MSRP $12.95

The Theory of Moral Sentiments
Adam Smith

QTY

This work from 1749. contains original theories of conscience amd moral judgment and it is the foundation for systemof morals.

Philosophy ISBN: *1-59462-777-0*   Pages:536
MSRP $19.95

Jessica's First Prayer
Hesba Stretton

QTY

In a screened and secluded corner of one of the many railway-bridges which span the streets of London there could be seen a few years ago, from five o'clock every morning until half past eight, a tidily set-out coffee-stall, consisting of a trestle and board, upon which stood two large tin cans, with a small fire of charcoal burning under each so as to keep the coffee boiling during the early hours of the morning when the work-people were thronging into the city on their way to their daily toil...

Childrens   ISBN: *1-59462-373-2*   Pages:84
MSRP $9.95

My Life and Work
Henry Ford

QTY

Henry Ford revolutionized the world with his implementation of mass production for the Model T automobile. Gain valuable business insight into his life and work with his own auto-biography... "We have only started on our development of our country we have not as yet, with all our talk of wonderful progress, done more than scratch the surface. The progress has been wonderful enough but..."

Biographies/   ISBN: *1-59462-198-5*   Pages:300
MSRP $21.95

The Art of Cross-Examination
Francis Wellman

QTY

I presume it is the experience of every author, after his first book is published upon an important subject, to be almost overwhelmed with a wealth of ideas and illustrations which could readily have been included in his book, and which to his own mind, at least, seem to make a second edition inevitable. Such certainly was the case with me; and when the first edition had reached its sixth impression in five months, I rejoiced to learn that it seemed to my publishers that the book had met with a sufficiently favorable reception to justify a second and considerably enlarged edition. ..

Reference   **ISBN: *1-59462-647-2***   **Pages:412**

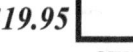 *MSRP $19.95*

On the Duty of Civil Disobedience
Henry David Thoreau

QTY

Thoreau wrote his famous essay, On the Duty of Civil Disobedience, as a protest against an unjust but popular war and the immoral but popular institution of slave-owning. He did more than write—he declined to pay his taxes, and was hauled off to gaol in consequence. Who can say how much this refusal of his hastened the end of the war and of slavery ?

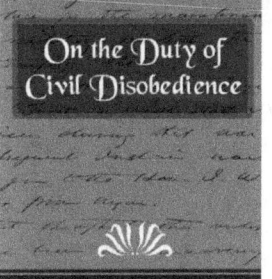

Law   **ISBN: *1-59462-747-9***   **Pages:48**

 MSRP $7.45

Dream Psychology Psychoanalysis for Beginners
Sigmund Freud

QTY

Sigmund Freud, born Sigismund Schlomo Freud (May 6, 1856 - September 23, 1939), was a Jewish-Austrian neurologist and psychiatrist who co-founded the psychoanalytic school of psychology. Freud is best known for his theories of the unconscious mind, especially involving the mechanism of repression; his redefinition of sexual desire as mobile and directed towards a wide variety of objects; and his therapeutic techniques, especially his understanding of transference in the therapeutic relationship and the presumed value of dreams as sources of insight into unconscious desires.

Psychology   **ISBN: *1-59462-905-6***   **Pages:196**

MSRP $15.45

The Miracle of Right Thought
Orison Swett Marden

QTY

Believe with all of your heart that you will do what you were made to do. When the mind has once formed the habit of holding cheerful, happy, prosperous pictures, it will not be easy to form the opposite habit. It does not matter how improbable or how far away this realization may see, or how dark the prospects may be, if we visualize them as best we can, as vividly as possible, hold tenaciously to them and vigorously struggle to attain them, they will gradually become actualized, realized in the life. But a desire, a longing without endeavor, a yearning abandoned or held indifferently will vanish without realization.

Self Help   **ISBN: *1-59462-644-8***   **Pages:360**

MSRP $25.45

www.bookjungle.com *email: sales@bookjungle.com fax: 630-214-0564 mail: Book Jungle PO Box 2226 Champaign, IL 61825*

QTY

The Rosicrucian Cosmo-Conception Mystic Christianity by *Max Heindel*　ISBN: *1-59462-188-8*　**$38.95**
The Rosicrucian Cosmo-conception is not dogmatic, neither does it appeal to any other authority than the reason of the student. It is: not controversial, but is: sent forth in the, hope that it may help to clear...　New Age/Religion Pages 646

Abandonment To Divine Providence by *Jean-Pierre de Caussade*　ISBN: *1-59462-228-0*　**$25.95**
"The Rev. Jean Pierre de Caussade was one of the most remarkable spiritual writers of the Society of Jesus in France in the 18th Century. His death took place at Toulouse in 1751. His works have gone through many editions and have been republished...　Inspirational/Religion Pages 400

Mental Chemistry by *Charles Haanel*　ISBN: *1-59462-192-6*　**$23.95**
Mental Chemistry allows the change of material conditions by combining and appropriately utilizing the power of the mind. Much like applied chemistry creates something new and unique out of careful combinations of chemicals the mastery of mental chemistry...　New Age Pages 354

The Letters of Robert Browning and Elizabeth Barret Barrett 1845-1846 vol II　ISBN: *1-59462-193-4*　**$35.95**
by *Robert Browning* and *Elizabeth Barrett*　Biographies Pages 596

Gleanings In Genesis (volume I) by *Arthur W. Pink*　ISBN: *1-59462-130-6*　**$27.45**
Appropriately has Genesis been termed "the seed plot of the Bible" for in it we have, in germ form, almost all of the great doctrines which are afterwards fully developed in the books of Scripture which follow...　Religion/Inspirational Pages 420

The Master Key by *L. W. de Laurence*　ISBN: *1-59462-001-6*　**$30.95**
In no branch of human knowledge has there been a more lively increase of the spirit of research during the past few years than in the study of Psychology, Concentration and Mental Discipline. The requests for authentic lessons in Thought Control, Mental Discipline and...　New Age/Business Pages 422

The Lesser Key Of Solomon Goetia by *L. W. de Laurence*　ISBN: *1-59462-092-X*　**$9.95**
This translation of the first book of the "Lernegton" which is now for the first time made accessible to students of Talismanic Magic was done, after careful collation and edition, from numerous Ancient Manuscripts in Hebrew, Latin, and French...　New Age/Occult Pages 92

Rubaiyat Of Omar Khayyam by *Edward Fitzgerald*　ISBN:*1-59462-332-5*　**$13.95**
Edward Fitzgerald, whom the world has already learned, in spite of his own efforts to remain within the shadow of anonymity, to look upon as one of the rarest poets of the century, was born at Bredfield, in Suffolk, on the 31st of March, 1809. He was the third son of John Purcell...　Music Pages 172

Ancient Law by *Henry Maine*　ISBN: *1-59462-128-4*　**$29.95**
The chief object of the following pages is to indicate some of the earliest ideas of mankind, as they are reflected in Ancient Law, and to point out the relation of those ideas to modern thought.　Religion/History Pages 452

Far-Away Stories by *William J. Locke*　ISBN: *1-59462-129-2*　**$19.45**
"Good wine needs no bush, but a collection of mixed vintages does. And this book is just such a collection. Some of the stories I do not want to remain buried for ever in the museum files of dead magazine-numbers an author's not unpardonable vanity..."　Fiction Pages 272

Life of David Crockett by *David Crockett*　ISBN: *1-59462-250-7*　**$27.45**
"Colonel David Crockett was one of the most remarkable men of the times in which he lived. Born in humble life, but gifted with a strong will, an indomitable courage, and unremitting perseverance...　Biographies/New Age Pages 424

Lip-Reading by *Edward Nitchie*　ISBN: *1-59462-206-X*　**$25.95**
Edward B. Nitchie, founder of the New York School for the Hard of Hearing, now the Nitchie School of Lip-Reading, Inc, wrote "LIP-READING Principles and Practice". The development and perfecting of this meritorious work on lip-reading was an undertaking...　How-to Pages 400

A Handbook of Suggestive Therapeutics, Applied Hypnotism, Psychic Science　ISBN: *1-59462-214-0*　**$24.95**
by *Henry Munro*　Health/New Age/Health/Self-help Pages 376

A Doll's House: and Two Other Plays by *Henrik Ibsen*　ISBN: *1-59462-112-8*　**$19.95**
Henrik Ibsen created this classic when in revolutionary 1848 Rome. Introducing some striking concepts in playwriting for the realist genre, this play has been studied the world over.　Fiction/Classics/Plays 308

The Light of Asia by *sir Edwin Arnold*　ISBN: *1-59462-204-3*　**$13.95**
In this poetic masterpiece, Edwin Arnold describes the life and teachings of Buddha. The man who was to become known as Buddha to the world was born as Prince Gautama of India but he rejected the worldly riches and abandoned the reigns of power when...　Religion/History/Biographies Pages 170

The Complete Works of Guy de Maupassant by *Guy de Maupassant*　ISBN: *1-59462-157-8*　**$16.95**
"For days and days, nights and nights, I had dreamed of that first kiss which was to consecrate our engagement, and I knew not on what spot I should put my lips..."　Fiction/Classics Pages 240

The Art of Cross-Examination by *Francis L. Wellman*　ISBN: *1-59462-309-0*　**$26.95**
Written by a renowned trial lawyer, Wellman imparts his experience and uses case studies to explain how to use psychology to extract desired information through questioning.　How-to/Science/Reference Pages 408

Answered or Unanswered? by *Louisa Vaughan*　ISBN: *1-59462-248-5*　**$10.95**
Miracles of Faith in China　Religion Pages 112

The Edinburgh Lectures on Mental Science (1909) by *Thomas*　ISBN: *1-59462-008-3*　**$11.95**
This book contains the substance of a course of lectures recently given by the writer in the Queen Street Hall, Edinburgh. Its purpose is to indicate the Natural Principles governing the relation between Mental Action and Material Conditions...　New Age/Psychology Pages 148

Ayesha by *H. Rider Haggard*　ISBN: *1-59462-301-5*　**$24.95**
Verily and indeed it is the unexpected that happens! Probably if there was one person upon the earth from whom the Editor of this, and of a certain previous history, did not expect to hear again...　Classics Pages 380

Ayala's Angel by *Anthony Trollope*　ISBN: *1-59462-352-X*　**$29.95**
The two girls were both pretty, but Lucy who was twenty-one who supposed to be simple and comparatively unattractive, whereas Ayala was credited, as her Bombwhat romantic name might show, with poetic charm and a taste for romance. Ayala when her father died was nineteen...　Fiction Pages 484

The American Commonwealth by *James Bryce*　ISBN: *1-59462-286-8*　**$34.45**
An interpretation of American democratic political theory. It examines political mechanics and society from the perspective of Scotsman James Bryce　Politics Pages 572

Stories of the Pilgrims by *Margaret P. Pumphrey*　ISBN: *1-59462-116-0*　**$17.95**
This book explores pilgrims religious oppression in England as well as their escape to Holland and eventual crossing to America on the Mayflower, and their early days in New England...　History Pages 268

www.bookjungle.com *email: sales@bookjungle.com fax: 630-214-0564 mail: Book Jungle PO Box 2226 Champaign, IL 61825*

QTY

The Fasting Cure *by Sinclair Upton*   ISBN: *1-59462-222-1*   **$13.95**

In the Cosmopolitan Magazine for May, 1910, and in the Contemporary Review (London) for April, 1910, I published an article dealing with my experiences in fasting. I have written a great many magazine articles, but never one which attracted so much attention... New Age/Self Help/Health Pages 164

Hebrew Astrology *by Sepharial*   ISBN: *1-59462-308-2*   **$13.45**

In these days of advanced thinking it is a matter of common observation that we have left many of the old landmarks behind and that we are now pressing forward to greater heights and to a wider horizon than that which represented the mind-content of our progenitors...   Astrology Pages 144

Thought Vibration or The Law of Attraction in the Thought World   ISBN: *1-59462-127-6*   **$12.95**

by William Walker Atkinson   *Psychology/Religion Pages 144*

Optimism *by Helen Keller*   ISBN: *1-59462-108-X*   **$15.95**

Helen Keller was blind, deaf, and mute since 19 months old, yet famously learned how to overcome these handicaps, communicate with the world, and spread her lectures promoting optimism. An inspiring read for everyone...   Biographies/Inspirational Pages 84

Sara Crewe *by Frances Burnett*   ISBN: *1-59462-360-0*   **$9.45**

In the first place, Miss Minchin lived in London. Her home was a large, dull, tall one, in a large, dull square, where all the houses were alike, and all the sparrows were alike, and where all the door-knockers made the same heavy sound...   Childrens/Classic Pages 88

The Autobiography of Benjamin Franklin *by Benjamin Franklin*   ISBN: *1-59462-135-7*   **$24.95**

The Autobiography of Benjamin Franklin has probably been more extensively read than any other American historical work, and no other book of its kind has had such ups and downs of fortune. Franklin lived for many years in England, where he was agent...   Biographies/History Pages 332

Name	
Email	
Telephone	
Address	
City, State ZIP	

☐ **Credit Card**   ☐ **Check / Money Order**

Credit Card Number	
Expiration Date	
Signature	

Please Mail to: Book Jungle
PO Box 2226
Champaign, IL 61825
or Fax to: 630-214-0564

ORDERING INFORMATION

web: *www.bookjungle.com*
email: *sales@bookjungle.com*
fax: *630-214-0564*
mail: *Book Jungle PO Box 2226 Champaign, IL 61825*
or PayPal *to sales@bookjungle.com*

Please contact us for bulk discounts

DIRECT-ORDER TERMS

**20% Discount if You Order
Two or More Books**
Free Domestic Shipping!
Accepted: Master Card, Visa,
Discover, American Express

www.ingramcontent.com/pod-product-compliance
Lightning Source LLC
Chambersburg PA
CBHW080951020726
47505CB00009B/2153